THE EMERALD BRACELET

ANDY STONE

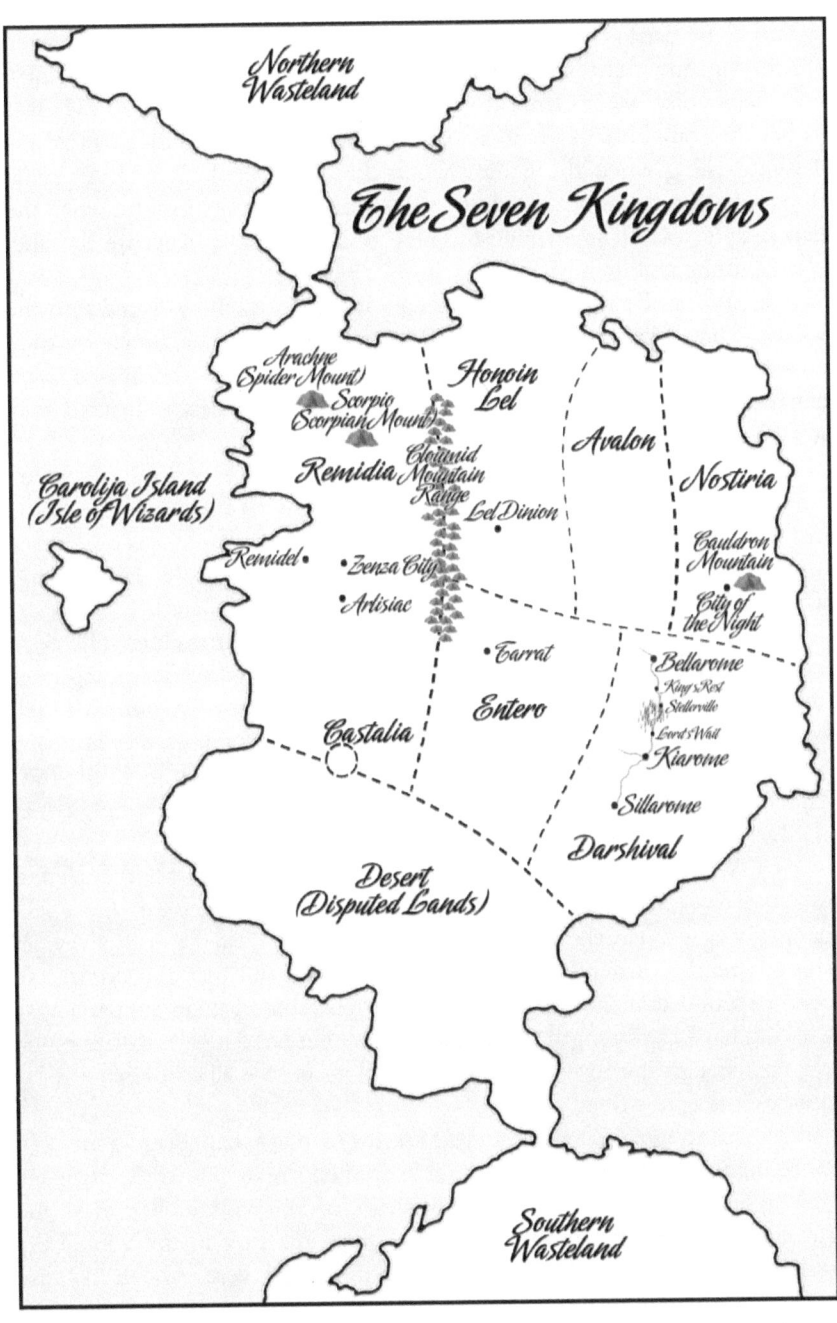

The Seven Kingdoms

Prologue: Disaster Strikes

The battle had not lasted long since the attack had been expected for a long time. The spell protecting Elhjem had been battered until it completely dispersed. Orric, the leader of Elhjem, had prepared his elves as best he could, but as much as they had been waiting for the attack there was no telling when the enemy would break through. The only certain thing was that the attack would come during the cover of night, when the dark magic was at its strongest. There was no way to evacuate the she-elves and the children.

When the shield finally broke a wave of orglin swarmed into the village. The disfigured creatures had been whipped into a frenzy by their masters. The spell-binders who had broken through the magic were exhausted. They would not be able to assist in the attack. Instead they would have to rely on the brute strength of the orglin.

The battle was short and vicious. There was no quarter given from either side. The elves well knew the ferocity of their enemies. Some of the elders had fought them in their younger years. There was no chance of retreat. The orglin would fight to the very end, to the very last one and would not stop until all the elves were completely annihilated.

The orglin's numbers far outweighed those of the elves. The odds were stacked against them, but they had the advantage of defending their homes. The first group of orglin fell to a barrage of arrows, but with each volley more and more of the creatures slipped through. It was not long before the archers had to come down from their perches and join the fray. The orglin were relentless in their attack, but the elves were just as stalwart in their defence.

When the dust settled and the splattering of blood had ceased, it was the elves who were victorious. The job of cleaning up the spell-binders was a much easier task. Most were too exhausted to run away, let alone defend themselves. They seemed so surprised that the orglin had been defeated that the thought had not even crossed their minds. Those who did have the strength to run away didn't get far. The elves were much swifter through the forest and it was not long before all of the enemy lay dead on the forest floor.

Although they were victorious the damage had been done. No more than a hundred of the elves had survived the battle. In the rampage the orglin had managed to destroy most of the village. Some of the stronger spell-binders had managed to light some fires in the huts. They were not enough to burn the entire village, but they were enough to cause some serious damage.

Orric looked over the mess that had once been one of the most beautiful places in the world. His soft blonde hair had started to grey with the stress and wrinkles started to line his face. It had been a long time coming but his great age had finally started to show on his body. The ground was scattered with dead elves mingled with dead orglin. The scene was like something out his worst nightmare. The worst part was that no one was able to get away. The orglin had surrounded the village leaving no room for escape for the children and she-elves. Everyone had to witness the slaughter.

He himself was covered with the sticky blood of the orglin he had killed. It was so dark red that it was almost black. His clothes were soaked and his skin was covered in it. The smell was almost enough to make him ill. If he wasn't still filled with such rage he would have been physically sick.

"We survived father, that is all that matters," Valen let a reassuring hand rest on Orric's shoulder. He didn't even flinch at the orglin blood that had soaked into his shirt and his muscular body didn't look at all fatigued from the ordeal.

"Where is Towen?" he looked around the remnants of the village. Most of the elves had grouped behind Orric, but there were some going through the dead bodies, looking for loved ones.

"I don't know father I haven't seen him since the fighting started. I am sure that he is around somewhere," there was very little reassurance in his voice.

Orric kept his vision on the scene in front of him. He didn't want to risk looking behind and showing the remaining elves the expression on his face. It was a mixture of rage and sadness. He needed to remain strong for the survivors. He wanted to speak to his Darziel, the Captain-of-the-Guard and as he looked out in front he saw him coming towards him. He was relieved to see he was still alive. Orric steeled and readied himself for the conversation; he knew it wasn't going to be pleasant.

Darziel was in much the same condition as the other elves, although he didn't seem to be covered in as much blood. As the Captain-of-the-Guard he was no stranger to fights, although there had not been many over the last few years. His light brown hair fell around his shoulders and was completely free of the orglin filth, only a few smears stained his face.

"A sore sight indeed my Lord," there was a grimace on Darziel's face when he saw Orric. Darziel's body was similarly covered in blood, but it looked much worse on someone else.

"Have you seen Towen?" Orric didn't have the heart to ask him anything else.

Darziel could see the look on his face. The information that he was about to give was not going to make him any happier. "I haven't seen him for a while, but I am afraid that he didn't make it," he was trying to choose his words carefully, but was failing miserably.

"It is not true," Orric kept his voice even. "He has to be around here somewhere. There are still elves coming back from hunting down the spell-binders."

"When the second wave came he was at the front of the defence. He fought valiantly, but there was nothing he could do. He was caught from behind by an orglin. He managed to drag it off his back and kill it, but he did not look good. I tried to get to his side, but we were cut off by a swarm of orglin. By the time the scene cleared I could not see him. There were no other elves where they had been fighting."

"It doesn't mean that he has fallen," there was a mixture of hope and anger in Orric's voice.

"No one could have survived what I saw," Darziel had already resigned to the fact.

"Get out there and look for him," Orric yelled.

"Father," there was uncertainty in Valen's voice.

Orric dropped to his knees. Towen had been one of his oldest friends. The elf had helped him on many occasions. He needed to stay strong for the remainder of the village, but the move was involuntary. His son kept his hand on his shoulder. The touch was somewhat comforting. He wanted to scream out, but that would solve nothing. Deep down he knew that Darziel was right. If Towen was still alive then he would have returned by now. Slowly he returned to his feet.

"Are you alright?" Valen was the first to notice the blood running down Darziel's arm.

The Captain of the Guard was trying his best to remain stalwart, but he was starting to wobble on his feet. It was clear that he had lost a lot of blood. His face had turned pale and he was sweating profusely.

"I'm fine, there's too much to do here," Darziel didn't hesitate to respond.

Valen knew it wasn't right. He looked at Orric, but his leader and father gave no response. Despite his concerns there was little time to argue. There would be time enough for Darziel to gain medical attention and until he asked for it, or needed it, Valen would have to accept his response.

"What are we going to do now?" Valen asked.

"We need to clean up this mess," Darziel replied. "We need to work on rebuilding the village."

"No," all eyes suddenly moved to Orric. "Our time here is done."

"But father. This has been the site of ancestors for thousand of years. It will not be that hard to dispose of the bodies and rebuilt the village. In a while this terrible sight will start to fade from our memories.

We will learn to laugh again," Valen sounded hopeful. His words almost made Orric change his mind.

It had not been an easy decision to make, but it was one that Orric had to. Ever since the attack started he knew what it was going to come down to. No matter how much they all wanted it they could not remain. Elhjem was a thing of the past and if there was any chance for a future then they would have to leave.

"I wish that this was correct. I know that we could rebuild, but this site is no longer habitable. The taint of the Evil One is thick in the air and on the ground. We shall never inhabit this place again." It was not exactly true, but he had to make his point. "It is time for us to move on. We have remained hidden in our shroud for too long. It is time that we join the world again," Orric was speaking very mysteriously.

Valen looked at Darziel, who still looked unsteady on his feet, and then at the remainder of the elves. The hope that had been on their faces was quickly gone. He could not work out what his father was doing. It was not the time to slip into a malaise. He was the leader of the village and he needed to start acting like it.

"This is no way to talk father. We need to remain positive," Valen thought that he was going to have to take command if his father did not change his mind. It was something that he did not want to do, but he would if it was necessary.

"There is nothing wrong with me son." A smile crossed Orric's face, but there was no humour in it. "It is time. It is long past time that we leave Elhjem." He turned and faced the other elves for the first time. "We have to join this war. I was a fool to think that we would be safe hidden in our village. Our first task is to pay tribute to those who have fallen. Then we shall travel to Jarrat."

"I don't understand what you are talking about father." Valen was confused.

"I must admit that you have me confused as well," Darziel agreed.

"I know where our path leads us now and that is to Jarrat. I don't know what we will find there, but I know that we have to travel there," there was not real answer in his words.

"But why should we all of a sudden pack up and leave the village," Valen was not happy with what his father was saying. "The rest of the world has shunned us for so long. We have proven we can survive on our own and that's what we should do."

"Be calm Valen, my son. It is true that world has shunned us, but we have also locked ourselves away." Orric paused for his words to take effect. "This was just a taste of what the Evil One can do. If he really wanted to he could have destroyed us without a second thought."

"If he could have then he would have. It makes no sense for him to let us live," Valen argued. "No, this was not a minor attack."

"I don't know why he only sent the force that he did. Maybe he underestimated us or maybe he just wanted to test our strength. Either way it is now irrelevant. It is our turn to make a move and this is the one we are going to make," full strength had returned to his voice.

Orric looked at Darziel. The elf was starting to understand what he was saying. He too was starting to feel the gentle pull towards the city of Jarrat. He didn't know the reason behind it, but he knew he had to follow it.

"Orric is right. We need to move to Jarrat. From there we will strike back at the heart of the Evil One. Nyrra will now know the true fury of the elves," Darziel's words brought a renewed hope to the other elves. He didn't know where they had come from, but he could see the effect that they were having.

Valen was still not convinced, but he could see hope amongst the group and that was something that he didn't want to extinguish. In the end he would have to trust that his father knew what he was doing.

"We need to get to work. Those who are injured need to be tended to," he looked at Darziel as he spoke, finally realising the elf's injury. "We need to give our fallen brothers and sisters their last rights and then we leave at first light," Orric's voice rose above the crowd.

There was a cheer from the elves. They suddenly had something to be excited about even if they didn't know what it was. They were doing something to avenge the death of their friends and family and that was all that mattered.

***

They had marched for more days than Hawthorne could remember. Finally he had reached his destination. Their travelling had been smooth until they passed over the boarder into Remidia. Things had not been that bad. There had been a number of small skirmishes, but nothing that could really be called a battle. All it managed to do, really, was to slow them down.

With each attack Gilgi urged Hawthorne to travel at a quicker pace, but Hawthorne was loathed to push his soldiers any harder. If his men were too tired when they were attacked there was less chance they would get away unscathed. The dwarf was so persistent that Hawthorne was forced to increase their pace. He was also eager to return to Remidel and his father's palace.

The prince sat high in the saddle. He had his hair freshly cut before they started out that morning and he had also shaved. It had been far too long since he had. He didn't allow his soldiers to look scruffy and he normally led by example. He wore his silver, ceremonial, breast plate with the Royal Remidian Army Crest, a fox head inlaid over a broadsword, engraved in the middle. He also wore a purple cape with the royal crest, a golden lion, prominent on its back. If he was going to return to his home he was going to look the part of its prince.

With the city in view Hawthorne could barely sit still in his saddle. There didn't seem to be an invading army in the surrounding land, but that still didn't settle his nerves and his strong jaw line remained set. Hawthorne only hoped that he was not too late. He would hate to think that Remidel was under control of the enemy. He looked to the north of the city where the royal palace sat, alone, on top of a small hill. The royal Remidian flags still waved proudly from the city's turrets.

"Bring the army in Derwin. I will ride ahead and announce our arrival," Hawthorne sounded excited.

"But your majesty, it is not proper. We should send a herald to announce your arrival," Captain Derwin spoke against his prince's wishes. He too had recently shaved, including his head. A large scar ran down the right side of his face, but the battle long forgotten.

"I know, but I don't want to wait. I am sure that everyone will understand," Hawthorne was about to ride forward when Gilgi came to the front of the line.

The dwarf had a stern look on his face. Even through his thick, brown beard they could decipher his expression. He was still the leader of the Western Dwarves Guild and he wasn't going to give up control. It was something that annoyed Hawthorne, but he always managed to agree with whatever the dwarf had suggested.

"You should wait Hawthorne," he knew exactly what the prince was planning on doing. "We don't know the state of play in the city or the palace. We should be careful until we know exactly what has been happening," his words were wise.

Hawthorne nodded his head. He knew that the dwarf was correct. If he rushed towards the palace and it was under the enemy's control then he would also be taken prisoner. If the city needed help then he wanted to be the one who delivered it.

"Very good. Have one of our scouts check out the palace. If everything is alright then he can let my father know that we have returned," Hawthorne spoke the order as if it had been his original idea.

Captain Derwin was much happier with his new edict. If the scout wasn't admitted into the city then they would know there was trouble. He quickly had a couple of scouts sent on ahead. If they managed to get into the city then he was confident they would be able to get into the palace and assess the situation with their presence unknown. If all was safe then they would report to King Faxon. If all was not safe then they would return to the army and report the situation.

The scouts disappeared into the distance and the army remained in position. The front of the army was in view of the palace, but not the entire army. Those inside the palace would not know the true numbers. It would be an advantage if they had to strike and although it would not be a complete surprise it would be more than they would be expecting.

The wait for the scouts to return was infuriating. All Hawthorne wanted to do was to enter the palace and speak to his father. There was much to do and little time to do it. Hawthorne knew that they had been right. There was no point running into danger. A few more hours wouldn't make any difference. It was better that he remained safe.

The light was fading in front of them when the scouts finally returned. They rode hard towards the army. There was no way to know if it was a good sign or a bad sign. Hawthorne's heart was racing as he watched them approach. With each second that passed his heart raced a little faster. His nerves were on a knife's edge as he tried to gauge their reactions.

"Sir, we have returned from the palace," the scout saluted as he reined in his horse in front of Prince Hawthorne, Captain Derwin, Gilgi and the dwarf's advisor Leo.

"Get to the point," Hawthorne would not stand on formalities. He wanted to know the situation in the palace and that was all that mattered.

"Sorry, your highness," the scout seemed somewhat annoyed with himself. "I have some great news. There has been no attack on the city. We have sent word to the King of your arrival. He is ready to receive you."

That was all the news that Hawthorne needed to hear and he breathed a sigh of relief. "Have the army set up camp down there," he pointed to a flat piece of land just down from the hill they were standing on. "You can approach the city in the morning."

Once he had finished speaking Hawthorne kicked his horse into a gallop. He was not going to waste another moment. He had missed his home more than he ever thought he would. He was also glad that he had made it home before they were under attack. Now he would be able to save his country from being invaded.

There was not the usual welcome for the Prince as he returned home. Faxon had not let anyone know that their Prince was returning, nor was there enough time to prepare anything too exciting. Hawthorne didn't mind not having all the festivities as normal. It meant that he would see his father sooner. He would be able to get all the information on the enemy's movements into his Kingdom.

The king was an older version on his son. Despite his growing age his body was thick with muscle. He blonde hair was kept neatly cut and his face was cleanly shaved. There could be no doubt where Hawthorne had learned his habits.

Faxon was pacing in his room when his son arrived. Hawthorne was pleased to see his father, but his father didn't seem all that pleased to see him. Hawthorne recognised the look and stopped as he approached. There was something in his father's eyes that wasn't right.

"What's wrong father?" Hawthorne asked slowly.

"I will ask the questions," he was using his Kingly voice. Hawthorne took a step backwards. "What are you doing back here and with the Remidian army?"

"I came back to protect my homeland. The battle in Avalon was just a trap to divert our power from the real battle. Nothing was happening in Avalon. It only made sense that they would attack Remidia," Hawthorne was a little nervous as he spoke. There was something accusing in his father's question.

"When the army left I gave General Jarwe strict instructions to remain with the Alliance until the war was over. Where is General Jarwe? Did he enter the palace with you or is he still with the army?" Faxon was doing his best to keep from raising his voice.

"Jarwe is still with the Alliance," it was the only answer Hawthorne could give. The cold reality of the situation was slowly sinking in. The decision to leave had been a mistake. At the time there seemed like there was no other option. Since he had finally made it home it dawned on him that he had erred.

"So you mean to tell me that not only did you disobey my order, but you also took my army away from my General?" Faxon could no longer keep his voice calm. "What in the Gods' name were you thinking?"

Hawthorne backed away even further. He recognised the look on Faxon's face and he didn't want to be within striking distance. "I thought that I was doing what was best for my Kingdom," Hawthorne was furiously thinking as he spoke. There had to be a way out of his current situation. He had been so happy to be returning home that it had not even crossed his mind that his father would be displeased with him.

Suddenly there was a knock on the door before Faxon could continue berating his son. Faxon thought about ignoring whoever it was on the outside, but he was suddenly curious to see who was there. The door opened and there was a page boy on the other side. He seemed nervous as he could obviously hear the sound of raised voices coming from inside.

"I am sorry to interrupt you your majesty, but there is someone here to see you. He said it is very important," the page boy's voice was shaken.

"I am not interested in seeing anyone else this evening," the harshness remained in his voice. "I still have much to discuss with my son."

The pageboy was about to leave the room when someone pushed passed him. At first Faxon was surprised, but when he looked down he saw it was a dwarf. He couldn't believe the gall of him to barge his way in.

"I am sorry for the intrusion, but we need to talk," there was something strange in the dwarf's voice.

Normally Faxon would have the dwarf physically removed from his room, but there was something different about the situation. He couldn't bring himself to speak the words. Instead he motioned for the pageboy to leave them alone. Faxon watched the dwarf walk around the room until his was standing to his left.

"I am Gilgi. I am in command of the dwarven army. We have travelled far to be here with your army. We believe that Remidia is under threat of attack," his words sounded familiar.

"Well Gilgi, you see that the situation is…" for a moment Faxon wasn't sure what he was going to say. The dwarf's words made perfect sense. When he thought about it his Kingdom was on the border of the Northern Wasteland. It made perfect sense that Remidia was the first place they would attack. "I think that you are right."

Hawthorne looked at his father with a strange expression on his face. He didn't know why he had so suddenly changed his mind. The thought troubled him for a moment, but then was gone. The thought was replaced by a feeling of relief that his father was finally seeing what he had seen. Something didn't seem right, but he wasn't going to question it.

"Very good then. I don't think there is much more that needs to be said. We have the army here ready for the attack. All we can do now is wait," there was a strange confidence in Gilgi's voice.

"I think it is time that we get something to eat. I am sure that you are hungry," King Faxon placed his arm around his son and moved out of the room.

Gilgi remained behind. He didn't want either man to see the broad grin on his face. He thought that it would be so much harder to take control of King Faxon. His son had been much harder to control. Now he had control of Remidel and it had been all too easy. The Great Lord would be pleased with the new development. He only wished that he was able to contact him. There was nothing more frustrating that not being able to contact the Great Lord.

When the euphoria of the situation died down he left the room. There was still much to be done, but everything was falling into place. He had secured the city and a large army for the Great Lord. He was sure that he was number one of all the Chosen.

***

Nyrra sat in the dark room in the farmhouse. He stared at the flames as they flickered in the fireplace. He liked watching the fire, it brought him some level of peace. He could still hear the muffled screams coming from the next room. The farmer, his wife and their small child were tied and gagged. Normally he didn't like being indoors, but he needed a place to think. The solitary farmhouse had been the best place for it. He also enjoyed punishing the farmer and his family. It was a small pleasure, but one that he was willing to take. Now he had to think about what his next move was. Things had not been going to plan. It was obvious to him that the ruse in Avalon had not worked. He could only assume that everyone there had been slaughtered.

He had chosen himself a facade that he assumed would be pleasing to the eye if anyone was to cross his path. The last thing he needed was to be discovered. His body was filled with muscles and he stood six feet tall. Blonde hair fell around his shoulders and his face was what anyone would call handsome. His eyes were a deep blue and anyone caught in their gaze would be spellbound. It was not the most subtle of disguises, but no one would know who he really was.

It had not be long ago that one of his General's had been murdered. Fenaroz had been one of the stronger of the Chosen. That was the reason why he had left him in charge of Darshival. King Unwin was strong willed and it would take someone with a great deal of strength to command him. He felt the day that he had been killed. There was a certain amount of pain that Nyrra suffered when one of the Chosen died. It was a physical pain, not an emotional one. He felt disgusted at the life as it was taken from the world. Two of the chosen had been destroyed and now one was off his radar.

He knew that Na'garoz had failed in his task. He was supposed to trap Alaric when he reached Bellarome. It had been a relatively simple task, but one that he failed miserably at. Since the Chosen had left Kiarome he had been out of contact. There was something disturbing about the fact. He didn't like it when they tried to keep things from him. That was the game they all played. He pitted the seven, now five, against each other, striving for his praise.

He had left Ra'naroz in Jarrat to get the answers from Alena and Eldred. The two had been less than cooperative, which he didn't overly mind. They were both strong and able to withstand more of his torture than most. He wished that he could have been there to watch his work, but there were more important things that he had to take care of. He could feel the Ruby stone. He could feel it calling to him. He didn't know why he couldn't pinpoint its exact location. Something had changed over the years. It was as if the stone didn't recognise him anymore and that was a disturbing development. All that mattered was finding the stone before the Cursed One did. If he found the stone first then he had won. There was nothing that could stop him with the power in his hands.

It was disappointing that he had lost control over Darshival, especially since he had two of the Chosen there. He was willing to let it go. He still had control over Entero and Castalia and if things went to plan he would have control over Remidia. He would still control three of the five. He had no doubt that the army would soon be on the move to Jarrat. Alaric would want to free his friends and that is where Nyrra had a little surprise planned. The pitiful creatures were all so predictable. They should let those who became captured pay the penalty for failing. They would never do it though and that is when he was going to strike. He only wished that he could be there himself.

Nyrra knew that it would not be long before he had to face Alaric again. Next time it would be face to face. This time one of them would not get away. Things were moving in the right direction. His plans were slowly coming to fruition. Once he had the stone in his possession he would take great pleasure in destroying the Cursed One.

The muffled screams had died down from the bedroom. Nyrra wondered what they were doing. He could sense their pain and anguish. He knew they had not escaped. It was time for him to be leaving. He had accomplished what he wanted to do. He looked at the fire and saw the flames dancing around. A smile crossed his face as an idea entered his mind.

One moment the room was dark and quiet, the next it was completely engulfed in flames. Suddenly the screams could be heard coming from the next room. The cloth gags that had been muffling the sounds were quick to go up in the flames. The pain and suffering in those cries made Nyrra laugh. The flames danced around him, but did not touch him. The scream grew louder and louder until they were suddenly silenced. Nyrra felt a euphoria that only came with the suffering of the wretched creatures.

Chapter 1: Cleaning

They had been in Kiarome for over a month. The cleanup of the city was taking longer than they had expected. Once word had run through the palace that the advisor had been killed his supporters scattered. They knew that it would only be a matter of time before someone started searching for them. In one sense it made life harder, but in another it made it easier. All they had to do was to go through the roster. Those who were no longer in the palace were assumed to be followers of the Evil One. It was hunting them down that would be the hard part. In a city as large as Kiarome there were many places for the enemy to hide so the army had set up a perimeter around the city to make sure that no one slipped out.

King Unwin was glad the have Alaric and Bern around. He respected the two men and was happy to let them make the decisions where the traitors were concerned. He felt betrayed by those who had been part of his household, but he also did not want to interrogate them. He was happy just to continue running his house and Kingdom as normal.

He blamed himself for the condition of his city. He had been enthralled by the Dark Knight Fenaroz and he allowed him to have the run of Kiarome. If he had been stronger then he would have been able to resist him, at least that's what he told himself. No matter how many times Alaric and Bern tried to convince him otherwise, he would not believe it.

The Dark Knight had taken away his will and his strength. Since its death his strength had returned, although he would always show the effects. His hair had turned grey and fine wrinkles covered his face. His moustache and goatee had also turned grey. The Dark Knight had not let him shave whilst under his control and it was one of the first things Unwin did with his freedom.

With each new traitor captured a new web of deceit was uncovered. The network of spies in Kiarome was a lot more extensive than what they had originally thought. Once captured it did not take long for them to tell all that they knew. With one Dark Knight dead and the other two gone the threat was the one in front of them. Although the fear of what the Evil One would do to them was great the imminent threat of what their captors would do was much stronger.

Sometimes Alaric thought that they were telling more than the truth. The captured felt that the more information they gave the greater chance they had of escaping a life in the dungeons. Alaric could easily see through those who were lying. As much as he didn't want to condemn them to a life in prison there were no other options. They had turned to the Evil One once before and there was no guarantee that if set free they wouldn't return. That was something that he couldn't risk happening. The suggestion was passed around that they should be put to death, but that wasn't something he was prepared to do.

Finding all the traitors in the city wasn't Alaric's only concern. As the days lengthened Alaric could feel the tug of the prophecy getting weaker and weaker. The feeling had been persistent, but it was not enough to draw him away from the city. Alaric knew that his time had not finished in Kiarome. No matter how strong the pull towards the prophecy had been the urge to remain was stronger. It was like he was the rope in a game of tug-of-war and the city was currently winning.

They would all have to leave soon enough, but they had to finish the task before them first. Alaric could not risk leaving a powerful enemy behind. He didn't think that Unwin would fall into the same trap, but he wanted to make sure. As much as he did feel empty without the prophecy he couldn't leave until the time was right.

It was a warm morning when Alaric was walking through the palace halls. He was on his way to another meeting with King Unwin. The king had insisted that Alaric be present at any major meetings. At first Alaric thought that it was an honour, but eventually he found it dull and boring. There was not much that he needed to be involved with. He thought that Unwin just liked having him there to show off to his officials. It had not taken long for Alaric's fame to reach everyone in the palace and then the city. It made it hard for him to go anywhere without being stopped. There had also been a number of assassination attempts, which in themselves made it easy to catch the rogue citizens, but it also made it very dangerous for Alaric. He wanted nothing more than to be on the road again.

Thankfully the meeting didn't last long. They discussed the latest traitors that had been captured in the last few days and what they were going to do to step up the search. Alaric did nothing but sit and listen. Unwin tried to get him involved in the conversation, but his mind was elsewhere. There was something that was bothering him. It was a feeling that had been with him ever since he woke that morning. He was glad to be out of the meeting and he wanted to speak to his old friend Bern. More to the point he wanted to speak to the spirit of Heryion who resided in Bern.

Unwin tried to speak to Alaric once the meeting was finished, but Alaric was quick to leave the room. He liked Unwin, but he knew what the King was going to ask him. It was to do with Princess Marina. Unwin's daughter, who had been spending a lot of time with Alaric. In truth Alaric enjoyed her company, but what he didn't enjoy was Unwin's questions on his intentions. He had no time to become romantically attached. There were too many things at risk for a lapse in concentration.

The princess herself seemed happy enough with the harmless flirting, and she didn't seem to want anything more. Alaric had thought about stealing a kiss, especially when she swished her raven hair back and forth in a playful manner, but he never did. It wouldn't be appropriate and he was sure Unwin would try and marry him off. The last thing he needed was a bride waiting for him or even worse following him around the Seven Kingdoms. That was enough to put any romantic thoughts out of his mind.

He found Bern in the war-room with the rest of the command group. His old friend from Arsiliac had always had a strong physique, but Alaric thought he looked more powerful than ever. His dark brown hair was slightly longer than it had been and he had started to grow facial hair.

It had been the first time that week that the command group had assembled together. General Jarwe sat at the head of the table. The Remidian General was still the commanding officer of the army, although he deferred as many decisions to Bern as possible. It had been a confusing time between Avalon and Kiarome and as much as Jarwe insisted the Bern was the rightful leader he would not accept the position. Jarwe scratched his freshly shaved head, showing only the minimum of hair, as Alaric entered. He wore a green tunic with a white dove over a wreath of maple leaves, his family crest. Alaric thought it was odd that he wasn't dressed in the livery of the Remidian Army.

To his left sat Duke Hadar a man who towered over Bern. His normally straight cut dark hair and beard had grown shaggy over the past few weeks. Despite the fact that he had retainers to look after his appearance he had refused their assistance. Since he had been investigating some of the seedier parts of the city he wanted to look the part. He didn't think if he was cleanly cut he would blend in with the other riff-raff. For the meeting he dressed in a light grey tunic with a red heart in the middle with two swords underneath, lying in opposite direction, his Ducal crest. He thought it would be a little too offensive if he wore the rags he had been in for the past week. The duke from Hondin Lel smiled when he saw Alaric enter the room. He had only seen him once since he arrived at Kiarome. The two had become friends when Alaric had been in Lel Dinion.

Next to Hadar was Lord Pernian. Pernian was the commander of the elvish component of the army. Like most elves he held his youth despite being much older than anyone else in the room. His long blond hair fell around his deep green tunic. There were no crests in the elven realms and the only other colour was a yellow trim. It was the first time he had met Alaric and he looked at the man closely, but did not acknowledge him.

Next to the elf was Captain Aimon from Entero, although no one noticed he sneered when Alaric entered the room. He was the only one in the room who wore a breastplate. There was no need for the armour, but he felt more comfortable in it. It gave him a sense of command over the others, even though his strength and physique rivalled anyone in the room. He made sure his shoulder length brown hair was freshly brushed and he looked the part of a leader.

On the other side of Jarwe were General Sorrell and his advisor Wojtek. General Sorrell, who had spent most of his adulthood in Kiarome, assisted the command group in the ways of the city. His commanding presence was undeniable and fine lines on his face showed his experience. Of all the commanders he had spent the most time in the army.

Next the Wojtek sat the two dwarves, Hulkan and Dorn. At the foot of the table sat General Bern. Bern, Alaric's oldest friend, had been given the rank of General since the battle of Avalon. He had broken the spell of the Evil One and ensured them victory. In truth it had been the spirit of Heryion who had ensured their victory, but Alaric was the only one who knew of his existence. The remainder of the command group referred to him as the entity. Even Bern did not know who he was.

Alaric sat at the spare seat between Aimon and Bern. He always felt uncomfortable sitting next to Aimon. He knew that the captain from Entero was in fact one of Nyrra's Dark Knights and that was a very disturbing thought. He wanted nothing more than to strike the Knight down, but Heryion had convinced him that it was better to keep him alive. It was a case of keep your friends close and your enemies closer. Even so Alaric didn't like being so close to the Knight. They had also decided that it was best not to inform the others. There was no telling what their reaction would be, Alaric liked that even less.

"Thank you for joining us," General Jarwe spoke first. "We have been in Kiarome for over a month without news of any attacks from the Evil One," Alaric saw Aimon flinch at the mention of his master. "One might think that this is good news, but I, on the other hand, find it quite disturbing. The soldiers are starting to become lazy and lazy soldiers can get up to quite a lot of mischief, especially this close to a city. I vote that we move the army away from the city. They have fixed the hole in the wall and the buildings that we were forced to demolish. There is nothing more productive that they can do."

"It is all well and good to move the army, but where would you have them move?" Lord Pernian asked, at little put out at what Jarwe was suggesting.

"We do not know where the Evil One will attack next. Until we know where he is hiding his army I do not think that it would be wise to move," Lord Hadar agreed with Pernian.

There was a slight rabble before Jarwe called for silence. There had been much debate about their next move amongst the group. This was the first time that it was brought up in committee and there were many opinions. Everyone wanted their opinion to be the first heard. Only Bern and Alaric remained silent. There seemed little point in talking whilst everyone was yelling at each other.

"I would like to hear what Alaric has to say." Suddenly all eyes move to Alaric.

"The time is coming soon for us all to leave. The last of the followers of the Evil One are being rounded up. Soon the city will be safe without us. For now I think that you are right Jarwe. Those who are not guarding the gates should be moved away from the city. At least a day's march I should think it will be enough to keep them out of harm's way," Alaric spoke his mind. It seemed the logical place to start.

"But where do we move them to?" Pernian re-asked his question.

"We move the army to the east," it was Bern who spoke.

All eyes quickly moved to him, waiting for him to justify his statement. Soon enough it was clear that he was not going to say anything. No one was sure whether it was Bern or the entity who had made the suggestion. Either way they all knew that when Bern made a suggestion or a command they should all listen, regardless of what they thought.

"Wouldn't that mean that we are heading toward Entero?" Aimon asked, almost too eagerly.

"I don't know yet, but east is the logical place to move the army for now," Bern replied without looking at Aimon.

Everyone was used to the vague answers and directives given by Bern, but no one really liked it. They trusted what he was telling them was the right thing, but they would still like more information. They were not in the position they were in because they simply accepted commands. Alaric was the only one who truly understood what was happening to Bern. He too had a feeling that he did not understand, but knew he had to follow.

"How long until we march?" General Sorrell asked, trying to keep the conversation moving.

Everyone was still pondering the suggestion and if they were left too long then the arguing would start again. It seemed as though Bern had made the decision and it was just a matter of accepting it.

"I do not know," Bern replied, somewhat downtrodden.

"You will be leaving by the end of the week," Alaric spoke and all eyes shifted again. "That will be enough time for you to be able to leave the city to look after itself. Unwin's strength has returned. If there are any enemies left in the city then he will be able root them out."

"You will not be travelling with us?" Jarwe's voice sounded just as surprised as everyone felt.

"For now our paths do not follow the same route, although our destination will remain the same," Alaric felt light-headed as he spoke.

"And where, pray tell, is this destination?" Aimon asked quickly.

"That I don't know exactly yet," Alaric was being just as frustrating as Bern. It was like someone was talking inside his head, although it was more of a feeling than any words.

The meeting continued in much the same way for the next hour. They were all hoping for more answers, but none were forthcoming. It was a long frustrating conversation. Eventually Jarwe called the meeting to an end. He could see, more so than everyone else, that nothing more was going to be achieved. At least they knew that they would be leaving soon. It wasn't much, but it did provide some comfort.

Once everyone had left the room Bern and Alaric remained behind. They checked to make sure no one was listening outside before they started their conversation. They were both keen to speak to one another. There had been little chance since Heryion had revealed himself and Alaric really wanted to speak with him again.

"So it seems that we shall be moving soon," Bern started the conversation.

As much as Alaric was hoping to speak with Heryion he didn't mind speaking to his old friend. The man that he had known growing up had definitely changed, but then again so had he. "You can feel it as well?"

"I have felt it for the last week. It has not been strong enough to warrant moving the army, but it's still there. It's been building over the last two days. I think that you are right we shall be moving by the end of the week," Bern explained.

Alaric didn't know how to approach the conversation with Heryion. He had promised the former small man, who had advised him through the hardest parts of his life, that he would not tell Bern the truth. He didn't like keeping secrets from his friend, but he had to trust that Heryion knew what he was doing. He didn't know his background, but he knew that Heryion had his part to play. He also knew that Heryion knew more about their current situation then he did.

"I am sure that we will know where we are to travel to when the time is right," Alaric didn't sound confident in his words.

"There is something that you are not telling me," Bern noticed the change in his tone.

Alaric really wanted to speak to Heryion first, but it seemed that he didn't have a choice. "Eldred and Alena have been taken to Jarrat," Alaric had already told Bern, but he thought it was the best way to start. "I think it's time that we set them free," he was uncomfortable speaking about his two friends. He knew that Nyrra would not be treating them with any respect. He hated to think about what torture he was putting them through.

"So it is true that you will not be travelling with us?" Bern sounded flat. He had hoped since Alaric had returned he would take control of the army. There was a strength in him that had blossomed since they had been apart. As much as Jarwe was back in the lead he knew it was only a matter of time before they started deferring decisions to him again.

"I have to leave you soon. The Dark Knight Na'garoz has the *Prophecy of the Stone*. If I am to defeat Nyrra then I need to reclaim the tome." The prophecy was deep in his thoughts.

"What about the stones?" there was a clear change in Bern's tone. Although Alaric had to look up he was sure that he was speaking with Heryion. "Have you used the Jade dagger yet?"

"No," Alaric was cautious about using the Jade dagger for the moment he wanted to limit the amount of people who knew about its existence, which was difficult considering the way Unwin had presented it to him. At least most people wouldn't know the significance of the jade stone in the dagger's hilt. If it was known that he had the *Jade Stone of Power* in his possession then the enemy would try and steal it. There was a chance the if King Unwin really knew what he had given away then he would ask for it back. Either way Alaric was happy to leave the Jade dagger safely in its chest. "I don't think that it is safe to use the dagger in the palace," Alaric had to qualify his statement.

"I know what you mean, but it is something that you should consider. The Ruby stone is out there and I have no doubt that Nyrra is searching for it. The other stones could also play a pivotal role in defeating him," Heryion gave some sage advice. "We thought that the battle was to be in *Crenallous*, but that wasn't the case. Now there is no telling how much time we have left."

"And that is exactly why I need the regain the prophecy. It will be written in there somewhere what we must do. We can't leave it in the possession of the Dark Knight for much longer. Eventually he will take it to his master," Alaric explained.

"There is no easy option Alaric," Heryion sighed. "Knowing the future will be all for naught if Nyrra gets his hands on the Ruby stone."

Heryion made a valid point and Alaric had a lot to consider and not much time to do it. He knew that if the army was to be on the march again within a week then he would have to be on the road in the next couple of days. When the army was on the move the citizens would man the walls to watch them leave, at least the Darshival component. There were rumours that King Unwin was planning some sort of festival. Alaric needed to leave in secrecy. As much as he didn't believe the Evil One's agents would see him leave he couldn't leave it to chance. The last thing he needed was for the Evil One to know where he was going. It meant that he would have to leave the rest of the Alliance in the dark. He couldn't risk Aimon finding out.

Before their meeting Alaric had made the decision to follow the prophecy instead of chasing the stones. He needed to get reassurance from it and that was the right thing to do. On the other hand Heryion made a lot of sense. If Nyrra found the Ruby stone before he did then there was nothing that he could do to win. The advice was only making his decision harder.

"I guess it couldn't hurt to get an idea of where the next stone is. Hopefully that will be the Ruby stone," Alaric agreed.

"It would make life a lot easier if we knew how to use the Jade stone to find specific stones," they still had no idea how the Jade stone worked. All they knew is that when the stone became illuminated it was pointing towards one of the other stones. There was no way to tell which stone it was, or how far away it was.

"What do you think that I should do?" Alaric sounded resigned.

"You know I can't tell you that. Only you will know which path is the right one," Heryion couldn't give him anymore advice.

"I know, but it still would be nice to get some idea that what I am doing is right," Alaric sounded completely deflated.

"Still I think that you are right. I think that we should rescue Alena and Eldred. I am sure that they are not enjoying themselves. I think that it would be better if you were with us. I have a bad feeling that Nyrra knows that we are coming," Heryion changed the subject. There seemed little point to carry on with their current conversation.

"Hopefully I will be able to meet you at Jarrat. It will take you a while to march the army that far. Once you reach Jarrat you will need to assess the situation before you attack," Alaric was glad to be speaking about something else, even if the topic was just as depressing.

"You are right. I have a feeling that this will be a much longer campaign than the one here in Kiarome," Heryion replied.

The two men thought for a moment. Both of them knew that they would soon have to part. They both had to think about things that they needed to discuss. Once Heryion left they would not be able to speak again before Alaric left. After a few minutes had passed it was Bern who spoke.

"What have you decided?" Alaric wasn't exactly sure what Bern was asking, or whether he knew that he hadn't been involved in the conversation.

"I still don't know. I can only hope that when the time is right I will know what to do." Alaric had decided that he shouldn't tell Bern the truth. It wasn't that he didn't trust his friend he just thought it was safer for everyone.

"So will you meet us in Jarrat?" Alaric looked at Bern carefully, trying to work out if he remembered any of the conversation that he had with Heryion.

"I hope so. There is more danger at Jarrat than we have faced to date. I would like to be there to help."

"I know. I can feel myself being drawn towards the city, but at the same time there is fear in my heart. The fear for what is waiting for us," Bern sounded excited more than afraid. He didn't seem to have noticed the fact that Heryion had taken control of his body.

His last statement caused Alaric to laugh out loud. It was a knee-jerk reaction and not one that he meant. Bern gave him a strange and then questioning look. Alaric went red in the face with embarrassment, although he couldn't stop laughing.

"I am sorry my old friend," Alaric spoke when he finally stopped laughing. "It's just funny how things end up. If you think a year ago we would have been sitting in your study discussing your crops and the current shipping rates."

Soon enough Bern was able to see the funny side. It was not all that long ago that the troubles of the world did not effect them. Bern's worst concern was with weevils in his grain. He stopped laughing when the reality of the situation returned. Regardless of where they had come from it was now their responsibility to make sure the Seven Kingdoms remained safe. That thought was enough to wipe away any humour.

"Yes, thank you Alaric. It is good to laugh, but we need to get back to more important things," Bern was grateful for the short interlude, but they needed to make a decision.

"I think that it is all but decided. In seven days you will lead the army towards Jarrat. You will need to make sure that the true reason why you travel remains a secret. There are only a few you can trust. There are spies with in the army and the last thing we need is for the enemy to know our plans," Alaric warned.

"I know what you mean. I will make sure that only a few know our real reason for leaving. I think I know who I can trust," Bern sounded reassured.

"Very good. Now Lord Richmond and his advisor Tancred will be joining your command group." It was a decision that would make a lot of people unhappy, no more so than the two men in question. There was no doubt that they would assume they would be travelling with Alaric. Despite their concerns they would have to assimilate into the Alliance command group.

"I don't understand. I thought they were bound to you. Wouldn't it be better if they continued to travel with you?" Bern was somewhat confused with Alaric's decision.

"They are good men. Lord Richmond ran Bellarome with a kind, but firm hand. Tancred is a wise man and will give you good advice. I must continue on by myself," Alaric explained.

"Don't get me wrong, I appreciate the addition of good, strong men." Bern thought for a moment. "Don't you think that they would be better to stay with you? I am sure that you could use someone to help you."

"I would have thought the same thing," Alaric replied. "It seems to me that I have to continue on alone. Don't ask me why because I have no idea. All I know is that when I leave Kiarome I will be leaving by myself."

"I don't think they will be too happy when they hear the news," Bern offered.

"They will listen to what I say. They won't have a choice," Alaric explained.

Before either of them could continue the conversation there was a knock on the door. The sudden sound came as a surprise to both men. Bern looked at Alaric who in turn looked back. Finally Alaric called for the door to be opened. On the other side was a young serving woman. She slowly walked into the room keeping her head down in a sign of deference.

"His majesty King Unwin has asked that you join him in the throne room," she kept her head down as she spoke, making her statement confusing.

"Which one of us does he want?" Bern asked the question.

"Why, both of you," she looked up briefly and smiled, a nervous smile, when her eyes met Bern's.

She quickly turned around and left the room. Alaric couldn't help himself. When she closed the door he burst out laughing. Bern was not happy with his reaction, but he could understand why he did it. It was an embarrassing situation, but he thought that the serving girl was a little more embarrassed then he was.

"I don't know what it is, but it seems that you have a cult following amongst the palace staff," Alaric teased.

"I don't know what you're talking about. All I am is civil to the staff. That is all," Bern's tone was defensive as he rose.

"You know exactly what I am talking about. All the single women on the King's staff want to date you. It is as obvious as the nose on your face." Alaric also rose.

"Still. I don't think that I'm the only one with a following," it was Bern's turn to tease Alaric. "The staff may like me, but what about the aristocracy?"

"Now you have me lost," Alaric didn't like where the conversation was headed as they made their way to the throne room.

"I see the ladies swoon around you when you meet with Unwin. More to the point I see how Princess Marina acts when you are around," Bern nudged Alaric in his side as he finished speaking.

"Now I know you are dreaming. There is absolutely nothing going on between the Princess and myself," Alaric was starting to go a lighter shade of red. He hoped that Bern did not see it. "She is a lovely child, but we are just friends," Alaric wished he hadn't said anything. It only made it sound worse.

"She is young indeed, but she is no child. Believe whatever you want, but there is definitely something sparking in her eyes whenever she sees you," Bern was happy that he had successfully changed the subject. "I wouldn't be surprised if you found her warming your bed one of these nights."

"That's enough!" Alaric snapped as he quickened his pace. If he had to listen to Bern's jibes then it would be for the least amount of time possible. He had to admit that he did notice Marina's attitude change whenever he walked into the room. Sometimes he caught her looking at him when she thought he wasn't looking. The thought disturbed him. It was not that she wasn't a very attractive women. In fact he thought that she was one of the most beautiful women he had ever seen. When she flicked her long black hair he almost lost his breath. Her smile could light up even the dullest of rooms.

"Alaric," Bern spoke when Alaric walked past the door to the throne room. He had been so deep in thought that he had not noticed what he was doing. "And you tell me that there is nothing going on," Bern shook his head as he opened the door.

Alaric was quick on his heels. He didn't want to be left waiting outside. He was relieved to see that Marina was not in the room. In fact the only person in the room was Unwin. It was unusual and made Alaric even more nervous than if the room had been full. He didn't know what the king had in mind, but he was sure that it was not going to be good.

"Thank you for joining me," Unwin stood from his throne when the two men entered.

"Of course, your majesty," Bern replied as Alaric looked around the room.

"Now I wish that you would call me Unwin. You two do not need to worry about formalities," Unwin had already spoken to them on the matter, but Bern still felt that he should. "At least not when we are in private."

"Why is it that you have summoned us?" Alaric asked when he was sure that there were no other surprises. He wasn't going to stand on formalities.

"I understand that you will be leaving soon," Bern was surprised that Unwin had already found out their plans. Then when he thought about it he was sure that Sorrell would keep his king informed. It really didn't matter much, it was only Alaric's movements that were to be kept secret.

"That is correct," Bern was not about to give any extra information away.

"It seems as though my daughter has it in her head that she wants to go with you," Unwin was straight to the point.

Bern looked at Alaric and almost burst out laughing and if Unwin wasn't in the room he would have. He couldn't believe what he was hearing. He thought that there was something going on between the two, even if it was one sided, now he knew it was true.

"I am sorry, but I don't quite understand," Bern was the one who replied as it was clear that Alaric was speechless.

"She is a very strong willed girl, I mean young woman. She has it in her mind that she had to repay you for saving our land. As for me I would much prefer that she stays here. She is my only child and since her mother passed away she is all that I have. When it is said and done it is my job to make sure that she is happy and I know that if she remains in Kiarome she will not be," Unwin didn't sound overly enthused with his request.

Bern looked at Alaric who shrugged his shoulders. They both knew why she had made the request. They both knew that once she was told that Alaric was not travelling with the army that she would change her mind. The only problem with that was that she would want to travel with Alaric. That was something that couldn't happen. It was not that he did not want her company on the road it was that his journey would be much to dangerous for her. He didn't want to have to worry about her safety.

"It is an unorthodox request," Bern didn't know what to say. He wanted to embarrass his friend further, but he knew that it would achieve nothing. "I do not know what she would do in the army."

"I thought much the same myself, but it was Marina who came up with her own solution," there was a wry smile on his face. "She is my daughter and is heir to the throne of Darshival. That being the case she has the right to ride at the head of the Darshivallian army. It would be the right of my son and therefore should be the right of my daughter."

There was not much Bern could do. Unwin was right. Even though the army was that of the Alliance he could not deny his request. Each of the individual armies had their own group of sub-commanders and Bern couldn't tell them how it was. The sub-commanders were paramount to controlling the different factions in the Alliance. He didn't want to lie to Unwin, but it was easy enough to qualify his response. Marina had asked to join the army, she had not asked to follow Alaric. He knew that it would be the only way to keep her from following him.

"Of course that will be fine. I am sure that it would be good for the Darshivallian component of the army to have such a figurehead." For a moment Bern remembered what had happened with Prince Hawthorne. There had to be a way that he could get around the situation happening again. "I don't know if you heard what happened with the Remidian army?" Bern would have to choose his words carefully so as not to offend him. Unwin nodded his head with an understanding look on his face. "My only concern would be if the Princess would want to lead the army away from the Alliance."

"I would make sure that she doesn't have the power to remove the Darshivallian army from the Alliance. I will assure you that you won't have the same problem with Marina." Unwin did not take offence to what Bern was suggesting.

"Then that will be fine. You can let her know that we will be leaving in seven days. She is more than welcome to ride at the front of the army if that is what she wishes." Bern hoped that he wasn't about to regret his decision.

Bern shot Alaric a look and he nodded slightly in return. The King didn't notice either gesture. Alaric knew there was only a slight risk that Marina would travel with the army when she realised that Alaric had gone. Since he was going long before the army she would realise before they left the city. At least that was what they were both hoping.

"Then we shall have a feast on the sixth night to celebrate your departure," Unwin sounded excited.

"No, thank you. I would much prefer to take it easy," Bern didn't want to be part of another feast, although he did enjoy the festivities.

"Don't be absurd." Unwin was not going to be dissuaded. "It would not be proper if I didn't give you send off that you deserved."

The king looked towards Alaric for a response. He didn't have the heart to tell the king that he would be leaving the city in two days. The least amount of people who knew what he was doing the better, especially if he didn't want Marina following him. He wanted to say yes, but again he did not want to speak for Bern. All his plans rested on his old friend keeping his secret so he didn't want to do anything that could jeopardise that.

"I suppose we could do something, but I don't want anything too extravagant." Bern resigned himself to the fact that he would have to do anything Unwin wanted if Alaric was going to leave the city unnoticed.

"I will make sure that it is as low key as possible." there was a look on Unwin's face that gave Bern no confidence at all.

Alaric was relieved when they left the throne room. He was glad that Unwin didn't suspect that he was leaving without the army. He was glad that Sorrell hadn't told him that part. He made a note that he would have to speak to Sorrell and make sure that he doesn't give away the secret. Bern also looked relieved to be out of the room. He was not overly happy with what had happened. He was sure that once Marina realised that Alaric had already left that she will realise that life in the army was not for her. With that thought in his mind he let himself smile. There were still two days for Marina to trap Alaric.

Alaric watched the expression on his friends face and shuddered slightly. He didn't know what he was thinking, but he knew that it was not good for him. He only hoped that he kept his thoughts to himself.

Chapter 2: Sneaking out

Alaric sat on his bed and looked at the box. He stared at the J engraved on its lid. Outside the sun was starting to rise. Originally he had wanted to leave during the night, but it would have been too hard to get Adelanta out of the stables, it would have caused too many rumours. Instead he had planned to visit the army or at least that is what he told Unwin. Once he was outside of the city Bern could arrange for someone to meet him with the supplies he would need for his journey. Alaric wished that he could say goodbye to everyone, but there was no chance of that.

He let his finger run over the box. It was the large J on the lid that was most intriguing. He knew that it stood for Jade, but it was the way it was carved into the wood that took his attention. He could not see any scores in the timber. It was as if the J had been pressed into the wood instead of carved. In the end all it was doing was keeping Alaric from what he was there to do. He had decided that it was time that he opened the box and at least have a look at the dagger. Once he was out of the palace he would have to be very careful about where he opened the chest. If the wrong person saw what was inside then he could get into a lot of trouble. He lost the prophecy by leaving it lying around. He was not going to make the same mistake with the Jade dagger.

Slowly he lifted the lid and as soon as he did he felt as though he could hear someone talking behind him. It was like a whisper, but he knew that there was no one there. The sound was like something brushing against the back of his head. He did his best to push the sound aside, but it still remained. It distracted him for a moment before he returned his attention to what was inside the box. The dagger looked almost perfect. The blade was a deep green and was made out of jade. It looked as though it had not been used before. The most captivating piece of the dagger was inlaid in the hilt. There was a perfect Jade stone. Something in the back of his mind was telling him to pick it up. He hadn't thought that far ahead. All he wanted to do was to look at the stone, but the desire to pick it up was almost overwhelming.

The buzzing in the back of his mind became louder. He knew that if he picked up the dagger the sound would stop, but he didn't want to give in without a fight. He was stronger than last time he had held a stone of power and he had to keep himself strong. He didn't know what was causing the buzzing, but he knew that it had something to do with the Jade stone. His experience with the Ruby stone was enough to tell him that. Slowly, but deliberately, he reached down and clasped the hilt of the dagger. Instantly the buzzing stopped. He smiled as he lifted it out of its box. The dagger felt so familiar in his hands. It was as if he had been missing a part of his body and now he was complete again.

There was something very unseemly about the situation. Slowly, at first, Alaric's eyelids started to flutter. The movement was involuntary. There was nothing that he could do to stop it, not that he tried really hard. Something was happening and he wanted to see what it was. He didn't feel as though his life was in danger. Eventually his eyes rolled up into his head until only the whites of his eye remained. He was still standing. He was completely rigid and, besides the eye flickering, completely motionless.

Suddenly Alaric was standing in a perfect field. The grass licked at his ankles as it swayed in the cool breeze. Small flowers popped up here and there. There was a sweet smell in the air. Alaric could not place the aroma, but it was pleasing to his nose. The situation was odd, but Alaric didn't seem to notice. The place was like paradise. He closed his eyes and took a deep breath before opening them again a looked around.

As he scanned the field his eyes locked on a solitary figure. At first it was too far away for him to work out who or what it was. Each time his eyes blinked the figure came closer and closer. It wasn't until she was right in front of him that Alaric realised that it was a women. Not only was she a woman, but she was the most beautiful woman he had ever seen. He also noticed that she was completely naked. Her long, curly, blonde hair hung down almost completely covering her breasts. Alaric took a moment to look her up and down, even though he knew that it was not the correct thing to do. When his eyes returned to her face she was smiling warmly. Her green eyes cut through him and he instantly felt embarrassed at what he had done, but the feeling quickly faded.

There was something about her that was very calming. He suddenly felt self-conscious as he looked down at himself, then he realised that he too was completely naked. He was about to try and cover himself when he realised that his naked body was not unattractive. He was covered with muscles, but they were not too overpowering. A lot of them had grown since he had left Arsiliac. He smiled as he looked at himself, before he realised what he was doing. Again he felt self-conscious and he didn't think that it was appropriate that he spend so much time looking at himself. He hoped that the woman standing before him didn't think that he loved himself.

"Hello Alaric," she spoke for the first time. "I am so glad that you could join me here," her voice was soft and sweet. It had a musical tone that filled his heart with joy.

"Where are we?" the question sounded appropriate, although he did not know why.

"We are somewhere private. No one will be able to hear our conversation," she was still smiling warmly as she spoke.

He looked around the field. There was no one in sight. Alaric did not know why, but he felt somewhat reassured by her statement. It seemed silly, but he was glad that no one could listen to what they were saying. He was also glad that no one could see the two of them naked. There was something very rewarding about being close to the mystery woman. She was looking at him like she was waiting for him to speak, but there was nothing that he wanted to say. As he remained quiet she seemed to get annoyed.

"I'm sorry, I don't know what to say." It was the truth.

"You are not at all what I was expecting," she took a step backwards and looked at him strangely. "I guess you are who I am supposed to meet." She gave a peculiar look that was more for herself than him. "What am I saying? I wouldn't be here if I wasn't supposed to be."

"I am sorry, but I still don't understand what is happening." He felt as though he should know. He knew deep down that something was off with the situation. "Would you please explain it to me?"

The smile returned to her face. Alaric wanted to know her name, but he also knew that he could not ask the question. It seemed like such a simple thing to do, but the words would not pass his lips. All he could do was to wait for her response.

"Time is running out," she paused as the words registered. "Nyrra is getting very close to finding Ruby."

The naming of the Evil One sent a chill down Alaric's spine. He visibly shivered as it happened. He wished that she had not mentioned him or the stone. Suddenly the field became duller. The grass now looked limp and the flowers looked faded. He was suddenly very afraid.

"Do not worry yourself, as I told you before, we are completely alone here. No one can touch this place," her words brought reassurance to his heart. "As I was saying, time is running out for you. If Nyrra finds Ruby before you do then all is lost."

He didn't know why, but he was unsure what she was saying was true. The words made sense inside his head, but there was something in her tone that made him suspicious. The feeling quickly faded away as she continued to speak. She was too beautiful to be a danger to him and he couldn't believe she was giving him false information.

"You must find Ruby first. There is a new world of pain if Nyrra finds Ruby before you," her voice was grave as she repeated her warning, but the warm smile remained on her face.

"I know that I have to find the Ruby stone," she seemed to cringe as Alaric mentioned the stone. He noticed, or at least thought that he did, and found it very strange. "I also have to find the *Prophecy of the Stone*. It is in the hands of one Nyrra's Dark Knights and I need to get it back."

"Ah yes. I sensed the Dark Knights have risen. I believe that it is Na'garoz who has the prophecy," she mused, as if to herself. "The prophecy is no never-mind. There is nothing that you can do with prophecy that you cannot do with Ruby. With his power you will be able to defeat Nyrra and all his servants."

Alaric thought that it was odd that she said 'his power', but he put it down to a slip of the tongue. There were more important matters to be dealing with than a simple mistake. The thought was already starting to fade from his mind as he looked into her deep green eyes. He didn't know what he was getting so worried about. He knew something had happened, but he did not remember what it was.

"You must rescue all seven of us," she was starting to become flustered. The smile left her face. There was a touch of panic in her voice. She quickly realised what she was doing and settled herself. Alaric had already forgotten what she had said before he had a chance to question it. "There is not much time left. The world is moving very quickly and there is no time to sit and wait. You have already spent too much time in Kiarome. The world is not waiting for you to make your next move."

"There was nothing that I could do," Alaric became very defensive. "I had to wait until I knew where to go next. Not only that but I had to help rout out the Evil One's agents. I could not leave so many enemies behind me. Now I can leave knowing that the city and the kingdom are safe."

"There are more important things at risk than just a city that more than likely won't be there in another thousand years. Kingdoms come and go with the sands of time, but if you lose then there will be more than a millennium of pain," her words were strict, as if she was speaking to a naughty child.

The thought returned to Alaric that she could not be trusted, yet there was sage advice in her words. His decision was not getting any easier. He knew that she was pushing him towards finding the stones and if he wasn't completely sure then her next comment sealed the deal.

"You have to forget about the prophecy. That book will lead you astray. You have to find the others. You must find the other six. It is the only way that you will be able to defeat Nyrra," she was more forceful this time.

"I will do what I can. I have the Jade stone now," as he spoke she did the strangest thing. At the mention of the Jade stone she screamed out loud. The sound echoed throughout the field. Alaric thought that his eardrums were going to burst. He didn't know why she was so upset, but he knew that it was something he had said. He wanted nothing more than to place his arms around her and comfort her, but he somehow knew that it would be inappropriate.

"I must apologise." The woman returned to her original serene state. "I don't know what came over me. Please continue with what you were saying."

"I…" Alaric couldn't remember what he was going to say. He knew that it was something important, but he couldn't remember what it was. "I don't know what I was going to say."

"That's okay, my dear. I am sure that it will come to you in time. Now speaking of time I think that ours is almost over," she almost cooed the words. "Now close your eyes."

Alaric didn't know what she was doing, but he couldn't resist. Slowly he closed his eyes. He trusted her completely and knew that she would do nothing bad. Slowly he felt her lips touch his. Suddenly there was a rush around him. When he opened his eyes he was back in his room in the palace. The Jade dagger was safely tucked away in its box. There was an impatient knock on the door, as if it was not for the first time.

"Enter," Alaric called out, a little dazed.

The door opened and there was a young man on the other side. He had a strange look on his face. "I am sorry, my Lord. I heard some strange sounds coming from inside and thought that you might be in trouble," he looked around the room as if expecting to see someone else.

"No, I am fine," Alaric acted as though nothing had happened, not that he knew what had happened anyway.

"But I heard," he sounded confused.

"Now if that is all," Alaric gave him a stern look.

Before he could leave the room Alaric called out. "What time of day is it?"

"It is mid-morning," the young man replied before quickly shutting the door. He had recognised the look on Alaric's face and wanted to be gone before he got into more trouble.

Alaric softly cursed to himself. He wanted to already be on the road. It would not be long before the others would start looking for him. He wanted to leave without speaking to the others. It would be easier for everyone that way. They would not be able to ask him to stay and Alaric would not have to make up an excuse why he could not. He also wanted to leave before Marina had a chance to find out. He had no doubts that she would try and follow him if she knew that he was leaving. The thought of having company was pleasant, but he knew that he could not have a princess travel with him. It would be too dangerous.

He remembered what must have been a dream. The thoughts were hazy inside his head. He didn't know how he could have fallen asleep standing upright. The last thing he could remember was picking up the Jade dagger. Then everything changed. He remembered the perfect field of grass and flowers. He remembered the beautiful woman, but he couldn't truly remember any of the conversations he had with her. All he could remember was that he needed to find the other six stones. That thought was thick in his mind.

Suddenly the door was pushed open without anyone knocking. Alaric spun round to see who it was and he was relieved to see Bern walk into the room. He was somewhat surprised to see him too and it was clear on his face.

"I was told that you were still here, but I had to see for myself. Why haven't you left? You know that sneaking out of the palace is going to be difficult, let alone leaving the city," Bern was speaking quickly, as if he was flustered.

"You don't want to know," it was Alaric's only answer as he didn't know himself what had happened.

Bern shook his head. It was not the response he was looking for. He thought about pushing harder for information, but there was no point. What was important was what Alaric was going to do next. The situation had become much more serious.

"So, what are you going to do now?" Bern sounded exhausted.

"I have to leave. If you can get Adelanta packed and out of the palace then I know a way I can leave undetected. I will be able to sneak out without anyone knowing," Alaric explained.

"What excuse could I have to take Adelanta out of the stables, fully loaded for a journey?" Bern didn't sound convinced.

"Tell them to mind their own business," Alaric snapped.

"You know that won't do. This city is full of gossip. That kind of information would be very valuable to a stable boy. It will not be long before the entire palace knows what we are doing. It will be just as bad if everyone thinks that I am leaving. The fact that I am taking your horse and you are missing means it won't be long before they realise what is really happening," Bern made perfect sense.

Alaric sat down at the table and lowered his head. He knew that it was not going to be an easy task getting out of the palace. He also knew that there was a way for it to happen. His original ruse of inspecting the army would only have worked if he had left at first light. By now the army would be continuing their hunt for the enemy. Suddenly an idea came to him.

"All you have to do is say that you have are going to spend some time with the army. That should be enough to keep the gossips from spreading too much information," Alaric seemed pleased with himself. "It makes more sense for you to be seeing the army at this time of day than me."

Bern thought about the new plan for a moment. At first he didn't think it was a good idea, but the more he thought about it the more he liked it. It was simple and effective. No one would doubt that he would want to spend some time with the army. He had been in the palace for over a month and spent no time with the soldiers.

"What is my excuse for taking your horse," Bern replied, not completely sure Alaric's plan was going to work.

"That is easy. Adelanta has been stuck in the stable for most of the time we have been here. He will be very keen to get out and stretch his legs. That is all that you have to say. You are taking him for some exercise," Bern cursed himself for not seeing the obvious.

"That makes sense. What about your supplies?" That was the biggest hurdle they needed to overcome. "You'll need a couple of pack animals and a good amount of supplies." Without knowing where Alaric was going he had to assume there would be none.

"Let me worry about that. I don't think I'll be able to take any pack animals with me. It will probably be better as I'll be able to travel faster since Na'garoz has a large head start." The feeling that he needed to find the stones disappeared as he spoke to Bern about his original plan. He could feel the prophecy to the south and there was an undeniable tug in its direction.

"I guess that all you have to do is pack your bags and we will get moving," Bern smiled.

Alaric nodded to the corner of the room. Leaning against the wall was a small pack. Sitting next to it was a bow, a quiver of arrows, a sword, a bedroll and another small bag filled with coins.

"You are travelling light," Bern commented when he saw the size of what he was taking.

"I don't need much. A change of clothes and some dried food. I will be able to hunt for most of my meals whilst I am on the road. I have enough money for when I reach towns and once that dwindles all I need to do is find a game of dice." There was an evil smile on his face.

"You don't want to get caught cheating at dice," Bern warned. "You will be hung from the nearest tree."

Alaric laughed at his warning. "Don't fear. I won't get caught and if I do I know how to look after myself."

Bern was not satisfied with the answer, but he knew that there was no point in arguing. There was nothing else he could do. Alaric had made up his mind. He knew that his old friend could defend himself, but he wasn't sure if he could defeat a mob of angry townsfolk.

The first thing he picked up was his sword. He felt much better with it hanging in its sheath from his belt. He then returned to where a black cloak was hanging on a wall. He dressed himself in the cloak with the hood hanging down his back. When he left his room he would pull the hood over his head. As much as it would look odd he didn't want anyone to recognise him. With a little luck he would just get some strange looks and no one would stop him. Once he was out of the palace grounds he would be able to relax.

"Now I think you are going a little too far," Bern commented when Alaric was dressed in the robe. "You will look too suspicious walking through the palace grounds dressed in that robe. It is too warm outside to be dressed in such a way."

"Be that as it may it will look even more suspicious if they see me with my sword. Once I am outside of the palace I will be able to use the cloak to blend in with the citizens," Alaric explained.

"Why don't you let me take your sword, as I am taking everything else?" Bern thought that was the logical way to do it.

"I don't think our little ruse will work if you have my sword. Everything thing else is believable, even if it is a bit of a stretch. No one will believe that you are taking my sword for a walk," Alaric explained.

"You're right, I didn't think about that," Bern sounded ashamed.

"That's alright," Alaric took the box from the table as he spoke.

"Do you want me to take that?" Bern asked, taking a step towards the table.

"No," Bern replied instantly, almost too quickly.

Bern retreated a couple of steps and raised his hands. He had known Alaric long enough to be able to recognise his moods, even if he had changed since they had left their hometown. There was a strange look in his eyes. It was only there for a moment, but it worried Bern. He knew what effect the *Stones of Power* could have on people. He hoped that Alaric was strong enough to control whatever urges were possessing his body.

"Sorry, but I will not let the dagger out of my sight," Alaric tried to explain. "It is not that I don't trust you, but I lost the prophecy and…" suddenly he remembered what the woman in his dream had said and he wasn't so sure he was doing the right thing.

"What is it?" Bern asked when he didn't continue with what he was going to say.

"Never mind. It is just a decision that I have to make, but one that I can make once I am on the road," Alaric was now unsure of his course. He had to decide whether the prophecy was more important than the stones.

"Good, then I think it's time we get you out of the city," Bern's voice was chipper.

Alaric nodded his head. He tied the box securely to his belt. He had to adjust his cloak a little so the box could not be seen. Although it wasn't comfortable wearing the box he could not just carry it around. Bern watched him carefully and gave him a nod when the box was completely hidden. He wasn't sure if his plan was going to work, but they had no other option. He let Alaric leave the room first before he called for a pageboy to carry his things to the stables. The boy would think that it was odd that Bern's things were in Alaric's room, but he didn't think that it would cause too much gossip. He was sure it would cause less than if he was carrying his own bags through the palace.

Alaric didn't get too far before he was stopped by a sweet voice calling from the hallway behind him. Alaric froze where he stood. The voice made his heart skip a beat. Not only because it was the one voice he didn't want to hear, but also because of its beauty. Slowly he turned around, but not before he replaced his look of horror with a smile.

"Where are you going?" although it was an innocent enough question Alaric became suddenly self-conscious.

"Just going out for a walk," Alaric tried to contain himself.

"Good. I was just about to go for a walk myself," Marina wrapped her arms and his right arm and started down the corridor.

There was nothing he could do. He was firmly stuck in her grip and he would have to be too forceful to get out of it. On the other hand he was happy to feel her touch. They had been spending a lot of time together when Alaric was not involved with state business. He had come to enjoy her company even though he knew that they could not take their relationship any further.

"So I hear that we will be leaving at the end of the week," she spoke as they walked towards the palace gardens.

"I wish that you would reconsider your decision."

She smiled sweetly at him and skipped softly for a couple of steps. "You know that my mind's made up. I don't know why, but I am draw to you," she blushed slightly as she realised what she said sounded like. "I mean, I feel as though I have to be with you," her words were only getting her into more trouble. "You know what I mean," she had gone a bright shade of crimson.

Alaric chuckled softly to himself. He knew exactly what she meant, but he was happy to see her embarrassed. She was very cute and none so more than when she was blushing. In some ways he was disappointed that she would not be travelling with him. She would definitely make life interesting. What he was about to embark on was too dangerous for her and he couldn't risk her life.

"What are you thinking about?" she asked, trying to change the subject.

"I am not looking forward to what is ahead of me," he spoke truthfully as they walked out of the palace. There was something about Marina that made him compelled to divulge more information than he wanted.

"That's alright. You know that I will be there to help you," she gripped his arm that little tighter as she spoke.

As they walked through the gardens Alaric almost forgot why he was there. When he remembered he knew that he had to get rid of Marina. It was not going to be an easy task since they were outside. It was something he should have done whilst they were still inside the palace. He led her to a vacant bench and offered her a seat. The gap in the wall was on the other side of the garden. If he could make up an excuse to leave her there then he would be able to escape. The only hard part was working out why he should leave.

"Would you like something to drink?" he asked after she was seated. He remained standing.

"That would be lovely. I will call for a servant," she looked around the garden to try and find a serving woman who she knew would not be too far away.

"Don't be silly. I have legs of my own. I will get it for you," Alaric tried to sound as casual and chivalrous as possible.

"Okay," she looked at him strangely, but then found his offer to be very sweet. "I will be waiting impatiently for your return."

"I will be back as soon as I can," he didn't like to lie to her, but there was nothing else he could do. It was the only way he could get away from her and Bern would be waiting for him.

His heart pounded in his chest as he walked away. He knew that she would be watching him as he walked back towards the palace. There was only one chance for him to escape and that was when he reached a small group of bushes. He would be hidden from her sight. From there he would have to be very careful to reach the hole in the palace wall. The garden was relatively empty which, although it made him more conspicuous, added to his advantage. There would be more chance of him disappearing with fewer eyes on him.

When he was sure that he was out of sight he started for the wall. There were a number of times when Marina would be able to see him. He moved quickly and carefully when he was out in the open. As he came into view he could see that she was still watching the place where he had disappeared. She kept her gaze on that spot, waiting for his return. He felt bad and for a moment thought about returning to her. She was really a beautiful young woman and he didn't like hurting her. He knew that she would be upset when he didn't return, but he was glad that she was not looking around the garden. The most important thing was for him to escape unnoticed. She would realise, in time, that he was doing to right thing by her.

It was a nervous walk to the palace wall. When he finally reached it he again had to make sure that no one was watching him. When he was sure he pulled the hood over his head and slipped into the bushes. The heat inside the bushes was much more intense than that of the garden and soon enough he had broken out in a sweat. He had expected that it would not be comfortable in the cloak, but he had hoped it would be a while before he started sweating. He didn't know when he was going to be able to bathe again and it was not a good start.

Once he was on the other side of the palace wall and out of the bushes it was much more pleasant, although it was more uncomfortable than the palace gardens. The city air was dusty and stale. There was no breeze blowing, not that Alaric would be able to feel the wind through his cloak. He kept the hood over his head as he walked through the streets to his meeting place. There was a small tavern near the Eastern gate where they were going to meet. He would have preferred to meet Bern outside the gates, but he couldn't think of an excuse for him to be outside without his horse. Once he was out of the city it didn't really matter who knew he had left. He would be able to get far enough away before word reached the palace.

No one noticed him as he walked through the streets. The black cloak hid his appearance. Even though he was sure that he was clear he couldn't help but look over his shoulder as he walked and he couldn't shake the feeling that someone was following him. He was only being silly, but he kept looking just to be on the safe side. With the hood covering his face he was able to watch the people around without them knowing it. No one looked as though they were taking any notice of him.

It wasn't until he reached the tavern before he could relax a little. He saw Bern waiting out the front with Adelanta. The horse seemed excited to see him. The white stallion flicked his head and stamped his front feet. Bern stroked his neck to settle him as Alaric approach. Bern was glad to see that Alaric had made it safely. It had been a tense wait. He looked behind Alaric as he walked towards him to make sure that he had not been followed.

"Thank you Bern," Alaric said as he approached.

"Are you sure that you're doing the right thing?" he asked as he handed over Adelanta's reins.

"I don't know, but I am sure that I would know if I was not. I think you already know that," Alaric knew that Bern was only asking the question the keep up appearances.

Bern knew the answer to his question before he had asked it. He knew that Alaric followed the same feelings that he did. He didn't know why, but he also knew that if they were doing the wrong thing he would know about it. It was reassuring as much as it was frustrating.

"When do you think I will see you again," it was his old friend, not the General, speaking.

"I'm not sure, but I have a feeling that we will meet outside of Jarrat. I think that you will need my assistance to rescue Eldred and Alena. There is something waiting for us in Jarrat and I don't think that it is going to be pleasant," Alaric's words were ominous.

Bern had to admit to himself that he knew what Alaric was saying. He had also been getting a feeling that there was something unpleasant waiting for them. He didn't know what it was, but he knew that it was something dangerous. That aside there was nothing else they could do. They had to go to Jarrat. They both knew that the city was under the control of the Evil One, much in the same way that Kiarome had been, but there was something extra waiting for them and only time would tell.

"Well I hope that is sooner rather than later," Bern shook his hand and then made his way back to the palace.

Alaric was sad to watch him go, but they couldn't remain in front of the tavern for much longer. People would start to notice them the longer they waited. There was nothing left for Alaric to do. He wasn't too nervous about leaving the city. At worst he would be able to tweak the guards' minds to let him leave. Adelanta was pleased to be walking through the streets with Alaric. He had missed his owner. Alaric chose not to ride the white stallion. He would wait until they were out of the city. He would be more noticeable if he was on the animal's back.

As he expected there was a large queue of people waiting to leave the city. Since the crackdown of those who were allowed in and out it was a common sight. There was no way that he would be able to wait at the back of the line. The way it was moving he would be surprised if those of the back of the line would reach the gate by nightfall, let alone be allowed out. He tried to his best to keep avoid eye contact as he led Adelanta to the front of the line. He received a few curses, but he kept his head down and ignored them.

"You!" a commanding voice called out before he was halfway down the line.

Alaric kept his head down and continued. He was hoping that the guard was not talking to him, although he knew that was not the case. No one else would dare attempt to cut in line. The guards were very strict and escorted any offenders to the cells for the night.

"I wouldn't take another step if I was you," Alaric paused and looked up. He didn't want to start any trouble. "That's better. Now I think you should turn around and go to the back of the line."

Alaric thought about opening the hood and showing his face, but he doubted that the guard knew who he was. If he did that then there was a risk that someone else would recognise him. He did not have time to waste. He would have to use magic to get through this situation.

"I need to leave the city. There is no reason not to let me go to the front of the line," Alaric's magic was subtle. No one would know what he was doing.

The guard seemed confused. He knew that he should not let the man in front of him continue, but he did not know why. All he wanted to do was to let the man pass and then continue on his way. Once he reached the gate he was someone else's problem. It was that thought that made the decision for him.

"Carry on then. I am sure you will not get the response you are after once you reach the gate."

The crowd lined up waiting to reach the gate could not believe what they were hearing. Instantly the cry came up by the many people trying to jump the queue. The guards were berated by almost everyone who was within earshot. Alaric slipped away before the guard realised what he had done. The guard would not be given a moments peace for the next hour or so.

Alaric chuckled to himself as he continued along the line. He didn't mean for the guard to receive abuse from the people waiting in the queue, but could not help but find the situation humorous. The funny side quickly left him. The poor guard would not be able to rest for a long time and he was only doing his job. In fact he was only doing the job that Alaric had suggested to King Unwin.

The thought of the guard left his mind when he reached the front of the line. There was a merchant arguing with one the guards. Behind him he had a wagon and a number of soldiers. The merchant, a man who had seen too many dinners, was red in the face. He was not happy with the treatment he had received. Alaric continued to lead Adelanta passed the merchant and the guards. He was almost through the gate when he was stopped by a dozen armed men.

"Where do you think you're going?" the lead guard asked.

"I mean no trouble. All I want to do is leave the city. I am a traveller by nature and have been locked up in the city for too long." Alaric hoped that he was able to speak his way out without using magic. One guard was easy, but twelve would take a lot more energy. He had no doubts that he could do it, but he was unsure whether he was able to mask all the residual energy. Although Tancred couldn't use magic he had an uncanny knack of being able to feel it. If Lord Richmond's advisor felt the energy then he would know that Alaric was out of the palace.

"No one leaves the city without the appropriate paperwork. The city is crawling with evil and who is to say that you are not one of them?" The guard lowered his pike until the tip was no more than a foot in front of Alaric's face. The gesture was definitely meant to be threatening.

Alaric found the move to be needlessly aggressive. He could see instantly that there would be no reasoning with the man. His first thought was to reach for his sword, but that would draw too much attention and there was a good chance one of the other guards would skewer him. He would have to use magic again to get his way and hope that he only needed to convince the one guard.

"I am not an agent of evil." There was a subtle ripple in the air, which no one but Alaric noticed. "There is no reason to keep me in the city. It would be just as easy if you let me pass."

The Captain of the Guard thought for a moment before he turned to one of his lieutenants. "What do you think soldier?"

Alaric quickly cast a second spell with the question. He couldn't risk one of the soldiers refusing him entrance. Since he had the upper hand he needed to keep it. If the soldiers turned on him then things would get nasty very quickly.

"I don't think that he is any threat to anyone. I don't think that there is any reason to keep him locked up in the city," the lieutenant replied, a glazed expression appeared on his face. No one noticed Alaric's lips moving at the same time.

"Very well then. On your way," the guards stood back and let Alaric lead Adelanta through the Eastern gates.

Once he was outside the city Alaric didn't waste any time in mounting the white stallion. Both rider and horse were happy. Adelanta had missed having Alaric on his back. The elven horse liked him. He pranced for a few steps to indicate his mood before settling into a light trot. He knew that Alaric wanted to be away from the city as quickly as possible, without looking too suspicious. They were both glad to be on the road again.

They had not travelled far before Alaric could feel the pull of the prophecy. It was somewhere out in front of him, but he wasn't sure exactly where it was. He had a feeling that he should be recovering the prophecy before he started looking for the stones. Before he could make a final decision another thought entered his mind. He should be looking for the stones and not worrying about the prophecy. He knew at some stage he would have to stop and check the Jade stone, but for the moment he needed to get away from the city. Any delay could cost him.

At mid-afternoon Alaric stopped by a small grove of trees. There was a small brook which ran through the middle which gave Adelanta a chance to drink and nibble on some grass. Alaric rested against a tree and opened his pack to find something to eat. He looked at the brook and wished that it was bigger so he could wash off the filth of the city. He would do his best regardless once he had finished eating.

Suddenly he realised that there was someone coming up from behind. He heard the sound of footsteps and horse hooves approaching through the grove. Alaric waited a moment before jumping to his feet and drawing his sword. He didn't know who had followed him, but he was not going to take any chances. When he saw who it was his heart dropped and danced at the same time.

Chapter 3: A Surprise Visit

"What are you doing here?" Alaric asked in surprise.

"I think you should lower your sword first. I would hate for you to skewer me by mistake." The smile didn't leave Marina's face.

Alaric blushed slightly when he realised that he still had his sword levelled at her. He quickly sheathed it before regaining his composure. The surprise was still clear on his face. He was sure that she had not seen him sneak out of the palace. There was no reason why she should be standing before him.

"I don't understand," Alaric started again. "What are you doing here?"

Marina led her beige mare towards the brook where Adelanta was drinking. The stallion seemed more interested in the new arrivals than Alaric. He watched the two approach before continuing to drink. The mare seemed a little nervous around the elven horse, a little different to her owner. Marina gently stroked Adelanta's mane before returning to Alaric. To Alaric's surprise the stallion didn't shy away from her like he did with anyone else who tried to touch him.

"You of all people should understand this situation." All Alaric could do was give her a confused look. "I had a feeling that you would be leaving today. Why do you think that I found you in the hallway? I already had my horse saddled and my bags packed ready to go. I just wanted to see if you were going to say goodbye."

Alaric felt a little hurt with what she was insinuating. "I couldn't say goodbye. It is important that no one knows that I have left. Now I guess that it doesn't matter."

"You really don't know me at all." It was Marina's turn to feel hurt, although she knew that he didn't really mean it. "I left my father a note that he will receive in the next couple of days, but by then we will be too far away for anyone to catch us."

Alaric let out a deep breath. There was a reason Marina was with him. He couldn't for the life of him work out why, but he knew she was meant to be there. Even since he had left the palace he had a feeling that he was missing something. Since she had arrived the feeling had completely disappeared. He only hoped they were doing the right thing. He didn't know if he could live with himself if anything happened to her and that was a dangerous thought. The thought was both exciting and disturbing.

"I guess there is nothing I can say," Alaric resigned himself to the fact that there was no arguing with her.

"It wouldn't matter. You could try to leave me again, but I will find you. If we are meant to be together there is nothing you can do to stop it." Marina continued to smile. She was very pleased with herself.

Alaric only half heard her words. There was something else plaguing his mind. The urge to check the Jade dagger was growing inside him, but he didn't what Marina to know what it was. As far as she was concerned it was just a pretty dagger that had been her family's legacy for a long time. For the moment he had to suppress the urge and continue on towards the prophecy.

"Where do we go from here?" Marina asked as Alaric stared at the wooden box on the ground in front of him.

"That is the burning question," Alaric's eyes didn't leave the box as he spoke. Despite his decision not to open it he could not shake the urge that he should.

"Do you want me to do it," hearing Marina's voice caused Alaric to snap out of his reverie.

"Sorry! What?" Alaric didn't understand the question

"You're staring at the box like whatever is inside might jump out and bite you if you open it. I know it's a pretty dagger, but it won't hurt you. I was just asking if you wanted me to open it."

"Don't ever touch this box," Alaric spoke harsher than what wanted to. "Sorry, but this is very important."

Marina took a step back and watched the box closely. She didn't understand why Alaric was getting so upset. The Jade dagger had been in her family for as long as she could remember. She had only seen it once before the day that it was given to Alaric. She couldn't see any reason why Alaric would be so protective of it.

Alaric returned his attention to the box. He wanted to hide it away in one of his packs, but he could not bring himself to move. The urge to open the lid became ever stronger and he knew that he couldn't resist. In the end he closed his eyes and let his hands do all the work. The familiar buzz in the back of his head returned when he lifted the lid. He opened his eyes to see the dagger resting comfortably at the bottom of the box. He made no further movement to pick it up. Picking up the box he hoped that he would not need to grasp the dagger for the stone to work. Despite his hopes he knew that he was going to have to pick it up and slowly he did so.

Suddenly a rush of power scorched through his body. He stiffened for a moment before he returned to normal. The movement shocked Marina, but she remained silent. She didn't know what was happening. When his eyes opened again Alaric looked down at the stone. There was a gentle glow in its centre. He was pointing it due east. When he moved it toward the north the stone lost any light, but when he moved it to the south the glowing intensified. It was at its strongest when it pointing almost due south.

"What does this mean?" Marina was in awe at the dagger.

Alaric quickly returned the blade to its box and shut the lid. When the lid was safely closed he breathed a sigh of relief before turning to Marina, as if he didn't hear her question. She noticed the look and re-asked it. Alaric wasn't sure if he should tell her the truth. In the end he figured that it would be safer for both of them if he told her what was happening.

"It is pointing to one of the other *Stones of Power*," he explained slowly.

"I don't think that I know what you are talking about," Marina was just as confused, if not more so, than before.

"I will have to explain to you later. Now we have to be back on our way," Alaric called to Adelanta who came to his master.

Marina wanted more answers, but she didn't want to hold them up. It was clear that Alaric wanted to be on the move again. She called her mare, but she didn't obey the same way as Adelanta. She was a little embarrassed, but Alaric didn't seem to notice. He was already riding out of the grove without waiting for her. Marina huffed as she mounted, but there was no reaction from Alaric. She wasn't even sure if he heard it and she scolded herself for acting like a spoilt princess. It might have worked with her father, but it seemed that Alaric wouldn't fall for it.

Alaric didn't wait for Marina. Once he was ready to go he started out of the grove. He had decided that until he knew exactly where the Na'garoz had taken the prophecy he would follow where the Jade stone pointed. For the moment they seemed to be going in the same direction and he was sure if he was making a mistake he would know about it.

Marina watched Alaric for a moment as she left the grove. He was riding erect in his saddle as if he had a purpose, although she thought that he looked somewhat disturbed. She wasn't sure what had happened in the grove when he touched the Jade dagger, but she knew that it was important. There was something more to the Jade dagger than just a royal artefact.

"Why are we travelling south?" It was not the question she wanted to ask, but she thought it was a good place to start.

Alaric kept his sight in front of him. It was not going to be easy explaining what they were doing, especially since he didn't fully understand it himself. He wished that he had Heryion to speak to, or Eldred. They were both very wise and always seemed to have the answers.

"One of the Dark Knight's has stolen the *Prophecy of the Stone*." Alaric decided that the explanation would pass the time. As much as he tried to concentrate on the prophecy the tug wasn't growing any stronger.

All he knew what that both the prophecy and a *stone of power* was somewhere to the south. "The *Prophecy of the Stone* is the one true prophecy."

"If it is the true prophecy then it should have told you that I was coming with you," Marina stuck her tongue out as she spoke.

Alaric wasn't in the mood for her playful attitude, he was quickly beginning to regret his decision not to send her back to Kiarome. There was little chance that she would have left him, but at least she would have known not to push him. He took a deep breath and settled himself before he continued. There was no point in making the situation worse.

"The prophecy isn't that easy to read. It is written in riddles and code," Alaric did his best to explain.

"Then why are we chasing after it?" Marina sounded confused. "If you can't understand what it says then it seems pointless trying to recover it. Let the Dark Knight have it and we can rejoin the army. Surely it's more important for us to be there?" It made sense inside her head.

Alaric wanted nothing more than to kick the flanks of Adelanta and leave Marina behind. The elven stallion would easily out run Marina's mare. Again he took a deep breath to calm himself before speaking.

"There are passages that I can decifer, but it seems only when I need to. Not only that, but the prophecy is ever changing, so there is no telling what insights might be written there now." Alaric waited for her to interupt, but there was no jibe from her. "But beyond that I'm connected to the prophecy. Just like you knew you were to follow me out of the city today I too know that I must find the prophecy."

The last part was the first part that made sense to Marina, even if she didn't really understand it. The feeling that she had to leave that morning was uncontrollable. Even if she didn't want to travel with Alaric she didn't think there was anything she could do to stop it.

There was something in his explanation that made Alaric's realise what he should do. He needed to get the prophecy back, there was no doubt in his mind. His meeting with the strange lady had dissappeared with the thoughts of chasing the stones. He would keep checking the Jade dagger from time to time, but his main focus was recovering the great tome.

They were travelling in open grassland in the southern part of Darshival. There were a number of small hills, but mainly the land was flat. All in all it was a pleasant afternoon for a ride. A cool breeze was blowing in from the west. Alaric had removed his black coat and was now wearing a loose fitting shirt and his riding pants. Marina was similarly dressed. She wore a more fitted shirt and riding pants. Alaric could not help but notice the subtle colouring on her face, when he eventually looked at her. There was something about her that made Alaric's heart flutter.

When he finished speaking he wasn't sure if Marina understood any better than before. She seemed to have some understanding and that was the main thing. She remained quiet after he finished. Alaric was happy enough with that. Alaric didn't think he could answer anymore of her questions. There would be time for talking later, but for the moment he just wanted to concentrate of the prophecy. The sensation was so subtle that he couldn't feel it when he was talking.

They rode at a trot for most of the afternoon. Adelanta kept the pace more so than Alaric. The white stallion knew how fast Marina's mare could travel and despite the fact that Alaric wanted to travel faster Adelanta wasn't going to push the mare any further. No matter what he did Adelanta would not go any faster and eventually he stopped trying. He knew well enough that when Adelanta didn't want to do something he wouldn't.

The open land gave them no shelter for their camp. Alaric kept riding past dusk and into nightfall, but in the end Adelanta chose where they were camping for the night. He could tell that the mare was struggling to continue the pace. Again Alaric wasn't happy, but again he submitted to Adelanta's will.

"That is a strange horse you have there," Marina spoke after Alaric had lit a small fire. He had taken some twigs from and small logs from the grove. Adelanta didn't seem too concerned with the extra weight.

Adelanta flicked his ears as he heard Marina speak about him. He didn't seem too happy with what she was insinuating.

"Adelanta is an elven horse," Alaric explained. "He is smarter than a regular horse." Adelanta was happy with what Alaric had said. "If he doesn't want to go any further I have to believe that he has a good reason."

"That is a lot of faith to put in a horse," Marina commented as she searched her pack for something to eat.

"You have to put your faith in something," Alaric shrugged off the comment.

There was not enough fuel to last the night and the evening air was starting to become cold. Originally Alaric had brought the wood purely to cook with, but soon enough he was grateful for the warmth. When they went to sleep the two of them were forced to huddle together. Alaric felt somewhat uncomfortable at first, but once he relaxed he found the situation quite pleasant. He lay awake long after Marina had fallen asleep in his arms. When he did finally fall asleep his dreams were pleasant, although he could not remember any of them when he woke in the morning.

There was no wood left for a fire in the morning. A thin layer of dew had formed on the ground and covered their possessions. Even though their bodies had kept them warm throughout the night they both woke feeling uncomfortably cold. They ate a quick breakfast before they were on the move again. The morning sun was refreshing on their bodies as they continued and it was not long before their bodies had been warmed through.

They stopped around midday for something to eat at the side of a small lake. The water looked clear and refreshing and the horses were both eager to drink. Marina sat at the bank and dangled her feet in the water. Alaric was a little disturbed at how relaxed she was. Their situation was less than pleasant. Alaric could not help but relax when he was around her and resigned himself to the fact that there was no point in upsetting her, just for the sake of it. Instead he slipped his boots and socks of and joined her by the lake.

"Do you know much about the terrain in this part of Darshival?" The land had not changed since they had left the grove. The lake was the only difference from the grassy plains and low-levelled hills.

"There is not a lot of citizens in the Southern part of Darshival," Marina started as if she was remembering something that she had been taught a long time ago. "It is due its proximity to the Southern wasteland and the jungle swampland of Southern Entero."

There was much contention on the ownership of the land at the southern most tip of the two kingdoms of Darshival and Entero. The land was inhabitable and therefore useless. There was no real reason to deny ownership, but for some reason the two kingdoms each claimed the other owned it. Any conversation held by Enteroites would claim that the land was part of the Darshival.

"After the swampland comes the desert that makes the border between the Seven Kingdoms and the Southern Wasteland," Marina continued. "Not many people have travelled to the swampland, let alone into it, so it is very hard to say if what the books say are true," Marina seemed quite happy explaining things to Alaric. She smiled as she looked at the crystal clear water. "There may be a few scattered farms in this part of Darshival, but there won't be any towns." She paused for a moment as she thought. "Sillarome isn't too far to the east though. We could travel there and rest tonight. It would be much better than another night out in the cold."

Alaric scowled at the suggestion. It had been a nice conversation until Marina mentioned the city. They were trying to remain inconspicuous and there was no doubt that Marina would be noticed.

Although Marina had told him he was sure that she had left without telling her father. King Unwin would be more than upset when he realised that his daughter had disappeared with him. The last thing he wanted was to get delayed in Sillarome.

"It's too far off our path." Alaric thought it better if he didn't scold her.

Marina's smile left her face. Never before in her life had she slept outside. As much as she enjoyed laying down with Alaric she didn't like waking up all cold and damp. It wasn't a pleasant feeling and one she could go without, but it seemed as though Alaric wasn't interested in discussing it further.

"Are there any other towns around here?" Alaric asked when Marina didn't speak.

"Anyone who lives out here basically survives on their own. There is a small farming community around Sillarome, but this far away makes trading difficult. I have heard rumours that there have been Southerners come to Kiarome, but I have never met them myself. Apparently they are not the most hospitable of people. I would suggest we avoid them."

Alaric had no intention of seeking shelter from anyone. Even if they didn't know who Marina was he couldn't risk anyone knowing where he was. At least it seemed she was happy enough to remain out in the open. It was one conversation he didn't have to have.

"How long will take for us to reach the swampland?" Alaric kept his gaze on the water as he changed the subject.

"If the maps I have studied are correct I would say about four or five days at our current pace." Marina did some calculations in her head and then nodded.

"Damn it," Alaric cursed.

"What's the matter?" Marina sounded concerned.

"I only brought enough food for about five, maybe six days. I had been relying on getting food on my journey."

"Can't you still get food?" Marina sounded confused.

"I don't know about you, but I haven't seen any animals here. If we can't find a town or a village to buy food then what are we going to eat?" Alaric was short.

Marina was a little hurt with his comment, enough for the smile to fade from her face. She knew that there must be a lot on his mind, but that was no reason to be rude. She thought back to her days of study and then the smile returned to her face. She sat for a moment and watched the water. She wanted Alaric to stew for a little while. It was her own small revenge for the way he spoke to her.

"I don't think that we have to worry yet. There are many animals that live in the grasslands of the south," Marina explained.

"Then why haven't we seen anything?" Alaric was just snapping for an excuse to snap.

"I think that I would like to bathe before we leave," Marina stood up abruptly. "I would appreciate it if you would give me some privacy," she said when he didn't move.

Alaric quickly scrambled to his feet when he realised what she was hinting at. There was a touch of red to his face as he left her in peace. The sullen mood he was in was suddenly replaced by embarrassment. The thought of bathing cheered his mood. He had been so transfixed by the water that he had not even thought about bathing. As soon as the thought entered his mind he realised how filthy his was. Most of the dried sweat and grim had come from the city, but there was still plenty from riding.

He spent his time, while he was waiting, scanning the country side for animals. On more than one occasion he almost let his eyes return to the crystal waters and the naked woman. Each time he stopped himself just before he saw anything. It didn't matter where he looked he could not see any animals. He could only hope that they were further south.

Before Alaric could find any sign of animals Marina returned from the lake. All she wore was a towel wrapped around her breasts and hips. He flushed we he saw her and his heart started to skip. Marina seemed to ignore his discomfort.

"I think that you should bathe as well, you are quite smelly," there was no humour in her voice, although she was teasing him. She scrunched up her nose to accentuate her point.

Alaric was quick to move to the water. He wished that he had brought a towel. He didn't know how he was going to dry himself after he bathed. Once he was in the water he didn't really care as it was quite refreshing and he wished he could stay in the lake for the rest of the afternoon. He knew, however, that time was already getting away from him and as soon as he was out of the lake he shook himself to remove as much water as he could before he dressed again in his dirty clothes.

Marina had already mounted her mare when Alaric returned from the lake. When she saw him walking toward her she tapped the mare in her flanks making her start to walk. He watched her as Adelanta walked up next to him. The stallion nudged Alaric with his head. In return Alaric stroked the back of his neck. "Don't ask me," he said before he mounted and continued after her. He stayed a few paces behind for the first half hour of their journey before he rode up next to her.

"What's the matter?" he asked slowly.

"There are a number of animals in the grasslands. Rabbits are bountiful, as are foxes. Although foxes will only come out close to the many groves of trees and generally only at night," Alaric was about to question the groves, but he thought better of it. "The main animal that we will find in abundance is the bison."

"The what?" Alaric had never heard of the creature before. He was wondering if she was making it up to mess with him.

Marina laughed softly to herself. "I think that you will have to wait to see one."

Alaric shook his head. He didn't understand Marina. One moment she was nice to him and the next he thought that she didn't want to know him. He had never known anyone to be that fickle. Bern had always told him that women could act in such a manner, but he had never believed him.

They rode for the rest of the day without seeing a single animal. The further they rode the grumpier Alaric became. Eventually Adelanta started to reflect his rider's emotions. He started jumping and snapping at the mare. This in turn caused Marina to become upset. She thought about scolding Alaric, but the look on his face told her otherwise. It was not a pleasant afternoon for anyone.

Again Alaric wanted to push hard into the night and this time Adelanta's bad mood meant that he was not looking after the mare. It was Marina, able to feel her mare struggling underneath her, who called for a stop. Alaric wasn't happy when and Adelanta also seemed annoyed, but there was nothing they could do. The stallion seemed quite happy to keep walking throughout the night, but no matter how Alaric felt he wasn't going to leave Marina alone in the dark. Whether he liked it or not she had become his responsibility and he would make sure she made it back to Kiarome in one piece.

Begrudgingly they huddled together again for warmth. The night air was not as cold as it had been the night before, but it was still cold enough to make them want to stay close. All in all they were both grateful for the extra heat. In the morning Alaric was quick to have them on the move again. There was a new sense of urgency to his movements. As the day progressed the rest breaks became more frequent and eventually Alaric called a halt as the sun was starting to set.

"There," Marina pointed to the top of a hill far away in the distance.

"What is it?" Alaric could see something standing on the top of the hill, but he couldn't recognise the creature. He thought that it looked like a cow or a horse, but there was something not right about it.

"That is a bison." Marina seemed somewhat pleased with herself.

It looked as though it would be a menacing creature and hard to kill. The bison didn't seem too worried as the two rode closer. Alaric wanted to continue to the hill. He was curious to see what the animal really was.

"It doesn't look that scary," Alaric commented.

"That is a female. The males have some fierce looking horns," she smiled again as he spoke.

Marina's spirit had lifted with Alaric's. He seemed a lot happier that there was something he could kill for food. His supplies were starting to run very low even though he was trying to stretch every meal, the even more annoying thing was that Marina had brought more food than he had. He thought that was one of the reasons why the mare was struggling to keep up the pace. She was carrying a lot more weight than Adelanta, although Alaric knew that was not the only reason. He knew that the elven horse could handle a lot more than a regular horse.

"I think that you should be careful," Marina warned as the approached the bottom of the small hill.

Alaric didn't think that there was anything to be worried about. The bison seemed peaceful enough. At a distance he thought that it was a cow, but up close he had to admit that the animal was larger than what he had expected. Although there were many similarities between the bison and some cows the differences were more noticeable. The mare snorted slightly at the sight and scent of the bison. The animal heard the noise and slowly looked up from where it was grazing. Although it didn't seem too perturbed by the new-comers it still moved from where it had been eating. Slowly it disappeared on the other side of the hill. Alaric was about to kick Adelanta to follow, but Marina called out to him.

"I wouldn't do that," the smile faltered a little and there was concern on her brow.

"It's getting away. If we want to eat a hearty meal tonight we have to make the most of this opportunity," Alaric had already picked up his bow and was now reaching for an arrow.

"Trust me," she winked and she continued on as she had been.

Alaric relaxed in the saddle, although he did nock the arrow. He wanted to be ready for whatever was about to happen. When they reached the summit of the hill Alaric nearly let the bow and arrow drop from his hands. The valley below him was covered in a sea of shaggy black. The bison they had seen on top of the hill had almost joined its brethren.

"Now you see why you shouldn't chase after a solitary bison," there was a hint of 'I told-you-so' in her voice.

"I still don't completely understand. They look peaceful enough," the creatures seemed so docile. Alaric thought that he wouldn't need to use his bow and arrow. He could just walk up to one of them and skewer it with his sword.

Marina shook her head. Although she had never seen a bison in her life she had been taught about them and read enough to know that they were not all that they seemed. She had seen drawings of farmers and would-be hunters being gored by one of the males. Their horn tips were razor sharp and deadly. Bison horns were prized amongst the ancient tribes. She had to admit to herself that she was enjoying give Alaric a lesson even if it was just on bison.

"How many bison do you think are grazing down there?" Marina took her chance to be arrogant.

Alaric looked, but could not accurately gauge the herd. In the end he just pulled a figure out of his head. "I don't know, about ten thousand."

Marina seemed impressed with his wild guess. "Now what do you suppose would happen if all ten thousand bison decided to charge at you at once?"

The question came as a shock. He hadn't thought about the chance of a stampede. As he looked down at the herd the horror of what Marina was suggesting sunk in. Even from a distance he could see the horns on the male animals. His heightened vision focused in on the horns making them even more vicious. He still had his doubts that the seemingly passive creatures could attack in such a manner, but it was not a risk he was willing to take.

"I see what you mean," Alaric spoke when he realised that he had been quiet for too long.

"Very good then. It is getting late in the day. I think that we should camp for the night and you can hunt in the morning. From what I have read they are more docile in the morning hours. I think that it will be safer then," Marina suggested, still with a hint of arrogance.

"I will take your word for it. There is a grove of trees off to the west. I think that I will be going and fetching some fire wood," Alaric was a lot less confident about hunting the bison, especially when there were so many grouped together.

"What grove?" Marina looked towards the setting sun, but could not see what Alaric was talking about.

"I think we should move away from the herd," Alaric ignored her comment and moved Adelanta away from the hill.

As they rode a short distance to the west Marina could finally see the grove just in front of the setting sun. It was still deep on the horizon and she didn't think she would have noticed it if Alaric had not already mentioned it. She looked at him, but there was no reaction on his face. She wanted to ask the question again, but she didn't think that she was going to get a response.

It was fair distance between their campsite and the grove. Dusk was upon them and it would soon be nightfall. Alaric quickly unloaded his packs and remounted Adelanta. Marina had done the same and was about to mount her mare.

"I think that it would be best if you stay here," Alaric called over his shoulder. He was about to ride off, but Marina was too quick to speak.

"The trees at least a league away and it is almost dark. Two of us will be able to bring back more wood than you by yourself," Marina put her foot into the stirrup.

"Trust me," Alaric smiled at her before signalling for Adelanta to go.

The white stallion instantly jumped into a gallop. It had been so long since Adelanta had been able to run that he could hardly contain himself. Marina was shocked to see at how fast he could run. Even her mare seemed surprised. Alaric had to hold on tight to the reins until he was able to settle himself. He was also glad to be moving at such a speed. The pace that they had been keeping had been annoying him.

Before they reached the trees Alaric tugged gently on the reins. He had seen something that made his heart fluttered. It took Adelanta a moment, but after a second tug he slowed to a walk. Alaric had seen a small rabbit jump out of the long grass as the two of them sped by. He knew well enough where there was one rabbit there were many more. Whilst there was still enough light he thought it would be a good idea to catch some food. He drew his bow and arrow and peered around the grass. It was not long before he saw what he was looking for. A small brown rabbit was nibbling on the grass no more than fifty feet away. Alaric quickly took aim, even as Adelanta was still walking towards the grove, and fired. The arrow flew through the air. The rabbit didn't know what hit it as the arrow sunk into the animals head and out the other side. The rabbit died instantly.

The sun was still up, if only just, and Alaric had shot three rabbits. Each time he killed one another would pop up near by. He was enjoying himself, but he knew that he would have start collecting wood. Once the sun went down the temperature would drop and Marina would start getting cold. He was also looking forward to eating one of the rabbits.

There was enough fallen wood on the ground that was easy for Alaric to collect. He knew he would have to do a second trip to get enough wood for the night and the next morning. If he was going to hunt the bison he would need a fire to cook the animal otherwise there was no chance of the meat staying edible for long.

"Do you know how to prepare a rabbit for cooking?" Alaric asked when he had returned and got a fire started.

Alaric wasn't sure if it was the light of the fire reflecting off Marina's face, but he thought that she was giving him a blank look. Alaric had hoped to make another trip to the grove whilst Marina prepared dinner. It looked as though he was going to have to skin and gut the animals himself. He should have known that a spoilt princess wouldn't be able to look after herself. Alaric was beginning to wonder what she was going to bring to the journey, besides being a hindrance.

"Never mind," he replied.

It was at that moment he realised he had not brought a knife with him. He looked at his sword, but that was too big to skin a rabbit. It might be handy for the bison, but it was no good for the small rabbits. He sat back and looked at the fire for a moment. Although the sword was too big and would not work well he didn't have any other choice. Suddenly a though came to him as he looked at the flames. The Jade dagger would be sharp enough to skin the rabbits. As much as he was not keen to open the box it would be a lot easier than trying to skin a rabbit with his sword.

He let his finger run over the lid. He liked the way the carved J in the middle felt. Marina watched him carefully. She thought there was a strange look on his face. She was worried that he was going to do something dangerous. Slowly he opened the box and a faint green glow came from inside. A buzz started in the back of his mind. He thought that was a good sign, although he really wanted to know why.

The dagger felt natural in his hand as he lifted it out of its box. He felt happy that he had decided to use the dagger to skin the rabbits. When the blade cut into the first animal Alaric felt a strange sensation ripple through his body. It was a feeling of elation. The dagger cut through the rabbit's skin with an ease that surprised Alaric. It was like cutting through butter with a hot knife.

Both the knife and his hands were covered in blood when he had finished with the three rabbits. Once he had finished he took a deep breath. He felt as though he had been in dream. When he realised what he had done he dropped the dagger to the ground and stepped away. It was not so much what he had done, but it was the manner in which he had. There was a raw joy that he could remember feeling. The emotion was so primal he could hardly believe that he had felt it. Marina had also noticed the change and was watching him with a worried look on her face. Once she realised that he had returned to normal she rushed to his side with a pouch full of water.

The rabbits lay in pieces on the ground. They had been stripped bare of their skin and then torn from the bone. It was obvious where the blade had slashed through the meat and where Alaric had ripped it with his bare hands. Thank fully it looked as though most of the meat was still suitable for roasting, although not as easy if it had been left on the bones.

"You should wash the blood from your hand and the blade," to her surprise when she looked down at the dagger she saw that there was no blood on the jade blade. She thought that it was a trick of the light, but as she looked closer she could see that it was not.

"Don't touch it," Alaric barked when he thought she was going to pick it up.

Marina shied away from his harsh words. She threw the pouch at him and then walked to the other side of the fire. She crossed her arms across her chest and then dumped herself on the ground. She wanted to yell at him, but she thought that her silence would be more powerful.

"I'm sorry, but you must never touch the dagger. It isn't safe and I would hate for you to get hurt," Alaric bent down and picked up the pouch. He quickly cleaned the blood off his hands.

Marina didn't reply. She was going to give him plenty of time to think about it. At least he could cook her dinner first. She had to admit that she had never seen the back end of where her meals came from. Seeing the little furry creatures being skinned and gutted made her stomach churn. Once the rabbits were cooking over the fire, however, her mind quickly changed.

Once Alaric had returned the dagger to its box his mood seemed to brighten. He noticed Marina's sullen mood, but did not know what caused it. He busied himself making sure that the rabbit meat cooked evenly and didn't burn. Once they were finished she seemed to brighten up. They were both hungry and happy to be eating fresh food.

"So will you help me hunt the bison in the morning?" Alaric finally broke the silence as they were eating.

Marina almost choked on the half chewed rabbit meat she had in her mouth. After she coughed a number of times she was ready to answer. "I think that you will need all the help you can get," she giggled after she spoke.

"Then it is settled. We will hunt in the morning."

Chapter 4: The Hunt

Hunting bison wasn't as easy as Alaric had thought, despite Marina's warnings. They were up at first light to try and get a jump on the animals. During the night the herd had moved on, leaving only a small number behind. With the smaller numbers the animals were more nervous than the one they had met on top of the hill. Without the safety of numbers the bison knew there was a greater risk of being killed. Unfortunately for Alaric and Marina they didn't know this fact and continued on horseback as they did the day before.

As soon as they crested the small hill the bison caught their scent on the wind. At first they looked up at the hill nervously, but did nothing. With the animals in his sight Alaric drew his bow as he started down the hill. Marina followed suit and also drew her bow. They weren't sure whether it was that movement or whether it was their approach that spooked them, but they were quick to move. They had only made it half way down the hill when the closest of the bison jumped slightly before running in the opposite direction. His movement caused the remainder of the herd to follow. Alaric was quick to kick Adelanta into a gallop. He was not going to let them get away.

"Wait!" Marina called after him, but it was too late.

The blood had already started to pump through his ears as the adrenaline coursed through his body and he couldn't hear what Marina was saying. Had he heard he would have realised that there was no point in chasing the beasts. It was not that they were quicker than Adelanta, but the fact that it was impossible to shoot an arrow with any accuracy whilst riding at a gallop. The bison would not be able to run as far as Adelanta, but if they were able to make it to the rest of the herd then they would be safe.

Marina did her best to catch Alaric, but her mare was no match for the elven horse. She continued to call out, even though she knew there was no chance he could hear her. Before he had a chance to shoot at one of the bison Alaric suddenly pulled Adelanta to a halt. It took a lot of will power to stop him from his charge. Marina pulled her mare next to him. A thin sheen of sweat covered the mare, but Adelanta looked much fresher.

"What?" Alaric sounded annoyed.

"Sorry," Marina was surprised at the question. "What are you talking about?"

Alaric looked more annoyed at what she was implying. He looked at her closely before he realised that she truly didn't know what he was taking about. "You have been calling out for me to stop ever since we started chasing the bison."

Marina had thought that he had not heard her calls. In the rush of the chase there seemed little chance he could hear her. The thought was odd, but she quickly put it out of her mind. There were more important matters to deal with.

The animals were still bolting away and soon they would be out of view. Alaric moved nervously in the saddle. He knew before long the bison would reach the rest of the herd and they would be impossible to kill.

Marina still looked surprised, but the realisation that he had been able to hear what she had been saying had sunk in. She looked down on the ground beside her mare as she tried to remember why she had been calling to him.

"The bison are running scared," she stated the obvious. "They are racing to reach the rest of the herd, which they will do if we keep chasing them. They won't stop until they reach safety or they collapse from exhaustion. If they reach the herd then the hunt becomes all the more dangerous. If it seems as though we are no threat to them then they will stop and assume that they are safe. Once they stop we will be able to sneak up on them."

Alaric had to admit that Marina's words did make sense. He didn't know if what she said was the truth, but he didn't know any better. The bison didn't look as though they were going to stop any time soon. They had already disappeared and there was no telling how far away the herd was.

It made sense that once they were out of sight then there was a chance they would stop. Although the terrain didn't lend itself to a sneak attack there was a chance he could shoot them from on top of the nearby hill without them realising they were there.

"Okay. We will ride to the base of that hill and then continue on foot from there," Alaric suggested.

Marina smiled at him as she gently kicked the flanks of her mare. Adelanta seemed to be a little annoyed at the slower pace. He also had a feeling that something was about to happen and he was going to miss out on it. He bucked his head a few times and tried to snap at Alaric. Alaric knew the reason why he was upset and in turn patted his mane. He whispered a few apologies to try and calm him.

"What did you say?" Marina asked when she heard him speak.

"Nothing," Alaric replied.

When the two of them reached the foot of the hill they stopped and dismounted. Alaric was about to start up the hill but Marina grabbed his arm and motioned for him to stay.

"From what I have read they had a very good sense of hearing," she whispered to increase her point. "We must be very quiet once we approach the top of the hill. If they are on the other side then they will hear us coming if we are not careful."

Alaric nodded his agreement. What Marina had told him made sense and he wasn't about to go against her word. He had already chased the animals too far away from their campsite and he didn't want to make any further mistakes. Originally the plan had been for them to catch a bison, prepare the meat and then be on their way again by lunchtime. There was very little chance of that happening now and Alaric doubted they would leave before nightfall.

Once they were nearing the top of the hill Alaric could feel his heart pounding in his chest. He didn't know why he was so nervous. There was something exhilarating about the hunt. He had never hunted an animal the size of the bison before. If the herd was waiting for them on the other side then there was a fair chance that they would not be successful. Not only that, but there was a more than reasonable chance that they could die.

They both crouched down low as they reached the top of hill. On the other side there was a small flat valley. To Alaric's relief the animals had not reached the rest of the herd, which was visible close to the horizon. They looked tired from the run and were breathing heavily. They didn't seem to notice the two on top of the hill. Alaric nocked an arrow and aimed at the nearest bison.

"What are you doing?" Marina did her best to keep her voice low.

Alaric shook his head before lowering his bow. "What do you think I am doing?"

"You will never make the distance from here," Marina whispered back. "There is a good chance that you will scare them into running away again."

"Just watch," a broad smile appeared on his face when he realised what she was saying.

Alaric returned the arrow to his bow, but remained in his crouched position. To make aiming easier he dropped to one knee. He would have much preferred to be standing, but he didn't want to risk scaring the bison. The closest animal was quite a distance away, but he was sure that he could hit it. He took aim. There was only a gentle breeze, but at that distance it would still affect the shot. Once he was sure that he had gauged the shot correctly he fired. The arrow arced in the air. Marina held her breath as she watched. As he suspected the wind started to drift the arrow towards the bison. The arrow struck just above its rump. Both Marina and Alaric dropped to the ground when they saw the arrow hit. The blow was not nearly enough to kill the animal. In fact the arrow was lucky to break the skin of the bison's tough hide. The animal looked around the valley and the surrounding land to see what had hit him. He looked more annoyed than anything else. Marina let out a deep breath when she realised that the bison was remaining in the valley.

"I told you that you were too far away," Marina sounded somewhat pleased with herself.

Alaric had to admit that he had overestimated his abilities and underestimated the bison's strength. He had not expected the animal to have such a tough hide. As he reflected it would be almost impossible to kill the creature with arrows. If there was any chance of killing the animal then he would have to hit it in the head and that meant a change of tactics.

There was no other place where he could get a shot at the bison without revealing himself to the creature. He drew his bow again, although he did not know why. It would be almost impossible for him to hit the bison, with enough power, in the head to kill it. Something inside him said that he should take the shot anyway. Marina watched him closely, but didn't speak.

Once the bison had stopped looking around Alaric took aim again. The animal had moved since the last shot so he could not gauge his new shot by his last. The wind had also picked up slightly, making the shot even more difficult. There was a chance he could scare the bison away, but after the animal's last reaction he didn't think that would be the case. Once the arrow was loosed they both held their breath. The arrow arched in the air and moved with the wind. Marina hoped that this would bring the animal down, but really doubted it would. This time the arrow struck high up on the bison's back. It sunk in a little further, but not enough to cause the animal any more than a little discomfort.

Three more shots and they were still no closer to catching their prey. Each time the arrow flew through the air and struck the bison somewhere on its body. Each time the blow was only superficial. Marina was still amazed at the skill it took to keep hitting it.

"What do we do now?" Alaric didn't want to waste any more arrows.

Marina didn't have any ideas. She wished she had remembered the part about bison being extremely hard to kill. She could only hope that Alaric could come up with an idea or else there would be nothing they could do. She had to admit to herself that she was starting to become worried that their supplies were not going to last.

Alaric stared at the bison with the five arrows sticking out of its body. He was sure that the only way to kill it was to strike in the head and that was going to be all but impossible. As he stared he realised that there was going to be another way. It was something that he really didn't want to do, but it was his only choice. Using magic seemed like it was cheating, but there was no other option. He didn't think that there would be anyone around with the power to feel what he was doing so there would be no reason to mask it.

He looked at the ground as he came up with an idea of how to kill the bison. He thought of sending Marina away, but he didn't think she would realise what he had done. Either way it was only a matter of time before she found out that he could use magic, if she did not already know. It didn't really make sense why he felt that way. The thoughts racing through his mind were only avoiding the real concern. He returned his gaze to the animals in front of him. The bison that had been shot five times already was still grazing in the same place place. If the animal was too stupid to realise that someone was trying to kill it then it deserved to die. That was the reasoning that convinced Alaric that he was doing the right thing.

Marina simply lay on the ground and waited for Alaric to come up with a solution. She watched him, instead of the bison. She could see that he was thinking hard as his brow was furrowed and his mouth was slightly turned down. Whatever he was thinking about didn't look good. Suddenly his look changed. There was a resigned expression on his face that didn't fill her with any confidence. She hoped that he was not about to risk his life. There were other animals in the south and there would be time to hunt before they reached the swamplands. She was going to speak, but Alaric moved onto his haunches. Whatever he had planned he was about to do it and Marina did not want to distract him.

Alaric stared at the bison as he started to draw in the energy around him. As he did he found that he already held quite a significant amount of energy. It must have happened subconsciously when the idea of using magic first came into his head. Even though he was sure that he was holding enough energy the feeling of drawing in more was euphoric. The energy of the land around him was magnificent. It was pure and untainted. He thought he could drift in the majesty for the rest of his life, but he knew that he could not. He had work to do and eventually, if he kept drawing in the energy, he would burn himself from the inside out.

When he was able to stop himself drawing on the power around him he was ready for what he had to do. He concentrated on the bison. There was a slight crackle in the air and then he could feel the bison's breath. He could feel the blood flowing through its veins. He could taste the grass that it was eating. He could feel everything that the bison felt. All of sudden everything stopped. The bison stopped eating, breathing and pumping blood. In one second it all stopped and the bison collapsed on the ground. As it did Alaric cried out a scream that gave Marina goosebumps. Not only that but it scared the other bison away from the valley. Again the animals were on the move, but that didn't matter anymore. They had their kill and that's all that they cared about.

When the scream died away Alaric took a deep breath. He sucked the air into his lungs as though he had not breathed before. His brow was covered in sweat and he looked deathly pale. As he tried to rise his legs gave way underneath him and he collapsed to the ground. The spell had taken more out of him than he expected.

"Are you alright?" Marina jumped up and rushed to his side. She lifted his head into her lap and gently stroked his hair, not that she knew if it was helping at all. "What happened?" She asked when he didn't respond.

"What happened?" she asked again when there was still no response.

Slowly the colour started to return to Alaric's face and his breathing returned to normal. The sweat was starting to dry from his face and he sat up on his own. He looked at Marina with a confused expression on his face. It wasn't until he saw the bison, lying dead in the valley, did he remember what had happened.

"It looks as though we've got our work cut out for us," Alaric smiled, ignoring the question.

Marina gave him an evil look. She did not understand him. One moment he was near death and the next he was making jokes, with no explanation for what had happened. She was glad that he was alright and that was all that she could hope for. There would be time for questions when they made camp for the night. There was a momentous job ahead of them and Marina was only just beginning to understand. Their camp was at least a league away, if not two, and they had no real way to get the bison back.

Alaric whistled for Adelanta to join him and the mare followed along after him. Marina was glad she didn't have to walk down to get her horse. She wished that she had a horse like Alaric. She liked her mare, but an elven horse was so much better.

They led the horses down to the dead animal. Alaric had been so focused on the hunt that he had not thought about how they would get the carcass back to their campsite. Slowly he scanned his surroundings to see if there were any trees. With a little luck he could send Marina for their things whilst he prepared the meat, but there were nothing in sight. All he could do was hope that Marina had the foresight to come prepared.

"Do you know how we are going to get this back to the camp?" Alaric was ashamed to ask the question.

"I have some rope, but I don't think the two horses will be able to drag it so far," Marina offered.

Alaric had to admit she was right. With the weight of the bison the two horses would only be able to make a few hundred paces at a time.

Not only that, but they would be too exhausted to travel once they reached the camp. He would have to come up with another plan.

Slowly an idea came to him. The problem with the bison was the weight. All he had to do was lighten the load. There was plenty of the bison that would be unsuitable for their needs. All he had to do was remove those parts and then hopefully the horses would be able to drag what remained.

Alaric returned to Adelanta and took his sword from its scabbard. Marina looked on in shock, not sure what he was planning. Without taking his eyes from the bison Alaric walked to the beast, swung his sword over his head and lopped its head off. With his elven blade and all his strength it only took one blow.

"What are you doing?" Marina squeaked before she spoke.

"If the bison is too big for the horses to drag then I'll just have to make it lighter." There was an evil grin on his face, but Marina thought he was putting it on for her benefit only.

Alaric thought about skinning the bison, but decided that the meat would need protection as it was dragged along the ground. As much as the pelt would make a great blanket, or even cloak, the meat was much more important.

"Come on, there is work to be done," Alaric called.

"What do you want me to do?" Marina was shocked at what he was implying.

"We need the roll the beast over so I can get at its underbelly," Alaric explained as he started to pull his arrows out.

Marina scrunched up her face at the thought of touching the dead animal. The blood was still pouring from its neck and was starting to smell.

"What about the horses?" Marina asked. "Maybe we could use them to roll it over?" She hoped he'd agree.

"That'll take too much time. By the time we tie it to the horses and they roll it over we could be on our way back to the campsite." It was a bit of an overstatement, but it got his point across. "We have already lost too much time. And we want to be back at the campsite well before night fall. We'll also need to get a lot more wood to cook all this meat."

It didn't take long for Alaric to realise he had underestimated the weight of the bison. No matter what they tried there was nothing the two of them could do to roll the beast. Alaric cursed himself for not listening to Marina in the first place. Although her motives had been self-serving she had been right. They should have used the horses in the first place.

Another half an hour had passed by the time they had rolled it onto his back. Even with the help of the horses both Alaric and Marina had to add their strength to move it. Things weren't going to plan and

Alaric could only hope that once he had removed the bison's organs it would be light enough to move. If not then he would have to carve it up even more and take back only a portion of the meat.

Carefully Alaric slid his blade through the middle of the bison's underbelly. The last thing he wanted to do was to pierce the stomach or other parts of the digestive tract. Although he had never slaughtered a bison, or even heard about them before a few days prior, Alaric worked his blade like a master butcher. When he was finished his arms were covered in blood, but he had achieved his goal. All that was left was meat, bones and the pelt.

Before he said anything he tested the weight. Although he couldn't lift it he felt as though it was considerably lighter. All he could do was hope that the two horses were strong enough to drag the carcass back to their campsite.

The ropes had been left tied to the horses and soon enough the carcass was ready. Even with the reduced weight getting it up the hill was a daunting task. Alaric and Marina needed to add their strength to help the horses. Once they were over the hill the rest of the journey was relatively easy. There were a number of other hills that they had to assist again, but none were as steep as the first one.

It took most of the day to return to the campsite and even Adelanta, looked as though he was going to collapse. Unfortunately for the elven horse his job was not yet complete. Alaric needed to return to the grove to gather more fire wood. They would need a lot more wood to cook the entire beast. It took a little persuading, but eventually Adelanta agreed to go along.

With the first load of wood Marina started the fire. As much as Alaric hoped she would start preparing the meat he knew she wouldn't. It would take time to skin the animal before he could start cooking it and the light was starting to fade when he returned with the last load of wood. It was time to start on the bison and he needed to remove the pelt. He thought about using the Jade dagger again as it made skinning the rabbits so much easier. He was about to reach for the box when he remembered the feeling that he had when he used the dagger. It was as if the dagger itself had a lust for blood. In the end he decided that it would be safer if he just used his sword. It wouldn't be as clean, but he didn't want to fight with the Jade stone again.

The job of skinning the bison was a lot more difficult than the rabbits. The animal's hide was ten times as thick and it was lucky that his sword blade was razor sharp. The size of the sword made the job much harder. With each passing minute Alaric thought about using the Jade dagger. It would make the job much quicker and cleaner.

Using the dagger the day before had taken him by surprise. It had been too easy for the Jade stone to take control of him. Even with the advantage of knowing what would happen Alaric didn't think he had the strength to fight it. In the end he decided to just finish the job with his sword.

Marina busied herself watering the horses and making sure they were comfortable. They had worked hard and they needed a little pampering. The truth was that Marina did not want to watch Alaric skin the bison. She gently brushed them down as they drank and nibbled on the grass. She didn't turn around until Alaric had finished skinning the animal.

"It's a shame we had to drag is so far," Alaric said as he looked at the tattered pelt. "It would have made a nice cover for the cold nights." There were great holes and gashes in the skin and it was no longer good for anything.

Marina had built a large fire, but it was still not large enough to cook all the meat at once. What had first started out as a simple hunting expedition had turned into a day long saga. It would be late in the night when the last of the meat was ready.

"It's done now," Marina commented as she sat by the fire. She was a lot happier with the meat roasting than when it had been raw. "This should be enough meat to keep us going for a while."

They would eat some of the bison that night and the rest they would wrap up in their supplies. They would eat the meat again for breakfast and then leave whatever they couldn't take with them. Alaric was beginning to regret not taking any pack animals with him. It would have been difficult getting them out of the city, but they would have been worth the hassle.

"Let's hope the wasted day was worth it. If your father has sent anyone after you then they would be a day closer."

There was little doubt that Unwin would have sent soldiers out to find his daughter, when he realised she was gone. They both hoped that it would have been at least two days, if not more before he realised. With all the action happening in and around the city it wasn't out of the question that they wouldn't see each other for days, if not weeks. The fact that Marina was planning on leaving with the Alliance, however, meant her father would want to spend time with her.

Alaric was exhausted when he sat by the fire. The day had taken its toll. It was the spell that had had the greatest effect on him. It had taken a surprising amount of energy to achieve his goal. As he sat and watched the meat roasting over the fire he wanted nothing more than to fall asleep. The heat from the fire made him even drowsier. There was nothing he could do. He had to stay awake long enough to prepare the meat. That was more important than sleep.

They ate their evening meal in silence. The day had been draining and neither of them wanted to waste energy on conversation. Marina stared at the flames and looked as though she was deep in thought. Alaric thought she looked quite beautiful in the firelight. He couldn't help but stare and was grateful that she didn't seem to notice. Eventually he returned his gaze to the fire. The last thing he wanted was to be caught staring. It would just lead to an embarrassing conversation that he didn't have the energy to have.

Marina was the first one to fall asleep as soon as she finished eating. Alaric was a little put out that she didn't offer to stay awake with him. Just when he thought he was happy for her company she had to remind him that she was a spoilt princess. In truth it was just that Alaric was jealous that he couldn't sleep, but he wouldn't admit that to himself.

After he had placed the two hind legs over the fire Alaric allowed himself to close his eyes. He wanted to get some sleep before the meat was ready to be changed. The only problem with his theory was that if he fell asleep he didn't think he was going to be able to wake. The feeling of sleep was overwhelming. No matter what he did he could not keep his eyes open. Slowly the power of sleep came over him and he drifted off.

Chapter 5: Continue South

Marina woke during the night just in time to save the legs from being burnt. Once she had removed them from the flames she thought of replacing the meat, but sleep was too overpowering. It would have to be a job for the morning. Alaric didn't wake until the sun rose over the horizon. He woke with a start and when he realised where he was he cursed himself for falling asleep. There was still meat they would need to roast and that meant they would lose even more time. For a moment he thought about leaving the rest of the uncooked meat behind, but he didn't know when he would get a chance to hunt again. Another hour or two could save another wasted day.

The sun was high in the sky when they were finally on the move again. With the added weight of the bison meat it was hard for Alaric to push the horses any faster. The day before had been hard on them and even Adelanta was still showing signs of fatigue. To make matters worse their water supply was starting to run low and by midday Alaric's mood was very morose.

They ate a quick meal in silence. Marina was quick to pick up on Alaric's mood and she didn't want to do anything to upset him further. Once they had eaten they were on the move again. Alaric had thought about eating in the saddle, but he knew the horses needed a break.

The further south they travelled the hotter the temperature became. It was a clear sign they were getting close to the swamplands the desert of the south. It didn't make for a pleasant ride and only furthered Alaric's foul mood.

Late in the afternoon they came across a small, shallow stream. Both the riders and the horses were relieved to see it. It had been a long time since they had drunk anything and their water pouches were almost empty. It was a little cooler by the water and Alaric thought about staying there the night, but there was still too much daylight left. Once they had watered the horses and filled their pouches they were on the move again. Marina had wanted to take the opportunity to bathe, but Alaric insisted that the keep moving. He snapped at her harsher than he intended and she sulked for the rest of the afternoon.

The sun had well and truly set when they finally stopped for the night. Alaric had pushed as hard as he could before calling for a halt. Even Adelanta was keen to keep going, but Alaric knew that it was time to call it a day. They would be able to get an early start in the morning. Their supplies would last them for a least a couple of weeks.

As they sat around the small campfire, after they had eaten and looked after the horses, Alaric looked the box containing the Jade dagger. If had been a few days since he had checked and the urge was almost overwhelming. In his mind he just wanted to make sure they were travelling in the right direction, but in fact it was something else. There was a hunger in his mind that he had felt ever since he had skinned the rabbits.

"Are you alright Alaric?" Marina asked, as she noticed a strange expression on his face. "Are you sure that is a good idea?"

"No, that's why I haven't opened it yet," Alaric's voice was cold.

"Do you remember what happened last time you used the dagger?" Marina wasn't even sure what had happened last time, but she thought it wasn't good. Something strange had happened and she knew the dagger was involved.

There was a vague memory of skinning the rabbits, but it was at the back of his mind. It was all that kept him from opening the lid and grabbing the dagger. Eldred had told him that the stones were dangerous. He had experienced that with the Ruby stone. There was no reason why the Jade stone should be any different. Despite the fact Alaric knew that he should check the dagger for the next stone. He could still feel the prophecy to the south, so he knew they were travelling in the right direction, but he still wanted to know he was following a stone.

"It doesn't matter. We need to know we are still heading in the right direction and the Jade stone is the only way to be sure." It wasn't exactly true, but it wasn't a lie either.

Without waiting for Marina to respond he opened the lid and was greeted by the familiar gentle green glow. Almost instantly he felt the buzzing in the back of his mind and quickly pushed it aside. Although he couldn't rid himself completely of the noise he was able to dampen it until it was almost unnoticeable. With the buzz taken care of he was able to concentrate on the dagger.

The sight of the dagger brought more doubts to his mind. The gentle, pulsating glow was slowly growing with each passing minute that Alaric didn't touch it. It was as if the stone was calling to him and that was a disturbing thought. Now that the lid was opened Alaric was starting to doubt he was making the right decision.

"Well? Are you going to pick it up?" Alaric could only just hear Marina's words. "Something doesn't feel right. Just find out the direction and put it away." If Alaric could hear her he would have noticed the subtle fear in her voice.

Taking a deep breath Alaric slowly picked up the dagger. As soon as he touched the hilt a rush of energy filled his body. The feeling was both exhilarating and frightening. He tried to shrug it off, but he couldn't, he wasn't even sure if he truly wanted to. A heat started to fill his head with ecstasy and his vision became blurred. The feeling was glorious and he just wanted to sink back in its majesty. Just before he could let himself fade away he felt two arms grip his shoulders and start shaking him violently. He could hear someone yelling at him, but he didn't return to normal before he felt a slap across his face.

"What are you doing?" Alaric sounded shocked.

Marina sat back a breathed a sigh of relief when she saw the recognition on his face. The panic was still clear and Alaric couldn't work out why. He knew something had happened, but he couldn't work out what it was.

"Something strange came over you. At first there was a blank expression on your face and then a look of evil pleasure. The Jade stone was lit up like a beacon. Anyone within ten leagues would have seen the green light. Whatever was happening I was sure it wasn't good."

Alaric noticed for the first time that he had broken out in a sweat. He didn't think that was a good sign. When he looked down at the dagger he noticed that the Jade was only just glowing. All he wanted to do was return it to its box, but he still had a job to do. Slowly he moved the dagger until it was pointing to the south. The stone glowed brightest when it was just pointing the western side of due south. Alaric was happy with the result and quickly returned the dagger to its box.

It wasn't until the lid was shut that Alaric realised how tired he was. Using the dagger had taken more of his energy than he had thought. In the end he was glad he did. If they were travelling due south then there was a chance they would ride right past the next stone.

Ever since he had left Kiarome Alaric had believed that he needed to chase the prophecy before worrying about the stones. As much as he wasn't about to divert from his original plan he had a feeling that there was a stone waiting for him along the way. Both paths were leading in the same direction and he needed to make sure he found the stone in question before chasing down Na'garoz and the prophecy.

"Thank you," Alaric finally spoke. "I'm alright now. I think we should get some sleep."

Marina wasn't happy with his response. She had hoped the get a better explanation, but she could see how exhausted he was and decided to let it be. There was something very wrong with the Jade stone. It was like it was trying to take control of Alaric and it looked as though it was winning. Marina didn't want to think what would have happened if she hadn't been there to bring him back.

In the morning Alaric was quick to have them in the saddle again. He wanted to avoid any conversations about the Jade dagger. The memory of taking it out was almost completely wiped from his mind. All he really knew what that they needed to skew a little to the west to stay on the right track.

The nights were getting warmer so they didn't need to waste as much fuel for their fire. The mornings were also warmer, which made it easier to rise. Marina certainly didn't like the cold nights and even worse, the cold mornings. Despite her need to question Alaric further she decided to wait. The fact that Alaric busied himself readying the horses and packing his possessions helped make her decision.

They rode for the rest of the day in silence only stopping for a quick lunch which was the only break that they had. Alaric kept the horses at a walk. If he pushed them any harder than they would need more breaks and that would give Marina a chance to question him. The questions would come eventually, but he would do anything he could to delay them.

Around mid-morning they came across another herd of bison. This one was much smaller than the first they had encountered. Although they didn't need to hunt for food it made Alaric relax a little, knowing that if they ran out there were still animals around. Along with the bison there were rabbits hopping around the plains.

"So what happened with the Jade dagger last night?" Marina asked when they had settled for the night. She wasn't going to let the opportunity pass.

Alaric stared into the flames of the small fire. As much as he knew the question was coming he still didn't have an answer for her. For the entire day he was happy for the memory to slowly disappear, but in the firelight he wanted it to return.

"I'm not sure," he finally admitted to her. "My memory of last night is sketchy at best."

Marina watched him carefully. Her initial reaction was that he was deliberately trying to be obtuse, but as she watched his face she wasn't so sure. There didn't seem to be any lie in his face and he genuinely looked as though he couldn't remember. That in itself was even more disturbing. If it was up to Marina they would throw the box away and be done with it, but that was not an option.

"There is something bad about the stone. I really don't think you should use the dagger again. It's much safer if you just leave it its box." Even as the words came out of her mouth she knew it was impossible.

Alaric didn't answer her. He had been thinking the same thing, but also knew it wasn't an option. They needed to find the stones and more importantly the Ruby stone before Nyrra. To achieve his goals he would need to use the Jade stone. All he had to do was learn how to control it. Although he couldn't remember what had happened he knew that control was the key.

To avoid any further conversation Alaric lay down on his bedroll and was soon fast asleep. Marina remained awake and watched him in the fading firelight. Despite their arguments and his brashness since she had joined him he still made her heart flutter. She wasn't foolish enough to think it was love, but there was an attraction that couldn't be denied.

It was half an hour before first light when Alaric woke in the morning. They were starting to make good ground and Alaric was keen to keep moving. The feeling of the prophecy was getting further and further away and Alaric wanted to close the gap. If he lost the sensation he wasn't sure he could get it back. They were in the saddle after eating a small meal, despite Marina's objections.

Alaric slowed the pace when the sun rose. He had pushed the horses hard and would have kept going, but something had changed. Until he could figure out what it was he thought caution was for the best. The last thing he wanted was to go charging into trouble. Adelanta also felt the difference. There was something on the air that the horse smelt, a strange scent. He was just as happy as his rider to slow the pace.

As they approached a large hill Alaric pulled on Adelanta's reins. The feeling that had been growing all morning was at its peak. The feeling was not bad, but it also didn't fill him with any confidence. Marina watched him closely, waiting for an answer.

"Why have we stopped?" she asked when no answer came.

"There is something on the other side of that hill," Alaric's voice was flat. He was trying to concentrate in the hope he'd get an idea of what was waiting for them.

"What do you mean? What is on the other side?" Marina was even more confused.

"I don't know. There is something on the other side of the hill. That's all that I know," Alaric looked at her and shrugged his shoulders. "There is only one way to find out."

They started up the hill. Adelanta was just as nervous as he was. There was no telling what was waiting for them on the other side. As they crested the hill he pulled on Adelanta's reins and he couldn't believe what he was seeing. Below them was a small village.

"I thought you said no one lives this far south?" Alaric asked.

Marina didn't know what to say. She looked down at the village in shock, it was like no village she had ever seen in Darshival. The houses were small huts made of mud bricks and thatch. They all seemed to be single roomed buildings with no main building.

Surrounding the village was only what could be called farmland, although there were no pens or paddocks, there were goats, pigs and some sheep. To both their surprise they saw bison wandering amongst the rest of the livestock without a worry in the world. There were people amongst the animals, but it didn't look like they were working too hard.

Suddenly the sound of a horn could be heard from the village. In the middle there was a small watchtower and there was a man looking straight at them. Instantly the men and woman all rushed back towards the village. They didn't seem to care if the animals remained or fled.

"I don't think this bodes well for us," Alaric said as he saw a small group of villagers rushing toward them. There were branding crude weapons and didn't look at all friendly.

"I don't suppose it would help if I told them I'm their princess," her tone was half sarcasm and half concern.

"I guess we will just have to wait and see, although I wouldn't lead in with that fact if I was you," Alaric smiled briefly as he spoke.

The group of villagers rushed up the hill, but they slowed as the neared them. There was something about the way they remained calm at the impending battle that worried Alaric. The group consisted of ten burly men dressed in crude clothing made from bison hide. All their confidence seemed to dwindle as they approached and they stopped altogether when they were three paces from the horses.

"What brings you here?" asked the lead man when it was clear no one was going to attack. There was a strange guttural tone to his voice. As he spoke Alaric felt a small buzz in the back of his mind.

Marina looked at Alaric with a confused expression on her face. Alaric ignored it and focused his attention on the men in front of him. As much as they made no move to attack they stood prepared for battle. Alaric knew that the wrong word could be disastrous and he needed to be very careful

"We are travellers passing through your land and we mean no disrespect." It seemed as good a place as any to start.

To Alaric's surprise he heard a gasp come from Marina. The confused look had strengthened on her face, but Alaric only gave it a passing glance. As much as he wanted to know what she was thinking he needed to concentrate on those before him. If any of them made a move to attack he needed to be ready to strike. He kept his hand on the hilt of his sword and hoped they wouldn't see it as a threat.

"You don't belong here. This is Kia'ra tribe land," it was becoming clear he was the chief of the village. He looked at them closely for the first time. He was concerned at the way they were dressed. He also saw the sword for the first time. "You are not from another tribe?"

"No, we are not from another tribe. We are just passing through," Alaric spoke softly.

"What are you saying?" Marina asked suddenly, as she did some of the villagers started brandishing their weapons.

"What are you talking about?" Alaric kept his voice low so he didn't upset the villagers any more.

"How do you know their language? I can pick up a few words from my time studying ancient Darshivallian, but you can understand and speak it fluently," Marina also did her best to keep her voice low.

Alaric didn't know what she was talking about. The tribesmen were speaking the main langue of the Seven Kingdoms. That was the only language that he knew. He shook his head and returned to the chief.

"What does your woman say?" the chief asked. "She speaks in a strange tongue."

Something very strange had happened. Alaric had not even realised, but when he thought about it things made perfect sense. The buzz he had felt in the back of his mind was a spell to allow himself to understand and speak the tribes language. With the chief's question he didn't think it was one of the tribesmen who had created the spell. Instantly his thoughts went to the Jade stone, but the dagger was safely locked in its box. The only other reasoning was that he had subconsciously created the spell. The thought was both disturbing and exciting.

"She was just asking if we could enter your village," Alaric lied. "It's getting late in the day and we would love some shelter for the night."

"I see." The chief thought for a moment before he decided that they weren't a threat. "Follow us."

The chief didn't wait for a response from Alaric. He motioned for the other tribesmen to lower their weapons and return to the village. Some of them didn't look impressed with his decisions, whilst the others look relieved that they didn't have to fight.

"Where are they going?" Marina asked.

"They have invited us to join them at their village." Alaric paused and thought. "There is a reason why we have come this way. I think we should see what they have to say."

Marina didn't like what Alaric was saying. She had a bad feeling that they were walking into a trap. Alaric didn't seem concerned at all and since she couldn't understand the conversation she had to trust his judgement. It was a new situation for her. In Kiarome everyone would listen to her and trust her judgement. Since she had left it was a different story.

Before they started down the hill Alaric dismounted and motioned for Marina to do the same. He felt it would be better if they entered the village on foot. The tribesmen seemed unusually nervous and he didn't want to do anything to further put them off guard. Something had happened recently to put them on edge and he needed to know what it was.

The feeling that they were doing the wrong thing only increased in Marina as they walked down the hill. She had a very bad feeling that they were walking into a trap. There was something about tribesmen that didn't sit right with her. She couldn't explain why, but she didn't want to enter the village.

"I don't think we should go any further," she spoke into his ear so the others could not hear, not that they would understand if they did.

"It's alright. I am sure that these villagers are friendly," Alaric didn't sound too worried, but he also kept his voice low.

Marina wanted to protest, but Alaric quickened his pace making it impossible for her to speak to him without the others hearing. His blasé attitude did nothing to ease her worries. They closer they came to the village the stronger the feeling became. The thought of mounting her mare and riding away crossed her mind, but she couldn't leave Alaric behind. She wished that he would listen to her concerns.

Once they were in the village that tribesmen left Marina and Alaric alone with the chief. He led them towards his hut without a word. Marina looked around nervously at the other tribespeople. They stared at the two as if they had never seen outsiders before. It made Marina feel very uncomfortable, whereas Alaric didn't seem to notice.

"This is my home. You are welcome inside," the chief finally spoke when they reached his hut. It was not huge, but it was the largest in the village.

"Is there somewhere we can leave the horses," Alaric wasn't worried about Adelanta, but he knew the mare would wander.

The chief looked around Alaric before raising his right arm and clicked his fingers. Shortly after the signal a rough looking man came to take the horses. Alaric moved to take his sword from where it was tied to Adelanta.

"You won't need your weapons," the chief spoke. "You are safe here."

Alaric let his hand slid off the strap, although Marina wished he hadn't. He was happy to leave his sword behind, but there was one thing he was not going to leave. He took the box with the Jade dagger. There was no change he was going to risk it being stolen. He didn't care what the chief said he would not relinquish the box.

"What's in the box?" the chief sounded suspicious.

Marina watched the two of them closely and tried to work out the conversation. Not being able to understand what was being said was extremely frustrating. She wanted to ask Alaric what they were talking about, but it wasn't the right situation. The last thing she wasn't to do was to upset the tribe's chief.

"It's a keepsake, nothing more, but one that I will not be parted with," Alaric was a little defensive. He hoped he had not offended the chief.

"Very good," there was a touch of understanding in the chief's voice.

. There was no door, just two bison hides hung down over the entrance. The chief pulled one of the flaps aside and motioned for them to enter his hut first. It was a sign of respect from the chief, although neither Alaric nor Marina knew it. They were suspicious as they walked passed him and into the hut. The chief followed closely behind once they were inside.

The hut itself was surprisingly homely and not at all what they were expecting. The hut was basically one room. It was very simplistic in design. At the back of the room was his bed. As Alaric looked closer he could see the headboard was made out of bison bones. The rest of the bed was concealed by the bison hide covers. At the front of the hut there were a small group of lounge like chairs. They, like everything else, were covered in bison hide. He took a deep breath as he lowered himself onto one of the chairs. To his surprise it was quite comfortable. He didn't want to think what the padding was made from. He sat the box on his lap and waited for the chief to be seated.

"Please wait here," the chief did not sit, but instead he made his way outside.

"What do you think that was all about?" Marina asked, her bad feeling was only getting worse.

Alaric was still looking around the room. He couldn't get his mind off the bison bones on the bed head. He heard the words, but didn't think much about them. Even so he thought he should respond. "I'm sure it's nothing," he let his fingers move over the carved J. He felt as though he should open the lid. The only thing that was stopping him was that he didn't want the chief to see what was inside.

It wasn't long before the chief returned. Alaric could hear him speaking with someone outside the hut, but he couldn't work out the words. Marina simply sat and watched him.

"Now I think it is about time that you told me the truth," the chief spoke harshly when he returned to the hut.

Alaric was taken by surprise by his harsh words. Things had been pleasant and they had done nothing to change that. From the tone of his voice Marina knew that the words were not friendly and she became extremely uncomfortable.

"I told you. We are travellers and we are just passing through. We mean no disrespect and we mean no harm. Truth be told we have already stayed too long." At first Alaric had thought he needed to stay in the village and gather information, but with the chief's change of attitude he wasn't so sure.

"If we offend you by being here then we are happy to keep moving." Alaric didn't think that his words were having any effect.

"He told me you would plead ignorance," there was a snarl on the chief's face.

A sudden realisation passed over Alaric, but he still needed the chief to confirm his suspicions. "Who told you?" he spoke the words slowly.

The chief laughed out loudly. The sound sent shivers down Alaric's spine. Marina sunk back in her chair to try and get away from the sound. Alaric let his head drop into his hands. He couldn't believe he had walked into a trap. He realised why Marina had been concerned and silently cursed himself for not seeing it himself.

"A friend of yours dropped by here not two weeks ago," the chief almost spat the words. "He told me that you would be coming this way." He paused, giving them a chance to confess their crimes. When it was clear that they were not going to speak he continued. "I know why you have come here." He paused again, but they remained silent. "How can you sit there and lie with such a straight face?" He was becoming enraged. "He told me that you would come here and claim that you were passing through. He told me that you would enter my tent armed with what is in that box. He told me a good many things." Although Marina could not understand what he was saying she knew that it was not good.

"The man was lying to you. We mean you no harm," Alaric spoke calmly.

"The man told us all about you. He warned us that you would try and kill me."

"Why would I do that?" Alaric sounded as defensive as possible. "I do not know you. I have no reason to kill you."

"That is what I thought at first, but it seems as though you have connections with Ter'go tribe. They have been trying to kill me for years. They think that with me dead they will be able to take over our land." the chief smiled a grim smile when he finished speaking. "If this is not true then what is in the box."

Alaric looked at the box sitting on his lap. There was nothing he could say. He had been set up. "There is nothing that concern's you in the box."

The chief looked angry for a moment, but then a smile crossed his face. He had Alaric where he wanted him. It didn't matter how strong Alaric was there was nothing that he could do. Outside was a group of his strongest warriors. It was only a matter of time before he would bring them in, but he wanted a little more information before he did.

"Why did Chief Esau send you to kill me?" the chief asked.

"I don't know Chief Esau," Alaric was starting to become frustrated. "Whoever this man was who came to see you is lying."

"He said you would say that." The mean smile remained on the chief's face. "He said that you would be aloof. I didn't believe him at the time but now I know he was telling the truth. Warriors!" he called out the men outside his hut.

Marina quickly rose to her feet at the sound of the chief's voice. She didn't know what he said, but she gathered that he was calling to someone outside. Alaric remained in his chair. He had a bad feeling that he knew what was happening and there was nothing he could do about it.

Six muscle bound, armed men, marched into the room. They were armed with crude spears and wore nothing but bison-hide loin cloths. By the way their held their spears it looked as though their strength was their only real advantage. With the stone tips on the spears it would take a skilled spearman to do any real damage. Despite the fact Alaric didn't want to start a fight. He had a feeling that was exactly what Ra'naroz wanted.

"You see there is no point in lying to me. I know all about you. Now I will give you one more chance to tell me the truth," the chief almost laughed he was enjoying himself so much.

"What is happening," Marina's voice was thick with worry.

"It's okay Marina. Whatever happens, just go along with it." Alaric kept his eyes on the chief. "I can see that there is no changing your mind. I could tell you that you have been duped, but I think you may already know this. We are simply passing through your village. We mean you no harm, but if you force us then you will regret it."

Alaric put the threat in to get the chief off guard. From the start of the conversation the chief had led the tempo and Alaric needed to change it. He doubted it would do him any good, but it was worth a shot. Anything that would gain them more time meant there was a chance he could come up with a solution.

"You say that you are passing through, but there is no reason for you to pass through. The only thing after our tribe is the jungle and there is no reason for anyone to enter the jungle." The chief was a little taken aback by Alaric's words, but he was still sure that he was doing the right thing.

Alaric didn't respond. There was nothing else he could say. The conversation was just going around in circles and there was no changing the chief's mind.

"Warriors?" the chief boomed.

"Yes, Chief Omri," the warriors spoke in unison.

They moved into position. Alaric had no choice. He had to rise from his chair. One of the warriors was waving his spear in Alaric's face.

Another guard moved around behind Marina, forcing her towards the exit. She looked towards Alaric and he made a motion for her to remain calm. He didn't think they mean to kill them, at least not for the moment.

"I do hope that we can resolve this pleasantly," Alaric held onto the box as he was ushered out of the hut.

They were marched to approximately the middle of the village. Waiting for them was a large cage made from bison bones. The sight made Alaric cringe again. Although he had killed and slaughtered one of the animals by himself he still couldn't get used to the sight of their bones used in such a fashion. The cage was large enough for them both to fit inside and a few more. The warriors forced the two of them into it.

"Give me the box," one of the warriors barked.

"I cannot give it up," Alaric kept firm.

Suddenly the warrior reached inside the cage and grabbed Marina. She screamed once, more out of shock than anything else. Alaric cursed himself for being too slow to stop it. He did not like the warrior manhandling Marina. A rage was growing and he could feel the energy filling inside him. He wanted to strike out, but he knew that wasn't going to help anyone.

"I will be getting that back," Alaric's voice was firm as he handed over the box.

Once they were locked inside four of the warriors left. The two remaining warriors turned their back on their prisoners. It was common practice amongst the tribes to give their prisoners no respect. They would not be acknowledged until the chief was ready to speak to them, or they were to be executed. It gave them some privacy, not that they needed it. The warriors couldn't understand a word they said to each other.

Marina rushed into Alaric's arms sobbing softly. It took Alaric a moment before he wrapped his arms around her. She let he her head rest on his chest. Alaric felt small comfort from her touch. He watched the warriors walk away with the box. There was no doubt that they were going to take it to the chief. He wished he had placed a spell making it impossible for the chief to open it, but his mind had been elsewhere. He didn't want to know what would happen if the chief picked up the box.

"What are we going to do?" Marina asked when she finally pried herself away.

"We have to wait." Alaric didn't really know what they were going to do. He walked to the edge of the cage and gripped the bison-bone-bars. It didn't take him long to realise that there was no chance he could break out.

Both of them went silent for a while. There was nothing to say. Neither of them had any ideas of how they were going to escape. The thought of what would happen if they didn't wasn't worth thinking about.

There was something that was wearing on Marina's mind. At first she didn't want to speak about it, but the more she thought about it the more she had to know.

"Why have we been imprisoned? What were you speaking about with the chief?" Marina kept her voice low, even though there was no point it made her feel better.

Alaric thought for a moment before he responded. At first he didn't want to tell Marina what had happened, but he thought that it would be better if she knew the truth. When it was said and done Marina was his travelling companion and she needed to know what they were up against.

"The chief has been lied to. Someone came by about two weeks ago and told the chief that we were coming. He made up some lies, or at least he twisted the truth," Alaric started to explain, although he didn't make a lot of sense.

"Who would know that we were coming this way? We didn't even know that we were coming this way," Marina sounded confused. She was trying her best to comprehend what Alaric was telling her.

"It's Na'garoz. He is the one who told Omri that we were coming. He is the one who told the lies."

"That still doesn't explain how he knew we were coming. I have studied the Dark Knights when I was younger. I don't believe that they have the power to predict the future, although the research was not definitive."

Alaric let out a deep breath and sunk to the ground. He let himself rest against the cage. When he realised what he had done he leant forward quickly before deciding that he was just being stupid. There was nothing wrong with leaning against the bison bones. All he was really doing was stalling in his explanation.

"He has the *Prophecy of the Stone*," he reminded her. "If he has worked out how to decipher it then he will know exactly what we're doing."

It was the first time Alaric had thought about it and the fact didn't bear thinking about. If the Dark Knight was able to read the prophecy then they were just walking into a trap. Na'garoz would be able plan an attack and there would be nothing they could do about it.

"So do you think he read about this first?" Marina asked. "Or did he read about us coming here and changed the prophecy to suit his own needs."

Her words made his head hurt. Alaric knew that the prophecy could change, but he didn't think that anyone could change it. It was an interesting theory and one he would have to try when he regained it. Until then he couldn't think about the consequences.

"The best thing we can do is assume that Na'garoz can't work out the words. He is still a long way away. I think if he was able to decipher the prophecy then he would have remained here to kill us. For the moment I think he was just guessing that we would be following the same path." It was a plausible excuse.

Marina wasn't overly happy with his response, but she wasn't going to push any further. There were more pressing matters they had to deal with.

"So what should we do now?" Marina asked, changing the subject.

"For now we wait and see what these tribesmen come back with." It wasn't much, but it was all he had.

Chapter 6: A Change of Heart

Chief Omri looked at the box the man named Alaric had given him. He couldn't take his eyes off the large J carved into its lid and wondered what mysteries lay inside. The strange man who had visited had told him that there was a great power inside the box. He started to shake slightly with anticipation. If what the man said was true then he would be the greatest tribal chief there ever was. He would be able to strike down his enemies once and for all.

For some reason he couldn't bring himself to open the box. There was something holding him back. He laughed to himself slightly for being silly. There was nothing for him to fear. He was Chief Omri. The glory of what was inside the box would be his. It was his destiny. Ever since he was a child he knew that one day he would come into great power. Without a second thought he flipped the lid open.

Omri let out a gasp of wonder when he saw what was inside. The small blade was almost perfect. There was not a single nick or scratch on it. It was the Jade stone inlaid in the hilt that took his attention. It glowed softly, creating a green effect throughout his hut. The gemstone mesmerised him as he stared at it. He wondered at how something so beautiful could exist in the world.

Slowly his hand reached down and picked up the blade by the golden hilt. At first a rush of euphoria passed through his body. The feeling was more powerful than anything he had ever felt before. He thought he was going to burst at the sides with joy. The feeling did not last long and when it faded it faded quickly. The air was sucked from his lungs as a feeling of dread passed over him. The feeling consumed him. He dropped to his knees in utter panic. As the air finally returned to his lungs he let out a blood curdling scream. The sound echoed throughout his hut and out into the rest of the village.

When the first of the tribesmen came to see what was wrong with their chief they found him curled up on the floor. The Jade dagger was firmly in his grasp and his knuckles had turned white. The Jade stone was glowing brightly and the chief was shaking slightly and did not look well. The warrior called out to him, but there was no response.

The chief's mind was still working even if his body was not. A pain like nothing he had felt before ripped through his body. He could see the tribe's men and women starting to fill his hut, but there was nothing he could do about it. Besides the subtle, uncontrollable shaking he was completely paralysed. There was one thought racing through his head. 'He had listened to the wrong man. He had been betrayed.' There was nothing he could do but hope for retribution.

***

They had spent the night in the cage. They were fed a miserly broth for their evening meal and that was all they had been given. They were given no blankets to warm themselves from the chill in the night air. It was not a comfortable night sleep and they were grateful for the morning sun.

"What do you think they are going to do with us?" Marina asked when she woke.

"I don't know, but I am sure they will not do anything rash," Alaric said.

"Isn't there something you can do?" It was clear what Marina was hinting at.

Alaric had thought he had been able to hide his magical abilities for Marina, but it was clear that he had failed. He was glad that she was able to realise the situation, but it didn't make things easier. It would have been better for him if she didn't know that he was able to escape at any minute. The thought had crossed his mind during the night, but the risk that one of tribesman would kill Marina was too great. He didn't think he had to abilities to kill the entire tribe and he really didn't want to test it. They weren't evil, they had just been duped by the Dark Knight. That wasn't enough to sentence them all to death.

"I can't," was all he could say. He was not ready for the conversation, even though he had gone through the reasons in his mind.

"I don't understand. I didn't think it would be too hard for someone with your power to break out of this prison," Marina sounded a little confused.

"It's complicated. Yes it would be easy to break out of this prison, but then it would be a matter of fighting the tribesmen," Alaric started explaining. "The tribesmen are not evil. They have been manipulated by Na'garoz. It's not their fault. I cannot kill them for this fact. It is just what Nyrra would want me to do. Needless death and destruction is his game, not mine."

"Couldn't you just knock them out or stop them from moving? There has to be something that you can do," Marina was starting to become desperate.

"I don't think that would work. It would take more energy than I have to be able to leave without hurting anyone. I think there would be *more* chance of us being killed if I tried that," Alaric spoke the truth. He didn't think that he would be able to complete the spells and still have the energy to leave.

Marina didn't seem to be happy with the answer, but it was clear that Alaric was not going to help. She didn't know what she was going to do. She had hoped Alaric was going to come up with a solution for them to escape, but it was obvious to her that she was going to have to do it.

"Don't worry too much about it. I am sure that a solution will arise soon," Alaric yawned as he stood and stretched.

Marina was not happy with his casual attitude. Their situation was more dire than he was giving it credit. His relaxed attitude did nothing to help her concern. Suddenly a dreadful sound could be heard coming from the direction of the chief's hut and Marina's attention was quickly diverted.

Instantly Alaric knew what had happened. He knew the moment the chief had opened the box and when he had picked up the Jade dagger. He didn't know for a fact what was happening to him, but he could guess. By the sound of the scream he was in a great deal of pain. Alaric felt for him, but there was nothing he could do trapped in the cage.

"What's happening?" Marina asked, her voice thick with concern.

Alaric shook his head. The last thing he wanted to do was explain what was happening to Marina. His mind was focused on the Jade stone and the effect it was having on the chief. There was little doubt they would be blamed and he would need to heal the chief if they were going to survive.

It was not long before a small group of concerned tribesmen came rushing to the cage. Alaric stepped up to speak to them. They whispered to each other before pushing an older looking man to the front. He was to be the spokesman. There was an obvious fear on his face. He didn't want to speak to the man in the cage.

"What have you done to Chief Omri?" there was a nervousness to his voice.

"I don't know what you are talking about," Alaric tried his best to sound surprised.

"Our chief is incapacitated. He picked up that dagger of yours and now he can't move. I'll give you one more chance to tell me what happened. If you do not then we will kill you both," his voice was too weak for Alaric to believe the threat.

"I don't think that is going to happen. By the sounds of it he has fallen into the little trap I set," it was a lie, but he thought it was better for everyone if they thought that he had done it and not the stone. "I am the only one who can set him free, but you have to release us first."

Alaric could feel his pain and knew that he was still holding the dagger. There was a feeling of hate coming from the hut that was undeniable. Deep down he felt sorry for the chief, but he couldn't help feeling annoyed that he was holding the dagger. Such a man didn't deserve to feel the power of the stone.

The man looked at the other tribesmen and whispered something. Alaric didn't know what he said, but the other tribesmen shook their heads. It was worth a shot, but Alaric didn't think it was going to be that easy. He was sure that eventually they would let him out, but it was a matter of getting Marina out as well. He really didn't want to hurt the tribesmen, but if they did anything to threaten his life or Marina's then he wouldn't have a choice.

"No, you tell me how to help the chief," the man didn't have anything to offer. He thought that if he told Alaric enough times that he would get the information he needed.

"I would if I could, but I have to be there to stop what is happening to him." There was no other way. He had to take the dagger from him and he couldn't risk one of the other tribesmen trying to remove it.

The man returned to the group. He didn't know what to do. He knew what Alaric was saying was correct, but he didn't want to let them out of the cage. If they escaped then there was no chance of saving the chief. The other villagers were just as confused as he was. In the end there was nothing more that they could do. They had to try and save the chief and letting Alaric go was their only chance. They didn't know how long the chief would remain in his current state before his body gave up.

"Fine. We will let you go, but your woman stays," the tribesman had a little more confidence in his voice.

It was not the best deal, but it was the best they were going get. When he showed them that he was not there to kill the chief he was sure that they would let them go. There was no way the Dark Knight's plan could work. At best it would only delay them a day. If that was the plan from the start then he had succeeded.

"I except your terms, but be assured that if any happens to Marina then your chief will suffer a much worse fate," they looked at him with confused expressions on their faces. Alaric wasn't sure why they were confused, but then he realised. "Make sure nothing happens to my woman."

They nodded their understanding and agreement. Alaric found it strange that they would not recognise Marina as a person. It was as if she was a possession. He shook his head as the lead tribesman opened the door to their prison. He thought about rushing him and trying to help Marina to escape, but there was a good chance that one of them would end up dead and that was not an acceptable risk.

The tribesmen, even with the two warriors standing guard, were very nervous until the prison door was shut. They were still wary with Alaric out of the cage, but they were more reassured with his woman safely locked up. The warriors stepped forward and stood either side of Alaric to make sure he didn't try and escape.

Alaric almost laughed when he saw Chief Omri lying on the floor. He was still convulsing slightly, which was the only sign he was still alive. His breathing was weak and heart was barely beating. His face was covered in sweat. There was nothing comical about his appearance yet Alaric's urge to laugh was almost overwhelming. He saw the Jade dagger in his hand and all humour left him. His hand was bone white as he gripped the hilt with all his strength.

"You fix him now," one of the warriors spoke, before menacingly waving his spear at Alaric.

Alaric crouched down beside the chief. He wasn't sure if he would be able to wrench the dagger clear, but he had to try. He could hear the gentle hum in the back of his mind, which was synonymous with the Jade stone. Suddenly the memory returned from the other night when the stone nearly took control of him and he pulled his hand back. He wondered if the stone could do to him what it was doing to the chief.

"You fix him," the tribesman barked before poking him in the back with his spear.

Taking a deep breath Alaric stood. He wasn't about to rush into anything. "Get me the wooden box," he commanded.

The box had been thrown across the room when the chief had started convulsing. Alaric thought about getting it himself, but thought the move might be taken the wrong way. It also gave him some command over the tribesman who quickly snatched up the box and handed it to Alaric.

Slowly Alaric touched the blade of the dagger. As soon as his fingers touched the blade the chief let his grip on the dagger drop. Alaric scooped it up before it hit the ground. As he did the soft hum turned into a loud buzz. Alaric grabbed at his head with his free hand. Slowly the sound started to subside. As it did Alaric realised that he was still holding the dagger. Suddenly the buzzing changed into an indistinct voice.

"Do not trust them. They are out to get you. Kill them all. It is the only way to set yourself free." The voice made sense. Alaric knew that he could kill them all before they even realised that they were under attack. It would be so simple. It would be easier than trying to talk his way out of the village.

"No!" Alaric spoke aloud. "I will not harm them."

At the sound of his words the tribesmen moved in close and levelled their spears at him. Alaric didn't notice the move, but the voice inside his head certainly did.

"See, they are coming to get you. If you don't strike first then they will kill you."

Alaric had to use all of his willpower to ignore the voice in his head. The words sounded very sweet and they made perfect sense, but he knew they weren't right. He forced himself to put the dagger back in its box. With the lid shut the voice inside of his mind disappeared. He took a deep breath before collapsing on a chair. It was at that moment he realised that the tribesmen had advanced on him. Without the dagger a wave of fatigued passed over him. The last thing he need was a battle.

"Wait!" Everyone was surprised to hear Omri speak. When the dagger was returned to its box his recovery had been almost instantaneous. "We have been duped." Omri walked to a chair opposite Alaric and sat. "This is not an enemy, he is a friend."

"Are you sure Chief Omri?" The tribesman asked in a rough voice. "This man tried to kill you."

"Harmi, are you stupid?" He waited for the rhetorical question to sink in. "This man didn't try to kill me. He tried to warn us and in the end he saved me." The tribesmen didn't look appeased. "When I was trapped I heard a voice in my head. It was soft and sweet. It told me some truths. The man who came here is pure evil. He told us lies because these two are chasing him. He wanted us to kill them for him. Now we will show them how grateful and apologetic we are."

The warriors lowered their weapons and stepped away from Alaric. They weren't exactly sure what Omri was telling them, but he was the chief and they had to obey him. Once he knew the threat was over Alaric visibly relaxed. Only Hamri seemed put out.

"If you wouldn't mind, I think my woman would like to be let out of the cage," there was a firmness to Alaric's voice. Although he was relieved that he did not have to attack he didn't want the others to know. Since he had the upper hand he had to keep the advantage.

"Of course. Move!" Omri snapped at the warriors and they quickly moved into action. "It seems as though I owe you an apology," the chief spoke when they were alone.

Alaric laughed. "I wouldn't worry too much. I know who it is who came to visit you and they can be very persuasive."

He could not remember much of the conversations that had been so clear in his mind. He knew that the man had deceived him, although he still did not know how he did it.

"We have mistreated you. What can I do to regain my tribe's honour?" the chief was very regretful.

"There is nothing to forgive. There is one thing that you could help me with." Alaric had a thought.

"What is it that you need? If it is something that I have then it is yours." Omri would do anything to help.

"Can you tell me anything you remember about your conversations with that man?" Alaric asked.

"It is the strangest thing. Before I picked up the dagger," he shivered as he mentioned the blade. "I could remember the words the man spoke to me. They were so sweet, but now I can't remember anything."

"It is quite important. Did he say where he was going? Did he mention anything about what he was planning?" Alaric was starting to become excited. He was so close. He could feel the prophecy calling out to him again. The sensation that had almost left him was growing stronger again.

Alaric reached out and touched the chief on the arm. He didn't know why he did it, but as he did he felt a subtle pulse of energy pass through his body and into the chief.

Suddenly something came back to him. The memory rushed back into his mind. His eyelids flickered for a moment before he spoke. "There is one thing that I remember. He mentioned to me that he was heading south. Now that I think about it I can't recall the conversation. Maybe I saw him leave to the south. Either way I am sure that he left to the south. I found this to be strange as the only thing that is south of here is the jungle. It's an inhospitable land. It is the end of the world. Some of my tribesmen have gone into the jungle, but none have ever returned."

Before Alaric could reply Marina came rushing into the hut. She flung herself into Alaric's arms. "What's happening?" there was a mixture of fear and confusion in her voice. She was sobbing gently as she pressed her face against his chest.

"It's alright," he gently stroked her long black hair as he spoke. "We have been set free. I will explain it to you later. For now I am trying to gather some information. Maybe you should have something to eat," he lifted her face off his chest before he spoke to Omri. "Is it possible for Marina to have something to eat," he was not comfortable to call her 'his woman'.

"Certainly," Omri called out. A young man entered shortly after. Omri instructed him to take Alaric's woman to be fed. Alaric thought about correcting him, but it wasn't worth the conversation.

"Thank you. Now please continue. Is there anything else you can tell me about the man?" Alaric was hoping for more information.

"There is only one other thing that I recall and that was quite strange. He carried with him a book. Although he was only here for a short time he would not let it out of his grip. Even when he sat down to eat he kept one hand on the book. I thought that this was odd," Omri mused.

Alaric thought on what he had been told. He knew that Na'garoz had the prophecy and there was nothing surprising about the way he treated it. It was no surprise that Na'garoz was heading south. Alaric could feel the prophecy drawing him in that direction, but what he wanted to know was why. He couldn't think of any reason why Na'garoz would take the prophecy south. There would be no one to help him there.

"Did he say anything about why he was travelling to the south?" Alaric asked, not really expecting a positive response.

The memory came rushing back to him, like it had before. His eyelids started to flicker and this time his hands started to shake. The sensation lasted for a lot longer this time. When Omri recovered he looked as though he didn't realise what had just happened.

"He did say one thing to me," Omri continued. "He said that he was travelling to a place, now what did he call it?" he made a sign of thinking. "Ah, that's right. He said that he was going to a place called the Southern Wasteland. I have never heard of the place myself. I thought that he might have been referring to the jungle, but he said that it was a land beyond the jungle. I didn't think he was telling the truth at the time, but now it does seem to make sense."

"Did he tell you what he was going to do in the Southern Wasteland?" Alaric asked.

There was no change in Chief Omri as he thought on the question. Alaric could see the frustration on his face. It was as if he was trying to remember something that was just out of his reach. He continued until he knew that it was not there.

"I am sorry Alaric. Each time that I think that I know the answer it's out of my reach. I don't think that he told me what he was planning on doing," Omri sounded upset.

Alaric watched him closely throughout the exchange. He knew there was something else. There was something about the way he reacted to Alaric's questions that wasn't quite right. It seemed more that he was fighting not to answer the questions than fighting to remember. A sudden realisation came over him.

"Do you mind if I try something?" The question was strange.

"Anything that I can do to rectify the situation," Omri didn't question what Alaric wanted to do.

"Just sit still and try to relax. I will try and make this as painless as possible," Alaric explained as he rose from his seat.

He squatted in front of Omri and raised his hand. The chief baulked for a moment, but quickly relaxed. A feeling of dread passed over him and he wanted to jump up and run out of the hut, but Alaric was blocking his path. He didn't know what Alaric was about to do, but he had to believe that he was doing the right thing. Taking a deep breath he calmed himself and relaxed.

Alaric wasn't exactly sure what he was about to do. Slowly he rubbed his hands together and then placed them on Omri's face. As soon as he their skin touched Alaric felt a small amount of energy pass between the two of them. There was something different about the energy than the first time. Alaric tried to concentrate on what it was, but the sensation disappeared before he could. Suddenly they both cried out in unison and then the hut went dark. The noise didn't reach those outside the hut, not that anyone could have done anything to help if they had.

"I was wondering how long it would take for you to join me here. It is good to see that you have underestimated my power. It is lucky for you that I have no intention of keeping you here," the voice was inside Alaric's head. He knew that it was Na'garoz.

"What do you want?" there was no concern in Alaric's voice.

"Straight to the point, I like that. Well here is the deal that I am offering. Leave me alone and I will make sure the prophecy does not end up in the wrong hands." Na'garoz gave Alaric his offer.

Alaric was about to point out that the prophecy was already in the wrong hands, but he didn't think that it was appropriate. Instead he had to ask the obvious question.

"Why would I trust you and why would you want to make such an offer?" Alaric asked.

"A fair enough question. I don't believe that there is anything that I could tell you to make you trust me. I can only tell you the truth and then you can make your own decision," the voice sounded reasonable enough, but it was also right. Alaric didn't think that there was anything that would make him believe a Dark Knight. "In light of recent events I do not think that I have backed the right team. You killed Fenaroz without much trouble and I assume you also did away with Morgoz. It seems to me that the Great Lord no longer has our back. If he is not going to look after me then why should I look after him? This seems like the best way out. I have something that you need, but also something that you don't want the Great Lord to get his hands on." There was something strange in his voice. Alaric knew that they were talking inside his mind, but there was still something strange. "I will keep the prophecy and stay in the Southern Wasteland until this is all over."

The words sounded true enough, but Alaric also knew that Na'garoz was trying to play with his mind. It seemed that Na'garoz was also underestimated him. He was not going to be fooled by simple tricks. He could also play the game.

"So if I leave you alone then you will no longer take part in this war?" Alaric reiterated what Na'garoz had told him.

"That is correct," Na'garoz thought for a moment. "Don't think that you can lie to me either. I am in your head and I know what you're thinking."

Alaric knew what he said was true. The Dark Knight was inside his head and would know what he was thinking. He couldn't lie, but he also couldn't tell the truth. There had to be away he could mislead the Dark Knight.

"Don't think you can be so clever. Remember that I hold the prophecy and I will soon know if you are still following me." Alaric imagined there was a sneer on the Dark Knights face, wherever he was.

There was something in the tone, or what he assumed was tone, that made Alaric suspicious. He quickly pushed the thought out of his mind before Na'garoz could realise he was thinking about it. He would need to be very careful.

"I know that you have the prophecy and I know how it works. What I don't know is what your motives are," Alaric returned.

"You will have to take me on face value, or mind value as it might be. Now time is running short and you need to make your decision," Na'garoz sounded worried.

"I will..." suddenly the room rushed back to Alaric.

The sensation caused Alaric to fall backwards. Omri was also shaken, but not nearly as much. The spell had broken so suddenly that Alaric had not been ready. There was a certain relief in his mind, although he wished he had received more information. The Dark Knight would know he was following and he still didn't know his reason behind running to the Southern Wasteland. He didn't believe that tale about not trusting Nyrra anymore. There would be an eternity of pain waiting for him if he even betrayed his master. There had to be another reason behind it. He thought about trying the connection again, but he knew it would do no good. Once the bond was broken there was no way to get it back.

"What was that all about?" Omri sounded confused.

Marina had been watching them, not knowing if she should try and help. There was nothing that she could do. As soon as the two separated Marina rushed to Alaric's side. It was her turn to try and comfort him. Alaric was grateful for the contact. The exchange had taken more out of him than he was willing to admit. The chance to rest was more than welcome, although he knew he could not stay for long.

"That was a little present that Na'garoz left behind for me," it was the first time that Alaric had used his name in front of Omri. He had intentionally left it out, just in case someone came looking for him, but it was too late.

"I can remember what happened now," Omri sounded surprised. The spell that Na'garoz had left behind had completely dispersed. "He did tell me something that he was planning."

Alaric was expecting such a response. The trap had been left in such a specific place. He didn't think that the information that he had given Omri would be creditable. It was still worth listening to what he had to say. Even misdirection would give him an insight into the Dark Knight's mind. If he was going to catch Na'garoz who was going to be one step ahead of him he had to use every advantage that he had.

"He told me that he was going to the Southern Wasteland to wait out the war. He said that he had been given a sign that was where he was supposed to be. He seemed somewhat nervous when he spoke to me." Omri was happy when he could clearly recall the events with Na'garoz. "There was something else." He paused, waiting for the inevitable response.

"What was it?" Alaric replied as he let he head rest back against Marina's chest.

"He spoke in another language to himself. It was a language that I have never heard before, yet I was able to understand every word. He said that there was something waiting in the wasteland. By the way he spoke it sounded as though it was important. I don't think that he realised that I was able to understand him and I don't know how I did. I think he was going to say more, but the way I was looking at him was making him uncomfortable. It was really strange that I was able to understand him."

Alaric gently pushed Marina aside and stood up. "Thank you for the information, but we have to be leaving."

"Please, don't leave right now. We still owe you a debt. We will kill a bison and feast on it tonight. There will be cava and dancing," Omri sounded excited.

"We have already lost so much time and really should be leaving." Alaric wasn't going to be dissuaded.

Alaric's body was still full of exhaustion from his ordeal with Na'garoz. Despite that he wasn't going to stay any longer than he had to. Unfortunately Marina had other ideas.

"We're not going anywhere Alaric. You can barely stand up," Marina spoke firmly and although she had no idea what had happened she knew he needed to rest. There was no chance he would make it an hour in the saddle. It would be much better if they rested in the relative comfort of the village. Marina would much prefer to spend the night indoors and in a bed, instead of another night on the ground. "Do you have somewhere Alaric can lay down? He needs a good rest before we leave again, which I think will be in the morning now."

"No, we must..." Alaric felt his legs go weak forcing him to stop what he was about to say. He steadied himself before speaking again. "Yes, I think that would be a good idea."

"Of course. There is an empty hut not far from here. You can both spend the night there," Omri smiled as he spoke.

Marina blushed slightly. Alaric was about to say something, but his exhaustion got the better of him. He couldn't think of anything more than to lay down and sleep. It was only just midday and it would be a long time before Marina would be tired. Until then Alaric would let it pass.

"Thank you and something to eat and drink would be great. We weren't given much in the cage," Alaric added as Marina put his arm around her shoulder to support him.

"Oh course," Omri shied away from the comment, although there was no malice in it. "I am terribly sorry for your mistreatment. Whatever you want, you shall have."

"Relax chief. There was nothing you could do. The Dark Knight has more power and magic than you have ever seen before." Alaric tried to calm him.

Omri thought on Alaric's words, not knowing how to respond. As much as his words were true the chief still couldn't get over the shame. There was a witchdoctor in the city, but that was as far as magic went. He didn't really understand what Alaric meant.

"Come on, let's get you into bed before you collapse," Marina broke the silence and started to edge Alaric towards the door.

The sight that met them was not at all what they expected. Hamri was standing with six warriors behind him all holding spears. Alaric and Marina felt concerned, but Omri didn't seem to notice.

"Just in time Hamri. Escort these two to Imari's hut," Omri commanded as he walked forward. It wasn't until no one moved that he realised something was wrong. "Why are you just standing there?"

"You have failed us for the last time Omri. You are no longer fit to be called chief. I am taking command of the tribe!" Harmi didn't falter. When he finished speaking the six warriors levelled their spears and took a step forward.

Chapter 7: Coup D'état

"You know the laws Hamri. If you want to usurp me then you need to battle me in single combat," Omri sneered.

After the initial shock Omri quickly composed himself. He moved to stand in front of Alaric and Marina. Normally he would have warriors to defend him, but that was not to case. After what had happened he wasn't going to let anything happen to his guests.

"It seems as though you have already ignored the old ways by letting this stranger take control of you and now you have sided with these other strangers. They all should have been killed on arrival." Hamri paused. "Now you will share their fate. They will be sacrificed to the Great on High tonight and so will you. Warriors!"

The warriors moved forward as Marina moved Alaric towards the back of the chief's hut. Without weapons there was little they could do against them, even though warrior's weapons were only crude. If Alaric had his strength he thought he could defeat them, but he was struggling to stand up. He thought about taking the dagger, but decided that would be more trouble than it was worth.

"I order you all to stop!" Omri yelled.

Although they did falter slightly none of them stopped their advance until they had the chief at spear point. They didn't seem too worried about the two standing behind. Hamri, on the other hand, recognised the threat they posed.

"Don't forget the other two and take the box away from them."

Alaric kept a firm grip on the box. He was not about to let it go again. Despite the fatigue a wave of adrenaline passed through his body and some of his strength returned.

"What are we going to do?" Marina whispered.

"I would rethink what you are doing," Alaric barked. "I have more power than what you can possibly understand." Although he didn't think he had the strength to cast any spells he had to act as though he could.

For a moment it seemed as though his bluff was going to work, but the warrior really didn't know what he was getting at. Only Harmi knew what had happened and even his understanding was limited. If they had known the danger they would have taken his threat more seriously.

"Don't listen to him," Hamri commanded. "Take his box and tie them up."

"You should make a run for it," Alaric said to Marina.

"I'm not leaving you."

Her sentiment was heartfelt, but Alaric wished she had listened to him. Since she couldn't understand their language she didn't know what they had planned. The last thing she wanted was to leave Alaric in his current state.

Two of the warriors stayed with Omri whilst the other four moved closer. Two went to Alaric. One kept his spear levelled at him whilst the other grabbed him by the arm. The other two moved on Marina. She wasn't about to go so easily. With a surprising strength she pulled away from the warrior and slapped him across the face. In turn the warrior smacked her across the face with the back of his hand. Although Alaric didn't see the attack he heard the strike and a rage started to build within him.

"I wouldn't do that again," Alaric growled.

The sound of his voice was enough to make the warriors pause. Hamri was too caught up in his own range to notice the danger that was before him. All he could see was his end goal, something that would never come to realisation.

"What are you waiting for? Grab them and let's get going."

Hearing the words made Alaric stiffen. He had hoped that his tone would have stopped them, but that was not going to be the case. Slowly the box slipped from his hands and crashed to the ground. For what he was planning he would need the use of his hands.

Quick as a flash Alaric grabbed the warrior, who was still holding his arm, by the wrist and twisted sharply. The warrior cried out in pain before crashing to the ground. Alaric turned his attention to the warrior with the spear who stood shocked. Quickly he grabbed the shaft and pulled the warrior towards him. When he was within striking distance Alaric punched him in the face. The warrior wobbled before dropping to the ground.

"What are you waiting for?" Hamri bellowed. "Kill them all."

Seeing their two fellow warriors lying on the ground, one unconscious and the other not willing to rise, caused the other warriors to rethink their plan of attack. It was obvious to them that they had failed. Even if they were able to kill Marina and Omri they doubted they would succeed against Alaric. One by one they turned around and marched on Hamri.

"We are sorry chief. What would you like us to do with him?" one of the warriors asked.

"Send him to the cage," Omri barked.

The warriors quickly moved into action. They didn't want to stay any longer lest the chief sentence them to death. One of the warriors also dragged away their fallen comrade. When they had all gone Alaric collapsed to his knees. The rage and all of his energy finally subsided. He didn't think he would have the strength to return to his feet.

"Are you alright?" Marina rushed to his side, but he pushed her away.

"I think I would like that hut now chief." There was a wry smile on his face. "But if it isn't too much trouble I think I'll need some help there."

The chief was about to speak, but Alaric waved him quiet. There would be time for conversation after he rested. It was all he could do to keep his eyes open.

Omri and Marina lifted Alaric onto his feet. With their assistance he was able to walk, albeit very slowly. It seemed to take forever to reach the empty hut and once he was inside he collapsed before he made it to the small bed. They had to carry him the rest of the way. Once Alaric was safely in bed Omri went to deal with the traitor. Marina remained behind to watch over Alaric.

It was dark by the time Alaric regained consciousness. He woke feeling somewhat refreshed, but deathly hungry and thirsty. His throat was so dry that he couldn't speak as he looked around the hut for something to drink. His movement stirred Marina who was sitting on the opposite side of the hut.

"Alaric?" Her voice was also hoarse, but hers from not being used. "Are you alright?" She slowly moved to the bed.

All Alaric could do was choke and make hand signals for water. Even in the dark it didn't take Marina long to realise what he needed. There was a pitcher of water and a pewter mug sitting next to his bed. She quickly poured the water and handed him a mug. The liquid hardly touched his mouth as he poured it down his throat.

It took two more mugs to quench his thirst. When he was finished he sat on the side of his bed. He still felt exhausted, but he needed to stretch his legs.

"I think some light would be good." The only light came from a fire burning somewhere outside the hut. Alaric really wanted to make sure all his things had been returned.

"That's what I thought as well, but there are no lamps or candles in the village. The only light is from the fires outside," Marina explained. "They have prepared a sacrifice for tonight," she sounded surprisingly excited. "The warrior who lead the failed coup is to be sacrificed to their god. Apparently it doesn't happen too often."

"I thought you couldn't understand them?" Alaric asked suspiciously.

"I can make out a few words and I got the rest by watching them." She paused. "I spent most of the day in here, but I had to get some fresh air."

Alaric didn't know why she had made the excuse and he quickly brushed it aside. He had more important matters to deal with. Despite what had happened he didn't want to see Hamri put to death. He needed to speak the chief before things went too far.

As soon as he was dressed he made his way out of the hut with Marina following behind. The only light came from a large fire in the centre of the village. It didn't take long for him to see that Hamri had been tied up to one side. Underneath the stake he was tethered to were piles of faggots. It was obvious how they were planning on sacrificing him. Alaric was relieved to see that they had not started. There was still a chance he could stop his death.

"Alaric!" Omri greeted him when he saw the two walking towards them. "I'm so glad you could make. We were just about to start and I didn't want you to miss out." He smiled.

"That's what I wanted to talk to you about," Alaric started, but he didn't get a chance to finish.

"There's no time for that. There is a chair for you over by the warriors. I figured that you would still be weak from your struggle."

Omri almost dragged Alaric to the other side of the fire. There was a large, throne-like, chair at the head of a group of tribespeople. Like all the other furniture it was made from bison bones and made Alaric feel very uncomfortable. Despite his concerns his legs were starting to wobble and he needed to sit down.

Once he was seated the festivities began. There was a circle drawn on the ground in what looked to be blood. Alaric wouldn't be surprised if it was and that didn't bear thinking about. He had to focus on the show before him. When he had the energy he would speak to the chief. For the moment it didn't look like they were in any hurry to sacrifice Hamri.

In the centre of the circle stood five warriors dressed in bison loincloths, with armbands and anklebands also made from bison fur. Their bodies had been completely shaved clean. The only hair that remained, which was on their heads, looked as though it had been treated with some oil. It hung down around their shoulders in wet strands.

Suddenly everything moved into actions. For the first time Alaric noticed there were tribesmen with crude drums on the far side of the circle. When the warrior started to move the men started to beat their drums. Every now and then one of the tribeswomen would screech. The first time Alaric heard he nearly jumped out of his chair. It took another three screams before he became used to it. He had to admit that dancing and the music was quite entertaining.

Marina stood behind Alaric and watched. As much as she wanted to make sure Alaric was alright she couldn't take her eye off the muscular bodies moving rhythmically before her. She had seen many entertainers in the palace, but nothing like what she was seeing. Whenever one of the warriors looked at her she felt her face go red. She hoped that no one would notice the change in the fire light.

To add to Marina's embarrassment she noticed that all the other tribespeople were only wearing loincloths, even the woman. She couldn't believe that all the women had their breasts showing to all the tribe. Sure, in the private bath houses in Kiarome the women would walk around topless, but there were never any men allowed. Suddenly she felt over dressed in her leather tunic and riding dress. The heat from the fire took away any cold from the night air.

When the warriors slowed their dance Alaric pushed himself to his feet. Although he was still exhausted he couldn't rest any longer. If they were going to kill Hamri when the warriors were finished then he would have to act quickly. Thankfully the chief wasn't too far away and he was able to make it to him without any assistance from Marina.

"This is wonderful chief, but I really need to speak with you!" Alaric had to shout to be heard over the ruckus.

"Don't be silly, the entertainment has just started. All you have to do is sit down and relax. Don't you worry, Hamri will be executed in due course." The chief didn't look at Alaric as he spoke.

"That is what I need to speak with you about," Alaric insisted.

"Very well." Omri didn't look happy as Alaric led him away from the fire.

"I don't think you should sacrifice Hamri," Alaric started when they were far enough away to talk. "It is not his fault that you were taken control of by the Dark Knight. The Knight is pure evil and would want this sort of reaction. You have to show him mercy," Alaric pleaded his case.

"I appreciate what you are saying, but there is nothing I can do about it now. It was Hamri's decision to try and wrest control from me and this is the punishment."

"Please Omri. You said if there was anything you could for me that you'd do it. This is what I want." Alaric was grasping at straws.

"If it was within my power I would change it, but there is nothing I can do about it now. He made his play for power and now he must suffer the consequences. If I didn't execute him then it would not be long before it will be me tied up. The tribe needs his death, it's the way it always been. There is nothing wrong with trying to take control of the tribe, but if you fail then that is the penalty. Hamri knew that before he made his decision and now he has accepted his execution," Omri explained.

It seemed there was nothing Alaric could do to change his mind. As much as he didn't want to see the tribesman killed he knew there was nothing he could do about it. He doubted it was the Dark Knight's goal to kill one man, but he wouldn't be upset with the result.

"Come on Alaric," Omri offered. "No one really likes the death part. It's the festivities that we are all here to enjoy."

Alaric lowered his head and walked back the others. His strength was slowly starting to return and he didn't want to sit any longer.

"Are you alright?" Marina spoke into his ear.

"I'll be fine," Alaric replied.

Alaric didn't want to talk. He was disappointed that when things were over they would still sacrifice Hamri. It was as if he had failed and the Dark Knight had won. He knew that wasn't really the case, but he couldn't help feeling it.

When the dancing finally came to an end the tribespeople moved into action. Long trestle tables and chairs were brought into the circle. It didn't take long for two long tables to be set. In the middle was a wider trestle table, with reinforced legs. A large bison, which had been roasting all day, was brought out by four large tribesmen. The table groaned under the weight of the great beast and just when Alaric thought its legs were going to snap the table settled.

It was time for the feast to begin and it reminded Alaric how long it had been since he had eaten. Since he had woken he had only drank water. Omri saved him the place of honour to his right hand side at the head of the main table. The chief thought about giving him the head, but he didn't think the rest of the tribe would understand. As much as he had secured his position by defeating Hamri he still needed to be careful. If he showed any sign of weakness then it wouldn't be long before someone else tried to take his place.

When everyone was seated and number of women came out from the darkness. Like the others they any wore loincloths, but there was something different about them. The cloths were not made out of bison hide, but instead it looked as though it was goat.

"Why are these women differently dressed?" Alaric ask Omri.

"They are slaves captured from other tribes. It is their job to serve us. As you can see they don't deserve the right to wear the bison hide. They wear the shameful goat hide that all servants wear." Omri smiled as he spoke.

The slaves walked around the table placing down large pewter jugs with the liquid Omri had called carva. There were also jugs of water for those who didn't drink carva, mainly the women and children. Alaric had to admit some of the slaves were quite attractive and he couldn't help but look at their almost naked bodies. When Marina realised she wasn't impressed.

"One would have thought you have never seen breasts before," she scolded.

Alaric blushed when he realised that she had noticed and quickly returned his attention to the chief.

"It would seem that if you help them as slaves it would give the other tribe a reason to attack you back." Alaric debated what he was going to say next. "And some of those women are quite attractive. I'm sure they would have husbands back in their own tribes?"

"Ah yes," Omri continued as one of the slaves poured him some carva. "Now be careful, this had a lot of kick to it," Omri warned before taking a sip. "It works the same way in all the tribes. Whenever one tribe takes slaves they are never married and never warriors. It is only ever young women and children who are taken as slaves. We keep them for a year and a day before they are returned to their own tribe. No slaves can be taken back before their time is up."

It seemed like a simple enough rule to Alaric, but he couldn't believe they all kept to it. "Surely not all the tribes stick to the rules? What if it was your son or daughter who was taken?"

Omri burst out laughing at Alaric's question. "My son is nearing the end of his year-and-a-day and my daughter was only taken a month ago. You see this is the way of our people. I myself was taken twice when I was younger. It is character building. It makes you appreciate what you have and makes you fight harder for those you love. None of the slaves are mistreated unless they refuse to serve their new masters. Occasionally one comes to us who believes they are not a slave. He is whipped until he or she becomes subservient. It has been the way of our people since the beginning of time."

Alaric nodded and took a draught from his mug before coughing uncontrollably. The liquid inside burned the back of his throat. Although the chief had warned him he had completely forgotten. His spluttering brought laughter from the entire tribe. Even Marina, who did her best not to laugh, had to snigger a little.

Before Alaric could speak the slave women brought platters of fruit for the first course. He was so hungry that he didn't care that he had looked the fool. Whilst they ate the first course there were slaves busy carving the bison. It was the meat that Alaric craved, but that didn't stop him eating the fruit.

Without any food in his stomach the strong carva had already gone to his head. The alcohol made him a little foggy, but he couldn't let the others know.

"Are you alright Alaric?" Marina asked when she noticed the strange expression on his face.

"I'll be fine," Alaric rubbed his head after finishing a small banana. "The carva was a little stronger than I thought."

Marina laughed softly. "That's why I'm drinking water." She smiled a little too sweetly at him, but he put it down to the alcohol.

"You may never be here again, why don't you live a little?" He wasn't sure where the words came from, but they were definitely his.

Marina looked at him carefully. There was definitely something playing about his little jibe, but she knew she shouldn't drink the carva. She had drunk wine plenty of times at her father's feasts, but there had always been someone there to make sure she made it back to her apartment unmolested. As she looked around she figured she was safe enough. None of the other men had taken any notice of her. As far as they were concerned she was Alaric's property and that in itself would keep her safe.

"I don't see you drinking anymore," she winked at him as a slave girl poured her a mug of carva.

Slowly she sniffed the liquid before screwing up her noise. It had a strange smell and she wasn't sure she wanted to taste it. When she realised that he was staring at her she knew she didn't have a choice. After watching his reaction earlier she only took a sip and despite her best efforts she started coughing. The alcohol was stronger than anything she had drunk before.

Again the tribespeople started to laugh at her reaction. At first she blushed before laughing herself. She raised her mug, said "Cheers!" before taking another sip. The second time she was able to swallow the vile liquid without coughing.

"Now it's your turn," Marina challenged Alaric as her head started to swim.

"I would be careful if I were you," Omri offered as Alaric took another drink. "It might not seem like much, but carva has a big kick to it. I would advise a full stomach before you drink anymore."

Just when he finished speaking the slaves were bringing the carved bison to the table. Along with the meat came a variety of vegetables. Alaric couldn't wait to fill his plate and start eating. The fruit had been a nice starter, but it didn't fill his stomach.

"I'm sorry Alaric, but I must say a few words before we start eating," Omri apologised just as Alaric was about to take a mouthful. As he stood the tribe went silent and the only sound was the fire crackling. "My fellow tribesmen and women!" Omri's voice boomed. "I stand here today because Hamri was unsuccessful in his attempt to usurp power from me." His words brought a roar from the rest of the tribe. He waited until the cheers died down before he continued. "Many have tried to kill me in the past and many will again in the future," his words brought silence again. "And I hope they do, as we deserve many more feasts!" Again the tribe cheered. Alaric hoped things would go quicker so he could start eating. He thought about sneaking some food, but since he was sitting next to the chief he didn't think he would get away with it. "Now the man sitting next to me has a lot to do with my victory today and that is why he sits at the place of honour. His name is Alaric and he is our most welcome guest and will be so until my rule comes to an end." There were a few more cheers, but not as many. "Now eat! And drink! Tonight is time to celebrate." The rest of the tribe joined in the cheer and when he finished speaking Omri returned to his seat.

As soon as the chief was seated Alaric started eating. He neither noticed nor cared that everyone else had raised their mug and drank to his and the chief's health. Marina only raised her mug and pretended to drink.

The meal went quickly and Alaric passed the time making small talk with Omri and then Marina. He thought about trying to convince Omri not to sacrifice Hamri, but he knew it would do him no good. The entire tribe was out for blood and nothing but the death of the traitor would sate them.

"I notice that there are only women and girls serving," Alaric started a new conversation. "Do you not have any men or boys as slaves?"

"Serving is no job for a man," Omri sounded surprised at the question. "The boys and men were the one responsible for gathering the wood for the fire. They will also help with the cleaning when the women clear the tables."

When everyone had eaten their fill the slaves returned to take the plates away. Everyone stood and the tables were separated and moved to the outside of the circle.

"What happens now?" Alaric asked.

"There is some more entertainment before we move on to the sacrifice." Alaric emptied his mug at the sound of the sacrifice. "Go easy on that, you don't want to be too drunk before the sacrifice."

Alaric wasn't so sure that was the case. Watching a man burn alive wasn't his idea of fun. He wanted to return to his hut and forget the rest, but he didn't think Omri would be pleased. The last thing he wanted was to make the chief look weak in front of the tribe. He also couldn't look weak himself. Not all the tribespeople were happy with his presence and he didn't want to give them any further reasons to dislike him.

Another group of warriors walked out into the circle. Two of them held six foot poles with material wrapped around each end. Another two had a length of rope and another stood in the middle simply holding a jug.

One of the warriors holding a pole walked towards the large fire. Carefully he placed one end close to it and to Alaric's surprise it burst into flame. When he returned to middle he lit the other pole and the ends of the ropes.

When they were all lit the warrior walked away from each, leaving the one with jug in the middle, and started to twirl the fire around in a magical display. Alaric had never seen anything like it.

"This is wonderful," Marina cooed beside him.

Alaric had to agree. He took a mouthful of carva as he started to relax for the first time. The fire twirling was mesmerising and he was quite content just to stare. One of the warriors with the poles moved into the centre and held one end up in front of the warrior with the jug. Slowly the warrior poured some of the liquid into his mouth. To their surprise he blew fire from his mouth. The tribespeople cheers, Alaric clapped and Marina giggled softly.

"More carva!" Alaric called out in the common tongue. He raised his mug and the slaves knew exactly what he was after, even if they couldn't understand him.

"Are you sure you should be drinking anymore?" Marina asked.

"It's festival, drink up!" Alaric slurred his words as he passed Marina his full mug and took her empty one. When it was filled he took another mouthful. The strong drink no longer burnt his throat like it had when he first tasted it.

The warriors continued until the flames finally burned out. That was the moment Alaric had been dreading. With the entertainment over it was time to move onto the sacrifice. He stood slowly as everyone started to make their way to the stake and Hamri's doom. His legs wobbled and he promptly fell back on his chair. The carva made his head swim and as much as he wanted to believe his weakness was due to the day's events he knew that wasn't true.

"Come on Alaric," Marina's words were slurred, or at least that's how they sounded to Alaric. "We have to get this over and done with."

Her words steeled his heart and forced him to his feet. She put her arm around him, just as much to steady herself as it was to steady him, and they followed the crowd. Omri led the way and he didn't seem to mind that they were mixed in with the tribe. The last thing Alaric wanted was to be brought to the fore for the sacrifice.

As much as they tried to stay in the middle of the tribe they were slowly bumped and pushed to the front. When they were finally there Omri signalled for silence and the sacrifice was ready to begin.

"Hamri, you have been charged with failing a revolt. If you had succeeded I would be burning and you would be chief. There is no shame in trying, only shame in failing. Do you have anything to say?" his voice boomed.

Hamri remained quiet, but he looked up for the first time. His lips were dry and starting to crack. He had not been given anything to eat or drink since he had been taken. His eyes were bloodshot, but not from crying. It looked as though he had been suffering for a while.

"Nothing to say?" Omri boomed again.

"I go to the Great Sky with a clear head and clear heart," Harmi's voice cracked has his tried to get the words out. His throat was dry and talking was difficult. "I did what I did for the good of the tribe and have no regrets."

Alaric wasn't sure he believed his last words as his head started to swim. He felt his stomach churn, but he refused to let anything come up. The urge to turn and run was almost unbearable, but he steeled himself nevertheless.

"Then we send you to the Great Sky with hope for your redemption. The Great on High will judge you and his judgement in final. If your heart is true then you will have a peaceful eternity. If your heart is not true then you will burn on the stake for all time." That was the end of his speech. When he finished two warriors brought burning sticks to light the faggots underneath Hamri.

"I can't watch." Marina buried her head against his chest.

There would be no shame for a woman to squirm, but Alaric would have to remain staunch. As the fire slowly started to light around the stake he felt flush in the face. As the fire intensified so did Alaric's face. The last thing he remembered was hearing Hamri cry out with pain. The warrior had waited as long as he could before crying out. The sound would stay with Alaric for the rest of his life.

Chapter 8: A Night to Forget

Alaric woke with a start and a roaring headache. The memory of his dreams had already faded, but he knew there was something that had woken him. Quickly he sat up in his bed and instantly wished he hadn't. The hut started to spin so he let himself collapse back onto the bone headboard. With the sudden movement his stomach started to churn. There was something inside him that wanted out, but he wasn't going to let it.

When his head stopped rattling and the room stopped spinning he suddenly realised where he was. The events of the previous day and night were still sketchy.

Feeling a little better he sat up and rubbed his head. A sudden shock filled his body when he realised he wasn't alone in the small bed. Quickly he jumped up and when he looked down he realised he was only wearing a very loose fitting loincloth. It took him a moment to recognise it as bison hide, but he had no idea why he was wearing it.

The night was still hazy in his mind and he wasn't sure he wanted to look around and see who was sharing his bed. There had been a lot for tribeswoman at the festival, but he couldn't imagine taking one to his bed. He remembered the carva and what a vile drink it was and the bile started to rise in his throat. He pushed the thought aside along with his stomach.

"Is it morning?" Alaric was slightly relieved to recognise Marina's voice, but only slightly. She sounded just as well as he felt. The memory was blurry, but he was sure she wasn't drinking as much as he was. Something had obviously changed.

"I'm afraid so."

He kept his back to her as he spoke, not wanting her to see him in his current state. The sounds of the bed covering being shifted could be heard from behind. Without looking he knew she was standing behind him. He looked around for his clothes, but they weren't there.

"I have to admit that the day started out very bad, but in the end it was quite fun. Even though I am the Princess of this Kingdom I had no idea these people existed. Sure we have all heard of the warrior tribes to the south, but I had no idea what they were like."

Alaric turned around when she finished speaking. He was about to respond, but then he turned around quickly. Marina was also dressed in the loincloth of the tribespeople and that was all she wore. Her breasts were complete exposed except for the odd strand of black hair flowing down. His heart rate started to rise and he could feel his face turning red.

"You didn't seem to mind last night," she tried her best playful tone, but struggled with her dry mouth.

Alaric wished he could remember what had happened. He hoped there was nothing untoward. It wasn't that Marina wasn't a very attractive woman, but he couldn't afford any romantic attachments. His mission was too important to get distracted by romantic issues. There may be a time where he had to choose between Marina and the prophecy and as much as it pained him he knew which choice he had to make.

Slowly he turned around. Marina had covered her breasts with her flowing black hair, which event after a night around a fire still seemed to shine in the morning light. Alaric wasn't really sure if it was better or worse. Ideally should would have found her clothes and dressed. It seemed as though she was revelling in his discomfort. It was at that point he realised his loincloth was started to slide down. The last thing he wanted was to reveal his own nakedness.

His clothes had been stacked on a chair in the corner of the hut. Without responding to Marina's taunt he moved to get dressed. With his back to Marina he quickly whipped off the loincloth and dressed in his riding clothes. He didn't care if she watched he just wanted to be fully clothed again.

"What happened last night?" Alaric asked as he turned around, grateful to see that Marina had also dressed herself. "I remember up to the sacrifice and then everything is blank."

Marina shivered at the mention of the sacrifice. She had kept her face buried against his chest, but there was nothing that could keep Harmi's screams out. Like Alaric it would be a sound that would stay with her for a long time. Her father had made her watch executions in Kiarome, but hangings were much quieter.

"After the sacrifice the tribe went back to the circle. Some of the warriors started to beat on their drums and the rest of the tribe got up and danced. Omri told you that we were welcome to join them, but we needed to wear their garb. At first I really didn't want to, but you were so persistent." She stuck her tongue out and smiled. If Alaric wasn't feeling so terrible he would have retorted, but instead he just waited for her to continue. "We drank and danced long into the night. I was so wonderful," she swooned. "It's such a shame it's morning already." The effects of the previous night returned. "I guess there's no chance of returning to bed?"

Alaric wished he could have said yes. The last thing he felt like was riding, but they had already lost too much time. He could feel the prophecy tugging at him, but it was so far away.

"We have to get going."

Outside they found of group of slave girls waiting for them. They all started giggle when they saw Alaric and Marina. Alaric didn't think it was a good sign, but he really didn't want to know why. If his memory didn't want to know then he was happy to accept it.

"Where is the chief?" he asked.

The girls giggled again before turning around and walking away. Alaric assumed they meant to take them to the chief and motioned for Marina to follow. The girls didn't look as though they wanted to speak and Alaric wasn't going to push them. The sooner they got to the chief the sooner they could be on the move again.

"Good morning Alaric," Omri greeted them with a smile as he stood out the front of his head. "I wasn't sure if we were going to see you today. You were hitting the carva fairly hard last night."

Alaric ignored the jibe. "Thank you for your hospitality, but we need to be leaving now. Are our horses here somewhere?"

The smile slowly faded from the chief's face. "I was hoping we might spend some time together and you could tell me of the rest of the world."

"I wish that I could Omri. I'm sure there is a lot we could learn from each other, but we have already dallied long enough. Our quarry had an extra day on us and that won't be easy to make up," Alaric explained.

Ormi nodded his agreement. "At least would you stay for something to eat?"

Alaric felt his stomach rumble and knew it was in no state to receive any food. As much as he didn't think being in the saddle wouldn't make him feel any better he thought it would be preferable to standing around.

"I'm sorry Omri, but we really need to get moving," Alaric replied.

"Do you think we could eat before we leave?" Marina asked, as if she could understand the conversation.

"There's no time," Alaric replied without turning from the chief.

Omri had someone send for their horses. In the mean-time he tried to convince Alaric to stay. Alaric did all he could to be polite before their horses finally arrived. They had already been saddled and packed with their possession and Alaric was grateful that he didn't have to waste any more time.

"I hope our paths meet again Chief Omri. If it does then I will certainly share some food, time and stories." Alaric felt a slight amount of sorrow for leaving.

"I will look forward to that day Alaric. Take care and I hope you find what you are looking for."

As much as she had enjoyed the previous night's festivities Marina had to admit she was happy to be out of the village. She still remembered the night they spent in the cage, but Hamri's scream would take a lot longer to disappear. Despite the memory she was happy to ride in silence. Alaric was in a sombre mood and she didn't want to do anything to upset him. The sun was high in the sky when Alaric finally allowed them to stop. His stomach made the final decision. He could feel the bile rising and knew if he didn't eat something then he would vomit uncontrollably.

Alaric stared at his food as they sat by a small stream. It was clear that he didn't want to speak. Something had been plaguing Marina's mind since they had left the village and as much as she wanted answers she knew better than to disturb him. There would be time for questions and it wasn't then.

Alaric stared to the south as they rode. Omri had given them a rough map of the surrounding area so they wouldn't run into another tribe. They both thought it best to avoid any further entanglements. Their path for most of the day led to the west with only a gradual turn to the south. Alaric had a bad feeling that they were heading in the wrong direction, but they couldn't risk falling into another of Na'garoz's traps.

An hour before nightfall they were finally able to swing around to the south. Alaric felt much more comfortable when they did. The prophecy was ever tugging at him and when he strayed, even a little, he felt sick in the stomach. He would have blamed the carva, but after he had eaten he had felt much better. There was no doubt it was the prophecy telling him they were heading in the wrong direction. All he could do was suffer through the discomfort and wait for the chance to get back on track.

Dusk was upon them when the jungle came into sight. Smaller awarra palms scattered around the sandbox trees which loomed up before them. The temperature and humidity had been gradually increasing since they left the village. The cool of the evening was a pleasant change and neither of them wanted to enter the forest before nightfall and set up camp.

Alaric busied himself setting a small fire and unpacking the animals. He would do anything to avoid the conversation he knew was coming. Throughout the day he saw Marina try and speak to him, but each time she had decided against it. He hoped if he kept busy then she would avoid it, but he knew he was only delaying the inevitable.

"What happened back in the Chief's hut?" Marina asked as they ate their evening meal.

Alaric had kept his eyes on the fire as he ate, hoping they would put Marina off speaking to him. There was nothing he could do to avoid answering the question. Slowly he started to explained, as best he could, what had happened.

"Na'garoz had left a spell in Omri's mind. It was a direct link to his conscious. When I touched him it unleashed the spell and I was drawn into a conversation with the Dark Knight." Alaric paused as he considered how much he was going to tell her. In the end he decided to tell her everything. "There is more to what Na'garoz offered," Alaric continued when he finished his tale. "He would never turn his back on the Evil One. Betrayal would be much worse than failure."

"Why would he offer his help to you then, or least offer to leave us alone? Surely their main goal is to kill you?" Marina asked.

The question had been plaguing Alaric for most of the day. Although he wasn't completely sure he had come up with a few theories. "At first I had no idea why he would be offering such a deal. There was no real reason for him to lie. The is a reason why he is travelling to the Southern Wasteland and more of a reason why he doesn't want us to follow him." Alaric paused as he thought over his reasoning. It was one thing to think it, but another to voice his suspicions. "I believe he is searching for one of the stones. If he can decipher the prophecy then there is no telling what information he could find. I think that is where the Jade stone is leading us." If that was true then the dagger was leading them in the right direction and he would no longer need to just follow the feeling deep inside him.

"Do you think the Ruby stone is there?" Marina almost bit her tongue as the words came out.

It was another question that had passed through his mind. "I don't think that is the case. If it was the Ruby stone then I'm sure Na'garoz would have sent for the Evil One. I don't think he would dare try and take the stone himself. No, I think there is another stone waiting for us in the wasteland. Which one? I have no idea. The Jade dagger will point to a stone, but it won't tell me which one." That was something that he wished was true. If he could control the Jade stone then he could find the Ruby stone instead of chasing shadows around the Seven Kingdoms and beyond. "We will need to make haste through the jungle. He had a long head-start and we need to catch him before he finds the stone."

"Do you have any idea what to expect in the wasteland?" Marina asked.

"I have no idea. I have poured many hours over the pages of the great tome, but there was no mention of the Southern Wasteland. In all my years of study I have never found anything on the wasteland except it is as the name suggests. It is a barren wasteland. Do you know anything about it?" Marina had spent a lot of time being tutored in the palace of Kiarome and Alaric hoped the wasteland was one of her subjects.

"Unfortunately there is little I can add to help," Marina replied. She really wanted to be of some use, but there was little information on it. "I don't know anyone who haa ventured there and returned to tell the tale. Every now and then some adventurers bravely, and foolishly, travel to the wasteland and are never seen again. If there are any books about it in the great library I haven't seen any."

"What about the jungle? Do you know much about it?" Alaric changed the subject when it was clear they were getting nowhere.

"There is little information about the jungle." That statement wasn't exactly true. There were plenty of books on the jungle in the great library, some were even accurate, but she had never taken much notice. "The vegetation is thick, with some huge trees. There is a lot of swampland and

some dangerous animals. Besides that it should be a walk in the park."
Her sense of humour was lost on Alaric.

"Then I think we should get an early night. There is no telling what we
will be dealing with in the morning."

They went to sleep with the thought of the unknown deep in their minds.
Marina wished she had paid more attention when her tutor was teaching
her about the jungle, but it had just been so boring. Eventually she fell
asleep with that thought in her mind. It took Alaric a little longer to fall
asleep. He could feel the prophecy calling to him and there was a new
urgency about it. For a moment he thought about waking Marina and
continuing, but sleep eventually overcame him.

They both woke early in the morning eager to be on the move as soon as
the sun rose. The jungle loomed up before them when the sun finally
crested the horizon. It was a complete change in scenery. The lush fields
stopped and the thick foliage of the jungle began. When they reached the
outskirts it was clear that they would not be able to ride. It was going to
be hard enough leading the horses.

The tropical trees grew high in the sky. Below the trees the undergrowth
was thick. Vines hung down from the trees creating a difficult path for
them to follow. Many shrubs and small trees dotted the space between the
larger ones. Alaric drew his sword when they entered the jungle. It was
obvious that he would have to cut his own path.

The morning continued slowly. The ground underfoot was uneven and
the undergrowth was thick. To make matters worse the temperature kept
rising. It was not long before Alaric had stripped down so he was only
wearing his pants. Even with his sword cutting through the undergrowth
by midday he had many scratches across his chest and back from the
many thorns and needles.

It was early afternoon when the ground started to soften. It was obvious
they were getting close to the swampland. Their travelling would become
even slower. The slow pace and the high heat were starting to irritate
Alaric. With each passing hour the travelling became slower and slower.
As the light started to fade they realised there was nowhere suitable for
them to camp for the night. The ground was uneven, covered with
shrubs, ferns and roots. To make matters worse ground was becoming
wetter and wetter. The dirt had become soft mud and there were ever
increasing pools of water.

"What are we going to do?" Marina asked as they looked around for
somewhere suitable to sleep.

"There was some dry ground not too far back. I think that is our only
option. I don't know about you, but I don't feel like a night in the mud,"
there was a slight amount of humour in his voice. Marina was glad he

could see the light side as his mood throughout the day had been gradually deteriorating.

The light had completely faded by the time they had cleared and area suitable for their camp. Even without the sun the temperature didn't drop. What the night did bring for them was a new variety of bugs. There were insects pestering them during the day, but nothing like what they were experiening. Before they had lost light altogether Alaric had managed to scavenge enough dry wood to light a small fire and that made the insect situation even worse.

"This is getting ridiculous," Alaric said as he slapped the side of his face. "How are we supposed to get any sleep like this? If the heat won't keep us awake then the bugs will."

"They do seem to be drawn to the light. Maybe we should put the fire out when we go to sleep?" Marina suggested.

When she finished talking they heard the sound of a large animal scream in the distance. Neither of them knew what it was, but they thought is sounded large and angry. Marina instantly shuffled closer to Alaric, but stopped before she touched him.

"Maybe we should keep the fire burning?" Alaric smirked as he asked the question.

"I have heard that fire will keep animals away because whatever that was it sounded hungry."

There was suddenly some movement in the trees above them and Marina jumped into Alaric's arms. She felt suddenly foolish for the act, but held onto him tightly nevertheless. Alaric had to admit that, despite the extra heat from her body, that he liked the feel of her body against his.

"I think we should stay close tonight," Alaric said as he gently stroked her hair.

Although the fear had gone Marina remained cuddled up to Alaric. It was the first real time he had shown her any real affection and she wasn't going to do anything to end it. Eventually Alaric released his hug and gently pushed her aside.

"I think we should try and get some sleep now," Alaric suggested as he suddenly felt uncomfortable.

Alaric fuelled the fire before lying on his bedroll. He hoped there was enough wood to keep the animals away as he couldn't build the fire too large. There was a lot of flammable vegetation around and the last thing he wanted to do was start a jungle fire.

It took a long time for either of them to fall asleep and it was a restless night. The insects were incessant and the high heat didn't waver. In the morning they both woke covered in sweat and bites. After a short meal they both keen to be on the move again.

The jungle canopy kept the heat in during the night and the morning it only became hotter. Alaric hadn't bothered putting a shirt on and soon enough Marina had to take hers off. Her milky white skin was covered in small red spots from where the insects had feasted on her. Even with her leather riding shirt they still managed to get through.

The further they travelled the more the ground started to deteriorate. It wasn't long before the dirt became mud and then a watery slush. The horses were starting to struggle just as much in the bad conditions. There was no doubt if they continued on their same course they would end up in one of the many swamps.

"This is ridiculous," Marina voiced what they were both feeling when they stopped to eat.

Alaric's shoulders slumped when she spoke. He was trying to remain positive, but there was no point. The water came half way up their legs and it was only getting deeper. It would only be a matter of time before their movement was completely hindered. Alaric had been so preoccupied with heading south that he hadn't been thinking. There was no telling how far they would have to travel to get around the swamp. He looked out in front and all he could see was water and trees.

"You're right. We have come too far," Alaric sounded resigned.

Alaric looked behind and all he could see was water and trees. He looked to the sky, but could not see the location of the sun through the thick canopy. When he thought about it he really didn't know if they were still travelling south. The only way he could truly gauge the right direction was to check the stone. It was not something that he wanted to do, especially in their current location. It had been quite taxing in the past to have the stone out of its box and if something went wrong he could very well end up face down in the swamp.

"I will check the dagger," he spoke more to himself than to Marina.

"Do you think that is such a good idea?"

"I don't think we have any choice. I believe that we are still travelling south, but it is hard to tell without the sun to guide us. Everything looks the same. There is every chance that we are walking in circles."

"If we were travelling in circles I doubt the water level would keep rising," Marina pointed out the obvious.

Alaric knew that was true, but he didn't care. It didn't change the fact that they could no longer continue going forward. Once they started changing direction they could end up anywhere. He still believed that it was the right decision. There was no other way to alleviate his concerns.

Before he could take the box from Adelanta something brushed passed his leg. The sudden sensation made him jump and cry out. He didn't know what it was, but it didn't feel nice. His sudden reaction surprised Marina and she looked at him and waited for an excuse. When he calmed down again he felt foolish. He was sure that it was just a fish, although it did feel long and slimy. The more he thought about it the more he thought that it was a snake. That made him even more uncomfortable, which in turn made Marina more worried. She started trying to see into the murky water around her.

"What was it?" she finally asked when Alaric refused to speak.

"What?" He only then realised that she was still looking at him. "Oh I am sure it was just a fish," his voice was nervous, which did nothing to reassure Marina. "But that is not the point. It is time to check the dagger," there was a little more confidence in his voice.

Alaric quickly opened the box without waiting. The buzz returned to the back of his mind, but he was quick to dismiss it. The Jade stone glowed slightly in its case before Alaric had even picked it up. The common rush passed through his body when he did and it was nearly enough to knock him off his feet. When the feeling passed he cursed himself for not being ready for it. Handling the stone was dangerous enough and he could ill afford to be complacent.

Slowly he moved the dagger around and when he did he was glad to see that they had still been travelling in a southerly direction. The only problem was that they could not continue that way. When he was satisfied he returned the dagger to its box. He thought he could hear something whining before he shut the lid. It was the first time it had happened so he was not sure if he had imagined it or not. He shook his head before returning his attention to Marina.

"Which way do we go now?" he seemed a little happier than before he checked the stone.

Marina was a little shocked by the question, but she had already thought of the best course. "I think we should head west."

It was Alaric's turn to look surprised. "Why west?" he had not expected such a definitive answer.

"The water, albeit slowly, is flowing from the east. That means that the source of the water is in the east, so it should narrow the more we travel to the west. Hopefully we won't have to back track." Her logic seemed to make sense.

Since Alaric didn't have any other ideas he had to go with Marina's. He started leading Adelanta to the west. At first the water level started to drop, but that did not last long. Shortly after they started again the water was almost up to their waist. Alaric was concerned that they had lost themselves in the middle of the swamp. He looked around, but there was no clear path out of the water. Safe passage out of the swamp could be in any direction.

"I don't think your plan worked," Alaric didn't mean to be offensive.

"Well I didn't see you coming up with any ideas," Marina was straight on the defensive.

"Sorry, I didn't mean to accuse you. I'm just frustrated. There is no telling which way is going to get us out of the swamp," Alaric apologised.

Marina had to agree that their situation was becoming dire. They could not stop whilst they were in the water and if they travelled once it was dark there was no telling where they would end up or what trouble they would get into. Looking around she realised there was no way to tell which way was which.

"I think that we should go north," Alaric resigned himself to the fact that they would have to retrace their steps. He looked around again, hoping to see something that would give them a sign. There was nothing. He didn't even have a feeling on which way he should go. The only sensation was the constant pull towards the prophecy.

"There has to be another way," Marina was even less excited about having to go backwards. "Besides, do you even know which way is north?" Marina looked around again, but couldn't figure out which way was which.

Alaric closed his eyes and concentrated. He felt the swampland around him. He could hear the multitude of insects buzzing around his head. Slowly he pushed those feelings aside and focused on the prophecy. It was the only way he could tell which way was the needed to go.

"We have to go north," Alaric did not sound happy. "It has to be the only way out of the swamp."

Marina was about to say something, but realised that it was no good. She had to admit that Alaric was right. They had to get out of the swamp.

It did not take long before they realised that north was also not the answer. At the start the water lever started to drop and their hopes grew, but that did not last long. The water level soon returned to waist height and was only getting deeper. To make matters worse what had previously been a soft swamp bed was turning into a quagmire. It was taking longer and longer to take each step. Eventually Alaric had to stop them again. Marina was shorter than Alaric and if the water kept rising she would have to start swimming.

"Now what are we going to do?" Marina asked when it was clear he was not just taking a break.

"This is starting to get ridiculous," his voice was thick with frustration.

"We keep heading north," there was confidence in Marina's voice. It was so surprising that Alaric turned to face her.

"What are you talking about? It is only getting worse the further north we travel." He didn't like what she was suggesting.

"We swim. I don't know why, but I still think north is the best way out of this mess." Alaric knew well enough that if someone had a feeling they should listen to it. He didn't think that it was the right choice, but he had no better ideas.

"If you think so," Alaric raised his hands in the air and continued walking. They had only been walking for another fifteen minutes before the water was too deep for them to walk. Swimming was easier for Alaric than it was for Marina. Alaric was able to let Adelanta's reins go and concentrate on swimming knowing that the horse was going to follow. Marina, on the other hand, had to keep a grip on her mare's reins. Even so she was comfortably keeping up with Alaric's pace.

The light was starting to fade and they could still not touch the bottom, at least not without putting their heads under water which neither of them wanted to do. To make matters worse both Marina and her mare were starting to struggle and Alaric was useless to help. He could do nothing more than keep his own head above the water. There was no chance for them to rest until they reached shallower waters.

Slowly Marina's head started to drop beneath the water. On her second time down Alaric heard her choke and gasp for air. Although she was a good few paces behind he heard her clearly. He was quick to swim to her side. He was not the strongest of swimmers, but he would do anything to save Marina. She disappeared under the water for the third time when he finally reached her. He had to grapple under the water until he found her. He did his best to pull her back above the water as well as keeping his own head up.

"Are you alright?" it was a stupid question, but he felt as though he should ask it.

"I think I might have made the wrong decision," she puffed the words. She felt weak in Alaric's arms. At first he thought that she was just a little tired, but soon enough he knew that she was truly exhausted. He didn't think that she would be able to swim any further. If she was going to survive Alaric was going to have to help. Adelanta had swum over to see if he could help. Alaric was quick to pass the reins of the mare over to him. The white, although after swimming in the swap he was almost grey, stallion understood. He was happy to take responsibility for the mare. The mare also seemed to be happier having Adelanta in the lead.

The travelling was slow, but they were on the move again. It took Alaric a while, and a number of underwater excursions, before he found the best way the transport her. The swimming was too demanding for him to enjoy being so close Marina. The adrenaline that was pumping through his body was all that was keeping him afloat.

Adelanta was the first one to touch the ground again. His excited whinny sparked Alaric's attention, which in turn nearly made him drop Marina. He had only seen Adelanta for a moment, but he knew the stallion had hit land. It was just as muddy and uncomfortable to walk in as the ground they had left, but that didn't matter. The sight only increased Alaric's pace. In his rush to be able to stand up he almost used up all of his energy. Even when he was able to stand they still had to travel to dry land. When his feet finally touched the soft muddy ground his legs nearly collapsed underneath him. If he wasn't still in the water he would have. Marina was just as grateful to be able to place her feet on the ground. Even the mud felt heavenly under foot. She still kept her arms tightly wrapped around Alaric. They were both happy to use each other for support. They could see the two horses a little way in the distance. They were already half way out of the water. They didn't want to get their hopes up, but it looked as though they were at the edge of the swamp.

The light had completely disappeared and they were still up to their waist in water.

"What are we going to do now?" Marina's voice was afraid.

Although they could hear the horses splashing in front of them they didn't want to move in the dark. It was bad enough trying to find their way with light.

Suddenly Alaric felt a strange itch on the back of his neck. At first he thought it was an insect bite, but when he scratched it there was nothing there. After a moment he remembered something that Eldred had done when they were in the dark. Slowly he created the spell and a small orb of light appeared in front of them. It was enough to see a few paces all around them.

"Wow! What is that?" Marina gasped in surprise.

Alaric laughed softly to himself before he replied. "Just a little spell. I really don't know why I didn't think of it earlier."

They were both dead on their feet when they finally reached dry land. The land itself was not so dry, but it was better than what they had been wading through. The smell of the swamp was still thick in their noses. As much as they had become used to it was still very unpleasant. The temperature remained warm and soon they would be dry again. The mud was not going to be suitable for sleeping, but they didn't have the energy to walk any further.

"We stay here," Alaric almost collapsed as he started to unload Adelanta. There were no arguments from Marina, in fact there were no words from her at all. Her breathing was laboured and she was struggling to unload her mare. Before she was able to untie her bedroll she collapsed to her knees. The sudden movement unsettled the mare. The horse moved away a few steps before she was comfortable again. She looked at her owner curiously, but made no attempt to help.

Carefully Alaric moved to her side. His own body was weak and he didn't want to risk collapsing himself. Neither of them would get a good night's sleep in the mud. The mare danced again as Alaric approached. He felt like slapping the creature, but he knew that would do more harm than good. He finished untying the bedroll and dropped it next to Marina. He didn't have the energy to help any further. If he did then he would not be able to untie his own bedroll.

He was about to move away when Marina collapsed onto the muddy ground. He could see that her eyes were still open, but there was nothing registering. Slowly he bent down and rolled out her bed. His next mission was not going to be that easy. It took all his energy to half lift her and half roll her into bed. When he finally got her into place he collapsed on the bedroll next to her. He didn't have the energy to move. He could hear her breathing next to him and it sounded very weak. Slowly and painfully he placed his arm around her. The movement was comforting to her and her breathing eased a little. Alaric held her a little closer. It was all he could do before losing consciousness.

Chapter 9: A Strange Meeting

They woke in the morning much the same way they had fallen asleep. Marina was somewhat surprised to find herself sleeping on Alaric's chest. She woke before Alaric did, but she did not rise. She was quite happy to stay where she was despite the discomfort of the muddy surface. It wasn't until Alaric started to stir did she move. She didn't want him to know that she had chosen to remain where she was.

Both of them woke somewhat refreshed, but still tired from the previous day's events. Neither of them were looking forward to what the day had in stall for them. They had no idea where they were supposed to go. There was no telling how long it would take them to walk around the swamp. It was going to be another long hard day.

"Are you feeling alright?" Alaric asked when they were eating breakfast. He was concerned at her condition.

"Yes," she seemed a little surprised at the question. It took her moment to realise why he had asked. "I didn't thank you for saving my life." She blushed at what she originally thought he was asking. "I don't know what I would have done if you didn't come to my aid." She smiled.

"That's not what I meant. You were exhausted yesterday and I just wanted to make sure you were feeling better." Alaric wasn't looking for gratification. "It's going to be another long day and I want to make sure you're up to it.

Marina blushed again. "I'll be fine. I am still a little tired, but I am sure I will be able to keep up." She became a little defensive.

Alaric was again going to tell her that was not what he meant, but in the end he thought better of it. The follow up conversation wasn't worth having. All he wanted to do was make sure she was feeling alright, but for some reason she thought that there was something underlying in his question. He smiled back at her as to not make her feel uncomfortable.

"I guess that we should keep heading west," Alaric busied himself packing up Marina's bedroll.

"I don't think that we have any other choice," Marina agreed.

They started off at a slow pace, but that did not last long. Marina hurried the pace thinking that Alaric was only travelling slowly for her. That was only half true. He didn't want to push her too hard, but he was also very tired himself. He didn't want to exhaust himself, but he also didn't want to slow Marina. If she was happy keeping up the pace then he wasn't going to be one to fall behind.

Even with Marina trying to quicken the pace the travelling was still relatively slow. The muddy ground made walking difficult and tiring. There was nothing they could do about it. They tried heading north for a little while to see if the ground would harden, but to no avail. Alaric didn't think the quagmire they were in was ever going to change.

At mid-morning a strange feeling came over him. He had a feeling they were getting close to something. It was strange because he didn't think that there would be anything in the jungle that would warrant the feeling. It started to annoy him after a while. He looked at Marina to see if she noticed anything, but there was no change in her demeanour. If she was feeling the same as Alaric she wasn't showing it.

The feeling grew stronger the further they continued. The route they were travelling slowly turned to the south as the ground hardened. By late morning they were no longer travelling in mud, but the vegetation had become thick again. It was not as bad as when they first entered the jungle, but it was still difficult to move. They were both grateful for not have to walk in the mud anymore and Alaric didn't mind having to cut away at the thick vegetation. He was just happy not to be wading in the swamp anymore.

All of a sudden they came to a small clearing. It was a small circle without any vegetation. The ground was raw, as if it had been swept clean. Alaric had a bad feeling that it was not natural. As soon as he stepped into the clearing he knew that he shouldn't be there. He turned around to speak to Marina and his heart sank. He had turned around with just enough time to see Marina sink to the ground. There was nothing he could do to help. He dropped Adelanta's rein and moved to help. He didn't take more than one step before he felt something stick into his neck. He reached up into feel what it was, but his hand didn't reach its location. His arm didn't have the strength to rise high enough. He tried to take another step forward, but there was no strength in his legs. Slowly a darkness came over him and he collapsed to the ground. He eyes remained open long enough to see a set of feet standing in front of him. As he saw the feet the feeling suddenly disappeared, it was replaced by a feeling of dread.

***

Alaric woke with a start and sat upright. His head started to swim and he couldn't focus on anything. He had to let himself lean back before he was sick. His lips were dry and he was deathly thirsty. He wanted to sit up and look at his surroundings when he remembered what had happened. Whatever had caused him to pass out was obviously what was causing his current state. He only hoped that whatever he had been drugged with would wear off soon.

It was a surprise to find that he was actually lying on a soft mattress. If he had been taken prisoner he would have expected to be on a hard floor. There was a glimmer of hope that he was not in trouble. That thought only lasted for a moment as the memory of how he came to be where he was returned. He didn't think that there was much chance of his captors being friendly.

"Is anyone there?" his voice was cracked and weak.

There was no reply. His head was starting to feel a little better. He didn't want to risk opening his eyes, but he had to see where he was being held. Slowly his opened them and tried to focus. His vision was still blurred. After a few seconds his eyes started to focus. Soon he could make out shapes and then he could see again.

The room he was in was not as all what he was expecting. The walls looked as though they were made out of vines tightly packed together. There were no windows, which he had expected, but there was nothing else that resembled a prison cell. There was a wooden door on the opposite side of the room, but there didn't seem to be any lock on it. The rest of the room was somewhat homely. There was a small table off to one side with two chairs around it. In the middle of the table was a small vase filled with multicoloured flowers. That was not at all typical of prisons and he had been in few recently. To his dismay Marina was not there. He hoped that she was being looked after as he was sure that she would be feeling as uncomfortable as he did.

Slowly he lifted himself into a sitting position. He eyes fluttered for a moment and the room seemed to spin, but he was soon back to normal. With stage one completed he thought he would try standing. As he stood he noticed that there was something lying at the bottom of his bed. He quickly realised they were in his possessions. He moved to see if everything was there. To his surprise he found his sword and the box containing the Jade dagger. His heart stopped when he saw the box. Slowly he picked it up. He was almost afraid to open it. If the dagger was missing, although he did not think that it was, he didn't know what he would do.

As he lifted the lid on the box he felt the familiar buzzing. He quickly shut the sound out of his mind. The Jade stone was glowing more than Alaric could remember. He thought about picking it up, but he doubted he would be strong enough to contest it. The last thing he wanted to do was to weaken himself even more. He had no idea what he was up against and he needed all his wits about him. It was hard, but he pushed the lid shut without touching the blade.

He dropped the box onto the foot of the bed before picking up his sword. He felt a lot better with it in his hands. As he did there was a gentle knock on the door. The sudden sound caused Alaric to draw his sword from its sheath. He took a fighting stance as he waited for the door to open. When it did not he relaxed slightly until there came another knock.

"Who is it?" it seemed the most appropriate response.

"I am Morna," a soft, gentle voice came from outside the door. "Is it alright if I enter?"

The question took Alaric by surprise. It was not at all what he was expecting. At first he didn't know how to respond, but then he regained his senses. "I am your prisoner, it's not up to me if you enter."

"Oh, dear," the voice was quiet and not meant for Alaric to hear. There was a moment of silence before the door was pushed open.

Alaric was again shocked as he saw who was on the other side. He recognised the face of an elf instantly. Her soft pale features were close to perfection. The beauty of the elves were unmatched. She wore a simple brown dress with the skirt around her knees. That was all she wore. Alaric simply stood and stared. He could not believe what he was seeing.

"Here," she spoke as she walked into the room. "You must be very thirsty." She walked to the table and place a tray on it containing a pitcher of water and a wooden cup.

Alaric suddenly snapped back to attention. His mouth was painfully dry and again he realised just how thirsty he was. He quickly moved to the table, taking his eyes off the she-elf for the first time since she had entered the room, and took the pitcher. He didn't bother filling the cup. He poured the water down his throat straight from the pitcher. Some of the water made it into his mouth, but most of it ended up running down his face. What did make it into his stomach quenched his thirst. When he was done he returned his attention to Morna, a little embarrassed at the way he acted.

"I am sure that you have a lot of questions, but it is not my place to answer them," her voice calmed Alaric a little.

He was about to ask a question, but then thought better of it. There was another question that was more important. It was a question that he knew Morna could answer. "Where is Marina and is she alright?"

Morna didn't seem surprised. It was as if he was expecting the question. "You need not worry about her. She is safe. I do not think she has regained consciousness. In fact you should not have regained consciousness," she sounded somewhat impressed. Alaric didn't know if it was compliment or not. "Now it is time that you come with me." She took half a step and then stopped. "You will not need that." She nodded at his sword, which he still held tightly. "You are free to come and go as you please. You are our guest, not our prisoner."

"Where are we?"

Morna didn't answer, but just walked towards the door. Alaric looked at the sword. He felt much better with it in his possession, but he couldn't justify taking it with him. Things were not working out like he expected. There would be more surprises on the way and he only hoped that they were nice ones. Once he had made his decision he dropped his sword and followed her out of the room.

The scene outside was not what he expected, not that he knew what to expect. They stood on a small landing about twenty paces up in the jungle canopy. The small vine hut was delicately built around the tree's limbs. As he looked around he could see many huts built around the trees, the larger the tree the larger the hut. Bridges made out of the same vines spanned between the trees. Alaric thought that he could have easily walked through the village without realising that it was above them. Then the realisation came to him. He was probably already underneath the village when they had been taken prisoner.

For the first time he realised that he was not dressed in the same clothes that he had been wearing through the swamp. He was dressed in soft, white, woven clothes. He wasn't exactly sure what the material was, but at a guess he would have said it was made with the same vines as everything else he had seen. Not only was he dressed differently, but he was also clean. Someone had taken it upon themselves to wash him before they redressed him. Not that he was about to complain about being clean again, but it was a disturbing thought.

Morna was already half way across the rope bridge to the next hut when she realised that Alaric was not following. She turned around and motioned for him to follow without speaking. The movement broke him from his reverie and he started walking. He still could not believe that an entire village had been built in the trees.

They passed a dozen different huts before they reached the one they were looking for. Alaric had to pause when he saw the size of, not only the hut, but the tree itself. The tree was massive. It had to be the largest tree that Alaric had ever seen. The hut, which was more of a large building, was even more impressive. It was built on three levels. One level was up and one was down from where they were standing. Unlike the other huts it also completely wrapped around the tree. Alaric guessed that this was the home of the head elf.

Morna waited for Alaric. She didn't say anything as she had already guessed his reaction. It was a common one for those who saw her father's hut for the first time, not that anyone had seen it for the first time for a long time. Once he had taken in the sight Alaric continued along the vine-rope bridge. He didn't know what was happening, but his feeling of dread was beginning to fade.

Once they were both at the door to the large hut Morna knocked. A voice from inside called out for them to enter. The voice sounded firm, but pleasant. He was sure that whoever was inside knew who they were. His heart started to pound as Morna opened the door. He was about to find out if he was a guest or a captive.

There was one elf waiting for them inside. He was older than any elf he had ever seen before. He had short cropped grey hair and his face had wrinkles, something he had never seen so prominent on an elf. Alaric couldn't hazard a guess at how old he must be. Although he looked old there was nothing frail about the elf. He stood quickly when Alaric entered the. Alaric could see the strength still remained in his body.

Morna was quick to walk over to the elderly elf and embrace him. She gave him a gentle kiss on the cheek before returning her attention to Alaric. The man stood in the entrance without moving. He didn't know how to take the situation.

"This is my father, Kilean. He is our leader. He will be able to answer any questions that you have, but first let him speak." Morna smiled before walking passed Alaric and leaving the room.

"Please have a seat," Kilean offered.

Alaric moved slowly towards the seat. There were so many questions that he wanted to ask, but he knew that he should do as he was told. There was something about Kilean that kept him quiet. It was a respect that he held for the ancient elf that he could not explain. Once he was seated he felt a little more comfortable.

"I must apologise for the way were brought you here. You must understand that we do not see too many people, so we have to take precautions." Kilean didn't think that it was the best way to start the conversation, but it had to be said. "We have been waiting a long time for you to join us." His next statement hit Alaric as if he had been struck in the head. "I know that you will find it hard at first, but I am sure with what you have already been through it won't be that much of a shock, Alaric."

Alaric had to admit that it wasn't that strange. He had been drawn to the village in the trees, he knew that. Ever since he had entered the swamp he had been pushed in only one direction. There was no other path he could have taken. That thought eased the tension he had been feeling. He was a lot more confident that the elves were there to help and not hinder his journey.

"As I am sure that you can appreciate these are troubled times and we need to be careful. As much as we thought we knew that it was you we have to be sure. The Evil One has many allies and we could ill afford to be trapped. We have one job to do. It is the reason why we have lived in the jungle for so long," Kilean looked to the left of Alaric as he spoke. He thought carefully about what he was going to say next. "You are also a day earlier than what we were expecting."

"So what is the reason that you have stayed in this forsaken place?" Initially Alaric missed what Kilean had said.

Kilean almost seemed shocked by the question. He paused for a few moments before answering. "There is time for that later. For now I will be happy to answer any other questions that you have."

There was only one question that he wanted answered. As he thought about it other questions came to his mind. He didn't know which one to ask, so he just asked the one that was foremost in his mind. "We are chasing a Dark Knight. Do you know if he has passed by this way?"

Kilean thought on the question. "I haven't heard of any strangers passing through our small village. If any of my elves had seen anyone in the jungle then they would have reported back to me. It is quite disturbing that you say there is a Dark Knight nearby. I will have some of my strongest warriors search the outlying area. I have to make sure that my village is safe," the old elf's voice was thick with concern.

He was about to rise when Alaric signalled for him to remain seated. "I don't think that you have anything to worry about. If you have not already seen him then I don't think that you will. He has a two week head start. I believe that he is heading to the Southern Wasteland." Kilean didn't look too reassured.

"Be that as it may I think that I will have someone take a look around. If he has passed here in the last two weeks then we will be able to find his tracks." Kilean relaxed. It was obvious that he was going to set his plan into motion after they had finished speaking.

Alaric liked the idea. If he could follow the same track that Na'garoz did then he would have the advantage. Even though the Dark Knight had the *Prophecy of the Stone* there was still a chance he could sneak up on him. Things were starting to turn around.

"I think that would be a good idea," Alaric added to reaffirm Kilean. "How long have you been living in the jungle," Alaric quickly changed the subject.

"As long as I can remember," Kilean explained, "my father brought us here when I was but a young elf. That was more years than I care to remember."

"I don't understand. How could you possibly have known that I was coming this way that long ago?" As soon as he asked the question he remembered the nomad tribe in Nostiria. They had known of Alaric's coming a long time before he was born. There was no reason why the elves would be any different.

Kilean laughed. "I thought this should also be something you would be used to by now." He paused and waited for a response from

Alaric. When none came he continued. "One day my father announced to the village that we were moving south. We had once lived in the Northern forest. My father was not the leader, but he spoke as if he was. The elves you will see here are those who left with him and their families," there was a brightness to Kilean's face as he spoke.

"You just upped and left your village?" the words came out before he had time to think. He hoped again that he didn't offend Kilean.

"My father was very passionate, but it was not that simple. The chief of the village did not like what my father was doing. He thought that he was trying to usurp his authority. Normally elves are not prone to the same problems as the men, but to our internal regret it seemed that we slipped into that category. The chief argued deep into the night and when morning came a decision had been made. Those who decided to leave with my father would be forever banished from returning. It was a last resort to try and keep anyone from leaving. My father pleaded with the others, but it seemed that the chief's words had taken affect. It was one thing to put their faith in an idea if they could return if it didn't work out, but quite another to place their entire life on it. In the end it was only a small number of us who left. My mother and older brother remained behind in the Northern forest. No matter what my father said he could not convince them to come. It was the hardest decision I ever had to make, but I knew that my father was right. I could feel myself been drawn away from the forest. There was nothing I could do to fight it," Kilean explained.

Alaric recognised the story. There were clear differences, but the overall theme was the same. It was what had happened with the nomad tribe. In fact if the obvious differences were taken out then the story was exactly the same. Alaric had a good feeling about his current situation. He didn't know what the outcome would be, but he no longer feared for his safety or that of Marina.

"I followed my father here, along with about twelve others. There were exactly seven males and seven females." That sounded like providence to Alaric. "We all felt the same pull towards this place. The feeling didn't go away until we reached this exact location," there was a warm glow on his face, but that quickly changed when he thought of what happened next. "The jungle was, and still is, a very dangerous and untamed place to live. At first we thought we would not survive, but soon enough we adapted to life here. It did not take us long to realise that there was safety in the trees. Not many of the creatures of the jungle dare to climb so high, but that is another story all together," he suddenly snapped back from his reverie when he realised that he had been rambling.

"There is one thing that I don't understand," Alaric was still thinking how he could word his question.

"What is it?" Kilean couldn't guess what he wanted to know.

"I have never known the prophecy to be wrong, even in the slightest. You said that I was day earlier than you expected. Can you explain what you mean?" Alaric was unsure that he really wanted to know the answer.

"I don't know how my father knew. He never did explain it me, but it was believed as fact. You were going to join us at the full moon festival. It is something we celebrate once a year on the first full moon of the celestial year." Alaric didn't fully understand what he was talking about. He had lost track of the days since he left Arsiliac, but he was sure that it was almost half way through the year and there had been many full moons in that time. Kilean saw the look on his face and thought that he needed to explain. "We do not follow the same calendar of man. We follow what is referred to as the celestial year. It is controlled by the cycles of the moon. Some years are longer and some are shorter, but that is not overly significant. It was for tomorrow that we planned the celebration. Now there is nothing that we can do. That in itself, though, is not such a bad thing."

Alaric was now completely lost. Kilean paused as he saw the look on his face. He wanted to give him a chance figure out what he was being told. When it was obvious that he couldn't and was not going to ask another question he continued.

"The poison that was in the dart that you were struck with hasn't completely worn off. Although you feel well now the drug has a delayed reaction. It gives us a chance to question those knowing that if they are truly evil they will be unconscious again soon. You will have a relapse, but there is no guarantee how long it will take. On someone normal it is usually about half an hour to an hour, but if there is one thing I believe in this world it's that you are not normal." Kilean wasn't going to say anything further. He didn't want to offend the Chosen One and he was definitely starting down that path.

His answer seemed to make sense. Even though he arrived a day early he would not be ready until the appropriate time. It was a stretch, but there was chance it made sense. He wasn't going to discount the prophecy just yet. There was a lot of information for Alaric to take in, but he couldn't get his mind off the real reason they were all there. He wished that Kilean would tell him, but he respected the elder elf's decision. He was the one who had left his home and family to meet and help him, so he had to trust his judgement. It still didn't make things any easier. There were other things that he wanted to know, but he knew that the longer they stay the further away the real answer would be. He also thought about Marina. He hoped that she was alright.

"Thank you for your candour," Alaric didn't know the best way to ask the question. "I would like to see if Marina is alright."

"Of course." Kilean almost seemed embarrassed. "She should be waking up any moment now."

As if by destiny the door opened and Morna entered the room. Alaric quickly hid the surprised expression from his face. No matter how many times it happened he didn't think he would get used to it. Sometimes he wished that the prophecy wasn't so prominent in his life, but then he thought what would happen without it and he didn't mind as much.

"Morna will you show Alaric to where Marina is?" Kilean didn't stand. He just motioned for Alaric to follow Morna.

Alaric rose from the seat and walked out. He didn't think that it was appropriate for him to speak as he left. He didn't know why, he just knew that it was the right thing to do. Morna didn't wait for him at the door and Alaric was just as happy to walk behind. He knew he wouldn't be able to help himself if they started talking. He could feel that it still wasn't time to ask. The only concern he could have was for Marina.

They took a number of different vine rope bridges until they reached the hut that Morna was looking for. It was similar in shape and size to the one Alaric had been staying in and most of the other huts. The only variables were in the size and shape of the trees. Morna waited at the door for Alaric to reach her. She made no movement to open it.

"I will leave you here. If she is still asleep then you should wait for her to wake. There is nothing that you can do to wake her." Alaric thought that it was funny that she referred to Marina's condition as sleeping. "I will have someone bring you food." She didn't wait for Alaric to answer. She simply left him at the door to the tree-hut.

Alaric watched her walk away with a confused look on his face before he returned his attention to the door. He was a little nervous on what he would find inside. Taking a deep breath he opened the door and walked inside.

He found Marina unconscious on a large bed. She had been dressed in a soft white dress made from the same material as Alaric's clothes. Her black hair was a complete contrast as it fell across the bed. Alaric let out the breath that he was holding and moved towards her.

As he sat down on the edge Marina woke with a start. She looked around in fright until she saw Alaric's face. When she did she wrapped her arms around him and drew herself close. It was at that moment that Alaric realised how thin the material was that Marina wore. It was so sheer that it was almost transparent. Alaric had to close his eyes in embarrassment as they held each other. Slowly Alaric drew Marina away from him. He could see that there was a tear in her eye. She was trying to be strong, but it was obvious that she was afraid. Alaric had to restrain himself from laughing. He knew that Marina would not find the funny side into their situation until she learned the truth.

"What is happening," Marina sobbed.

"It's alright." He held her close again as she looked as though she was about burst into tears. "There is nothing to fear. We are amongst friends."

Marina pushed herself away from Alaric when the words came out of his mouth. "What do you mean that we are amongst friends? I don't know any of my friends who would drug me and kidnap me." The fear had completely gone, leaving a mixture of confusion and anger.

"I know. I thought much the same as first, but it is true. It was just a case of mistaken identity. They had to be sure that we are who we say we are, but that is all taken care of," Alaric tried to explain as best he could.

"How would they know who we are?" Marina picked up on what he was saying.

"That is a long story, but let's just say that it is part of our destiny." Alaric didn't think that it would be wise to tell her everything.

"Okay, be that as it may, can you tell me whom it is who has captured us?" Marina moved back in the bed so she could get a better look at Alaric.

"We are not captured." the look on Marina's face showed Alaric that she didn't want to argue the point. She would make up her own mind in due course. "We are the *guests* of the elves." There was no other way to put it. He didn't know what her reaction would be. He knew that some people really didn't care for elves.

At first there was little reaction on her face as she thought about what Alaric had just told her. When the information sunk in a warm smiled appeared her face. She giggled with glee before throwing herself back into Alaric's arms. He didn't know what to think.

"That is wonderful. I have never seen elves before," there was something uplifting in her voice. "I have heard that they are beautiful. Can I see one now." She pushed away from Alaric and came to her feet. It was as that point that she realised what she was wearing. Her first reaction was to hide back under the covers, but her excitement at seeing an elf was too powerful. "I have read many books on elves and seen many pictures, but I have never seen one in person."

Marina was making her way to the door, but Alaric quickly cut her off. There was more to his story that he needed to tell her and she wasn't going to like it. Regardless she was going to have to listen to his judgement.

"There is more that you need to know." Alaric blocked her exit.

"What? I want to see the elves, get out of my way!"

"The drug that they used to knock us unconscious has a side effect." He thought that was the best way to put it. "After an hour or so we will become unconscious again. There is no telling how soon it will hit. I think that it would be best if we stay here. It will be dangerous for us to be outside if we collapsed." Alaric had yet to tell her they were in tree houses and that was the main threat to their lives if they lost consciousness.

Marina looked at him, trying to gauge the truth of his words. Initially she thought that he was keeping her inside because there was no way she would be able to walk out the door. She was still suspicious about their circumstances, but she did not think that he was lying. Slowly they both moved back towards the bed and sat down together. Marina still watched Alaric closely to try and catch something in his face. Alaric didn't seem to notice. There was something else on his mind. Ever since he had mentioned the effects of the drugs he had started to feel somewhat dizzy. It had started slowly, but was becoming worse. He didn't know how long he was going to remain conscious.

"What did you say?" Alaric puffed the words. He knew Marina had spoken, but he had no idea what she said.

"I asked are you okay?" the words seemed to be far away, as if she was speaking from the back of a long tunnel.

"I am fine, thank you for…" Alaric didn't get a chance to finish what he was saying. His eyes rolled back into his head and he collapsed onto Marina's lap.

Marina smiled. At least she knew that Alaric wasn't lying. She gently stroked his short blonde hair. His breathing was heavy, but he looked at peace. After a couple of minutes had passed she thought that she should put him into the bed. It took a little effort to lift his legs and put him into place. He was a dead weight and didn't seem to want to move. By the time she finished she was puffing slightly. When she was done she looked toward the door. Alaric had warned her not to leave, but she really wanted to see what was outside. Everything he had said had been true, so in the end she decided that she would trust his judgement. She didn't know what was outside, but she would wait until Alaric woke.

She sat by a small table that was on the opposite side of the room to the bed. There was nothing else for her to do, but watch the sleeping man. She didn't mind though. Ever since she had met Alaric she thought he was very handsome. There were no other feelings initially, but the more time they spent together the more she was growing to like him. There was a definite physical attraction between them, at least that's what she thought. She thought that Alaric felt the same, but she was not going to be the one who made the first move. As a princess she was used to male suitors vying for her attentions, but so far Alaric had ignored all her subtle signals.

Slowly she felt the affects of the drug return. She looked towards the bed where Alaric still lay. There was still plenty of room and she didn't think he would mind sharing his bed. He was the one who had shared her bedroll when he didn't have the energy to move. When it was said and done he was really sleeping in her bed. The more she thought about it the more the effects of the drugs took hold.

It was all she could do to take one step after another. Her head swam and she hoped more than anything else that she would remain conscious long enough to reach the bed. With her last amount of energy she made it. She half dived and half fell in and when she finally came to rest she was unconscious again.

Chapter 10: A New Moon

They remained asleep for the rest of the day and all of the night. Alaric was the first to wake and found Marina's head resting on his chest. His arms were wrapped around her and he was holding her tightly. Taking a deep breath through his nose he realised that her hair had been scented with flowers and for a moment he forget where he was. When he remembered the events leading up to their current situation he slowly lifted her head from his chest and lowered it onto a pillow. When he was completely detached from her he stood. Although he wasn't completely sure he felt as though someone had changed his clothes whilst he was sleeping. It was a disturbing thought.

At some stage during the night an elf had come and brought them some food for when they woke. Alaric had not eaten for an entire day and was ravenous. A side-effect of the drug also added to his hunger. It felt like he hadn't eaten for a week. Without a thought for Marina he made his way to the table. The smell of the food drew him towards it and there was nothing he could do to resist.

Surprisingly there were a number of plates filled with fruits and cold meats. Alaric didn't have a care for where the food had come from, since they had seen nothing really that edible since they entered the jungle. He didn't care where the food came from, he was just happy it was there.

Alaric was half through his first plate of food when he heard Marina stir from behind him. The noise made him cringe. He hoped that she didn't berate him for not waking her. She would be just as hungry and there was a good chance she would be upset that he had started eating without her.

"Where are we?" She asked sleepily as she made her way to the table.

"We are in an elven village in the jungle to the south of Kiarome." As much as he knew she would remember eventually he felt he should explain.

Marina sat without really taking any notice and filled a plate with food. She couldn't believe how hungry she was and there were no other thoughts in her mind. As she slowly started to fill her stomach the memories returned and she realised exactly where she was.

"What do we do now?" She asked in-between mouthfuls.

Alaric really didn't want to answer any more questions. He was still hungry and he didn't want to stop eating. In the end he decided that he had to answer her.

"I don't really know. I guess when we finish eating we should go and find someone. Hopefully we can get a few more answers. Kilean wasn't too forthcoming yesterday," Alaric replied before he continued eating.

When they had finished eating Alaric was the first to stand. As much as Marina wanted to leave she wasn't going to move without Alaric. Despite Alaric's assurances and her desire to see an elf she wasn't completely sure they were safe. His explanation had been weak and there was nothing to make her believe they were truly safe.

As they neared the door the excitement of the previous day returned to Marina. It had been a dream of hers since she was a little girl to meet an elf. She had heard rumours of elves visiting Kiarome, but her father had never allowed her into the city to see if they were true. She thought that her dream would never come true. Since it was about to happen she could hardly control her excitement.

Alaric slowly opened the door. "I hope that you are not afraid of heights."

"I'll be fine." She smirked as he didn't realise she had already looked outside.

As soon as she took a step out onto the rope bridge something felt wrong. She had spent many hours on the palace walls watching the people below, but there was something different about the rope bridge. It swayed subtly as they stepped onto it. Marina took one more step before stumbling backwards uncontrollably until she fell into Alaric's arms.

Instantly she felt foolish and pushed herself away from him. She made a scene of straightening her dress to hide her embarrassment and Alaric took a step backwards to give her some room. Alaric thought that she huffed to herself, but he could not be sure. Marina kept her head high as she made her way out of the hut again.

To her disappointment she could not see any elves walking along the many vine-rope bridges. She didn't wait for Alaric to decide which bridge to take. It had been embarrassing enough to stumble and she was not going to defer to him. She had no idea where she was going, but she was happy to be out in the open. Being outside meant freedom and freedom meant they weren't prisoners.

As she neared the end of the first bridge she suddenly froze. The moment that she thought was not going to happen was finally there. A she-elf was standing out the front of the small hut at the end of the bridge. Marina couldn't move. She didn't know what to do. Her heart was racing and she could feel her face become flush. When the she-elf saw the two of them a smile appeared on her face making Marina even more bashful. Alaric, on the other hand, didn't miss a beat. He walked passed her without noticing she had stopped.

"It is good to see you again Alaric," Morna greeted him.

Marina was within earshot, but she still could not bring herself to move. It was the first time in her life she had reacted in such a manner. Normally it was the other person who was afraid to meet her. She had always thought it was stupid the way people felt around her, but she now knew exactly how they felt.

"And you Morna. Thank you for the food. I don't think that I have been that hungry in a long time."

"What do you think of it?" Morna asked when she could see the question already brewing inside his mind.

"It was very nice, but I would like to know what it all was. I haven't seen anything edible since I entered the jungle," Alaric wasn't sure if he really wanted to know the answer.

Morna smiled as she recognised the look on Alaric's face. "Of course you have." She winked once. "There is food everywhere if you just open your mind and your eyes. The meat is easier to find than the fruit. The fruit is high in the trees, although there are some small berry bushes hidden in the thicker undergrowth."

"I know that you must be kidding about the meat," Alaric didn't think that it was possible that it was so easy to find meat in the jungle.

Morna laughed jovially. She found the questioning quite humorous. "I think you need to broaden your perspective. I know that we do not have the animals that you are used to eating, but that doesn't mean that what we have isn't just as good. Now before you make judgement on our staple diet let me remind you that you just ate it." Morna paused before she gave her answer. "Snake is what is abundant in the jungle. If we are lucky we also have alligator, but they are a dangerous animal and very hard to catch."

Marina started coughing as she heard what she had just eaten. She almost gagged at the thought of eating a snake. Snakes were vile, evil creatures. They were the pets of the Evil One. It was the reaction that made Morna take notice of her for the first time.

"I see that your companion is awake. Are you going to introduce us?" Morna refrained from laughing again.

"Ah, yes, sorry, this is Princess Marina of Darshival." Alaric thought she would get more respect if he used her full title, he was wrong.

"A princess, well, it has been a long time since we have had a princess here. I must apologise that we have not better prepared for your arrival." Marina recognised the sarcasm. Alaric was also aware of the fact and wished he had not said anything.

"Now I am sure there are more important things we can be doing than talking out here." Alaric said as he tried to ignore Morna's comment.

Marina remained were she was. She was no longer stationary due to her awe of the elf, but because of the rage brewing inside of her. She couldn't believe that the elf was so rude to her. It was not only that, but the fact that Alaric didn't defend her.

Alaric couldn't look at Marina. He could feel her anger on his back, but he was between a rock and a hard place. He didn't want to upset Marina, but he also didn't want to offend Morna. The only way he could get around the situation was to try and ignore what had happened.

"Well, as a matter of fact there is very little for you to do. The festivities don't start until the sun sets tonight." Morna had a broad grin on her face. "You are more than welcome to travel around, but there are certain areas that you are not allowed to see before tonight. Don't worry though, anywhere you are not supposed to go will be blocked off by guards," she sounded as though it was the simplest thing in the world.

It was at that stage Alaric noticed that the jungle floor below them was a hive of activity. Elves scurried around like ants before the rain. Alaric was curious to know what they were doing. It didn't look like it was normal day-to-day business.

"What are they doing down there?" Alaric asked and Marina looked down for the first time and saw what he was talking about.

As soon as the words left his mouth he knew that he was not going to get the answer he was looking for.

"They are preparing for the festivities, of course," Morna thought it was the most obvious answer.

Alaric thought about rewording his question, but he knew that it would be no good. His interest was piqued. There was a reason that the elves had travelled into the jungle to meet him. There had to be a very good reason why they would reside in the most inhospitable place in the six kingdoms. He really wanted to know, but knew that he would have to wait until nightfall.

"Speaking of which I must keep going. Now remember, don't go anywhere you are not supposed to," Morna was about to leave, but she could see that Alaric had another question.

"How do we get down to the ground?" Alaric was keen to get back down. It wasn't that he was afraid of heights, but there was something unsettling about being so high up.

"That is one of the places you are not allowed to go," Morna smiled before walking away.

Once the elf was gone Marina walked to where Alaric was still standing. Alaric knew by the look on her face that she was not happy. Alaric wished that he had said something to defend her, but there was no changing the past.

"Can you believe the attitude of that elf?" Marina's tone was harsh. "Who is she to say that we can't leave? I thought you said that we were not prisoners. It doesn't sound that way to me." Marina was just looking for any excuse to belittle the elves. Her left eyebrow was already raised. No matter what Alaric's response was she was not going to be happy.

"There is a good reason why they are doing what they are doing." Alaric didn't going into detail.

"That doesn't tell me anything. There is something that I don't like about this situation. I don't know how you can remain so calm. They are planning something and I am sure that it is not good. You know I have read stories about cannibals. They eat people." She didn't really know why she mentioned it, but it seemed a good way to put doubts in Alaric's mind.

"Let's go back to your hut, there is quite a bit that you need to know. Maybe once you know this you will not be so harsh." Alaric didn't wait for her response before he started back towards the hut. He wasn't overly happy with her attitude, but he figured an explanation was the easiest way around it.

Marina stamped her foot in a sign that she was about to throw a fit. It was something she had always done when her father wouldn't let her do something that she really wanted. More often than not it worked like a charm, but it seemed that it had not effect. Alaric didn't even seem to notice. The fact was that Alaric did notice and he did his best not to laugh. He had seen little children do the same thing. It was the first time he had seen an adult do it and it looked ridiculous. He had to admit to himself that she was very cute when she did it and it did ease his displeasure.

In the end she had no choice but to follow Alaric. The last thing she wanted to do was to be outside by herself. She had been so excited about meeting an elf, but now she wished that she hadn't. They were like nothing that she had read about. The elves she had read about were kind and beautiful creatures. She had to admit that the she-elf had a certain amount of beauty about her, but she was crueller than she thought she would be.

Alaric had already seated himself with a strange look on his face when Marina entered. Marina was still upset, but the short time she had spent by herself had given her time to calm down. She was still not going to let Alaric off so easily. He should have defended her on the bridge and it would take a lot of apologising for her to forgive him.

He motioned for Marina to have a seat. It reminded her of when she had been a bad girl and her father had sat her down to speak to her. Whenever it had happened she always left feeling sad. She was not ready to let Alaric do the same thing.

"What is this all about?" she remained standing as she spoke.

"Please, sit down and relax." Alaric was not going to start until she was seated. He wasn't about to play the game with a spoilt princess. There were more important matters to deal with and the sooner she realised the better.

Marina thought about throwing a tantrum, but in the end she decided that it would do no good. Alaric had the same look on his face as her father had. She didn't want to give Alaric the upper hand and it was clear he was not going to relent. She needed to know what he knew and there was no other way to find out.

Once she was seated Alaric explained to her what Kilean had told him the day before. At first she didn't want to believe, but the more he explained the more it made sense, or at least as much sense as it could. There were still holes in his stories and she wondered if he was keeping something important from her. He claimed that Kilean had not explained everything and that they would find out later, once the sun had set, but she didn't completely believe him.

"I don't understand. Why would he not give you any more information?" Marina pressed, hoping to catch him out in a lie.

"I tried, but as I explained there was a chance I would lose consciousness, which I did. I'm sure if there was something important then he would have told me." Alaric wasn't even sure if he believed his own words, but there was no other explanation.

"But..."

"That is enough," Alaric's voice was firm. He had enough of Marina's attitude. "There is no more information. I am just as frustrated as you are, but there is nothing we can do about it."

Despite the tension neither of them left the room for the rest of the morning. Around midday an elf came with another platter of food, similar to the one that had been left for their breakfast. Alaric didn't hesitate to start eating. Marina, on the other hand, sat and stared at what was in front of her. She could imagine the snakes wriggling around in her stomach. The thought alone almost made her wretch. The fruit, however, looked very appetising. She didn't know what an alligator was, but she was sure that it wasn't worth eating. It was only when Alaric had finished did he realise what Marina was doing. He shook his head, but didn't say anything. Things were still tense between the two and he didn't want to make matters worse.

Alaric couldn't stay in the hut for the rest of the afternoon and there were hours before the sun would set. He didn't want to be around Marina, it would only be a matter of time before he snapped at her and that would probe nothing.

"I'm going for a walk," Alaric spoke softly. He hoped that she didn't decide to come with him. He was about to offer, but decided against it. That would only add to the risk.

Luckily Marina remained quiet as Alaric rose from the table. She still had a sulky expression on her face and that made Alaric want to leave even more. He couldn't believe, with everything that had happened to them, that she could behave in such a manner.

The temperature was pleasant as he walked along the vine-rope bridges. He was surprised that it wasn't uncomfortably hot like the rest of the jungle, especially since they were so high up. He also noticed for the first time that there were no insects buzzing around his head. All in all it was a pleasant afternoon for a walk.

After fifteen minutes he came to a tree that didn't have a hut around it. Instead there was a landing encircling the tree. Alaric thought it was a good a place as any to stop for a break. He leaned against the railing and looked out at the jungle before him. For the first time he saw a number of brightly coloured birds flying through the jungle canopy. He had never seen such beautiful birds in his life. It seemed there was some beauty in the jungle after all.

"They are parrots," the voice came from behind Alaric and made him jump slightly.

Turning around he saw a young male elf standing behind him. Although he looked young Alaric couldn't hazard a guess at his true age.

"That one there is toucan," he pointed to a black bird with a yellow bib and a large multicoloured beak. Alaric thought it was a wonderful looking bird.

Something caught the corner of his eye before he lowered his gaze. It took him a moment before he saw a large, cat-like animal lying in the corner of a large branch. It had a yellow coat with black spots. When it yawned Alaric saw two rows of razor sharp teeth. He wondered if it was the creature they heard the other night.

"She is a leopard, a beautiful, but very dangerous animal. If you see one then move away as quick as you can, without making any sudden movements," the elf warned.

Alaric was about to respond when he felt something land on his shoulder. He jumped in surprise and was about to grab whatever it was when the elf spoke to him again.

"Relax Alaric, that's just a monkey. It won't do anything to harm you." His words calmed Alaric.

Slowly he moved his head until he could see it. A surprisingly man-like face, with large black eyes, was staring back at him. Its body was covered in a fine brown fur and a long tail wrapped around his arm. When it was clear it wasn't going to attack Alaric reached up to pat its head.

Before he could reach it the monkey jumped from his shoulder back into the trees.

"Don't worry it takes a while for the monkeys to get used to you. I'm surprised it was comfortable enough to land on your shoulder."

The elf didn't wait for a response from Alaric before continuing on his way. It seemed as though Alaric had received all the information he was going to. He spent a few more minutes on the landing before carrying on his journey.

It was late in the afternoon when he returned to the hut and found Marina sitting there waiting for him. Nothing really had seemed to have changed since he had left. He wondered if she had remained there for the entire afternoon. The thought quickly left his mind and another entered. Since they had been turned around in the swamp and then taken by the elves he had not checked the dagger. They would need to be on the move again soon and it would be best if they knew where they should be headed.

The elves had brought the box to Marina's hut when they realised that was where he had lost consciousness. Alaric hadn't noticed until he returned. He trusted the elves and he didn't think they would try and steal the stone. For whatever reason they had come to the jungle they were there to help him.

Alaric let his fingers run over the J. The intricacy of the engraving always fascinated him. Marina had moved to the bed on the other side of the hut when she realised what he was planning. Once she had settled she suddenly wished that she hadn't moved. He was about to open the chest and she really wanted to see the perfect jade stone inlaid in the hilt. The feeling had crept up on her and caught her by surprise and it took all her will power to remain seated.

Alaric didn't notice the pair of eyes on him. All he could do was to concentrate on the box and the inevitable battle of wills that would come when he opened the lid. He couldn't give the Jade stone any advantage. With each battle it was growing stronger and Alaric had to be even more careful.

When he opened the lid he was able to block the buzzing sound almost before it started. It was a small battle, but one he needed to win. He was sure in time he would be able to block it out before it came, but that would come. For the moment he was just happy to see the dagger and yet he hesitated. There was something in the back of his mind telling him to shut the lid. He pushed the thought to the back of his mind and snatched up the dagger.

Instantly a mind-numbing scream filled his head. It was not like anything he had experienced before, but he was unable to cry out. The Jade stone was glowing brighter than he had ever seen. Alaric grasped his head in a vain attempted to stop the pain. Marina watched him closely, but she was oblivious to what was truly happening. The pain ripped through Alaric's body and there was nothing he could do to stop it. His body was frozen with agony.

Through a great effort Alaric was able to gain some of his sense back. The intense pain still ripped through his body, but he was able to move again. He lowered his arm and was about drop the dagger back into its box when the screaming stopped. Alaric sucked in a deep breath as the pain rushed from his body. When it was gone it was like it had never been there. All that remained was an unpleasant memory.

Taking another deep breath Alaric turned the blade around and strengthened his grip on the handle. When he did he was expecting to the Jade stone to dull down, but instead the it held its intensity. He moved the blade around, but the stone didn't change. Alaric let out his breath. Something was wrong and without its help there was no chance he would reach the stone before Na'garoz.

He turned the dagger over and over in his hands. He moved it backwards and forwards, but there was still no change. Nothing he tried could change the intensity.

Suddenly there was a voice calling to him in the back of his mind. At first he couldn't understand the words, but soon enough he could hear what was being said.

"Stop them! Don't wait! They are out to get you. Take it now! Take it now! Take it now! Take it now!"

The words kept repeating inside his mind getting louder and louder. The words were yelling inside his head when he finally pushed the dagger back in its box and shut the lid. As soon as the lid was shut the voice was extinguished. The strain had caused Alaric to sweat slightly. Marina was surprised to see it. From where she sat it didn't look at though Alaric had moved too much at all. She was going to ask him if he was alright when there was a sudden knock on the door.

Morna didn't wait for a response from inside and just pushed the door open and walked inside. Alaric was glad that she hadn't walked in a minute earlier. He didn't want to elves to know about the Jade dagger. As much as they knew there was something in the box he didn't want them to know exactly what it was.

"It is time," was all she said before walking out of the hut.

Alaric had not even realised that the sun had set. Marina had lit the two lanterns on the walls when it became dark, even though the Jade stone sufficiently lit the room. The excitement overpowered the feeling of dread. Their entire reason for being in the tree-village was going to be revealed. He knew that his excitement was nothing compared to what the elves were feeling. This was what they had been living their lives for.

Marina had already started making her way to the door as Alaric thought about what was before them, as she waited and grunted slightly at him. The sound broke him from his reverie and he realised that he was keeping everyone waiting, not to mention that he was delaying what he had been waiting for.

Outside the village was lit by many torches both outside the huts and along the bridges. One thing was different about that night. The jungle floor was also lit. A pathway of lanterns showed the paths they were supposed to take. Morna had already disappeared leaving to two of them to make their own way. A ladder waited for them at the end of the bridge. Alaric was sure that it had not been there earlier in the day.

The path was easy enough to follow. There was no other way for them to travel without stepping into the darkness. Once Alaric had set foot on the jungle floor the sound of distant music could be heard. It was mainly drum beats, but Alaric could also hear subtle woodwind instruments.

It wasn't long before the path led them to the clearing where they had been shot the day before. It had been completely transformed. It was covered with candles and towards the back a small podium was set up. It was covered in some sort of leathery material. Alaric couldn't hazard a guess what it was. Kilean was standing on the podium wearing a mask, but Alaric couldn't gauge what it was supposed to be. He was the only one in the clearing and the music came from somewhere behind him. Besides the paths there were no lights in the rest of the jungle. Alaric stopped when he reached the clearing, he didn't want to step inside without being invited. There was a strange ceremony about to happen and he didn't want to do anything to ruin it. Marina stopped behind him.

"Step into the circle, Chosen One," Kilean boomed at the top of his voice when he realised Alaric was waiting for him. His voice sounded stronger than Alaric would have thought possible from the elderly elf.

Alaric realised that there was a circle drawn into the ground almost completely covering the clearing. He took three steps in before stopping. Kilean made a sign that made him stop. It took him a moment before he realised that Marina had followed him in. He didn't think that it was appropriate for her to be there.

"I think you should wait outside the clearing," Alaric kept his voice low.

"But…" she was about to protest, but the look on his face told her not to. She slowly retreated backwards out of the circle.

Although Alaric could not see outside the clearing he knew that the jungle was filled with elves. The thought made him somewhat self-conscious. They were all watching him, or at least that is how he felt. He wished that he could retreat out the back with Marina, but he knew that wasn't the right thing to do. He steeled himself and waited for the ceremony to begin.

"We have travelled a long way," Alaric jumped at the suddenness of Kilean's words. "We have travelled for a long time. Now the waiting is over. This is why we are here and this is our salvation."

There was a roar from the surrounding jungle. Alaric only then realised how nervous his was. It was a positive sound, but it made him very uncomfortable. It was obviously necessary for Kilean to make his speech. There were a lot of elves that would need appeasement for leaving their home. He only wished that he would hurry up and get to the point. Alaric had been waiting all day for answers and the ceremony was insufferable. He took a calming breath and waited for the cheering to die down before Kilean spoke again.

"We have left our brothers and our sisters. We have left all that we have known," his speech continued on the same way for almost five minutes. Alaric was really starting to get frustrated. "But now is our time," the change of tone brought Alaric's attention around. "This is what we have been living for all these years."

His words were a cue for someone to step into the clearing. A younger looking elf walked in from behind the podium. He held a small round tray aloft from his left hand. On top of the tray was a small pouch that looked to be made out of velvet. Alaric didn't think that it had been made in the jungle. Whatever it was Alaric assumed that it had been taken from the Northern Forest. Things were starting to make a little more sense. There certainly would be animosity between the two factions if Kilean's father had stolen a valuable artefact. His interest was piqued.

"This is what brought us into disrepute. It is also the moment that we have all been preparing for all these long years," Kilean's voice was joyous. It also had a touch of anticipation. Initially Alaric couldn't work out what it was and then it struck him. Kilean didn't know what was in the pouch. Whatever it was that his father had taken was unknown to him and possibly the rest of the elves. This only made Alaric's anticipation grow. "Now is the time."

The jungle went suddenly quiet when Kilean stopped talking. It was as if the entire jungle was taking a breath, waiting for what was soon to be revealed. Alaric knew that it was his time to step forward and receive his prize. Slowly he joined Kilean on the podium. He knew that all eyes were fixed on him and that made him very self-conscious. Alaric reached out to grab the velvet bag, but withdrew before he touched it. It was as if he was afraid that his hand was going to be bitten off by some unseen creature. As he did there were multiple gasps coming from the jungle.

"What is in the pouch?" he sounded afraid. He didn't know why, but he couldn't bring himself to take the pouch.

Kilean whispered so no one besides Alaric could hear. "I do not know. The only person who knew what was in it was my father. He stole it from the Northern Forest, from our fellow elves. He said that when the time was right all will be revealed. Now the time is right and it is up to you to reveal its secrets."

Alaric still wasn't sure. He returned his attention the small velvet bag. The longer he stared at it the more he did not want to touch it. It was as if the bag, or what was inside, was trying to repel him. He didn't know if it was a good sign or a bad one. One thing he did know was that he could not avoid the inevitable. He didn't want to think of what would happen to the elves if he refused their gift.

Kilean lifted his mask to get a better look at Alaric. He had a concerned look on his face. Things were not going to plan, not that he actually knew what the plan was. They had been waiting for the celebration for over a century. It was all they had to do whilst they waited. The only thing that was truly prophesised was that Alaric would arrive and they would give him what was in the pouch. There was nothing that actually explained how it was supposed to play out. In their planning it had been perfect, but they had never actually had the pouch. Now he was afraid that it was not going to happen.

"Take the pouch," Kilean spoke through clenched teeth so no one could see him speak.

Alaric was still unsure, but the look on the elderly elf's face convinced him otherwise. They had left their families and travelled leagues and leagues. That thought was enough to refill his confidence. Without a second thought he reached out and took it. As soon as he touched it a warm sensation passed through his body. It only lasted a second, but it was definitely there. The concern of what was inside the pouch returned, but it also gave him more of an idea of what is was.

"Open the pouch," again Kilean kept his voice low. "We have been waiting a long time for this."

Now that he had figured what was inside he was even less enthused about opening it. After what had just recently happened with the Jade stone he didn't want to have to go through it again and not in front of all the elves. On the other hand he was interested to see which stone was hiding inside. The one thing he knew was that it wasn't the Ruby. It also explained why the Jade stone had reacted the way it did. That thought gave Alaric a lot more hope for the future.

"Open it," the call came from somewhere in the jungle. The elves were starting to become restless. Alaric could only guess how they were feeling, but it was still no reason why he should rush in.

Suddenly the chant was taken up by a number of other elves. Soon the entire jungle was engulfed in the sound of the elves. It did nothing to ease Alaric's nerves. If anything it made him move tense. Kilean was quick to realise that the chanting was not helping the situation.

"Quiet," his voice boomed out into the night. His voice was enough to instantly silence the other elves.

Alaric was grateful for the silence, but he couldn't take his eyes from the velvet bag nestled in his left hand. He knew that he had to open it for more reason than just for the elves. Whatever inside was the reason he entered the jungle. He could not move on until he knew what was inside, or more to point which stone.

Chapter 11: A Disrupted House

The palace had been in disarray when they realised that Alaric had left. That was nothing compared to what happened when they realised the princess was also missing. At first King Unwin was furious. He accused Alaric of kidnapping his daughter. Although he knew that it was a childish accusation he didn't care. He threatened to have the entire army command brought up on charges and hung in the palace square. It was Bern who was eventually able to calm Unwin.

Bern simply explained that Marina was a grown woman and was fulfilling her destiny. The king was not happy with Bern's excuse, but in the end he had to accept it. He had accepted the fact that she was leaving, but he had thought that it would be with the army. He thought that he would have a chance to say goodbye.

King Unwin was not the only one who was distraught with Alaric and Marina's disappearance. Richmond and Tancred were the worst. They had it in their mind that they would travel with the Chosen One into the depths of destiny. They were the first to try and race after him. Again it was up to Bern to try and defuse the situation. His words alone were not enough to convince the two that their destiny, at least for the moment, was with the army. In the end he needed a little assistance from Heryion, although Bern himself didn't know it at the time.

It had been a crazy day, but in the end Bern was able to appease everyone. He was relieved that Alaric was able to escape on his own. It had been disturbing when he had heard that Marina had gone with him. Alaric was embarking on a dangerous mission and he didn't think that a princess would be up to the hardship. On the other hand if Marina wasn't supposed to be with Alaric then there would be no chance of her finding him. It was that thought that helped him fall asleep.

The day after Alaric and Marina had left the army command group met in Unwin's war room. It was the first time in the history of Darshival that there was a meeting in the war room without the King being present. It had been decided that although Unwin was the ruler of the land he was not directly associated with the Alliance and should therefore be kept from the meeting. At first he didn't like the idea, but when General Sorrell promised to update him once they were finished he permitted them the use of the room.

The first matter was appointing a new leader for the army. A lot had changed since the Alliance was formed and they believed that it was time to change the old guard. It had already been discussed and agreed upon, but it was yet to be made official. It had all been done in secret from Bern. They figured that the transition would be smoother if he didn't know in advance.

"Thank you for your confidence in me, but I have no idea how to lead and army. I really think that Jarwe should remain in command and if he no longer wishes to then there are a lot of more worthy candidates around this table," Bern objected when they asked him.

When the entity took control of his body there was no doubt he could lead the army, but he had no control over that. When it was just Bern he was still the farm owner from Arsiliac. He knew he looked the part. His hours of working in the field had built strength into his body, which had only grown since he had left. It wasn't his physical presence that was the problem, it was his knowledge of warfare and that was to say that he didn't have any. He couldn't in his right mind officially take the position.

"You were the one who saw through the ruse of the Evil One in Avalon. No one else could see through the evil fog and realised that it had all been a ruse. If it wasn't for you then there is no telling how long we would have remained waiting there. You were the one who brought us to Kiarome where a Dark Knight had taken control of the King. There is no one around this table who is more worthy to lead the army," Jarwe rebutted.

If that was true then Bern wouldn't have had an issue accepting control. Everything they gave him credit for was the result of the entity. He wanted to explain that to them, but that would lead to too many questions. All he could do was reiterate the fact that he wasn't suitable enough.

"I don't know enough about warfare to be the General..."

"You have the best advisers in the Seven Kingdoms to help you, General," General Sorrell interrupted before he had a chance to continue.

"Exactly right!" added Hulkan. "We wouldn't be doing this if we didn't think you were up for the job. This isn't a game we are playing. We need you in command. Deep down you must know this is the right decision?"

Bern had to admit to himself that Hulkan was right. Despite not knowing what he was doing it did feel right for him to be in command. Regardless of how much he protested he knew the others wouldn't stop until he accepted the position, but he wasn't going to tell them they had won. Instead he remained silent and let the question float away.

"I think that it's time to put it to a vote." Jarwe was chairing the meeting. "All those in favour?"

There was a flurry of hands across the room. All hands were raised except for Bern's. Aimon, even though he didn't look happy with the decision, also raised his hand. Bern shook his head. He had been quite happy to assume command when it was necessary, but he was much happier with Jarwe being the official leader. Deep down he knew that it was the right decision. It was time for him to step up and take command.

"Thank you for your confidence in me," Bern stood as he felt he should make a speech. He was about to continue when Jarwe cleared his mouth and shook his head.

"Now we should get down to business. You can make a speech when we announce it to the army," Sorrell interrupted.

Bern took his seat again a little embarrassed with his reaction. There was little time to hold on ceremony and it's not like the others needed his reassurance. It had been their plan all along to make him general, he realised. The discussion had just been a ruse to make Bern more comfortable with the arrangement. Since it was over it was time to move onto more important matters

"We have remained in Kiarome too long. There is no telling what the Evil One has been doing whilst we have been stationary," Duke Hadar spoke when Bern didn't speak. "We have done all that we can."

"We should have moved by now," Hulkan spoke. The dwarf's voice was deep and resonant.

"And where do you think we should have gone?" Jarwe asked the question. The Remidian General did not sound happy with what Hulkan was insinuating. "Pray tell. Do you know where we should march?"

Hulkan was about to speak, but he knew that he didn't have an answer. It was the main reason why they were still in Kiarome. If they knew where to go then they would have marched. After the first week they had either captured all the traitors or they had gone to ground. There was little that they could do that the royal army couldn't achieve.

"It has not been a waste of time," Sorrell spoke. The Darshivallian General did not like what was being said. "We can ill afford for Kiarome to be captured again. We had to root out as much of the enemy as possible. Now that Kiarome is free again we can safely move on. One of the key points of warfare is never leave an enemy behind you. That way you can not be attacked from both sides at once." His reasoning was true, but he also didn't want his homeland left in ruins.

"I think that it is time that we hear from Bern," the argument lasted for ten minutes before Jarwe spoke again.

"Thank you, General," Bern didn't want to interrupt. He figured that his solution would be all the more powerful. There was no real reason behind it, but he thought that it might strengthen his position. "We now have a course to bear and a reason to march." He paused as his words sunk in. "We are to head east, towards Jarrat."

"Jarrat, why Jarrat?" Aimon asked quickly. The words came out of his mouth before he had a chance to think and he instantly wished that they hadn't.

"I thought you would be happy to hear that we are travelling to Jarrat. Wasn't that what you wanted us to do?" Jarwe disliked the captain. Ever since he had tried to take control of the Alliance Jarwe had not trusted him. He had been trying to lead the Alliance towards Jarrat from the start and his sudden change of heart didn't make any sense.

"Yes, but I am concerned at the reasoning behind his decision." It had been no secret that Aimon did not like Bern. The rest of the command just thought he was trying to be difficult.

"I believe there is a Dark Knight in control of Jarrat." Again Bern paused to let the revelation sink in. "There is a great evil over Jarrat and it is our duty to remove it."

There was a great cheer from the remainder of the command group, except for Aimon. They finally had another purpose. It might not be the main reason why the army had been gathered, but it was something more constructive. It would give the Alliance a purpose again and that was something it definitely needed.

"There is more," Bern had troubled himself on whether to reveal the second part of his plan. He knew that there was a traitor in their midst and he wasn't entirely sure he wanted to share the information with them. In the end he decided it was better they all knew. The traitor would already know what he was about to say anyway. "Two of my friends have been taken prisoner in Jarrat. It is our duty to free them."

There was a mixed reaction from the command group. Some seemed complacent, others seemed annoyed and Hadar and the two dwarves seemed concerned. It wasn't the reaction Bern was looking for, but there was nothing he could do about it.

"I do not believe we can take the time or the risk to rescue two people. I am sorry to say this, but there are more important tasks for us to take. I know the dungeons of Jarrat and they are a maze under the palace. It could take weeks to search them all and then that doesn't mean that we will be able to find our way out again. I am afraid that it is too risky. Your friends will have to help themselves," Sorrell didn't want to sound harsh, but he believed in his words.

"Who is it that has been taken?" Dorn asked what the three of them all wanted to know. He already had a bad feeling her knew who they were.

"Eldred and Alena have been captured. I think it was a ploy to lead Alaric to Jarrat and away from his true mission." Bern was the only one who knew where Alaric had gone. He couldn't tell the others, not that they would be able to follow now, but it was what they had both decided. He wished he hadn't mentioned his name, but he just had to continue with what he was saying and hope no one would bring up his whereabouts. "We cannot leave them to be tortured by the Evil One. They are more important than you can imagine."

That thought settled in all their minds. Although some of them still thought that it was not a good idea they had to agree with Bern. There could be no worse fate than to be in the clutches of the Evil One. Hadar and the two dwarves could only imagine what fate had in store for them. The pain they would be going through didn't bear thinking about. All they wanted to do was rush to Jarrat and rescue them, but they knew rushing wasn't an option. They would need the strength of the army behind them and the army couldn't move fast enough.

"Why wait until now to make the decision to rescue them?" Hadar had a deep relationship with Eldred. The two had been friends for a long time. He had a great respect for the wizard who he had known since he was a child. "How could you leave them to be tortured like this?" With each word Hadar's voice rose. The more he thought about the situation the more it didn't make any sense.

Bern didn't know what to say. He knew the large man was right, but there was also more to the situation than they could possibly know. He could see there was no response that would appease the Duke. In the end he had to be as honest as possible.

"Believe me when I tell you that it pains me greatly to leave the two where they are. Alaric also feels bad, but unfortunately there is nothing we can do. We are all slaves to the prophecy and we must go where it leads." A lot of the confidence had left his voice. He wished he could have given them a more positive response, but there was no other reason.

"So when do we leave," Hulkan's voice was also somewhat aggressive.

"We leave in four days," there was no doubt in Bern's voice; although he knew that no one would be happy.

"What do you mean, four days?" Hulkan snapped again. "We should be moving now. It will not take long to get the army to move."

"Be that as it may we are marching to war." Bern was ready to defend himself. "We cannot take this lightly. What we are about to embark on is more dangerous than anything we have done so far." His words of doom caught everyone's attention. "We need to make sure that we have enough supplies for a long campaign. We can not rely on a quick victory like we had here."

"Bern speaks the truth." Jarwe was the first to understand what Bern was saying. "We are not ready to march into the unknown. We need to restock our supplies before we leave." He was basically just rewording what Bern had already said.

"Then why are we waiting here?" there was a hint of urgency in Aimon's voice. "We should be getting ready to leave," his words came as a surprise to everyone.

He had been the only one who was not happy with Bern assuming command of the army. He argued the point, but in the end realised that he had no choice. He was forced to vote in favour of Bern at the meeting. If he didn't then he knew that he would be forced out of the command group. If nothing else he needed to remain in the position he was in. It was the first time that he had agreed with any decision that Bern had made and it came as a shock to everyone.

"Aimon is right," Jarwe agreed. "We should get organised. The men will be excited at the prospect of being on the move again. The fact that we are moving towards battle will excite them even more."

"Good, then it's settled." Bern was glad that they were all in unison again. "I think we should be careful in what we tell the army, especially those from Entero. I don't think that they will be happy to hear that we go to battle with their kinsmen. Aimon," he turned to the captain from Entero. "I trust that you will be able to speak to your men and make them understand that we have no other choice."

"Of course. If the Evil One has taken control of Jarrat I don't think that they will mind. I am sure that they will fight harder and more passionately then anyone else," Aimon sounded proud to be an Enteroite.

"There is more to it than that." Although Bern knew that Aimon was a Dark Knight he didn't want him to know and that meant treating him like the Captain he was pretending to be. "You will have to fight your own countrymen."

"Why would they fight for the Evil One?" Aimon didn't sound convinced, he was also playing his part.

"The same reason why those soldiers in Kiarome were about to fight against us. Your Queen is in the thrall of the Evil One and your kingdom men will do what she commands," Bern could see that his words were having their effect on all of them. "It is much easy to control the person who controls the people, than to try and control the people."

"I see. This is indeed disturbing," Aimon had a pensive look on his face. "I will have to be careful what I tell my troops."

Bern did his best not to look too carefully at Aimon. If the Dark Knight was to figure out that Bern knew what he was then he would lose any little advantage he had. If he was going to learn the mind of the Evil One then he would have to keep Aimon close and if that meant sharing their plans it was a sacrifice he was willing to make. He would just have to be very careful what he told him.

"I think that we should get to work," Bern suggested before anyone had a chance to speak. "There is much to be done and not a lot of time to be doing it. We need to be ready to march on the morning of four day's time."

Everyone was keen to have a purpose again. As much as they were all grateful they didn't need to attack Kiarome there was still a sense of need for battle. They had been travelling across the Seven Kingdoms and had yet fight a decent one. The battle in Avalon had been a ruse and once the spell had been broken it was almost over before it began.

"Lord Richmond... Tancred, would you stay behind for a moment? There is something that I need to discuss with you," Bern waited for them almost to be out of the war room before he spoke.

They returned to the table as the others left the room. Bern made sure that they were alone before he started to talk. What he had to say to them he didn't want anyone else to hear. It was very important that it was only the two men in front of him who heard what he had to say.

"I know that you wanted to travel with Alaric, but unfortunately at this time your destiny lies on a different path." He thought that it was the appropriate way to start the conversation.

"We understand the prophecy more than you know. If it is our destiny to travel with the Alliance then that it what we shall do. I am sure that our paths will cross with Alaric again," Tancred didn't sound impressed with Bern's words.

"I am glad that you understand the situation." Bern was clearly relieved. "Now I must ask you to do something for me."

"Whatever you need. You are the commander and we will do what you say," Richmond spoke before Tancred had a chance. He didn't know what his advisor was going to say, but he didn't want to risk offending Bern. He knew that Bern and Alaric were close. Staying with Bern was the only way they would be reunited with Alaric.

"Thank you. What I need you to do is not difficult. I believe that there is a traitor in the army," he waited for his words to sink in. It was obvious when they understood what he had said. "I need you to keep watch of Captain Aimon," Bern went straight to the point. He could come right out and say he was a Dark Knight, but he still needed someone to keep an eye on him. The two newcomers seemed to be the best choice. "I need to know if he is the one who is siphoning information to the enemy."

"How do you know it is him?" Tancred asked.

"I don't know for sure. That is why I need you to keep and eye on him. If I am wrong then I need to know who the traitor is."

"We will do our best, but why have you asked us? I am sure one of the others would be better qualified," Richmond asked.

"You are new to the group. Aimon has had confrontations with most of the command group. If he thinks you are on his side he might just trust you. Alaric told me something about the intrigues of your kingdom. He also told me on what happened when he first arrived in Bellarome. I think that you are perfect for the job," Bern explained.

"We know of Aimon's treachery. It is hard to say whether he is a traitor or whether he was just concerned about his own kingdom," Tancred did not sound convinced.

"That is true, but it's not the point. The point is that you are new and it is possible that Aimon will take you into his confidence. Just don't be too obvious with what you are trying to do," Bern offered some advice.

"This is nothing new to us," Tancred was full of confidence. "We know how to get on Aimon's good side. We will do out best to find out what he's up to."

"Be very careful. If my hunches are correct this is a very dangerous man. If he gets wind of what you are doing there is a good chance that you will end up dead. More to the point I don't need him knowing that I am onto him. It is very important that he continues to believe that we do not know who he is." Bern had to give them the warning. It was not as simple an assignment as they thought.

Bern's words took effect. There was something in his tone that made the other two believe what he was saying. The extra fear only made their assignment more exciting. Just getting to know someone was boring. The chance of death was a real challenge. They were both happy to have something important to do since they had lost the Chosen One.

"We will not let you down, sir," it was all Tancred could do not to stand and salute.

"Very good. Now go and get prepared to leave. There is a lot to do," Bern dismissed them as was appropriate to his new position.

They were both glad to leave the war room. Although Alaric had only just left they both felt lost without him. It was good that they had something important to keep them busy. The intrigue was just what they needed and they were the perfect people for the job.

Once he was alone Bern was able to relax. Like everyone else he wished that Alaric was still with him. Despite the fact that they had grown up together in the same small village there was something powerful about him. Bern wished that he shared the power, but that just wasn't the case. There were unknown horrors waiting for him and he would have to be strong to survive. Everyone was looking to him for answers and there was nothing he could do to oppose it. He knew that hiding in the war room was not going to help. Before he could stand there came a knock on the door.

"Enter," Bern called without thinking.

"Sorry to disturb you General, but King Unwin would like to see you." A young pageboy stood nervously in the doorway.

"Thank you. I will be along shortly." The pageboy didn't know whether to wait of leave. In the end he let the door shut before racing down the hallway.

Bern knew that Sorrell had gone straight to Unwin and told him what they were planning. What he didn't know was how Unwin was going to react. It was not going to be easy on Kiarome. What they would need to get them through to Jarrat would put Kiarome in a near state of famine. It was not something that he wanted to discuss with the King.

He sat in the war room for another minute before he decided to leave. He knew that he was not making his life any easier by making Unwin wait. It was a tense walk through the palace corridors. He didn't know if it was deliberate, but the corridors were completely empty. It didn't make his journey any easier.

When he arrived at the throne room he found a complete contrast to the corridors. There was a myriad of people milling around in front of the throne. Bern had only been expecting Sorrell and Unwin. What he saw in front of him made him worry even more. The group of people was not a good sign.

"Thank you for joining us," Unwin spoke when he saw Bern enter. As soon as Unwin spoke everyone else was suddenly silent.

"Of course, your majesty. What can I help you with?" That was as formal as Bern would ever be.

"General Sorrell has informed me of your decision. I have to admit that it is a very bold one," King Unwin continued.

"Excuse me General. The Honourable Hugh d'Genz, Minister of Civic Affairs," a short, plump, aging man spoke from somewhere in the crowd. Unwin shook his head. "How can you expect us to give you what you have asked for? It will cripple the city. There is no way we would be able to recover. Both our economy and our people will suffer," he sounded very smug.

Bern's shoulders lowered a little. The last thing that he wanted to do was to deal with bureaucrats. There were much more important matters for him to deal with. It was obviously important to Unwin, although Bern didn't know why the King couldn't explain it himself. When it was said and done Unwin was the ruler, but Bern had to respect his wishes.

"I appreciate your concerns Hugh," he made a point of not using his official title, "but it is necessary for us to take these supplies. The most important thing in the Seven Kingdoms is to defeat the Evil One. We do not wish to see your people forced into poverty, but it may be necessary. We all have to do what ever it takes," it was a common speech, but generally not an effective one. Bern found that those who believed in what he said generally didn't ask the question in the first place.

"That is all well and good for you to say," there was a great deal of arrogance in his voice. It was obvious that the councilman was about to rebuff his statement. "You are the one who will walk away with all our food and, by the looks of it, half of our treasury. We will be left behind with nothing. What happens when we run out of food? Our people will start dying off, that's what will happen." Hugh was not going to be swayed so easily.

"Then answer me this question," Bern could understand the man's point-of-view, but he didn't have any time for the accusations. "What will happen if we fail against the Evil One's army? I will tell you quite confidently what will happen. His pestilence will wash over the land and no one will be safe. Sure you will have money and food, but there will not be anyone alive to spend it or eat it. I know that this situation is hard, but I can assure you that it is completely necessary," Bern kept his voice firm. He wanted to yell at the fool, but he couldn't lose control.

His words gave the crowd something to think about. Despite their truth it was not a guarantee that if they did not supply the food and money the world would come to an end. There was still a chance that Hugh could have his cake and eat it too. The thought was still strong in Hugh's mind, although he knew his supporters were starting to wane. He would have to come up with a new plan of attack if he was going to win.

"Right Honourable Conrad d'Weise, Minister for Foreign Affairs," a new speaker introduced himself. "It seems to me that we are bearing the brunt. What are the other nations prepared to donate?" There was a round of agreements from the crowd. Hugh was grateful for Conrad's response.

The question was not completely unreasonable. Bern had to give himself a moment to think on it. His delay in answering brought a rabbled response from the councillors, even the ones who had supported the move. Unwin waited for a moment and then called for silence. The room was instantly quiet after his voice boomed throughout.

"This problem has not been laid solely on you shoulders, although I am sure that it seems that way now. We do not have time to wait for supplies to come from the other Kingdoms. Entero is under the control of the Evil One. He controls not only Oriana's land, but her army as well. We have to move now or we risk the enemy sinking his teeth into more land. We don't know what his plans are, but we can ill afford any delays," Bern spoke passionately.

There were a lot of mumbles from the crowd. Some were agreeing with what he was saying and others were refuting it. There was no easy answer to the problem. Bern knew with every answer there would be another question and things continued that way for the next hour. Every time Bern answered there was someone else with another question. Sometimes the same question was re-asked. Ultimately it was still Hugh d'Genz who chaired the debate for the opposition. Eventually Bern began to lose his patience. He didn't seem to be getting anywhere with them.

"Okay, gentleman," Unwin interrupted as Conrad was about to ask another question. "I have let you speak with General Bern about what is happening. Now the debate is over. There is much for all of us to do if we are going to survive these dark times. We must prepare for the upcoming hardships."

"Yes, your majesty," Hugh was the only one who spoke. "But we have not decided on a course of action."

King Unwin stood to reply. "I told you when you asked for answers that was all that you would receive. We did not come here today to change the course that we have already started on," Bern was in shock when he heard what Unwin had said. The King had kept that fact very quiet. If he had known then he would not have wasted the time, although he knew that was why Unwin did not tell him. "This forum was just so you all had a better idea of what we are trying to achieve."

"But, your majesty," it was Conrad's turn to risk the wrath of his King. "It is not right that we are the only kingdom to have our resources diminished. If we win this war against the Evil One then we will be open for attack from stronger nations. At the very least will be at their mercy."

"Your concerns are warranted, but it is not your place to complain. It is now your job to work out how we are going to survive. Now that you have your mandates what are you doing standing in my throne room?" his voice boomed throughout the room. There was no doubt that he wanted them to leave.

Both Hugh and Conrad, who had been the two strongest voices in the meeting, both thought about protesting further. If they couldn't tell by the look on Unwin's face, the fact that the guards slowly started to make their way towards the group of bureaucrats was enough to tell them it was time to leave. There was no point in spending a night in the cells. That would prove nothing for their cause. In the end they had to file out with the rest of the councillors.

"I am sorry I didn't tell you earlier," Unwin had motioned for Bern to stay when he made a move to leave. "I didn't think that you would be as convincing if you knew that nothing was going to change. It is important for the survival of my kingdom that my subordinates know what we are working towards. They will do their jobs a little better now."

Bern thought about telling Unwin what he thought of his tactics, but in the end he knew that the King was only doing what he thought was right. He was the one who was going to have to stay behind and watch his subjects suffer. It was not going to be an easy task, running the city once the army left.

"That's alright, but I fear that I have been here too long. There is still much to be done before we are ready to leave. I don't know if you have heard, but I am now in command of the Alliance." Bern didn't know why he felt that he needed to tell Unwin that.

"Yes, I am aware that was the result of your meeting this morning. I think that is a good thing. There is no doubt that you are the best man to lead the army to victory," there was no humour in Unwin's voice.

Bern didn't know if he was serious or joking, but that was irrelevant. What was pertinent was the fact that he had work to do.

"I will have to take my leave." Bern didn't wait for Unwin to give him permission to leave.

"Will you do one more thing for me?" Unwin asked before Bern could take more than a couple of steps.

"Whatever you need," Bern held his tongue as he replied.

"Will you send word to me if you hear from Alaric and my daughter. I know that you will be in contact with them before I am. Tell Marina that I love her," there was a sadness in Unwin's voice that matched his face. It did not seem right on the King's face.

"I will," was all Bern said before turning away and leaving the room. There was still much to be done.

Chapter 12: On the Road Again

On the morning of the fourth day since their meeting the Alliance was ready to march. Bern sat on Tormenta at the front of the army. The elven stallion seemed a little uncomfortable with his new rider. He had never been comfortable with anyone accept Eldred. Tomenta noticed there was something different about his current rider. There was a commanding presence about him that didn't seem quite right. Tormenta decided that he would wait and see what he was like before making any rash judgements.

Bern wore the golden breastplate they had given him in Avalon. The crest of the Royal Remidian family was engraved in the centre and a purple cape flowed behind. It was on the insistence of the other commanders that he wore the armour. All he wanted to wear was his leather jerkin and riding pants, but they said it would be inappropriate. No matter what he said they wouldn't listen to him. He was the General of the Army and he needed to look the part.

General Jarwe and General Sorrell sat upon their own horses by his side. The rest of the command group were back with their respective armies. The sun was shining as it bridged the horizon and there was a cool breeze. All in all it could not have been a better morning to start the next stage of their journey.

"Shall we?" Jarwe asked as Bern stared out in front of them.

"I think so," Bern replied without changing his view. "Would you do the honours?"

Jarwe raised his hand high into the air and signalled to his flagman. That was all that was needed to get the huge army into motion. The flagman waved his flag back and forth, in what looked to be in a random motion, but was in fact a signal that rippled throughout the army. Bern was the first to start moving. He gently kicked the flanks of Tormenta causing him to move.

It would be a solid two week march for them to reach the border between Darshival and Entero. From there it would be at least another two weeks until they reached Jarrat. It was not going to be an easy journey. The pure size of the army made it impossible for them to travel along the highway. They best they could do was to try and stay on flat ground.

Bern was pleased at the time they had made when they set up camp for the first day. The campsite stretched out as far as the eye could see. The back of the army was at least a league away from front of the line. The hardest part was being able to keep an eye on everyone and making sure that the men didn't get up to no good. Gambling and fighting would be rife amongst the men and with the diversity of the army it would be worse than usual. It was not only the men from the different kingdoms, but it was also the difference in races. There had been a long history of hatred between the dwarves and the elves and although they only made up a small component of the army they could be just as volatile.

The command tent was set at the very front of the campsite. Normally it would be set deep within the army for protection, but since there was no imminent threat they were happy to set it at the front. The command would meet there for the evening meal each night before returning to their own factions. It gave them to a chance to discuss any concerns as they arose. If anything was bothering the men then they could nip it in the bud before it spiralled out of control. A bad rumour could easily shatter the men's moral.

Bern was grateful to be out of the breastplate. He never felt comfortable in armour and the golden one was only for show. In the morning he would have it packed away and dress in something more comfortable for riding. He didn't care what the rest of the army thought. He was the General and he made the decision. It was bad enough that he had to spend the first day riding in it.

The tent was the first to be erected and they all gathered inside when the sun had finally set. A large table and chairs were set in the middle and their food had already been placed on platters. It was a little more extravagant than Bern would have liked. They had just pillaged Kiarome of most of its food and he felt bad having such a feast before him. There were a variety of roasted meats and vegetables. Fruits and chesses were also laid on the table for dessert. Bern would make a point of telling his pages that they would be on the same rations as the rest of the army.

"We made good time today," Jarwe spoke as he started his meal. "We will have to move fast if we are going to make it to Jarrat in time."

"In time for what?" it had been a throw away line from Jarwe, but Aimon was curious at his answer.

"In time to defeat the Evil One. In time to save Entero," Jarwe didn't sound impressed with what Aimon was implying.

"How do we know that we are not already too late?" Aimon sounded morose. "We have not heard anything from Entero in a long time. How do we know that we are not just wasting our time?"

"I thought you of all people wanted to return home," Jarwe was beginning to raise his voice. "I thought you would want to try and save your kinsfolk?"

"It's not that," Aimon became defensive. "It is just that all this talk about saving the Seven Kingdoms has me thinking. What if all this is just an elaborate trap? I think that we need some more information before we go running towards potential doom."

"I think you are a little too late," Hadar spoke from the other side of the table. "There is nothing that will stop this army from moving towards Jarrat."

"All I am saying is that I think we should send scouts to Jarrat to make sure that we are not needlessly moving into a trap. I have plenty of good men that could sneak into the city unnoticed. Wouldn't it be better to know what we are facing?" Aimon's words made sense.

The first thing that came to Bern's mind is what happened when Aimon suggested the same thing as they approached Kiarome. The Dark Knight had taken soldiers to the city to scout the situation. Only Aimon had returned. At first Bern had his doubts, but the more he thought on it the more it became obvious that Aimon had killed them. Not only that, but he believed Aimon had betrayed them to the other Dark Knight's in the palace. There was no chance he was going to let him loose in Jarrat. At the moment they had the power of surprise and he wanted to keep it that way for as long as possible.

"I think this has merits," Lord Pernian spoke next. "We really do not know what we are walking into. I don't mean to doubt your visions, General Bern, but I would be a lot happier if we had a first hand account of the situation."

There were a number of muffled agreements from around the table. It was clear that Aimon was going to suggest that he go with his men. To everyone else it would be the logical choice. Aimon knew the city and knew where to look for information. The last thing Bern could allow was for him to leave the army. Not only would they risk betrayal, but he would also not be able to keep an eye on him. He really needed to know which of the Dark Knight's he was up against.

"I think we can ill afford to send someone into the lion's den," Bern spoke slowly as he tried to think of a reasonable excuse. It was a precursor to his real agenda.

"How can you say that?" Aimon sounded more surprised than anything else. "We need all the intelligence we can get. I don't see how we can do anything but..."

"Aimon is right," Richmond interrupted. "We need to gather information on what is happening in Jarrat. We were lucky in Kiarome that Alaric was there. This time he is gone and we can't rely on his return. If we are going to fight a Dark Knight then we will need any advantage we can get."

"At the moment the Evil One doesn't know what we are doing," Bern knew that it was a lie, but it also led towards his excuse. "If you send someone in and they get caught how long do you think they would remain silent under interrogation. It is more of an advantage for us to remain a secret for as long as possible."

There could be no arguing with Bern's logic. Aimon's shoulders sank as he knew that he had been beaten. There was no chance of him officially getting into Jarrat before the army. He would have to think of another way to get around Bern.

"Once we get closer to Jarrat I am sure there will be an opportunity for espionage," Jarwe added when nobody spoke.

Once everyone had finished eating the meeting ended. There was not much to discuss as they had only been travelling for a day. As the journey continued their meetings would continue for longer. For the moment Bern was happy that they were not all staying around. He wanted to have a chat with Richmond and Tancred. He called for them to stay behind before they left the tent. He waited for everyone else to leave, including the servants, before he spoke.

"Have you managed to gather any information on Aimon?" he kept his voice low. Although there was no one else in the tent it didn't mean that there wasn't anyone listening outside.

"No more than what we already know. He is shifty and conniving, but I don't know if he is an agent of evil," Tancred also kept his voice low.

"You need to give us some more time. It's only been day. Hopefully what was said here tonight will help us gain his confidence," Richmond added.

"Unfortunately we don't have any more time. My plans for you have changed. It seems as though Alaric trusted you, so I will trust his judgment," Bern knew they were trustworthy, but he still had to make it seem they needed to earn his trust. "Aimon is right. We need to get information from inside of Jarrat."

"But you said that it was too dangerous," Tancred let his voice rise for a moment, before he realised what he was doing.

"I know what I said, but that was only for Aimon's sake, or whoever the traitor is. I need you two to sneak away from the army and go on ahead to Jarrat. I will make up an excuse that you had to return to Bellarome, so no one will know what we are up to. That way we will be able to stay one step ahead of our enemy," Bern explained.

"Or it could give us a chance to flush out Aimon," Tancred started.

"What do you mean?" suddenly Bern had a feeling that this was not going to be the greatest of ideas.

"If Richmond and I confide in Aimon with your idea then there is a chance that he will reveal his plan to us. If he thinks that we are his allies then he might get us to do his bidding. If we can work out what he is planning then it will give us the upper hand," Tancred had a wry smile on his face as he explained his plan.

"That sounds very risky," Bern was not sure.

"This is nothing new. What you have to understand is that Darshival is full of intrigue, especially in the nobility. We will be able to convince Aimon that we are on his side, without revealing that we know he is playing for the other team," Tancred added.

"Don't forget that we don't know for sure that Aimon is the traitor. If this goes wrong then there is a chance the real traitor will hear of our plans." As much as Bern wanted to tell them that Aimon was the traitor he knew it wasn't the right thing to do. He thought he could hear the entity speaking inside of his mind, telling him that it was a bad idea.

"I have been doing a little investigating on the remainder of the command group and it seems that your hunches are correct. The others all seem committed to the cause," Richmond replied. "I think that Aimon is the only one who could possibly be a spy."

"What you have to remember is that the enemy will not reveal itself so easily. Don't be so quick to discount the others, although I do fear that you are right," Bern took a deep breath. "I don't think that it the right thing to do, but I am happy to trust your judgement on this one."

"We will not let you down. This way we will be able to get a better insight into the enemy." Tancred was happy with Bern's response.

"I hope not," Bern didn't sound impressed.

"We will leave in the morning," Richmond stood and was about to leave when Bern stopped him.

"I don't think you should leave so early. Give it a couple of days. That way it won't be so obvious to the others," Bern suggested.

The other two couldn't argue with his logic. It would be rather suspicious if they disappeared the day after they discussed sending someone into Jarrat. The extra time would also give them a chance to get more information out of Aimon. Bern had to admit that the idea was growing on him. It added to the risk of their mission, but if he was able to put a spy into the midst of Nyrra's network then he would have the upper hand.

When the other two left the tent Bern was completely alone. It was the first time he had time to himself since they had left that morning. It would be the first of many long days on the road. There would be no time for rest until they reached Jarrat and from there things would only get worse. They would have to lay siege to the palace to save Alena and Eldred. Bern felt sad as he thought about his two friends being tortured in the bowels of the Entero Royal Palace. He wanted nothing more than to rush in and rescue them, but he knew that was not the best way to do it.

Even once they reached Jarrat it would take them a long time to free them.

The thought going through his head was only starting to depress him. He decided that he would take a walk through the campsite before going to sleep. For some reason he brought comfort to the other soldiers when they saw him. He guessed that was just the result of being the commander.

The night air was fresh, almost cold. There was something in the air, but Bern couldn't put his finger on it. It was almost like there was a sense of anticipation. It didn't sit well with him. As he walked through the campsite there was nothing to warrant the feeling.

***

Tancred and Richmond left the command tent together. They were both excited that they had a real mission again. They had both felt that Bern had asked them to watch over Aimon to keep them out of his way. Now they knew that it was a real assignment and they had to admit to themselves that they were a lot happier. Now they really had something to sink their teeth into.

They walked through the campsite until they were sure that they were alone. There was much for them to speak about and they knew that they could not let anyone else hear.

"What do you think of Bern?" Tancred asked when they were sure they were alone. He ran his hand through his short brown hair, which was well overdue for a cut. He wondered if there would be time before they left.

"I don't know. On one hand he seems to know more than he's letting on, but on the other hand he doesn't seem to know much at all. It is very confusing," Richmond replied his age showing on his face. Despite being the same age as Tancred his showed more lines on his face. He too felt that he was in need of a haircut.

"What about this new mission of ours?" Tancred asked.

"That is another enigma. There is no doubt that we need to get intelligence from Jarrat, but I don't know if it needs to be such a secret," Richmond replied.

The two men stood in silence and thought for a moment. There was a lot of information to digest. Their lives had suddenly become much more complicated. They knew that they would be in danger whem they embarked on their journey with Alaric, but they had no idea where it would lead them. The both had to admit that they would prefer to be with Alaric, but there was nothing they could do. The prophecy, for whatever reason, wanted them to help Bern and that is what they had to do.

"Do you think that Aimon is a traitor?" Richmond asked suddenly.

"Bern thinks that he is and I have to admit that he is acting strange. On the other hand I have always thought that Enteroites are strange people," Tancred replied.

"I know what you mean, but I think there is something off with Aimon. He doesn't sit right with me," Richmond wasn't afraid to voice his opinion "Some of his mannerisms belie what he is saying. On one hand he wants the army to stay away from Jarrat and then he is happy for it to move in that direction."

"I know what you mean. He certainly is a contradiction. I think we should go and have a talk with him. I think he will be very interested in knowing what Bern just told us," Tancred winked at Richmond when he finished speaking.

Richmond returned the wink before starting towards the Entero area of the campsite. The different nations and races within the army kept to themselves at night, as much as possible. It was the only way to keep the mayhem to a minimum. It also made it easier to find someone when you needed them. They found Aimon outside his tent staring at the sky. He was watching the stars intently, as if they were telling him a story.

"What can I do for you gentlemen this evening," Aimon asked when he noticed the other two men standing before him. The thing that annoyed Richmond was that he hadn't looked away from the sky. There was something very suspicious about his attitude.

"We have some interesting news," Tancred got straight to the point.

Since Bern had given them the instruction to spy on Aimon they had managed to get close to him. Aimon had to admit that he had found it quite comforting to have friends within the command group. Since his attempt to usurp power the other commanders had been quite cold and standoffish towards him. Richmond and Tancred didn't seem to have to same opinion of him as everyone else. They also seemed to disagree with a lot of Bern's decisions. He knew there was someway he could use that to his advantage.

"Come into my tent. We will have enough privacy there," Aimon could tell that something had happened when he left the meeting. He knew that Bern had kept these two men behind for some reason. If he played his cards right he would get all the information that he needed. "Would you like something to drink?" he offered when they were inside his tent.

There was a young man standing at the back, next to him was a small table with a pitcher and a number of pewter cups. The man had a blank look on his face.

"Please sit," there were a number of chairs to one side of his tent.

The two men were surprised at the lavishness of his tent. It was unusual for one man, even if he was a Captain and the leader of the Enteroite army. Both Richmond and Tancred only had a tent that was sufficient for them to sleep in. Either way they were not going to be rude. They both took a seat and accepted the offer of a drink. Again to their surprise they were giving a cup of vintage red wine. It was a lot nicer than what they expected in the middle of the army.

"I have to admit that I have grown used to some of the finer details of life. I know it is strange in our current situation, but if I can't share a nice drink with friends every now an then I don't want to go on living," Aimon spoke warmly, as if he was having good friends over to his house for supper. "Now tell me what it is you have to say."

There was nothing right about the situation, but they couldn't go back. Aimon sat back in one of his chairs, his shoulder length brown hair looked faultless. Neither of them knew when he would have time to have it washed and cut. He was dressed in a red silk shirt and trousers. It seemed completely out of place for a Captain in a mobile army.

"What about him?" Tancred pointed to the man at the back of the room, after taking another mouthful of the wine.

"Don't worry about him. He will not repeat anything that is said here," there was nothing but confidence in Aimon's voice.

Tancred took another look at the man. There was still the same blank look on his face when they entered. That helped him to believe what Aimon had told them. He wasn't even sure if the man could hear the words they were speaking, but there was something very disturbing about the whole thing.

"Very well," Richmond spoke when it was clear that Tancred was not going to. "What do you know about Bern?" If they were going to get Aimon to trust them then they had to give him and excuse. If they just blurted out the information then it would look too suspicious.

"I know that he is reputedly the best friend of the Chosen One," it almost seemed as though Aimon were about to choke on his last words. "There are many rumours about his true origin. One story, which I seem to be hearing more than any others, is that he is a farmer from a small village in Zenza. One thing I can tell you for sure is that he has no military background. That is obvious by the decisions he makes. If the command had listened to me then we would already be marching on Jarrat. Now it is too late," Aimon sounded disgusted.

"I know what you mean. Kiarome was in no danger. Let's face it, it didn't take us long to get into the city," Tancred fuelled the rage inside of Aimon.

"You're exactly right. Bern is gong to lead us to destruction. We need to get information from Jarrat. It is the only way that we can get in," Aimon took a long drink from his cup before calling for a top up.

"Well that is not exactly true," Richmond looked at Tancred before he continued to speak. "It seems to me that Bern suspects that there is a spy in the command group. Can you believe it?"

"Did he say who it was?" Aimon was suddenly interested.

"No, but I think he suspects either Jarwe or Pernian," Richmond replied quickly, almost too quickly.

"I see," Aimon added pensively. "That is indeed disturbing news."

The further the conversation continued the more Tancred and Richmond came to believe that Aimon was indeed the traitor. They also knew that their ruse was working.

"On the other hand it means that Bern trusts both Tancred and myself. He wants us to travel to Jarrat and try and gather some information." Richmond knew that they had Aimon right where they wanted him.

Aimon thought for a moment as he took another drink. "That is very interesting news." Aimon thought again about what he was going to say next. "It seems that I may have underestimated Bern." Aimon paused and thought again. "Things are going to be dangerous when you reach Jarrat. You will need my help if you are going to return safely."

"What are you talking about?" Richmond feigned confusion.

"If what Bern says is true, then right now Jarrat is the most dangerous place in the Seven Kingdoms. Remember that Jarrat is my home city. I still have friends there, friends who will be able to help you," Aimon sounded excited.

Richmond and Tancred both moved closer, as if waiting for some piece of secret information. When Aimon didn't continue Tancred felt as though he should speak.

"How can you help us?" The trap had been set.

"I will write you a missive to give to one of my closest friends. For now that is all that I can tell you. There is more treachery out there then you know. You must keep what I tell you here secret. If there is a spy in the command group then they must not hear about this," Aimon warned as he drained his cup. "Now you should be going. If you are found here then people will start asking questions. Come and see me tomorrow night, after the sun sets."

Both Tancred and Richmond knew when their time was up. As much as they both wanted more information they knew not to push. There was no doubt that Aimon did not suspect their true motives and they didn't want to do anything to jeopardise it. They both quickly drained their cups and left the tent.

Once they were outside they both let out sighs of relief. They didn't realise how tense they had been until they were outside. They were both grateful that they had survived the meeting without giving anything away. Soon enough they would know Aimon's true intentions. Then they would be able to give their own false information.

When they were back at their own tents they felt free to talk again.

"Do you think that he's the enemy?" Richmond asked when he was sure that no one was within earshot.

"I don't know, but it's not looking good. He did seem very excited when he heard that there was a traitor and it wasn't him. I hope that he is on our side, but I doubt it very much," Tancred replied.

"I know what you mean. We should report to Bern," Richmond added.

"I don't think that would be a good idea. If Aimon is the spy then I am sure that he will be watching us very carefully," to emphasis his point he looked around nervously. "We will have to speak to Bern tomorrow night. I am sure that he will call for us to stay again. That way it won't be as obvious."

"So what do we do now?" Richmond asked.

"I think we should both go to bed. I think that would be the logical thing to do. Anyway I am feeling rather tired and I am sure that once we get moving there will not be much chance for rest," Tancred suggested.

Richmond had to agree. What was ahead of them was not going to be easy. It was still early in the night, but that didn't matter. Once they left the army they would be travelling against the clock and there would be no time for rest. Speed would be their only advantage. That thought in itself was enough to make him tired.

"I think you're right. Sleep sounds like a wonderful idea," that was the last thing they said to each other that night. They both knew that the morning would bring an entirely new set of problems.

Chapter 13: Make Haste

In the morning the army was on the move at first light. There was no time for Tancred or Richmond to speak to Bern. The General had made himself strangely unavailable. Throughout the day he made sure that there was no opportunity for either man to speak to him alone. There was something very disturbing about his attitude. It was almost like he was deliberately avoiding them. Aimon also made a point not to speak to the two men throughout the day. Richmond and Tancred were basically left to their own devices. It seemed that no one wanted to speak to them. At the end of the day, however, that all changed.

The command group gathered again for the evening meal once the sun had set. Again there was little to discuss besides the regular day-to-day business of the army. Tancred and Richmond were silent throughout the discussion. With so many in the tent it was not hard for them to go unnoticed. Once the meal was finished the tent slowly started to empty.

Richmond and Tancred waited almost until everyone had left before they made their way to the exit. They made a point of making sure Aimon was still in the tent when they did. They wanted to make sure that he knew it was Bern who asked them to stay. It would be less suspicious that way. Aimon also waited to see what Bern was going to do.

"Richmond and Tancred," Bern spoke when they were almost out of the tent. "Would you mind staying for a moment? There is something that I need to discuss with you."

"Of course General," Tancred was relieved to hear Bern's voice. As he walked back to the table he made eye contact with Aimon. The captain's eyes told a story in themselves.

Once they were sure they were alone Bern spoke. "I take it that you both went to see Aimon last night?"

"Yes General. We felt that it was necessary to set the trap," Richmond kept his voice low as he spoke.

"Don't worry. No one will be able to hear what we are saying," there was something noticeably different about Bern's voice. Both Richmond and Tancred had heard about the entity that possessed Bern's body from time to time, but this was the first time they suspected it was true. "I need to know what he told you."

"He said that we are to meet him again, two hours past sundown. Then he will give us a letter to take to a friend he has in Jarrat. He said that his friend will help us escape if we get into any trouble," Tancred explained.

"I doubt very much that will happen. You have to believe me when I tell you that. He is more dangerous than you think. By making this decision you have made your mission all the more difficult," there was a touch of dread in his voice.

"What are you talking about? Last night you told us that you suspected him of being a spy. Now you are telling us that he is much more dangerous than that. I think you owe us an explanation," there was concern in Tancred's voice.

"Unfortunately that is all that I can tell you about Aimon, at least for now. If you knew the truth I don't know if you would be able to continue on your current course and that I believe would be worse," there was nothing that Bern was saying that was filling them with any sense of confidence.

"Well if you can't give us anymore information, what is it that you wanted to talk about?" Richmond sounded annoyed with the situation.

"I am sorry. Please believe me when I say that I didn't want to get the two of you into this situation. I know you have followed the prophecy religiously. Now it is time for the prophecy to ask more of you, maybe even the most of you," again Bern didn't say much. Richmond was about to speak, but Bern silenced him with a wave of his hand. He was not finished with what he wanted to say. "Once you leave here tonight we will not speak again until you return from Jarrat."

"Do you mean for us to leave tonight?" Tancred spoke before Bern could continue.

"No. You will speak to Aimon once you leave here. He will give you the message. From there you will return to your tents and retire for the night. In the morning you will continue on with the army. Instead of adjourning to the command tent you will disappear into the night. You must leave as soon as night falls. You will have to have fresh horses and all your supplies ready to go by then. I will make sure that you can leave unnoticed. I will also give the excuse that you both had to return to Bellarome. I will make up some sort of emergency," Bern explained.

"If we just leave on nightfall we will be seen leaving," Tancred protested.

"I will make sure that you leave unnoticed. All that you have to do is head due west until the army is out of sight. From there I am sure you will be able to remain ahead of the army," Bern explained further.

Tancred wanted to ask what he meant, but he knew that he would not get a response. There was something happening that wasn't right. The situation was spiralling out of control. Just when they thought they understood one lot of intrigue it completely changed. He had to admit, that life in Bellarome was a lot simpler than this.

"What do we do with the letter?" Richmond asked, trying to change the subject slightly.

"Take it with you. I wouldn't advise giving it to the intended person, but that will be up to you. I would suggest that you be very careful with it. You never know what sort of traps can be set," Bern was being mysterious.

"What are you talking about? What sort of traps could someone set in a letter?" Richmond asked.

"When you work out that answer then you will have a greater understanding of what a mess you are in." There was nothing but seriousness on Bern's face. "For now you must go to meet with Aimon. He will be expecting you."

At Bern's reminder they realised that if they didn't leave they would be late for their meeting with Aimon. It seemed to be very fortuitous for Bern. There was no more opportunity for the others to question him and there were still many questions to be asked.

"I thank you for your help in serving the prophecy." Bern stood in an effort to end the meeting.

"We always do our best to serve," the words came out of Tancred's mouth before he could stop them.

The two men walked away from the command tent feeling somewhat disheartened. Their situation had just become a lot worse and they didn't even know how. Things had been seemingly going in their favour, but Bern put an end to those thoughts. There was something strange about the way that Bern had been speaking. It gave them pause to believe the rumours. Not only that, but there was something not right with Aimon. It seemed that the Captain from Entero was more than just a traitor. There was nothing they could do, but continue on with the original plan. Perhaps that's what Bern wanted all along. It was a warning without a warning.

The two of them walked in silence towards Aimon's tent. They were both pondering what Bern had told them, or more so what he had kept silent. There was a lot more to his words than what had been said, but neither of them could work it out. They were still deep in thought when they arrived at Aimon's tent. They waited outside until he came to get them.

"I wasn't sure if you were going to make it, come in," his voice was friendly.

As they entered the tent they had to forget about their conversation with Bern. If they dwelt on it then Aimon would realise that they were onto him. The best they could do was to forget Bern's warning and pretend that nothing had happened.

"Would you like something to drink?" Aimon offered. The same young man stood in the corner with a pitcher of wine.

"Yes please," Richmond sounded grateful. He thought it was the best way to keep up pretences.

"No, thank you," was Tancred's response. After Bern's warning he was suspicious of Aimon's motives.

Aimon looked at him. Something twitched on his face. It was so sudden that Tancred wasn't sure if it had even happened. Aimon settled himself quickly before sitting. He handed Richmond a cup before taking one for himself. He seemed to relax a lot when after he had taken a sip of his wine.

"Now what was it that our esteemed leader had to say to you tonight?" Aimon's voice was friendly.

"Not much. He just wanted to make sure that we knew not to speak to anyone about what we are doing. He also said that we should leave tomorrow night," Richmond was quick to answer, a little too quick for Tancred's liking.

Richmond took a long drink from his cup when he finished speaking. It was almost like talking was too much of an effort for him. On top of what Bern had told them this made Tancred extremely worried. He was concerned that there was something in the wine. If they weren't careful Richmond could give away their entire plan.

"Do you have the letter for us?" Tancred spoke before Aimon could continue his line of questioning.

"Ah, yes," Aimon motioned for the young man in the corner of the tent. The servant quickly moved into action and brought over a sealed envelope. "Now I must warn you not to open the letter. It contains information that only my friend will understand. If the seal is broken then he will know that someone had tampered with it and your life will be in great danger. Believe me when I tell you that this is of the utmost importance." Aimon took another drink from his cup. When he was finished he handed the missive to Tancred. "You must find a good friend of mine by the name of Coyne. He works in the city's market district. He has a small farriers business. Mainly he shoes horses for merchant wagons, but that's not the point. You will find him at the southern end of the main square. There is a small stable and a shop front. He will be able to give you all the information that you need."

"We will search him out as soon as we reach the city. I am sure that he will be able to help us with all we need," Tancred spoke again, just before Richmond was about to say something. "Now I think we should be going. If Bern finds us here he will think that something is up."

"Of course, you are right," Aimon stood as he spoke and finished his cup. "You are very brave men. I am sure that you will return to us safely with the news that will help us win the war," the irony of what Aimon was saying was not lost on Tancred.

Tancred stuffed the envelope into his coat pocket as he stood. Richmond finished his wine before standing himself. He looked a little unsteady on his feet. Aimon seemed a little perturbed that their meeting was being cut short, but he didn't say anything. It seemed to Tancred that they were involved in an intricate game of cat and mouse. The only question was who was the cat and who was the mouse.

"Now remember. Don't speak of our meeting to anyone until you reach Coyne. He will be able to assist you," Aimon waved to his servant for another wine.

Tancred quickly ushered Richmond from the tent. It seemed as though they left with Aimon being none the wiser. Richmond looked a little worse for wear. He stumbled as Tancred helped him from the tent. It wasn't until they were far enough away that the two of them spoke.

"What happened back there?" Richmond's voice sounded weak.

"I think Aimon put something in the wine," Tancred helped his friend through the campsite. "I think that he was trying to find out if we were double crossing him."

"Good thing that you didn't drink any then," Richmond didn't sound as though he truly understood the situation. His mind was still covered in the fog of the drug.

"I think that you need to sleep off whatever it was that he put in your drink," Tancred was almost carrying Richmond as they continued. Whatever drug Aimon put in the wine it was still taking effect. If he couldn't make it back to their tents then things would start looking very suspicious.

Tancred breathed a sigh of relief when they made it back and he was glad when he was able to place Richmond on his bedroll. He loved the man who he had served so graciously back in Bellarome, but sometimes he wondered if he was cracked up to being a Lord. He knew Richmond was a smart man, but sometimes he got himself into dangerous situations. If it wasn't for Tancred then he would have been assassinated a long time ago.

Once he was sure that Richmond was not going to get up to any mischief Tancred made his way to his own tent. Before he was able to retire for the night he was stopped by General Jarwe. Who had a concerned look on his face. Tancred had a bad feeling that it was not going to be a friendly meeting. He knew that he would not be able to leave without being confronted by someone in the command group.

"I am sorry to bother you," Jarwe spoke softly. "There is something that we need to discuss."

"Of course, General. What is it that I can help you with?" Tancred kept his voice level. He didn't want to give anything away.

"There is a concern amongst the command group at the reason behind your meetings with Bern. I'm sure that it is nothing, but since you are the last to join us I thought that it would be a good idea to speak to you first," there was something underlying in Jarwe's words that Tancred couldn't put his finger on.

"There is nothing to be concerned about," Tancred wasn't going to give any information away without being asked. It would be too obvious a deception if he did.

"What is it that is so important that he can not speak to everyone about it?" Jarwe cut straight to the point.

"It is exactly the opposite," Richmond and Tancred had already agreed upon their response. "All Bern was looking for was information about our encounter with Alaric. He was interested in hearing what he had been doing."

"That is odd. I would have thought he would have had plenty of time to discuss things with Alaric when they were in the palace together," Jarwe didn't completely believe Tancred's lie.

"I don't know about that. Maybe Bern wanted to get someone else's point of view. I guess you will have to ask him if you want to get the answer," Tancred was trying to be as nonchalant as possible.

"I suppose you are right," Jarwe didn't sound convinced, but he didn't have enough reason to push Tancred harder. "I will let you get back to what you are doing."

Tancred was glad to see the back of Jarwe. There would be no rest for him the following day, so he was keen to get as much sleep as he could. If they were going to get far enough in front of the army then they would have to ride hard into the night. It was still early, but he felt as though he could easily sleep.

In the morning they were on the move again at first light. It would be the same for the Alliance until they reached Jarrat. They would march for the full length of the day, stopping only briefly to eat the midday meal. At the end of the day they would only stop with enough time to set up camp. In the morning they were up well before dawn to eat a light meal and pack down the camp. Only the commanders and the next in command had servants to set up and break down their tents.

The day passed much the same as the previous two. The army marched for as long and as hard as it could with Richmond and Tancred riding nervously at the front of the line. With each moment that passed they came one moment closer to leaving. Once they had left the army there would no longer be a threat of discovery by Aimon, but that was the least of their concerns. Infiltrating Jarrat was going to be no easy task.

When night fell Tancred and Richmond found their new mounts and then continued on in front of the army. To their surprise they were able to ride past the guards without being stopped. They didn't know how Bern had managed it, but they weren't about to look a gift horse in the mouth. They were just grateful to be away without being caught.

A full moon was in the sky giving them enough light to ride without needing to use torches. Tancred was sure that if the army was to see two torch lights moving in the distance then they would become suspicious. Bern's lie would only work if the rest of the command didn't know which direction they had left.

It was well past midnight when they finally stopped for the night. Neither of them had spoken since they had left the army. The night air was thick and they feared that their voices would travel on the wind. They rode as fast as they could in the moonlight, which was to say not very fast. Once the sun had risen they would be able to keep a much quicker pace.

"I guess there is no turning back now," Richmond spoke as they settled down for the night.

"There was no turning back when we left Bellarome," Tancred sounded sour.

They found a small grove of trees to shelter for the night. The trees would hide their fire, and also provide some wood. The night air was crisp, but not uncomfortable. The fire was a nice comfort they needed for their first night away from the army. It also gave them some light.

Tancred pulled the envelope from his pocket and placed it on the ground in front of him. He looked at the envelope for a moment, thinking on what he should do.

"Do you think we should open the letter?"

"I don't think that's a wise idea," Richmond replied as he went through his packs for something to eat. "Remember what Bern said to us?"

"I know, but it was not a definitive answer. He said that there might be a trap. I don't think Aimon suspects that we are not on his side. Therefore I don't think there would be any reason for him to set a trap for us," Tancred was not convinced.

"Here," Richmond tossed Tancred some dried meat. He took a bite from his own food before speaking again. "If we keep the letter intact then we might be able to get some insights from this Coyne person."

Tancred chewed on the meat as he thought on Richmond's words. It was not a bad idea, but he knew that there was something wrong with it. "If we show Coyne the letter without reading it first we run the risk of letting the enemy know exactly what we are doing."

Richmond looked at the fire and then looked at the letter. He was looking for an answer. Finally he spoke his mind. "I think you're right, we should look at the letter."

"But a minute ago you said it was not a good idea," Tancred starting to have doubts.

"You're right. We have to open the letter to see what Aimon is up to. If we have all the information then there is still a chance we will be able to play Coyne," Richmond stared at the envelope.

"Okay. I'll open the envelope, but I think you should stand back. If there is a trap I don't think we should both be caught in it," Tancred suggested.

Richmond thought for a moment. His old friend was right. There was a chance that opening the letter was a mistake. If it was then there was no point in them both becoming trapped. As much as he didn't want to put his friend in danger they had to know what was inside.

"Okay," Richmond stood and left the grove. He made sure that he could still see Tancred from where he was standing. He needed to make sure that if something went wrong that he was still in a position to help.

Tancred took a deep breath as he picked up the envelope. All of a sudden it seemed as though it had doubled in weight. It felt heavy in his hand. Something weighed on him as he considered opening the envelope. A sudden feeling of dread came over him. Something really didn't want him to open the letter. He hoped that this was just the trap that Bern had warned them about. If it was then there was nothing to worry about.

Slowly Tancred slid his finger between the paper and the wax seal. The seal broke easily as he pushed his finger through it. Immediately a wave of energy passed through the grove. Richmond could only stare in amazement as the energy rippled towards him. Once he was struck he fell to the ground, completely unconscious. The energy had an entirely different effect on Tancred. He was at the source of the power and the one who had set off the trap. His eyes rolled up into his head and his eyelids started to flicker. He remained in his sitting positions. The only sign that he was still alive was the slow rise and fall of his chest. The reality around him suddenly changed, although at first he was completely unaware of it.

***

"I told you not to open the envelope," the voice echoed in the space around Tancred.

His opened his eyes, but everything was pitch black. He looked all around, but he could not see anything. It was as if the grove had been sucked out of existence. The voice repeated its last statement. Tancred had to cover his ears at the sound that resonated inside his head.

"I'm sorry," even though he couldn't see who was speaking he knew the voice belonged to Aimon and that didn't seem at all out of place. "I couldn't help myself," he didn't know what to say to make things right.

"Why did you open the letter?" the voice echoed again.

Tancred tried to think of an excuse, but his mind seemed to be clouded. He didn't know why, but he felt as though the truth was the only thing to say. He knew that it wasn't right, but he didn't care. "We think that you are the traitor," Tancred could have cursed himself as the words came out of his mouth, but there was nothing he could do to stop them.

A sudden wave of hatred passed through the air. The feeling was almost enough to knock Tancred to his knees. The wave made his bones shake. For a moment he thought that his whole world was going to collapse. His breath was suddenly sucked from his lungs. The pain that followed was like nothing that Tancred had ever experienced before. His head ached and his body trembled. The feeling only lasted for a moment before it instantly disappeared, but it was enough to knock the breath out of him. Tancred gasped before the dark air filled his lungs.

"That is to be expected," Tancred thought that he heard the voice curse to itself. "I shouldn't have been so trusting."

"I am sorry to have deceived you. It will not happen again," Tancred grovelled; although he didn't know why. The situation didn't seem to make any sense and yet it seemed like the most natural thing in the world.

"I am sure that it will, but that is a story for another time. Now we have to get down to business," there was something evil in Aimon's voice. Tancred still waited eagerly for his words. "You will now work for me. You will not mention any of this to your partner. He will still think that you are working for Bern. Do you understand what I am saying?"

"Yes, my Lord. I will do what you wish," the words came out of Tancred's mouth unbidden. "Tell me what you command."

"That's good to hear," Aimon laughed loudly. The sound echoed around Tancred's head before it was instantly cut off. "You will read the letter to Richmond. You will agree that I am a traitor. In fact you will agree with everything Richmond says about me. What you will not tell him is about this meeting and our arrangement. Do you understand?"

"Yes, my Lord," Tancred responded in a monotone voice.

"You will suggest that you use the information contained in the letter to your advantage. You will seek out Coyne under the pretence that you will use him to gain information. You will give Coyne the information that is contained in the letter. Then I will contact you with further instructions. Do you understand?" Aimon's voice was sickly sweet inside his mind.

"Yes, my Lord," Tancred couldn't believe the words that were coming out of his mouth.

"Good. Now return to your friend and forget that you have been speaking to me," Aimon was about to leave when something crossed his mind. "Know now that I am your master. I will be watching you."

Tancred wanted to scream out, but nothing left his mouth. There was nothing that he could do. His body was completely immobile as the darkness slowly started to fade.

***

Suddenly Tancred was back in the grove staring at the flickering fire. Richmond had also regained his consciousness. He gave Tancred a strange look. The shadow that had been looming over Tancred suddenly disappeared when he regained his senses.

"What was that?" Richmond finally asked when Tancred didn't speak.

"What do you mean?" Hearing Richmond's voice broke him from his reverie.

"Something happened," Richmond wasn't sure of himself as the words came out of his mouth. "When you opened the letter, something happened."

"Nothing happened," Tancred replied, a little surprised at Richmond's question. "I only just opened the envelope."

Tancred's response didn't seem right, but the more Richmond thought about it the more it made perfect sense. He didn't know what he had been talking about. He couldn't even remember the question that he asked. All that he wanted to know was what was inside the letter then they would know one way or another if Aimon was indeed a spy for the enemy.

"Read it then," Richmond's voice sounded eager.

The words brought Tancred around to the letter in his hand. Suddenly he remembered what he was doing. He was about to reveal that Aimon was a spy. He knew this before he read the first word.

Coyne,

If you are reading this letter and the seal has been broken then you will know that the people delivering it have betrayed me, if the seal has not been broken then the people before you are true to our cause. You can trust them as friends and know that they speak on my behalf.

More important than that is the information that is contained in this letter.

The army of the Alliance is heading in your direction. By the time this letter reaches you the army will be about two weeks from your door step. There is much that you need to prepare for. The most important thing is to let the prince know that we are coming. I will do all that I can from my end, but I fear that my influence is becoming weaker and weaker.

I trust you and only you with this information. It is up to you to make sure that we do not fail. You must tell the prince to dispose of the prisoners. They threaten everything that we work towards. If they are alive when we reach the city I fear that all will be lost.

Your Lord
Argoz.

"What do you suppose that means?" Richmond asked when Tancred finished reading the letter.

"I don't know," Tancred let the letter slip from his hands into the fire. Instantly it was engulfed with flames.

"What are you doing," Richmond was about to reach for it, but he realised that he was already too late. "That was the proof that we needed that Aimon is indeed the traitor."

"There is nothing in the letter that we did not know already. Our mission is not to out Aimon as the traitor. It is to work out what the enemy is up to. That letter could only get us in trouble." It was not the real reason why Tancred disposed of it, although it was the one he truly believed. The real reason was that there were words in the letter that he did not want Richmond to see.

Richmond had to agree that Tancred was right. If the letter fell into the wrong hands then they would know that they had betrayed Aimon. One thing that puzzled Richmond was the person who signed the letter. Tancred had seemingly brushed over the name Argoz. It was a name that Richmond had never heard before.

"Who do you think that Argoz is?" Richmond asked.

"Who?" It was as if Tancred had only heard the name for the first time. "I don't think that it's really important. The important thing is what we are going to do with the information that we have?"

"For one thing I think we should stay well away from this Coyne character. I think we will be able to gather enough information without getting involved in more intrigue," Richmond suggested.

"There is one thing that I don't understand," Tancred seemed to back to his normal self. "Well there is more than one thing that I don't understand, but there is one that stands out the most. The letter makes a reference to speaking to the prince. Now we both know that Oriana only has two daughters and neither of them are married. So who is this prince that he writes about?"

Richmond thought on every possibility. He had to admit that he didn't know very much about the internal workings of the Entero Royal family. He did know, however, that Oriana had been looking for a suitable husband for her first born daughter for a long time, but had yet to find anyone. Now he was not so sure.

"It is indeed a disturbing statement. I am sure that it will all become clearer once we reach the city," Richmond added. "What we need to do is to work out our next plan of attack."

"You are right. I think that the best way for us to gather information is to befriend Coyne. He is obviously working for the enemy. He will be able to give us the information that we need," Tancred suggested.

"I don't know if we should be getting involved so closely with the enemy. I'm sure there are other ways for us to gather information."

"That is true, but unfortunately we don't have time to assimilate ourselves into Jarrat. We need to get the information and we need to gather it quickly. The only way is to use the resources that the prophecy has laid before us." Tancred still pushed his own agenda.

Richmond had to accept the fact that Tancred's words were true. He still did not like the idea of trying to trick Coyne, but it would be the easiest way to make contact. They still had plenty of time to come up with a better plan. He wasn't sure if the easiest solution was the best, but for the moment he had to go along with what his advisor suggested.

"I guess that you are right. For the moment we will pretend to be followers of the Evil One. If we can gain Coyne's trust then it is possible that he will share information with us," Richmond resigned. "For now I think that we should get some rest. The sun will be rising soon and we will need to be on the move. The last thing we want is to oversleep and allow the army to catch us."

There was very little chance of the army catching them. They would have to sleep for the rest of the day for that to happen, but it was still important for them to be up and dawn. They would be able to travel faster during the day. The thought of sleep washed over both of them and soon they were both sound asleep.

Chapter 14: Jarrat

Jarrat was the smallest of the capitals in the Seven Kingdoms. The main reason was due to its proximity. The city of Jarrat was nestled in the Entero Forest in the heart of Entero. Along with being the smallest, it was also the newest. It had been literally cut out of the forest. As the city grew the residents simply cut down more trees, which worked on two levels. Firstly, it created more room to build and secondly, it gave them the materials to build with. The city was almost completely built out of the large pine trees of the forest. Over the years some of the city's richer inhabitants had stone, marble and other materials shipped in from around Entero and even from some of the other kingdoms. As the city grew a large wooden wall had been build around it for defence.

When the city was recognised as the capital of Entero King Leroy III built a castle and moved his residence to Jarrat. He had his castle built out of stone brought down from the foot of the Cloumid Mountain range. It took almost all his life to see it completed. King Leroy III only lived for six years in his newly built castle and it became a monument to his rule. His subjects truly loved him to transport the materials to build his castle such a distance. It had been built atop a small hill to the North West of the city and looked down upon the city as a loving mother would a child.

The large forest that encased the city was its major defence. No army could stay regimented to reach the city. There were roads connecting the city to the rest of the kingdom, but not wide enough to bring a full army. At most the highways would allow twenty men to march side by side. There were only four roads leading out of the city, one to the east, one to the west and two to the north. All roads had outposts scattered throughout the forest. No approaching armies could use the roads undetected.

There was a large open grassland to the north of the city where livestock roamed during the day. It was the only place where an invading army could station themselves for battle. It was where the Alliance was aiming to reach.

The journey for Richmond and Tancred from the Alliance to Jarrat was somewhat uneventful. On the third day since they had left the army they reached the Jarrat-Kiarome highway. It was the most logical road for them to enter the city if they were going to use their real identities. They figured that it would be easier to gather the information if they used their true identities then assumed ones. It was more likely that they would be granted entrance into the castle as a nobleman and his advisor. They doubted that anyone would know much about Lord

Richmond in Jarrat. They certainly wouldn't know they were part of the Alliance.

They had met a few merchants on the road, but less than they had expected. The closer they came to the city the busier the road should have become, but instead it was just the opposite. There seemed to be less and less people on the road as they approached the city. They didn't expect the city to be running as normal, but things seemed strange. Rumours from Kiarome said that it ran much the same as normal with the Dark Knight in control. They hoped that Jarrat would be in much the same state.

In was mid-morning when they passed through the Northern gates into Jarrat. The Jarrat-Kiarome highway passed through the only open space near the city. The fields they passed were empty of livestock. Neither men thought it was a good sign.

"What should we do now?" Richmond asked as they led their horses through the streets of Jarrat.

To their surprise they were not stopped at the gates to the city. The guard didn't really seem interested in them as they walked through. They didn't know if that was a good sign or a bad sign. If they were preparing for war then there was no way they would be able to just turn up and stroll through the gates. That meant that they didn't know the Alliance was on its way.

"I think we should find somewhere to stay," Tancred was a little nervous at the ease of their entrance.

"There is a nice inn by the commerce district. I have heard that it's a comfortable place to stay. It is called the Merchant's Nest," Richmond explained as they walked through the streets.

"Don't you think that a merchant's inn is a little down class for a nobleman? If we are to keep up the pretences of being visiting nobles then were should stay somewhere better," Tancred suggested.

Richmond was a little annoyed at Tancred's use of the word pretence. He was still a Lord and his family name would still hold sway in court. He was not sure that Queen Oriana would know who he was, but he was sure that someone would know the name Lord Richmond d'Edelmann. The Edelmann family name was synonymous throughout the Seven Kingdoms, or at least that's what his father always told him.

"Do you have any suggestion then?" Richmond asked.

Although Tancred had never been to Jarrat there was an inn that came to mind. He didn't know how he knew its name and more importantly he didn't know how he knew its location. All he knew was that it would be a more suitable resting place for a nobleman. He was sure that it was the inn they were meant to stay at.

"There is another inn in the commerce district. It's called the Royal Watchman. I think it will do nicely," Richmond watched Tancred closely for a moment. He thought about inquiring as to how Tancred knew of such a place, but then thought better of it.

"Okay, we will do it your way," Richmond didn't think that it really mattered where they stayed. There was something strange about Tancred's insistence of the location of the inn that didn't sit right with him. In the end his put it down to tiredness from the long ride and pushed the thought to the back of his mind.

Tancred led the way through the streets. Although Richmond was sure that Tancred didn't know where he was going his advisor was doing a good job of finding his way. It wasn't long before Richmond had no idea where he was. He would have stopped to ask for directions, but Tancred was moving like a man possessed.

The sun was high in the sky when Tancred stopped them outside a lavish looking inn. The sign hanging to the left of the door had a crown and a pair of glasses carved into it. Richmond knew it was the Royal Watchman. How they got there without directions was a question he was afraid to ask. He had been involved with the prophecy long enough to know that some questions would always remain unanswered.

They were met at the door by a young stableboy. He gave the two men a questioning look. Neither of them were dressed like nobleman. The boy knew better than to ask questions of his elders. It would not be the first time that he had been beaten for refusing to serve someone because they did not look as though they could afford his service.

"Would you like me to take your horses?" the boy sounded bored.

"Stand straight boy." The stableboy was leaning against the side of the inn. Richmond's harsh words brought him to attention. If he didn't believe the man was a noble before he did now. One thing Richmond couldn't abide was rudeness. "See that our horses are well looked after and make sure that our bags are taken to our rooms. It has been a long journey and I don't wish to be kept waiting."

"Of course, sir. Go right inside and the master will take care of you."

The stableboy almost fell over himself as he made his way toward the horses. The sooner he was out of their way the less chance there was of repercussions for his attitude. If the two men told the owner of the inn there was no doubt he would receive another beating and that was something he would do anything to avoid.

The two men waited out the front until the stableboy left. Richmond smiled at his friend when they were alone. "I haven't had this much fun in a long time."

"He certainly needed a boot up the behind, but I think that we should continue inside. I would hate for the stableboy not to have anywhere to place our bags," Tancred added.

Tancred entered the inn and then held the door for Richmond. Their plan would be more plausible if they acted like nobleman and his advisor. It would be expected of Tancred to look after his Lord. Neither man was happy with the situation, but they had played their roles for so long that it came naturally.

"Greetings to you," a man dressed in a dark blue suit greeted them. "I am the owner of this establishment. My name is Gage Aubergiste and I am your servant." There was nothing sincere about his words, it was a rhetoric that he had spoken over a thousand times.

Gage was younger than they had been expecting. He would have been no older than thirty. Richmond could only guess that his parents had died and left him the inn. It would have it advantages though. A younger man would be more likely to be helpful than an older one.

"Very good," Richmond pushed his way passed the man an into the inn's common room. He would leave Tancred to close the deal. It was what would be expected.

"I am sorry, my Lord has had a long journey. Due to the current state of things in Darshival he had to ride by horseback. You have no idea how grumpy he is going to be now," Tancred kept his voice low as if he was telling Gage some great secret.

"Of course, I understand completely. If you don't mind me asking, who is your Lord? I don't see a crest on his shirt." There was a certain amount of suspicion in Gage's voice. It had not been the first time that someone had come to his establishment posing as a nobleman. It was only when it came to paying for the bill did they reveal their true identity.

Tancred knew exactly what he was talking about and in truth he would wonder if the man was truly the innkeeper if he didn't ask the question. It was a perfect opportunity to lie, but that would prove nothing. For the first time the truth played better for their intrigue.

"He is Lord Richmond d'Eldermann of Bellarome. He is the cousin of King Unwin," that was all Tancred needed to say. He didn't need to embellish too much or else Gage would become suspicious again.

Gage looked at Richmond carefully before returning his attention to Tancred. He would need some more information before he truly believed who they were. Again Tancred was expecting the question.

"What is he doing in Jarrat?" he kept his voice low as Richmond had made his way within earshot.

"That is not something that needs to be discussed in public. If I could get our rooms sorted then maybe we could go somewhere to talk,"

Gage had walked right into his trap. As Gage would think that he was gaining information when in fact he would be supplying Tancred.

"Of course. The royal suite is available," Gage started dry washing his hands in anticipation.

"Ah, I don't think that will be necessary. I think when you hear my tale you will understand what I mean. For now we will take a standard room for the night. I am sure we will be staying longer, but who's to tell?" as much as he wanted to keep up the pretence they only had a limited amount of gold.

"Whatever your Lord requires, but I would ask for a gold coin as a deposit." He still didn't truly trust them.

"Would a Darshivallian half crown be suitable," Tancred flicked the coin out of his hand and into the innkeeper's.

Gage's eyes bulged for a moment at the sight of the coin. The gold half crown was worth two Enteroite golden crowns. It was more than enough to pique his interest. Little did he know that it was the only gold half crown they possessed. Tancred had taken it for such an occasion. There would be no doubt in Gage's mind that they were who Tancred said they were.

The innkeeper quickly placed the coin inside his coat pocket. When he was done he greedily rubbed his hands through is light greased brown hair. The excitement was clearly printed all over his face. He looked around quickly until he saw the man he was looking for.

"Gilles, find these men a room," an elderly looking man walked over to the desk and started to flick through the papers. A moment later he returned with a key, which he placed in Gage's hands.

In the moment of distraction Tancred signalled to Richmond. He knew immediately what Tancred wanted him to do. All he had to do was to wait for the right moment.

"Gilles, make sure that little scamp takes their bags straight to their room," Gage referred to the stableboy. "I am sure that his lordship would like to rest from his travels and he will not want to be disturbed."

Richmond couldn't believe his luck. It was just the excuse that he needed to leave the room. He knew that Tancred was up to something that needed privacy. When it was said and done he was tired from their journey and any excuse to rest was a welcome one.

"I think that I will retire for a while. See that I am not disturbed," Richmond made it sound as though he didn't hear their conversation and rest was purely his idea.

"Of course, my Lord," Tancred made a show of subservience. "Now if there is somewhere we can talk?" Tancred spoke once Richmond had left the common room.

"My office is through there," Gage pointed to a small doorway behind the main desk. "I will see that we have some refreshments brought in." Since Tancred had given him the half crown he was more than happy to help.

Tancred moved into the office while Gage went to kitchen to get some food and drink. He would, of course, be adding the price to their account, but that wasn't something he was going to discuss. Tancred made himself as comfortable as he could as he waited for him to return. He looked around the office to see if he could gather any information about the innkeeper. The office was small and tidy. There was a small pile of papers on his desk that looked to be a list of food required for the meals. There was a ledger on the other side of the desk and that was it. A calendar hung on the wall behind the desk with some letters scrawled on it that didn't make any sense. If nothing else Tancred worked out Gage was a shrewd and organised man. He would have to be very careful if he wanted to gather information from him.

The innkeeper returned, followed by two young serving women. One, the younger of the two with long blond hair, brought a pitcher of ale and two tankards. The other girl, with short brown hair, who had similar features to Gage, carried a platter of fruit and berries. Tancred was pleased to see the sight. They had not eaten before they reached the city and he was becoming hungry.

"Would you see that Lord Richmond is also fed," Tancred asked.

The dark haired girl bowed her acknowledgment before looking at Gage for confirmation. The innkeeper did his best to hide his agreement from Tancred. He didn't want the man to think that his staff was second guessing him. There was coin to be made from his new arrivals and he didn't want to do anything to upset them.

"Please," he passed a tankard of ale, which the blonde girl had poured. "Eat and drink."

"Thank you," Tancred took the tankard and drank deeply. The cool drink felt good as it slid down his throat. He ate a few pieces of fruit before he returned his attention to the job at hand. "Now you asked what brings us to Jarrat. I am afraid that it is troubled times that brings us to your doorstep."

His opening piqued Gage's attention. Although intrigue was not as rife in Entero as it was in Darshival a pertinent piece of information could be just as important. The information Gage was about to receive could increase his standing, at least amongst his own friends. He waited for Tancred to continue.

"There are troubles in Darshival," Tancred paused as the look on Gage's face changed.

"I have not heard any news about troubles in Darshival. Now I admit that I don't have as many merchants stay here as some of the other inns, but I am sure that I would have heard."

Tancred understood why Gage was keen for information. It was obvious that the local innkeepers would get together and gossip. Those with the most important information would be treated better than those without. He still found it very hard to believe that nothing had been mentioned about the troubles in Kiarome. As much as the Alliance had tried to stop anyone leaving the city he was sure someone would have got through. On the other hand if nothing had reached Jarrat then there was still a good chance they didn't know the Alliance was on its way. Tancred knew that he had to be very careful.

Gage could hardly contain himself as he waited for Tancred to continue. Tancred couldn't continue with his original plan. He made a scene of drinking and eating as he thought what to say next.

"Now I can only tell you what I have heard, but that is disturbing enough. My Lord and I live in Bellarome, and I fear that is the next city to be invaded." He quickly changed his tact.

"Invaded!" Gage had to cover his mouth as he blurted out the words.

"Have you heard of the Alliance army?" Gage nodded that he had. There wouldn't be many who lived in a major city and didn't know that the Alliance existed and Tancred figured it was safe to mention it. "Now it was my understanding that the army was formed to defeat an enemy most foul, but the reality is much different. The Alliance marched on Kiarome and took control from King Unwin," his words would do nothing to help the Alliance when it arrived, but it would give him the cover that he needed to gain information from the enemy. "I believe that the army has been formed to gain control of the Seven Kingdoms," Gage was sitting on the edge of his chair. It was obvious that he believed every word. "It will only be a matter of time before the Alliance controls all of Darshival. Then I would imagine that it will be marching on Jarrat."

His last words gave Gage cause to think. "No one has ever attacked Jarrat. I do not think that this Alliance would come after us."

It seemed that the innkeeper didn't know his history all that well. It was true that no one had attacked Jarrat in a long time, but there were a few years that it was under the subjugation of Darshival. King Eugen II invaded Entero and managed to secure the city for a year and a half before returning it. He figured that there was little gain for his own Kingdom in holding the city and was happy to have his soldiers returned home. He had proven his strength and there was peace between the two kingdoms for the remainder of his reign.

"That is exactly what we thought in Darshival, now the kingdom is in disarray." There was no going back on his story. "And is the reason why me and my Lord have ridden here." Tancred paused as he could see that Gage was thinking deeply. His words were having their effect. Soon it would be well known that Lord Richmond and his advisor Tancred were seeking refuge from and evading army. "We are seeking an audience with Queen Oriana. We wish for asylum until the Alliance has been defeated. We do not wish to be slaves of a ruthless overlord."

"This is indeed troubling news. I am sure that our good Queen will offer you sanctuary. Our walls will not be as easily breached as Kiarome's." Tancred let the jibe pass without comment.

"That is good to hear," Tancred continued to eat and drink as he let Gage continue to process the information. He needed to be careful of how to ask his next question. "Do you know anything about the Alliance?"

Gage made a show of thinking. "I haven't heard much, but there is a meeting of local innkeepers and tavern owners soon. If anything is happening I am sure that I will be able to find out then."

"One thing that I don't understand." Tancred would have to tread very lightly with his next line. "If there is supposedly this great evil coming to attack us then where is it?" It was against what he had previous suggested, but he needed to float the idea to see Gage's response.

"That is true. I have heard stories of the Evil One breaking out of his prison in the Northern Wasteland, but I have yet to see any sign of him. His coming was supposed to bring about the end of the world, but I think you are right. I think it was just an excuse for someone to create a super army and take control of the Seven Kingdoms," Gage was basically repeating what he had already heard. The innkeeper would be more useful than Tancred had first believed.

"I wouldn't discount the idea completely," Tancred kept his voice low, as to only allow the information into Gage's subconscious.

"What did you say?" Gage was deep in thought and didn't know if he heard Tancred speak or not.

"I think that I will go and see what my Lord is up to. I am sure that he will need some assistance with something." It was as good an excuse as any to leave the room. If he remained any longer there was a chance that he would undo the good work that he had already done.

He didn't need to ask the question before he left. He knew that Gage would seek him out once he had met with the other innkeepers. At least he would be able to get the gossip around the city. For the real information he would have to gain entrance into the castle. If the situation was as dire as he thought then that would not be an easy task.

When he reached their room he found Richmond sitting in a chair, eagerly waiting for Tancred to return. The room itself was quite spacious, more so than what he had wanted. He knew that he would be spending more coins than he had intended. There was nothing he could do about it. Part of the reason why Gage was willing to do so much was due to the fact that he was a greedy little man. If he was going to get the information he needed from the innkeeper then he needed to keep up pretences.

"Did you found out anything?" Richmond asked as soon as Tancred had closed the door behind him.

"Nothing yet, but I think that Gage will be a good little spy. The best thing is that he will not even know what he is doing. I have fed him some misinformation. I wouldn't be surprised if he was out telling someone now," Tancred sounded pleased with himself.

"That is good news. Unfortunately I don't have anything to offer. I have been locked in this room since we arrived," there was a petulant tone to his voice.

"You know that there was nothing I could have done. I am sure that Gage would not have opened up with you around. You have that effect on people." Tancred would not let Richmond's morose mood spoil his.

"You know that it's not me, but my title that people don't like. I just wished for once that I could play the advisor and you could be the nobleman," Richmond mused aloud.

"I am sure you would be at home agreeing to my demands. I sure you would love bowing to my every whim," there was only a slight amount of mocking him his voice.

"I am not that bad," Richmond was straight on the defensive. "It's not like you haven't been in command in the past."

"That is one thing, but it is completely different to playing a nobleman. It is much easier for you, since you are the one with all the experience," Tancred's words did make sense. He was more than happy with their current situation and didn't really want to change their dynamics.

"Very well. What are we going to do now?" Richmond didn't sound any happier.

"I think that we should find Coyne," the words came out of Tancred's mouth before he had a chance to think.

"I don't think we should rush into that." Richmond still wasn't sure if it was the right thing to do. "I think we should try and get some more information about him before we jump to any decisions."

His words made sense, but Tancred couldn't get the urge out of his mind. He could always leave without Richmond, but then he would need an excuse. No. He would have to wait until Richmond was ready, but it couldn't hurt to do a little recognisance first.

"You're right. We should go to the commerce district and see what we are up against," Tancred felt a little better, but it still didn't appease his compulsion.

The two left the inn via the back door. They didn't want anyone to see them leave. As much as they didn't think anyone knew why they were there they didn't want to take any chances. It was possible that Gage would have them followed. It was a little paranoid, but they had to be safe.

The commerce district wasn't too far away from the inn they were staying, but it took them longer than it should to reach it. Neither of them wanted to draw attention to themselves by asking for directions and that meant taking a couple of wrong turns. They were in no hurry and were happy to wander around the city watching the citizens go about their daily business. Once they had arrived at the commerce district it was easy for them to find the farrier's shop.

The main area of the commerce district was a market square. Inside the square many different stalls were set up selling anything the residence of Jarrat could want although not many food stalls set up as that was reserved for the market district. Most of the trade was in fine clothes, jewellery and other forms of luxury. Only the wealthy could shop in the market square.

Around the outside were many small shopfronts. It was on the Southern side of the square, as Aimon had instructed, that they found the farriers shop. He had a small shopfront with a stable next to it. They were able to get a good view of the shop from within the market square. They only had to move from stall to stall in an effort to look like they were simply shopping.

They saw Coyne working in the stable as they made a show of looking at some bolts of silk. They could see that he was fashioning horseshoes from his small furnace, but there were no horses in the stables. He was a large man with a closely shaved head. From their distance it was hard to judge all his features, but it looked as though there was a piece of his right ear missing. He wore a thick leather smock to protect him from the heat of his furnace. There was nothing out of the ordinary about the man. If they did not already know that he was an agent of evil they would have never guessed. He worked like anyone else in his job. For a moment Richmond wondered if it was the right man.

"Do you think that's him?" Richmond asked finally, when he was sure no one was paying any attention to them.

"There is no doubt," a smile crossed Tancred's face that Richmond could not see.

Chapter 15: A New Deceit

They spent a good part of the afternoon watching Coyne go about his day-to-day business from the various stalls. They couldn't stay too long at any individual stall or they would start to look conspicuous. Richmond even bought a new shirt so they had something to carry around with them. It cost a little more than Tancred wanted to pay, but he had to go along with the ruse. Richmond was the noble and it would be out of place if he didn't buy something extravagant.

As they watched they realised there was nothing out of the ordinary about Coyne. Occasionally someone would come by with a horse that had thrown a shoe or something else that needed fixing, but all he did was quickly fix the problem and send them on their way. All in all it was a relatively boring afternoon. It was a little disappointing. They didn't know what to expect, but they thought more would have happened.

Once they had returned to the inn they kept themselves inside their room. Tancred was happy to hear that Gage had already left for his meeting. He didn't want to have to speak to him again, at least not before he had more information. On the plus side the innkeeper had instructed his staff to give them whatever they wanted. It made ordering food for inside their room a lot easier. Again Tancred knew it was going to cost them, but that was the last thing he was thinking about. All they needed was to buy supplies for the return journey to the Alliance. The rest would go to the innkeeper, whether it covered their entire bill or not.

In the morning Tancred woke with a new purpose. The Gage would have had his meeting with his fellow innkeepers. Tancred was keen to find out what information he had brought back with him. Again he would have to leave Richmond behind. He knew that his old friend would not be happy.

"Where are you going?" Tancred had tried to leave whilst Richmond was still asleep.

"I have to speak with Gage. I need to know what he discussed with the other innkeepers," Tancred explained.

"Just wait a moment. I'll come with you." Richmond started to rise from his bed.

"No," Tancred was a little too quick to react. "Gage will not open up if you are there. We discussed this last night." Tancred didn't want to have the same conversation again. "This is something that I must do alone. There will be plenty of time for you to do your thing once we get inside the castle. I am sure that being a Lord will have its advantages then."

"Well, what am I supposed to do until then?" Richmond almost sounded like a spoilt child.

"Stay here, relax and try to stay out of trouble." Arrogance seemed the best way to counter Richmond's sulking. "When I get back I will tell you what happened."

Tancred left the room before Richmond had a chance to reply. He could understand why Richmond was frustrated, but he couldn't understand why he was complaining. There was nothing Tancred could do about it. If he was going to get the information they required then he would have to do it alone.

Gage was standing by the front desk talking to a young couple who looked as though they were leaving. By the expression on Gage's face he didn't look too happy. No matter what he said he couldn't convince the couple to stay. In the end he handed them back their deposit and they left. Tancred saw the opening he was looking for.

"Is everything alright?" Tancred asked as he casually walked to the desk.

Gage looked surprised and then embarrassed. He didn't realise that there was someone else in the room. When he saw it was Tancred he seemed relieved. At least that was a promising sign.

"I am sorry Tancred, I didn't see you there. The common room is empty now. Will you join me for some breakfast?" He sounded nervous.

"Yes, that would be nice. It seems my Lord still requires his rest." The jibe on Richmond wasn't really necessary, but he was still a little upset with his attitude.

Gage led Tancred into the common room. As he had said the room was completely empty. Tancred found it to be strange. Although breakfast was not the busiest time of the day he would have expected there to be some patrons. He was slowly starting to understand why Gage had been upset with the couple who had left.

"It is awfully quiet," Tancred initiated the conversation. He figured if he could get Gage started with small talk then it would be much easier to get the information that he needed.

"I know," Gage let his head drop as the realisation washed over him. "It has been quiet for a long time."

"Why is it so quiet?" it was obvious that Tancred was going to have to push for answers.

"Things have been quiet in the city ever since Queen Oriana took a new suitor. Prince Leroy he is called, or at least that is what he calls himself. We all doubt that is he is a real prince. Ever since he has been in the castle the trade in Jarrat has slowed. There are fewer and fewer visitors, which doesn't make my life any easier. It is the same throughout the city." Tancred was really starting to get some useful information. "I hate to say this to you, but I don't think that you are going to get your amnesty from the Queen."

"Why do you say that?" Tancred pushed again when Gage paused.

"The castle has been shut off to visitors. No one is allowed in or out these days." The story sounded all too familiar. "I don't think that you will be given the chance to speak with her."

Tancred took a sip of the tea that had been brought for him. The news was not good. There would only be a certain amount of information to be gained in the city. To get a true sense of what was happening they would need to get into the city. Things were only going to get harder.

"What about your meeting last night?"

"It seems what you said is correct," Gage seemed happier to be speaking about something else. "The city of Kiarome has been taken over by the Alliance. The rumours coming out of Darshival are all different though. It is common belief that one of the Evil One's servants was in control of the city at the time of attack. It is said that he had enslaved King Unwin. It was only a matter of time before the Evil One would mobilise the Darshivallian Army and march on Entero, not that they would have gotten far mind you."

"I have heard that rumour as well and I can assure you that is all that it is." He didn't like spreading the rumour, but it was necessary to their plan. "King Unwin was never under the thrall of the Evil One. He has always been a wise and kindly ruler. It is all lies made up by the Alliance to try and justify their actions."

"That is what I told the others. I told them of your arrival and your search for sanctuary. They were interested to hear your views. In fact I think they would like to hear from you directly."

Tancred thought for a moment. It could be a good opportunity, but with a bombardment of questions he might also become unstuck. The last thing he wanted to do was to undo all his good work. Their main reason for entering the city was to gather information, not to give misinformation.

"That sounds good, but I do not think my Lord would appreciate it. I am sure that he would be upset if he knew I was speaking with you." He was able to kill two birds with one stone.

"I understand."

"What is the general consensus on the Alliance?" again Tancred changed the subject before Gage could dwell on his response.

"It's hard to say. I believe that the down turn in business is due to the attack on Kiarome." It was becoming obvious that Gage would believe everything Tancred told him. "I think that is why no one is visiting the city. If the Alliance is on its way here then I think we need to prepare for battle."

"I am sure that the Alliance will not be moving here for a while," Tancred was trying to reassure Gage. He didn't want the innkeeper to start anything stupid. He was playing a dangerous game. If he said the wrong thing then he could easily ruin everything they were working towards. "I don't think now is the time to panic. I am sure if the Alliance was marching on Jarrat you would have heard about it by now."

The blonde serving girl came in with a platter of food. Again it was full of fruit. If he hadn't had meat the night before Tancred would start wonder if there was anything else to eat. He was glad at the distraction. It was the first time he was unsure where he wanted to conversation to go. The food gave him a chance for silence and to think of what to say next.

"So tell me more about the man who calls himself Prince Leroy?" Tancred thought it was time to try and gather some pertinent information on what was happening inside the castle. "You mentioned last night that you weren't sure he was all he made out to be."

Gage had a pensive look on his face. It looked as though he was trying to remember what he had said. Something didn't seem right to Tancred, but he gave the innkeeper the benefit of the doubt.

"I don't think I said anything like that." Gage looked around nervously. "The Queen's suitor is a blessing to the city."

Tancred didn't know how to respond. He knew Gage had been unsure of the Prince the night before, but he had completely changed his tune. There was something very nervous about the him. Everything inside of Tancred said he should let it go, but he needed more information.

"But I thought things started to go badly for Jarrat when the Prince moved into the castle?" Tancred spoke carefully.

"Not at all. Things haven't been better since he arrived. The problems in the city are completely unrelated." There was no confidence in his voice, but Tancred decided not to push him further.

"I still think that we should try and gain an audience with Queen Oriana. Do you know anyone who might help us gain access to the castle?" Tancred shifted the conversation slightly.

Gage thought as he ate a piece of melon. It was obvious that he didn't, but he didn't want Tancred to know. "There is no one who comes to mind, but I can ask around."

Tancred didn't think any trouble could come of Gage asking for help. He knew the innkeeper would use their names and that would only prove to help their story. The more people who knew who they were and why they were there the better chance they would gain entrance to see the queen.

"I would appreciate it if you would," Tancred stood as he spoke. "Now I think that I should see if my Lord has woken. He will be very taken aback if I am not there." Tancred reached down and took the half eaten plate of food. He knew that he would be paying for it in the end so he had no qualms. Gage looked a little taken aback, but he didn't say anything.

Tancred was glad to be away from Gage. He had gathered some useful information, but the man was not doing everything he wanted. If he wasn't careful then he might cause Gage to do something silly. If the man was able to gather enough support against the Alliance then there would be trouble once the army arrived. All he wanted to do was to get the idea into the enemy's head that Lord Richmond and Tancred supported their cause. Although everything was not going to plan, things were still looking up. If he could convince Coyne that they weren't spies then there was a good chance they could get the information they needed.

He found Richmond staring out of the small window towards the stables. He didn't look impressed when Tancred entered the room, although that did change when he saw the fruit. He ate hungrily as Tancred sat and watched. As he ate Tancred explained what had happened with Gage. Richmond waited until he had finished eating before he spoke.

"It's a dangerous game you play. You have to be very careful if you are going to play both sides. Inevitably one side always loses out," Richmond warned. "I guess there is nothing we can do about it now. What is the plan for today?" he sounded less grumpy than when he first woke.

"We need to meet with Coyne. I see no other way to gain entrance into the castle. I believe that this Prince is an agent of the Evil One. The innkeeper was acting very strange this morning. Last night he didn't think the Prince was who he said he was and this morning he denies everything. If I'm not mistaken he was told something last night in the meeting that made him change his mind. If my suspicions are correct then Coyne is our only chance to gain entrance into the castle," Tancred explained.

"Then what are we waiting for?" Tancred was concerned at Richmond's new attitude. He had known Richmond for a long time and he knew that such a sudden change in composure was not a good sign.

It took them longer than they thought to find the farrier. Coyne was not in his shop as they walked by. All that they found was a sign on his shopfront door with the picture of a man walking. It indicated that he was out, but there was no indication on when he was going to return. They eventually found him at the other end of the market buying some new tools. They carefully followed him back to his shop, making sure he didn't see them. They didn't want to confront him in public. What they had to discuss had to be done in private.

Just before Coyne reached his shop he spun around and charged at the two men following him. In his right hand he was brandishing a mash hammer that he had just purchased. In the large man's hand they knew it would only take one blow to the head to kill them.

"Tell me what it is you want?" there was a mixture of rage and concern in Coyne's voice.

"We have a message for you." Tancred raised his arms to defend himself, but no attack came.

Coyne had the hammer ready to attack, but when he heard the words he stopped. He also realised that other people in the market were starting to look at them and he suddenly felt self-conscious and wanted to be out of prying eyes. There was something very strange about the two before him and he had a bad feeling that he didn't want to be associated with them.

"I see," he looked around quickly. "Come inside," he quickly ushered them inside his shop before sliding the door bolt across. He kept the hammer in his hand as he did not completely trust the two men standing before him. "Who is it that sent the message?"

"A man by the name of Aimon," Richmond spoke before Tancred had a chance.

"Sit down," it was not a request. It was obvious that Coyne was not going speak until they were seated. He paced back and forth, tapping the hammer against his hand as he waited for them to sit. "I don't know any Aimon," he stood over the two as he spoke. "I think you should tell me what this is all about or else I will have to dispose of you," his voice was full of menace.

Richmond looked confused, but Tancred remembered what he had read in the letter. "You might know him as Argoz," Tancred almost whispered the words.

The look on Coyne's face changed so suddenly that Richmond almost fell off his chair. He still looked at the two suspiciously, but the murderous expression had left his face. Richmond tried to remember the name that Tancred had spoken, but he had already forgotten it. He thought about asking, but decided that it would look too suspicious.

"I see and do you have a letter for me?" there was knowing in his voice.

"We have no letter. The message that he gave me was too important to put down in words," his lie was convincing.

Coyne looked at the two men, trying to gauge a response by their faces. After a moment he decided the let Tancred speak. He would wait and listen to the message before he made his judgement. He was not convinced that they were who they said they were. Argoz had told him that all communications would be in writing. There was something suspicious about the two before him. One seemed to know what was happening, but the other seemed a little unsure of himself.

"We are here to tell you that the Alliance is on the way to Lel Dinion," they had both agreed that the best move was to try and divert the enemies attention. "They fear that there is a conspiracy to overthrow King Lisle. You must be wary though. Once the army finishes with the Lel Dinion it is likely to move towards Jarrat."

Coyne didn't look convinced. He didn't understand the reason why Argoz would send a message that everything was alright. It didn't make any sense. The last thing he wanted to do was to let them know that he didn't trust them. The fact that they knew who Argoz was the only doubt left in his mind. They would not know his true name if he didn't want them to.

"This is indeed good news. We are not yet ready for an attack." Coyne wasn't going to give much away.

"There is one more thing," Richmond added. "We must get a message to the Prince."

Tancred could have jumped up and strangled Richmond. He knew they were on a thin thread with Coyne. Mentioning the Prince was not a smart move. He really was starting to wonder if Richmond remembered anything about espionage. If he wasn't careful he was going to give away their true motives. They needed to gain the farrier's trust before they asked for any favours. There was still plenty of time before the Alliance arrived.

"Really, that does seem odd. All messages for the Prince come through me. I don't know why he would suggest you meet him yourself." Coyne wasn't sure if they were telling the truth. "What did you same your names were?"

"I am Lord Richmond and this is my advisor Tancred." They had agreed to use their real names, a decision that Tancred no longer believed was the right one.

Coyne thought for a moment. He recognised the names, but couldn't place from where. He paced back and forth for a moment before something clicked inside his head. A smile crossed his face briefly before it returned to its previous rock hard façade.

"It seems that you are making quite a name for yourselves," there was no humour in his voice. "I have already heard the rumours that you have been spreading. It seems that you are not too fond of the Alliance?" Coyne was still not convinced of their motives.

Richmond recognised the tone in his voice. He had not been pleased when he heard what Tancred had been saying, now he knew why. He doubted that Coyne was going to believe their lies. He wished that he had brought his sword with him. It was only then did he realise that

Coyne was the only one in the room with a weapon. It might have only been a mash hammer but he was sure that Coyne knew how to use it.

"That's correct," Tancred was not giving up. "I believe that the Alliance is just a ruse for a ruthless dictator to take control of the Seven Kingdoms."

"Hmmm…" Coyne made a sign of thinking as he continue to pace and continued to tap the palm of his left hand with the hammer. "Something doesn't make sense. If you don't believe the Alliance is who they say they are then how would you know Argoz?" Richmond recognised the name again, but again he couldn't hold onto for more than a second. He also knew that they had been caught out.

"I see that you are as smart as Argoz said," Tancred was not defeated. He had been prepared for such a situation. "Of course I do not believe that it is the purpose of the Alliance, but it doesn't hurt to spread some rumours. From what I gather things are on a knife's edge here in Jarrat. A little piece of misinformation might just be the thing to tip the scales in our favour." Richmond was impressed that Tancred did not miss a beat. He was grateful that he didn't have to speak himself, because he was sure as soon as he spoke he would give them away.

It was obvious that his words were having their effect. Coyne was visibly starting to relax. He was still suspicious on Lord Richmond, but he was sure that Tancred was on the level. He would still have to be careful what he said. It would be better if he could speak to Tancred alone.

"Well I thank you for your time," something suddenly changed in Coyne. He moved to the door and slid the bolt back. "I think it's time that you leave."

Richmond was about to protest, but Tancred motioned for him not to. Something had happened and Richmond didn't know what it was. Tancred had moved away from the original plan. Richmond knew that things had not gone to plan and Tancred had covered well, but something was still not right.

"What happened back there?" Richmond asked when they were heading back towards the inn. "I don't quite understand."

Tancred chuckled to himself. "I am sorry my old friend. I had to think quickly. At first Coyne was able to see through our ruse. Now he is not so sure. I believe that he thinks that I am true and you are false. It is something that I have been working on. I think that he will open up more to me when I go back and see him later."

Richmond stopped walking. Tancred took a number of paces before he realised that Richmond had stopped. The alley they were walking down was deserted, so no one was there to notice. Tancred let his shoulders drop as he knew Richmond was going to complain again.

"This was not part of the plan," Richmond sounded upset.

"You cannot believe that everything was going to work to the plan. You should know as well as anyone that the best laid plans never come to fruition. It is our ability to adapt to the current situation that makes us master tacticians." It was a simple rule of espionage, yet it still did not ease Richmond's concerns.

"This is not a game of intrigue. We have never faced an opponent such as this. I do not think that we should deviate from the plan. We do not know what the enemy is thinking. If we become separated then there is no telling what will happen," Richmond was beginning to think that there was something wrong with his old friend.

"It's too late now," Tancred turned to walk away, but Richmond grabbed his arm. "I must go alone. Coyne trusts me know, but he is still unsure about you. Don't worry. I will make sure he knows that we are on the same path."

"I still don't think it is the right thing to do." Richmond would not be convinced so easily.

"It's the only way to get into the castle," Tancred spoke through clenched teeth to stop him from yelling. "We need to get into the castle if we are going to truly find out what the enemy has planned."

Richmond let his arm go and Tancred started walking away. Although his words made sense Richmond knew that there was something wrong. Tancred was continuing on a dangerous path. All Richmond could do was to wait. Tancred would not be swayed.

They returned to the inn for the midday meal. Gage was excited to see them, although he gave them their privacy. Like everyone they had met so far he only wanted to speak to Tancred alone. Richmond also picked up on the fact. It was not the first time that Tancred had played the part of the poor advisor to the miserly Lord to gain someone's trust. Normally it didn't worry him, but for some reason it didn't seem right. It was almost as if Tancred was deliberately trying to cut him out.

Tancred only stayed long enough to eat. He knew that Coyne would be waiting for him. Richmond decided that he would do his own snooping throughout the city. Tancred warned him not to go anywhere they had already been. It was important that they kept the ruse going if they were going to be successful. Richmond begrudgingly agreed. He knew how to assume a secret identity, but the risk of crossing paths with someone they would meet again would be too great. He would have to play to role of curious, yet ignorant nobleman. The chance of gaining any true information was unlikely.

Coyne was tapping mindlessly on a horseshoe when Tancred returned. He had been waiting for the man to return and couldn't focus on his regular work. When he saw Tancred arrive his quickly dropped what he was doing and moved into his shop. Once they were both inside he shut the bolt on the door. What neither of them saw was the man watching them from inside the market. When he saw them disappear into the shop he moved away.

"What is the true message that my master sends?" Coyne looked around the room nervously as he spoke, as if he was expecting to see something jump out of the shadows.

There was a glaze of sweat on Tancred's face and his skin was pale when he replied. "The Alliance is on its way to Jarrat. It will be here in about two weeks. There is much that needs to be prepared. I must get in and speak to the Prince," Tancred spoke in a monotone voice.

"This is indeed disturbing news." Coyne dry washed his hands as he thought on the information. "I do not wish to bring such news to the Prince. He will not be happy and trust me when I tell you do not want to be around him when he is upset."

"You will not have to speak to him. I will give him the message. All you will have to do is make sure that Richmond and I can gain entrance into the castle." Tancred was struggling with his word. Someone them were his own and others came unbidden.

"I can not get both of you into the castle. I could get you in, but not both of you," Coyne's hand started to shake slightly.

"This won't work if you can't get us both in. Richmond is already suspicious of my motives. If I tell him that I will be going alone then he would know that something is wrong," Tancred's logic was impeccable. He knew that it would not take much to convince Coyne that he was right. The man was obviously not too smart.

"The prince will not be happy," Coyne looked around nervously again, as if someone was watching them.

"He doesn't have to know. All you have to do is to get us into the castle. I will do the rest," Tancred was starting to become annoyed. "What he won't be happy about is if he doesn't get the information I have for him."

Coyne was trying to think. The pressure of Tancred's steely gaze was not making it easy. He couldn't doubt that the man before him was an ally. The information was what he was expecting. The problem he had was getting the man into the castle. He had been told not to speak to anyone about the prince. He had only met the prince once, but that was enough. The man scared him almost to death. The last thing he wanted to do was to go against the prince. He had not met Argoz, but he had heard about him. By all accounts he was just as scary as the prince. He was between a rock and hard place.

"I am sure it's not that hard," Tancred sounded impatient. He clicked his fingers in front of Coyne's face to regain his attention. "All you have to do is get me into the castle," he repeated.

"Of course, I will do what I must to serve the Great Lord," Coyne was sweating under the pressure. "It will take me a day to make the arrangements. At noon tomorrow you should see a woman by the name of Emilie by the North-Western gate. You will know who she is when you see her. Be there at noon and don't be late," Coyne spoke quickly, as if he spoke too slowly he wouldn't be able to finish.

"What does Emilie look like?" Tancred asked.

"This is all that I can tell you. Now it is time for you to leave. If we get caught then you do not want to know what the punishment is," there was fear in Coyne's voice, that was obvious.

When Tancred was out of the shop the cool air hit his face and nearly knocked him off his feet. The conversation he had just had with Coyne was already a blur. He knew something important had happened, but he couldn't remember what it was. All he could remember was that he had to meet a woman by the name of Emilie. He had no idea what she looked like, but he was sure that he would know her when he saw her.

There was not much he could do until noon then next day. He wished he remembered more because he knew that Richmond would grill him as soon as he returned to inn. With that in mind he decided to do some sightseeing. He hoped that it might jog his memory.

***

Richmond followed Tancred to the commerce district. He could see that his old friend was deep in thought. It was not often that he could trail Tancred and not have him notice. That was a worrying sign. He watched him enter the farrier's shop before walking away. He turned down an aisle and instantly bumped into someone walking the other way. He could feel the man's muscles as they bumped into him. Richmond was about to apologise, but the man had already disappeared into the crowd. He looked around, but he could not see who it was. He shook his head and continued walking. He couldn't believe that someone would bump into him and not stop to apologise.

The thought was in his mind as continued to walk through the stalls. There was nothing of any significance that took his eye, not that he was there to shop. He was dressed in his travelling clothes. Without being dressed as a nobleman the stallholders didn't pay him much attention. He much preferred it that way.

As he walked around he tried to eavesdrop on the many conversations happening around him. Unfortunately nothing was relevant to his investigation. After an hour of wasted time Richmond decided that he would get something to eat. The food stalls in the commerce district were few and far between, but eventually he found a stall suitable for his needs.

As he reached into his coat pocket to find a coin to pay for his food he felt a small folded piece of paper. The old woman who had served Richmond shook her fist at him when he didn't pay instantly. The movement brought him around from his short reverie and he passed her a small copper coin. It was more than enough to pay for what he bought. He had already turned and started walking away before she could get his change. He was concerned at how the paper managed to find its way into his pocket. He was sure it wasn't there when he put on his coat.

When he was away from the crowd Richmond reached back into his pocket and casually pulled out the paper. He did not know why, but he figured it was important. As he pondered the idea he remembered the man who had bumped into him in-between the stalls. He pulled the sheet of paper out of his pocket and looked at the words written on it. 'Open this in private'. He quickly returned the paper to his pocket when he read the words. As he did he looked around the stalls to see if anyone was watching him. All of a sudden he felt very self-conscious. The only place he would find solitude would be back at the inn. He only hoped that Tancred had not returned. He had a feeling that the letter would reveal some answers to his concerns.

Once he was back at the inn he made his way quickly to his room. The innkeeper had attempted to speak to him, but he simply ignored him. He didn't deliberately mean to be rude, but he could not wait to open the letter. It was all that he could do to make it back to inn without reading it. He had the letter out of his pocket before he had opened the door. Once it was closed and he was sure that he was alone he unfolded the piece of paper.

Lord Richmond,

I am sorry to have to introduce myself this way, but unfortunately things are moving out of control. I am called Duke X and I am the leader of a small group loyal to the crown. As I am sure you have already guessed by now Queen Oriana is the prisoner of the Evil One. More on that matter I cannot write in this letter.

The second problem we have is your friend. We believe that he is working for the enemy. I know it is hard for you to believe, but it is important that you take my word for it. Your friend can not know of this letter.

I implore you to meet me tonight, once the moon is full in the sky. Meet me in the forest to the west of the city. You should have no problems leaving through the Western gate. I will make sure of it.

When you have finished reading this note, destroy it. It is of vital importance that it does not fall into the wrong hand. The lives of you and your friend are at risk.

Duke X.

Richmond read the letter again when he finished, just in case he missed something important. Once he was done he ripped it into little pieces and stuffed it into one of his packs. When the lantern in his room had been lit he would burn it. Until then he was sure it was in a safe place.

No longer than a minute had past since he disposed of the letter then the door opened and Tancred walked in. There was a strange look on his face which disappeared when he saw Richmond. Richmond looked at his friend closely. He could not forget the words written in the letter. He had his suspicions about Tancred, but he refused to believe that he was a traitor. There had to be another reason for his strange attitude.

"How did you go with Coyne?" Richmond asked when Tancred was seated.

Tancred's face went blank for a second before he twitched. He had been struggling to remember his meeting with Coyne since he had left the farrier's shop. Now he seemed to remember everything, or at least he thought he remembered everything. The memories in his head were not all together real.

"He believes that we are his allies. He is going to arrange for us to gain entrance into the castle to see the Prince. We have to meet a woman by the name of Emilie. She will make sure we get in. From there Coyne has assured me that the prince will listen to what we have to say. It looks as though our little ruse has worked." A smile appeared on his face.

Richmond was not convinced. He hated to doubt his friend, but there were too many reasons to. The words that came out of his mouth didn't sound plausible. He didn't know why, but it sounded as though his speech was rehearsed. Either way he could not let Tancred know he suspected him. He would play along, like a good little ignorant Lord.

"That is good news. Now we will really be able to get the information that we need," he hoped that his voice didn't sound too fake. Tancred didn't seem to notice.

Chapter 16: Duke X

Richmond lay awake in bed until just before midnight. He could hear Tancred breathing in the next bed. He couldn't risk sleeping in case he missed his meeting with whoever Duke X was. He was excited to get some vital answers. Their mission had gone seriously off course and he needed to get it back. There was a risk that he was walking into a trap, but he felt as though he was doing the right thing.

The rest of the inn was quiet which aided him in leaving. Thankfully there was no one up to ask him any questions about where he was going. He didn't know if he would be able to come up with a plausible excuse. Either way he was sure that it would get back to Tancred that he had left during the night. He knew that Tancred had befriended the innkeeper and the man would do anything to please him. It was good in a sense, but annoying in another.

The streets of Jarrat were only half lit. It seemed odd that better care wasn't taken for a capital city. Although it was a worrying sign it did give Richmond enough cover to move through the streets unnoticed. He didn't know what would happen if he got caught, but since there was no one else around he figured that it wouldn't be good. His heart started to pound as he crept from shadow to shadow.

He reached the Western gate as the moon was high in the sky. To his surprise there were no guards on watch, but he knew there was no way a gate would remain open and unguarded throughout the night. There had to be guards somewhere and he could ill-afford to get caught.

Richmond remained in the shadows and watched the gate closely for any sign of movement, but none came. He was loathed to walk out into the open, but then he remembered what was written in the letter. The Duke had said that he would arrange for him to leave through the Western gate.

Richmond held his breath as he walked out into the dim light around the gate. The first step was the hardest. He paused and he could hear the blood pumping through his head. The seconds seemed to pass like hours as he waited. When he was sure that he had not been set up he continued on.

The fact that there was no one around made the walk even more nerve-racking. It was eerily quiet; the only sound was his footsteps on the packed dirt road. He thought at any moment the guards would come running out to arrest him. The fear was deep in his mind as he passed through the gates.

It wasn't until he was through and in the shadows of the wall did he hear someone behind him. He let a sigh of relief when he realised that they did not know he had passed. He wondered at his luck. He knew that someone had moved the guards away from the gate, but he had no idea how they had done it.

Since he was outside the gate he felt a lot safer, although normally that would not be the case. Generally being outside the city walls at night was the last thing someone wanted to do, but the fear of bandits was far from Richmond's mind. He was excited at the prospect of meeting his destiny. He had a good feeling that he was about to meet an ally and that was something he didn't expect to find in Entero.

As he was deep in thought he walked off the highway and into the forest. He didn't know exactly where he was going, but he was happy to let his feet guide him. He had to put some faith in fate, he had to believe that the prophecy would guide him.

He had not been walking long in the forest before he heard a twig snap from somewhere behind him. Suddenly his heart stopped and he could not breathe. It was only then did he realise that how tense he had been. He froze where he stood. When his heart started beating again he could feel it thundering within his chest. The fear of who was behind him kept him from turning around.

"You are late," the voice whispered.

Richmond relaxed, but only slightly. It would not be long before he found out if he had made the right decision. If not he didn't think that he would live long enough to regret it. Slowly he turned around. In the dark of the night he could only see the outline of a cloaked person. The voice sounded male, but at a whisper it was hard to be completely sure.

"Who are you?" was all he could say.

"There will be time for that later," the whisper was soft, feminine. The thought that it was a woman who had come for him, that made him a little more comfortable.

She walked passed and motioned for him to follow. He was lucky to catch the hand movement in the dark. What light the moon had given was almost completely blocked by the trees. Richmond quickly followed. If he lost her in the dark he didn't think that he could able to find her again.

They walked through the forest for over half an hour, which seemed like hours to Richmond. They took a number of turns along the way. In the end Richmond had no idea where they were. When they finally reached their destination Richmond could see a number of torch lights through the trees. He was about to meet the mysterious Duke X.

They entered a clearing and in the centre a large fire burned brightly. It took Richmond a moment to adjust to the new light. Coming from the darkness of the forest into the clearing was blinding. When his eyes became focused he saw a rag-tag group of people standing around in small groups. They didn't seem to take any notice of the newcomers. Men, woman and children all huddled around the fire dressed in whatever rags they had left the city in. Although they looked poor there was a certain spark in their faces. A man standing with a group of people looked over when Richmond and the woman entered the clearing.

The man was dressed in similarly tattered clothes as the rest of the group, but there was something different about him. He held himself in a manner that didn't suit his appearance. Richmond had no doubts that the man had been noble born. Then it clicked. The man must be the mysterious Duke X. He had messy brown hair, the despite the tatters looked freshly trimmed. His facial hair was also overgrown, but somehow it looked deliberate. There was definitely more to the man than met the eye.

"Hello, Lord Richmond I am Duke X," Richmond was surprised that he didn't give his real name, or at least his real alias. "I thank you for coming here. I know that it is a risk," there was strength in his voice, which also belied his appearance. "If your companion finds out you are meeting with me then your life will be in great danger."

"You didn't give me much choice. There were some very interesting accusations in your note." Richmond wasn't going to act impressed. He had already decided that he would play things as defensively as possible. He didn't want the Duke to know that he already suspected his friend. "It is very presumptuous to assume that you know me and my advisor when we have only been in your city for a couple of days."

"Your arrival has not been as secret as you would have liked. It seems that your advisor has been making your presence known. He has also been speaking to someone who is on our watch list for friends of the enemy," Duke X kept his tone level. He did nothing to hide their conversation for the others around the fire. "He is spreading the rumour that you are on the run from the Alliance and are looking for asylum. It is also said that you are trying to gain entrance into the castle. That in itself is a dangerous task and if we are right about your friend then it is something we cannot allow. The Queen is in the thrall of the Evil One's minions and we can't allow them to get any more information."

Richmond looked at him carefully. He didn't like what the Duke was saying, but he had to admit he was right. If somehow Tancred had turned evil then the last thing he could do was lead him into the castle. On the other hand it might make things easier for him to gain entrance. In the end he needed to get the information back to the Alliance. It would only be a matter of time before the enemy knew the army was approaching. It was impossible to take Jarrat unawares.

"It is you that asked me to come here, so I am assuming that you have an offer or information for me. If not then I have a very expensive bed going cold," Richmond kept his uncaring persona. He was not going to fall into the trap of giving away any information. Although he believed they were allies he couldn't be completely sure.

"That's all well and good, Lord Richmond, but we have to make sure that you are the person who we think you are." Duke X indicated to a small group of men.

Before Richmond could react one of the men had a sword drawn across his neck. The movement was so sudden that Richmond didn't know how to respond. Another man took his sword out of its sheath and then checked him for any other weapons. The sword blade was touching the skin of his neck giving him very little opportunity to struggle. When he was finally released he was less than impressed.

"Why bring me out here if you are just going to insult me?" Richmond had lost his composure. He did not like being manhandled. "This is an outrage. I come here in good faith and this is the way you treat me. I hope that you have a good explanation for yourself," Richmond raised his voice. He didn't care who heard. He figured they were far enough away from the city.

"I am sorry Lord Richmond, but we have worked too hard not to be cautious," there was little apology in his words. "We can't have you armed in case you are not who we think you are."

"You could at least tell me your name," Richmond did his best not to lose his temper completely as he spoke between clenched teeth.

Duke X started laughing, which he continued for longer than Richmond expected. "I think I'm going to like you Richmond," it was noticeable that he had dropped the Lord. "Again I will tell you that trust is a big issue. The secret of my identity is vital."

"Then it seems as though we are at an impasse," Richmond was standing strong.

"I am sorry to have bothered you now," Duke X turned his back on Richmond and started to walk away. "I will see that you are taken back to your inn."

"Wait!" Richmond knew that he had no choice. Duke X had played the game much better. He was still curious on what information they had. "I will answer your questions, but first tell me what you are doing out here?"

"What?" Duke X turned around.

"You are not the only one with a perilous mission. I have to be sure that you are who I think you are," there was no lie in Richmond's voice. He had to try and get the upper hand and the only way to do it was to gain information.

Duke X thought for a moment. "Okay," he nodded to the men who were still standing around Richmond. They all moved away, giving him some space. "We are here because for one reason or another, our lives have been touched by the Evil One," he paused, waiting for the information to sink in. "We are here to stop what he is doing to our kingdom." He kept his answer brief. Like Richmond he didn't want to give too much away.

"What is he doing?" It was information that Richmond desperately wanted and it was the perfect opportunity to ask.

"All in good time, but now it is time for you to tell us what you are doing in Jarrat?"

Richmond thought about lying, but if they were who they claimed to be then lying would be more detrimental. He was sure that if they were agents for the Evil One that he would know. By the looks of them they were indeed refugees from the city. One of them had to be the first to trust the other and it seemed as though it would have to be Richmond. There was only a certain amount of time before he would have to return to Tancred. If he continued to play the game then he would achieve nothing.

"We have come here from the Alliance army to do some reconnaissance. We have heard that the Evil One controls the city and need all the information we can get," Richmond explained.

"Then why have you been meeting with the farrier Coyne? He is well known to be a support of the Evil One," Duke X came straight out with the question.

"That is a long story," Richmond was hoping that excuse was enough, but by the look of the Duke's face it was not. "We believed that there was a traitor in the command group of the Alliance," he wasn't sure if he should be telling the Duke, but he knew that it was the only way he would get to know what he needed. "General Bern commissioned me to root out the traitor and befriend him. The traitor instructed us to meet with Coyne and give him information about the army's movements. We decided that it would work out best if we gave him false information. That is why we met with him. We also figured that if he thought we were on his side then it would easier for us to gain entrance into the caslte."

"I see." The Duke stroked his beard as he pondered Richmond's words.

"Now I think it is time that you tell me what is going on here?" Richmond saw his opportunity and took it.

"Okay. Things have not been right in Jarrat for a long time. It happened slowly at first. People started disappearing. It was rumoured that they were taken in the middle of the night to the castle dungeons. Most people just believed that people were leaving the city, but when someone finally investigated it was not the case. All their possessions remained in their houses. Those who had families claimed there had been no reason for the missing to run away. It wasn't until the Queen's Guards came marching into the city that the investigations were suddenly shut down. It seemed odd, but no one would argue with them, at least not until after the first man was arrested. His wife had disappeared and he wouldn't accept what the guards told him. At nightfall he was hung in the city's main square. It had been over a century since anyone was put to death in the city square. Once that was done no one questioned the Queen's Guards again and the investigations were put to rest.

It was around this time that it was rumoured that the Queen had taken a new lover. He is known as Prince Leroy, although we do not believe that is his real name. At first everyone was happy that the Queen had a new consort. It has been almost ten years since the King died. Soon enough it was apparent, at least to some of us, that the Prince was evil. Not only that, but he had Oriana in his thrall. She would do whatever he asked of her and soon enough it was clear that he was running the kingdom.

One of his first edicts was to shut down the castle. Anyone who disagreed with his rule was sent to death or worse. No one who was loyal to the Queen was allowed to remain in the castle. It was surprising the number of traitors who had taken up residence there." The Duke stared at the fire as his spoke.

"What can be worse than death?" Richmond asked to fill the silence.

"I'll answer that one." A man stepped up from around the fire. Richmond hadn't even notice him and jumped slightly at the sudden movement. "My name is Jerome. I have been loyal to the Queen and her family all my life. One night I was in a local tavern and I was a little drunk. I got into an argument with someone about the new Prince. I said that I thought he was an agent of evil. It seems that I said it to the wrong person, or a little too loudly. When I came home the next night I found my wife and son dead. That is how I came to be here," the man had a blank look on his face as he spoke. "You asked what was worse than death. You make up your own mind. I was quite happy to take my own life, but the Duke saved me. If it wasn't for this little group of rebels I would not be alive today. He gave me the means for my revenge."

"Thank you, Jerome," there was a certain amount of sympathy in his voice, but also some annoyance. Jerome had said more than what the Duke would have liked. "Now you get the idea of what's been happening."

Richmond felt sick in the stomach when he heard Jerome's story. He could only think of Kiarome and what their citizens had to put up with. He had heard stories from his capital city, but they were nothing like this. The more he heard about Jarrat the more he wished that the Alliance was already there.

"The problem is now that the people are so afraid of the Prince that they are starting to believe that he is their saviour. No one would openly oppose him now, besides us that is, but we are not strong enough to take on the castle guards, let alone the entire army. We do what we can, but I am afraid that it is a losing battle. Now the rumours that you are spreading about the Alliance being led by an evil overlord is not doing anything to help. In fact it seems as though you are working against us. This is the last thing we need," Duke X sounded annoyed.

"Tancred thought that it was a good idea for us to gain the trust of the enemy," Richmond knew how lame it sounded as soon as the words left his mouth. "We also didn't want the enemy to mobilise its army. That's why we are spreading the rumour that the Alliance is moving on Bellarome."

"It seems that your friend is playing you for a fool." The Duke looked directly at him to gauge a response. It was obvious that Richmond didn't appreciate his words.

"I think you better tell what you know about Tancred. Remember that you asked me here so I can only assume that you need my help," Richmond spoke calmly.

Duke X wasn't overly happy with Richmond's response, but there was little he could do. He had bluffed Richmond earlier and won, but he didn't think he could again. There was obviously a close relationship between the two men, more so than there should be between noble and advisor. He would have to be very careful if he wanted to keep Richmond on side.

"As I said to you earlier, we have been watching Coyne very closely. Your friend went to visit him yesterday," the Duke spoke.

"I know that. I told you that we are playing him to gain entrance into the castle. I think that you might be a little paranoid." Richmond was starting to believe that the Duke didn't know what he was talking about. Of course it would look suspicious for them to visit an agent of evil, but that seemed to be the only evidence they had.

"If you would let me finish," Duke X didn't appreciate being interrupted. "Not only have we been watching Coyne, but we have been listening to him as well." The revelation sent a chill down Richmond's spine. "Your friend has betrayed you. He has told Coyne that the Alliance is on the way here. He is working for the enemy."

Suddenly Richmond felt week at the knees at the words sunk in. He had suspected that something was wrong with Tancred, but he never really believed that he was working for the enemy. He suddenly felt as though he was going to bring up the contents of his stomach.

"It's not all doom and gloom." Duke X tried to comfort him. "The man who was spying on Coyne and your friend used to work in the castle. Let's just say he has seen things that most ordinary people haven't." Richmond only half heard what the Duke was saying. He couldn't believe that Tancred was an agent of evil. "I don't think that your friend has turned." It was his last comment that caught Richmond's ears.

"What do you mean?" He still felt sick, but there was a new feeling of hope.

"Have you heard of the Dark Knights?" Duke X asked.

"Yes. We have run into one or two of them in our time," Richmond wasn't sure if he wanted to continue with the conversation. If Tancred was a Dark Knight he wasn't sure if he could keep going.

"Good, then I won't have to explain too much," the Duke continued. "I believe that the traitor you spoke of earlier is in fact one of these Dark Knights, as is the Prince." Richmond let out a deep breath when he heard the Duke's words. He was so relieved that Tancred was not a Dark Knight that he didn't care about the repercussions of what he had said. "I believe that your friend is under the thrall of your traitor."

"If that is true, what can I do about it?" Richmond asked quickly.

The Duke lowered his head. "I am afraid there is nothing you can do about it, unless you're a power wizard. If your friend is strong of mind he might be able to break the bond by himself, but I doubt that very much. No one I know has been able to do that and I have known some strong people. The only other way is if the Dark Knight relinquishes his hold and I believe that the only way he will do that is if your friend is dead."

The hope quickly left Richmond's body. "Then why have you told me this?" he was no longer thinking laterally.

"Use your head Richmond. I have heard stories of your land and the intrigues that you play. To be a noble you have to play the game." the Duke could see that Richmond's mind was slipping away. "I would not have believed that you could be defeated so easily." The words brought Richmond around.

"I have not been defeated," there was little confidence in his voice. "I just don't know what to do."

"You must use this information and remember your mission. There is more at stake than just your friend," the Duke paused as the information sunk in.

Suddenly Richmond realised that he was being silly. He was a slave to the prophecy and if it needed him to keep an eye on his advisor then that's what he had to do. He had to believe that there was a reason Tancred had turned or been turned and there was a chance to bring him back. They had been through too much together and he couldn't believe that it was Tancred's fate to die a traitor.

"What can I do with this information?" strength returned to his voice.

"You can keep and eye on Tancred once you are in the castle. There is no doubt that he will try and get information to the Prince without you knowing. You can use this information to your advantage. If Tancred can play both sides then there is no reason why you can't either. Turn this disadvantage into your advantage and there may be chance you can help your friend after all," the Duke's words were mysterious.

Richmond had a lot to think about. Things were becoming a lot clearer. In once sense he was glad that his friend had not betrayed him, but the fact that Tancred was being controlled by a Dark Knight filled him with dread. They had always known it was a dangerous mission, but not once had he thought either of them could be manipulated by the Dark Knight. It seemed their ruse wasn't has good as they thought it had been. They should have known the enemy would be a lot smarter than they had given them credit for. It was their arrogance that had caused their current situation.

"You must go now," the Duke spoke suddenly, breaking Richmond from his thoughts. "It will be getting light soon and you will need to be back in bed before your friend wakes. If he realises that you have left then he will become suspicious."

"Thank you for the information, Duke X. Would you tell me your name?" Richmond was interested more than anything else.

"As I told you before, keeping my identity secret is of the utmost importance. Hopefully one day we will be able to walk in the castle grounds, free to know one another. Until that day we all have our tasks ahead of us," the Duke spoke strongly.

"Come," it was the same soft feminine voice that first spoke to him in the forest. "We must get you back to the city."

Once they were away from the campfire it again took Richmond a moment to adjust to a change in light. The woman didn't wait for him. He only just had his eyesight return to see her disappear into the dark. Without waiting he hurried after her, in the general direction she was heading. If the sun was due to rise soon he needed to hurry back to the inn. He didn't know what he would say if Tancred realised he had left.

Again it was a long walk back to the city. They twisted and turned through the trees so Richmond would not be able to find his way back. He tried to remember the way, but in the dark there was no way he could retrace his steps. Before Richmond knew he was out of the forest and onto the highway. He turned to thank his guide, but she had already disappeared back into the forest. He looked around a number of times before he realised that he was completely alone. The night air was eerily quiet. He suddenly felt very self-conscious. It was like there were a hundred eyes watching him from inside the forest. Just before the feeling overpowered him he started walking towards the city.

As he approached the Western Gate he noticed again that there was no one around. The spaces on both sides of the gate were completely empty. It was a little too perfect for his liking, as he stood just outside of the light. He had a bad feeling that he was about to be set up in a trap. If he got caught then everything that he had gone through earlier that night would have been for nothing.

Taking a deep breath Richmond stepped into the light. He couldn't move past that first step. His heart was pounding and he held his breath. After a few seconds had past he let it out. No one had made any attempt to capture him. When he was sure that he wasn't been watched he started walking towards the gate. It was another nervous walk through the gates, but he made it unscathed.

Once he was out of the light he was able to relax. It was the first time he had relaxed since he had left the city earlier in that night. All he had to do was to return to the inn unnoticed. That was the easy part. With the streets still deserted there was no one to watch what he was doing.

The inn was dark when he returned, but he knew dawn was just around the corner. He was thankful for the cover of darkness. There was no one inside when he entered the inn. He crept through the hallway until he reached his room. He slowly opened the door, trying no to create any sound. When it was open he crept into the room.

Inside he could hear Tancred sleeping soundly in the other bed. Richmond crept to his bed and climbed on top. Only when he had returned to the inn did he realise how tired he was. He would need to get as much sleep as he could. If they were going in to the castle he would need all his wits about him. He fell asleep with that thought in his mind.

***

Tancred was lying in bed when he heard the door open. He opened his eyes and could see it was Richmond without moving his head. He wondered where his friend had been. It was late in the night when he woke and realised that Richmond was gone. As the dim light of dawn crept through the window he didn't know how long Richmond had been gone, but he knew it was a long time. He was sure Richmond would tell him when they rose, but if he didn't then he would know that something was wrong.

Although Richmond had crawled into his own bed there would be little time for sleep. Tancred thought about rising himself, but then

Richmond would know he was awake. If he was going to get the answers he wanted then he would have to play dumb. They would be gaining entrance to the castle soon enough and he didn't want Richmond to know what he knew.

Chapter 17: Emilie and Amilie

Richmond and Tancred spoke very little the next morning. Tancred had hoped to speak to Gage, but the innkeeper was nowhere to be found. There was still more information he wanted before he entered the castle, but there was nothing he could do. As they ate their morning meal he waited for his friend to explain his late night rendezvous. His curiosity was piqued, but he didn't want Richmond to know that he knew. He would keep an eye on his friend and he was sure that the answer would reveal itself eventually.

Richmond made an effort not to watch his advisor too closely. The last thing he wanted was for Tancred to know he was onto him. Things were going to be dangerous enough as it was. There was some reason the Dark Knight wanted them together or he would have made Tancred kill him in his sleep.

Just before midday they left the inn and made their way to the North-Western gate. Tancred didn't know what the woman they were looking for looked like. He had no idea how he was going to find her. It was that thought that kept him from speaking to Richmond as they walked through the streets. He knew that if they started talking then he would have to ask about the previous night's activities and that would distract him from his current task.

The North-Western gate had once been the busiest of the city's gates. It held the main traffic between the city and the castle. It was also the entrance to the Remidian-Entero highway. All goods coming and going between Remidia and Entero would come to Jarrat first before being shipped to other parts of the kingdom. It seemed silly as there were a number of small towns and villages along the route. But the law had been passed many years ago. It allowed the Crown to tax all the goods coming and going between the two kingdoms. Since the Prince had arrived in the castle he had stopped all trade along the highway from Remidia. Since he had locked down the entrance to the castle the North-Western gate was almost empty. A few guards stood around lazily and didn't look too interested as the two men approached. There was no sign of any women, let alone the one they were looking for.

"Where do you think you're going?" one of the guards asked as they neared the gate. "No one is allowed through here without a specific order from Prince Leroy," the guard didn't seem too interested.

Richmond looked at Tancred, hoping that his advisor had an answer. Although the guards didn't look too dangerous there was no telling what they would do. Both Richmond and Tancred wore their swords, which could easily provoke an attack.

"Stand down, Belden. These two are with me," a slurred woman's voice called out from behind them.

Both men spun around to see who it was. The woman before them was not at all what they expected. She was dressed in a dirty, ripped, blue dress. There were dirt marks all over her clothes and face and her light brown hair was tattered and looked to have a number of serious knots in it. She looked as though she had spent many years living on the streets, if not her entire life. Although there was one strange thing that Tancred noticed. Most street urchins were missing at least one of their teeth, but he saw a nice white set of teeth as she smiled at them. Tancred hoped that it was not Emilie, but he knew that it was.

"You have no business here, hag. Be off with you." Belden picked up a small stone and threw it at her.

Richmond was a little surprised at the hag comment. The woman was definitely rough around the edges, but with a hot bath and some new clothes he thought that she would be quite attractive.

"Come with me," she kept her voice low as she walked past them.

Richmond and Tancred were a little surprised by her words. She kept walking towards the gate even though the guards were starting to become interested. Tancred looked at his friend and shrugged his shoulders. He hated to take it on faith that Emilie knew what she was doing, but they had little choice. Coyne had told them that she would get them into the castle and they had to believe him. Even if he was playing them they had no other options.

"Stand aside," she snapped at the guards. "I have work to do and you know not to get in my way."

All the guards started laughing. "I don't think you boys know what you have gotten yourselves into. She will eat you both alive," Belden spoke in-between laughs.

The guards stood out of Emilie's way as she led the two men out of the city. Richmond eyed the guards carefully as he walked past. He didn't fully trust the woman and he didn't want to be skewered by surprise, but they made no move to stop them. After Emilie had spoken they returned to their lazy stance.

They made it through the gate unharmed. The walk to the castle was only about half a mile, but before they got half way Emilie stopped to speak to them. She came close to Tancred and placed her arm around him seductively. She did so for the sake of the guards, who were still watching them.

"I understand that you are friends of Coyne's," she whispered into his ear.

"I take it that you are Emilie?" Tancred asked in return.

She giggled at the sound of her name. "If you want me to get you into the castle pass me a number of coins," she continued to whisper.

"Coyne didn't say anything about payment," Tancred pushed away from her. He didn't want to waste their limited coin.

Emilie quickly moved closer to him. "I don't think you quite understand how it works," she gave Tancred a knowing look, but he didn't understand what it meant. "My cover is a whore," as soon as the words left her mouth Tancred suddenly understood. He instantly went red in the cheeks.

"I understand," Tancred took his money pouch out of his pocket. He removed two copper coins and placed it in Emilie's hand.

She looked at the coins closely and then scowled. She was obviously not happy with the contribution. "You are lucky the guards can't see. There is no way they would believe that I would work for two copper coins," she slid the coins into her one dress pocket that didn't have a hole in it.

Once she had been paid she let Tancred go and they started making their way back to the castle. Richmond looked at Tancred who just stared back. There was nothing for it but to follow the strange woman.

"You know I am not really a whore," Emilie spoke as the other two men kept a pace behind. "It just makes it easier for me to come and go with strange men if the guards think that I am."

Tancred knew that there was something off about Emilie's appearance. Someone who worked as a street whore would not have such well maintained teeth. He didn't know why, but that thought made him feel a lot better.

"How are we going to get into the castle?" Tancred asked when they were walking side-by-side.

"Simple," Emilie gave him a cheeky smile. "We walk up to the front gate and then walk straight through."

"We heard that no one is allowed entrance into the castle," Richmond added from the other side.

"Of course, but if you know the right people you can do anything, and it seems you know the right people."

There was something about Emilie that didn't sit right with Richmond. She was certainly not all that she made out to be. Although she had already admitted to her facade being fake there was more to her than met the eye. Richmond knew he would have to be careful with what he said around her.

It was a short walk between the city and the castle walls. There was no more conversation between them. Richmond had hoped they would talk, but if they did there was a chance they would give something away. He was walking into a very dangerous situation and he had hoped to gather some more information.

The guards by the castle gate looked more ready for action than those by the North-Western gate. They looked even less impressed when they saw Emilie approach with two men. Richmond didn't like their chances of gaining entrance. The large castle gates were closed and the portcullis was down. None of the guards made any attempt to open either.

"Be gone, wench," one of the guards snapped at Emilie. "The Prince has informed us that no one is to be admitted today."

"I think you should check again. You know that I am not to be kept standing out in the open. My friends and I have a meeting with the Prince," her voice was cold as steel.

"I know what business you have with the Prince and do not believe that it involves these two men," he looked at Richmond and Tancred with disgust. "Now be gone or I will have you killed and your heads placed on pikes as a warning to others." The guard was not going to be persuaded.

Emilie thought for a moment. She looked at the guards and then at the other two. Eventually she shook her head. "Okay boys. It looks like we are not going to be able to go sightseeing in the castle," she nudged Tancred as she spoke.

Tancred instantly understood what she was doing, although he did not know why. He grabbed her by the shoulders and spun her around until she was facing him. The sudden movement confused everyone.

"We paid for a castle tour and that is exactly what you will give us," Tancred shook her as he spoke.

"Take it away from the gate," the guard barked as he drew his sword.

"Come on," Emilie spoke. "Let's take it into the forest," she smiled at the guards before taking Richmond and Tancred by the hand and leading them away. "I know another way you can get your money's worth."

"Where are we going?" Tancred asked when they were out of earshot.

"There is more than one way into the castle. I had hoped that we could have walked through the front door, but it seems that is no longer an option. It doesn't matter anyhow. I have been given leave to let you in the back door, so to speak," she winked at him when she finished speaking.

Richmond's ears pricked up when he heard the words. A secret way into the castle would be most useful. Besides taking over the city from the Evil One they had to rescue their friends. There would more chance of that happening if it happened before the attack. He walked a step behind and watched Tancred closely. Despite all the information he was still hopeful Tancred wasn't an agent of evil, but he was still looking for anything that might prove his theory.

The castle backed up to the forest, which both helped and hindered its defence. The trees made a siege from the Western side impossible, but they also shielded invaders. The King who designed the castle figured that one or two invaders were better than the entire wall coming down. It still made it difficult for someone to attack, but it also made it easier for someone to sneak into the city.

"Since the Prince arrived into the castle he has made sure that the Western wall has been manned day and night," Emilie explained as they continued along the highway. She would not deviate from the road until they reached the forest. "Unfortunately for him there is a hole in the wall that he doesn't know about. It's what I use to sneak in and out of the city."

The news was both good and bad. If Emilie was an agent for the Prince, then it should be well known if she indeed had a secret way into the castle. Richmond had his doubts on her authenticity. He had a bad feeling that she was leading them into a trap. There was still nothing he could do. They had gone too far and there was no turning back.

Once they had reached the forest Emilie made her way along the castle wall. The trees gave them cover from the guards on the wall above them. She checked the wall at regular intervals. And whenever she did, the two men looked at the wall to see what was there. It was obvious that she was checking for some sort of markings to direct her to the hole in the wall. All either of them could see was a number scratches in the stones. They had to be what she was looking at, but they could not work out what they meant.

Soon enough Emilie came to a stop. To both men's surprise she started to pull off her tattered rags. Both men turned away, but not before they saw her naked thighs. As they did they heard her laughing. There was something magical in the sound. They both wondered at her inhibition and what she was going to do for clothes once she had finished undressing.

"There is no need to turn away," she giggled as she spoke.

Tancred opened his left eye a crack and breathed a sigh of relief when he saw that Emilie was in fact fully dressed. He had no idea how she had got changed so quickly or where she had found the clothes. She had discarded her old tattered rags on the ground. She was now dabbing away the dirt marks on her face with a cloth. Once she had finished cleaning her face she pulled a hairbrush out of her dress and started brushing her hair. The task was a lot more difficult than the cleaning of her face. Her hair had been deliberately matted and tangled. The two men watched without knowing what to say. All they could do was to watch in silent awe.

When Emilie had finished her transformation neither man could believe the woman in front of them was the same person. She wore a pale blue silk dress that fitted her body more snugly than her previous dress. Tancred had though that she was quite portly, but in her transformation he could see otherwise. It then struck him that she had been wearing the silk dress under her tattered rags. Her face was beautiful and her blonde hair was longer than either of them expected.

"Are you two boys going to stand there and stare all day or are we going to enter the castle?" Emilie's voice was a lot softer then it had been and she no longer slurred her words.

Tancred knew how she would get into the castle without the Prince knowing. She had one persona for the front door and one for the back. Emilie noticed the realisation on his face and smiled.

"It seems that you might be smarter than you look," she winked at Tancred as she spoke. She had done that same thing when she was dressed as a whore, but this time it made Tancred blush. "I use Emilie the whore as a way to get in and out of the city unnoticed. Sometimes I can get into the castle, but most times I get rejected. I must admit it is much easier to move around in my current persona."

"So who are we speaking to now?" there was a playful tone to Tancred's voice. Richmond watched the exchange carefully.

"You are speaking to the Lady Amilie," she giggled when she revealed her alter ego. "I am well thought of in the Royal Court and a close friend to Queen Oriana herself."

"It is a pleasure to meet you Lady Amilie," Tancred bowed before taking her hand and kissing it.

Richmond shook his head. Anyone would have thought they were on a nice romantic outing, not about to embark on the most dangerous mission of their lives. The two of them were just looking at each other, not speaking.

"Do you think we could continue today?" Richmond had a scolding tone to his voice, like he was speaking to a couple of naughty children.

"Of course," it seemed as though Amilie had forgotten that he was there. "It is not far now."

Richmond held Tancred's arm as Amilie continued along the wall. When he was sure that she was out of earshot he whispered to Tancred.

"Don't forget that she is working for the enemy."

"I know, but as the old adage goes 'you catch more flies with honey'." He smiled at Richmond before removing his hand and following after Amilie. He quickened his pace until he was walking next to her.

Richmond watched them for a moment and shook his head. He hated to think of what Tancred meant by his last comment. There was no time for romance, although he might have been right. They needed to get all the information that they could get and sleeping with a member of court might speed things along. The fact that she was playing for the enemy didn't fill Richmond with any confidence. Before the two could get too far away Richmond moved to catch up.

Amilie checked the wall another three times before she brought the group to a halt. Richmond looked at the wall, but he couldn't see anything. He wondered why she had stopped. He couldn't imagine she was going to change her appearance again. She looked at the two men and recognised they had no idea where the hole was.

"Good thing you have me with you or else you would be marching up and down these walls for the rest of your lives trying to get in," it was an exaggeration, but she made her point.

"Is this where we enter?" Richmond didn't like the tone of her voice.

"Follow me," she winked at Tancred again, seemingly ignoring Richmond's words.

Amilie walked towards the wall. Just before she reached it she turned to the left. To both men's surprised she started walking downwards, as if she was walking down stairs. As they moved closer to the wall they realised that there was a hole and a set of stairs. When they stepped back they could no longer see it.

Tancred started after Amilie, but Richmond waited a moment. He wanted to make sure the he could remember that place in the wall. He was sure that he would have to use the secret entrance again. It would be no good to sneak the army into the castle, but it would be enough to make a rescue attempt. Getting Eldred and Alena out of the dungeons was just as important as reclaiming the city. He waited until the other two were out of sight before drawing his sword. He made a scratch above the hole. It was not large, but he was confident that he would be able to find it again. Once he was done he made his way down the stairs.

The stairs led deep underneath the castle. Richmond guessed that they were at least twenty feet under the castle grounds. At the bottom they came to a small tunnel. It was high enough for them the walk upright, but it could only accommodate one abreast. By the time Richmond made it to the bottom the other two had disappeared into the darkness. Without thinking about what might be on the other side, Richmond made his way into the tunnel.

There was a stale smell in the air. It was obvious that the tunnel didn't get much wind blowing through it. The ground felt grainy under his feet. He wished that he could see what was around him. He could feel the walls were close on either side and he could sense that the ceiling was not far away from his head. He wished there was more air flowing through the tunnel as he was finding it hard to breathe. He wasn't claustrophobic, but he felt as though the walls were going to come down on top of him. As he looked behind he could see the dim light from outside the city walls slowly disappear. Once that was gone there would be no light left. The only other sound, besides his breathing and his footsteps, were the sounds of the others walking somewhere in front.

"Hurry up," Amilie called from somewhere in the dark. "We need to be out of here quickly."

"Why is that?" Richmond heard Tancred ask as he tried to quicken his pace.

"That is something that I am sure that you would rather not know about," there was nothing cute in her voice.

Her ominous words made Richmond quicken his step even more. He stumbled a few times in his haste, but he remained on his feet. Whatever would happen if they lingered Richmond didn't what to find out. He much preferred to have skinned knees then to face the unknown. In his hurry to reach the others he wasn't taking any notice of his surroundings. Before he could stop himself he went crashing into Tancred, who in turn went crashing into Amilie and awkwardly the three of them tumbled to the ground.

In the confined space of the tunnel getting up was not easy. As they fell their arms and legs became tangled together. They all tried to get up at once and that only made matters worse. In the dark there was no way to tell what was happening besides touch. Eventually, after a lot of effort and muttered curses, they all returned to their feet.

"Do you want to be a little more careful? We don't want to look like we've been trekking through a dirty tunnel," Amilie snapped at Richmond.

Both men brushed themselves down. They had no idea if they were dirty or not and they knew that Amilie couldn't see them, but they made the effort anyway. Richmond felt somewhat embarrassed for causing the fall.

"Now you will both have to wait here whilst I check to see if the coast is clear," Amilie spoke at a whisper. "Try not to speak as your voices will carry."

She didn't wait for either to answer. The sound of bolt being pulled aside could be heard from in front of them. As the door opened a small glimmer of light was let into the tunnel. The sudden light blinded them until the door was shut again. Richmond was happy that Amilie had left the tunnel. There was something about her that made him uncomfortable and he didn't like how his friend acted around her.

They both did as they were told and remained silent until she returned. It was a short wait before they heard the door swing open and when it did they both shielded their eyes again. Amilie had a scolding look on her face.

"Come on you two. Do you want to stay in that tunnel all day?" there was a playful note to her voice.

Her words hit the mark and the two men hurried out of the tunnel. Richmond had to admit that he was a lot happier outside the tunnel. Even though they had come out into a small basement room it felt to Richmond that they were in a wide open space. He looked at the other two who didn't seem to notice the change. Tancred looked at Amilie, keen to find out what would happen next.

"This basement comes out at the castle stables. We should be able to enter the castle grounds unnoticed. Once we are there we will be able to walk around unhindered. It is assumed that any one in the castle is supposed to be there," Amilie explained.

Tancred nodded his head in response. She didn't look to see if Richmond understood what she had said. Instead she turned her back on the two men and walked towards a small flight of stairs at the opposite side of the basement. At the top of the stairs there was a small trapdoor. Richmond thought that he was only just going to be able to fit through.

On the other side of the trapdoor was an empty stall at the back of the stables. Except for a number of horses the stables were completely empty. Amilie visibly relaxed when she saw that there was no one there. She walked casually out of the stall and motioned for the other two to do the same.

It seemed that it had been a while since the stables had been mucked out. There was a strong smell of horse manure in the air. They all had to walk carefully so as not to stand in anything. Normally they would not be noticed walking around the castle, but if they stunk of horse droppings then there was little chance of them being unnoticed. Besides that, they didn't want to have to smell like a dirty stable for the rest of the day.

The stables opened out into a large courtyard and a hive of activity. A multitude of soldiers were moving around. Richmond thought that they looked as thought they were preparing themselves for battle. They didn't seem to notice the three walking towards the castle despite the fact there were few citizens in sight.

"They ready themselves every day. The Prince is sure that there will be an attack on the castle any day now," Amilie explained.

"What about the city?" Richmond asked. He kept his voice low as they passed by the soldiers.

"What do you mean?" she asked. She didn't seem to notice the soldiers.

"I haven't seen any soldiers in the city. If he is expecting an attack then why isn't he fortifying the city?" there was a touch of suspicion in his voice.

Amilie suddenly stopped walking and looked at Richmond. She had a very suspicious look on her face. Tancred had taken a number of steps before he realised they had stopped. He wished that his lord would take his advice and keep his mouth shut. Ever since they arrived in Jarrat Richmond had been trying his best to ruin all the good work he was doing. There would be time to press Amilie for answers, but walking through courtyard was not such a time.

"Why would you ask that?" there was an accusatory tone to her voice.

Richmond suddenly had a bad feeling that she was going to realise that he was not who he said he was. It seemed like a simple question. If they were expecting an attack then it would make sense to fortify the city. He thought he had been obviously making small talk, but it seemed Amilie was more suspicious. He would have to be very careful as he continued. One wrong word and he could end up in the dungeons with Eldred and Alena.

"It would make sense to fortify the city if he was expecting an attack. An invading army would not just attack the castle. They would take the city as well," it was Tancred who spoke. Richmond was suddenly grateful for his friend.

"Oh," Amilie said. "I see," was all the explanation she gave before she continued towards the castle.

Richmond remained standing in the courtyard by himself for a moment. The situation seemed strange. Amilie had seemingly accepted Tancred's answer, but Richmond was not sure if that was the case. He watched her walk away, but she did not look back at him. He half expected her to stop and call the soldiers to attack him. When she didn't he started after them.

The large wooden doors leading into the castle were unguarded. Again Richmond was surprised, but as Amilie had explained once you were inside the castle then everyone assumed that you were meant to be there. Richmond tried his best to blend in and not look suspicious, but he didn't think that he was doing a good job. The situation was just a little too discerning for his liking. He couldn't help feeling self-conscious.

Once they were inside the castle they got away from the hurrying soldiers of the courtyard and instead were swamped by servants and low officials. It seemed as though the castle was just as busy as the courtyard. Richmond felt a little better that the men and women racing around were not armed.

Amilie paused once they reached the end of the first corridor. It was as if she was looking for someone in particular. When it was clear she didn't find them she continued. The two men followed behind her. Tancred had walked beside her when they first entered the castle, but Amilie had cautioned him to walk behind. It would look better if Amilie was in the lead by herself.

"Lady Amilie," a male voice growled from behind them.

Amilie's shoulders suddenly tensed. Richmond did not think that it was a good sign. He didn't want to turn around in case the man wasn't friendly. His voice definitely did not sound friendly and after Amilie's reaction he was even more convinced.

"I thought it was you," the man spoke when Amilie turned around. Richmond and Tancred walked past her before turning around themselves. "Where have you been?"

"Lord Reynard!" she sounded surprised. "I have been walking in the courtyard. It is all that I can do now that I am not allowed out of the castle."

"Don't be sassy Amilie, it is not a becoming trait," Lord Reynard was an older man. The lines of age were starting to show on his face and there were flecks of grey in his short brown hair. "You know that you were due to attend the morning court. You would want to have a better excuse for missing it."

Amilie took a step forward and gave Reynard a cheeky smile. Richmond thought that she was very effective in using her beauty to her advantage. If the situation was different then Richmond thought that he might have tried to court her himself. Since he knew that she was an agent of the Evil One there was no chance. He even cursed himself for thinking in such a manner.

"I need to see Prince Leroy," Amilie ignored the question.

Reynard was a little annoyed at her elusiveness, but he ignored it. His question hadn't been that important anyway. He was a little perplexed at her statement though. Something strange was happening and he really wanted to know what it was. He didn't know who the two men were with Amilie. With the changes in the castle any knowledge was power and one thing that Reynard wanted was more power.

"The Prince has left the castle. He is out on important business. He didn't say when he was going to return. It seems to me that this is something that you should already know," he watched her carefully for a response.

Amilie was a little surprised, but she didn't show it. It was the first time that the Prince had left the castle since the lockdown. The man didn't seem to know many people outside of the castle and in fact inside as well. She didn't know who he would be visiting outside of the castle walls. She did know that Reynard was looking for some advantage over her and that was one thing she was not going to give away.

"Of course, it just slipped my mind," she lied. "You know how vague I can be at times," she giggled softly as she spoke.

"Hmmm," Reynard didn't sound convinced. "Anyway, Queen Oriana as requested you visit her."

"Then what are you doing standing here wasting my time?" Amilie did well to hide her surprise. She had once been very close to the queen, but since the Prince had arrived she had not spoken to her once. "I am sure that Queen Oriana will not appreciate being kept waiting."

Lord Reynard became suddenly very self-conscious. He still didn't know who the two men were standing with Lady Amilie, but he assumed that they were the reason she was being summoned. If the queen found out that he had detained them for longer than necessary then there was no telling what would happen. More and more of the noble families were ending up in the dungeons. The last thing he wanted to do was to give the queen a chance to imprison him and his loved ones.

"Hurry along Amilie. You do not want to keep the queen waiting. You know how angry she gets these days," Reynard's voice was gruff.

It took all of Amilie's self-control to contain herself from laughing. When she was a little girl she had like Lord Reynard. The man had slipped her lollies when she was supposed to be studying. She doubted now that he remembered. The man seemed so different when she was all grown up.

"What does Queen Oriana want?" Tancred asked as the continued down through the castle, once Reynard was out of earshot.

"I don't know," she couldn't hide the concern in her voice.

Amilie didn't think that it was going to be a good meeting. She really had no idea why the Queen would want to speak to her. The fact that it was on the same day that she was sneaking the two men into the castle couldn't have been a coincidence.

"I am sure that we will find out soon enough," she added as an afterthought.

"Do you think that it is a good idea that Tancred and I come with you. I am sure it would be better if we kept a low profile until the Prince returns," Richmond wasn't keen to meet Queen Oriana. He knew that she was under the thrall of a Dark Knight and he didn't know how he would handle seeing her that way. He remembered seeing King Unwin is such a condition and it was not pleasant.

Amilie stopped walking when she heard Richmond's words. She made a sign of thinking before she spoke. "I think that you might be right. You can wait in my quarters. You will have all the privacy you need." Richmond visibly relaxed although no one else noticed. The other two were already continuing along the hallway. Amilie's quarters were on the other side of the castle, which meant they had to pass by a lot of people to get there. Every now and again someone would stop to speak with Amilie. Most she could brush off saying that she was in a hurry, but some of the higher ranking nobles she could not. They all wanted to know who her new friends were. She was able to deflect their attentions by simply saying they were guests of the Prince. Even though some did not believe her they were not going to take that chance. They all knew how easy it was to be sent to the dungeons and the rumours spreading around the castle of what happened beneath the ground was enough to scare even the most stalwart of men.

"Please make yourselves comfortable. I will try and return as soon as possible," she spoke once they were safely inside her quarters. She winked at Tancred before leaving.

Richmond listened at the door as her footsteps faded away. He wanted to make sure that she was not able to hear what he was about to say. When he was sure that they had privacy he turned his attention to his old friend.

"I think you should be careful," even though they were alone he kept his voice low.

Tancred had started exploring his surroundings. He continued his rummaging for a moment before turning to face Richmond. "What are you talking about?"

"Remember why we are here. She is working for the enemy," Richmond reminded him.

"I know," Tancred held up his hand defensively. "There is no harm in being nice."

Her allegiances were not his only concern. He was still worried about Tancred intentions. He knew that his friend was under control of one of the Dark Knights, but he didn't know how much of his friend still remained.

"I have seen the way you have been looking at each other and I don't think that it is just friendship," Richmond scolded.

Tancred frowned. He didn't like what Richmond was saying. He was dedicated to their cause and there nothing was going to distract him from their goal. He had to admit, even if only to himself that the thought had crossed his mind. Once she had cleaned herself and changed clothes she was quite attractive. At that point he realised that Richmond was watching him closely.

"There is nothing between us. We are here to get information from Prince Leroy and that is it. Once we get what we came for then we make our way back to the army," Tancred didn't sound convinced with his own words.

Richmond frowned at him, but didn't say anything. He didn't believe a word that came out of Tancred's mouth. He knew that there was a romantic connection between the two and he had a bad feeling that no good was going to come of it.

Before they had a chance to continue the conversation there was a knock on the door. The sudden sound made both men jump. They looked at each other, not sure whether they should answer it or not. When the knock came again Tancred made his way closer to the door. He looked back at Richmond before calling for them to enter.

The door was slowly pushed open and young man entered. He looked surprised to see the two men in Lady Amilie's room. Although he was told to collect them he didn't believe they would be there.

"Queen Oriana has requested you join her in the throne room," the man sounded nervous as he spoke.

Chapter 18: Queen Oriana

The throne room was filled with people. Richmond had been nervous enough about meeting the queen, but the scene put him on the verge of panic. He didn't know if he could contain himself if Oriana's condition was anything like Unwin's had been. The last thing he needed was to create a scene, but he was relieved to see that she sat purposefully on her throne. It was a fair indication that she still held some of her senses. A glimmer of hope filled his body.

Queen Oriana was a lot younger than Richmond had been expecting. He estimated that she could be no older than forty and she still held all of her beauty. A slight amount of colouring hid the small wrinkles that came with time. Her brown hair fell down around her on either side of her shoulders. She wore a yellow flowing dress and atop her head was a golden crown with a sapphire in the centre. Richmond thought that she was very attractive.

Lady Amilie stood next to the throne. She had a concerned expression on her face when she saw the two men arrive. She did her best not to look at the reaction on Oriana's face. She tried to sneak a look out of the corner of her eye, but she could not see. The two men were the reason why Oriana had called Amilie to the throne room. It had not been the original reason, but when she heard about the new arrivals she could think of nothing else.

"Welcome to my castle," Queen Oriana was the first to speak. "What brings you to my domain, Lord Richmond," she spoke directly to Richmond and seemingly ignored Tancred.

Tancred was used to this treatment. Richmond was of noble birth, so he always received the most attention. In high circles it was common for him to be forgotten, ignored or unseen altogether. That was the price for being Richmond's advisor. He was happy enough with that. It meant that he was able to listen and gather information. It was amazing what some people spoke about in front of him.

"We come here to seek refuge," Lord Richmond spoke with a commanding, but deferential tone. "Darshival is under siege and we seek asylum within your walls," the lie was weak, but they had both agreed it was the best plan if they were discovered.

"That is not the story I hear," the Queen looked at him suspiciously. "In fact it is just the opposite. I hear that Kiarome has been liberated by the Alliance. Is this not true?"

"That is a matter of opinion. We believe that the Alliance is not working on our behalf, but instead is working for its own personal gain. We believe that the Alliance is trying to take control of the Seven

Kingdoms. It is for this reason that we have come seeking your aide," the lie sounded reasonable enough and it got Oriana thinking.

Oriana was about to speak to Richmond when she stopped. She turned to Amilie and whispered something to her. Richmond wished that he could have heard what she said, but there was no chance. Amilie looked at the two men before answering the Queen. Her words were also silent to Richmond.

"It seems as though you are not the only one who believes that the Alliance is out for domination," she made another pensive look. "I think that what you say may be true, or at least that you believe it's true. I do not know if the Alliance is indeed an agent of evil, if it is trying to take over the Seven Kingdoms then my soldiers are already lost. If that is the case then their next logical step would be to march on Jarrat," her logic was impeccable, which annoyed Richmond. There was no other way he could prove his reasons for arriving in Jarrat. In the end he had given Queen Oriana an excuse to fortify the city.

"That does sound right," Richmond had to choose his words carefully. "The last I heard was that the Alliance was still in Kiarome. I don't think that they have any plan on moving for a while. It is one of the reasons that I came here. I hoped that you would send an army to Kiarome and return control to Unwin." Richmond knew that Oriana would not entertain the notion. There was no chance she could believe that the remainder of her army was enough to attack the Alliance. The only chance she had was in defence.

Queen Oriana watched him closely as she thought. She knew that there was no way she could send soldiers into Darshival, not without the approval and support of the other three Kingdoms, and she didn't think that would happen. She still thought that the Alliance would be moving on Jarrat sooner or later. If that was the case then she could not weaken her own defences more than they already were. She didn't want to offend her guests by answering too soon so she kept up the pretence of thought.

"I am afraid that I do not think that I will be able to help. Believe me when I say that I wish I could. It is not quite that easy to move and army across borders," she was about to continue explaining, but she saw the knowing look on Richmond's face. He had hoped that it would stop whatever she was about to say.

Richmond couldn't tell if there was anything wrong with Queen Oriana. She seemed to have all her senses. If that was the case then there was a chance that Prince Leroy was not a Dark Knight. He felt a moment of hope flitter through his body. It only remained there for a moment as there were too many things that were consistent with the opposite.

"I must protect my own people. It is my responsibility to look after my people," she added.

"I understand your majesty," Richmond bowed in response. He hoped that it would end the meeting.

"Tell me more about the Alliance," the Queen spoke just as Richmond was about to leave.

The question caught him by surprise. He didn't really know what she was expecting from him. He stood there silently before he knew he had to say something. The longer he remained silent the less chance they were going to believe his lie.

"What is it that you want to know?" it was all he could think of as he tried to conjure up a convincing lie.

"Why are they trying to conquer the Seven Kingdoms?" there was a touch of doubt in her voice that Richmond recognised instantly.

"I am not sure how much I will be able to tell you. The Alliance passed by Bellarome without stopping. It seemed as though they were planning on rushing Kiarome without worrying about the smaller cities. All I can tell you is what the rumours have brought to my door step." He thought that was the best way to get away with his lies. If he didn't stand by them then he could not be blamed if they were found not to be true. "I don't know why they want to take over the Seven Kingdoms, but I have heard that there is an overlord who is greedy for power. He is spreading lies about an invasion by the Evil One. I believe that is how he is recruiting new soldiers. Then, when you think that they are working for you, he turns around and invades. At that stage there is nothing you can do, but surrender. I am sure that he will send an emissary here offering to protect you from some unseen evil. It is at this point he will attack. You will not see it coming until it is too late," it was a variation on the lie they had already been telling. He was quite impressed with himself when he finished speaking.

The Queen had a strange expression on her face. It was half way between thoughtfulness and horror. Richmond tried to keep as calm as possible, although his heart was starting to pound and his palms were sweating. If Oriana saw through his lies then he was sure that he would end up in the dungeons. Not only that, but it would make things even harder for the Alliance.

"You don't have to worry about me. I am well protected here in my castle. Prince Leroy has informed me of the Alliance and the evil things that they do." At the sound of the Prince's name the throne room became suddenly silent.

Richmond suddenly became very self-conscious. He felt as though all the eyes in the room were fixed on him. In fact all the eyes in the room were fixed on the Queen. Neither of them had spoken since everyone had gone quiet. Richmond wasn't sure if he was supposed to answer her or not. He was sure that she had not finished speaking. When it was obvious that she was not going to continue Richmond felt as though he had to speak.

"Do you think that we could discuss matters in private?" He made a sign of looking around the room, as he did all the spectators were suddenly busy speaking amongst themselves. They all kept watch out of the corner of their eyes.

Queen Oriana also looked around the room. She noticed that everyone, even though they were trying not to, was still watching her. She herself had nothing to hide, but she could understand why Richmond was suddenly so nervous. She thought for a moment before she spoke again.

"I think that we shall retire to my chambers. I feel as though I need something to eat. I think tea would also be in order," she looked around for a serving maid. When she couldn't see one she became annoyed. She brushed it off and spoke to Amilie. "Take our guest to my chambers. I will be there shortly."

Amilie was about to say something, but the Queen dismissed her with a wave of her hand. She knew well enough not to push the point. If Oriana didn't want to speak with her then she just had to accept it. She motioned for the two men to follow her as she walked away from the throne. Even though Oriana had just invited Richmond she figured that he would want Tancred to tag along.

The Queen's chambers were at the end of the throne room. A set of large mahogany double doors were plan in design, but that was part of their beauty. As Richmond walked through he thought they were magnificent in their simplicity.

Once they were alone Richmond was able to relax. Oriana's official chamber was a large room and at the far end was a large table with a number of official looking documents stacked on top. There was one chair at the far side of the table and three on the other. Amilie led the two men to the table where she sat down. Tancred instantly sat next to her. Richmond held back, he did not like the situation. His friend had protested that there was nothing between the two of them, but he did not believe it. He wondered if maybe it was something to do with the spell Argoz had cast on him.

Richmond walked slowly to the end of the room and sat in the chair on the other side of Amilie. She didn't seem to notice him. Her attention was completely on Tancred. The two were looking into each others eyes with stupid smiles on their faces. Richmond had to put an end to it.

"What do you think about the Queen?" he asked.

Amilie's body stiffened for a moment. She seemed somewhat annoyed at the sudden question. "You must be very careful what you say to her," she warned. "She has not been the same since the Prince arrived."

The warning seemed odd to Richmond. If she was indeed an agent of evil then it didn't make any sense for her to give them such a warning. Richmond thought for a moment that maybe there was more to Amilie than met the eye. Whatever it was he didn't like the new situation they were in.

"It's the Prince who we wish to speak to, but I will take your warning on speaking with the Queen. We will make sure that we are as brief as possible and don't give away too much information," Richmond tried not to be rude, which he only just managed.

Before they had a chance to say anything further the door opened and a page boy entered. He promptly announced the arrival of Queen Oriana. The show was completely unnecessary, but Oriana insisted on the formalities. It was her right to be introduced when entering a room and she was going to use it. All three of them stood when she entered. If they did not then they didn't want to think of what the Queen would do.

"Please be seated," the Queen said once she herself had sat down.

The three sat almost in unison. Now that the Queen was in the room Richmond felt very uncomfortable. She held a presence that was very unsettling. He assumed that it was due to the spell she was under as he had been in the presence of royalty before and not felt such a way.

"What is it that you plan on doing if the Alliance come here?" Richmond asked, when no one else spoke.

Queen Oriana seemed taken aback by the question and Richmond was beginning to regret asking it. Amilie had warned him about her, but he just blurted it out. Slowly her face started to soften and he relaxed slightly at her new demeanour.

"That is for the Prince to decide. He is in charge of the protection of the city. I have every faith that he will do the right thing," she had a glazed look on her face, as if she was trying hard to remember something. "He will look after me."

Richmond didn't like what he was hearing. There could be no doubt that she was under the thrall of the Dark Knight. She didn't seem totally sure of herself and Richmond hoped that the Knight's hold on her was not complete. He didn't know how he could use it to his advantage, or even if he could.

"Where is the Prince?" to everyone's surprise it was Tancred who asked the question.

"And who might you be?" the Queen looked at him suspiciously, as if seeing him for the first time.

"This is my advisor, Tancred," Richmond spoke for him. He thought about explaining further but Oriana had already returned her attention to Tancred.

"The Prince is out of the castle on business," the Queen watched his reaction closely. "I do not ask him what he does. I trust him completely."

Richmond did not like where the conversation was going. He knew that his friend would not simply accept her answer, but would keep pushing until he got the answers he was looking for. There was no telling what would happen if he continued to push the Queen. He only hoped that he had enough sense to keep his mouth shut.

"When do you expect him back?" Richmond nearly hit him across the head when he continued to speak.

The Queen looked at him with a stunned look on her face. Richmond assumed it was at Tancred's boldness, but the real reason was completely different. It seemed a simple enough question and one that she should know the answer. It seemed as though the answer was hidden away somewhere within her mind, but she just couldn't locate it. The feeling was disturbing to her.

"Are you alright, your majesty?" Amilie asked when Oriana didn't respond.

"Yes, my dear," the expression on Oriana's face suddenly changed. Her confusion was replaced with what could only be described as doting. "Thank your for you concern. I think that I would like to have a lie down now," she looked upon Amilie as she would her own child.

If there was any doubt of Queen Oriana's condition before it had completely gone. Although Richmond didn't know what she was like before the Dark Knight arrived he knew that it wasn't like this. She wouldn't have stayed Queen for long if she was. Although intrigue was not as prominent in Entero as it was in Darshival the people of Entero would not accept a vague ruler.

Both men were watching Amilie as Oriana stood from the table. She didn't know what to say. The Queen walked out of the room whilst they remained seated. It wasn't until she was gone that Amilie herself stood.

"What are we going to do now?" Richmond asked before rising himself.

"I think that it would be best if you remain inside my quarters for the rest of the day. The castle will be a buzz with your arrival as it is and I don't think we need to give them anything else to gossip about," Amilie announced.

Richmond couldn't argue with her logic. He also thought that it would be better for them to remain as anonymous as possible. The more contact they had the more chance they had of giving themselves away. All Richmond wanted to do was to speak to the Prince and then get as far away from the castle as he could. He had a bad feeling that something terrible was going to happen. The more time they wasted the less chance the army had to formulate their plan. There was a lot riding on the information that they had to retrieve.

They walked quickly through the castle to avoid having to speak to anyone. Whenever someone tried to speak to Amilie she simply lowered her head and ignored them. If they were stopped by anyone then it would not take long for a crowd to form. Once that happened there was no chance of making it to Amilie's quarters, she would have to deal with them another time.

They all relaxed when they reached her apartment. Richmond felt a lot more comfortable when they were alone with Amilie. He didn't think that it would be the case, seeing as she was an agent of the Evil One. She was a lot more pleasant than he had originally thought. He could see why Tancred was attracted to her.

"Do you have any idea on how long it will be before the Prince returns?" Richmond asked when they were safely inside.

"It is hard to say. From what I have gathered he hasn't told anyone what he is doing."

Richmond didn't like the tone in her voice. There was something that just didn't seem right. "Well that is just great!" both Tancred and Amilie turned their full attention to him. "We have to speak with him. You work for him. You should know when he's getting back," Richmond didn't know where the words had come from, but they seemed appropriate.

Amilie was taken aback at his harsh words. She looked towards Tancred for support. He didn't know why Richmond had suddenly turned on her, but she was not going to let him get away with it. It was not at all in tune with their act and he could risk everything.

"What are you saying? Amilie has been very good to us. There is no need to speak to her in such a manner." Tancred felt like comforting her further, but he knew it would gain a negative response from Richmond.

"She works for the evil bastard," the words came out of Richmond's mouth before he could stop.

The words had a greater effect than Richmond had expected. The rage was clear on her face. She stormed up to Richmond and puffed herself up in an effort to look ferocious. Richmond took a step back as he thought she was going to walk right through him. It was his turn to be taken aback. He suddenly wished that he hadn't said the things that he had. As far as Amilie knew they were also agents for evil and acting on the behest of a Dark Knight. Richmond's words had just proven otherwise. If word got back to the farrier then it would only be a matter of time before

Aimon knew they were playing him false. All he could do was wait and hope he could fix the problem he had created.

"I do not work for the Prince," she spoke through clenched teeth. "I am loyal to the Queen." It was Amilie's turn to say something that she wished she hadn't.

A look of horror appeared on her face. She had revealed her true allegiances and as she already knew that could be disastrous. The Prince had already imprisoned anyone who openly supported the Queen and not him. Those who were left supporting Oriana did so in secrecy. She had a bad feeling that she had revealed herself to the wrong people. They had already claimed to be followers of the Prince and they seemed nervous around the Queen. She didn't seem to notice the meaning behind Richmond's outburst.

"I didn't mean that," she moved away quickly from Richmond, but her retreat was blocked by Tancred.

"What are you talking about?" he asked, with a concerned tone in his voice.

"Nothing," she kept her face down to avoid giving away her true feelings. "It was a slip of the tongue, nothing more."

"I think that it is time that you are honest with us," Richmond kept his voice level. He was excited at the thought of finding an ally within the castle, but he wanted to make sure before he told her the truth. "Tell us everything or else we will tell the Prince when he returns."

"Richmond!" Tancred could see the fear in her face. "We will do nothing of the kind. Here," Tancred brought a seat over for her to sit on. "Have a seat." He waited for her to be seated before he continued. "You can trust us. We are not going to tell the Prince anything."

Amilie relaxed slightly, but she wasn't completely convinced. She looked at Richmond with a worried expression on her face. Richmond couldn't help himself, but laugh. The thought that she was afraid of them turning her into the Prince was funny. All along he had been careful of what he said around her for fear of exactly the same thing. He knew that the laughter was inappropriate and quickly stopped.

"So if you are not in league with the Prince, what are you doing sneaking us into the palace to see him?" Richmond settled himself before he asked the question.

Amilie didn't know how to take Richmond's reaction. The laughter was more confusing then anything else. She realised that she had no option, but to answer their questions. The only problem was how much she should tell them. She was unsure if they were indeed members of the enemy and thought carefully before she spoke again.

"I am loyal to Prince Leroy," her words convinced no one.

There was only one way they would get the truth out of her and that was to reveal their own allegiances. The only problem was that neither of them was completely sure of Amilie. She seemed innocent enough, but that could just be a ploy to catch them out. The last thing they could do was to reveal themselves and risk ruining everything they had done. took the decision out of Richmond's hands.

"You can relax Amilie, we are not here to help Prince Leroy," Richmond could have crossed the room and run Tancred through with his sword. There was nothing he could do. The cat was already out of the bag. If he made a scene then there would be no chance of taking it back. "Please, if we are going to trust you then you have to be honest with us," there was a softness in his voice that did nothing to calm Richmond's nerves.

Amilie looked at Tancred and then at Richmond. She tried to gauge the truth by the look on their faces, but they gave nothing away. They were both waiting for her to speak. It was enough to make her very nervous, but she had no other choice. The slip of her tongue would be enough to see her tortured in the castle dungeons if the Prince ever found out. Her only chance was to trust the two men before her.

"Okay, it's true," she lowered her head as she spoke. She didn't have the heart to look them in the face. "I am not a servant of the evil Prince Leroy," she figured if she was going in she may as well jump all the way. "It is all that I can do to keep myself from screaming," her words came out in a hurry. She was afraid if she stopped talking then she wouldn't be able to continue.

"Calm down," Tancred finally spoke as she continued to ramble. He walked to her side and placed a reassuring hand on her shoulder. "It's alright, but I don't understand. If you are loyal to the Queen then why do you sneak traitors into the city?"

She looked up and smiled. She was beginning to believe that they were on her side. "All those who showed defiance to Prince Leroy were quickly disposed of. Those of us left knew that there was only one way to stay alive. I found that once the castle was shut off there was still a need to get people in and out. It seemed as though I am one of the only people who know how. The Prince doesn't care how I do it, he is just happy that I can. Although I have to do his bidding, it means that I can remain here and keep an eye on Oriana," Amilie seemed relieved that she had confessed.

"That still doesn't make any sense," Richmond decided to add his thoughts. "If the Prince is the one who shut the gates then wouldn't he be able to open them for those he wanted to gain entrance. It seems a little silly to have someone sneak them in. I would have thought you would only have to sneak people in who are opposed to the Prince."

There was a moment of silence as Richmond's words settled on the other two. It was something that Amilie had never questioned. If she had questioned the Prince's motives then she would end up in the dungeons and that would help no one.

"I guess you would need to ask the Prince that," Amilie sounded annoyed. "I don't dare question his motives."

"Enough of that Richmond," Tancred scolded him. Amilie is a prisoner here and doing what she can to survive. She is one of the only people left in the castle loyal to Queen Oriana."

Richmond wasn't completely convinced, but he wasn't about to start and argument with his advisor. There were more important matters at stake. For the moment he was prepared to go on faith. They had more important matters to deal with and it seemed Amilie was a friend.

"Now I think you should tell me what you are doing here?" Amilie took the opportunity to change the subject.

Tancred was about to speak but Richmond stopped him. He wanted to talk to his advisor before he gave away all their secrets. Even if Amilie was who she said she was there was no reason to tell her everything. Their safety hinged on certain things not being made known. They had to keep some secrets from her and Richmond was afraid he was going to reveal too much.

"I don't think we should tell her anything," Richmond whispered to Tancred at the other end of the room.

"What do you mean? She's on our side."

"I believe her, but it will only make life harder for her if she knows what we are doing. If the enemy finds out then there is no telling what he will do to her," Richmond's words made sense.

"I suppose that you are right. I don't think it is the best plan, but I will defer to your judgement," Tancred's words were condescending.

"I think that is would be best if you know as little as possible about what were are doing here," Tancred said as though it was his idea. "It will be safer the less that you know."

His words only piqued her interest. She could tell by the look on Richmond's face that Tancred wasn't going to divulge any further information, but she was not going to let it pass. There would be another opportunity for her to press them and she would wait until then to get her answers.

"I think that it is best if we leave it at that," Richmond added. "I think that we should have our own rooms made up. We will need to wait here until the Prince returns." Richmond wanted to take the temptation away from the two of them.

"Of course," Amilie seemed a little put off by his words, but she didn't say anything. "The Queen has already ordered guest rooms made up for you. Housing is tight at the moment so I dare say that some minor noble will be sleeping with a friend. I am sure that they will not be happy with the situation," she paused and thought for a moment. "I will have someone check to see if they are ready."

Richmond didn't think that sounded right. With all the nobles who had been removed by the Prince there should be plenty of vacant rooms. He was about to say something, but then thought better of it. Amilie had already started to leave and he was happy to see her go. The longer she stayed the more likely it was that Tancred would reveal too much information.

When she was out of the room Tancred moved closer to Richmond. Despite the fact that they were alone he didn't trust anyone in the castle. There were many places someone could hide and listen to their conversation and he still didn't completely trust Amilie.

"What are you doing?" he spoke as quietly as he could.

"I don't know if we can trust her." Richmond replied.

"She risked a lot to tell us the truth," as he finished speaking they heard the sound of a bell ringing in the distance. It was a signal that Amilie was soon going to be returning to the room.

When Amilie returned there came a knock on the door. She called for them to enter and a skinny man came in. She advised him that they wanted to know if the men's rooms were ready and he quickly disappeared.

They waited in silence until the man returned. Amilie could tell that there was some tension between the two men. She wanted to ask questions, but thought better of it. She didn't want to start any trouble. Her relative safety made her nervous enough without risking it further. If they were not who they said they were then it would not be long before she was joining the others in the dungeon. That was a thought that wasn't worth thinking about.

"The rooms are ready. They will be staying in Lord Alain's quarters. I can show you if you like?" the man had a soft voice.

"No, thank you. That will be all," Amilie smiled at the man as he left the room.

"I think we should go now," Richmond suggested.

"I will show you the way." Amilie said as she walked towards the door.

The two men followed quickly behind. Tancred gave Richmond a dirty look as he walked past. He clearly did not like Richmond's attitude towards Amilie. He told himself that it was because she was now an ally, but that was not the reason. He felt as though there was a connection between himself and Amelie and he wanted more time to explore it. He had loved Frida back when he was Tancred of Bellarome, but that life seemed a life-time away. The nurse had been dear to him, but he knew that relationship was over. If he ever returned to Bellarome he knew she would have moved on. She was a beautiful woman with strong ties to the nobility. She had been a nurse inside the palace for many years. It would not be long before she found someone else to warm her bed.

Their rooms were a lot nicer than they were expecting. At the entrance there was a main room with brightly coloured paintings on the wall. Many couches with soft cushions lined the room with a table and chairs for dining to one side. Two bedrooms and a bathing room lead off from the main room. Richmond was a little concerned at the lavishness of their accommodation. It was much more than it should have been. He didn't think that there was much hope of them sneaking in and out of the castle relatively unnoticed. It would not be long before the entire castle knew they were there.

Amilie looked as though she wanted to stay in the room, but Richmond quickly ushered her out the door. He didn't want to create any opportunity for slip ups. He knew he was going to hear about it from Tancred, but it was something that he was prepared to suffer.

"Are you jealous?" Tancred asked as soon as the door was closed.

"What are you talking about?" Richmond tried to sound as disinterested as possible.

"Why are you being so aggressive towards Amilie? She had done nothing but help us. Now that we know she is not an agent for evil we should be able to confide in her."

There was something in Tancred's tone that irritated Richmond and he had to let him know. "Do you realise how important our mission is?" he started yelling until he was able to control himself. He didn't want anyone walking past to realise what they were talking about. "Just because she said she is loyal to the Queen doesn't make it true. She may be a spy for Prince Leroy trying to gain information from us. What we are doing here is too important. We cannot risk ruining everything because you want to scratch an itch," the last comment was unnecessary and counterproductive.

"If you honestly think that I would ruin everything for a woman then you don't know me at all," Tancred sounded hurt, but he still managed to keep his voice in check. "I think that I am going to go for a walk around the castle," even as he said it he knew that it wasn't an option.

Richmond moved so he was standing between Tancred and the door. Whatever he did he couldn't let Tancred leave. At the moment their safest bet was remaining in their room until the Prince returned.

"You can't leave," Richmond crossed his arms across his chest.

Instead of starting another fight Tancred sat in one of the lounge chairs. He might have to stay with Richmond, but he didn't have to speak to him. He knew that his friend was right, but he wasn't going to let him know it. He could well use the time to think. He hadn't been thinking properly since they arrived in the castle and he didn't know why.

They remained in Lord Alain's quarters for the rest of the day. To their relief the evening meal was brought to them. They were both worried at the thought of a state dinner. It would just be another opportunity for the Queen to get information from them. They didn't want to speak to anyone until they reached the Prince. Only Tancred wanted to speak to Amilie again. He resisted the urge and they both went to bed early.

***

Richmond woke late in the night. He could see the moon high in the sky outside his window. Sleep was still thick in his mind and he wanted nothing else to return to its comfort, but something was not right. There was a reason why he woke and he had to investigate further. He couldn't sense anyone in the room, so that was not the reason. Slowly he came to his feet. He had to take a moment to settle himself before he started moving around.

Once he was out of his bedroom he realised why he had woken. The door to Tancred's room was half open. Even though it was dark he knew that the bed was empty. He cursed softly under his breath. He knew exactly where his friend had gone. He was going to risk everything for his little romance.

As the thought rolled around in his mind he considered going to Amilie's apartment and accosting them. His hand was almost on the door handle when he decided not to. In the end he had to accept that whatever was done was done. There was no point in barging in and making a fool out of himself. He would wait until the morning before he confronted his friend. He only hoped that he was doing the right thing.

Chapter 19: Prince Leroy

In the morning Richmond woke to find Tancred sitting in the main room. He looked as though nothing had happened the previous night and smiled at Richmond as he entered the room. It was obvious that he had no idea that Richmond knew of his midnight tryst. Richmond wanted to see if Tancred was going to own up to what he had done before he jumped to conclusions.

"I slept well last night. It is amazing what a decent bed will do," Richmond made the comment as casual as possible.

"I know what you mean," there was a large smile on Tancred's face. Richmond didn't know how much sleep he actually got last night, but he looked refreshed.

Richmond paused and waited for him to continue to speak, but Tancred had said all he was going to say. Richmond hadn't resigned the fact, but he didn't think Tancred was going to divulge the information he was after. He wanted to openly accuse Tancred, but instead he remained quiet.

"Have you heard any news about the Prince's return?" Richmond asked after a long silence.

"No," Tancred seemed surprised at the question. "I have not seen anyone since yesterday. I am sure that Amilie will let us know when he arrives."

Richmond had to bite his tongue. The words were a lie. He knew they were not all lies, but the important ones were. He wanted to throttle his old friend, but again he kept his anger in check. He would wait and see what information he could get before he accused him. He didn't like playing his old friend. They had been through too much together, but he had no choice. Tancred was not himself and Richmond could not take any risks.

The two remained in their rooms for the rest of the day. Their meals were brought to them, but that was it. There was no sign of Amilie and no word about the Prince. Richmond had thought that they would have had more visitors. He was sure that the populous of the castle would have come fishing for information. What he didn't know was that the Queen had decreed that no one was to disturb them, under Amilie's insistence.

Again that night Richmond woke to find Tancred had left the room. He considered going to Amilie's apartment and confronting the pair, but again he thought better of it. He wanted nothing more than to get the truth out of them. Instead he returned to bed and slowly returned to sleep.

The next day continued in much the same fashion. Richmond awoke to find Tancred sitting in the main room. When he asked about how he slept Tancred replied the same as the day before. Again Richmond wanted to confront him and again he remained quiet.

Besides someone coming for their meals no one else entered the room until later in the afternoon. There was a gentle knock on the door. Both men sat up quickly when they heard the sound. It was too early for the evening meal, which meant that it was someone to see them. Tancred looked at Richmond who in turn looked back at his advisor.

"Enter," Tancred finally spoke.

The door was pushed open and Amilie entered the room. Tancred seemed as concerned as Richmond at her arrival. There was only one thing that it could mean. They were both as nervous as they were excited as they waited for her to speak.

"Prince Leroy has returned," she didn't wait on formalities. "He has requested that you see him."

"Did he say where he has been?" Richmond asked, curiously.

"It is not for me to ask and I wouldn't advise you asking either. If he wants you to know something you can be sure that he will tell you. Asking questions is one of the quickest ways to end up in the dungeons," she didn't look at Richmond when she spoke.

Richmond could tell that she was deliberately not making eye contact with either of them. He also noticed that Tancred was trying his hardest not to look at her. If there was any doubt that there was something going on between the two of them it was now gone. He could sense the tension between them and the only way to break it was to speak.

"I suppose we shouldn't keep him waiting."

"Follow me," she replied before turning her back on them.

They both waited for her to be out of the room and earshot before they rose. Richmond held Tancred back as he started towards the door.

"We must be very careful with what we say. We do not want to give anything away," Richmond watched him closely as he spoke.

"Of course," was all he said before shrugging off Richmond's grip.

Amilie was already half way down the corridor when they left the room. She didn't seem too interested in waiting, she knew well enough not to keep the Prince waiting. At least if she arrived then she could announce them as they caught up. It was clear that she was shaken as she approached. It was as if she was approaching some unseen horror. In truth she was afraid of the Prince and would do anything to avoid being in his presence.

They walked though the corridors until they reached the Queen's personal apartments Tancred and Richmond had caught up with Amilie and when they did she quickened her pace. If it wouldn't look too suspicious she would have happily started to run. She wanted to introduce the two men and then get as far away from the Prince as she could. She never felt comfortable in his presence. She felt as though he could see into her soul and at any moment he would discover her true alliances.

She knocked loudly on the door when they had arrived. There was a short pause before a voice called out for them to enter. The man's voice was a lot softer than they had expected. Amilie motioned for them to wait outside until she called for them to enter. When she was sure that they understood she entered the room and shut the door behind her. There was only a short wait before she returned.

"The Prince will see you now. Remember to be very careful with what you say. I don't want to be visiting you in the castle dungeons. I will meet you in your rooms when you have finished." She leaned forward ever so slightly, as if she was going to kiss Tancred on the cheek, before she remembered where she was and pulled away.

Richmond waited for Tancred to enter the room. It was usual for Tancred to introduce Richmond when they were meeting foreign dignitaries, but he wasn't sure if it was appropriate. If Amilie had already introduced them, which he was sure that she had, then there was a chance that Tancred would offend the Prince. In the end Richmond walked into the room and Tancred quickly followed behind. His Lord didn't look happy.

"It's a pleasure to meet you, your majesty," Richmond spoke quickly before Tancred had a chance. He bowed slightly as he spoke hoping that it was sufficient.

Prince Leroy was lying around a large pile of cushions at the far end of the room. Two young women dressed in sheer satin dresses were standing on either side of him. He was a lot different to what they had expected. His light blonde hair hung down around his shoulders. His features were fair and not at all rough as they were expecting. He was very pretty. That was more disturbing than if he had been a deformed monster. He wore a red silk shirt with the top few buttons open revealing a muscled chest.

"You may leave." He casually waved the two women away.

They walked straight for the door. Richmond noticed that they both had blank expressions on their faces. He doubted that they would remember anything that was spoken, but he was happier that they were not in the room. There was something very unsettling about them.

"Now I understand that my brother has sent you to see me," he was not about to beat around the bush. Richmond was taken back by his forthrightness. "Do not look so surprised. Argoz might like to play games, but I like to get straight to the point. My emissaries tell me that you are both on the level, but I will be the one who decides. Be assured that if I don't like what you tell me you will both end up in the dungeons."

Richmond looked at Tancred who in turn returned his gaze. Neither of them knew what to say. They both thought that there would be some small talk before they got down to the hard facts. There would be little chance to gain any useful information if things remained the same. They would have to proceed very carefully. It seemed the Prince knew more than what they had hoped. On the plus side they didn't have to explain themselves and that was going to be a tough task.

"He wanted us to tell you that the army is heading north to Hondin Lel. They were planning on coming here, but Argoz was able to convince the other leaders that the real threat was to the north. I can't guarantee that they won't return, but for now the threat is gone," Richmond's heart was pounding as he spoke.

Prince Leroy looked at Richmond closely. He was trying figure out if his words were true or not. As he looked something caught his attention from the corner of his eyes. He quickly looked at Tancred and then back at Richmond.

"This doesn't seem to make any sense." Richmond failed to notice him look at Tancred. "Why would my brother send you here to tell me that no one is coming?"

Richmond was afraid that would happen, but he had his next answer already prepared. "He didn't want you to unnecessarily prepare for battle. He figured that you would assume the army was coming here and make preparations. He just wanted you to be informed."

Prince Leroy took his time again to mull over the words. He waited for an opportunity to look at Tancred without Richmond knowing. He made another sign of thinking before he continued to speak.

"I see. That was very thoughtful of him, but I do not believe that to be true." His face didn't give anything away.

"I can assure you that I would not lie to you. I am a faithful servant of the Great Lord and would do nothing to subvert him." Richmond had learnt enough about the followers of Nyrra to sound like one.

"Calm down," there was no expression on the Prince's face. Richmond could not tell what he was thinking. "I have no doubt that you are telling me exactly what my brother wanted you to say. That is not to say that it is true." He paused again and tried to gauge a reaction from their faces. In contrast there was still nothing on his face. "I don't think that he would necessarily tell you the truth, especially if you are going to have to lie to me. He would know that I would be able to tell if you are lying." That was obviously not true as he could not tell that Richmond was indeed lying.

"What are you going to do?" Richmond couldn't help himself. He had to ask the question. He hoped that the Prince did not take offence. Luckily it seemed as though he had taken a liking to Richmond.

"I will prepare for battle, that is what I will do. I will continue to fortify the castle," again there was no expression on his face. The look was quite discerning.

"But I do not think that the castle will hold against the might of the army. Wouldn't it be better if you just leave?" Richmond was playing it by ear. It was a big risk, but one he had to take if he was going to get any answers.

"Don't be concerned," for the first time a smile crossed his face. "I have a few tricks up my sleeve."

Richmond was waiting with bated breath, but Leroy was not going to divulge his plan so easily. He wasn't sure whether he should push his luck and ask another question. He didn't think it would be long before his questioning would get on the Prince's nerves, but he had to ask.

"What is it that you have planned?" he tried to sound as interested and excited as possible. He thought it was the best way to keep the Dark Knight interested in the conversation.

"Let's just say that there is a surprise waiting for them in the forest when they arrive. When they least expect it I will attack with a force they will not be expecting." He suddenly paused to think. Richmond wasn't sure if he was supposed to respond. The Prince continued before he said anything. "I don't think that I should say any more. If Argoz is trying to subvert me then it is best that you don't know what I have planned."

"Of course. I do not think that he is trying to subvert you. I am sure that he is telling you the truth," Richmond was pushing his luck, but he figured that the Prince was not going to send him to the dungeons.

"Be that as it may but I think that I will ere on the side of caution. Now is there anything else you can tell me of any use?" it was clear that he wanted to finish the conversation.

Richmond was relieved that the meeting was almost over. It had been short, but he felt as though he had received some valuable information. He had pushed his luck and he had survived. As much as he wanted to know what the Prince was planning he didn't want to push it any further.

"I am sorry, my Prince. There is nothing more that he asked me to tell you," Richmond lowered his head, a sign of deference, as he spoke.

"Very well then. I think that you should go now." Richmond and Tancred made their way to the door. Before they reached it Leroy spoke again. "Don't leave the castle. I will need time to think of a response. If Argoz is planning a ruse then I shall give him one of my own," there was something evil in his voice that made Richmond shiver.

"Of course," Richmond was about to leave, but there was something else that he had to say. "We will have to leave soon if we are going to catch the rest of the army."

He waited for a response, but there was none coming. When he was sure that Leroy was not going to answer him they both left the room. Richmond let out a deep sigh of relief. He looked at Tancred who also seemed relieved at being outside the room. The two men walked back to their apartment in silence. There was no one else in the hallways, but Richmond felt as though there was someone watching. He couldn't shake the feeling until he was back inside the apartment. Just when he thought that he could relax he saw Amilie sitting on a lounge chair.

"Is it all done?" she asked when neither spoke.

"Yes," Richmond spoke when he saw Tancred was about to say something. "I think that it is time that we leave the castle."

"Good. I will arrange for something to eat. There's no point leaving on an empty stomach." She didn't wait for anyone to argue with her logic.

"We can't leave yet," the words were cold as ice coming from Tancred's mouth once they were alone. Richmond looked at him in shock and waited for him to speak again. "There is something that we are missing," his voice had returned to normal and he relaxed slightly. "There is something that he is hiding and we need to find out what it is."

"There is no telling how long that will take. It is not like you can openly ask him. The army will be approaching soon and we need to get what information we have back to them. We must leave," Richmond didn't like what Tancred was suggesting. They had been lucky to gain the information that they had. The longer they stayed in the castle the more likely it was they would end up in the dungeons.

"Leave it to me," there was something sinister in his voice. "I will have all the answers we need by morning. If I don't then we can leave anyway."

Richmond wasn't happy with his answer. He wanted to scream at his friend, but he knew he couldn't say anything. He couldn't reveal what he knew about him. He didn't even know if Tancred knew. He didn't know if he fully trusted his advisor, but there was nothing else he could do. The last thing he needed was to leave Tancred alone with the Dark Knight, but he didn't think he had any other option. Even if he said no he knew his advisor would find some way to see him, just like he had with Amilie.

"Okay. If you think that you can be careful enough." He paused before a thought came into his mind. "If you end up in the dungeons I won't be able to get you out. I have to get back to the army."

Tancred sneered at him. He was about to say something, but decided that it was not necessary. He would let Richmond have the last word on the matter. There were more important matters to deal with. What he was about to do was going to be very dangerous. There would be time for conversation later. For the moment he needed to get some rest.

"I am going to get some sleep, it is going to be a long night," Tancred didn't wait for Richmond to answer.

Richmond watched Tancred walk away. The part that worried him the most was that he didn't know if his friend was still in control. He knew that it was not a good idea to let him go. He only hoped that he was doing it for the right reasons. As he considered what to do next there was a knock on the door. The sound made Richmond jump as he was deep in thought. He took a moment to settle himself before he called for the door to be opened.

Amilie casually walked back into the room. Richmond was somewhat put out that Tancred had gone to bed. He wasn't overly fond of Amilie. Even though she was no longer a threat to his safety he didn't like what was happening between her and Tancred. The last thing he wanted to do was make small talk, but it seemed as though he didn't have an option.

"Where is Tancred?" she suppressed the urge to smile as she spoke.

"He has gone to bed," Richmond spoke in an off-hand manner. He hoped if he sounded disinterested enough she would leave him be.

"What?" she sounded surprised. "It is not even dark outside and the food will be here soon."

"I'm not his keeper. I can only imagine that he hasn't been sleeping well." Amilie didn't catch the jibe. "I'm sure he'll eat something when he wakes. Is there anything else I can help you with?"

She had a strange look on her face, as if she was thinking about something. When she realised he asked her a question she blinked a couple of times before returning her attention to him.

"Sorry, what did you say?" she asked, a little embarrassed.

"I can only assume that there is something more," although he could not be completely sure. "Is there something that you want?"

"Ah, yes, there is," it was as if she was trying to remember. "There is someone who wants to speak to you."

There was a sudden knock on the door that interrupted their conversation. Richmond couldn't believe the timing of the serving women who had brought their food. It was not the time to pause things.

Richmond didn't like the sound of what Amilie had said. There was no one in the castle he wanted to speak with and no one who should be searching him out. He had a bad feeling that something bad was going to happen. As much as he wanted to know the answer he had to wait for the servants to leave.

"And are you going to tell me who it is?" he finally asked when they were alone again.

"A minor noble by the name of Xarles Dúc, he is a Count or a Duke or something like that," there was something in her tone that made Richmond very suspicious.

"I don't think that I wish to see anyone else today," Richmond shrugged off the request.

"I am afraid this is not just a simple request. It is very important that you meet Xarles. He has a message for you," Amilie did her best not to sound desperate.

Richmond thought for a moment. There was every chance that this was a trap. He didn't know what Tancred and Amilie had discussed in private. There was still a chance that she was working for enemy. It would not be unthinkable for them to lie. If that was the case then he was about to walk into a trap. On the other hand there might be some valuable information.

"Okay, I will meet with Xarles," Richmond finally agreed.

"Good. Let's get going," Amilie turned around and walked out.

Richmond waited for a moment. He didn't want her to think that he was in a hurry to meet her nobleman. The man, whoever his was, could wait. He would not be summoned like a pageboy. When he left the room he found that Amilie had not waited for him. She was already half way down the corridor. He had to quicken his step not to lose her once she rounded the corner.

They found Xarles on the other side of the castle. He was talking to a man and two women. The conversation seemed to be light-hearted. When he saw the two approached he quickly said his goodbyes and moved to greet them.

"Good afternoon Lord Richmond, I am Duke Xarles Dúc," he dipped his head in an informal bow. "I am glad that you could meet me at such short notice."

Richmond dipped his head in return and as he looked up again he swore that he had met Xarles somewhere before. His shoulder length blonde hair seemed somewhat out of place. His face was very familiar. It was smooth, as though it had been shaved recently. The most familiar thing was the man's voice. It seemed softer than he remembered, but it was still familiar.

"It is good to meet you Duke Xarles," Richmond replied, still trying to place where he knew that man.

"I thank you for coming here. We should go to my quarters and speak," Xarles motioned for him to follow.

It was his first words that made Richmond think and then it finally came to him. In Entero Charles was spelt with an X. Duke Xarles was Duke X. When it was said and done it was not a clever pseudonym. By the look on his face it gave away what he was thinking.

"There will be time for that later. For now we need some privacy," the Duke whispered as he spoke.

"Yes, of course," Richmond replied as they started walking.

Amilie followed them for a short while before Xarles told her to leave them. Richmond was a little more comfortable that he knew who Xarles was. All thoughts of a trap left his mind. He was very interested the hear what Xarles had to say to him. Neither of them spoke until they reached his quarters.

The Duke's quarters were smaller than Richmond expected. There was a bedroom and a small sitting room. It seemed as though the Duke had to use the communal bathing house whenever he wanted to wash up. It seemed strange, but there were more important matters to deal with.

"I have heard that you have had a meeting with Prince Leroy," Xarles started the conversation.

He moved to a small round table with a teapot sitting on top with two chairs around it. He poured two cups, without asking Richmond if he wanted one, before taking a seat. When he saw Richmond was still standing he offered him a seat and a drink.

"Sorry, my manners are a little on edge these days. Please, have a seat and some tea. It's about the only good thing in the palace these days." Xarles smiled as he did his best to make Richmond feel comfortable. "Now is it true that you have been to see the Prince?" he re-asked the question when Richmond was seated.

"That is correct." Richmond sipped his tea, trying to hide that fact that he didn't want to give away too much information.

"What is it that he told you?" Xarles seemed annoyed at having to ask.

Richmond slowly started to explain what Leroy had told him or the lack of information therein. The Duke listened intently nevertheless. He thought that there might be something underlying in his words. The threat of a surprise did not please him.

"Did he say what he had waiting?" Xarles asked.

"No. I pushed as hard as I dared, but he would not reveal anything to me. Tancred is going to see what information he can gather tonight."

At the mention of Tancred's name Xarles became very uncomfortable, but Richmond didn't notice the change in his demeanour. He continued to tell Xarles how good Tancred was at espionage. It wasn't until he stopped talking did he realise that something was wrong.

"What is it?" he asked when Xarles didn't speak.

"I have warned you already about your friend. He is not himself and should not be trusted. There is no telling what he will say to the Prince. He is not himself. He is an agent for evil. You are in more danger than you know. Have you told him anything about me?" Xarles warned.

Richmond silently cursed himself. In his rush to give Xarles information he had completely forgotten that Tancred was under the thrall of Argoz. In the end there was no way around it. He knew he shouldn't let Tancred speak with the Prince, but there was also nothing he could do to stop it. If he did then he would give away that they were not agents of evil and the Prince would know that they were trying to give false information.

"No. I told you that I would not mention you or the others and I will not. I do not think that he will betray me to the Dark Knight. He may be under the control of one of them, but he is still in there somewhere. I am sure that he will not betray me." He was trying to convince himself more than the Duke.

"You must get back to the army. The information that you have will be vital to the attack," Xarles didn't sound happy.

"I will go back to our rooms and make sure that he doesn't visit Leroy," Richmond turned to leave, but Xarles stopped him.

"I fear that you are already too late," Xarles replied. "Even if he is still in your rooms there is nothing you can do to change his mind. Unless you watch him all night he will leave as soon as you fall asleep."

"Then I will remain awake for the entire night," Richmond snapped.

Xarles shook his head. "You really don't understand what you are up against, do you?"

Richmond looked at him, but didn't know what to say. That was all the answer that Xarles needed to prove his point.

"I guess that now is as good a time as any." Xarles paused for a moment before he continued. "If Leroy wants Tancred to leave unnoticed then that is exactly what will happen. He will use magic to put you to sleep, or worse. I have no doubt that he would know that another Dark Knight has control of him. Tancred will be drawn to Leroy and there's nothing we can do to stop it."

Richmond nodded his head as Xarles spoke. He had not understood where the Duke was going with the conversation, but as soon as he heard the words he knew exactly what he was talking about. He quietly cursed himself for not realising himself. Sometimes it was good to be thought an idiot, but he didn't think that this was one of those times.

"You are right. Well I suppose there is nothing left to do I may as well go back to my room and wait for the inevitable," there was a touch of sarcasm to his voice.

"Don't despair too much. There is plenty for you to do. You just have to pick the right time to do it. You will know what I mean when the time comes," Xarles ignored the tone in his voice.

Richmond was starting to resent the way that the Duke was speaking to him. He knew more about the situation than Xarles gave him credit for. He didn't like being spoken to as if he was a child. He restrained himself from making any rude comments. There was no point in getting into an argument with the man. He didn't think that Xarles would see the point anyway.

"I will go back to my room now, unless there is something else you wish to tell me," his tone was almost daring Xarles to say something.

The Duke simply wished him a good evening and a safe trip back to the army. Richmond was a little disappointed that he didn't get a chance for a verbal fight. He was sure that he would have been able to win a battle of wits. Either way he was happy to be on his way back to his room. He wanted to speak to Tancred, but he knew that it would be counterproductive. He would have to let Tancred visit with the Prince and hope he didn't give away too much information.

***

Tancred walked through the empty corridors of the castle. It was not the first time he had done it, but that night he was travelling to a new location. He could almost feel the warmth of Amilie's touch as he thought about her, but not even that could distract him from his destination. He walked as though he was in a dream. He could feel his legs lifting, one after the other, but he had no control over them. He knew where he was heading and he knew that he had no choice. There was something calming in that thought, although he knew there shouldn't be.

He paused once he reached the door. His arm reached up, but his hand didn't touch the handle. It was as if it was his last chance for redemption. He knew that it was not the case and it was inevitable for him to open the door and enter the room. Even so he still paused, as if he had a choice.

"You may enter," a cold voice called from inside the room.

It was clear to him why he had been waiting. He was waiting for permission to enter the room. He didn't know why he needed permission as he was sure that it was Na'garoz himself who had summoned him. It was of no consequence. If he waited outside pondering the idea then he would be in even more trouble. He knew that Dark Knight's didn't like being left waiting so he opened the door and walked inside.

"I see you have come," Na'garoz spoke to Tancred after he shut the door. "I was not sure that it was you when we spoke earlier, but now I am."

Tancred could hear the words, but he could not comprehend them. He still felt as though he was in a dream. He didn't know what he was going to do. He couldn't think of an appropriate response, but then his lips started to move.

"Of course I was going to come. Did you think I would just leave you to be destroyed?" the words came out of Tancred's mouth, but they were not his own.

"Well, the thought did cross my mind." Na'garoz thought for a moment.

As Tancred looked at him he thought that the man standing before him was different to the one he spoke with earlier in the day. He couldn't pick the difference, but he knew that it was there.

"But now that you are here we can get down to business," there was nothing pleasant in Na'garoz's voice. "What is it that you have come here to speak to me about?"

"The army is on its way here." Tancred paused as the information sunk in. "It should be here in less than two weeks."

Na'garoz did not seem surprised at his statement, which upset Tancred, although he did not know why. He knew that the situation was not right, but he couldn't do anything to change it. He wanted nothing more than to turn and run, but his body would not move.

"So you have come here to warn me? That is very considerate of you," there was a suspicious tone in his voice.

"I do nothing for you," Argoz's voice spat the words. "I do what I do for the Great Lord."

"Very good, it seems as though you are being honest with me. Now we can continue," Na'garoz's voice didn't soften. "What is it that the army is planning?"

"It's hard to say. They are waiting for information from this one and his friend," the words coming from Tancred's mouth didn't even sound like him. His heart pounded when he realised what he had said. He had just given away their secrets and more than likely sentenced them to death.

"You must have some idea of what they are going to do," Na'garoz pushed him for information.

"They will attack. I know that much. There is nothing else about the approaching army that I can tell you except to be prepared," there was something else in his voice.

"You are holding something back." Na'garoz wasn't easily swayed.

"You are holding two prisoners, friends of the Cursed One?" Argoz asked.

"What of them," Na'garoz snarled, not overly happy at the insinuation.

"I believe that they will try to rescue them."

"Of course they will try to rescue them. You are slipping my brother. Your time amongst these mere creatures has softened your brain."

"Be careful who you insult brother. I may only be here in spirit, but soon enough I will be here in body as well. You don't want to make an enemy of me." Argoz did his best not to raise Tancred's voice.

"Keep yourself calm. These walls have ears."

"Is your grip on this Kingdom that frail?" Argoz sneered.

"There are traitors everywhere, you should know that. It is best if they don't hear what we are talking about."

The conversation was going nowhere and Argoz knew he would have to get Tancred back soon. They would need to be on their way back to the Alliance. He knew his brother would want to put them to death, but he still had a use for them.

"You should dispose of your prisoners now whilst you still can." Argoz returned the conversation. "That last thing you want to do is lose them back to the enemy."

"Don't you worry about them. If, on the off chance, they are able to breech my walls I'll have a little surprised waiting for them."

Argoz wasn't sure with his response, but in the end it wasn't his concern. If Na'garoz lost the two prisoners then the Great Lord would not be happy. That would only prove to help his own cause.

"What is it that you want?" Na'garoz was getting tired of the conversation and needed to bring it back to his favour.

"When you wipe out the Alliance I want to you to tell the Great Lord why you won." There was a sneer on Tancred's face.

"Okay," Na'garoz was a little quick to answer.

"You know that I will not accept your words. You know what I need." Tancred smirked.

Na'garoz produced a dagger from behind his belt. He looked at the blade for a moment before he drew it across his wrist. Slowly blood started to drip from the wound. A dozen drops hit the floor before the wound closed over. With the blood on the floor he passed the blade to Tancred who took the blade and looked at the blood on it. He looked at both side before licking one side before returning it to Na'garoz who promptly licked the other side before returning to his belt.

"There, that should be sufficient," Na'garoz almost growled his words as he kept the smile from his face. He would surely tell the Great Lord why he had won, but that didn't necessarily have anything to do with Argoz. The information that he provided had not been that useful and he doubted it was pertinent to his success.

"There is a traitor in your midst," Argoz added as he was about to leave.

"I know that. There are many traitors in the castle. You are going to have to do better than that," Na'garoz scoffed as he finished speaking.

"The Lady Amilie is still loyal to the Queen. She placates you so she can stay close."

Na'garoz started pacing as the information started to sink in. He had trusted Amilie with more than one secret. Now he didn't know what to think. "What about the other one?"

"He is an enemy. He doesn't know who I am though," Argoz was sure of that.

After another moment of introspectiveness Na'garoz spoke again. "I will have him taken to the dungeons. I will find out exactly what he knows. He will pay for her treachery. I will have him killed. I don't think he will have any information worth keeping him alive for," Na'garoz's was starting to go red in the face with rage.

"I don't think that you should be so rash. If you kill Richmond then this one will know that you know who they are. If that is the case then he might guess that he is my slave. If that is the case then he will report back to the army and everything will be for nothing," Argoz spoke carefully.

Na'garoz had to think again. His rage was starting to dissipate. He knew that his brother's words were correct. As much as he wanted the hang Richmond from the main gate as a warning to all other spies it would prove nothing. He could, however, still have Amilie tortured. That will be very enjoyable. He almost started drooling as he thought about it.

"Okay, I will let him live, but Amilie will be in the dungeons by dawn," he licked his lips.

Argoz repressed the urge to shake his head. He knew if he did he would upset Na'garoz. Normally he wouldn't mind, but he was too close to risk losing his advantage.

"We need her free until after we leave the castle. She can get us in and out unnoticed,"

"I can get you in and out of the city," Na'garoz argued.

"I know you can, but don't you think that Richmond will find it strange if we just wander out of the city." He wished that he didn't have to explain everything to his brother. "Don't do anything for two days. Once I have left the city you are free to do whatever you want." There was something inside of Tancred that was crying out. Fortunately the sound did not make the surface. All he could do was listen and cringe. "Now I think that I should return to my room. This body requires sleep."

"I think we are done here," Na'garoz was still thinking about torturing Amilie.

Tancred didn't need an excuse to leave. Even though Argoz was still leading the body he was starting to relinquish control. Since he had finished with his brother he didn't need the body anymore. He needed to return to his own body. There was more work he needed to do before the army reached Jarrat.

Tancred suddenly regained control as he was walking back towards his room. He didn't really know why he was walking through the corridors. The last thing he could remember was returning to their rooms after meeting with Prince Leroy. There was a strange feeling of dread that almost overwhelmed him. It was almost enough to knock him to his knees and make him break down and cry. The feeling stayed with him until he finally fell asleep.

Chapter 20: Escape from Jarrat

Tancred woke in the morning and felt as though he had not slept at all. There was a fog over his mind that he couldn't shake. For the life of him he couldn't remember what had happened the night before. He had a bad feeling he had done something wrong. The thought was thick in mind as he rose from his bed.

He found Richmond and Amilie waiting for him in the main room to their apartment. The sun was shining through the window, although it had only just risen. He could feel the tension as he walked into the room. He looked at them both suspiciously before taking a seat.

A platter of food sat on the table in front of them of scrambled eggs, crispy bacon and warm toasted bread. The smell should have been enough to increase Tancred's appetite, but he couldn't think of eating. There was a pain in his stomach and he didn't think food would help. It looked as though the other two didn't have the same problem. They had already cleaned their plates.

"What were you talking about?" he asked when no one spoke.

"Nothing exciting," Richmond replied before Amilie had a chance to speak. "More to the point, what did you find out last night?"

Tancred suddenly grasped his head as a great pain ripped through it. The feeling only lasted a moment before he returned to normal. "Nothing exciting," was all he could say. He was sure that something had happened. He knew that he had left the room, but that was it. The most frustrating part was that he knew it was important. He strained to try and remember, but nothing came to him.

"Nothing happened!" It was all Richmond could do to stop himself from yelling. "You risk everything and come back with nothing. I find it hard to believe that you could be gone for half the night and have no information for us."

Tancred couldn't look at the other two. His head was sore and he was missing his memories from the previous night. He knew they were inside somewhere, but he just couldn't find them. Whenever he thought they were close they would disappear again. The feeling was enough to make him cry out in frustration. The sudden noise worried the other two.

"I think we should get moving," Amilie's said. "It is early in the morning and there won't be too many people about. The longer we wait the more chance we have of being caught."

Although Richmond wanted to stay and get answers out of Tancred he knew she was right. It was more important that they get what little information they had back to the Alliance. It would not be long before they were in position to attack and they needed to know the situation in order to make a plan.

"Let's get moving," Richmond added.

As much as Tancred didn't want to rise he was happy to be on the move. Once they left the room there was no chance for discussion. The chance of someone hearing them talk would be all the deterrence they needed. He hoped by the time they were out of the castle he could remember what had happened. The feeling was infuriating.

Amilie led them out of their apartments. Richmond let Tancred walk in front of him to keep an eye on him. Something had happened the night before, he knew that and he didn't trust him. Tancred was under the spell of a Dark Knight and that in itself was a worrying sign. He wasn't sure what he was going to do. Until Tancred was able to confide in him there was nothing he could do. He definitely couldn't speak to him about anything important.

The corridors were nearly empty. A few servants rushed around, getting things ready for the morning meal. Besides them there was no one else around. It was much better for them that way. The word of the strange visitors and their meeting with Queen Oriana and Prince Leroy was all over the castle. Anyone of any standing would want to speak with them. Just to be seen with the strangers would increase someone's standing in the castle, if only for a short time. They needed to leave the castle unnoticed. It made life easier for everyone concerned.

Richmond concentrated on where they were going. If he was going to sneak back into the castle, which he had a feeling he was going to, then he would need to know his way around. He knew where the dungeons were so all he had to do was to work out how to get to the apartments and more importantly how to get to the secret entrance in the castle wall.

The courtyard outside the main castle doors were still patrolled by many guards. Luckily the soldier didn't take any notice of them. The soldiers knew better than to get in the way of the nobles left in the castle. The Prince didn't suffer anyone being accosted by the guards. More than one had been sent to dungeons for such an act. It was well known that if someone was in the castle grounds then they were meant to be there and didn't need to be questioned.

Without a second thought Amilie led them away from the castle towards the stables. Richmond felt very self-conscious as he walked through the courtyard despite the fact that the soldiers were making a point not to look at them. Although no one was taking any notice he felt as though there were a hundred eyes locked on him. He was glad once when they were inside again.

There was no one in the stables as they made their way to the stall with the secret trapdoor. Even though there was no one around Amilie had to check every stall in turn. The last thing she wanted was to be half way down the trapdoor and someone poke their head over a stall gate and see them. When she was satisfied there was no one in the stables she lifted the trapdoor and ushered the other two inside.

Once they were underneath the stables Richmond was about to speak, but Amilie motioned for him to be quiet. She gave no reason but continued towards the tunnel door. She produced a key and unlocked the door which was bolted shut on the other side. With a little effort the key turned and the bolt slid open.

Richmond shuddered as she pushed the door open. He could see the darkness down the tunnel and he remembered the last time he walked down it. He did not like the thought of going back into the tunnel with the walls and roof so close to him. The thought of it made him start to sweat.

"Quickly, inside and remember to be as quiet as possible," she whispered.

Tancred was the first to plunge into the darkness. Richmond took a deep breath before stepping into the tunnel. Once Amilie had entered she shut the door behind her and returned to bolt to its place. Richmond felt the walls close in as the darkness encased him. He felt Amilie's hand on his back giving him a gentle push forward. There was something comforting about her touch, which stopped as soon as he started moving. He was about to stop again, but the thought of staying longer in the tunnel did not appeal to him.

Richmond moved along as quickly as he could in the dark without falling over or running into Tancred. He knew that Tancred was somewhere in front of him, but he did not know how far. He took a deep breath as he steadied his pace. All he wanted to do was get back into the light. The darkness was suffocating him.

It did not take them long to reach the end of the tunnel. Tancred led the way out into the open air. The forest outside the castle walls was almost as dark the tunnel itself. Since they had entered the stables clouds had moved across the sun. The thick tree cover added to the darkness. Richmond was somewhat unhappy with their gloomy surroundings, but he had more important things to worry about than the weather. He looked around for any points of reference that would help him return. The only thing he could see that would be of any help was the marks he left on the wall and even they would be hard to find again.

Once Amilie had joined them outside he stopped what he was doing. He didn't want her to know that he was trying to remember the secret entrance. She didn't seem to take any notice of him when she rose from the tunnel and he looked through the undergrowth for the small bag that held her rags. It only took her a few minutes to make the change from Lady Amilie to the street whore. Tancred couldn't help but think that she was still beautiful. Richmond, on the other hand, thought that it was a more appropriate appearance.

"Come on, ya two," she spoke with the same drawl as when they first met her. "We gots to get ya into the city," she had a broad smile on her face as she spoke.

Richmond gave Tancred a look before following after her. Tancred shook his head and smiled before continuing himself. He didn't understand why Richmond didn't like Amilie. She had a good heart and had helped them more than she should have. He would have to have words with Richmond once they were alone. When they returned to the city he would have to treat her with more respect.

They walked in silence along the edge of the castle wall. They were not worried about being overheard they just didn't have anything to say. Tancred wanted to speak with Amilie, but he didn't want to do so in front of Richmond. He didn't know if or when he would have the chance to again, but with Richmond in earshot he felt self-conscious. He didn't want his friend to know of the relationship they were having. Although it had only been a couple of nights he felt as though there was a real connection between the two. He had no idea where his journey would lead him after they had liberated Jarrat, but he was hoping she could come with him.

Richmond had been able to relax whilst they walked with the protection of the trees to hide them. It wasn't long before Amilie moved them away from the castle wall and any chance of being seen by the guards. Once they were back on the highway and out in the open his tension returned. There was no one else on the road and the soldiers on the castle walls didn't seem to pay them any attention. Again Richmond couldn't help but feel that someone was watching them. The tension increased the closer they came to North-Western gate.

"Well, what do we have here?" Captain Beldon asked as the group approached. "You have been gone for a quite a while. I think you should tell me what you have been up to," it was clear that the Captain-of-the-Guard recognised the two men with Emilie.

"I know that you are a deviant, but this is too much, even for you," her voice was slurred with a cheeky tone to it. "If you want me to tell you tales that will cost you a silver mark," she added.

Beldon thought about slapping her across the face, but he could not with the two men as witness. He didn't know what the relationship was with the three and Prince Leroy, but he didn't dare risk enraging him. He had only gotten to the position he was in because his predecessor did something to upset the Prince. He didn't know the full story, but by the rumours he had heard he wasn't sure if he wanted to know the truth. The last thing he wanted to do was end up in the castle dungeons.

"Move along," he decided that it wasn't worth the argument or risk to his life. He might lose a little face with his men, but he would keep his head on his shoulders. "If you stand there any longer I will have you arrested," it was an empty threat.

Emilie thought about giving him a snide comment, but in the end she thought better of it. His last command might be to have her executed. As much as she believed that the Prince would not allow it he may not hear about it in time. That was not a risk she was willing to take. Instead she ushered the two men through the gate and hurried after them.

Once they were out of view of the guards Emilie stopped them. She looked around nervously and when she was sure that no one was around she spoke in a whisper.

"This is as far as we go together," she looked at Tancred as she spoke. "You will have to find your own way out of the city. I cannot help you get out of the Eastern Gate. They do not know me over there," she wanted to say more, but not in front of Richmond. She wished that he would leave, but she could not ask him.

"Thank you for all of your help," Tancred spoke before Richmond had a chance to say anything. "I will not forget what you have done for us. Be assured that we will be back soon and then everything will be all right," he didn't completely believe his words, but he thought that they would ease her suffering.

"Now go. I don't think it would be good if we are seen talking together. I am just a lowly street whore after all," she winked at Tancred again before turning away and disappearing into the city.

Tancred looked at Richmond and waited for him to speak. He had his own ideas of what they should do next, but he wanted to hear what Richmond had in mind. Things were becoming tense between the two and he wasn't sure why. It was as if his Lord didn't trust him anymore. He had no idea what he had done to upset him. Even if he knew he had snuck out to see Amilie in the middle of the night that couldn't be enough to put him out of favour.

"We should head back to the inn. Hopefully the innkeeper hasn't already sold our possessions," was all that Richmond said. If he had a plan he was not going to reveal it.

They both set off together. It took them a moment to find their bearings, but once they knew where they were going it didn't take them long to return to the inn. It was mid-morning when they reached to the Royal Watchman. Richmond would have liked to spend some time, alone, in his room, but that was not going to happen. Since they had all the information that they needed, or at least all they were going to get, there was no reason for them the stay. They would have to leave the city as soon as possible.

They were met as they walked through the door, by the innkeeper. Gage looked surprised as he saw the two men enter. When he heard they were heading into the castle he didn't like their chances of returning. When there was no sign of them for two days had had assumed they would not return. He stood there, staring for a moment before he regained his senses.

"It is good to see you two again," he paused as he thought about what he was going to say next. "I was so worried that something had happened to you when you didn't return," he looked around nervously. "I will have your room ready shortly if you would care to have something to eat while you wait?"

"I think we would just like to get going," Richmond wasn't in the mood for small talk. "I think that we have already spent too much time in Jarrat," he was deliberately trying to be as rude as possible. Some of it was to play the part of nobility, but most of it was to make himself feel better.

"Ah, I see," there was obviously something wrong as Gage struggled to find his words. "I'm afraid the Prince isn't as accommodating as you might think. If it is amnesty you are after then I'm sure someone in the city could look after you. I don't think you needed to be running off so quickly." Gage was desperately trying to get another day or two out of the pair. "The forest surrounding Jarrat is no safe place these days. I have heard stories of children being taken by all sorts of nasty creatures. The roads to Remidel or Lel Dinion would not be safe for you."

Richmond sighed. He had tried to get away without any further delay, but that didn't seem like it was going to happen. He would have to leave it for Tancred to try and explain where they were going.

"Now that I think on it I will have something to eat before we leave. Tancred see that the good innkeeper is paid and have our horses saddled and read to leave once I have eaten." Richmond dismissed them both with a wave of his hand. The conversation was going nowhere and he wasn't it the mood for futility. Tancred had been happy to deal with the innkeeper in the past and could do so again.

"I'm sorry for my Lord. He has been in a foul mood ever since we left the castle. It seemed he didn't believe us when we told him the Prince wouldn't allow sanctuary for anyone," Tancred didn't his best to cover for Richmond. The last thing he wanted to do was to make small talk with Gage, but in the end it was his job. He would need to leave a convincing lie that Gage could spread amongst the other innkeepers.

"That is certainly alright. I understand. I am surprised that you were able to get into the castle in the first place. You'll have to tell me your secret."

Although it was a throwaway comment, but there was something in the way he was looking at Tancred that pressed for a response. He couldn't tell the innkeeper the truth. Amilie's safety was paramount and once Gage knew it wouldn't be long before the rest of the city knew. On the other hand a lie could be just as dangerous. If Gage told the wrong people the wrong thing he could end up dead and that was something Tancred didn't want that on his conscience.

"That is a story for another time," Tancred brushed it aside as best he could. "My Lord will be keen to leave as soon as he's finished eating and I wouldn't mind filling my stomach myself."

"Of course. It'll be a long ride to... where is it you will be heading next?" Gage hid his questions in idle banter. Tancred had to admit he was impressed.

"I think his Lordship is planning to ride back home to Bellarome." There was little point in lying. Someone would see them leave to the east. "What you said was right. It will be too dangerous riding towards one of the other capitals."

"But what of the Alliance?" Gage pushed.

"We'll just have to see what happens. I feel that Lord Richmond will surrender Bellarome when the army arrives. There is no way we can survive against a siege. I'm afraid there is little option."

"Surely there has to be another way."

Gage was starting to get on his nerves. He was openly pushing for more information and that was not a good thing. It would only be a matter of time before he slipped up. There was a lot on his mind and he didn't want to get distracted.

"If you could have our possessions taken to our horses and have them prepared for us to leave that would be greatly appreciated," Tancred changed the subject abruptly.

"Of course." Gage paused for a moment. When Tancred didn't realise what he was getting at he continued. "If you would be so kind as to settle your account?"

"Ah, yes." Tancred pulled out his coin pouch. He made a sign of weighing it in his hand before tossing it towards the innkeeper. "That should be enough, plus some for supplies for our journey home."

Gage wasn't about to trust him without counting the coins himself. His friendliness would only go so far. Tancred couldn't begrudge him that, but the time delay was frustrating. If the innkeeper wasn't satisfied with the payment there was little he could do about it. There were no more coins to make up any shortfall.

"It seems a bit light, but I guess since you didn't stay in your room the last couple of nights I can let it slip," Gage wasn't going to show any appreciation, even though there was more than enough to cover their expenses. "Your horses will be ready shortly. If you would like to join your Lord I will have another plate of food brought out for you."

It seemed that there would be no more pleasantries now that their transaction had been completed. Tancred was a little annoyed, but there was not time. He wanted to eat before they left and it wouldn't be long before the horses were saddled and ready to leave.

Tancred met Richmond in the common room. He was already half way through his meal when Tancred sat down. It was obvious that Richmond was keen to ask a question, but his mouth was full of food. Tancred thought about taking the opportunity to escape what was going to be an uncomfortable conversation.

"Did the innkeeper have any last minute information for you?" Richmond sounded strangely pleasant. It was not at all what Tancred was expecting,

"Unfortunately not," Tancred started as his meal arrived. "He was more interested in what we've been doing, that and getting paid. When our transaction was complete he didn't seem to have time for conversation. In fact if I didn't know better I would have thought he was in a hurry to get rid of us."

"I can certainly understand. It's not like we've been model patrons."

Tancred smiled and shook his head. He had to admit that he was starting to enjoy himself. He had missed spending time with his old friend around a good meal. For an instant he almost forgot the dire situation they were in. They wouldn't be truly safe until they returned to the army and even then it would only be for a short period of time.

"What should we do whilst we wait for the innkeeper to return?" Richmond asked when they had finished eating.

"I don't think that Gage will be much longer, but I wouldn't mind an ale before we leave," Tancred suggested.

"That is best idea I have heard in a long time," Richmond had to agree. It would be a long time before they could sit in an inn and drink. There was no guarantee that they would even be able to do it again.

When the serving woman returned Tancred made it seem as though their inconvenience would be less if they had something cool to drink. He also had to hint at the ale to make sure they didn't receive something non-alcoholic.

"What do you think is taking so long?" Richmond asked when they finished their first ale.

"I have a sneaking suspicion the innkeeper didn't think we were going to return." Tancred paused and let the thought sink in. "I think he might have started to sell our possessions. I'm sure he's out chasing everything that he managed to get rid of."

Richmond had to laugh. There wasn't much in the way of value in their packs, but obviously there were some things he had been able to sell. He hoped it wouldn't take too long as they needed to be on road.

They had finished two ales and were about to order another when the innkeeper returned. He was puffing and there was sweat on his face. He tried his best not to look flustered, but he failed miserably. Both Tancred and Richmond had to contain their laughter. If they gave away the fact that they knew what Gage had been doing then there was a chance that he would expect them to pay. They wouldn't pay either way, but it was easier if they didn't start a fight.

"Your horses are loaded and ready for you to leave," he struggle to speak without panting.

"Thank you," Tancred spoke whilst Richmond played the part of a disgruntled nobleman. "I will make sure that I tell everyone of your hospitality," Tancred hoped if he ignored the delay then Gage wouldn't feel the need to explain.

It seemed as though Gage was just as happy to let the delay slip by unnoticed. He had managed to get back most of their possessions. There were a few items of clothes that had already been sold, but they were not important. All he wanted to do was to get them away. The further away they were when they realised the less chance that they would return.

"You are too kind. Let me show you to your horses." Gage ushered them out of the common room.

It was almost rude the way he showed them out of the inn. If it had been normal circumstances then Richmond would have said something, but he was just as keen to get out of the inn as Gage was to be rid of them. In the end it worked out well for everyone.

They found their horses waiting for them at the front of the inn. Richmond didn't wait to mount his horse and Tancred gave Gage a slight nod of the head before he mounted his. The innkeeper quickly disappeared back inside once they were both mounted. He didn't want to give them another opportunity to catch him out.

"How are we going to get out of the city?" Tancred asked Richmond as they rode through the streets towards the Eastern gate.

"I had hoped that you might have some ideas on the matter," Richmond had thought about their escape, but had not come up with any solutions. "I think that we will just have to wing it when we get there. We had no problems getting in through the Eastern Gate, so let's hope it's the same on the way out."

Neither man liked to idea, but there was nothing else they could do. They could only hope that it was not going to be as difficult as the North-Western gate had been. They both became nervous as they approached the gate. There were a number of guards milling around and they became more attentive when they realised that the two men were approaching.

"Halt!" one guard spoke when they arrived at the gate. "No one is allowed through the gates."

"We wish to leave the city. We are not residents of Jarrat. We are from Darshival and wish to return home," Tancred hoped that it would work, although he never really believed that it would. It was more a starting point than anything else.

"I don't really care where you are from. No is allowed out of the city, so no one can exit the city." The guard looked around to make sure that the other guards were there to support him.

"I am Lord Richmond of Bellarome. If you do not let me through you will create an inter-kingdom incident. I do not think that Queen Oriana will appreciate you for forcing her into war," his voice was firm, but it did not have the desired result.

"That is all well and good, but it is Prince Leroy who calls the shots now and he says that no one can leave the city." The guard would not be dissuaded.

Suddenly a feeling came over Tancred. At first it was like an itch in the back of his mind. As it continued it soon became a compulsion. He had a feeling that there was something in his coat pocket. Eventually he couldn't control himself. The feeling was overwhelming. He knew that Richmond was pleading their case with the guard, but he had no idea what they were saying. As he reached into his pocket he felt a soft sheet of folded paper. He could not for the life of him remember putting it there. It was at that moment that the guard realised what he was doing.

"What have you got in your pocket?" The guard had drawn his sword as a precaution, just in case he was going for a weapon.

"What?" Tancred was suddenly broken from his reverie. "This? Nothing," he pulled the piece of paper out of his pocket as he spoke.

"Let's have a look at it."

Tancred didn't want to hand it over, especially since he had no idea what was written on it, but he had no choice. His arm reached out and he passed the guard the note. When his arm returned the intense feeling disappeared.

The guard had a smug look on his face as he took a couple of steps backward and opened the folded piece of paper. As he read down the page there was subtle change to his demeanour. The smugness was quickly gone from his face. As he came to the bottom of the page his hand started to shake. Fear was clearly written across his face.

Richmond gave Tancred a questioning look who in turn shrugged his shoulders. Tancred had no idea where the letter came from let along what was written in it. The only thing he knew was that it was having a desired affect. He dared to hope that they were going to be let out.

"I am sorry, sir," there was a quiver to his voice. "It seems that I have been mistaken. You two are free to leave whenever you want," he stepped out of their way as he spoke.

Again Richmond looked at Tancred and again he shrugged his shoulders. There was nothing else he could do but to kick his horse forward. The guards watched in awe as they passed through the gate. No one, except for the one guard, knew what was in the letter. Once he had finished reading it the guard, much to everyone's surprise, ate it.

"What was in that letter?" Richmond asked when they were away from the gate.

"I don't know." Tancred looked back over his shoulder to see what was happening back at the gate.

The other guards had converged on the one guard to find out what was in the letter. Even from a distance it was obvious that the guard was not revealing any information. Tancred had to wonder to himself what was in the letter and why it had such an effect on the guard. He felt as though he should know the answer. It was part of his memory block from the night before. He knocked the side of his head as if that was going to help, but nothing happened.

"I think that we should get moving. The army will be reaching the edge of the forest any day now," Tancred didn't wait for Richmond to answer. He kicked his horse into a trot. It was going to be a long ride.

Chapter 21: Returned

It was early in the morning when Richmond and Tancred rejoined the Alliance. The army had made camp the night before just outside the forest. One of the night scouts had brought word that they had seen Richmond and Tancred's campsite. The men were asleep at the time and the scout had decided that it would be better if they rested. The command group had decided that it was better to wait for them to arrive before entering the forest. Once they were inside the forest it would be difficult to keep track of the army. They needed to have a solid plan before they moved any further and the only way they were going to do that was to get information from Richmond and Tancred.

There was a buzz throughout the entire camp when they arrived. Word quickly spread once they reached the army. The march from Kiarome had been long and uneventful. They had expected, or more so hoped for, a number of small skirmishes. The arrival of Tancred and Richmond was the first change since they had left Kiarome and they brought a feeling of hope with them. The army had a new sense of purpose.

Even the command group had become despondent as the march continued. Their malaise had nothing to do with the lack of action like the other soldiers, but more impending battle that weighed heavily on their minds. Without the information from Richmond and Tancred they doubted they would be able to win, or at the very least they would lose more men than they should. When they reached the forest they thought the chance of the two men returning was getting less and less. They had decided that they would wait for a full day before heading into the forest. Luckily they didn't have to wait that long.

Tancred and Richmond had ridden hard since they left the city, partly because they wanted to get the information back to the army and partly because they wanted to be away from Jarrat. There was no telling what would happen if they ran into soldiers along the way. Tancred checked his pockets and there were no more mysterious pieces of paper to save them. When the other elven scout greeted them in the morning they were more than relieved. They knew that the army would be close to the edge of the forest.

Once they were back with the army they felt the same excitement that the soldiers did. Finally their hard work was going to come to fruition. Relief and nervousness mixed with the excitement. The information that they gained was not great and they could only hope that it was enough to help them win.

Despite everyone's eagerness for the meeting the command group allowed them to bathe. They had ridden hard and only stopped to eat and sleep. They had all decided that it would be a much more pleasant meeting if they washed the grime away first. There was limited water for bathing, but they all agreed it was well worth it.

The command group was already assembled when Richmond and Tancred arrived, freshly cleaned and dressed in finery suitable to their position. They would have to change once they were on the move again, but they were both happy to be out of their riding clothes. Everyone was on the edge of their seats as they entered the tent.

"It is good to see you again," Bern stood and spoke. "Please be seated."

There was a lavish breakfast spread out on the table before them. They had been on tight rations since they left Kiarome and everyone had decided that the news would be better served on a full stomach. No one had touched the it as they were waiting for the guests-of-honour to arrive. The food in front of them was very tempting, but they all had to resist.

"Thank you," Richmond's voice was weak.

They were both tired from their journey. They had also been on slim rations and the sight of the food before them was almost overwhelming. They both filled their plates before starting to eat. As much as everyone was dying to hear what had happened they were just as happy to be eating. It was mid-morning and they were all hungry.

Richmond started explaining what they had learnt inside the city. Everyone listened intently as he recalled the information. He left out the part about Duke X and his small group of insurgents. He was also very careful about what he said about their time inside the castle. He knew that Aimon was the Dark Knight Argoz and didn't want to give too much away. When he was finished a quiet came over the group.

Once the information had time to rest Tancred started his tale. He had different information that he had picked up by speaking with Gage. The private conversations he had with Coyne and Prince Leroy he kept to himself. It wasn't that he wanted to keep them secret it was that he couldn't remember them.

"So now we have to decide what we are going to do?" Bern spoke when they had finished.

The statement was met with silence. Although the information was useful there wasn't a great deal they could do about it. The most disturbing part was the surprise that the Prince had in store for them. It would have been great if they had more information. Instead they would have to proceed and hope they weren't marching into a trap.

"Is seems as though we have to get into the castle and kill this Prince Leroy," Sorrell suggested.

"That will not be easy," Hadar added. "There will not be a chance for a siege."

"What do you mean?" Bern asked.

"There might be plenty of wood to build the siege engines, but there is no ammunition. Besieging the castle is not going to be an option," Hadar explained.

"Then what are we going to do?" Bern didn't sound like the great General of the Alliance.

"The gates are strong, but I think that we could break them with a battering ram," Jarwe suggested. He had only visited the city once many years ago, but he remembered the castle quite clearly.

"There is no shortage of trees," Richmond added.

"I would much prefer to come up with another idea of getting into the castle," Bern looked as though he was thinking intently as he spoke. "To walk up to the gate with a big tree would be fatal to a lot of soldiers. We would lose a lot more than we would gain. Not to mention we leave ourselves open to attack from the city and whatever this 'surprise' is that the Dark Knight has waiting for us."

"That is true, but I can't see there being another option," Jarwe continued.

The discussion continued for the next hour. Ideas were passed around, but no one came up with a better one than the battering ram. In the end they decided that it would be their main plan of attack, at least until someone came up with a better option. They would have continued to debate the matter, but they had to keep moving. The army was excited, but that would only last for so long. If they remained where they were then the army would become restless again and that would only start trouble.

Bern really wanted to have some time alone with Richmond and Tancred, but that would look too suspicious. As he watched them during the meeting he knew there was something they were keeping to themselves. There was something different about Tancred. It was as if he was holding back, but not by choice. He knew that they wouldn't reveal anything pertinent in front of Aimon, but that wasn't the reason.

When the meeting finally came to an end Bern thought about asking them to remain, but too much time had passed. It was past midday and the army needed to be on the move. There would be little chance for conversation on the road so Bern would have to wait for another opportunity.

Slowly the army started moving into the forest. The journey would be a lot slower until they reached the city. The wagons had to travel around to the highway as the denseness of the trees made it impossible for them to move with the rest of the army. It also meant the army itself had to travel close to the highway to receive their supplies at the end of the day, it also decreased their chance of a surprise attack.

The command group gathered again at the end of the day for the evening meal. They had found a clearing just before dusk that would be suitable for their tent. The rest of the army marched until nightfall. It was the only way they could make up the time they would lose marching through the forest.

They discussed further plans for the attack, but again came up with no new ideas. In the end the meeting became rather heated. The tension was getting to everyone. It would not be long before they reached their destination and if they didn't come up with a better idea then a lot of soldiers would needlessly lose their lives. That thought weighed heavily on everyone, but no more than it did on Bern.

Finally Bern called for the tent to be emptied. They were getting nowhere and he worried that it would not be long before weapons were drawn. The sound of their voices travelled outside of the tent and the last thing they needed was for the rest of the army to find out about the dissention in the command. Their spirits were still high, but they would start getting nervous the closer they came to the city. If they knew about the problems in the command then their moral would drop considerably, some would even use the cover of the trees to desert.

Richmond lingered behind as everyone left. The others were so self-obsessed that they didn't realise. Bern could have hugged him, but that would have been totally inappropriate. He looked around for Tancred, but he had already left. It seemed a little odd, but Richmond didn't seem to care.

"Things are starting to fall apart. It is a sign that the Evil One is winning," Bern said, he didn't look at Richmond as he spoke.

"It's worse than you think," Richmond's words sent a chill down Bern's spine.

As the days had past the entity that had invaded his body was starting to merge with his own personality. He could remember things that he had no right to. The memories didn't make a lot of sense to him and he knew they were not his own. On the plus side he was more confident as the leader of the army. The entity provided him with the military background that he would otherwise not know. It still didn't make him feel comfortable, but it was better than not knowing anything.

"What do you mean?" Richmond had Bern's full attention.

"It is as you feared. Aimon is the Dark Knight Argoz," Richmond paused and let the information sink in. "That is not the worst of it. Tancred is under his control. I don't know exactly how it works, but I don't think it happens all the time. I believe that my friend is still in there somewhere, it's hard to explain. The point is that I think that he has given information to the Dark Knight who calls himself Prince Leroy. If I am right then he knows that we are on the way."

"That is indeed terrible news," Bern stopped in mid sentence. Richmond thought he saw a change come over him, but he was not sure. "It sounds as though Argoz has placed a mind trap on your friend. It is a simple enough trick, but very effective. He can control Tancred from wherever he is in the Seven Kingdom, although the further away the harder it is. He can see what Tancred sees, hear what Tancred hears, but most importantly he knows what Tancred knows. It seems that I was a little hasty when I asked you to spy on Aimon." Richmond didn't think that it was Bern any more. He had heard stories about a mysterious entity, but he doubted their validity. It seemed as though he was wrong. "It is not ideal, but all is not lost. There was only ever a slim chance that we would arrive unnoticed." Bern paused to think. "Now that we know what we are up against we can use this to our advantage."

"Do you think Argoz will be in contact with Prince Leroy again?" Richmond was starting to lose the conversation. Bern was talking about something that he didn't understand.

"No. I do not believe that he has control of anyone in Jarrat. What I mean is that I should be able to get the information from Tancred's mind. As much as he won't be able to remember what he did when Argoz was in control it will all be stored in his subconscious. All I have to do is unlock it," Bern still looked as though he was deep in thought as he spoke.

"How will you do that?" Richmond was completely lost.

"That is not important." Bern felt as though he had said too much. "Is there anything else from your mission that you would like to discuss with me?"

Richmond didn't want to be dismissed, but he felt that he shouldn't continue his questions. Bern needed to know about the Duke. He knew that it would be invaluable to their success.

"There is a small group of insurgents in the forest west of the city." Richmond went on to explain about Duke X and what he was doing.

"This is promising," Bern spoke when Richmond had finished. "We may not need to kill the innocent people of Jarrat after all."

"I wouldn't get your hopes up. The Prince has Queen Oriana enthralled. As much as they would not go to war for the Prince they would definitely go to war for the Queen. I think there will be a good number of soldiers waiting for us once we reach Jarrat."

"So it seems as though we will have to do battle," the hope that had entered Bern's voice was gone again. "If only there was another way into the castle. If we could kill the Dark Knight then this war would be over, just like Kiarome."

"There is another way into the castle," Richmond had thought hard about telling anyone about the hole in the wall. It was the only way into the city without being noticed and pivotal if they were going to get the prisoners out alive. "There is a hole in the Western wall of the city. It leads down into a tunnel that comes up at the back of the stables. It is only small, but it's unguarded."

Bern thought on the news. A glimmer of hope returned to his face. "This is indeed good news. Do you think we could slip the army into the tunnel?"

"It is possible, but I do not think that we would get many men through before we are found. Once the stables are full there is no other place for them to hide. If we are lucky we might be able to take the castle gates before they realise we are inside. With the gates open there should be no problems in taking the castle," Richmond explained.

"Good. I think it would be best if you check on Tancred now. I will think about what you have told me and hopefully I will be able to devise a plan," Bern dismissed Richmond.

Richmond wanted to ask more questions about the hold Argoz had on Tancred, but Bern had already risen from the table. He motioned for Richmond to do the same. There was nothing else for him to do, but what Bern told him. Begrudgingly he rose from the table and left the room.

Things had just become a lot more complicated, yet there was also a glimmer of hope. There was a chance they could save the lives of those Enteroites who believed that they were doing the Queen's bidding. Bern had a few days left to devise a plan, but he doubted it would be long enough.

***

When the meeting had broken Tancred made his way to Aimon's tent. He didn't know why, but he felt compelled to meet with the Dark Knight who was posing as the Captain from Entero. He didn't even know that Richmond had not left the command tent. All he knew was that he had to speak with Aimon.

Once he reached the tent he waited outside until Aimon called for him to enter. It seemed odd that he knew he was there even though he had not contacted him at all. The thought only stayed in his head for a moment before it disappeared.

"It is good to see that you have returned unharmed," Aimon greeted him warmly. "Now let's get down to business. What is it that you have found in Jarrat?"

Tancred knew that something was wrong. He knew that he shouldn't be divulging information, but there was nothing he could do. Even as the words started coming from his mouth he knew that he was making a mistake. His heart was filled with dread as he recalled his time in Jarrat. He tried to hold back information, but he was not strong enough. It was as if it was being pulled from his brain.

When Tancred finally finished he felt physically sick. It took all of his self-control to keep from retching. Aimon, on the other hand, had a big smile on his face. He knew that he had gained a wealth of knowledge. There did seem to be something that Tancred was holding back, but he didn't think that it was anything important. It was more something that he suspected. Aimon put the thought aside. He had everything that he needed and he had enough to destroy his brother. One way or another he would gain the upper hand.

"That is good. You have served me well. Now you can go and remember to keep your ears open. We are amongst the enemy and any information will helps us," Aimon spoke with a harsh voice.

"Yes, my lord," the words did not seem right.

Tancred rose and left the tent. It wasn't until he was over half way back to his own tent did he fully regain his consciousness. His head was ringing and he had no idea what he was doing out and about. The last thing he remembered was leaving the command tent. The next memory was walking through the mass of trees and tents back to his own. He knew that something important had happened, but he couldn't for the life of him remember what it was. He felt a lot happier when he was inside his tent. Nothing else could wrong, at least for that day.

The vanguard was on the move before first light. The second battalion to move started at dawn. The command group was on the move shortly afterwards. The forest made it impossible for the army to move together. If they did then they would soon start falling over each other. It was going to be a slow, painful march to the city.

The army started to stop about an hour before nightfall. It would be almost midnight by the time the entire army had managed to setup camp for the night. As per usual the first of the tents to be erected was the command tent. Even though the command group was scattered throughout the army during the day they would come together on dusk for their regular meeting.

There were no new suggestions on their impending battle. Bern did not bring up the secret entrance into the castle or any of the other information Richmond had given him the night before. He could neither speak candidly in front of Aimon nor Tancred. In the end it worked out rather well. As much as he wanted to discuss his idea with the others the longer the enemy thought they had no plan the better. There was no way that they could counteract their plans if they didn't know what they were.

Once the meeting was over they all left the tent. Bern had arranged with Richmond to bring Tancred back half an hour after everyone had left. He didn't want Aimon to know what they were up to. There was a wealth of information stored inside Tancred's head and he was keen to get it out. Bern himself wouldn't be able to gather the information, but with the aide of Heryion's spirit he would.

"Do you know why you are been brought here?" Bern's voice was sombre.

Tancred looked from Bern to Richmond and back again. There were serious looks on their faces. He really had no idea why he had been brought back into the command tent. He thought that he had covered everything the night before.

"No, but by the looks on your faces it is not good," Tancred replied slowly, trying in vain to gauge a reaction from their body language.

"Good. I think it would be better if we left it that way," Bern smiled.

"What is he talking about, Richmond?" Tancred was starting to sound worried. He trusted his old friend, but things had been very strange recently and he was beginning to doubt who he could trust.

"I think that you should tell him." Richmond looked at Bern.

Bern looked at the two men and thought. His shoulder's dropped for a moment as he came to a decision. "I suppose, but he cannot keep the information."

"What is going on?" Tancred's voice rose as he stood from his chair. "I'm not going to stay here unless you explain what is happening."

"Okay, okay, sit down and relax. There is nothing untoward happening here," Bern waited for Tancred to sit before he continued. "You have been put under a spell from Argoz, who you know as Aimon. I am sure that you have noticed by now that you have been missing pieces of your days. There is an explanation for that, but it is not really simple. At sometime Argoz placed a mind trap on you. Now most of the time you are in control of your body and mind, but when Argoz wants to he can take over. You will be slightly aware of what is going on around you, but you will retain no conscious memory of it. The most you will feel will be a feeling that you should be remembering something, but no matter how hard you try you won't be able to. Does that sound about right?"

"Yes, but what does it mean? Will I be in his thrall for the rest of my life?" Tancred continued to sound worried.

"If we don't do something to stop it then you will be in his control for as long as he wants. I doubt he would keep you forever, but the bad news is that Dark Knights are renowned for killing their puppets when they have finished with them," there was little humour in Bern's voice. "I guess they don't want the information to ever get out," he added as an afterthought.

"Then do it! Whatever you need to do, do it, get him out of my head," Tancred was starting to panic.

"I am afraid that I can't do that, not yet anyway," Bern knew that it would not go down well.

"What!?" both Tancred and Richmond cried out at the same time.

Bern knew they were going to react like that and had his excuse ready. He didn't know if they would accept his reasoning, but in the end they really did not have a choice. There was nothing they could do about it. The information and misinformation that Tancred could supply was invaluable. He would have to remain under the spell of Argoz at least until they reached Jarrat. Then Bern would consider calling on the power of the entity to try and remove Argoz's hold on him when the time was right. He only hoped that the entity would comply.

"I need the information that he had gathered for Argoz. I know that it is risky, but it is a risk that I am willing to take," Bern was emotionless in his explanation.

"I won't do it," Tancred stood and was about to leave, but Richmond blocked his path.

"Bern is right," Richmond spoke softly, hoping that he would not have to physically restrain his friend. "We need to keep Argoz believing that we don't know who he is and what he is doing. It is the only way he will continue to do what he does and in turn give us an insight into the enemy's plans."

Tancred couldn't argue. Deep down he knew that made sense, but he didn't like the thought of what was to come. He could vividly remember the feeling of complete helplessness when he was in Argoz's control. Leaving was not going to help matters. He needed Bern to help him. There was no one else who could reverse the spell.

"Okay. Do what you have to do," Tancred sighed.

"I need you to relax your mind. The mind block will try and stop what I am doing. If you do not relax then I will not be able to succeed. The longer this takes the more chance Argoz will find out what I'm doing," Bern's voice was deadly serious. "Now close your eyes."

Tancred did as he was told. He closed his eyes and tried to relax his mind as much as possible. It was not as easy as it sounded. Something was buzzing inside his head. It was as if whatever it was knew what Bern was going to do. Tancred, on the other hand, had no idea what to expect.

"Visit a safe place," Bern's voice was calm and monotone. "Somewhere from your childhood. Somewhere you were happy."

Tancred thought about the house that he grew up in. He could smell the fresh bread baking in the oven. His mother always made sure that there was fresh bread in the morning. Something wasn't right though. He couldn't put his finger on it. The more he focused on the inconsistency the further it got from him. His mother was calling him to the table for breakfast. The bread smelt so good. He wanted nothing more than to smear it with butter and honey. As he started to walk towards the table it started to move away from him. The situation didn't seem right, but he continued to walk anyway. No matter how far he walked he could not reach the table. He started to run, but as he did the table moved even further away. Although he knew that something was wrong he continued to move after the table.

"Now tell me who you are?" Bern kept his voice as monotone as possible.

"I am the vessel of Argoz the Great," Tancred's voice seemed different to Richmond.

Tancred's eyes were shut, but he seemed as though he could see the other two quite clearly. He looked from one to the other. The sight was very disturbing to Richmond. Bern, on the other hand, didn't seem to notice. He was more concerned about the questions he was asking.

"You recently journeyed to Jarrat. There you visited many contacts. Tell me who you spoke to and what you said," Bern's voice remained calm.

Tancred recalled his conversation with Coyne first. There was very little useful information from that conversation. Nevertheless Bern's attention did not leave him. Richmond was amazed at how patient he was being with Tancred. In truth it was all Bern could do to keep the spell going. If he interrupted Tancred then he would lose his control and that would be the end of it. Once the connection was gone there was no way to get it back without Argoz knowing what they were doing.

"Who else did you speak with?" Bern asked when Tancred finished speaking.

"I... I don't know. I don't think that I spoke with anyone else," Tancred's voice was strained.

Bern knew that he would have to be very careful once he reached his meeting with Prince Leroy. The information would be carefully stored inside his mind. Argoz, although he would not be expecting someone to pull the information from his memory, would not make it easy. There would certainly be traps set for any probing of Tancred's mind and if he was not careful then he would end up being caught.

"You went somewhere," Bern gently probed. "You went into the castle. You had another meeting," Bern was careful not to mention the man's name.

"I don't know. I feel as though there was something else, but I don't know," there was an obvious strain on Tancred's face as he tried to think.

"It is really important that you remember," Bern tried to push a little harder. "There is something there and you have to find it."

Sweat started to appear on Tancred's brow. The strain was getting worse. Richmond wasn't sure if Tancred could handle the pressure. He didn't know what would happen, but he knew that it wouldn't be good. Messing with a man's brain could have serious repercussions.

"Yes, there is something. Where is it? There it is? I met with someone. An old friend? No I don't think that we were friends. More of an acquaintance I think. I can't quite remember his name. I think he wanted to be called Leroy, but I know that is not his real name," Tancred stopped talking, as if that was all he could remember.

"His name is not important, but what you spoke about is. Do you remember what you spoke about?" Bern did his best to keep his voice level.

"Of course," there was a sudden change in Tancred's tone.

Slowly Tancred started to repeat his secret meeting with Prince Leroy. Richmond sat in shock as he listened to the words that came out of his friend's mouth. The worst was when he revealed the secret allegiances of Lady Amilie. He could only imagine what would happen to her. On the other hand he was pleased that he didn't reveal the secret entrance into the castle and some of their other secrets.

When Tancred finished his story his suddenly snapped out of his dreamlike state. His skin was flush and he looked as though he was going to faint. Richmond wasn't sure if he should help so he remained where he was. He would wait for Bern to say something before he would move again.

"Are you alright?" Bern asked, his voice had returned to normal.

"What just happened? I feel a little light headed," Tancred rubbed his head slowly.

"Nothing much. You just got here. I wanted to ask you if there was anything from Jarrat that you wanted to tell me. Just in case you forgot to mention it yesterday. You only just sat down when you stared to feel dizzy," Bern explained as he poured Tancred a mug of water.

Tancred continued to rub his head. The explanation didn't sound right. He felt as though he was missing something, but it only lasted for a moment. Once it was gone a feeling of calm came over him. The feeling that had plagued him for the last few days that he was forgetting something important had disappeared.

"No, I didn't miss anything yesterday. I don't think that there was anything important," Tancred replied.

"Very good, I just wanted to be sure," Bern called out to a serving man. Bern had to yell for the man to hear. "Tancred is not feeling the best. See that he makes it back to tent alright."

The man helped Tancred from his chair. Tancred had a question in his mind, but that soon disappeared. The thought of returning to his tent and retiring for the night was overwhelming. There was nothing more that he wanted to do.

Once Tancred was out of the tent Bern turned to Richmond. "This is disturbing news."

"I fear that Lady Amilie will be dead by now," Richmond replied.

"I can only hope," Bern didn't qualify his statement which upset Richmond.

"She risked everything to help us. How can you be so cavalier about her situation?" Richmond sounded offended.

"I know what a Dark Knight can do. Especially when they feel betrayed," the words echoed through Richmond's mind and haunted his sleep.

Chapter 22: Return to Jarrat

It took another five days for them to reach Jarrat. The army remained a good way back in the forest so as to not alert the city to their location. It was late in the day and there was no time to draw up plans to attack. Although the secret of surprise was no longer there they didn't want to announce their arrival. Only the command group rode to the edge of the forest to see what lay before them.

The city and castle looked rather peaceful. No one would have guessed that they were on the verge of a battle. The only sign was that the gates to the castle were locked shut, but the gates to the city were still wide open. If they wanted to they could march into the city and take it over night. On the other hand it could be a trap and that is one thing they didn't want to walk into. Bern knew that the Dark Knight had a surprise waiting and he couldn't rush into anything that would get people killed, regardless of which side they fought on.

The command group remained at the edge of the forest for the rest of the day and into the night. Throughout their entire stay they did not see anyone leave the city or the castle. The only people they saw were the soldiers guarding the castle walls. They couldn't see exactly, but from what they could, the soldiers didn't look as though they were expecting an attack.

Eventually the group retired back into the forest. Sentries were set up all around the forest. Not that they had seen anyone outside of the buildings, but if anyone was unfortunate enough to wander into the trees then they would be taken prisoner. They could not risk anyone knowing they were there. Bern couldn't give away any information that he had learned from Tancred and as far as the rest of the command group new their arrival had been in secret.

"What are we going to do?" Aimon asked when they returned to the command tent. "We need to be ready to strike at first light."

"The last thing we can do is rush into a battle that we know very little about," Jarwe almost spat at Aimon as he spoke.

Tensions had been rising over the days. The closer they came to the city the worse things became. Even with the information gathered no one had been able to come up with a decent plan.

"It seems as though the only way we are going to get into the castle is to break down the gate," Bern added.

The argument continued late into the night. Eventually the command disbanded. Although they had not decided on a plan of attack they needed to get some rest. The conversation was not getting anywhere and a good night sleep could be the solution to their problems. Only Bern and Richmond remained after everyone had left. It would not be long before the other commanders became suspicious of their meetings, but once they had started their attack on the castle it didn't matter who knew.

"What do you make of it?" Bern asked. He seemed to have more energy than Richmond had expected.

"There is something not right here," it was an obvious response. "We know for a fact that the Dark Knight knows that we are coming and yet he doesn't make any real attempt to defend himself. The question we need to ask is why he would want to invite us to attack?" They were finally getting somewhere. The only problem was that they couldn't speak amongst the rest of the command group.

"That is the key. It seems as though he wants to draw us out into the open." Bern was starting to follow Richmond's line of thinking.

"We know that he has a surprise planned for us. I can only imagine that it would be a secret army stashed somewhere in the forest. The scouts have yet to uncover anything, but I have a feeling that they are there," Richmond continued. "If Leroy knows of the secret passage into the castle then there is little chance of us attacking from there."

"That doesn't give us much option in rescuing Eldred and Alena. It sounded as though it was the best way to get into the city unnoticed. We really need to get them out before we start to attack," Bern sounded worried. "We can't risk the Dark Knight killing them once he is under siege."

"There is only one way that I can see this working. We have to strike at the same time," Richmond added.

"I don't understand, what do you mean?" Bern was starting sound tired.

"If Leroy knows of the secret passage then he will have soldiers posted there. If we start attacking the front of the castle then there is a good chance the soldiers will move away. If they don't believe we are striking from behind then there is no point wasting soldiers protecting the rear," Richmond continued to explain.

Bern thought for a moment as Richmond's words started to sink in. The solution was so simple he was somewhat embarrassed that he didn't think of it himself. A smile crossed his face.

"That will work out perfectly. We can get a small group together without letting Aimon know. As far as he is concerned we will be assaulting the front of the castle. We will sneak a small contingent of men in through the back to rescue Eldred and Alena," Bern explained his plan. "Once they are safe then we can destroy the Dark Knight."

Richmond liked what he was hearing, but then something crossed his mind. There was something that they were both missing and that could be the difference between winning and everyone dying.

"Once we get into the castle what happens if we run into Leroy. I saw what a Dark Knight is capable of when we were in Kiarome. If it wasn't for Alaric then we would all be dead," Richmond explained. He didn't want to be the bearer of bad news, but he thought that it would be better to bring it up sooner rather than later.

"That is a very good point. It is more than likely to be a suicide mission. We are damned if we do and damned if we don't," Bern didn't sound enthused.

"Would Eldred be able to defeat a Dark Knight?" Richmond asked as a though crossed his mind.

Bern had to think. Eldred was a powerful wizard, there was no doubt about that, but could he defeat a Dark Knight? "To be honest, I don't know. He would definitely stand a better chance than any of us. The only problem is that he may not have the strength to fight. Remember that the Dark Knight has him prisoner. There must be something stopping him from fighting his way out."

Richmond hadn't thought of that. It was obvious that if Eldred could defeat the Prince then he would have already. The hope of succeeding was starting to wane. If they could not beat the Dark Knight then there was little point in starting the battle. All they would end up doing was killing their allies as well as themselves. There had to be another way. Like Kiarome they needed victory without battle, but that was looking less likely by the minute. Richmond didn't think they could be as lucky twice in a row. Eventually the army was going to have to fight and it seemed that time was soon.

"We need Alaric," Bern mused, almost as if he was talking to himself.

That was the only answer. They needed Alaric. The only problem was they had no idea where he was or when he was likely to return.

***

Prince Leroy lay is his bed with the Queen sleeping gently beside him. The moon shone through the open window. Despite the dropping temperature the Dark Knight enjoyed the cold. It wasn't that he felt the temperature, but the way the others reacted to it. The Queen's skin had already pimpled and she was starting to shiver slightly in her sleep.

Earlier that night he had received the news that he had been expecting over the last couple of days, the Alliance had finally reached Jarrat and it would only be a matter of time before they attacked. Unfortunately he didn't receive any news of what that attack might entail. He had a sneaky suspicion that his brother was keeping information from him. He was part of the decision making group in the army and he should know what they were planning. All he could tell him was that they still had no idea what they were going to do.

The last thing he was worried about was the army attacking the castle. He had the entire Enteroite army, or at least those who were in Jarrat, assembled. At the first sign of attack he would open the gates and send them out to die. There was no advantage to him in keeping them safe inside the castle. He had no misconceptions that the Alliance was more powerful than his army, but that was always going to be the case. Even behind the walls they were at risk; it would only be a matter of time before they were breached.

If he was purely relying on the city's soldiers then it would all be over and he would have abandoned the city before the Alliance arrived, but that wasn't the case. The soldiers from the city would just be a diversion. He had a surprise for the Alliance and one that would see it decimated.

The thought of the chaos he was about to cause made him drool. He quickly wiped his mouth and looked around, but of course no one was there. The Queen was still asleep and no one was allowed into their chamber during the night. It made it much easier for Ra'naroz to roam around the castle unnoticed and that's exactly what he needed to do. The big problem he had was the two prisoners he had in the depths of the dungeons. The Alliance would try and rescue them and if they breeched the walls they would succeed. That was something that Ra'naroz couldn't allow.

Slowly he rose from his bed and dressed. He wore a black velvet shirt and matching trousers. He liked to wear black the best, but there seemed less and less opportunity for him to dress in such a colour. His multitude of servants and maids would choose his clothes in the morning. At first he thought about sending them all to the dungeons, but the Queen had assured him that it was a necessity of his position. As the days wore on he had started to enjoy the fact that someone would come and choose what he was going to wear for the day, but a black cloak wasn't suitable for the Prince of Entero.

The corridors were empty. On the eve of battle everyone was spending what time they could with their loved ones, at least those who had loved ones in the castle. Those who had family in the city could do nothing to see them. All they could do was hope that they were safe. The rumours had already started through the castle that the Prince had decided to give up the city to the enemy and it seemed as though the rumours Richmond and Tancred had started had managed to hit their mark. Those locked up in the castle believed that the Alliance had arrived to invade and the Prince was just going to give them the city. There was no telling how may would die or be raped or both before their desire for mayhem was sated.

Prince Leroy knew the rumours were false, but he wasn't going to ease their minds by telling them otherwise. Even though he knew that Richmond and Tancred weren't truly on his side he could have kissed them for what they had started. It was always going to be difficult to convince Oriana and her soldiers to attack the Alliance, but that had all changed. No one needed the command from the Queen to prepare for a battle. Most of the soldiers had been expecting a siege, but there were few complaints when they were told that they would meet the Alliance in open battle. Things had worked out better than Ra'naroz could have ever dreamed.

He didn't come across anyone until he reached the door leading down to the dungeon. Two soldiers stood guard. It was at the Prince's command since his prisoners had arrived that there was always to be two soldiers guarding the door. No one was allowed into the dungeons without the Prince's expressed permission. At first there had been a lot of prisoners, but it had grown less and less with each week. Lady Amilie had been the only one in the last fortnight. The only other visitors were the servants bringing food to the guards and prisoners and then it was the same two boys each time. Ra'naroz couldn't risk anyone trying to free his most valued prisoners.

The two soldiers moved the side of the thick oak door with thick iron bands for reinforcement. It would take an almost impossible effort to break the door down from the other side. One of the soldiers produced a large iron key, unlocked the door and then pushed it open. He groaned under the effort of moving the great door.

The door opened to a flight of stone stairs leading downwards. There was no landing for anyone to try and gain any purchase on the door. It was just another precaution to stop anyone trying to escape. As far as dungeons came it was one of the most secure in the Seven Kingdoms.

As the bottom of the stairs he came out in a well lit common room. A number of guards lazed around, waiting for their shift to start. None of them looked overly keen to start their work for the night. It wasn't until they realised who had joined them did they jump to attention. One thing the Prince couldn't abide was laziness from his guards. It was one of the easiest ways to end up on the other side of the bars. Luckily for them his mind was on his prisoners and he didn't seem to notice.

"I believe that your prisoner is asleep, but if you wish we can wake her up. She has yet to reveal anything of importance, but I don't think she's far away. I'm sure you'll be able to break her, your majesty," the head guard spoke very quickly as he tried to guess why the Prince was there.

Ra'naroz had left for the dungeons with the expressed intention to visit Eldred and Alena, but at the mention of the traitor things changed. He didn't imprison her immediately once Tancred and Richmond had left the castle. Since he knew she was a traitor he wanted to see what she was doing. The exercise was fruitless and he soon got sick of playing games. All she seemed to do was get herself close to the Queen. That in itself wasn't enough to warrant sending her to the dungeons, but since he knew she was a traitor anything she said to the Queen without his knowledge was potentially dangerous. In the end he decided that torture was the way to get the information that he wanted, but he had not been to the dungeons to see to the task himself. With the Alliance on the way he needed to concentrate on his hold over the Queen. Since he was already in the dungeons he figured a little detour couldn't hurt. There was nothing the Queen could get up to whilst she was sleeping.

Another reinforced door lead into the first level of the dungeons. This was where those who were on a light sentence were kept, at least before the Prince arrived. Now they were filled with those who couldn't be housed in the lower levels.

Lady Amilie had been taken to the third level where there was more open space for those who were to be tortured. The cells were packed close together and allowed its occupants to hear those who were being interrogated. It also gave the added bonus of fear.

Again the guards jumped to attention when the Prince arrived. Normally the other guards would have announced his arrival, but the Na'garoz had not given them time. Again the guards were lazing around, the torturing done for the day.

"I want to see the new girl," he barked at no one in particular.

One of the guards jumped to his feet. "Yes, sir!" He was about to salute, but then remembered the Prince didn't like it. "I will take you to her cell."

They walked down a dimly lit hallway cut into the rock below the castle. There was a thick smell of blood and excrement in the stale air. The pungent aroma brought a sense of euphoria to the Dark Knight. He had spent too much time in the castle with the constant smell of perfumes and flowers. As much as he had grown accustomed to those smells, at times he even enjoyed them, he was much more at home in the filth of the dungeon. He smiled at the thought at what had caused such a stench.

"This is her cell," the guard said.

Na'garoz waited a moment before he spoke. "And do you want me to open it with my teeth?"

The guard fumbled in his pockets until he found the key. When he pulled it out he nearly dropped it before he struggled to push it into the key hole. He was starting to sweat as the Prince stood back and watched. He wanted nothing more than to strike down the weak creature, but that would be hard to explain. In the end they were doing his bidding and that was enough to keep him alive. There were plenty other creatures around that he could kill, including the one he was about to meet.

"You can leave us now."

The guard moved quicker than his large frame should have let him. There was nothing he wanted more than to be out of the Prince's sight. It would only be a matter of time before he ended up in one of the cells. In his hurry to leave he didn't even think how the Prince was going to lock the cell when he was finished.

The cell was dark and the only light came from outside the corridor, but Ra'naroz had no problems seeing clearly. His Dark Knight eyes quickly adjusted to the change in light. He was used to the dark. The smell that plagued the lower levels increased as he walked into the cell. He couldn't help himself as he breathed in the pungent aroma. If there was anyone else around it would have looked suspicious.

In the corner a woman was huddled, trying to protect herself from the chill of the underground. At some point she had managed to fall asleep, but she woke again as soon as Ra'naroz entered her cell. She shied away from the light and tried to retreat into the walls.

"Please, not again, I don't know anything," she whimpered.

Ra'naroz could feel the fear emulating from her. Obviously she didn't know who he was or her fear would have doubled. He could see for the first time that she was completely naked. The remnants of the nightgown she was wearing when she had been taken was torn to shreds and scattered around the cell. The nightgown had been ripped when she was whipped for the first time and the rest had been torn from her body when the guards came to ravish her.

Dried blood had congealed on her back. Ra'naroz could see the bruises and blood on her thigh from her other attacks. He had never understood the carnal pleasures of the bodies he had used over the years, but that had changed when he met the Queen. There had been something about her that raised his spirits, but he had never thought of taking her in such a manner as the guards had taken Amilie. Just the idea made him want to return the Queen's bedroom, but he had more important matters to deal with.

"Please, just let me sleep!" Amilie continued when there was no response.

When the door had been opened she had instantly feared the worst, but since there had been no response there was a glimmer of hope and Ra'naroz knew exactly how to exploit it. A few months back his only option would be pain, but his life inside the castle had changed that. He had watched how the vile little creatures interacted with each other and had learned that sometimes information was gained from being overly nice opposed to overly evil. He didn't completely understand the concept, but he knew enough to give it a try.

"Hush now," he cooed. "You must be freezing. Here."

A large bear skin rug materialized in his hand. As he approached she cringed away from him until he knelt down and wrapped the rug around her. From a distance he hadn't noticed, but up close he could see that her face was puffy and her eyes closed over. He had to admit that he was impressed that she hadn't revealed any information.

"Now child, I am here to rescue you," Na'garoz cradled her is his arms as he spoke. The feeling was uncomfortable to him, but he knew it was the right thing to do. "First you must tell mr why they have imprisoned you here?"

Amilie was about to talk, but instead she started coughing uncontrollably. Ra'naroz just waited and rocked her gently. When she finally stopped coughing she was able to speak, her voice dry and cracked. "Do you have any water? I haven't eaten or drunk anything in what must be days, although it's hard to know down here."

"Of course my dear," Ra'naroz was started to get irritated with the niceties. He just wanted the information and he didn't seem to be getting anywhere. Taking a deep breath he conjured up a tankard of water and handed it to Amilie.

She drank down the entire tankard followed by another bout of coughing. When she finally finished she felt somewhat better. The cold had numbed her body from the pain and the warmth of the rug was slowly starting to bring it back. The whip marks across her back started to sting. Her face started to throb and there were very few other parts of her body that didn't hurt.

"Now, please. If I am to help you then you must tell what you have done," Ra'naroz kept his voice as soft as he could.

"What do you mean?" Amilie tried to look up at who her saviour was, but she couldn't see in the dark through her puffed eyelids.

"What have you done to be brought here? Tell me who it is you've been speaking with and I'll take you to them."

Amilie tried to pull away, but her body was too weak even though he held her gently. If it wasn't for his support she would have collapsed on the floor. There was little fight left in her, but she would still not give away any information, at least until she knew who she was speaking with.

"I have been wrongly accused. I am loyal to the crown and always have been. There is nothing I can tell you. Please, take me out of here," she whimpered despite trying to keep her voice hard.

"All you need to do is tell me the truth and I will set you free. I know you have been playing the Prince for a fool. You have betrayed him and you need to confess. It's the only way I can help you," impatience was creeping into his voice.

"Who are you?" Amilie tried her best to see, but she still couldn't make out who it was.

"I'm your friend. Don't you remember who I am?" Ra'naroz sounded offended.

Amilie was about to speak, but then thought better of it. Something wasn't right with the situation. The pain ripped through her body making it hard to concentrate, but she knew she shouldn't reveal anything. If it was indeed a friend then they would already be on their way out of the dungeon.

"I think not," she did her best to sneer. "You are no friend of mine. Do whatever it is you came to do and be gone. I have no time for your lies."

At the sound of her sharp words Ra'naroz jumped to his feet and in doing so dropped her to the ground. She cried out in pain as her body hit the hard packed floor. If it wasn't clear before she knew it was no friend standing before her.

"Very well," Ra'naroz raised his voice. "If you really want to know who I am?" Suddenly the cell was full of light. Even though Amilie could only see through thin slits the sudden light was enough to blind her. It would take some time before she could see who was there, but by the sound of his voice she thought she already knew and her heart was filled with fear.

Slowly she felt herself being lifted from the ground as the rug slid from her body, but it wasn't by strength. She could feel no hands underneath her. It was pure magic that moved her into the position the Dark Knight wanted her in. She floated a foot off the ground and her head nearly touched the ceiling of her cell. Her ankles pressed together and her arms were spread out as if she was nailed to a crucifix.

"Now you will know who I am," Ra'naroz sneered.

Amilie felt something strange on her face. At first it was a gentle heat, but quickly it started to intensify. Soon enough there was no pain on her face and slowly she was able to open her eyes. She didn't know if it was by her desire or the Dark Knights, but she could see who was standing before her. Prince Leroy had an evil expression on his face. Amilie had no idea what he was thinking, but she knew it wasn't going to be pleasant. She hoped he would just kill her and not torture her anymore.

She had already endured more in the last few days than most people did in their entire lives.

"So you have decided to come and do your own dirty work," there was strength in her voice that came as a surprise to him. He thought she had been broken, but it seemed not to be the case. "I was wondering if you had the stomach for this." She knew there was no truth to her slander. The Dark Knight was capable of much worse. "I will not tell you anything it will not be..." Her threat was cut short has she felt something grip around her throat and she could no longer breathe. Finally, she thought, the pain was going to end. She had succeeded in goading the Dark Knight into killing her. Just when she felt her life slipping away the grip released and air rushed into her lungs. Again she started to cough uncontrollably.

"Did you really think I was going to let you off so easily?" He paused, not really expecting a response. "I have seen many of your kind come and go and none of them have gotten the better of me."

"Do to me what you will. I will never betray the Queen." She forced a smile on her face.

"We shall see then."

Amilie suddenly cried out in pain as she felt something cut into her left breast. A tickle of blood appeared just above her nipple. Slowly the cut started to moved and snaked its way across her breast and then down along stomach before it finally stopped. Blood trickled down from the wound. She continued screaming for a full minute before the pain suddenly disappeared.

"You see? I can make you suffer or I can make you feel better. All you have to do is tell me what I want to know and all the pain will be gone. I can heal your scares and it will be like nothing ever happened."

The offer sounded so sweet and Amilie nearly accepted, but she still couldn't betray everything she had worked to save. She had endured a lot of pain and she would endure whatever he had for her. There was nothing he could do to make her talk.

"Is that the best you can do?" She laughed. "I had worse from your pitiful little slaves."

An invisible hand slapped her across the face. The blow stung more than she had thought it would and it left a warm sensation on her cheek. The blood still ran down from the wound he had cause and she thought, with a little luck and time, it might be enough to kill her.

"It seems as though I've been too easy on you." He paused and though about what to do next. "Let's see how you like this one."

For a moment nothing happened and there was a glimmer of hope that whatever he was planning had failed. That feeling quickly disappeared as she felt a warm sensation on her right foot. At first it was pleasant, but gradually the heat intensified. When she looked down she could see a flame burning softly into her skin. The fire didn't climb up her leg. It focused all its heat on her foot and ankle. It took a second for the pain to register, but when it did Amilie cried out like she had never done before. There was a whole new level of pain that was coursing through her body. Just when she thought she was going to lose consciousness the fire stopped. The pain still remained, but its intensity waned. When she looked down her right foot was a charred stump.

"Now I ask you again, what have you done to betray me? Who have you been speaking with?" He continued his questioning.

"Just do what you came here to do 'and be gone. I'm not telling you anything," her voice was weak despite her effort to remain strong.

Instantly she wished she had just remained silent. Slowly her left arm started to twist. The pain grew and grew. Her throat was already sore from screaming, but she knew eventually she would not be able to control herself. She had already started screaming when the sound of her bones snapping resonated around the cell. It was at the point the Dark Knight released his pressure.

"This is your last chance. I have been going easy on you so far. Next time I will not relent. You will suffer until you lose consciousness and when you wake you will suffer even worse. I can keep you alive for years."

It was no idle threat, but she had gone so far it would not be for nothing. Her sense of patriotism was absolute and she would happily give up her life to save her Kingdom. Whatever he was going to dish out she would accept.

When there was no answer Ra'naroz continued. Amilie felt the same tightness around her throat as before. A glimmer of hope returned when she thought he might be ready to kill her, but that was not his intention. He was playing with her as he thought of what torment to place on her next.

Suddenly something changed. There was a shift in power. It was subtle, but undeniable. Ra'naroz forgot about the woman before him and reached out to try to figure what it was. He couldn't believe that his brother would try such a thing. Argoz had positioned himself nicely in the enemy and wouldn't do anything to risk that.

When his attention returned to Amilie he cursed loudly. She still hung in the air but her head was facing the opposite direction. The distraction had caused him to break her neck. Normally he would have savoured her death, but that had not been his intention. Eventually she would have broken and revealed the other traitors in his court.

He had to put that thought behind him. There were more important matters for him deal with. His brother had told him there was no one with the sort of power to cause the disturbance that he had felt. There was no way his prisoners could have done anything. They were safely protected from using any magic.

The thought of his prisoners reminded him of the reason he had come down to the dungeons. They would have to wait. He was sure that they would be secure where they were. Things had become more dangerous for him and he needed time to prepare.

He let the body drop to the ground as he left the cell. The torture had been pleasing to him, but the joy had already disappeared. If he was going to survive he would need a better plan.

Chapter 23: The Sapphire Ring

Alaric was grateful to be back in his hut, alone. Marina had almost begged him for her to join him, but he had insisted that she leave him in peace. He didn't know whether she wanted to see the stone in private or whether she was truly afraid to be by herself. In her defence the elves had not been polite to her, even when they were enjoying the festivities. She had been shunned and since Alaric was the centre of attention she spent most of the evening by herself. He felt bad telling her to go back to her own hut, but he wanted to spend some time alone.

He had opened the velvet bag only once to look inside. Once he knew what it was he quickly pulled the bag shut. He was somewhat surprised at its contents. As much as the elves also wanted to see what was inside he refused to show them. There was much complaining until Kilean ordered that Alaric be left alone. The treasure was his and what he did with it was his business. His order did not go down well with the other elves. They had left their homes and families for what was in the pouch and since it had been delivered they wanted to know what it was. Eventually they settled down to enjoy the festivities. It was a wondrous occasion for them and they would not spend the entire night sulking.

The party continued late into the night. Most of the elves still remained even after Alaric said he was going to bed. Just because the guest of honour was leaving didn't mean that they had to finish. Their purpose had been fulfilled and they were not going to let anything dampen their spirits.

Once Alaric was back in his hut amongst the trees he dropped the velvet pouch on the bed in front of him. It bounced once before it came to rest. He looked at it, as if he was afraid of it. In truth he was concerned. What was inside was not what he was expecting, although it was what he was hoping to find. With that knowledge he wasn't sure if he wanted to open it again.

The urge to open the velvet bag was stronger than the one telling him not to. Slowly he picked it up and opened the strings. A gentle blue glow came from inside, but there was something different. There was not the usual buzzing in the back of his mind when he let a *Stone of Power* out in the open. The Sapphire stone had a calming effect on him that he had not noticed when he had initially looked at it as he had quickly tied the pouch shut. With each passing second he was more comfortable to let it out of the pouch that had kept its power dormant.

The Sapphire stone was a lot smaller than the other two he had seen. The stone was set in a small golden ring. Slowly he tipped it out onto the bed. He was still unsure whether he should pick it up or not. What he wanted to do more than anything else was to put the ring on, but he knew that it was not his senses speaking to him. He had to be sure that it was safe to wear it before putting it on. The feeling was almost overwhelming.

Carefully he picked up the ring, making sure he did not touch the stone. It felt cool to his touch and not at all what he was expecting. He had never felt such a calm in his life. He felt as though nothing in the world could harm him. The feeling of euphoria was almost as disturbing as the voices that had followed the other stones. This form of persuasion was a lot more convincing and a lot more subtle. The feeling that the ring belonged on his finger was overwhelming.

A bead of sweat appeared on his brow as he struggled with the urges inside him. He knew that as long as he kept the stone outside of its pouch he would eventually slide onto his finger. That urge won sooner than he expected. He didn't even realise he had done it until the ring was on his right middle finger. It seemed so natural and the feeling of calmness only increased. He knew that the feeling was not real, but he didn't care, it was wonderful.

A feeling of hope coursed through his body. He felt as though he could do anything. The feeling could not last forever and he needed to find a way to control it. He had yet to succeed with the other two stones, but he was getting better. The Jade stone still tried to control him, but it was becoming less effective. If he was going to defeat Nyrra then he had to learn to control the power before him. He wished Eldred or Heryion was there to teach him.

The ring felt right on his finger. It felt as though nothing else in the world felt right. He stared at the perfect blue sapphire, transfixed by its beauty. He couldn't bring himself to look away. He felt as though all his troubles were washed away in its blueness. Suddenly there was a knock on the door which drew his attention away from the ring.

"Enter," he called out without thinking.

As the door opened he placed his hand behind his back. He didn't want whoever it was to know what was in the bag. He wanted to keep the Sapphire stone secret, the least amount of people who knew about it the better. He wasn't sure how much he could trust the elves. Even though they were the ones who had given him the stone they may not have been so quick to give it up if they knew what it was.

To his surprise he saw Marina walk into the room. He had been quite specific when he told her not to join him and was a little upset that she had ignored him. He would give her the benefit of the doubt before scolding her. He wanted her gone as quickly as possible and he figured that would be the best way to do it.

"What can I do for you?" there was a slight amount of nervousness in his voice.

"What are you doing in here?" she sounded as though she was still clouded by sleep.

There was something wrong. As he looked closer at her it seemed as though she had just woken. He almost let his hands slip to his side before he caught himself. Looking at the pouch on the bed he wanted to return the ring, but he didn't think there was a chance without Marina seeing it.

"I think the point is what are you doing here? I specifically asked you to leave me alone tonight," he harshened his voice slightly, but it was all for show. The truth was that he was actually pleased to see her, but he was getting lost in the stone and he didn't know how he was going to get out.

Marina looked around the room as if she was lost. When her eyes fell on Alaric she spoke. "I was sleeping. I wasn't going to come here, but then something woke me up," she sounded as though she was starting to regain her senses.

"What was it?" Alaric was now intrigued.

"I don't know. I woke suddenly with a voice inside my head," she suddenly doubled over and grabbed at her head. The movement was so sudden that Alaric didn't know what to do. As quickly as she had moved she just as suddenly returned to normal. "I had a sudden feeling that something was wrong. It's hard to explain. There was no one in the room, but I could hear someone speaking. When I looked outside there was no one there. Then I suddenly got the urge to come here. Even as I walked along the bridges I could hear the voice. As I approached your hut the voice became louder although I still could not understand what was being said. When I entered the voice suddenly stopped, although it feels as though there is a buzzing in the back of my head. Just when I think I know where it is it moves. It is really quite annoying."

Alaric listened to her intently and couldn't believe what she was saying. It was a situation he knew all too well. The stones had been speaking to him, but it seemed as though the Sapphire stone wanted to speak to Marina. He knew that there was more to the Princess than he had originally thought, but he did not know the true extent.

"I don't know what you are talking about?" he was not about to try and explain it to Marina, especially since he really didn't understand it himself.

She gave him a suspicious look. Although she didn't know what was happening she did not believe for an instant that Alaric did not. For a while they stood on opposite sides of the hut and stared at each other, each waiting for the other to crack. In the end neither of them knew what they were waiting for the other to say.

"I think that you should return to your hut. It's late and we will have to be on the road in the morning," he didn't know if they would be able to leave, but he thought that it was a good enough excuse. He could feel the prophecy getting further and further away and he needed to start the chase again.

A sudden look of fear crossed her face. Alaric took a half step backwards until he was hard up against the bed. There was nothing that should have caused such a reaction. The light in the room seemed to dim for a moment and a feeling of unease came over him.

"I don't want to go back to my room," her voice was soft, almost like a small child.

"What do you mean?" Alaric was confused by her response.

"I don't know," she replied honestly. "All I know is that I cannot go back to my hut. Would it be alright if I stay here tonight?" she sounded as though she was about to burst into tears.

In the diminishing light Alaric thought that her face had changed. He blinked his eyes once and she returned to normal. He simply put it down to the dying light playing tricks on him. Her black hair hung around her face and Alaric thought that she looked quite pretty. The decision that he had to make was not if he wanted her to stay, but whether he wanted her to see the ring. There was little chance of keeping the Sapphire stone secret if she stayed. He wanted to send her away, but there was something inside him saying that he wanted her to stay.

Before he spoke he looked at the bed. "I don't think that there is room for the two of us in the bed."

"That's okay. I can sleep on the floor," she stepped closer to Alaric as she spoke. "I don't know what it is, but I do not want to be alone," the light dimmed even more as she moved closer.

She was almost in Alaric's arms when she noticed a blue glow from behind his back. The light caught her attention and she couldn't think of anything else. She stopped where she was and stared. When Alaric realised what she was looking at he tried to back away. The only problem was that he was already hard up against the bed and had nowhere to go.

"What do you have behind your back?" the light was all but sucked out of the room when she asked the question.

The calmness that the ring had brought on was gone and he felt a sudden surge of panic. There was now no way for him to hide the stone from her anymore. With a sigh of regret he moved his arm from around his back and showed Marina the Sapphire stone. When he did the light suddenly returned to the room and the sapphire started to glow brighter. Marina instantly stepped backwards, though it was not in fear, but to give her a better look at the ring.

"Is that…?" she let the question fade away.

"It is the *Sapphire Stone of Power*," he explained, without going into any detail.

"It's beautiful," she stepped forward again. This time she touched Alaric's hand and moved it closer to her eyes. It was like she was inspecting a friend's engagement ring. "It's the most beautiful thing I've ever seen, although it doesn't look like something a man would wear." It was a strange comment, but Alaric let it pass.

She had seen the Jade stone when Alaric was checking for directions, but she reacted quite differently to this one. The Sapphire stone transfixed her. Alaric wished that he could get away, but he was not prepared to climb up onto his bed. There was a strange look on her face and he thought he saw some drool form in the corner of her mouth, but when he looked again there was nothing there.

Suddenly, without warning, Marina wrapped her arms around him and kissed him on the lips. He was lost for a moment in the embrace. When she let him go he fell back onto the bed. He didn't know what to think. There was a warm feeling inside his chest. She looked down at him with a strange look on her face. Alaric didn't know what she was thinking. Before he could move she leapt from where she had been standing and landed on top of him. He was so surprised with her sudden movement that he didn't know what to do. In the end he relaxed and let her take control. The last thing he could remember was the sweet smell of her hair.

***

In the morning Alaric awoke as the sun light crept through his window. It was then that he realised there was someone in the bed next to him. When the initial shock passed he remembered that Marina had stayed the night, but the rest of the night's events remained hazy. There was something wrong with his memory, but he knew that something important had happened. He couldn't for the life of him remember anything after he returned to the hut from the festivities. Although it should have seemed strange to him that Marina was in the bed, it seemed perfectly normal.

The next shock came as Alaric pulled the sheets back and realised that he was completely naked. Still no memories returned, but he was starting to guess what had happened. He was too afraid to look under the sheets to see if Marina was wearing anything. The thought made him smile, but he quickly returned to the job at hand. He looked around the room until he found his clothes hanging on the back of a chair. He made sure that Marina was still asleep before carefully making his way across the room. Once he was dressed he breathed a sigh of relief.

It would not be long before they would have to be on the road again. Na'garoz still had the prophecy and he needed to get it back. He was sure that there was valuable information he was missing out on and he felt lost and alone without it. He knew that the Dark Knight had travelled into the Southern Wasteland. He could still feel the prophecy drawing him. Although he could still not point to the location he knew that the ancient tome was somewhere to the south. The fact that it was too far away for him to pin-point meant that Na'garoz must be in the wasteland.

Suddenly he remembered the gift he had been given the night before. He looked to his finger and a bolt of fear shot through his body. The ring was missing and he had no idea what he had done with it. He looked wildly around the room, but to no avail. He saw the empty velvet pouch on the floor next to the bed. It was obvious that the ring was not inside.

Frantically he started looked around the small hut, trying not to wake Marina in the process. He looked under the bed and all around, but there was no sign of it. He looked towards the ceiling as if the answer might be written somewhere up there. He couldn't believe that he had been so careless. He had already lost one of the *Stones of Power* he couldn't afford to lose another one.

"Looking for something?" a soft voice came from the direction of the bed. There was a playful tune to her voice.

Alaric jumped slightly. He had been so involved with his search that he had forgotten there was someone else in the room. He quickly looked down at her. At first all he saw was her naked shoulders. Then he saw the top of her breasts which just showed above the covers. The sight almost made him blush until he noticed that she was waving her fingers at him. At first he didn't know why she was doing such a thing, but then the light reflected off something on her middle finger. As soon as he realised what it was the blood rushed to his head.

"What are you doing?" his voice rose louder than he intended, but there was nothing he could do to stop himself.

The sudden outburst caught Marina by surprise. The smile dropped from her face and she was suddenly aware of her naked skin. Normally it wasn't an issue for her, but she suddenly felt very self-conscious and she quickly covered herself with the blanket. She couldn't understand why he would speak to her in such a manner. It had been such a beautiful night, but he seemed to have completely changed.

"What are you talking about?" she sounded confused and defensive.

Alaric restrained himself from running to the bed and ripping the ring from her finger. He tried to remember how she got the ring, but he couldn't. The only thing he could think of was that she had taken it when he was asleep. That thought made him even more suspicious. He could feel something bubbling inside of him. It was a rage that he had never felt before. The feeling had a power to it, he knew that much. He didn't know how he could tap into that power, but he didn't think that it mattered. He could feel the power starting to take control of him and he liked it.

"Alaric?" fear came from the voice across the room, but Alaric didn't hear it. All he could hear was the power rushing around his body. He didn't know what he was going to do with it, but he knew it was going to happen soon. "Alaric?" She moved closer to him, but still there was no response. She had a sheet wrapped around her as she left the bed.

His hands started to shake and his face was stern. His entire body was rock hard. It was clear that something wasn't right with him, but she had no idea what it was just that it was something to fear. She thought about reaching out and touching him, but she didn't know how he would react. The last thing she wanted to do was to provoke an attack. Instead she screamed at him to calm down.

Just when Marina thought that he was going to burst her screams finally got through. Alaric heard her calling his name. The rage was suddenly sucked from his body. As it left his knees started to shake and he almost collapsed to the ground. When he finally steadied himself he saw the terror still written on Marina's face. Although he couldn't remember what had happened he knew it was his fault. One way or another he needed to get the Sapphire stone back in its pouch.

"What's wrong?" she asked, taking a step backwards when she realised that he was able to support himself.

"Why do you have the ring on your finger?" he spoke between clenched teeth as it was all he could do to keep his anger under control. He couldn't believe she had stolen the ring in the middle of the night. She knew how dangerous the *Stones of Power* could be. The ring wasn't a simple trinket.

Marina seemed even more confused. Alaric thought that it was a simple enough question. He thought about asking it again, but he decided that it would be better to wait. If he had to re-ask the question he didn't know if he would be able to contain his rage. All he could do was stare at her with an enquiring look on his face.

"I don't understand. You gave it to me last night. Don't you remember?" it was clear in her voice that she was not lying. "You told me that it was no ring for a man to be wearing and it would look much better on a beautiful woman."

It was Alaric's turn to look confused. He turned away as he tried to think about what had happened the night before. He remembered Marina walking into his room and he also remembered showing her the

Sapphire ring. The rest of the night was hazy. He knew something had to have happened for them both to wake up naked in the same bed. As much as he didn't believe he would just give away the ring nothing was making any sense. As much as they had spent the night together in the tribal village they had been intoxicated, but Alaric had not eaten or drunk anything that might have altered his awareness. All he could think about was returning to his hut and looking at the Sapphire stone.

"I need it back," he replied without answering her question.

Marina took another step backwards and placed her hand behind her back. At the same time the Sapphire stone started to glow. It was clear that she did not want to relinquish the stone. The rage started to build inside of him again. It was difficult, but he was able to keep if from taking over his body a second time. The power surged and it felt good, but Alaric knew he could not let it win. He would get the ring back, but he would not hurt Marina in the process.

"You gave it to me. You told me that I could have it. You have to remember," the fear had returned to her voice.

Alaric took a step forward before he spoke again. "Give me the ring," his voice was rough and guttural. The sound took Marina by surprise. She wanted to back away, but for some reason her legs wouldn't work.

"Please, you have to remember," Marina sounded deathly afraid.

"All I know is that I need the stone back. This is very important," Alaric was suddenly not so sure of himself. There was something in the back of his mind telling him that was he was doing was wrong, but he pushed it aside.

The stone's glow increased in intensity. It seemed to be mimicking Marina's fear. The more the she felt it the stronger it glowed. Alaric was so focused on Marina he didn't notice the ever growing blue glow behind her. If he did he would have realised the danger he was in.

"What are you doing?" Marina's body had gone completely stiff. It sounded as though she struggled to speak and there was something different about her voice.

Alaric didn't know what was happening. He could still fill the power inside him, but he had made no move to use it. There was a slight scratching in the back of his mind, but it was so subtle that he just ignored it. He had no idea why Marina was doing what she was doing. He could only put it down to the Sapphire stone having some kind of reaction on her.

As he looked at Marina he could see that she was completely motionless. Her face was contorted, but he couldn't work out if it was from fear or pain. The intensity of the blue glow continued from the stone until the entire room was lit. Alaric wanted to reach out and comfort her, but he had no idea what he could do. Even her chest wasn't rising and falling with breath or a heartbeat. Alaric didn't think it would be long before she died.

Just when he thought she would die he felt something change inside of him. There was a sharp pain in his head and his heart started to race. As it did Marina was suddenly able to move again. She stumbled forward and gasped for breath. Her hands moved to her neck as if she had just been choked.

When she finally looked up there wasn't fear or relief on her face like Alaric had been expecting. Instead her face remained completely bank. Alaric had to take a step back as he saw a fire in her eyes that belied her expression. There was something dangerous about her and he needed to be careful. The blue glow hadn't decreased and he could see the Sapphire pulsating on her finger. Alaric was transfixed by the glow as she reached out towards him.

Alaric only just realised what was happening before it was too late. He looked into her eyes and could only see the whites. Whatever was controlling her body did not look happy. He only just managed to release the protective spell as a shot of blue light came from the Sapphire. The light hit an invisible shield about an inch from Alaric's face. The impact was enough to send him flying across the room until he crashed into the far wall, but the light didn't break through. If it had it would have engulfed him in blue flame.

Despite the fact her pupils had rolled up into her head she could still see what was happening, although she had not control over her body. She couldn't believe what she had done, but there was nothing she could do to stop it. Eventually, when it was clear that Alaric's shield would not be broken, the light stopped.

"I don't think you realise the potential of the one," the soft feminie voice came within Alaric's head.

"What are you talking about?" Alaric used his mind voice, although he had no idea who he was speaking with.

"Just be warned. You have won this time, but next time you won't be so lucky."

When the words ended Marina doubled over in pain and the light faded from the stone. After Alaric was sure that he was no longer in danger he rushed to her aid. For a moment he thought she was going to vomit, but slowly she returned to her upright position. Alaric wasn't going to take any chances as he helped her to the bed. He could only assume that the Sapphire stone had taken control of her body and use her for the attack. The alternative wasn't worth thinking about. He couldn't believe that she would try and kill him.

Alaric took the opportunity to gently pull the ring from Marina's finger. When she felt Alaric touch the ring she tried to pull away, but the ordeal had left her weak. Alaric was as gentle as he could be, but he also couldn't remove the ring quick enough. Once it was off her finger he suddenly felt very calm. He knew it was a false feeling brought on by the Sapphire stone and as much as he wanted to bask in its serenity he knew he had to return it to its pouch. With a great effort Alaric moved across to the pouch, picked up, stashed the ring inside and then pulled the strings tight. When the ring was safely inside its pouch Alaric felt that a great weight had both been lifted and added to his shoulders.

"Are you alright?" he asked, his voice hoarse.

"I don't know. What happened?" again a question was asked that couldn't be easily answered. Since the stone was returned to its pouch her memory of what had happened disappeared.

Alaric didn't know what to say. He was used to the effect of the *Stones of Power* on himself, but he had no idea what effect they would have on someone else. The last thing he wanted to do was voice his suspicions. The less that Marina knew about the stone the better. It seemed to have an affinity with her and that was a disturbing thought. Until he knew more about the stone he would have to be very careful with it. He couldn't let it out of his sight around Marina, which would make sleeping very difficult.

"I don't really know," was all Alaric could reply. It wasn't really a lie, but it definitely wasn't the truth.

Marina watched him suspiciously. She had a feeling that he knew exactly what had happened. She was about to speak, but then thought better of it. Whatever had happened had knocked her around and seemingly Alaric as well. She thought that it was better to leave it alone, for the moment. She couldn't even remember why she was in Alaric's hut or what time of day it was.

She sat on the bed and let her head rest on the palms of her hands. She wanted answers, but she had no idea what the questions were. The last thing she wanted was for Alaric to think that she was losing it. All she could do was hope that she could remember before Alaric questioned her.

Alaric sat next to her and wrapped his arm around her. With the Sapphire stone safely tucked away the memories were starting to return to him. At first it was just from the ceremony, but then the events of later that night also started coming back. At first he blushed, before he realised that Marina no longer remembered. Their encounter in the morning was all starting to make sense to him. After their passion had died down Alaric had felt compelled to give her the ring. At first he could believe that he had given it to her, but there could be no doubting his memory. Everything she said was true and he could finally understand why she had been so confused. It seemed that it was Marina's turn to forget and Alaric wasn't sure he wanted to remind her.

"I think I might need to remind you what happened last night." Marina had decided she could take whatever it was he was going to say. She was sure she hadn't overdone things like Alaric had at the tribal ceremony, but there could be no other explanation for her memory loss.

Alaric had moved to the table and sat down. He didn't want to be holding on to her when he went through the gory details. In fact he wasn't sure he wanted to go through any details. He could remember her reaction to the Sapphire stone and thought it was better if he kept it a secret from her. The longer he could keep it from her the safer they would both be. He didn't think she had hit him with all the power of the stone, but there was no telling what would happen if she unleashed it. He doubted he was strong enough to defend himself if that ever happened.

Before Alaric could speak there was a knock on the door. Alaric looked guiltily at Marina before he called for whoever it was to enter. Alaric could have kissed whoever was on the other side for interrupting them and he called out a little too quickly. Marina knew he was avoiding the question, which made not knowing even more frustrating.

Alaric was relieved to see Kilean on the other side

"Good morning chief!" Alaric did his best to sound cheerful, but failed miserably.

"Were you expecting someone else?" Kilean misinterpreted Alaric's tone.

"Ah, no chief, it was just that I was hoping that it was someone with breakfast." Alaric spoke quickly in an effort not the offend him. "I'm very hungry, but it is an honour to see you."

"Well I have some good news for you. There is a lavish breakfast in my hut. It would be my honour if you would join me," Kilean didn't seem to notice Marina in the room until she shifted uncomfortably. "And of course you are welcome as well."

Marina wasn't completely sure she was welcome. She had not received the warmest of welcomes since arriving in the village in the trees. The elves had been somewhat shorthanded with her compared with how they treated Alaric. Despite the fact, however, she was too hungry to worry about formalities. It was a thought that she never thought she would have. As a Princess she was always treated with respect and never went hungry. If Alaric had refused to explain the previous night then she would have had him flogged. It seemed as though that life was so far away that we she wasn't even sure if it had been hers.

"Thank you, chief, it would be my honour to join you," the Princess knew how to speak with people of power.

Kilean didn't seem to notice that Marina was dressed only in a bed sheet. He didn't really see her at all and he didn't respond to her pleasantries. His gaze never left Alaric.

"I will meet you in my home when you are ready," he didn't wait for Alaric to respond.

Alaric waited for him to leave the room before he spoke again. "We should hurry. After we eat we need to be on the road again. The Dark Knight has too much of a head start and we need to make up ground."

"If you would excuse me I think that I should dress before going outside," Marina had a cheeky smile on her face. "Unless you want me to walk around as I am?"

Alaric went red in the face. He had forgotten that she was still naked under the sheets and despite the events of the previous night he still felt uncomfortable. He didn't know where to look, but he still didn't leave his chair. She watched his reaction carefully, as if she was trying to read his mind. When she knew that he was not going to leave without further instruction she spoke.

"I think that it would be best if you leave the hut. I will meet you outside," the smile remained on her face as she spoke.

There was something about Alaric's discomfort that she found reassuring. It was obvious that she still remained oblivious the events of the previous night. For some reason Alaric felt somewhat offended, but he couldn't let her know.

Alaric quickly stood. He scolded himself for not realising that was the only answer to their situation. He looked around quickly to see if he needed anything before leaving the room. He had to admit that he was happy to be outside again. Things were really starting to become tense between them, for more reasons than one. The cool morning air felt refreshing on his skin.

Inside the room Marina let the sheet fall away from her body. As she stood, completely naked, in Alaric's room she almost hoped that he would return, for whatever reason. When he did not she continued to get dressed. She was a little disappointed that he didn't take to opportunity to see her naked.

Chapter 24: The Journey Continues

There was more food than the three of them could eat, but Kilean was not going to skimp. He knew that Alaric would have to leave and he would make sure he did so on a full stomach. He wished the Chosen One could stay longer or he could travel with him, but he knew that was impossible. He could not leave his fellow elves and he could not take them with him.

"So how did you find the festivities?" Kilean started making small talk as they ate their breakfast.

"It was a little overwhelming, I have to admit," Alaric replied when he finished what he was eating.

"I know what you mean. I think that the elves appreciated the chance to relax. Some of the younger elves were still going when the sun started to rise. It was a great relief for our destinies to finally be revealed," Kilean explained.

"What will you do now?" Alaric kept the conversation going. The more they continued to speak the less chance that the Sapphire ring would be brought up. No one had seen what was inside the pouch, but Kilean would want answers.

"We will stay. There is no place for us with our brethren. It was quite clear that when we left that we would never be welcomed back," Kilean didn't sound upset. He had made a life for himself and his elves in the jungle and as far as lives went it wasn't that bad. They were far enough away for the Evil One not to take any notice of them, at least not until he had wiped out everyone else. If Alaric failed in his task then there would be nowhere safe in the Seven Kingdoms. There would be nowhere to hide.

Alaric felt a buzzing at the back of his neck. He looked down at the pouch, but the Sapphire stone was safely protected. The Jade stone was locked away back in his hut and he would definitely know if someone had managed to open it. There was something not right with what the chief had just said to him. He didn't know what it was, but he was hopeful that the answer would come soon.

"I would have thought that the other elves would have wanted to leave the swampland. Even if you don't return home there has to be somewhere better than this," Alaric hoped that if he kept the conversation on the same track that he would realised what was wrong.

"I know that it doesn't seem as though the jungle is a homely place, but what you have to remember is that it has been our home for a long time. We have grown accustomed to living in the jungle. It can be quite a beautiful place once you get used to it," Alaric didn't believe what Kilean was saying, but he didn't want to argue with him. If that was what he wanted then Alaric would have to let it be, but the feeling in the back of his mind didn't go away. If anything it became stronger.

"I can understand your feelings towards this place, but do you think that is the right decision. I am sure that some of the other elves would like to leave," Alaric had to continue until he knew what to do.

"That's a good point," Kilean took a moment to think, taking a mouthful of food to try and hide the fact. "I am sure that most of them will feel the same. This is our home and we are going to stay."

A shiver ran down Alaric's spine. The feeling that something wasn't right was ever growing inside him. The elves could not stay in the jungle. He didn't know where they had to go, but he knew that they could not stay. The elven chief seemed as though he had his heart set on staying and Alaric didn't know what he could say to make him change his mind.

"I have to tell you something and I don't think that you are going to like it," Alaric hoped if he could prepare Kilean for the news ahead he would accept it. "You have to leave the jungle," he blurted out.

Kilean was taken aback by his outburst, but he did not seem surprised. He took a moment for the words to settle before he spoke again. "I thought that this might be the case. I had hoped that we could stay, but I really didn't think that it would be possible."

"What are you talking about?" it was Alaric's turn to be taken aback.

"I know there is a war happening. That is the reason that we are here, to help with that war effort. I thought that once we handed over the pouch to you that we would be finished. We have suffered a lot to get here, but I know that it is only the beginning. We will go were you tell us," Kilean didn't sound upset, instead he sounded uplifted. It was like he had a new lease on life.

Suddenly a revelation came to Alaric. He knew where the elves must go, he only hoped that he wasn't too late. He felt reassured by telling himself that he could not have arrived any earlier. It had been ordained that he would arrive and receive the Sapphire stone on the first full moon and that is exactly what had happened. That thought brought him great comfort.

"There is a battle brewing in the north. You must take your elves there and help," Alaric felt a little light headed as he spoke.

"I feared as much, but I am sure that my brothers and sisters are keen to leave the jungle. I don't know whether they will be willing to go to war, but they came here for a reason. I know that it is the prophecy speaking again. I can feel something tugging at the fabric of my life. At first I didn't want to believe it was there. It is drawing me to the north and I am sure that even if you didn't tell us we would still be leaving." He looked around his home with sadness in his eyes. It was only there for a moment, but Alaric saw it.

"I will try and make things as easy as possible for you," Alaric wasn't sure if that would help, but it was all he could do. "The battle will take place at Jarrat."

Kilean thought for a moment before he spoke again. "I am sorry. I don't think that I know Jarrat."

Now Alaric was confused. He didn't understand how Kilean could not know of Jarrat. He would have almost had to pass right through it to get to the jungle from the Northern Forest. He didn't know what to say. Luckily for him that Marina did.

"Jarrat is only a relatively new city. I don't think it would have been around when Kilean entered the forest," Marina continued to explain, as best she could, the location of the city. It took a while, but in the end she was comfortable that the elder elf would find the way.

"I've been dying to know Alaric," Kilean started when Marina finished. "What was it that was inside the pouch? I've been holding onto for more years than I can remember and I've never looked inside."

Alaric knew that the question was going to come eventually. As much as he wanted to keep the stone a secret, especially from Marina, he felt the he owed him that much. Kilean and his fellow elves had risked their lives to bring it to him. He knew if he was in Kilean's place he would want to know as well.

"It's the Sapphire *Stone of Power*," Alaric said.

A silence fell over the hut that Alaric wasn't sure was completely natural. He could see the look of wonder on Kilean's face. He wondered on Marina's reaction, but he didn't want to look at her. As much as he wanted her to remember some things of the previous night that Sapphire ring wasn't one of them.

"I knew it would be something important, but I had no idea it was a *Stone of Power*," there was awe in his voice. "May I see it?" He was almost too afraid to ask.

"I'm sorry." Alaric had already decided that he wasn't going to open the pouch. He couldn't risk Marina getting it again. Although he remembered giving the stone to Marina he had no idea why and that was something that disturbed him. "It is no mere trinket to be gazed upon. The *Stones of Power* are more dangerous than you can imagine. Even I have trouble controlling them at times," Alaric bit his tongue. It was a piece of information that he didn't want to reveal. If Kilean didn't pick up on it he knew Marina would, eventually.

"I understand," Kilean seemed disappointed, but it seemed that he wasn't going to push it any further. "I guess we should all be on the move now."

Alaric was surprised that Kilean ended the conversation so abruptly, but he had to admit that they should be back on the trail of the Dark Knight.

"I think you are right. Once we have finished here we should be on our way."

"Where will you go?" Kilean asked.

"We head south," Alaric replied as he placed the last piece of fruit into his mouth.

"But there is nothing south of here. About a day or two's walk and you are at the border of the mainland and the wasteland," Kilean sounded surprised with Alaric's answer.

"That's where we are going," Alaric wiped his mouth with the linen napkin when he finished eating. "There is a Dark Knight that we have to deal with before we can do anything else." He thought about telling him about the stolen prophecy, but he decided against it. He didn't know how the elf would take the news. It was best he just focused on the task at hand.

"Surely he is not a threat in the Southern Wastelands. Why do you bother taking such a risk? I have been to the borders of our lands on a number of occasions and I dare not risk crossing over. There is nothing, but death on the other side. I wouldn't be surprised if the Dark Knight you speak of is already dead," Kilean didn't sound happy with Alaric's plan, or lack of it. He had hoped that their paths would have joined.

"I know that it sounds risky, but it is what we have to do. We cannot leave an enemy behind us, especially one as powerful as a Dark Knight," Alaric did his best not to go into specifics.

"I guess there is no changing your mind," Kilean knew there was no point in continuing the conversation. "I took the liberty of replenishing your supplies. If you eat sparingly you should have enough for about a month, bear that in mind when you travel into the wasteland. If you are there any longer than a week and a half there is a good chance that you will run out of food," Kilean's warning struck home.

Alaric hadn't thought about food and water once they crossed into the wasteland. He knew that he could find food on the mainland, but the wasteland was another story. There were no words that could express how grateful he was. All he could do was say thank you.

"There is another gift that I have for you," Kilean said. "I know the stones can be a handful, at least that is what I have been told. There are more things we have to give you besides the Sapphire stone." Alaric's attention had been drifting, but hearing the words snapped him back. He couldn't believe there was another stone, he had not thought there was one in the first place. "There was also this. I didn't understand until now the reason for it. I know you have been carrying the Jade dagger in a wooden box and that has silenced the effect it has on the world." Alaric couldn't believe what he was hearing. Kilean had more knowledge on the stones than what he had expected. "I also know that there will be a time when you need to draw on that power quickly and easily and keeping it in the box is not suitable." Alaric was starting to wonder where he was going. He didn't know that Kilean had looked inside the carved box with the Jade dagger inside. He didn't know whether to feel upset or not. He would have to wait and see before he made his decision.

"Anyway, here it is."

Kilean passed across the table a small velvet sheath. It was made out of the same material as the pouch the ring had been in. It had been designed to completely cover the Jade stone once the dagger had been slid inside. There were a number of runes sewn into the pouch. Alaric wasn't sure if the material would remain intact with the dagger's blade sliding in and out, but he was grateful all the same. Anything to help his mission was worthwhile trying. Alaric attached the sheath to his belt before he returned his attention to the chief.

"I think that we should be moving. We have a lot of ground to cover and not much time to cover it. I think that you should start to tell the rest of your elves that it is time to leave," Alaric rose as he spoke.

Kilean also came to his feet before he spoke. "I think we both have a lot of work ahead of us." He smiled even though the comment was ominous. "It has been a pleasure to meet you Alaric, and you Marina."

They all said goodbye before Alaric and Marina left the hut. They collected their possessions from their tree huts before meeting on the jungle floor. A young looking elf met them there and led them to where the horses were waiting. The two animals looked happy and refreshed, especially Adelanta. He was from an elven breed of horses and he felt at home amongst the elves. Alaric thought that he looked sad to go but that changed once he saw the two of them approach.

Alaric felt good to be back in the saddle, although he knew it would not last long. They had only ridden for half an hour before the undergrowth became too thick for riding. Alaric was disappointed to be off Adelanta's back. He felt comfort in the horse underneath him.

Neither Marina nor Alaric had spoken once they had left the tree top village. They kept a southerly path as Kilean had told them to travel due south as much as they could. If they strayed too far to the east or the west then they would end up in trouble. Kilean didn't say specifically what that trouble was, but by the way he spoke it was not worth finding out.

They still wore the thin clothes that the elves had provided them. The thin material was surprisingly robust and easily protected them from the many thorns and needles from the various plants. Not only did they protect their skin from being scratched it kept them cool as the temperature increased. Alaric even thought it would be hotter if they removed their clothes.

They stopped early in the afternoon for the midday meal. Alaric pushed on as far as they could before stopping to eat. Although Marina was not complaining he knew that she needed to rest. Despite the large breakfast he was also becoming hungry and tired. They had not been travelling for long, but the thick undergrowth made it more difficult than travelling in the open, it was more the battle with Marina and the Sapphire stone that had drained his energy. Marina was also suffering from the effects.

"What do you think we will find once we cross the border into the wasteland?" Marina asked as she ate.

"I was going to ask you the same question. Between the two of us you are the only one who has studied geography," Alaric smiled as he spoke. "In short I have no idea what to expect. I have heard stories from merchants passing through my home town. They claimed to have heard from someone who had heard from someone who knew someone who had crossed into the Southern Wasteland and never returned. The stories seemed so unreal that I never believed them. Now that we get closer I am starting to wonder if there was in fact truth to the stories," he let the thought drift away.

"Have you checked the Jade dagger to see if there is another stone in the wasteland?" Marina asked when she had finished eating.

Since he had received the Sapphire stone he had not thought to check the dagger again. In his rush to leave he had left the dagger in its box and forgotten all about the sheath which was still attached to his belt. Without answering Marina's question he rose and walked to where Adelanta was grazing. The white stallion didn't seem to take any notice when he took the box from his back. He returned to Marina and sat down.

Alaric prepared himself when he opened the lid. Each time it was getting easier, but he also knew he couldn't be complacent. He knew given a chance the stone would try and take over him. He took a deep breath before he opened it.

An intense screaming filled his head even before he touched the dagger. It was so painful that all he could do was slam the lid shut and the screaming stopped instantly. As much as he was expecting the stone to put up a fight he couldn't have imagined such a reaction. Even without the screaming Alaric's head still ached and he let it rest against his hands.

"Are you alright?" Marina finally asked when Alaric hadn't moved for over a minute.

Alaric slowly lifted his head. He didn't know what he was going to tell her. "I just had a pain and thought it better to close the lid." It was a twist on the truth that he hoped would satisfy her.

"I know the stone is having an effect on you Alaric," Marina sounded concerned. "I've seen it every time you open the lid."

Alaric had to smile. "Yes, you are right. There was a screaming inside my head. It disappeared when I closed the lid. Something has changed with the Jade stone. I've never felt anything like it before."

Marina thought for a moment before she spoke. "Do you think the Sapphire stone has anything to do with it?"

Alaric didn't know how to respond. The last conversation he had with Marina was that she didn't remember what had happened the previous night. He had hoped that the memory wouldn't return, but it seemed as though that wasn't the case.

"Why do you say that?" Alaric stammered.

When Alaric had opened the chest Marina's memories came flooding back. Her mind opened and it was like she had never forgotten. She seemed a little perplexed with Alaric's question, but she continued nonetheless.

"I'm not sure exactly how things work, but when I was wearing the Sapphire ring I felt a great calm wash over me. It was like nothing I had ever felt before. I just wonder if it might have the same effect on the Jade stone."

Alaric didn't like what he was hearing, even though it did make sense to him. He had tried to keep Marina away from the power of the stones, but it seemed as though she was learning on her own. He silently cursed himself for giving her the ring.

"I guess it could be worth a shot. I'm not going to get anywhere with the screaming in my head." Alaric wasn't so sure it was good idea, but he had a compulsion to agree with her.

Alaric fingered the pouch in his pocket for a moment before he slowly pulled it out. Although it was inevitable there was something holding him back. Despite his compunction something was telling him it was the wrong move. Marina watched him eagerly as he played with the pull strings.

"Come on Alaric, what are you waiting for?" Marina couldn't hold back.

Without waiting a moment longer Alaric pulled back the strings and pulled the ring from its pouch. This time the feeling of calmness didn't wash over him like he was expecting. Instead he felt as though he was going to bring up his meal. The feeling was almost overwhelming and it was all he could do to remain conscious. He swallowed deeply before pushing down the nauseous feeling.

"Are you alright?" Marina asked when he didn't say anything. There was a slight amount of anticipation in her voice that Alaric missed completely. If he had heard it he might have changed what he did next.

"Here you take it. I don't think I can hold onto it anymore."

Alaric almost threw the ring at Marina in his rush the get rid of it. As soon as it left his possession he felt much better. The nausea disappeared just as quickly as it came. When he looked up at Marina she had already slid the ring on the middle finger of her left hand. The Sapphire stone glowed a gently as Marina looked at it lovingly.

Just as he was about to speak he thought better of it and he didn't think Marina would hear him anyway. Until he checked the Jade dagger he was happy to let her be. The thought of trying to get the ring off her again didn't bear thinking about. Instead he focused on his main goal, which was the box sitting on his lap.

Alaric slowly let his finger run over the engraved J. Marina was so focused on the Sapphire ring that she didn't notice what Alaric was doing. If he wasn't so focused on the box he might have been concerned with the expression on her face. It was as if she was looking at a long lost lover, but he was too concerned with his own task.

Taking a deep breath Alaric prepared himself to start the battle again. He would not be caught off guard again and he started to draw in some energy around him in preparation. When he was comfortable he slowly opened the lid.

To Alaric's surprise the screaming did not come again. It seemed as though Marina was right. Although he wasn't completely sure there didn't seem to be any other explanation. The Jade stone glowed dimly, almost timidly. If Alaric did not know better he would have thought it was being shy. From what he knew about the Jade stone it was like the big brother of the stones. Jade was the God King who brought the world together and the Jade stone was a link between the other stones.

When he was sure there was no danger Alaric picked the dagger up from its box. Instantly the hilt felt warm in his hand, which seemed odd. As he thought on it he felt as though the stone was angry. When he saw the subtle glow he thought it was from nervousness, but that didn't seem to be the case.

"You can't trust her," the voice came inside his mind followed by what Alaric could only think was a snarl.

"What are you talking about?" Alaric was taken by surprise.

"You can't trust her. She will betray you. She was never trustworthy."

Alaric didn't think the words made any sense. There was no way the stone could know Marina. He knew that the stones could be treacherous and he pushed the voice out of his mind. He wasn't interested in useless conversation. He needed to see the direction of the next stone and then get on the move again. When the light faded they would have to rest. They couldn't travel in the jungle after dark, it was too dangerous.

He pointed the dagger to the south. At first nothing happened and Alaric instantly thought that the Sapphire stone was the stone they were chasing. He was both relieved and annoyed at the same time. They were heading into the wasteland to retrieve the prophecy and all being well destroy another of Nyrra's Dark Knights. Alaric wanted to achieve that goal and leave as quickly as he could. He didn't want to then have to go chasing around for another stone. There were still things he had to do on the mainland and he was quickly running out of time.

When nothing happened as he moved the dagger across the southern plane he thought about returning it to its box, but then a thought changed he mind. He turned around allowing the dagger to cross west to north to east. To his surprise and chagrin the stone didn't glow any brighter.

"What are you doing?" Alaric used his mind voice. As silly as it sounded he figured it was the only choice he had.

"I don't have to help you. If you ignore me then why should I do anything for you," the voice sounded sullen.

Alaric knew he had to overpower the stone, but he had no idea how he was going to do it. With a little niceness he might be able to talk it around, but he really didn't believe that would work. At the very least the conversation would buy him time as he figured out what to do next.

"You will do as I command. I am the Chosen One. I am the one to control all the stones and defeat the Evil One. You can help me by your own choice or I can force. Believe me when I tell you that you want to take the first option." Alaric had no idea if he could do anything to hurt the stone, but he felt he had to offer the threat.

There was silence. Although there was no noise Alaric knew that the voice was thinking. He would need to remain strong if his bluff was going to work. The voice was in his head and he knew that it could sense, at least on some level, know what he was feeling.

"Very well. I will help you this time, but mark my words. Before this is over she will betray you." After the warning his head went quiet.

When he looked down at the stone he could see that it was still glowing softly, but there was something different about it. He slowly started to move the dagger back around to the south and the glow started to increase in intensity. Alaric didn't have to wait for its intensity to peak to realise it was pointing to the south. It seemed as though there was another stone waiting for them in the wasteland. When he was confident the job was done he quickly returned the dagger to its box and shut the lid.

"Why didn't you use the sheath?" Marina asked.

Alaric jumped, slightly, when he heard her speak. He had not realised that her attention had returned to him. There was a concerned expression on her face that really didn't fit the situation. There was no way she could have known what he had just been through. Then he realised that the Sapphire stone was glowing a little brighter than it had when he handed it to her. As soon as he saw it the stone reduced its brightness until it was almost completely gone.

"I don't know. I guess I feel for comfortable with it in its chest. It's a case of out of sight out of mind." It was the best he could do.

Marina simply nodded her head before looking lovingly down at the ring, which had moved from her middle finger to the ring finger. Alaric cringed at the thought, but kept his mouth shut. They needed to keep moving and he didn't think it was going to be a short conversation. In fact he would be just as happy to avoid the conversation altogether.

"We need to keep moving. At this rate we have no chance of being outside the jungle before nightfall."

Marina had to admit that Alaric was right. As much as she wanted more information she couldn't argue with his logic. Even with the light clothes the elves had given them it was still uncomfortable in the forest. As much as she wanted more answers she wanted to be out of the jungle. She would press him for answers when they stopped for the night.

The travelling for the afternoon was slow. The ground soon became soft underfoot. With each step Alaric was concerned they were going to run into another swamp, but they managed the day without seeing any water.

Alaric found some wood to use for a fire. The evening air was not that cold, but he felt as though a fire would be good all the same. The fire did not have the desired effect that Alaric was after. Instead it managed to draw in the many bugs and small insects from the jungle around them. They were clearly attracted to the light.

"So are you going to tell me what happened with the stone's earlier today?" Marina swatted at a couple of bugs as she spoke.

Neither of them had noticed that sudden, albeit gentle, glow of the Sapphire stone at the mention of the stones, nor did they notice the insect that got fried in its light. Alaric was staring the fire doing his best to ignore the bugs that were buzzing around, taking their turns at biting. At first Marina wasn't sure he had even heard her question until he looked up from the fire. The flames reflected off his eyes and the darkness seemed to shrink away from him. Marina shook her head and put it down to tiredness.

"I don't know. What I do know is that it's dangerous for you to wear the ring." Alaric let his comment float away on the night air. Marina didn't look happy with what he said and when it was clear she wasn't going to speak he continued. "I'm not going to take it from you, but you need to think about what I've told you. The *Stones of Power* are treacherous and dangerous. You might feel comfortable with it on your finger, but it has an agenda that you can't possibly understand."

It was Marina's turn to stare at the fire. She kept her eyes low to avoid Alaric's. There was nothing that Alaric had said that made any sense to her, but she still felt somewhat ashamed. She couldn't believe that there was anything untoward with the Sapphire stone. She never felt more alive than when she had slipped the ring over her finger. It was like she had been asleep for her entire life and had only just woken up. The only thing she was happy with was the fact that Alaric wasn't going to try and force it from her again. The memories had returned from the last time it happened and she really didn't want to hurt him.

"I'll be alright," Marina finally said.

Alaric was happy to let the conversation pass. He really didn't want to speak any further. It had been a long day and he wanted to sleep. Before he could he would have to do something about the bugs. There would be little chance for them get a decent night sleep with the insects eating them.

"I'll take care of that." It was as if Marina knew exactly what he was thinking.

Slowly the Sapphire stone started to glow brighter and brighter. The light shone out in a dome around her ring. Whenever a big hit the light there was a sizzling sound and the bug disappeared in a puff of smoke. Although the blue light disturbed Alaric he was glad the insects had been taken care of. The light continued until they were both covered. It seemed as though the horses were having the same issues.

Marina was a little put out that Alaric didn't even bother to say thank you as he lay down to sleep. She didn't exactly know what she had done, but she knew she had helped.

Unlike Alaric she didn't go to sleep when she had finished eating. Instead she sat by the fire and stared at the ring. The stone's glow had dampened once the blue glow had been completed. She wondered at its beauty for a long time before sleep finally overcame her.

In the morning they both woke refreshed. Marina was pleased to see that Alaric seemed to be in good spirits. She had been worried at their abrupt conversation that he might still be sullen. Despite his apparent revival they didn't speak during their morning meal and as soon as they were done he had them on the move again.

Alaric picked up the pace early in the morning. They didn't know how much further they had to travel before they reached the border between the two lands, but he wanted to reach it by nightfall. He had a bad feeling that time was creeping away from him. If the Evil One found the Ruby stone before they returned then it would not matter what they did.

By mid-morning the dense undergrowth started to grow lighter and the ground became harder. Soon enough they were able to mount their horses again. Alaric pushed them hard, but they were still inside the jungle when they stopped for the midday meal. The heat was starting to become uncomfortable and the elven clothes were losing their affect. Alaric hoped they would get some relief once they were out of the jungle, at least until they crossed over into the wasteland. There was no telling what things would be like then, but he didn't think they would be pleasant.

It was close on dusk when they walked out of the jungle. As much as they were both keen to be out, the sight before them did very little to lift their spirits. The land immediately before them was sparse grassland. The soil underneath was white sand. There was the odd palm tree here and there, but nothing else. There was a salty smell in the air that neither of them had ever smelt before, but they both knew that it was coming from the sea. Although they could not see the water they knew they were close.

"I think we should camp here tonight," although Alaric was happy to be out of the jungle the thought of sleeping in the open was not encouraging. He liked the cover of the trees and he didn't know how long it would be before he would feel safe again.

Marina was just as happy to stop. There was no telling how long it would be before they could rest again. The wasteland was a dangerous place and they would need to be constantly vigilant. Despite the growing dread as they approached the wasteland she had to admit that it was quite a pleasant place to camp. There were a cool breeze blowing in off the sea and the sand was soft underfoot.

Alaric returned to the jungle to gather as much wood as the horses could carry into the wasteland, which wasn't a lot. With the food they had received from the elves their burden was already great with the added weight of their riders. Alaric had made a decision that they would used the horses as pack animals and walk themselves. It seemed as though it was the best way to survive.

"But if it's going to be that hot in the wasteland why do we need more wood?" Marina asked when Alaric had returned and settled for the night.

Although Alaric wasn't completely sure he figured that the wasteland would be similar to Nostiria, hot during the day and freezing during the night. He had no doubts that they would need firewood to survive.

"It couldn't hurt to be prepared for the worse. The last thing we want to do is be stuck in the wasteland and wish we had wood for a fire."

Marina nodded in agreement. She didn't like the thought of having to travel on foot, but she could understand his reasoning. The wood could be the difference between life and death.

"Do you think we're going to make it?" Marina asked as she stared at the reflection of the flames dancing on the Sapphire stone.

The question took Alaric by surprise. He had been trying not to think about the fact that there might be a chance they would not make it out of the wasteland. The stories were that no one had ever returned. He had heard rumours of brave men venturing into the wasteland in search of fame and fortune. The stories he had heard about the wasteland was enough to curdle his blood, although if no one had ever returned he didn't know how the stories could be true.

"I don't know," he spoke after he had been silent for a long time. "All I know is that we don't have a choice. If we let Na'garoz find the next stone and keep the prophecy then we have already lost."

His words did nothing to reassure Marina, although she was not really listening to his reply. Her focus remained on the stone on her finger. Alaric was staring into the flames, deep in thought. The thought of what lay before them was all they could think about.

Chapter 25: Into the Unknown

They were both woken by the sun in the morning. The thought of what was ahead of them kept them from rising, but soon enough the heat from the sun forced them out of their bedrolls. They suffered the discomfort for as long as they could until Alaric eventually rose. Marina knew that she could not remain in her bedroll. The last thing she wanted was for Alaric to have an excuse to leave her behind. As much as she didn't want to enter the wasteland the thought of being left behind was worse. She could feel the prophecy pulling her south. She knew that she could not resist that urge no matter what she did.

Once he was up he didn't waste time. They ate a light breakfast before they were on the move again with the smell of salt water thick in the air. A slight cool breeze was the only thing that was stopping the day from becoming unbearably hot. The elven robes that had kept them relatively cool in the jungle had little effect out in the open. Alaric thought about removing his shirt, but the memory of their last night with the elves had made him suddenly very self-conscious. He didn't want to do anything they might provoke those feelings inside of Marina.

Although Alaric had never been to the beach himself he had heard stories. Inside the taverns in Zenza City he had heard of the wondrous holidays people had taken by the beach. If it wasn't for the impending doom that they were approaching he would have thought that the ride could have been pleasant. The white sand between the blades of grass looked soft and pretty. He wanted to take off his boots and let his feet feel the softness, but there was no time for frivolities. If he stopped he wasn't sure that he could keep going.

As they continued the grass became thinner and the sand became more prominent. By mid-morning they reached the top of a small sand dune. The sight on the other side of the dune both excited and scared Alaric. No more than half a mile away was the deep blue water of the sea. Small whitewash peaked the waves before they broke along the beach.

"Have you seen anything like this before?" Alaric asked in awe.

"Only in books. But they don't give it justice," Marina shared Alaric's awe, but there was something else in her voice. There was an emotion that Alaric could not put his finger on. "Do you think that we could go closer?" she asked, in an almost pleading tone.

"I don't think that we have any choice. The causeway is just down there."

A small strip of land bridged the Southern Wasteland and the Seven Kingdoms. It was high tide and the causeway was mostly covered making it narrower than usual. From that distance it was hard to even see. It took Marina a moment to see where Alaric was pointing.

"How are we going to get across? It looks no more than a couple of feet wide," Marina's voice was tense.

"I don't know, but there is only one way to find out." Alaric didn't wait for a response. He gently tugged on Adelanta's reins and started down the other side.

Marina wasn't so keen to follow and she waited on top of the dune. Something inside her told her not to move. All she could do was stare at the beautiful blue water. There was something mystical about the sea that had her captivated. She didn't want to stop looking, but she knew that she could not let Alaric get too far away. The thought of coming closer to the water was enough to get her to move.

It was not long before they could hear the sound of the waves crashing against the beach. Marina thought the sound was very soothing. She closed her eyes as she walked with a subtle smile on her face. Alaric didn't take any notice of her. He was too focused on the small stretch of land in front of them. It was the last chance he had to turn and run, although he knew that it was not an option.

Once they arrived at the start of the causeway Alaric stopped them. It was not that Marina was a dozen paces behind, although he would have stopped if he had noticed, it was that he wanted a chance to think. It was the worst thing he could have done. All it did was make him even more nervous about crossing. Marina, on the other hand, could not get the sights and sounds of the sea out of her head. Again Alaric didn't notice the look on her face. If he had he might have been concerned. Instead he was more concerned with the trail ahead of him.

As Marina neared the causeway she realised that her estimation of two feet was thankfully wrong. Instead it was three paces wide with waves lapping at its shores. The water was shallow at its sides and offered no risk of them being swept out to sea. Alaric still looked at the causeway with concern. It wasn't the causeway that had him worried, but what waited for them on the other side.

Alaric tried to see what was waiting for them, but despite the short distance he couldn't see anything. It was as if there was a haze at the end of the causeway. When Alaric tried to focus on what was before him the images seemed to shift. All he could really see was the narrow strip of land and the water to either side. He had a bad feeling that there was nothing but death waiting for him on the other side of the border.

In the end it was not Alaric's order to cross the causeway, nor was it Marina's, that started them on their way. It was Adelanta, who was followed closely by Marina's mare. Alaric was still staring, trying to focus, at the other side when he realised Adelanta was leading him across. The sudden realisation made him stumbled and he nearly fell into the water.

The white stallion turned his head and snapped at Alaric as he tugged on his reins to regain his balance.

Alaric's heart started to beat faster as they approached the wasteland. He thought about turning Adelanta around and retreating back to the mainland, but he wasn't sure that it would do any good. The stallion seemed focused on reaching the other side. He was grateful to have Adelanta's strength leading him.

As they reached the half way point an eerie fog rolled in off the sea. It was so thick that Alaric could not see more than two feet in front of him, the feeling of dread doubled inside of him. He looked around nervously, as if something was about to step out of the fog. It was then that he realised that he could no longer see Marina. The only way he knew that she was there was the gentle clopping of her mare's hooves behind him. He could only hope that she was following.

The waters lapping the side of the causeway had kept Marina calm as they continued towards the wasteland. The fog had not only blocked her view of the water, but also the sound and she suddenly felt very nervous. Terror filled her heart and all she wanted to do was turn her mare around and hurry back.

In the end it was only Adelanta who kept them moving forward. The mare was just as scared as Marina, but she would not stop following the stallion. Even if Marina had ordered her to turn around she would not. Knowing that Adelanta was in the lead was the only thing stopping the mare from going crazy. His strength kept them all on the right path.

Suddenly Alaric felt the scent of magic in the air. In an instant his suspicions were confirmed that the fog was not natural and neither was the fear that they were feeling. At first he thought that it might be Na'garoz trying to keep him from crossing the border, but that thought was quickly discarded. He could still feel the tug of the prophecy and it was still a long way away. He could not envisage Na'garoz letting the ancient tome out of his sight and the magic felt somewhat different. It felt older, somehow, more natural. For some reason that thought made him feel a little better. He closed his eyes and took a deep breath, savouring his surroundings. All of a sudden the feeling of dread disappeared. A new feeling of calm came over him. It didn't take him long to realise what was happening. The magic only worked through his optic nerves.

"Alaric?" he heard Marina's panicked voice from behind him. He was tempted to open his eyes as he followed behind Adelanta, but he caught himself at the last moment. "I don't think I can make it. I am going to turn around," there was pure terror in her voice.

"It's alright Marina," there was a smile on his face as he spoke. "Close your eyes. You will feel much better."

"What are you talking about?" Marina didn't sound appeased.

"Just close your eyes and you will know what I am talking about."

Marina was shaking uncontrollably with fear and for a moment she thought her legs were going to collapse under her. She didn't think that they were going to make it to the other side, but she still decided to do what Alaric wanted. She reluctantly closed her eyes. She couldn't understand why he sounded so calm. Slowly the fear started to leave her body. She couldn't believe that it was true. She almost opened her eyes again, but the memories of the fear she had been feeling quickly changed her mind. She was finally starting to feel normal again and she didn't want to risk anything changing that. Her renewed confidence reassured her mare, although she could tell that her horse was still frightened. Marina wished she could cover the mare's eyes, but that would never work. She had to rely on the mare to keep them on the right path.

It wasn't until the tingling sensation of the magic had ended that Alaric was comfortable opening his eyes again. To his relief he found that they had crossed into the wasteland and the mist had dissipated. He gently tugged on Adelanta's reins and waited for Marina to reach them. Marina kept her eyes closed and it wasn't until her mare stopped did she realise they were safely across the causeway.

Their relief didn't last long as there was an entirely new horror before them. For a moment Alaric wished that he had kept his eyes closed, but he knew he couldn't do that forever. Sooner or later he would have to face the wasteland and with time against them sooner was the only real option.

"This can't be good," she spoke without really thinking about what she was going to say.

Alaric couldn't take his eyes off the desolation that was before them. The earth was a dusty yellow with shards of jagged rock, a slightly darker yellow, jutting out all around. Alaric couldn't work out if the rocks were trying to enter the ground or trying to bust out. There was not a tree or any other sign of vegetation as far as the eye could see. The only sign of life was the sea which quickly disappeared to the left and right. If the trial of crossing the causeway wasn't enough to change his mind then the land before him really tested his resolve.

"Which way should we go?" Marina asked when Alaric still did not move. She didn't seem as concerned with the desolation in front of them as Alaric.

"I don't know," he spoke, almost breathlessly, as he continued to stare into the wasteland. "I knew that it would be bad, but I had no idea it would be like this. I have travelled into Nyrra's domain and I thought that was bad, but at least there were small signs of life here and there, but this is much worse. I don't think we are going to find any signs of life."

"I don't think that is a good attitude to take. We need to keep wary of our surroundings. Remember that Na'garoz has been here for probably the best part of a week. For him to survive that long means there has to be something to sustain him. If that is the case then there is no reason why something else couldn't live here," Marina's words made sense. Alaric was surprised at her sudden change of attitude. A few moments prior and she was ready to run back to the mainland.

The next problem they would have was the heat. The sun beat down in a cloudless sky. The mist had been refreshingly cool, but since it was gone the sun would take its effect. Even in the light elven clothes the heat beat down on them. Alaric knew that it was only the beginning. The further south they travelled the hotter would become.

"We should get moving. I think that we are going to need to find shelter before nightfall," Alaric said.

"Why is that? I am sure that it will be warm enough outside," Marina didn't see the point in finding shelter. She only guessed that Alaric was concerned of animals hunting at night. As much as she suggested that they kept their wits about them she didn't truly believe that there was anything living in the wasteland.

"You could be surprised," Alaric recounted the time he had spent in Nostiria. "During the day it was sweltering, but at night it was deathly cold. Anyone caught out after nightfall did not live long enough to see morning. I can't guarantee that it will be the same here, but I wouldn't be surprised if it was. The scenery and the temperature are very similar. Either way I do not want to take that risk. One mistake like that and we could end up dead."

Marina took his words on board, although she still thought that he was being a little paranoid. She could not believe that a place as hot as the wasteland could ever cool down. It was not yet midday and the temperature was almost becoming unbearable. If Alaric had not already mentioned shelter for the night she would have suggested it for the day and that they should travel in the cool. She did not like the sound of having to travel during the heat of the day.

"So which way should we go?" Marina asked when they still had not moved.

Alaric thought about taking the Jade stone from its chest, but he didn't want to go through the strain. He could sense the prophecy in the distance. Although he could not pinpoint its exact location he was comfortable in its general positioning. They would continue south. He was sure that sooner or later he would be able to take a more direct route.

Once they were on the move again the severity of their situation started to sink in. Alaric had been so relieved that they had managed to cross the causeway that he didn't really care about what was before them. He knew that the land was destroyed, but he didn't realise the full extent.

"I think it's time to don the thick robes we have to protect us from the sun." Alaric said after they had been walking for an hour.

Despite the intense heat radiating from the sun he had avoided suggesting the robes. He could already start to feel the sun burning his skin and he couldn't risk it any longer.

It was shortly after midday when the temperature started to become unbearable. Both Alaric and Marina were covered in sweat, not only the two of them, but their horses as well. Adelanta was trying his best not to show that he was starting to struggle. Marina's mare, on the other hand, had no compunction to hide her discomfort. Alaric was also starting to feel uncomfortable and looked around for somewhere for them to rest, but that land was barren. If the heat became any worse, and Alaric was expecting it to, he didn't think they would survive the day.

Alaric kept his eyes open for somewhere they could escape the heat as they continued to trudge through the sandy ground. The only shaded places were under the jagged rocks sticking out from the ground, but Alaric didn't think that they would be much use. The difference in temperature wouldn't be that great. They needed to find a cave, not only that, but it might be their only chance of survival. Alaric looked around but he couldn't see anything that even vaguely looked like a cave. Just because there were caves in Nostiria whenever they needed them didn't mean that they would be in the wasteland. The more he thought about it the more he doubted that there would be. Nostiria, even though it was a veritable wasteland, it was designed to be inhabited. The wasteland, on the other hand, was not.

It was an hour later when Marina collapsed to her knees. It was the soft thud that made Alaric turn around. He turned around just in time to see her mare also drop to her knees. They both looked exhausted and Alaric feared that they had travelled too far. He looked around in one last, vain effort to find shelter. As he expected there were only the jagged rocks. He had no other option. He had no doubt that if they stayed out in the sun that they would die. Their only chance for survival was to hide in the shade of the rocks. Alaric didn't like their chances, but there was nothing else he could do.

With Adelanta's help he moved Marina to the shade of the closest rock. Moving the mare was a different story. There was not enough room under the rock for the horses and the two of them. The next rock that was suitable for shade was over fifty paces away. Alaric tried to get the mare onto her feet, but she did not move. Her eyes were glassy and she was covered in sweat.

"Come on, Adelanta, we have to get her into the shade," Alaric was desperate.

Alaric wiped his brow and started to unload her burden. The last thing he wanted to do was overexert himself, but he couldn't let the mare die. Only they needed shade, it didn't matter if their possessions remained in the burning sun.

Adelanta took a tentative step closer until his head was over the mare's. He snorted once and waited for a response. Even without her load the mare didn't seem interested in rising. It was almost like she had already given up. When no response came Adelanta stamped his foot. The mare flickered her ears and looked up at the stallion. All Alaric could do was stand back and watch the show. He had no idea what Adelanta was doing, but he hoped that it was working. The stallion's next move took everyone by surprise. He reared up on his hind legs and whinnied at the top of his voice. Sweat flicked from his body and mane. The move was what was needed to raise the mare. Slowly, and shaken, she stood. Adelanta remained close by, just in case she needed assistance.

With the mare on her feet came the slow journey to the shelter of the rocks. When they were passing Marina, Adelanta snorted and flicked his head towards her. Alaric knew exactly what he meant and did not need to be asked twice. Alaric took a couple of packs from the stallion and disappeared into the shade of the rock.

The shade was surprisingly refreshing. The temperature was still hot, but it was no longer life-threatening. After he caught his breath he focused his attention on Marina. She was still lying where Alaric had left her. Her face was pale and covered in sweat. Strands of her black hair stuck to her face. In a strange way Alaric thought that she looked quite beautiful. If it wasn't for her laboured breathing he would have thought that she was relaxing on a summer's afternoon. He quickly put the thought out of his mind and he rummaged through his possessions until he found one of the water pouches. Despite the fact that they had been trying to preserve their water supplies the pouch was almost empty. If they ran out of water then they would be dead for sure, but he still had to try and rehydrate her. His mouth was dry and he wanted nothing more than to drain one of the water-pouches himself.

To his surprise he found that the water was still cool to touch. He thought that he better test the water temperature first expecting it to be close to boiling. Hot water could make her sick and that would defeat the purpose. Unbeknownst to Alaric the elves had replaced their water pouches. The elven ones were able to keep the water cold when their originals ones would not have.

Gently he lifted Marina's head off the ground. She slowly opened her eyes and smiled when she saw Alaric's face. The effort was clearly laboured.

"Drink slowly," Alaric kept his voice soft as he started to pour some water into her mouth.

He continued until she had drunk her fill. There was no point in saving water if Marina was going to die in the process. Once she had finished Alaric took a number of small drinks himself. He didn't drink his fill, but he was sure that he had drunk enough to keep himself going. When he was finished he tried to make himself as comfortable as possible.

He looked out at Marina's possessions and hoped that they would remain safe. Before he relaxed he had made his way to the edge of the shade and he could feel the intensity of the heat from the ground. It had increased since they had reached the safety of the rock and he didn't think he would last long if he tried to reach the packs.

After drinking Marina remained lying on the ground. Alaric let her head rest in his lap and gently stroked her hair in an attempt to comfort her. He was relieved that her breathing had returned to normal. There was still a layer of sweat on her body, but it was not as bad as it had been. Alaric was confident that she was going to be alright. The horses would need watering, but there was nothing he could do until the temperature started to drop again. It would not be a pleasant afternoon for the two animals, but he was confident they would survive.

When the sun started to wane Alaric thought that he would brave the heat to look after the horses. He thought that he would be safe enough. He was sure that the intense heat of the day would have passed, but he was wrong. He took one step out of the shade and he could feel his skin starting to burn. He quickly jumped back into the safety of the shade and regretted not putting on his thick robe again. A tendril of smoke wisped from his arm. His initial reaction was to pour soothing water onto it, but he refrained at the last moment. He would have to suffer through the pain. They could not afford to waste the water.

He peered around the edge of the rock to see if he could see how the horses were doing. He could see them just before he had to leave the safety of the shade. They were both lying under the protection of the rock. It looked as though Adelanta was comforting the mare. The sight made Alaric smile. They were both trying to make the best of a bad situation. He only hoped that they could hold out until he was able to get to them.

When he returned to Marina he found that she had fallen asleep. She looked so peaceful. Alaric was happy to let her sleep. It was not like they had anything else to do. He would like to sleep himself, but he knew he had to remain awake. As soon as it was safe to leave they would have to keep moving. In Nostiria the cold of night came on quickly. So quick that those caught outside had a greater chance of dying than what they had of surviving. The shade was nice during the heat of the day, but he didn't think the rocks would give them any protection during the night. That thought weighed heavily on his mind.

Every fifteen minutes Alaric poked his arm out of the shade to see if the temperature was dropping. Each time he quickly retracted it as it started to burn and his frustration continued. The only plus was that Marina was able to rest, but it did nothing for Alaric's nerves. It wasn't until the sun finally set that Alaric was able to leave and check on the horses. He was relieved that the temperature had not dropped that much, but he still felt as though they needed to find a better shelter.

"It's time to get up," Alaric gently woke Marina after he had fed, watered and loaded the horses. "We have to keep moving."

Marina slowly came awake. She looked up into the darkness, as if she was trying to figure out where she was. It took her a moment, but she finally worked out who was looking down on her. When she did a serious look crossed her face.

"What happened?" she asked slowly.

Alaric started to explain, but then he stopped himself short. He really didn't have time to waste. Once they reached the safety of shelter he would continue his explanation. He helped her to her feet and to where the horses were waiting for them. When he was happy that she was steady on her feet he started them south again.

It did not take long for him to realise that his thinking was flawed. Although the full moon was enough for them to see the ground in front of them it was not enough to scan the land for a cave. There was no way to tell what was more than a few paces around them. The only way they would find a cave would be to stumble across one. The temperature was still hot as they walked into the night, but Alaric was not sure how long it was going to last.

There was another option, but he was not sure that it was one he was willing to risk. He could magically enhance his eyesight so he could see further than what was natural. The only problem was that he was too exhausted. He didn't think that he had the strength to create the spell and then mask it. The last thing he wanted was to announce to Na'garoz that he had entered the wasteland. He was sure that the Dark Knight was expecting him, but he didn't want to give anything away. The longer he could keep his enemy guessing the better.

They had only been walking for about two hours before Alaric felt the chill of the night on his skin. The temperature was dropping quickly, a little too quickly for his liking. He had no choice. He had to use a spell to check his surroundings. If there was no shelter then he didn't think they would survive. At the rate the temperature was dropping it would be freezing before midnight.

"What is that?" Marina's voice distracted him just as he was about to start his spell. There was hope in her voice and that caught his attention.

He looked in the direction he thought she was pointing. In the darkness he could not see what she was talking about, although there was something itching in the back of his mind. He didn't know if it was a good sign or a bad sign. He continued to look in hope that he would see what she was talking about, but it was too dark

"What are you looking at?" Alaric was almost ashamed to ask.

"I don't know, but I think we should take a look," she sound somewhat excited.

She steered her mare off the line of where Alaric was leading them. At first the mare didn't want to leave Adelanta's side, but eventually she had to do what Marina instructed her to. She was a little nervous until Alaric steered Adelanta in her direction. With the white stallion back by her side the mare was a lot more confident.

As they neared their destination Alaric could see what she was talking about. Besides the rocky protrusions the land had been relatively flat. What was before them seemed like a small hill. Alaric's heart started to race. If there was a hill then there was a chance that there was a cave. There was a good chance that they would not die of exposure.

"I think that there is a cave up ahead." Alaric no idea how Marina was able to see so far ahead. He could only just make out the hill. "It looks as though it will be big enough for us to spend the night."

Once they reached the foot of the small hill they could both see that there was a small entrance to a cave cut into its side. They were so excited that they had found somewhere to stay that they didn't stop to think that there might already be someone or something inside.

The light of the moon only just poked into the entrance of the cave. The rest of the cave was pitch black. Neither Alaric nor Marina could see in front of them and there was no way they could continue without some light. It was up to Alaric to create a light spell. He was confident that he would be able to do it and also mask the spell. What he had to do would not take a lot of energy and soon enough he would be able to rest.

Alaric reached out and touched Marina getting her to stop. It was not long before a small ball of light floated in the air a pace in front of them. The sudden light made Alaric blink. Marina had to put a hand in front of her eyes to block its brightness. It took them a moment to adjust their eyes and when they did they could finally see what they had gotten themselves into.

The cave was larger than they had expected. There was a short entrance tunnel before it opened into the true cave. It was twenty paces deep and ten paces wide. There was more than enough room for the four of them and they were all grateful to be out of the cold. The sun's heat filtered through the rocks during the day and created a warm environment during the night. By morning the cave would be cold again, but that was something that they would have to worry about later. For the moment they were happy that they were in a warm, safe place.

Once they were seated it didn't take long before they were both shivering. The warmth of the sun was already starting to leave the cave. Alaric quickly unpacked their things from the horses. The thin blankets that accompanied their bedrolls were little comfort, but it was better than nothing. They were both thankful that they had loaded some wood on the horses and not decided to ride. It wasn't long before Alaric had a small fire burning in the centre of the cave.

"Do you think that we are going to survive this?" The warmth was returning to her body and she was no longer shivering.

"I don't think we have any other choice," there was little comfort in his words. He had to admit to himself that he was thinking the same thing. He didn't know how they were going to get out of the wasteland. There was only so long the wood would last and once it was gone he didn't know what they would do.

Marina had noticed that Alaric's attitude had lost all of its strength. When she had first met him in Kiarome he was oozing confidence. His confidence had waned, nearly on a daily basis, as they approached the wasteland. It was more worrying for Marina than what lay before them. She was sure that if he did not regain his strength that they would certainly die. He would need all his wits to defeat the Dark Knight. She only wished she knew what she could do to help.

"I need to get some sleep. Hopefully we will get some answers in the morning," he sounded even more downtrodden.

Marina stayed awake a little longer after Alaric had fallen asleep. The sleep she had got during the day still refreshed her. The fire slowly dwindled until it extinguished completely. Despite the impending cold they couldn't use all the wood in one night. Although the cave was completely dark she still looked down at where he was sleeping. Since she couldn't see him she had to imagine what he looked like. She hoped that the next day would bring a new hope. She didn't know how long she herself could remain positive, not that she was doing such a great job, with Alaric feeling the way he did.

Slowly Marina fell asleep with those thoughts racing through her mind. She had to figure out a way to lift Alaric's spirits. As she drifted off to sleep no ideas came to her. Throughout the night her dreams were haunted by the question that plagued her. She knew that there was an answer was in there somewhere, but when just when she thought it was in her grasp it disappeared.

Chapter 26: A New Day

Alaric woke early in the morning. The cave was still dark and the heat had completely gone. It was not as cold as it was outside, but it was still very uncomfortable. Although he could not see her he knew by the sound of her breathing that Marina was still asleep. He crept out of the cave to see what it was like outside. He didn't get to the mouth of the tunnel before he had to turn around and go back in. The temperature was too cold for him to go any further. He thought about lighting a fire, but figured that it would be hot enough, soon enough.

"What is it?" Marina asked when he returned.

"It's too cold outside," he shivered as he spoke, vibrating his speech. "We are going to have to wait for the sun to rise before we can leave."

"What about a fire?" Marina reflected his shiver.

"We need to save the wood. There is no telling how long it will take to reach the Dark Knight. I can still feel the prophecy, but I can't feel its exact location."

They both understood what that meant. They could only travel from sun up to early afternoon. Time was their enemy and it just became even stronger. Any hope that remained was slowly dissipating.

Alaric recreated the light ball from the night before so at least they could see each other. Since Marina was awake there was no point in remaining in the dark. At least they would be able to eat before the sun rose and not waste any more time. Once the sun was up they would have to leave. In the time remaining they would have to prepare themselves.

Alaric busied himself preparing the animals and their meals in an attempt to avoid conversation. Marina was still concerned about Alaric's attitude and saw straight through his acts. The sleep seemed to have regenerated him somewhat, but he still seemed downtrodden. She knew that she had to say something, but she didn't know what. If she didn't say the right thing then she could make matters worse.

"Are you feeling alright?" she asked and then cursed herself silently for asking such a stupid question.

"I'm fine, why do you ask?" Alaric said as he loaded the horses. He had hoped he could avoid her until dawn, but that was not going to be the case.

Marina had hoped that her question might have led a little further than it did. She didn't know what to say. There was no way around it. All she could do was to come right out and say what she was thinking. The last thing that she wanted to do was to bring light to the situation, but if it helped then it would be worth it. It wasn't until Alaric turned around that she realised that she had not replied to his question. He looked as though he was about to say something, but he stopped before he spoke. It was obvious that he was not going to speak first.

"It's nothing," she couldn't bring herself to say the words.

"Then I think that you should get ready. We will be moving very shortly," Alaric didn't sound impressed.

There was very little for Marina to do to get ready. It was not like there was anywhere for her to bathe. All she had to do was put her robe on and she was ready to go. She made a show of trying to comb the knots out of her head to look busy. That seemed to satisfy Alaric and it did give her something keep her mind off her problems.

It did not take long before a small sliver of light crept in through the entrance tunnel. It was all that Alaric needed to get them moving again. The wait inside the cave was excruciating and he couldn't wait to be outside. They had to make as much ground as they could before they would have to find another cave.

The air was still fresh when they exited the cave. Alaric could already feel the heat of the sun on the back of his neck. He would travel for as long as he could without donning the thick cloak, but it seemed as though that would not be long. There was no doubt that it would not be long until the travelling was unbearable again. He had to take advantage of the cool conditions to push as hard as he could. He thought about lightening the loads of the horses and riding them, but they needed everything they carried. It would only be another day or two before the wood dwindled enough for them to ride again.

Marina kept her mare a step behind as she watched Alaric closely to see if there was any change in his demeanour. He kept a look of pure determination on his face. Marina couldn't tell what he was thinking. She didn't think that his attitude had changed. It seemed as though he was racing towards a grim end and the thought made Marina even more worried. She knew that she would have to speak to him when they had a chance to stop.

Alaric kept trekking through midday. Marina was hoping to stop for something to eat, but Alaric seemed determined to keep moving. Again the heat was starting to get to all of them. Alaric could sense that there was another haven somewhere in front of them and he didn't want to stop until he reached it.

The mid-afternoon sun beat down on them. Both Marina and the mare were starting to struggle. Alaric didn't seem to notice the other two. If it wasn't for Adelanta, Alaric would have marched them all to death. He was so focused on finding shelter that he didn't notice everyone was failing.

There were no caves in sight, but again there were plenty of rocky outcrops to provide shade. Adelanta simply stopped in front of one and refused to go any further. Alaric tugged on his reins, but that would not get him to move.

"I think that this is as far as we can go," Marina's voice was dry. It sounded as though she was really struggling to speak.

It was the sound of Marina's strained voice that brought Alaric back to reality. It was only then that he realised how hot it had become. His focus on the task ahead helped to block out the intense heat, but he was quick to realise that it would not be long before their skin would start burning off their bones. Even in the thick robes of the elves there would be nothing they could do to stop from burning.

"Of course," Alaric quickly led them into the shade of the rock.

Adelanta seemed impatient as Alaric unloaded him and then the mare. Marina simply collapsed once she was in the shade. Despite the fact that she wanted to help Alaric the heat had beaten her down and she could not move any more. The only thing stopping her from losing consciousness was the fact that she needed to confront Alaric. She was happy for the chance to catch her breath whilst he unloaded the animals.

Once Alaric had finished unloading them Adelanta led the mare to their own rock. Alaric was much happier once he was in the protection of the shade. His skin retained the heat and it was hard to cool down. He wanted to pour cold water over his arms and face, but he knew that he couldn't. There was nothing he could do to relieve the heat. All he could do was try to relax and wait for the sun to set. Then it would be another dash for shelter before they froze to death. He was already starting to regret his decision to follow Na'garoz into the wasteland. He was sure that there was another way for him to get the prophecy back. Na'garoz would have to come back to the mainland eventually.

"What are you thinking about?" again Marina was hoping that he would offer her something, even though the question was weak.

"What?" Alaric didn't hear the question. When Marina re-asked it he thought carefully about his response. "I don't know if I made the right decision to come into the wasteland. I am not even sure if I am going to live to regret this."

Marina took a deep breath. She had to admit that she regretted bringing up the conversation. She was still struggling with the heat and she needed all her energy for what she had to do. Since she had started there was no going back. She had to break Alaric from his malaise.

"You have to stop thinking about that," her weakened state made her words less effective. She paused to catch her breath, which Alaric took her being finished with what she was saying. In the end she was happy that he took the opportunity to speak.

"I don't know what you want from me. We are still so far away from Na'garoz. I don't know if we are going to make it. We can only survive for so long on the rations we have set ourselves. There is every chance that we could die of dehydration before we run out of water," Alaric's words brought no joy to Marina.

"Stop that!" Marina started coughing as she raised her voice. Her throat was dry and yelling was not an option. "This is not the Alaric that I…" she let that thought trail away, but continued speaking before Alaric could think of a word to end the sentence. "It is not the Alaric that I met in Kiarome," she hoped that she covered her mistake. "We will not die here," she was struggling to speak, which made her statements lose their effect. "You need to be strong if you are going to defeat Na'garoz."

Alaric turned away from Marina and looked out at the wasteland. He heard her words, but they had little effect. The surrounding land was much worse than Marina's words. He didn't know how she could be so positive with all the desolation around them. He knew that there must be something in her words, but he couldn't see what it was.

"I think you should save your energy. This heat is not good for either of us," it was a fair sign that Alaric didn't want to continue the conversation.

Marina hated the fact that she had given him the opportunity to quit the conversation, but she had to admit that he was right. She didn't have the energy to keep up the conversation. She would have to give it another try once they reached their stopping point for the night.

The day drifted away slowly. Marina tried to get some sleep, but she couldn't. Her mind was still thick with the questions she would have to ask. She was not looking forward to the conversation.

Again they had to wait until the sun had set before they were able to set out again. They were not gone long before Marina suddenly reined her mare to a halt. Alaric continued a short way before he realised that she had stopped. He was a little annoyed, but he returned to speak with her.

"What is it?" he asked, trying to keep his voice level.

"I don't know. All of a sudden I felt something." She seemed to be concentrating on something other than Alaric.

"What is it that you felt?" Alaric was a little more annoyed at having to ask the question.

"It's hard to explain. It feels familiar, but I don't know exactly what it is." Alaric thought he saw a smile appear on her face. If it wasn't for their current situation he would have thought that she was beautiful in the moonlight. He thought that she glowed slightly.

"Anyway, we should keep moving. It will be getting cold very soon," Marina didn't wait for Alaric to answer.

Alaric remained where he was for a moment and shook his head. He didn't know what Marina was doing. She seemed to be all over the place and he really did think he should be following her. He couldn't understand women at the best of times and the princess seemed to be the hardest to understand of all the women he knew. She didn't even seem to notice that he was not following her. Adelanta wasn't prepared to wait any longer. It wasn't until he felt the tug on the reins before Alaric realised that Adelanta had started moving. If he didn't follow suit then he would have to let the reins go and that wasn't something he was prepared to do.

Alaric remained a couple of paces behind Marina despite Adelanta's insistence that they catch up. Every now and again she changed direction with no explanation of where she was leading them. Alaric was not sure if she knew where she was going, but it was better than nothing. He had no idea where to find the next cave, so he just remained silent and followed obediently. The only feeling he had was the gentle tug of the prophecy and he knew that wasn't leading them towards a cave. For a change he was able to follow instead of having to lead. He was able to relax, ever so slightly, not being in control.

Again they were close to freezing before Marina finally found them a place to stay for the night. The cave was slightly larger than the one they had staying in the night before. Again Alaric had to create a ball of light for them to see. There was another small chamber at the back of the cave that looked as though something had been living there. Alaric's initial reaction was to leave, but they had not seen any other sign of life since they had entered the wasteland. Alaric did not want to wait to find out what sort of creature could survive in such a place. The only problem was that they could not longer leave the cave. Marina assured him that if there had been something there that it would be long gone. Whatever it was would have to already be there if it was going to survive the cold of the night. Although she wasn't completely sure it did make sense to her.

Once they had eaten and settled down for the night Marina decided that it was time to have the conversation that she had started earlier in the day. She needed to break Alaric from his malaise. She didn't know how long it would take for them to find Na'garoz, but she knew she could not risk waiting. As much as she did not want to have the conversation she knew that she had no choice.

"Please, tell me what is bothering you?" Marina asked as she nestled into her bedroll.

Despite the fact that their fire had almost burned out Alaric extinguished the spell that created the light ball. Marina wasn't sure if he had done so to avoid the conversation, but she wasn't going to let it go. When there was no response she decided to push him further,

"You need to snap out of it Alaric."

Alaric was surprised at her hard words, but he knew she was right. He sighed before he spoke. "I don't know. Ever since we entered the wasteland I have had a feeling that we are not going to survive. I know that it's stupid, but I can't help it," Alaric sounded defeated as he confessed.

In the fading firelight Marina could the see the look of resignation on his face. She was afraid that he had already given up. There was no real answer to his problem. All she could do was to try and give him comfort.

"We have made it this far. I am sure that we are not meant to die here in this desolate place," Marina steeled her voice. She had to believe the words herself if she was going to convince him.

"I suppose that makes sense, but there is nothing to say that we will survive," there was a small spark in his voice, but it was gone all too quickly.

"I am sure that the story does not end here. Why would the prophecy put you through so much just to end your life in the wasteland," her words were starting to convince herself as much as they were convincing Alaric. "It doesn't make any sense. We were meant to come into the wasteland. I can feel it and I don't think it was to die. I am sure that the prophecy will reveal itself soon. All we have to do is remain positive," she was afraid to look in Alaric's direction. She was afraid that he would see through her words and see her true feelings.

Alaric thought about what she said. Her words made sense and that made him feel a little better. He did have a sense that he was supposed to be in the wasteland. The feeling of dread was slowly starting to lift and he also did not think that the prophecy would want him to die in such a manner. The thought was pleasing to him. He knew he couldn't rely solely on the prophecy to keep him alive. That would be naïve, but it was reassuring to think that the prophecy was on their side.

"The more that you think on it the more it makes sense," Marina continued. She knew that she was having a positive effect on Alaric's mood. "The prophecy has brought us here for a reason. Until we realise that reason we have to keep out spirits high." Even in the failing light of the fire neither of them noticed the Sapphire stone had started to glow gently as Marina spoke.

Alaric knew that she was right, but it was easier said than done. Although he did feel a little better the feeling of dread still weighed heavily on him. The thoughts bounced around inside his head as he tried to sleep. The only thing that kept him calm was the sound of Marina's gentle breathing. He found it hard to believe that she was being so strong, whilst he was falling apart. It was that thought that was in his mind when he finally fell asleep.

His dreams were pleasant and he woke in the morning, refreshed and ready for what the day had for them. He lit the orb, but kept it low until Marina awoke. She was pleased to see that his spirits had lifted as he busied himself readying the animals.

"You look more like your old self," Marina started as she ate her morning meal.

"I feel much better," initially Alaric didn't acknowledge the part that Marina played. When he saw the look on her face he thought that he better. "Thank you for what you did last night. If it wasn't for your words I don't know what I would have done," he embellished a little.

His words made her blush. As much as she wanted him to acknowledge what she had done when she heard his words it made her embarrassed. Alaric did the right thing and pretended that he didn't notice. Marina was grateful for that.

"What's the plan for today?" Marina wanted to change the subject. She was not really expecting much of a reply as she was sure it would continue on much the same as the previous two.

"I need to focus," Alaric paused as he took the last mouthful of his breakfast. "That is the mistake that I have been making," he continued when he finished eating. Marina wasn't sure what he was talking about, but she didn't want to interrupt him. "I have been able to feel the prophecy."

"You have mentioned this before," Marina spoke softly. "But I don't understand what you are getting at. Isn't the prophecy still too far away?"

"That's what I have assumed, but now I am not so sure. I think that Na'garoz might be having a hand in it. I can't be completely sure until I try, but I think that he is masking the prophecy. If I concentrate enough I should be able to get around his spell, but more importantly he shouldn't be able to notice. There is a connection between me and the *Prophecy of the Stone*. I have forgotten how powerful that link can be. If I can regain that connection then it should give us more direction," there was a spark in Alaric that Marina had not seen in a long time.

"Then what are you waiting for?" Marina's voice was uplifting. "The sooner you do this the sooner we can get going again."

Alaric was about to say something, but then thought better of it. He crossed his legs and sat with his back straight. He didn't know why, but he felt more comfortable in that position. He closed his eyes and slowed his breathing. Marina watched him closely, but she could not see anything change. Meanwhile there was plenty going on inside Alaric's mind. He relaxed his body so he could concentrate more on his mental power. The prophecy was still somewhere to the south, but he could not pinpoint its exact location. He had assumed that it was because the prophecy was so far away, but now he was not so sure. The sense of the prophecy could have been anywhere from a couple of paces to a hundred leagues away. Until he was able to pinpoint the location there was not much point in them moving.

Slowly the light orb started to fade and Alaric's face started to turn pale. Marina thought she should help him, but stopped herself before she came too close. She had to accept that he was doing the right thing and she didn't want to break his concentration. Slowly she felt something brush against her shoulder and she jumped in surprise. When she looked around there was nothing there and she just put it down to the tense situation playing tricks on her.

Although his exterior was starting to look weak, internally he was fine. His mind was searching for the prophecy as his body drew on small amounts of energy around him being careful not to draw anything from Marina or the horses. He panned out in the space around him. He could not see anything, but he could feel if he was going in the right direction. Already he was feeling the prophecy becoming clearer. The distance was starting to become less and less. His breathing started to become laboured as his scanned the vast nothingness around him. Slowly he was starting to struggle to stay in control of what he was doing. He knew that he was getting closer to his goal. Just when he thought he had found what he was looking for his concentration was suddenly broken. As his consciousness returned to the cave he collapsed on the floor.

At first Marina didn't know what to do, but that quickly passed. She rushed to where was lying and lifted his head off the floor. His face was still pale and his eyes were shut. She rested his head in her lap and gently stroked his hair. She didn't know what else she could do. The thought of pouring water on his face crossed her mind, but she didn't think he would appreciate the waste of their supplies.

The ordeal had drained Alaric, but he knew it was something that he would soon get over. It did not take long for him to recover, yet he remained in Marina's lap. There was something very comforting about her touch. He knew that it was not yet sunrise, so there was no hurry for them to move. Marina seemed content taking care of him, so he didn't see the harm in what he was doing.

"Are you alright?" Marina asked after they had been sitting there for a while.

"I should be in a moment or two," Alaric kept his voice weak, even though he was feeling better.

Marina smiled as she looked down at him. She didn't realise that he was feeling better. She just liked being this close to him. The thought returned to the night they spent in the tree hut and her smile broadened. She had to admit that it was one of the happiest nights of her life. She wished that she could spend more nights like that, but she knew it would not happen again for a while. The wasteland wasn't really the right setting for what she had in mind.

"I think that we should get moving now," Alaric lifted his head as he spoke. It just so happened that his decision to move coincided with the sun rising.

Marina didn't want to move, but Alaric had already started to rise. She felt a little sad to be on the move again. There had been a breakthrough with Alaric and she didn't want to leave. The cave had retained more heat than the one they stayed in the previous night. It was still quite pleasant and she knew that the outside would very soon become hot.

"So what happened? Did you locate the prophecy?" Marina asked as they walked out of the cave.

Alaric didn't want to speak of his failure. He knew that he was close, very close to finding what he was looking for. He only hoped that it wasn't Na'garoz who blocked his search. If he had then there was a good chance that he knew they were in the wasteland. There was a big difference between the Dark Knight assuming they were coming for him and him knowing. Once he knew they were there then he could prepare for them.

"Not in so many words," Alaric spoke when he realised that Marina was staring at him. "I am closer than I was last night, but I still cannot pinpoint its exact location."

Marina wasn't sure exactly what that meant. She couldn't read from his body language if it was a good sign or a bad sign. Alaric wasn't sure himself. He could sense that the prophecy was not as far away as he had originally thought. That in itself was a good sign. They did not want to go further into the wasteland than they had too. The more they had to travel the less chance they had of being able to return. The direction of the prophecy was not any better. All he could say was that the tome was somewhere to the south. One thing he knew for sure was that they were not going to find it that day.

The day passed much the same as the previous two. The landscape had not changed at all. The rocky outcrops were the only shade they could find during the afternoon. Alaric pushed them as far as he could before they had to stop. They again rested for the remainder of the afternoon under the rocks. They were both exhausted from the heat by the time it was time to stop. Neither of them thought that they would be able to travel any further. Alaric was feeling the worst he had felt since he had entered the wasteland. The morning's effort was harder than he had thought.

Once again they had to wait for the sun to set before they were able to move again. Again Alaric let Marina lead the way. Like the night before she moved as though she was possessed. Alaric was concerned, but he had more concern for their safety. Once they were safely in a cave he would ask her. It was now his turn to look after her. He much preferred it that way. He was glad to have his strength back, mentally if not physically.

Marina led them through the darkness until they reached a cave. Alaric still had no idea how she was able to find the caves in the darkness and she did nothing to ease his concerns. The temperature was not quite as cold as it had been the previous two nights. Alaric was tempted to keep moving, but Marina insisted that they stop.

The cave was much warmer than the one they had stayed in the previous night. It seemed the further south they travelled the hotter things were getting. Alaric only lit a small fire to cook their food. He was confident that they would not need the fire for warmth throughout the night.

"Now it is time for you to tell me what is happening?" Alaric didn't know how to broach the subject, but Marina had pushed him and he was going to do the same.

"What are you talking about?" Marina asked as she was busying herself with her bedroll.

"Please stop," Alaric needed her full attention. He walked over and gently pulled her to her feet. "This is important. Something is happening to you and I need to know what it is."

"I don't know what you're talking about. There is nothing happening to me." Alaric thought that Marina seriously believed what she was saying.

"I don't really know how to explain this, but once we start travelling in the evening you seem to go into some kind of a trance. I'm not quite sure how you do it, but you always manage to find us shelter for the night. I want to try and understand what is happening." He was beginning to become concerned.

Marina thought for a moment. She didn't like the way Alaric was looking at her. She didn't know what he was talking about. They had just stumbled across the caves each night. To her recollection she had been following Alaric's lead. She didn't like what he was implying.

"I think that you are the one that has been in a trance. Now if you don't mind I am very tired. I would like to get a good night's sleep," her tone was harsh.

Alaric was taken aback by her response. He could not quite understand why she was being so defensive. The fact that she wanted to sleep and she hadn't even eaten didn't make sense. He watched as she made an effort to cover herself in her bedroll. The scene reminded him of a naughty child sent to bed without their supper. He almost laughed, but he thought that would not improve the situation.

"Are you just going to stand there watching me or are you going to put out the light," she huffed when Alaric did not react to her command.

"Of course, your majesty, but don't you think that it would be a good idea to eat first," Alaric put on his best mocking voice.

The sarcasm was not lost on Marina. She promptly sat upright and scowled at him. Her cheeks were flushed, even more so than the sunburn that already inflicted them. The smile on Alaric's face only made her mood worse. She did not appreciate being mocked.

"Wipe that smile from your face. You are impressing no one," Marina was starting to babble. "If you have nothing better to do I am sure I could find something to keep you busy," the rant made no sense, which only added to Alaric's amusement.

If it wasn't such a serious time Alaric would have been quite happy to tease her further. She was right that they had to go to sleep soon. He had a feeling that the next day was going to be especially taxing and he needed answers.

"What is it that draws you towards the caves?" Alaric re-asked the question. He kept his voice level in an attempt to appease Marina.

"I told you that I don't know what you are talking about. I have no idea how we find the caves." Suddenly Marina felt a warm flash in her face. Neither of them noticed that the Sapphire stone was starting to glow.

"Please Marina," Alaric was starting to become desperate. "I need to know."

The tone in Alaric's voice brought worry to Marina. She truly did not know what Alaric was talking about. She tried to hide it behind her tantrum, but it didn't work. She didn't know how she was going to make Alaric understand.

"I think that I would like to sleep now. I will eat in the morning," Marina's voice was flat.

Alaric stared down at her as she lay down again. She rolled over so her back was facing him. She knew that he was looking at him, but she didn't care. She felt suddenly depressed with what Alaric had done to her. She wanted nothing more than to fall asleep, which she couldn't do with the light still on, but she didn't have the heart to speak to Alaric again.

Marina eventually fell asleep shortly after Alaric extinguished the light. He deliberately kept the light on until he had eaten and looked after the horses. When he was finished he felt guilty at such a childish trick and went to sleep feeling disappointed with the night's events.

***

Marina woke in the middle of the night. The cave was pitch black. She could hear the gentle breathing of Alaric and the two horses. She knew they were in the cave, but she could not guess their exact location. The thought puzzled her for a moment before it washed away. There was something else that caught her mind. Something that was more important. She felt was though someone, or something, was calling her and she felt compelled to follow.

Even though there was no light in the cave Marina had no problems picking her way through the dark. She walked for what she thought was almost an hour. She did not think that the cave was that big, but she did not hit a single wall. The thought seemed strange to her, but it soon washed away. She had to focus on the task in front of her. She had to find who was calling to her. That was all that mattered.

Turning a corner in the cave, she couldn't remember there being any corners in the cave, she noticed that there was a gentle blue light somewhere in the distance. She knew that the light would deliver the answers that she had been looking for. As she neared a feeling of ecstasy came over her. She thought that she would explode with joy and she didn't care if she did.

She walked into the blue light without thinking that there could possibly be any danger. As she did the feeling of bliss settled. It still remained, but it didn't grow any stronger. She rubbed her arms and her chest as she was as if she was bathing in the light. She wanted to cover herself in its majesty.

Suddenly she felt another presence. She looked around nervously, but she could not see anyone. She was afraid that whoever it was would take away the blue light and the feeling of bliss. That thought made her panic for a moment before the feeling of ecstasy took over again. She forgot about what had made her afraid and returned to basking in the light. The thought of the other presence left her mind.

"Why have you come here?" the voice echoed around her, yet the voice was soft and feminine.

The voice didn't bother Marina. In fact the sound of it made her even more content, if that was possible. She could not see anyone around the light, but she knew that they were there. She could feel someone on the edge of her senses. It was as if they were on another plain of reality. The thought should have made her upset, but it didn't. She was quite happy with her situation, although she did not know the answer to her question.

"I don't know. You summoned me, so I came," it seemed as though it was the obvious response.

She thought she heard the sound of laughter in the distance. It was as if someone was cackling at her. The sound made her suddenly feel self-conscious. She wanted to step out of the light and back into the darkness. The only thing that stopped her was the fear that her feeling of pure joy would dissipate. She remained where she stood and waited for the voice to speak again.

"It was not I who summoned you here. It was you who summoned me. I have come here on your bidding," there was a touch of mocking in her voice.

"I don't understand," Marina was confused. She had followed the call towards the blue light. She did not create it, did she? "What do you mean?" her voice was small, like a child's.

A sense that the woman was thinking came to Marina. She didn't know where the sensation had come from, but she understood its meaning. When it suddenly disappeared she knew that she was about to speak again.

"You have questions for me, that is why you summoned me here," the voice now sounded like a mother trying to calm a restless child.

"I do not know who you are. How can I have questions for you?" Marina was still confused.

"Think, my child. You will know what it is you want," Marina thought that there was a touch of impatience in the voice.

The last thing Marina wanted to do was to disappoint the voice. She had to reason out the riddle. There was a reason she had been drawn into the light, but it completely eluded her. Why would she call a meeting with someone she had never met before? If she had been thinking properly she might have asked who was in the wasteland. As she thought the blue light washed over her and she relaxed again. She knew the answer was somewhere in her mind, but it was so hard to concentrate. When she thought she was close to finding the answer another wave of bliss washed over her.

"I know," she blurted suddenly.

"Very good. Relax and explain it to me," the voice spoke softly.

Marina hadn't noticed how excited she had become. She took a deep breath before speaking again. "Alaric wanted to know how I find the caves at night. I didn't think that I was doing it, but now I am not sure. Can you tell me?" Her true question was underlying in the question she asked.

"You know the answer already. You do not need to ask that question of me. Think harder." It was not the response that she had expected.

Marina tried to think again. If that was not the right question then what was? How could she already know the answer to her first question? The questions raced through her mind, but no answers came to her. She wished that the voice would just answer the question that she knew

Marina had to ask. It would be so much easier, but she knew it would not happen that way. For whatever reason that voice wanted her to work it out herself.

It took what seemed hours to Marina before the question dawned on her. When it finally did she wondered why it had taken her so long. The question itself seemed so simple. She was almost embarrassed to ask it. She should not have taken so long to realise what it was.

"Who are you?" she asked softly.

"Very good my child. I knew that you would realise in the end," Marina thought that she heard the sound of soft clapping somewhere in the distance. "You and I are joined by a bond that no other could possibly imagine. We are two and we are one. There is no one that can break that bond, now that we are joined," the voice didn't really answer her question.

"I can feel the bond," she could, although she did not know what it was. "But that does not explain who you are."

"No, I guess that it doesn't, but you already know what it is that you are looking for. You do not need me tell you. I fear that our time is up," the voice almost sounded sad.

Marina was about to speak again, but the blue light suddenly blinked out. Before Marina knew what she was doing she realised that she was sitting upright in her bedroll. Alaric had recreated the light orb and was busying himself making breakfast. Marina looked around for any sign of her friend, but there was none.

"Good morning Marina, did you sleep well?" Alaric's voice was cheerful, although Marina did not know how to answer the question.

Chapter 27: Friend and Foe

Marina was quiet during their morning meal. She was not sure if what had happened during the night was real or just a dream. As she looked around the cave it became more and more apparent that it had just been a dream. The cave was not big enough for what she had done. The only problem she had was that it seemed so real. The memory remained in her mind whereas a dream would have already started to fade. Alaric didn't seem to notice her reverie. For some reason he was excited about the day's journey. Marina didn't notice or else she would have questioned his renewed vigour.

"It is time for us to keep moving," Alaric spoke when they had both finished eating.

Marina didn't respond. It was only then did he realise that she was deep in thought. He waited until he had the horses packed before he spoke to her again. He hoped that by the time he had finished she would have broken from her reverie.

"Are you alright Marina? You haven't said a word since last night." Alaric was starting to become concerned. He hoped that she wasn't still sulking.

Marina suddenly realised that Alaric was looking down at her and suddenly felt very self-conscious. She blushed slightly, which was hard to see under the sunburn, before getting up. She hoped that Alaric didn't ask her any questions. She still didn't know what to make of everything. There was a feeling that the answers were not that far away and all she had to do was think about them and everything would become clear. She didn't think that would happen if Alaric pestered her.

"Yes, sorry, I was just thinking," she hoped that would be enough to appease him. "I am ready to go now," she added quickly before Alaric could speak.

She jumped to her feet and moved over towards her mare. Alaric simply watched her leave the cave and wondered what she had been thinking about so intently. Something had happened to her during the night, he was sure of that. He hoped that she would tell him sooner rather than later. He would let it go for a while, but eventually he would have to ask her if she did not tell him herself.

Alaric was content to be on the road again. He felt refreshed. He had a new lease on life. He could feel the prophecy and he knew that it was close. He still couldn't tell exactly where it was, but he knew that it was only two or three days away.

They had been travelling for about two hours when Alaric gently tugged on Adelanta's reins. Marina had been deep in thought throughout the walk, but she stopped as soon as Alaric did. She didn't know why he had stopped, but she didn't want to give him another reason to question her. She was concerned that was that reason why he had stopped them. She still remained and waited for Alaric to speak first.

"There is something out there," he looked towards the horizon as he spoke.

Marina looked to where Alaric was looking to try and see what he was talking about. The horizon was only half a league away, broken up by a small hill. There was nothing but sand and the occasional rock as far as the eye could see. Marina stared until her eyes became sore. As much as she didn't want to speak she had to ask the question.

"I don't see anything. What are you talking about?" she whispered.

Alaric put his finger up to his lips. "Just wait and see," he whispered so quietly that she only just heard him.

She wished that he had told her what they were waiting for, but she was afraid to speak again. Whatever it was Alaric didn't want them to hear what he was saying. That could not be a good sign. She doubted whatever was coming was going to friendly.

The wait was excruciatingly long. Marina was sure that Alaric was imagining things. They had not seen any living creatures, animal or vegetable, since they had crossed into the wasteland. She doubted very much that there was anything approaching them. She was about to start moving again when she saw something shimmer on the horizon. She almost fell over when she saw an animal walk up the hill. It was hard to see from the distance exactly what it was, but she could see that it stood and walked on its hind legs. It looked as though it was covered in fur, but she could not be sure.

"I think we should go and see who it is," Alaric suggested as he started Adelanta to a walk.

"Wait!" Marina did her best to keep her voice low.

Alaric's body went stiff when he heard her voice. He thought about continuing, but he thought it was better if he heard her out. He pulled on Adelanta's reins and then waited for Marina to join him.

"What's wrong?" he tried to keep the annoyance out of his voice, but he failed.

"I don't think that we should just rush over to whatever that is. If it can survive in such a harsh land I don't really think that is going to be friendly. I dare say such a creature would be hungry. It is not as if there is plenty of food out here. I think would she give it a wide birth," Marina's voice was thick with concern.

Alaric considered her words for a moment. He had to admit that she did make sense. There was nothing to say that the creature before them wouldn't try and eat them once they came closer. It made more sense than anything. The smart thing to do would be to turn around and run, but that had been the smart thing to do ever since they arrived in the wasteland. He had a feeling that the creature did not want to harm them. He didn't know why, but that was enough to convince him to continue. The only problem he had was that he didn't know what to say to Marina.

"I don't think that he want to hurt us." Alaric's defence was weak.

"And what would you be basing this fact on?" Marina was starting to raise her voice.

"Just a hunch. Come on, this will be fun," there was a playful tone in Alaric's voice that annoyed Marina.

Marina did not have a good feeling. She could not believe that Alaric was being so cavalier. She also knew that there was nothing she could do to change his mind. She thought about returning to the safety of the cave, but she didn't think that being alone would be any safer. All she could do was follow and hope that Alaric knew what he was doing.

The creature on top of the hill didn't make any move towards them. It seemed content to let the two of them approach in their own time. The closer they came the more Marina doubted they were doing the right thing. She could see that the creature was in fact covered with rough, brown fur. It was larger than an average man and its muscles could be clearly seen underneath its fur. Even from that distance she did not think the creature looked friendly. She wanted to stop and turn around, but Alaric continued on. His strength of resolve did nothing for Marina's nerves. She could not understand how he could be so calm.

Alaric would not be dissuaded, even if Marina had said anything. As they neared the creature he was not sure if he had made the right decision. The fact that it made no attempt to either attack nor run away was a reassuring sign, but the creature's appearance was another story. As they approached Alaric could see that the creature had sharp claws on its hands and feet and its teeth looked razor sharp. He didn't know what he was going to do if the creature turned hostile. He had his sword, but the creature's hide looked thick. He wasn't sure if he would be able to scratch the surface. He started sweating and it was not just because of the intensifying heat.

Alaric was starting to have second thoughts as they neared the creature. He wondered if he had made the right decision, but there was no turning back. Forward was the only way his legs would carry him. It was the only way they were going to achieve what they came for. He was sure that he would know if they were walking into a trap. That was enough to reassure him. His next problem was how he was going to communicate with the creature.

"Welcome to our land," the creature spoke with a rough voice. He knew that it was a different language different to that spoken in the Seven Kingdoms, but he understood it perfectly.

At first Marina didn't understand the words. It was a rough, guttural language. As she stood back by her mare the words suddenly started to make sense. She didn't know how it happened, but she knew what he was saying.

Alaric turned to see how she was coping. He recognised the look on her face, that meant she knew what was being said. He was happy that he didn't have to explain. Neither of them noticed that the Sapphire stone was softly glowing.

"My name is Caleb. I am a member of the Heji," Caleb explained. "We have been watching you ever since you arrived in our land."

His last comment hit a nerve with Marina. He didn't seem to be a threat and she couldn't help herself. "How can that be true? We have not seen anyone." Alaric wished that she hadn't said anything.

"I think that we know how to travel our land without being seen by strangers," Caleb seemed a little annoyed at what Marina had said. "We could have easily left you out here to die." Alaric didn't think the last comment was necessary.

"I'm sorry. I didn't mean anything," Marina quickly apologised.

"That's alright. I get a little touchy sometimes. We are not used to the way of strangers. I will continue. We saw you enter the wasteland. It has been a while since someone had broken through the mist between our two lands," Caleb didn't get the chance to continue.

"So it was you who created the mist?" Alaric interrupted.

Caleb lowered his head and dropped his shoulders. It was obvious he was not used to such questions. He took a deep breath before he returned his gaze to Alaric. He had to remember that the foreigners had different customs. He thought that life to the north must be very frustrating. If everyone interrupted like the ones before him then it would truly be an annoying place to live. He quickly shook the thought from his head and returned his full attention to Alaric.

"Of course we did not create the mist. It is a natural barrier between our two lands. It has been there for as long as I can remember." Alaric didn't think that sounded right, but he did notice something strange about the magic. He thought that maybe Caleb could be correct. "It is safer for everyone that the barrier exists. We were not meant to live in each other's lands. This is what makes our meeting quite an unusual occurrence."

There were so many questions that Alaric had to ask, but he knew that it was not the place to be having such a meeting. They needed to find shelter before it became too hot. Caleb didn't seem too worried about the heat. Alaric would have thought with his thick coat of hair he would be very uncomfortable.

"I appreciate the candour," Alaric didn't want to offend the Heji. "But I think that we should keep moving."

"Of course, what was I thinking?" Caleb seemed more upset with himself than anyone else. "There are many more of my kin who want to meet you," his words sounded dangerous. "We should make it to our home by nightfall."

Caleb turned and was about to start down the other side of the hill when Alaric spoke. "There is one problem with that," Alaric waited for Caleb to face him before he continued. "We can only travel until early in the afternoon. After then it is too hot. We have to wait until nightfall and then we can continue."

"You, what?" there was deep concern in his voice. Alaric was taken aback by his tone.

"We travel at night time until we reach the safety of the caves." Alaric was trying to gauge a reaction by Caleb's face. He had no idea what the Heji was thinking.

"In the caves?" Caleb sounded even more shocked.

"Of course. It gets too cold for us to stay outside," Alaric didn't see what the problem was.

"I see why none of your kind survives in our land," Caleb looked even more surprised.

"What do you mean?" Alaric asked.

"I will tell you as we continue. We need to move quickly," again Caleb's words were ominous.

Now that it seemed they were safe Alaric took a moment to unload the wood from the two horses. He had a feeling that they would need to ride if they were going to make their destination before they fried.

Caleb's stride easily kept pace with the two horses. In fact it seemed as though he was slowing himself so the horses didn't have to rush. Alaric felt as though he should push Adelanta quicker, but he wasn't sure if Marina's mare was up to the challenge.

"Night time is extremely dangerous in this part of the world. We don't move around outside, unless it is really necessary. There are all numbers of dangerous animals that prey on the darkness. They hunt for their food during the night and they are very efficient. I do not understand how you were able to move around unmolested," Caleb kept watch on the land in front of them as he spoke.

"We didn't see any creatures during the night. You are the first." Marina wasn't sure what to call him, so she decided to skip over the description. "We have seen nothing since entered the..." she was going to call it the wasteland, but she thought that might sound condescending.

"This land," she hoped \ her slips did not offend the large creature. Alaric seemed to be comfortable with him, but she was not so sure. He was such a large, strong creature that if he wanted to kill them she didn't think there was much they could do to stop him. When it was said and done they didn't really have a choice. They needed assistance if they were going to survive.

"That is not to say that there wasn't something looking at you. I do not know why they did not attack, but I can assure you that they were out there. The fact that you visited their nest to sleep at night is even more perplexing. I would have thought that you would have been ripped to shreds when they realised that someone had been sleeping in their cave," there was no humour in Caleb's voice.

Marina nearly fell of her mare when she heard Caleb's words. She didn't realise that they had been sleeping in a creature's cave. More to the point she didn't realise that the creature would more than likely kill her. Alaric, on the other hand, didn't really seem concerned. He continued to sit high in his saddle.

"I cannot tell you the reason." Alaric wasn't sure if it was by design or just by pure luck. "All I know is that we were given a wide berth."

Caleb couldn't help himself. He had to break his view of his surroundings to look at Alaric. He couldn't believe how casual the man was. He was just told that he had been minutes away from a painful death and he just simply brushed it off. He knew that they were special to survive such a long time and to travel so far, but there was something else. He didn't know what it was but he knew that it was there.

They continued on in silence for the rest of the morning. Caleb didn't look as though he was planning on stopping to eat. Alaric wanted to eat and he could only imagine how hungry Marina was becoming. He didn't want to say anything whilst Caleb was so keen to keep moving. He didn't know how far away they were from his home, but if they were able to make it before things became too hot then that would be a great achievement.

Unfortunately they were still a least an hour away when Alaric called for a halt. Caleb seemed annoyed, but there was nothing he could do. When Alaric showed him how their skin was starting to burn he understood. They quickly found a small group of rocks to use for shade.

"I will leave you here. This is a dangerous part of our land. I will make sure that there is nothing hunting us," Caleb didn't wait for Alaric to respond. He could tell that he would struggle to speak.

Alaric passed the water pouches to Marina. She looked as though she was ready to pass out. She drained two half filled pouches before she stopped. There was not much water left for Alaric to drink. He drank a few small mouthfuls, just enough to stop him from losing consciousness. Even though they had seemingly met a friend he didn't know if there was going to be any water. He had not seen Caleb drink since they had met. He wasn't sure, but there was a chance that he did not need water to survive.

"I need to know," Alaric started on the conversation once Caleb had disappeared. "How is it that you keep finding the caves?"

Since they had continued riding in silence Marina had the opportunity to reflect on her dream. She had come to the conclusion it was not a dream. She could still remember the events as if it had truly happened, only she knew that it was impossible. There was no way that it had. The cave was not big enough. She knew that it wasn't a dream, but she had no idea what it truly was.

It had taken a while, but eventually the answers came to her. The realisation, which should have made her happy, in fact had the opposite effect. There was nothing she could do about it. She knew that her lot had been set. Her fate was now intertwined with the Sapphire stone. Alaric had once said to her that she would need to give him the stone, when the time was right. She had agreed at the time, but things had changed and she didn't think she could. She did not think that the ring would be so easily parted from her finger. She had hoped that Alaric would have forgotten his line of questioning when he had met Caleb.

"I can feel the water," Marina kept her head low as she spoke. Her voice was stronger than both her and Alaric would have thought. Alaric thought that she was going to continue. She opened her mouth, but no words came out. She thought that it was better if Alaric asked the obvious question.

"What are you talking about? There is no water. There has not been any water since we entered the wasteland," his words were little more forceful than he had intended.

"There is water," Marina's voice had lost some of its strength. "There is water underground. I can feel it flowing through the underground streams. The caves go down, so the feeling is stronger as it comes closer to the water. I could tell you exactly how far away the Heji's home is. It's underground, like the caves we have been staying in. It is a lot closer to the water supply though. I wouldn't be surprised if there is a water source running through their cavern."

Alaric listened to her words. Her voice sounded gloomy, like she was reflecting on a sad occasion. It took Alaric a moment before he realised what she was talking about. Then came another dilemma. He knew that he should not have let her keep the ring. There seemed to be a bond growing between the two and he didn't like it. He knew that the stones could be devious and they should not be trusted. His experience with the Ruby stone was a prime example. The Jade stone had not been much better. He could only imagine what the Sapphire stone was doing to Marina. He didn't think that she was built to handle such a thing and could easily fall under its spell.

"I think that I should take the ring back now," Alaric hoped that she would just hand it over, although he wasn't going to hold his breath.

Marina looked at the ring on her finger. She heard Alaric's words, but it was as if he was calling to her from the bottom of a well. She didn't want to answer, but she knew that Alaric would not let it lie. She could not give him the ring, even if she wanted to. She only hoped that he would understand.

"I can't," was all she could say as she continued to look at the ring. The Sapphire stone had started to glow at the mere mention of giving up the ring. There was a menace to the glow that Alaric didn't notice. He was too busy focussing on Marina and he still didn't like what he saw.

"At least return the ring to its pouch. I am sure that will make things better," Alaric suggested, knowing that he couldn't push her too hard.

At the sound of Alaric's suggestion Marina suddenly heard an ear-piercing scream. The sound echoed throughout her head. She put her hands up to her ears in a vain attempt to block the noise, but she quickly realised that sound was inside her head. No matter what she did she could not block out the sound. Just when she thought her head was going to explode it disappeared. The next thing she knew was that she was in Alaric's arms. Not only that, but she could feel a certain amount of power radiating from him. She had no idea what it was, but she knew that she didn't want to be anywhere else in the world. She felt safe and secure in his arms.

"I am sorry. I didn't realise that would happen," Alaric gently rocked her and stroked her hair.

"Could you hear it?" she asked, her voice weak.

"No, but I know what you are going through." He was sure that he had done the right thing, even though Na'garoz would have to be completely blind not to have noticed. He reacted too quickly to completely mask the spell. "I will not ask you to relinquish the ring," as he finished speaking she could feel the power leave him.

At first she thought the screaming was going to come back. She knew that he had stopped it, although she did not know how. With the power leaving him so did the spell that he had created and that meant that the screaming could return. She was relieved that it did not. Whatever he had done had worked. Alaric knew that it was the Sapphire stone and he knew how to stop it. He knew exactly what the stone was after.

"We have a problem," he continued. "It seems as though the Sapphire stone has a hold over you and it doesn't want to let go."

Hearing Alaric's words made Marina pull away from him. She didn't like what he was insinuating. It was true that there was a connection between her and the stone, but it was not all one sided. She felt an affinity with it and it was a beautiful thing. Just because Alaric couldn't work out the stones didn't mean that she couldn't. There was no way that she could believe the Sapphire stone was trying to control her. If anything it was trying to help her. It had helped her to find the caves and without it they would already be dead.

"What's the matter?" Alaric was surprised at her reaction.

"I don't think you realise the connection between the stone and I. It is not all one sided. I can feel the stone. I know that I can control it," Marina's words were a shock to Alaric.

He didn't know what to say. He had misjudged Marina, but he didn't think that he was completely wrong. He didn't think that Marina knew what she was getting herself into. There was strength in her that he had not seen before, but he didn't think that it would be enough to overthrow the stone's power. He could tell that there was nothing he could do, at least not for the moment.

"I apologise," Marina was making Alaric feel very uncomfortable. "I did not mean to offend you. I was only thinking of your wellbeing," he felt like saying more, but did not want to risk offending her.

Marina thought about berating him further. There was something about what he said that infuriated her, but she didn't know what it was. A rage started to burn inside her. It didn't really make sense. She didn't think that there was anything wrong with his words, yet the feelings were bubbling up inside her and they were almost ready to burst.

"Don't say anything," Alaric spoke before Marina had a chance. He could see that she was going to yell at him. He didn't really mind, but he had a feeling that someone or something was coming. If it was not friendly, then he wanted them to remain anonymous in their shade.

She could tell by the look on his face that she should remain quiet. There was something wrong and her anger could wait. She was relieved that she didn't speak. As she reflected on her feelings she realised that she was being silly. Alaric was trying to help her, not make her feel insignificant.

They waited in silence as Alaric stared out in front of them. He knew that there was something coming, he just didn't know how far away it was. Just when he was about to give up he saw a figure on the horizon. From the distance he couldn't make out what it was, but he knew that it was too small to be Caleb and therefore he didn't think it was another Heji. That made him worried. Caleb had warned them about the dangers of the other creatures in the wasteland. He didn't think that the creature on the horizon was friendly. The more he looked the more he was sure of it.

Even from a distance it looked as though the creature was sniffing the air. Alaric did not like the look of it. Even if they were able to hide from its sight it looked as though it could sniff them out. He didn't have the energy to get into a fight and he hoped that the creature couldn't pick up their scent.

Slowly the creature started walking towards them. As it neared Alaric thought that it looked like a lizard, only it was much bigger than any lizard that he had seen or heard of. I moved slowly and with purpose towards them. Every now and again the creature stopped and smelt the air. It seemed to be following its sense of smell more than its sight. Its movements were excruciatingly slow. It took almost an hour to cover the distance between them and the horizon, although Alaric estimated that the horizon was at least half a league away.

The closer the creature came the less Alaric thought that it might be friendly. It had a pointed head and was covered in hard scales. It looked as though it was covered in plate armour. A forked tongued flicked every now and then. It reminded Alaric of something he had seen before, but he couldn't think of what or where. One thing he knew for sure was that the creature was moving ever closer towards them. Then he realised the horses were much closer to the creature than they were. He felt suddenly hopeless. Being unable to leave the protection of the shade he could do nothing to help the horses. They would have to defend themselves. Alaric didn't think that they would be able to defeat the creature. It almost made him sick the thought of the horses being eaten by some wicked creature of the wasteland.

Before the creature came within a hundred paces Alaric realised that there was someone else on the horizon. He peered into the distance, completely ignoring the advancing creature. It took him a while but he recognised a Heji coming towards them. He could only assume that it was Caleb, returning to see them.

Suddenly the creature seemed to notice that there was something else on the horizon. It caught a scent on the wind and suddenly stopped. The creature's sudden movement caught Alaric's attention. He didn't think the creature looked happy at Caleb's arrival. He returned his gaze to Caleb, who didn't seem to notice the creature that was only fifty paces from the horses. It moved its head from the Heji to them and back again. Alaric thought that it looked as though it was trying to make a decision. He wanted to call out to Caleb, but he didn't think that it would do any good, he was too far away to hear him. All it would do was let the creature know exactly where they were. In the end he remained silent and hoped that things would work them out for themselves.

The creature hadn't moved for fifteen minutes as Caleb approached. It seemed as though it couldn't decide on where it should go. It showed no sign of fear, only indecision. Alaric wasn't sure if Caleb was walking into a trap. Either way there was nothing he could do. He hated being so helpless.

In the end it was the creature that made the first move. It looked to its left and right before disappearing. Alaric was surprised at how quickly the lizard-like creature could move. It was only then that Caleb seemed to notice. He was still too far away to see clearly, but Alaric thought he looked as though he was a little nervous. Alaric was too happy that the creature had decided to disappear to care about the reason why. He relaxed as waited for Caleb to approach.

The Heji was carrying two bundles under his arms. It was late in the afternoon when he reached the two of them. Alaric guessed that there couldn't be much more than an hour of light left. Alaric was glad the see the Heji return. After the sighting of the strange reptilian creature he much preferred to see Caleb.

"We have to keep moving," Caleb spoke when he reached the rock they were sheltering under. "It will be night soon and we must not be out of the open."

"That is all well and good, but we cannot travel until the sun sets. Our skin will burn if we leave the safety of the shade," Alaric explained.

"Cover yourself with these and you will be able to make the journey," Caleb dropped one bundle in front of Alaric and the other in front of Marina.

Instantly Alaric recognised that it was a pelt of some sort. As he opened it he realised that it was not that of a Heji, which he had originally thought it would be. It was from a creature that he didn't recognise. He wondered at how many different animals could survive in such a place. There was a strange smell coming from the pelt. He could see Marina scrunch up her nose out of the corner of his eyes.

"It doesn't matter. The horses will still not be able to handle the heat," as much as Alaric didn't want to drape himself in the skin of such a dead animal, he really wanted to leave. Caleb's attitude did nothing to calm his nerves.

"I think you will find that the horses will be fine," Caleb didn't sound at all concerned.

Marina wanted to voice her own objection, but Alaric waved her silent. Now that they had started to see the creatures of the wasteland he was starting to believe Caleb's warnings. If the night was as dangerous as he said then it would be better if they kept moving. Holding his breath

Alaric wrapped himself in the pelt. There was also a smaller pelt to protect his head and face. He was loathed to put it on, but he knew that Marina was watching him. If he faltered then it would give her an opportunity to complain.

The smell inside the suit was revolting. Alaric did all that he could to stop from dry retching. Again he knew if he did then Marina would refuse to don her own pelts. He took a tentative step out in the sun and was surprised to realise that it actually worked. The temperature rose considerably, but his skin did not feel as though it was going to ignite.

"Come on Marina. We need to keep moving," Alaric tried to keep the revulsion out of his voice.

Marina still hadn't put on her pelts. Alaric couldn't blame her. She had lived the life of a princess. It could not be easy for her to wear such a disgusting piece of clothing. There was only so long he could wait before he became annoyed. The fact that Adelanta had already left the shade and was walking towards them, made him impatient. He was able to lead the mare out which meant that Alaric should be able to lead Marina, at least it was in his mind.

"Come on Marina," his voice was overly harsh.

"Okay, okay," Marina knew she had waited too long.

Holding her breath Marina wrapped herself in the pelts and walked out of the shadows. She instantly wished that she hadn't. As soon as she breathed in the true stench of the pelts filled her nostrils. She couldn't contain herself from dry retching. It was all she could do to keep what was left in her stomach inside her. She wasn't sure if she was going to be able to continue. The smell was overwhelming and starting to make her dizzy. She thought she was going to pass out. Just as she thought she was going to lose consciousness a sudden wave came over her. The smell completely disappeared and she felt normal again. She looked up at Alaric to see if it had been his influence, but he was busy loading the horses. It quickly struck her who, or what, had made her feel better. She quietly thanked the Sapphire stone in her mind.

Caleb waited, impatiently, for Alaric to load the horses. He looked around nervously. The arrival of the reptilian creature had made him nervous. If Alaric had been paying attention he would have made an effort to load the horses quicker. Marina was too busy with her own feelings to worry about anyone else.

It was not long before they were on their way again. Caleb was much happier once they were on the move. The horses were able to withstand the intense heat, but they could not carry the packs and the riders at the same time. Alaric was happy to walk, but Marina was not so accommodating. She started to complain, but the others had already set a firm pace.

Marina trudged behind the four of them. She was sweating more and more, struggling to keep up with their pace. The heat was really starting to get to her. She could feel the stone and if she had been able to think straight she would have attempted to use its power, but all she could do was remain upright. Eventually the stone did what she had been hoping it would do. She felt the pelts become suddenly cold. The sweat was soon off her body and she was able to catch up with the others. She had a bad feeling that all the help she was getting from the Sapphire stone was eventually going to cost her more than her life.

Chapter 28: The Heji

"This is the entrance to our land," Caleb announced when he suddenly stopped.

The sun had almost completely set, but they still wore their pelt suits. Alaric had wondered at what animal had made such a pelt, but in the end he decided it was probably better that he didn't know. The pelts had served their purpose well. Even though the smell was enough to make him gag he was grateful for the protection.

"What are you talking about?" Alaric looked around, but all he could see was sand. The nearest rocks were over a hundred paces away. A bad feeling was starting to rise in his stomach. "There is nothing here."

Caleb started to laugh, or at least Alaric assumed that it was laughter. It was a guttural, growling sound and for some reason the sound made Alaric feel very uncomfortable. He looked across at Marina, but it was impossible to gauge her reaction as she was still covered in pelts.

"This is a very dangerous land. Do you think it would be wise to have a welcome sign on the entrance?" Alaric thought there was a smile on the Heji's face.

Alaric suddenly felt as though he was a school child, learning a lesson for the first time. He still could not see the entrance, but he knew that it was not far away. He stretched out his senses to see if there was magic in the air, but he could not feel anything. He thought, given enough time, he could find the entrance, but Caleb was waiting for him.

"Shall we go then," Alaric did not know how else to respond.

"You may want to close your eyes. This can be quite a disturbing experience for this first time," Caleb warned as he started to walk forward.

Alaric didn't know what he was talking about until he realised Caleb was slowly starting to shrink. At first Alaric didn't know what was happening. He thought that the Heji had found a way to shrink themselves before he noticed that the sand now covered his knees. If he continued the way he was going he would soon suffocate in the sand and if he didn't there was no way that Alaric and Marina could survive the decent.

"Just remember, if you start to feel panicked just close your eyes. I will let you know when you pass through," Caleb explained as he disappeared further into the ground.

Alaric couldn't believe what he was seeing. Marina, on the other hand, didn't seem too worried. In fact she knew what was on the other side, or underneath as it were. She could feel the water nearby and it was calling to her. The Heji disappearing into the ground was strange, but she was prepared to take it on face value. Slowly she started to descend behind the large creature.

Alaric wanted to take a deep breath before he started his own descent, but he could not stand drawing in the filth of the pelts. He would have to trust that Caleb was telling them the truth. As soon as he took a step forward and his feet dropped into the ground he felt a sudden rush of magic. He felt a tingling sensation around his ankles and a cold sensation rushed through his body. He didn't want to take another step, but Caleb had already disappeared and Marina was already covered up to her waist. He took one last look around before realising that there was nowhere else for him to go.

Marina was strong right up until her head was going to dip under the ground. She stopped just as her head was the only part of her that remained visible. She looked around to Alaric for support. He didn't know what he could do. He wasn't too happy with the situation himself. He didn't know how he was going to build up the strength to plunge his head into the ground himself. The magic didn't feel right to him. He had no idea what would happen once they were completely submerged.

"I don't think that I can do it," Marina had seemed so strong. "Something doesn't feel right to me. I have a bad feeling."

Alaric wasn't sure he could do anything to comfort her. He was sure that she felt the same. He didn't know if he wanted to continue himself. He definitely didn't know what he should say to Marina. As he remained silent Caleb poked his head out of the ground. Alaric wasn't sure, but he thought that there was a confused look on his face.

"What are you two doing?"

"I don't think that we can go any further," the words sounded wrong as they came out of his mouth.

"What are you talking about? The sun has almost set. We have to be inside before it completely disappears," there was fear in Caleb's voice.

It was that fear that got Marina moving. If such a creature was afraid to be outside in the dark then there was no way that she wanted to stay out. She turned away from Alaric and when Caleb moved out of the way she disappeared completely. Alaric wasn't as worried at Caleb's warning. He looked around nervously, but there was still no sign of other creatures. In the end knew that he didn't have a choice. He had to follow where Marina and the horses had gone. He could not go on by himself.

Slowly he started again. With each step the feeling of dread increased. He could feel the bile starting to grow in his stomach. He thought that there was a chance he was going to be sick. He was up to his neck and he was sure that the feelings were at their worst. He could not think that they would become stronger. Closing his eyes was the only way he was going to be able to go any further. Still he could not take a deep breath, so he only closed his eyes before stepping under the ground.

As soon as he was completely underground the feeling of dread completely disappeared. It was so sudden that he almost lost his step and tumbled forward. In doing so he was forced to open his eyes. He was surprised to realise that he could easily see. He had expected to be cloaked in darkness, but instead it was a lot brighter than it was outside.

In front of him was a tunnel leading downwards. Where he was standing he could still see the sky, which was all but black. It was the tunnel that was radiating light. The fact that he wasn't covered in sand brought a sense of relief and he was keen to continue. The tunnel was very alluring. He could just see Marina in the distance before she disappeared.

With the danger of burning alive gone Alaric removed the pelts. He thought about dumping them on the ground where he stood, but then decided that it would be rude. He finally took the deep breath that he had been longing for. It was not as rewarding as he had thought. The smell of the pelts was still thick on his robe and he fought down the urge to retch as he continued down the tunnel.

The ceiling of the tunnel glowed a bright white and clearly lit the tunnel below it. Alaric tried to see what was causing it, but it was too bright. The more he looked the less he could see. In the end he had to return his gaze straight in front of him. He would have to ask Caleb when he caught up to them. With that thought in mind he quickened his pace. He no longer wanted to remain so far behind.

The tunnel sloped downwards for about fifteen minutes before it came to an end. Alaric could see the others waiting for him. Even though they were waiting neither of them gave him any attention. Marina was focused on something in front of her and Caleb was judging her reaction. Alaric's curiosity was piqued. He thought about increasing his pace to a run, but he didn't want to draw any unnecessary attention himself. Whatever had Marina so engrossed would just have to wait.

"Hurry Alaric, you are not going to believe this," Marina called when she heard Alaric approach.

As Alaric neared the end of the tunnel he could see that it opened up into a massive cavern. He could see that the cavern roof was also emitting the same light as the tunnel. He could only imagine that was what Marina was staring at. It wasn't until he reached the entrance that he realised just how wrong he was.

He almost had to take a step backwards as he looked out into the cavern. The sight took his breath away. Below them, over a hundred feet beneath them, was an entire world. Alaric could not believe what he saw. The cavern was larger than the eye could see. Below them was a fully live forest. There were trees, streams and a multitude of birds flying around. He had a feeling that below the forest canopy would be a number of small animals. The more he looked the more he could not believe it. Towards the far end of the cavern he could see a small village. The huts were made out wood, obviously cut from the trees of the forest. A larger building was on a platform of rock sitting above the roof line of the rest of the village. Alaric assumed that this was chief's house.

The first thing that Marina noticed was the main river, cutting almost through the middle of the cavern. Its source was at the far end of the cavern. A great waterfall streamed down behind the chief's house, far enough away so that it did not get the house or the village wet. There were also many streams that drifted away from the main river. Marina felt a joy in her heart that she had not felt in a long time. She knew what had drawn her towards the cavern. She was thankful that she didn't let the bad feeling deter her.

"This is the land of my people," Caleb announced when Alaric joined them.

"It's amazing," Alaric was in awe. "How did this happen?"

"I'll explain as we descend," Caleb motioned for them to follow him. "It will be night time soon." Alaric really wanted to ask how that could be, but Caleb had already started to move.

To the left of where they were standing was a path leading down towards the forest. Alaric quickly moved so he was walking besides the Heji. Marina followed behind with the two horses behind her. She was quite happy to let Alaric take the lead. She was still dumbfounded by the sight before her. She could not believe that such a place could exist.

"How does the light work?" Alaric remembered the question that he wanted to ask. He figured that if he let Caleb start explaining things then he would forget to ask him.

Caleb chuckled to himself at the question. He took a brief look towards the roof of the cavern before he spoke. "It is a moss that grows only on the roof of our home. It soaks up the heat from the rocks and that is what gives it light. When it becomes warm it starts to glow. The hotter it becomes the brighter it gets. When it cools down then it will lose its light. It gives us day and night. We are a few hours behind the outside world, but our day lasts just as long."

Alaric looked up in awe. The fact that something like that existed at all was amazing. It did seem to make some sense. If it was impossible to live above the ground then something had to be suitable for them to live below it. The moss light was just a necessary phenomenon.

"That is amazing," Alaric responded when he returned his attention the Caleb.

The descent into the forest took longer than Alaric expected. The path zigzagged its way down the wall of the cavern. At times it levelled out before it started falling away again. Alaric thought that its length was somewhat unnecessary. When he asked Caleb the Heji looked happy to explain.

"It was designed this way specifically. If an enemy finds its way down to our land then they have to take the long road down to the forest. It gives us a good chance to defend our home. In fact nothing has ever made it to the forest floor, unless by our design," there was a certain amount of pride in Caleb's voice.

Alaric had to admit it was an ingenious idea. Although it took them an insufferable amount of time to reach the bottom of the cavern Alaric could appreciate its design. Nothing would be able to sneak through. Once they were on the ledge overlooking the cavern they were in view of the entire village. It was the perfect defence.

"So how did this place come to exist?" Marina asked the question from behind them. She had been listening intently to their conversation and had a few questions of her own.

Alaric was about to ask a similar question. There were many that he needed to ask, but that one seemed to be the most pertinent. He was a little annoyed with Marina as he was the one who wanted to ask thm.

"There will be time for all your questions, but this is not it. We need to move quickly now if we are going to make it to the village before nightfall," as Caleb spoke he started to quicken his pace.

"Why? Are we in danger?" Alaric sounded surprised, but also quickened his pace.

"Of course not," Caleb stopped suddenly at Alaric's question. "We are completely safe here," he faced Alaric as he spoke.

"I am sorry," Alaric apologised. "I didn't mean to offend you."

"Of course not. Now let's keep moving. I think it would be a good idea if you ride your animals again." Caleb started off again.

The two of them mounted before following after Caleb. The Heji kept a brisk pace and even the horses had to move at a canter to keep pace with him. There was not much time to enjoy the scenery as they sped by, but what Alaric saw he thought was not quite right. It looked as though the forest was sick. The leaves on the trees were wilting and the flowers looked faded. It was like the entire forest had a disease. Alaric wanted to ask, but he knew that it was not the time. Caleb looked too focused to answer any more questions.

The light was starting to fade as they reached the outskirts of the village. They had yet to see any sign of any other Heji. Marina was beginning to wonder if Caleb might be the only one left alive. If that was the case then she didn't like the consequences of what they were walking into. As they walked past the first of the wooden huts the sound of drums beating could be heard in the distance. That was enough to put aside Marina's worries for the moment, but she still felt somewhat uncomfortable. The bad feeling had gone once she was completely underground, but the memory still remained. She could not help but think that there was a reason she had felt such a way. She looked over towards Alaric who sat straight backed in his saddle. There was no concern of his face or in his body, which helped Marina to relax.

Alaric was engrossed in his surroundings. The wooden huts were of a design he had never seen before. He wondered why they had rooves on them. It was not like they needed to keep the weather out. They were strangely ornate in design and not at all what Alaric was expecting.

As they continued through the small village the beating of the drums became louder. It was obvious they were getting closer to the noise. It sounded to Alaric that there was some kind of ceremony happening.

"Each evening we celebrate the setting of the sun, or the going out of the moss light as it may be," Caleb slowed his pace as he spoke. "This is the reason why we must hurry. It will not be long before the lights go out," after speaking he quickened his pace again.

Alaric could understand why he was in such a rush. He didn't know what would happen if they did not make the celebration, but he didn't think that it would be good for Caleb. Riding through the streets, approaching the festivities, made Alaric very nervous. He doubted he could overpower Caleb if his attentions were wicked let alone an entire village of Heji. He could only hope that they were indeed friends. Caleb had done nothing to earn his mistrust, but he still had his doubts.

The festivities were taking place, as they always did, on the ledge out the front of the chief's house. There was a small flight of stairs cut into the stone leading towards the ledge and Caleb suggested that the horses remain at the base. Alaric trusted that Adelanta would be able to look after Marina's mare. He wasn't sure if he liked the idea of leaving the horses alone, but he did not want to offend the Heji.

Alaric walked closely behind Caleb when the reached the top of the stairs. The last thing he wanted to do was to stand out. He wasn't sure if he wanted the other Heji to know he was there. As soon as they stepped foot on the precipice the drumming stopped and all the Heji looked to where they were standing. Alaric had never felt so more self-conscious in his life. Marina was feeling the same. Even standing behind Caleb and Alaric she still felt as though every eye was on her.

"Come forward, Caleb," the chief was sitting on a throne, cut from stone. It was placed at the back of what looked to be a meeting square. His voice boomed and seemed to echo throughout the entire cavern. "We have been waiting for you to return."

When the chief finished speaking the only light from above blinked out and the only light came from the many fires lit around the square. The Heji looked even more terrifying in the glow of the flickering fires. Alaric did not want to go any further, but when Caleb started to move he felt compelled. He thought that he might still be able to hide behind the great creature, but that was not going to be an option. Caleb led them toward the chief. All the Heji, who had previously been jumping and celebrating, backed out of their way. In the end it was a like a guard-of-honour, although Alaric didn't think it was their intention. When Caleb stopped in front of the chief the other Heji closed in around them in a semi-circle. The move made Alaric feel even more nervous. He thought that he could feel a certain amount of hostility coming from them.

"So what have you brought before me?" there was no softness to his voice, not that Alaric thought a Heji could talk like that.

Caleb bent down on one knee before rising again. Alaric followed suit and Marina followed him. The last thing he wanted to do was to upset the chief. He had a bad feeling that he was going to have to do some fancy talking to remain alive.

"Chief Abram, I bring you two survivors, as is the way," Caleb let his voice boom, but not as much as Abram's.

"Ha, it is our way, but do we even know what that means anymore." There was a half cheer from the Heji around them. Alaric did not take this as a good sign. "We have put our faith in the way of our forefathers and it has led us to disaster in the past. Will we not continue down this path again?"

There was another cheer from the Heji. This one was much louder as the entire group of Heji roared at the chief's words. Alaric felt as though the circle around them had started to close in on them. Something was happening, but he didn't know what it was. It was as if they were on trial for something they had not even done. He wanted to speak, but for the moment he knew he had to let Caleb speak on their behalf.

"I know that we have been betrayed before, but I believe that these two are here to help us," Caleb's word caught Alaric by surprise.

"We can not risk another betrayal. We must dispose of these two," Abram looked at them with disgust in his voice.

Marina was about to speak, but Alaric silenced her with a hand on her shoulder. He wanted to give Caleb every chance before he spoke. If there was a chance they could work it out amongst themselves then it would be all the better. He hoped it would work out that way, but he did not truly believe it.

"We have already been betrayed. We need the help of these two if we are going to recover the lost treasure," Caleb was not gaining any ground. "Let us hear from them. They can tell you what you need to know."

"That is impossible," Abram looked and sounded shocked. "No outside can speak our language. That was the sign of the betrayer. Are you trying to tell me that these two also understand our words?"

"That is exactly what I am saying. Not only can they understand, but they can speak our words too," Caleb explained.

"Is this true?" the Chief spoke directly to Alaric and Marina.

"It is true," was all Alaric said.

"How can this be?" There was now a hush over the entire village. Abram's words floated away and disappeared in the distance. "Answer me!" Abram demanded when no one responded.

"I do not know. We have been able to understand Caleb ever since he met us. Unfortunately I can not explain it," Alaric wished he knew to explain further. He didn't think that his answer would appease anyone.

"They are traitors," one of the Heji called from the crowd. His words were met with cheers from the others.

"Be calm," Alaric had to cover his ears as Abram yelled. "There is no need to reduce ourselves to a rabble." He quickly regained control of the crowd. "Now, I have one question for you. Give me a reason not to have you put to death?"

It was not what Alaric was expecting. He wished that Caleb had given him some warning. He wished that he could have prepared his answers. Something bad had happened in the past and it seemed as though they were getting the blame. If he knew what it was it would be easier to defend himself.

"I feel as though someone has betrayed your trust," it seemed as though the best way to start. "I am afraid that I know nothing of this. We ourselves have followed someone into the..." he was going to say wasteland, but he didn't think he would gain any friends that way. "... into your land, someone who has betrayed us. We mean you no harm and if there is anything we can do to help you then we would certainly be willing to help."

His words caught Abram by surprise. He was not expecting such a response. Abram had to choose his words carefully. "No one survives the harshness of our land. I say that the man you have been following is well and truly dead by now. It seems as though you have wasted your time." Abram watched Alaric closely to see his reaction.

"I do not mean to be rude, but I know that he is still alive," that was all Alaric was going to say.

Alaric's words brought mumbled voices from the crowd. He did not know why, but they seemed interested in what he said. He noticed that Abram started to look uncomfortable. Alaric didn't know if it was a good thing or a bad thing, but he knew that the chief was not as confident as when they first met. Abram broke his gaze from Alaric and returned it to Caleb.

"How can this be true?" he didn't wait for Caleb to respond. "If what this man says is true then you know what it means?" he let the question settle over the crowd.

"I am aware, my chief. This is the reason that I brought the two back here," Caleb spoke as softly as his gruff voice would allow.

"Very well. I think that we have said enough here tonight. I think that we should all go away and think on what has been achieved," Abram's voice carried throughout the square and down into the village. "We will reconvene at darkness tomorrow."

As much as the Heji wanted answers they would not get any that night. They would all respect the decision of their chief. No one would dare speak against his wishes. Caleb was the only one who had the authority to question Abram, although if the chief was firm there was nothing he could do. He was only really there to give Abram a different point of view.

"What shall we do with these two?" Caleb asked as the Heji went back down to their village.

"They shall spend the night locked in the cell room," Abram didn't wait for Caleb to respond. He stood from his throne and returned to his house.

"What does that mean?" Marina spoke, but only loud enough for Alaric and Caleb to hear.

"Follow me," was all that Caleb said.

He started off down the stairs to the rest of the village. Alaric and Marina followed closely behind. Marina wanted to talk, but Alaric didn't want to be left behind. He had the feeling that Caleb was the only Heji who didn't feel intense hatred towards him. There was no telling what would happen if they were left alone.

They collected the horses when they reached the bottom and Caleb led them along the cliff wall away from the village. There was a small hut on the edge of the village where Caleb was leading them. Alaric found the sight somewhat promising. There was a chance that they weren't going to be locked up for the night.

Once they had unpacked the horses the animals were left to roam the village. Alaric wanted to ask if there was somewhere to stable them for the night, but he didn't think there was much chance. Caleb was happy to let the animals wander freely and Alaric was not going to argue. He didn't think that they could get up to much trouble. He was sure that Adelanta would look after the mare.

The inside of the hut did not have the feel of a prison cell. Even though it only had the bare essentials it had a homely feel about it. There were two beds at the far end of the hut and a table and chairs at the front. There was a small fireplace to one wall and a window on the other. There didn't seem to be any locks on the door or window. Alaric doubted that it was indeed a prison.

"You will remain here for the night," Caleb didn't enter the room, he remained in the doorway as he spoke. "Be warned. Do not leave the cell room. You do not want to run into any of the other Heji."

"What is going on?" Alaric asked the question before Marina had a chance. "Why didn't you tell us that we were going to be attacked," Alaric assumed that Caleb was on their side.

Caleb looked confused at the question. A realisation crossed his face before Alaric spoke again. "Just because I don't believe that you are our enemy doesn't mean that I am right. Surprise is the best way to get the truth out of someone. I had to be sure of your intentions."

Alaric was surprised to hear such insight coming from such a creature, but his shock only lasted for a moment. He needed answers to his question and it looked as though Caleb was about to leave. "And do you believe us?"

"I do believe you are telling the truth, but unfortunately for you I do not have the final say. It is up to Chief Abram to decide your fate," Caleb's words were sombre.

"What have we done? What are we being accused of?" Marina could help herself. She wanted answers.

"I have already said too much. I am not supposed to give you any information. That is the ruling from Chief Abram," Caleb looked around nervously as he spoke. "There is wood next to the fireplace. Do not wait too long before you light it. It becomes very cold, very quickly. I know that your kind do not do so well with the extreme temperatures of our land. There are temap leaves in the basket over there. If you use the stone and bowl to crush them into a paste you can use then on your burns. I don't know if it will work, but occasionally a young Heji will get his skin burnt out in the sun. The pulp from the crushed leaves help. Now I think that you should get some rest. You will need all your wits in the morning."

Caleb simply shut the door behind him. There was no sound of a bolt being slide shut or any locks being locked. Marina's initial reaction was to open the door and run for safety. The only thing that stopped her was that Alaric remained where he stood. He made no attempt to leave. His first movement was towards the fireplace. He took Caleb's warning very seriously.

"What are you doing Alaric?" Marina almost sounded shocked. "The door is not locked. We should get out of here."

Alaric chuckled to himself as he moved a number of small logs into the fireplace. Once he was happy with what he had done he returned his attention to Marina. He could tell in an instant that she was not happy. Even though her face was badly burnt Alaric could tell that she was turning red. He couldn't help, but chuckle again.

"What is so funny?" Marina spoke between clenched teeth.

"I am sorry. I know that this is not the time for humour, but I just couldn't help myself." Marina still didn't understand what was so funny. "I don't think that there is any point in trying to run away."

"And why is that?" Marina was so worked up that she wasn't thinking straight. It was a mixture of anger and fear.

"There is nowhere for us to go. I am sure there are not even guards posted outside of the door. It is night time outside and that means that it will be getting very cold, very soon. We have no idea where the next safe cave, or even if there is a safe cave nearby. This is the safest place for us to be at the moment."

Marina could not believe that she had not thought about it herself. Embarrassment made her turn another shade of red. She quickly moved to the basket of temap leaves. She thought that if she busied herself with the leaves then her embarrassment would disappear. Alaric thought that it was very cute. He liked the occasions when Marina acted like the little princess that she was, or at least had been. That life was a long way away and Alaric didn't know if she was ever going to get it back. The thought made him sad.

"I am sorry." He spoke for the thoughts in his head, not the comments he had made.

Marina chose to ignore him anyway. She had already started to grind the leaves. She hoped that Alaric didn't notice her embarrassment, although she had a feeling that he did. She had to admit that the thought of easing the pain of her burning was a pleasant thought. She had managed to block out the feeling, but she could still feel her pain growing.

With Marina preparing the salve Alaric returned his attention to the fire. He was just as happy to the let the previous conversation drift away. He looked around, but he could not find a flint or a tinderbox to light the fire. He could feel the temperature already starting to drop. When he realised there was nothing there he returned his focus on the wood in the fireplace. He didn't have to draw any power to create the small flame required to start the fire and in a second the small logs were burning brightly.

"This stuff really works," Alaric jumped at the sound of Marina's voice. He had been lost in the flames.

He turned around to face her and nearly jumped back into the fire. The sight was more than a surprise. Her face was covered in a sticky white paste. It was Marina's turn to laugh at Alaric's misfortune and it was Alaric's turn to blush.

"Don't worry, I am sure there is enough for you," Marina teased.

Once she had spread the paste over all of her exposed skin she started grinding again. She had used almost half of the leaves in the basket. She hoped that there would be more when it came time to reapply as that the paste was doing its job.

It was not long before they were both covered in white paste. Alaric had to admit that the salve was like a miracle cure. Alaric's pain had also started to intensify. When they were finished they took the chairs over to the fire and sat down. They ate a meal to satisfy their stomach and it was only then did Alaric wish they had stopped to fill their water pouches. There was enough to keep them sated, but only just. When they finished their meal they had also finished the last of their water.

"Do you think they would mind if we got some more water?" Marina asked.

"I don't think that would be a good idea. Until we know what we are up against I think that we should do all that we can to keep Abram happy. I think that Caleb was right. We should get some rest." Alaric stood from his chair before he realised that sleep was not going to be so easy. He quickly returned to his chair. "I think I might wait for the paste to set first."

Marina chuckled to herself. She had used creams on her face before and already knew how difficult it was sleeping and keeping the sheets clean, or that fact that it was next to impossible. She did not want to tell Alaric that she didn't think that the salve was going to dry anytime soon. She was happy spending time with him in front of the fire. Besides the fact that they were in a pseudo-prison cell it was quite romantic. She moved her chair until it was next to Alaric. It took her a short while, but eventually she was able to snuggle up to him. What ever happened in the morning was not worth worrying about. For the moment Marina was happy to be in Alaric's arms.

Chapter 29: Judge, Jury & Executioner

The morning came around all too quickly. The paste remained on both Marina and Alaric, but it was only left in patches. Alaric was amazed to see that the skin that was showing on both him and Marina had been completely healed. There was no need to reapply the salve. He didn't know what was in the leaves, but he was definitely going to ask if they could take some with them. There was no telling what else the leaves could heal. Not only that, but he saw a number of plants and flowers on their way to the village that he had never seen before.

Caleb came to check on them shortly after they had risen. He wanted to make sure that they were comfortable and had everything they needed. He seemed to be a little more confident than he had been the night before.

"We are completely out of water. It would be great if we could fill our pouches in your river. Also we would like to wash the paste from our bodies," Alaric explained.

"Oh no, don't do that," Caleb sounded shocked at Alaric's suggestion. "The water doesn't react well with the temap leaves. If you put water on your skin before you have removed the leaves' juice you will end up with a worse burn than when you started. Most of it should just flake off. The rest should come off if you just rub your skin a few times."

Alaric tried what Caleb suggested. He picked at the dried paste on his left arm. To his surprise it peeled off quite easily. Underneath there was a sandy residue left behind. He didn't think it would be too hard to remove it all. He was about to start when he realised that Caleb was waiting for his attention.

"Your first request is easy enough. If you give me your water pouches I will fill them for you," Caleb offered.

"It is no problem. We can fill the pouches ourselves," it was only after the words had left his mouth did he realise what he had said.

"You still are not allowed to leave the cell until you are summoned by Chief Abram. I will bring the pouches back to you shortly," Caleb explained.

Alaric thanked Caleb as he passed him the pouches. Marina was busying herself with removing the paste. She was scratching furiously to remove the sandy residue. It had been too long since she had been able to bathe and she would not pass up the opportunity.

"Be careful, or you'll scratch you skin right off," Caleb warned before he left. He didn't wait for Marina to respond.

She took his warning and slowed down her scratching. She had just been excited to see her milky skin, even though it was a lighter shade of brown. All the redness and peeling skin had disappeared. It took a while, but eventually they were both able to completely remove the paste from their skin. Alaric thought that Marina had a glow about her. He couldn't take his eyes off her. He was thankful when Caleb opened the door before she realised what he was doing.

"Drink your fill. Lord Abram has summoned you. We will leave once you have quenched your thirst," Caleb sounded very sombre.

"Could we not bathe before we go?" Marina asked. "I'm sure things would go a lot better if we didn't stink from days of travel."

Caleb shot Alaric what he could only assume was a questioning look. It took him a moment to realise that he had no idea what Marina was asking him.

"I don't think Abram really cares what we smell like," Alaric responded to her.

It took Marina a moment to realise what Alaric was saying and when she did she felt somewhat foolish. She had to remember that her preconceptions on life were completely different to what was before her. Despite the realisation she still wanted to bathe. Her freshly healed skin was starting to itch and the grime from their trek through the wasteland was weighing heavily on her. She would not feel right until she had thoroughly cleaned herself.

Both Alaric and Marina were glad to see the pouches filled with water. They did not hold on ceremony before pouring the water down their throats. With the river nearby they no longer had to spare their water supplies. To Alaric's surprise he didn't need to drink as much as he expected before he was satisfied. He could tell by the expression on Marina's face that she also felt the same. He wanted to ask Caleb, but he didn't think the Heji would have an answer. It was the only water they had so they would not know anything different.

"Now there are a few things that I must warn you about," Caleb started as he ushered them out of the cell. "What you must remember is that you are on trial. Anything that you do to upset Chief Abram will be held against you. The first thing you must do is bow down on one knee. That is very important. If you don't do that then the trial will be over before it begins. Once the trial starts you must not speak until Chief Abram asks you a question. Even if you do not like what is being said about you. Even if what is being said is a lie, you must not speak. When you do speak you must look Chief Abram directly in the eyes. Even if it is someone else who asked the question your gaze must not leave the Chief's when you are talking. Once you have finished speaking then you can look around. I will do all that I can to help, but ultimately it is Chief Abram's decision."

"What are we being tried for?" Alaric asked when Caleb finished speaking.

"That I cannot tell you, it will be revealed in due course. It is best that we don't speak from here on," Caleb quickened his pace so he was walking in front of them.

Alaric did not like the sound of things. He didn't want to admit it to himself, but there was a chance that he was going to have to fight his way out. He could not let them become permanent prisoners of the Heji, or worse. He didn't know how he was going to overpower so many of the great creatures, but he was sure there would be a way. He was so deep in thought that he didn't realise that they had assembled again. Chief Abram was seated on his throne at the head of the square. All the Heji were assembled around him with a large enough space in between for the two prisoners.

It was only at the last moment did Alaric's senses return to what he was doing. He saw Marina down on one knee. He could hear the Heji murmuring around him and quickly he dropped to his right knee and lowered his head. His heart was suddenly racing. He hoped that he had not already ruined their chances of escape.

"Stand before me, those accused," Chief Abram's voice boomed.

Alaric and Marina came to their feet as ordered. Alaric's attention was fixed on Abram. He had not come up with a solution to their problem, but he could ill afford to let his concentration lapse. There was still a chance he could talk his way out. If only he knew what they were accused of then he could plan a defence.

"You stand here accused, what say you?" Abram announced.

Alaric was taken by surprise by the question. He had no idea what to say. Until he knew what he was accused of he could not give a reasonable response. "I am afraid Chief Abram..." Alaric didn't get the chance to finish his statement.

"The prisoner is afraid," a Heji called out from behind him. It was followed by a cheer throughout the crowd.

Alaric was about to look around at who had spoken, but then he remembered Caleb's warning and kept his gaze on Abram. He could feel the eyes of all the Heji burning into his back. It took all of his concentration to remain focused on what he was doing.

"So you admit to what you have done?" Abram asked.

"I do not admit to anything," Alaric had to choose his words carefully. He did not what to give the Heji another chance to attack him. "In fact I do not know what I am being accused of. It seems as though there is a case of mistaken identity."

"Do you dare accuse me of being mistaken?" Abram boomed his words and all the Heji went suddenly quiet.

It seemed to Alaric that it didn't really matter what he said. Abram was set on twisting his words to his own purpose. The best thing

Alaric could do was to remain calm. He didn't think that losing his temper would help their cause at all. It seemed as though the Heji were trying to bait him into giving something away. The plan might have worked if Alaric had anything.

"Of course not, Chief Abram. I would not dare subvert your command," Alaric hoped that his words were not going to enrage him further. "I am sorry…" Alaric rued his choice of words.

"The prisoner is sorry for his crimes," another Heji roared from the crowd and was followed by thunderous applauding.

"So you do admit to what you have done?" Abram kept the advantage.

"I cannot admit to something when I don't know what it is I am accused of, Chief Abram. I know that you are a wise and powerful ruler," he thought that if he praised the chief then there was chance he would get him on side. "I you would kindly tell me what it is I am supposed to have done then I could tell you one way or the other. Until then I am," he was going to say afraid again, but decided against it at the last moment, "going to be unable to give you any more information."

Chief Abram had to think on Alaric's words. He had lost his advantage and was not sure how he was going to get it back. There was something in Alaric's words that made him think. He had to reassess his plan of attack. If he waited too long then he risked losing the support of his fellow Heji. He could see them all waiting for his response to Alaric's words.

"Very well. You give me no choice, but let it be known that your punishment will be a lot worse if you do not confess." He paused, giving Alaric a chance to speak. When there was no reply he continued. "You have been accused a supporting someone who stole a very important artefact of ours."

"But we have only just arrived," it was Marina who spoke and instantly wished that she hadn't.

"Who do you think you are to interrupt me while I am talking?" Alaric thought about responding, but figured that the question was rhetorical. If he spoke then he would only make matters worse. "Such insolence is punishable by death." He let the thought settle in their minds before he continued. In truth he was grateful to Marina for giving him the upper hand again. "I will be merciful since you do not know the rules of our land, but be sure that this will be the only time." He paused again and let everyone realise what he had done. When he was satisfied he continued. "You stand accused of assisting in a most abhorrent of crimes. How do you plead?" Alaric was hoping for more information, but at least he knew that they had nothing to do with the crime they were being accused of.

"I can tell you that we are not guilty of such a crime. I am sorry if one of my kind has wronged you, but I can assure you that we had nothing to do with it," as Alaric spoke it dawned on him who it must have been. He suddenly became very excited and deeply concerned. Whatever it was that had been stolen must have been important for Na'garoz to risk his life. Now that it was in his possession it was not a pleasant thought. "If you can give me some more information then maybe I can help you."

"Just because you claim that you are innocent does not mean that we believe you. This trial has only just started," Abram really didn't know how he was going to get the two to confess. Normally when he asked for a confession he got it. "We have never seen someone from your land in over a thousand years. Now we have seen three in less than month. Our most treasured possession and the basis of our life has been stolen. Our very existence is on the brink of disaster. Now what would you think?"

Alaric was slowly starting to piece things together, but he was still missing some vital pieces of the puzzle. At least he was starting to get Abram rattled and that was a good thing. If he could keep fishing he might get the entire story. The only thing he really wanted to know was what the treasure was, but he didn't think it would be that simple.

"We are not with the other one you saw, the one who is responsible for these atrocities. If it is who I think it is then we too are trying to catch him," Alaric stopped there. He didn't want to give away too much information.

"That is easy enough to say," Abram was losing ground again and he didn't like it. "If this is indeed the same person then I think that you could explain what he looks like." Abram was pleased with his quick thinking.

Alaric should have seen the question coming. He didn't know how he could explain it. He knew that Na'garoz would no longer look like the innkeeper Emil. He had no idea what form he would have taken. Normally, when in doubt, the truth was the best course, but he didn't know if that was the case. The truth was even more unbelievable than a lie could be. He just didn't know if the Heji were ready for the truth.

"That is not as easy as you might think?" Alaric was trying to buy some time to think about what he was going to say.

Abram could see that he was stalling. He knew that he was getting the better of his opponent. Whatever happened he was not going to let Alaric win. He would get the truth if it was last thing he did. With the advantage he needed to stay on the offensive.

"So it seems as though you are in league with the thief. I can see right through your stalling tactics." The crowd was starting to become boisterous again.

Alaric didn't have a choice. If he was going to get them out of trouble then he would have to tell the truth.

"This is not going to be easy for you to understand, but it is the truth," Alaric started to tell the story of the Evil One and what was happening on the mainland. He tried to keep it as brief as possible, but that was not easy. There was a lot of information to pass on, both past and present. "And that is why we are in your land. The Dark Knight who stole your treasure has stolen something from me. I need to get it back as much as you need to get back your treasure."

The story had taken up most of the morning. Even with Alaric trying to keep his account brief the story went for over three hours. To his surprise Abram was riveted by his words. He hoped the other Heji felt the same way. He wanted to look around, but he took Caleb's warning to heart and kept his gaze on Abram. It was difficult not letting his eyes drop for three hours. Occasionally he paused, just so he could rest his eyes, but for the most part they were locked on the chief's.

"That is a very interesting tale," Abram didn't know what to think. The story went on a little too long to for it to be a fake, but then he really didn't know the ways of the outsiders. He had to take time to deliberate. "I need some time to think about what you have just told me. I will pass my judgement tomorrow morning. Until that time you will be confined to the cell again."

It was clear that the proceedings were over. Chief Abram stood from his throne. As he did the other Heji quickly cleared the square. They knew well enough not to be around when their chief was in such a mood. Alaric and Marina waited until Caleb came to take them away. By that stage the square had been completely vacated. Abram didn't waste any time in returning to his house. He had a lot to think about.

"Do you think that he will believe Alaric's story?" Marina asked as they walked away from the square.

"That all depends on whether he was telling the truth or not," Caleb kept his gaze out in front as he made the jibe.

"I am pretty good, but I could not keep a lie going for that length of time. I know that it sounds totally unbelievable, but it is the truth. That is how bad things are on the mainland." Alaric also kept looking in front.

"Then I am sure that he will make the right decision," Caleb replied.

They walked the rest of the way in silence. Again Caleb kept a pace in front of them to avoid conversation. He looked as though he was deep in thought, although Alaric really didn't know if that was what he was doing.

"No one will come here until tomorrow morning when Chief Abram is ready to see you. If there is anything that you need then let me know now, otherwise you will be confined here again," there was little sincerity in his voice.

"No thank you. I think that we will be fine," Alaric noticed that the wood they had burnt the night before had been replaced. The temap leaves had also been replaced, although they no longer needed them.

"I would like to take a bath in the river," Marina pouted, to little effect.

"You can't leave the cell until I come for you," Caleb sounded a little put out at the request. "Now if that is all?"

"Then can you bring us some water to bathe?" Marina wasn't going to be dissuaded so easily.

Caleb seemed to be struggling with the idea. It wasn't until Alaric realised that the Heji had no idea what Marina was asking for did he step in.

"Marina would like a large tub of water so she can clean her skin," Alaric explained.

"Very well, I think I have just the thing. I will be back shortly." Caleb still didn't seem to understand, but he knew exactly what they wanted.

It wasn't long before the door opened and Caleb returned. He carried in his arms a large pewter tub filled with water. Alaric thought even with Marina's help that he couldn't lift the tub, let alone carry it over distance. He wondered at how strong the Heji truly were.

"Is there anything else you need?" Caleb asked.

"What about food?" It seemed Marina was not going to simply let things end. "Our supplies are starting to run low and I see that your trees are laden with food. I also notice some animals on our ride in. I assume they are for eating?"

Caleb didn't respond. Once the tub had been left on the floor he left the prison cell. As soon as he was sure Caleb was out of earshot Alaric started to berate Marina. He couldn't believe she was being so confrontational.

"Caleb might be our only friend in this place, why are you trying to goad him?" Alaric did his best to remain calm. He had no doubts that there were Heji outside their cell and the last thing he needed was for them to think there was dissension between them.

"I'm sure I don't know what you're talking about," Marina feigned ignorance. "He asked if we needed anything and I simply responded." Marina walked to the large tub and ran her fingers through the water. "Do you think it might be a bit much if I asked for the water to be heated?" Marina winked at Alaric and gave him a cheeky smile before he had a chance to respond.

The situation was too dire for Marina to be playing silly games. If Abram didn't believe his story then they would both end up dead. He wanted to scold her for her blasé attitude, but Caleb returned before he had a chance to speak.

He carried a basket full of strange looking fruits. Alaric had to admit they did look appetising and he could only hope that they were edible. Just because the Heji were able to eat it didn't mean that they could.

"Is there anything else I can get you?" Caleb's voice was gruff. Alaric couldn't tell if he was annoyed or whether it was just his normal tone, he hoped it was the latter.

"No, thank you. That will be fine," Alaric shot Marina a stern look when he finished talking.

"Very well. I will see you in the morning," Caleb didn't wait for a response from Marina. He simply shut the door after he left the room.

"Turn around Alaric. I'm going to clean myself now," Marina snapped, like she was speaking to one of her servants.

"But..." Alaric didn't know what to say. He had need her naked before, but it was not an argument he wanted to use. In the end he sat down, facing away from her.

He thought he heard her giggle softly at his discomfort as he heard her clothes drop to the floor. Suddenly his heart started to race at the sound of her splashing in the water. The urge to turn around was almost overwhelming, but he steeled himself and kept staring at the wall.

It didn't take long before the splashing stopped and he could hear Marina rifling through her packs. Suddenly a smell of roses filled the room. The scent was almost enough for Alaric to turn around, but he caught himself at the last moment. Despite the surprise he had to admit that the smell was pleasing to him.

"What's that?" Alaric brought himself to ask.

"Oh, this?"

Marina's questioning tone forced Alaric to turn around. He was grateful to see that she had already slipped on one of the sheer dresses the elves had given her, although he wasn't completely sure there was much difference between the dress and her being naked. He eyes quickly moved from her body to the small vial she held in her left hand.

"Yes, what is that smell?"

"It is rose oil," Marina explained although it was the most obvious thing. "I had almost forgotten that I had packed it back in Kiarome." She absently tossed it back into her pack. "I think you could use some yourself," she scrunched up her nose as she spoke.

"I think I'll pass, but I will clean myself." Alaric walked over the tub. The water already looked filthy, but it was better than nothing. He was about to undress when he realised that Marina was still watching him. "If you don't mind?" Alaric raised an eyebrow at her.

"Fine, fine!" She raised her hands in the air in a defensive manner before she walked to the other side of the room. It was her turn to sit and stare at the wall.

After Alaric had bathed and change his clothes he joined Marina. He thought about asking Marina for the rose oil. Although he felt clean without any soap he did still smell, but he really didn't want to smell the same.

"I think that the trial is going well," Marina said when he was seated. She had started picking at a large round fruit with a prickled green skin and revealed the bright pink flesh inside.

Alaric picked up another fruit of the same variety before he spoke. "I don't know. It's hard to say what they are thinking. I hope that Abram believed me. If he doesn't I don't know what we are going to do."

Marina thought for a moment when it was obvious that Alaric wasn't going to continue. Alaric stared at the fruit, but his thoughts were on the trial. If he hadn't been so pensive he might have noticed the subtle change on Marina's face.

"Don't you worry about it. I have an idea that I think will work," her tone was slightly off, but Alaric was more focused on what was said, not how.

"What?" was all he could say surprised at her statement.

"If things don't go to plan then I think that I could get us out of here," Marina didn't look at Alaric as she spoke. She stared at the half eaten fruit in her hand.

Alaric noticed, for the first time, that the tenderness had suddenly left her. There was hardness about her that he had not seen before. That was enough to pique Alaric's interest. He had seen glimpses of hardness before, but this was different. He didn't know if it was time to get concerned.

"Would you mind sharing your little secret," Alaric asked, she suddenly held his full attention.

"What?" Marina broke her stare and looked at Alaric. "Oh, I don't think that I want to give anything away. I think it would be better if you didn't know."

Alaric didn't like the answer, but he didn't know if he was ready to have an argument. There were more important things for him to worry about. They had not finished their conversation from the other day. Her current state was just another symptom and Alaric needed to get to the bottom of it. If it was what he thought it was then she could be in great danger, but it also might be too late.

"It's the Sapphire stone," Alaric blurted.

"What is?" Marina didn't respond the way Alaric had expected. She was not at all rattled by his sudden statement.

"The stone is starting to take control of you." He couldn't back away from the conversation. His only move was to continue forward.

Marina had to stop and think about his comment. There was truth to his words, she knew that. The only problem was that she didn't really want him to know. She could feel the Sapphire stone. It was almost like the small gem was a part of her. She didn't know how she was going to respond. She had to tell him something, but she could not reveal to him to entire truth. She tried to recall the conversation they had in the heat of the day. Even though it only happened the day before it felt as though it had happened a lifetime ago.

"It is not taking control of me," she almost laughed as she spoke, even though it was not a joke. If she played it that way she might be able to get Alaric to believe her. "I can feel her presence. She is with me, but she is not taking control of me."

Her words brought alarm to Alaric. The way that Marina referred to the stone as she and not it was disturbing. Not only that but the way she spoke was also worrying him. He didn't think that it was her natural tone. He wasn't sure if it was the stone speaking through her, but he knew that it wasn't completely her. Until he could be completely positive he had to be careful how he approached things.

"I think that is good, but I still believe that the stone is trying to take control. Think about your words. Think about what you are saying. If you delve deep into yourself you will see what I am talking about," there was a certain amount of urgency in his voice. He thought that would be the best way to get her to open up.

Once he had finished speaking Alaric noticed that the Sapphire stone was gently glowing. If he was not looking directly at the stone he would not have noticed it. That in itself was a worrying sign. He didn't think that Marina was consciously drawing on the stone's power. He hoped that she was subconsciously. If she was then there was a good chance that she could regain control. If it was indeed the stone taking control, as he expected, then it was going to be harder, much harder.

Marina didn't like what he was insinuating. She didn't want to look inside herself. She knew that she was in control. She could feel the stone, but it was not a bad feeling, it was joyous. She wasn't sure if she wanted to let that go. Feeling so free could not be a bad thing. She felt as though she could take on the Evil One himself. She could not remember feeling so free.

"There is nothing wrong with me. I am in control of my own life," the stone was starting to glow a little stronger.

Alaric could sense the Sapphire stone on the edge of his reality. The feeling he received was hatred. He could feel it coming from the stone. He could only imagine what Marina was feeling inside. He thought that she might be lying to him to protect herself from the wrath of the stone. There was certainly a bond growing between the two and the longer he let it go the harder it would be to break it.

"Okay, if you say so. I didn't mean to upset you. I am just concerned for you wellbeing," he hoped that would appease her.

Marina looked confused. She did not know how to take his comment. The Sapphire stone slowly started to lose its intensity until it finally blinked out. Alaric was surprised to see such a response. He thought about pressing her further, but then decided against it. There seemed little point in spending the rest of the day arguing.

"I can think of a much better way we could spend our time," Marina winked at him as she spoke. The sapphire stone suddenly started to glow much brighter.

Although Alaric wasn't sure exactly what she was getting at he did feel a lot better about their situation. Slowly it dawned on him what she was talking about as she slowly stood and sidled over to him. Before he knew what was happening she was sitting on his lap, stroking his hair.

If he was not already lost in her eyes Alaric would have realised that the situation wasn't right. The feel of her light weight on his legs felt comforting and he gently caressed her long black hair. He had to admit that the smell of the rose oil was very alluring. He could only imagine how bad he smelt, but that thought soon left his mind as Marina brought her lips together with his. The passion he felt overwhelmed him as he returned her kiss as passionately as he could. Before long they were wrapped in each other's arms, rolling around on the floor. A deep blue light washed over their bodies

***

When they were finished Marina decided it was time for a nap. She tried to coax Alaric to bed with her, but he had too much on his mind. He tried to work out how they had made it to where they were. One moment Alaric was concerned for her safety and the next they were in each other's arms. It wasn't that he was complaining, but it did seem an odd turn of events.

He thought about taking the ring from her finger when she was asleep, but he had a feeling that as soon as he touched it she would wake up. There was nothing he could do to take it from her. It would be up to Marina to relinquish the stone and he hoped she would do so when the time was right.

Alaric spent his time trying to focus on the location of the prophecy, as there was nothing else for him to do. Being confined to the cell was no interesting task. At first the prophecy seemed to be further away than the day before. He thought that maybe Na'garoz was travelling deeper into the wasteland. As he concentrated on its location he realised that it was just a spell to mask its location from him.

He meditated on the fact for over an hour before he figured out what was happening. Once he was able to break through the fog he could see the strands of magic that Na'garoz had placed in front of the prophecy. He had to rest once he had made the realisation. The meditation had taken a lot of energy from him. It took great power and concentration to seek out the breakdown of someone else's spell, especially when it was cast such a distance away. He would need to rest before he attempted to unravel it.

His next dilemma would be once the spell was unravelled then Na'garoz would definitely know he was close. He comforted himself with the fact that he believed that the Dark Knight already knew he was there, not that it was much comfort. It had been his one advantage over Na'garoz and it was gone.

He rested for almost another hour before he prepared himself for the upcoming ordeal. He knew that he would have to be careful in what he was about to do. He was sure that the Dark Knight would have set traps along the way. If he was not extremely careful then he could end up frying himself from the inside out.

The first thing for him to do was to get into position. He sat on the floor in front of the fireplace and crossed his legs. He kept his back straight and his head up. Physical posture would be very important once he attempted his spell. Even though a lot of what he was doing would take place away from his body the strain on his physical self would be immense. It was quite possible that his body could die while his consciousness was in the distance. It would not be good for him to return to a dead body.

Taking a number of deep, even breaths Alaric pushed out with his senses until he could feel the threads of magic. It was a lot closer than he had expected. He didn't know if that meant Na'garoz was getting closer or he was getting better. Either way it really didn't make much difference. His consciousness was completely separated from his body. The ability to do such a thing was no small feat.

He plucked at the threads of the spell as a harpist would pluck on a string. The spell was surprisingly complex for what it was. Alaric knew that he would only have one chance to break the spell. If Na'garoz knew what he was doing then it would be easy for him to block Alaric. He would also have to be wary of any traps the Dark Knight had placed on the spell. It was something sorcerers and wizards would do to try and prevent their spells from being unwoven. It took a greater amount of energy, but it was a necessary form of protection.

If Alaric had been a lot closer to Na'garoz then it wouldn't have taken so long to figure out the spell. The distance created its own problems. The weaves that he saw were a lot more jumbled than they should be. As he delved the spell he wasn't sure if he was doing the right thing. He had one chance and if he failed then he would not get another.

Sweat started to appear on his brow and his body started to shake. His consciousness had no idea what his body was going through. If he had realised he might have stopped what he was doing as the true test had not even started. Slowly he started to pull on the strings to see if there were any traps. There were two that weren't very well hidden and would be easy for Alaric to remove.

Taking what he thought was a deep breath in his consciousness he started to unravel the spell. Once he started he had to move quickly. First he dispelled the traps and then he went to work on the rest of the spell. Within a matter of seconds the spell had been dispelled. Without a second thought he quickly returned body before Ra'naroz could find him.

When he had returned to his body he realised the extent of what he had been doing. He had remained in his seated position although his body had already started to slump. As soon as he was one again his body collapsed to the floor. He was completely drained of energy. He could not move a muscle. It took all of his remaining energy just to breathe. There was nothing he could do to pick himself up from the floor. All he could do was remain where he was and hope that he had enough energy to remain alive.

It did not take long before a great pain rushed through his body. It was not from the spell that Na'garoz had created, but from the energy he had expended. His body had been tense for most of the time he was trying to unravel the threads. It was only since he had finished that it started to relax and therefore truly suffer the consequences. He was so exhausted that he could not even scream.

The pain remained intense for the next ten minutes. Alaric wished that there was something that he could do to stop it, but he couldn't. Eventually the pain started to ease, but that did not mean much. The agony was still unbearable. He lay in silent pain for the next hour before he could finally start to move again. All he wanted to do was to crawl onto the bed and try and sleep. Even though he was able to move again it was still a great effort for him to crawl across the floor and climb into bed.

Once he was on the bed he started to feel a little better. The problem was that he was deathly hungry and thirsty. If he raised his head he could see their water pouches and the fruit on the table at the far end of the room. He knew that there was no way he would be able to make it over there. He looked across to where Marina was still sleeping. He didn't know how she was feeling, but he didn't think that it could be any worse than him. The only way to get food and water was to wake Marina, even though he wanted to let her sleep.

"Marina! Marina! Wake up Marina," Alaric's voice was hoarse. He wasn't sure if he would be able to speak loud enough for her to hear him.

He wanted to call out again, but he was already panting for breath. He didn't know if his lungs were up to another round. He watched her intently, as best he could with his head on the pillow. After a few seconds had passed he was grateful to see her eyes open. Once she realised that Alaric was staring at her she became a little surprised.

"Why are you staring at me?" The look on his face was making her uncomfortable. There was something in his gaze that was not quite right.

"I am sorry. I will explain to you shortly, but first can you please get me some food and water?" Alaric's voice sounded weak.

It was the weakness in his voice that motivated her to move. She was going to tell him to get his own meal and that she was not his nurse maid, but decided against it. It was a serious concern that he sounded so weak. When she had gone to bed he was in a such a relaxed state that she couldn't imagine what had happened.

At first she placed the food and water on the small side table next to his bed. She quickly returned to her own bed when she was done. She had also gathered herself some food and water. When she was finished she looked over to see if Alaric was alright. She was surprised to see that he had not touched his food or water. At first she was going to berate him for wasting her time, but she refrained. She sensed that there was something seriously wrong with him and she didn't want to fuel the fire.

"Are you not hungry?" she kept her voice soft.

"I can't," he paused and caught his breath before starting again. "I can't lift my head. Can you please help me?" his voice was still weak.

"Of course I can," although she wanted to know what was wrong with him she would wait until after he had eaten.

She gently sat down on the bed next to him. She had a mission to get Alaric better. When she was comfortable she lifted Alaric's head onto her lap. She started by pouring a little water into his mouth and then a little more. When she was sure that he had drunk enough she started to feed him.

The meal lasted for almost an hour. Even the act of chewing and swallowing drained his energy. Marina didn't mind though. She was happy to look after him. She was always happy to be close to Alaric. There was something she found calming about his presence. When he had finished eating she remained on the bed with his head in her lap. She slowly started to stroke his hair. She was quite happy to stay there and forget about their current predicament. It wasn't until Alaric lifted himself up into a seated position did she stop. Alaric had to admit that he was very comfortable, but he couldn't remain there forever.

"Will you tell me now why you are so weak?" Marina asked.

Alaric thought about lying, but decided that she deserved the truth. "Na'garoz created a spell to block his location and the exact location of the prophecy. If we are ever to find him then I had to remove that spell. It seemed as though it took more energy than I had anticipated, but it is done now. The spell is gone."

"So you can feel where the prophecy is?" Marina asked.

Alaric had to admit that he had not felt anything since he had removed the spell. There was no energy inside him to do anything. Since he was able to move again he thought there was no better opportunity to try again. He could only hope that his plan had worked.

Chapter 30: Judgement

It was a long night in the cell. Alaric thought that he would simply be able to feel the prophecy, but his full strength had yet to return. In fact he was still feeling the effects of the ordeal. The ability to sit up in bed was the full extent of his strength. If he had attempted to stand then his legs would have collapsed underneath him. In the end he just let himself collapse back on the bed.

Alaric was concerned that given enough time Na'garoz would realise that his spell had been broken and would replace it. Alaric had done all he could to avoid the Dark Knight from knowing what he was doing, even though it took more energy to accomplish. If Na'garoz was in control of the spell then he would have felt pain, but he had left it to run its own course giving Alaric the chance to keep it from him.

Before he could say anything else Alaric's eyes glazed over. There seemed to be no life in them, but they remained open. For a moment Marina thought that he had died. Tears welled up in her eyes before she noticed his chest rise and fall again. It was slow, but there was definitely movement. She let the tears roll down her cheeks, but they were more for relief than sorrow.

Marina did her best to keep Alaric comfortable without really knowing how he felt. She noticed that his skin had become extremely hot. Gently she dabbed his skin with water in an attempt to regulate his temperature. It wasn't until the room started to become cold did Alaric's skin follow suit.

When she was sure that Alaric was alright Marina tried to light the fire. It was obvious the sun had well and truly set and the moss light had been extinguished. She had stacked the wood in the fireplace before she realised there was nothing for her to light it with. She had watched Alaric light the fire the night before, but she did not understand what he had done. The thought of the Sapphire stone entered her mind, but she had no idea how to use it. She tried to concentrate on the stone, but it didn't seem to be listening. If she had the power she could have commanded the Sapphire stone to create a fire, but it would be no easy task. Being the water stone it did not like fire and would do anything to avoid it. All Marina got in return for her trouble was silence.

As the night set in the cell became colder and colder. She didn't know how she was going to stay warm. She didn't think that body warmth was going to be enough. She didn't think that Alaric would survive the cold of the night in his current condition and there was a no guarantee that she would survive either. The only thing she could do was to go out and try to find help. She did not want to risk leaving the cell, but she didn't think that there was any other way.

Just before her hand touched the door knob she felt a warmth inside her. She didn't know exactly what it was, but it made her feel safe. Without warning the wood in the fireplace suddenly burst into flame. Marina spun around when she heard the sound of fire crackling. Her initial reaction was to look to see if Alaric was up, but when she saw that he had still not moved she had to think again. Her second thought was not as pleasing as the first. She looked down and saw the Sapphire stone glowing softly. A scowl crossed her face as she tried to get in contact with the stone. There was still no response.

Marina waited a moment before trying to contact the stone again. She had no idea what response she was looking for, but she would know it when it happened. When nothing happened she stamped her left foot and pouted. She did not know why she did it, or who she was expecting to gain a reaction from. She was not one to give up and that was how she signalled her intentions, at least it had been when she had lived in the palace. It was the reaction of a spoilt princess and something that she was trying to remove from her life. When she realised what she had done she was glad that Alaric was still unconscious.

It was just before midnight before Marina eventually fell asleep. She continued to watch over Alaric, occasionally mopping the sweat from his body. It was only when his eyes would no longer stay open did she crawl into bed. She did not want to sleep before he woke, but in the end she did not have much choice.

Marina did not sleep the entire night. Every so often she woke to check on Alaric. When his lips were dry she poured water into his mouth. When he was drenched in sweat she bathed his body. When he murmured in his sleep she comforted him. In the morning she woke tired to find that Alaric was still unconscious. Although it was still not a good sign she took comfort in the fact that he was no longer sweating and the colour had returned to his face. The next problem would be when Caleb came to get them. She did not know what he would do if he found Alaric unconscious. She did not think that Abram would bear the excuse.

As the morning wore on no one came to get them. Marina sat, nervously, by Alaric's side. With each passing moment her tension grew. She did not think that she would be able to survive the trial without Alaric by her side. If things went wrong then she knew what she had to do, but it would be Alaric's strength that would get her through.

It was just before midday when there was a knock on the door. The sudden sound made Marina jump. She had been focusing so hard on Alaric that she did not notice that someone had arrived. She did not know why they knocked. Caleb had always just entered as he pleased. She did not think that it was a good sign.

"Enter," she called out when she regained her senses.

A Heji pushed the door open and entered the cell. Although he looked similar to Caleb, Marina knew that it was not him. Even though she thought that all the Heji looked angry, or ferocious, she could tell that there was a certain amount of animosity radiating from him. She did not know why he was there and not Caleb, but it confirmed her original bad feeling.

The Heji took two steps into the cell before it noticed that Alaric was still in bed. He looked confused, or at least Marina thought that it was confusion. It did not take him long to realise what was happening. When he knew that Alaric was not about to wake up Marina thought that an evil look crossed his face.

"It seems that I have come at a fortuitous moment." He took another step closer. One more and he would be on top of her.

His advance had Marina worried. She did not want to leave Alaric alone, but she also needed to defend herself. Whilst she was pressed against the bed there would be nothing she could do. Before the Heji moved again Marina took a step away.

"Don't make this harder than it needs to be." There was no doubt that the Heji was having evil thoughts.

"I don't understand. Chief Abram has not made his decision yet." Marina was trying to buy some time, not that she really knew what she was going to do with it.

"That is just the problem. Chief Abram should have made a decision by now. He should have made the decision to have your lives ended. He is growing weak." The Heji took another step towards Marina. She backed away in turn, but there was not much further she could go. "It is because of his weakness that our entire lives are at risk. Not only our lives, but our entire world. I have been chosen to make sure that he doesn't do it again."

"We are not your enemy. If there is any chance of recovering the stolen property then we are your best bet." Marina walked backwards until she touched the wall.

"You have already said that, but it is not something that we believe. We will not risk further destruction to our land." He took another menacing step forward. Marina didn't think that there would be any more words.

Marina had no idea what she was going to do. The great creature towered over her. She thought that one swipe of his mighty arms would see her dead. A sudden wave of fear rushed through her body. Her legs started to shake as she waited for him to attack. Just as he was about to move forward again they heard a movement from behind them. The Heji spun around quickly to see who it was. Marina tried to see, but the great creature blocked her view. She thought about moving, but she didn't want to draw any attention to herself.

"I don't think that you want to be doing that," there was strength in Alaric's voice, strength that Marina was surprised to hear.

"I was wondering when you would join us. I must admit that I would have liked to do away with your friend before you, but in the end as long as you are both dead it really makes no difference," the Heji had lost none of his confidence.

"Do you really think that you can defeat me?" Alaric's voice was as cold as ice. Marina was almost afraid to hear his words.

"It looks as though we are about to find out," the Heji didn't sound perturbed by Alaric's confidence.

"You will not!" the voice boomed from the doorway.

Both Marina and the Heji jumped in surprise. Alaric didn't seem phased by the new arrival. In fact he seemed pleased with it. A broad smile crossed his face. It didn't take long before the Heji knew that he was in trouble. Caleb stood in the doorway and it was clear to all that he was not happy. Marina wanted to move to Alaric, but she still didn't want to draw attention to herself.

"I might have thought to find you here Jacob." Caleb made no move into the room. He could sense that things were already on a knife edge. He didn't know what his fellow Heji would do if he thought that he was cornered. His main concern was to make sure that the two were safe. "It was only a matter of time before you tried to wrest control from Chief Abram."

"It is time for new leadership," Jacob turned to face Caleb. He completely ignored Alaric and Marina feeling no threat from them. Marina took her opportunity to move out of harms way and over to Alaric. "Abram is weak. He has brought us to the brink of disaster. Now it is up to me to bring us back and killing these two is the perfect start."

"It is not your decision to make." Caleb would not be swayed. "Until Chief Abram dies he will rule the Heji. There is nothing that you can do about it."

Jacob took a slow, deliberate step towards Caleb. Caleb remained where he was. It was a common tactic of the Heji to find out if their opponent was serious. If Caleb had stepped backwards, like Marina had, then Jacob would have known that he was bluffing. It was obvious that Caleb was not going to back down and he had to be careful. He had made his power play and he could not take it back. Once Chief Abram found out what he had done he would be sentenced to death.

"I have support amongst the other Heji. They know that he has caused us pain. I think you will find that it will be you who faces death," Jacob said, not as confident as he had been.

"Well I think that it is time to see your fate. Chief Abram has made his decision." Caleb made no move into the cell. He wasn't sure exactly how far Jacob would take things. He wished he had brought support.

Jacob had to think quickly, something that he was not renowned for. He had been painted into a corner and he didn't know how he was going to get out. There were only two choices. He could surrender or he could fight his way out. If he could kill the three of them then his plan still had a chance of succeeding.

He made a move towards Caleb. He figured that his fellow Heji was the most imminent threat. Caleb had no choice but to move backwards. He knew that Jacob was going to attack and he needed room to defend himself. Running away was not an option, but if he could aim the fight towards the square then there was a chance he could gain assistance. There was no way his supporters would stand up in front of the chief.

Jacob charged towards Caleb and grabbed him in a bear hug. The fight had begun. It did not take long for Caleb to break the hold. Then the fight was really on. The two Heji struck at each other with their massive fists. Some of the punches connected and others missed. Marina was amazed that they were still standing. The power behind their blows was amazing. They were so focused on each other that they had forgotten about Marina and Alaric. That was Jacob's mistake.

Alaric was not bluffing when he had asked the question. He was confident that he could beat Jacob. It seemed as though he had completely recovered from his ordeal the day before. As much as he wanted to see who the stronger Heji was, he didn't have the time.

Marina felt a sudden jolt in the air. She did not know what it was, but she knew something was going to happen. Once it happened Alaric moved so he was out of the cell and had a better view of the two combatants. Then Marina realised what the jolt was. Alaric was doing something. She followed Alaric until she was standing right behind him.

"Wait Alaric!" Marina kept her voice as soft as she could. "You don't want to risk hurting yourself again."

"I'll be alright," Alaric didn't face her as he spoke. He was too busy concentrating on the sight in front of them.

There was a strain on Alaric's face that he was trying to hide. Marina was suddenly worried. He had only just woken from an ordeal that nearly killed him. She had no idea how he had the energy to do what he was about to do. She didn't think that Alaric would have the energy to do anything once he was done and she wasn't sure it was worth the risk. Once Jacob had been dealt with they still had to contend with the trial. There was no telling what decision Abram had made, but if it wasn't favourable then they would have to fight for their lives. Despite her concerns she knew there was nothing she could do to dissuade him.

It was obvious when Alaric released his spell. He was glad that Caleb was fighting, it meant that he didn't need such a powerful a spell to stop Jacob. When the spell was finished Jacob was trapped mid-motion. He was pulling back his right arm ready for another strike. It was unfortunate for Jacob that Caleb's fist was already coming towards him. Caleb struck him with a force more powerful than what he was expecting. That was also was bi-product of the spell.

Caleb didn't know what surprised him the most, the fact that Jacob was frozen in time or the fact that he was still standing after his attack. It was the perfect time for him to take advantage, but he didn't know what to do. The expression on Jacob's face was the only thing that moved on his body.

"What have you done to me?" he exclaimed.

Alaric walked around the Heji until he was facing him. Caleb was more than happy to move out of his way. He was almost in as much shock as Jacob. It was all too easy for Alaric and it was time for him to play a little. He wanted to make sure that Jacob fully understood the danger he was in.

"I warned you, but you didn't listen." He started to walk around the Heji. With Jacob unable to move his head he had to follow Alaric with his eyes. It gave Alaric a chance to walk out of his line of sight for effect. He felt as though it would give his words more power. "Now you will see the power that I have," he said from behind Jacob.

"I do not think that this is going to help you," Caleb warned when he regained his senses. "If Chief Abram deems you as a threat then he will certainly have you executed."

That was exactly what Alaric wanted Caleb to say. He wanted to put into Jacob's head that he could leak the information to Chief Abram. If that was the case then he might be able to save his own hide and have Alaric executed in the process. In doing so Jacob would reveal the chief the extents of Alaric's power without him having to show it. If he was forced to attack the chief then he did not think he would have able to save themselves from the rest of the tribe.

"I don't think that Chief Abram will mind if I punish a traitor. This is just the beginning. You have no idea what I can do to you," Alaric spoke directly into Jacob's ear. He had to stand on his toes and he was still too short for the move to be completely effective.

"That is enough!" Caleb didn't want to get to close to Alaric. There was not telling what the man was capable of doing. The last thing he wanted was to enrage him further. "You do not know our ways. Now we need to get to the square. Chief Abram needs to speak to you."

Alaric had proven his point. As much as he wanted to make Jacob sweat he had done what he needed to do. There was no doubt that Jacob would speak in the meeting. He was also positive that the Heji would not try anything until he had allies around. The next plan was going to be even harder to accomplish. He only hoped that Marina was ready to do what needed to be done if he failed.

"Very well," Alaric released the spell. He stumbled slightly, but Marina was the only one who noticed. She was glad to see that he was still standing.

When the spell was lifted Jacob fell backwards. The force of Caleb's blow was stored up just waiting for a chance to be released. Caleb was surprised to see such a reaction. His opinion of Alaric had completely changed. He was starting to wonder if he had made the right decision in supporting him. It would not matter soon enough. Chief Abram had made his decision and that was all that mattered.

Jacob remained on the ground. He didn't know what to do. The delayed reaction for Caleb's punch shocked him. He knew that he had been beaten. He didn't really understand how, but he knew it was true. He would remain down until he was told otherwise. Either way he did not like his chances of seeing nightfall. He figured that he had a better chance of surviving facing Abram than trying to attack again.

"Get up you disgrace," Caleb stood over Jacob as he spoke. "I should kill you myself, but it will be Chief Abram who decides your fate."

"I knew you wouldn't have the courage to finish the job yourself," Jacob took a chance at having a last dig at Caleb.

"He might not finish the job, but you can be sure if you do not keep quiet I will," Alaric's voice was stone cold.

Jacob was not going to chance his luck any more. He had said what he had to say. The walk to the square would give him time to think on what he was going to say to Abram. His doom was not certain, but he would have to be very careful. As Caleb grabbed him by the scruff of his neck and pushed him forward an idea came to his mind. He smiled to himself and continued towards the square. He would have his revenge.

They walked in silence. Caleb walked closely behind his new prisoner. He wanted to avoid contact with the other two. Their fate was in the hands of the chief and he was happy to leave it that way. There was little chance he would be able to defend them anymore. Their actions, one way or another, would seal their fate.

The square was a buzz. They could feel the atmosphere as they climbed the stairs. Alaric didn't know if it was a good sign or not. He knew that some of them were out for his blood. He just didn't know if there were any who supported their cause. When it was said and done it was just Abram's opinion that mattered. The other Heji would form their opinions based on his. With Jacob's failed attack there was a chance that he had lost all of his support. It was doubtful that anyone would follow the leader of a failed coup.

Caleb ushered Jacob to the place in the square that had been reserved for Alaric and Marina. He was going to out the Heji as a traitor before Abram past judgement on the other two. He didn't know how that would affect things and he didn't care. Abram was surprised to see the two of them arrive before the prisoners. He didn't look happy with the situation.

"What is the meaning of this Caleb? Is this how you transport prisoners? Let them travel behind you and escape on a whim?" his voice was abrupt.

"I am sorry Chief Abram, but something important as arisen," Caleb was about to continue before Abram spoke again.

"I do not take this lightly Caleb. I do not see how anything could supersede my judgement." He wasn't going to make it easy for Caleb.

There was nothing else for Caleb to do, but to get straight to the point. Unfortunately it was Jacob who spoke first. He was not going to let Caleb get the upper hand. If he was going to survive he had to be quick.

"I caught these two trying to escape. They were half way out of our land when I found them. When I brought them back to the cell Caleb jumped me. It seems that he was the one who helped them to escape. The three of them overpowered me." The scene didn't completely make sense, but he hoped that it would be enough to convince Abram.

"Is this true?" Jacob's statement took Abram by surprise.

"Of course it's not true," It was all Caleb could do to keep from throttling Jacob. He didn't really know what else he could say to convince Abram.

"These are serious accusations. If that is all that you have to say then I will have to find Jacob's words to be true." Abram did not truly believe Jacob, but unless Caleb defended himself there was nothing he could do.

The allegations had taken Caleb by surprise. He had not thought that Jacob could be so deceiving. Underestimating an opponent was the best way to be defeated. That was something that he had learnt at a young age. He could not believe he had walked straight into a trap. He thought that it was too late to tell the truth. It would seem like it was he who was making up lies.

It was Alaric who moved into the square and addressed the chief. Caleb wanted to tell Alaric that what he was doing had a death wish, but he wanted to hear his words. Being unable to speak himself he had to rely on Alaric to defend him. He wasn't sure how things got so out of hand. It should have been a glorious occasion, someone arriving from the Northern land.

"I am sorry to interrupt Chief Abram, but I feel that it is my duty to explain to you what really happened," Alaric started to speak.

"Chief Abram, are you going to let this outsider speak to you this way. Not only is he an outsider, but he is also on trial for his life." Jacob didn't want to let Alaric speak.

Abram thought for a moment. As he did the crowd started to become restless. Some of them knew what Jacob had done and they also did not want Alaric to speak. Although they would not be in as much trouble as Jacob they did not want anyone to know what they had done. The rest were just surprised with the turn of events. It was not at all what they were expecting.

"I will let him speak. I am interested to hear what he has to say," the crowd became even more vocal when Abram spoke. Those who supported Jacob's claim shrunk back into the crowd. The fact that Abram was going to give ear to Alaric's account was not a good sign. "You will all be quiet, now!" his voice boomed throughout the square and everyone was suddenly quiet.

"We were not trying to escape," Alaric thought that it would be pertinent to point that out from the start. Jacob was about to interrupt again, but was silenced by a look from Abram. "It was Jacob who came to get us. He came to kill us. He did not believe that you were making the right decision. He wanted to do away with us before you made your judgement," Alaric's words brought a roar from the crowd. It seemed that no one believed his words.

"You will all be quiet!" Abram boomed. It seemed as though he was the only one who was interested in what Alaric had to say.

His words had more power than Alaric had expected. The entire congregation was suddenly quiet. None of them would go against the word of their chief. The Heji's power was absolute. There had never been a coup in the existence of the Heji. What Jacob was trying to do was unheard of in their society.

"He is trying to usurp your power. He has a group of followers and this was his chance to gain control. With a show of decisive force he would rule the Heji," Alaric paused and waited for the words to sink in.

It was obvious to everyone that Abram was taking Alaric's words seriously. Marina wondered if he was using a spell to convince the Heji chief. The thought had crossed his mind, but he wanted Abram to come to the conclusion on his own. It would be easier if that was the case. Otherwise Alaric would have to continue to keep the spell going and he had more important things to spend his energy on.

"Hmm. This is indeed a serious allegation. What do you have to say, Caleb." It didn't sound like Abram needed much more convincing to believe Alaric's words.

Caleb had hoped that he would not have to speak. "I am afraid to say that it is true."

Jacob knew that those Heji who had supported his claim would very quickly be changing sides. He knew that he was not going to gain any support from his co-conspirators. His only chance of survival was to make a run for it, but that was not really an option. He did not think he would make it off the square.

"What do you have to say for yourself?" Abram addressed Jacob.

He didn't think that there was any point in trying to defend himself. He knew that Abram believed the outsider. All he could do was to try and convince him that he was wrong. If he could get Chief Abram to change his mind and understand what he was trying to do then there was still a chance that he might survive. It was not going to be easy.

"Don't you see what you are doing to us? It started when you let the last outsider into our land. He stole our treasure and has risked destroying our world. What I did, I did for all of us. These outsiders cannot be trusted. They will be the ruin of us and they must be destroyed. What I did was for the safety of our people and if you can't see this then you do not deserve to be chief," he kept the strength in his voice right up until the last statement. It was in that statement that he started to fade and thus gave Abram the advantage back.

"I have heard enough. I do not believe for one second that your motives are genuine." Abram did not have to think about what he had to say. "You did this to try and seize power. This is something that is unforgivable. Yes we made a mistake in trusting the first of the outsiders, but it is written in our laws that we must take in anyone who survives for more than a day. There is nothing we could have done and there is nothing we can do. If nothing else we are bound by tradition. Now what you have done goes against everything we believe in. It would do me no greater pleasure then to watch you being ripped to shreds, but I do not believe that will prove anything." There was a glimmer of hope in Jacob's eyes. He should have known that Abram would not have the courage to put him to death. He would spend a few days in a cell and then he would be out again. "I cannot, however, turn a blind eye to what you have done. Your dissention risks causing more damage than what the outsiders have done. That cannot go unpunished." A hush came over the crowd. "For your crime I can't sentence you to death. The most I can do is have you banished from our land," that in itself was a death sentence. Any hope that Jacob had felt was now gone. "Henceforth, Jacob shall be known as the 'Lost One'. He is now lost to us. Now escort him out of our land."

Jacob looked around nervously. He wanted to run, but the other Heji had already closed in around him. There was no chance for him to escape, not that there was anywhere for him to run to. They all knew that he could not survive more than a week outside of the cavern. It was a crueller way to die, but in their society it at least gave him a chance to survive.

"What about the outsiders?" Jacob called over the crowd as he was being ushered away.

His words caused everyone to stop. They had been so carried away with what had just happened they had forgotten their reason for being there. Abram had hoped that they would have left without his answer. His decision had become even harder and with Jacob's revelations he didn't know how they would react to his judgement. He wanted more time, but he knew that it would not be wise for him to defer.

"I have to find the outsiders innocent of the charges." There was little reaction from the Heji. No one really knew what to expect and no one could work out if it was a good decision or a bad one. "There is not enough evidence that they are in league with the first outsider. Now it is time to dispose of the guilty party."

In the end the Heji were happy with what had happened and they quickly moved away from the square. They wanted to get rid of the traitor, especially those who had been on his side. Abram knew that he had co-conspirators, but he did not think that they would try anything again. He could not in good conscience attack the other Heji. He knew now to be wary and that was good enough for him.

It was not long before it was only the four of them alone in the square. Abram had stepped down from his throne and stood in front of Alaric. Caleb had taken a few steps backwards, but remained on the square. He wanted to tell Alaric to do the same thing, but he could not speak. He was too relieved that everything had worked out for the best. Marina stood back with Caleb. She wasn't sure what Abram wanted, but she knew that he wanted to address Alaric.

"Thank you," a smile crossed Abram's face. "I don't think that I can thank you enough. I have had my doubts of Jacob's loyalty for a long time, but there was no proof. There was nothing I could about him and his followers. Now I think they will settle down."

Caleb was in shock. He had never heard Abram speak so candidly. He had to wonder about the outsider. He was having an effect that he could not believe. In that moment he thought that there might be a chance for the Heji to survive.

"That is perfectly alright. I am here to help. I am just glad that you finally believe that," Alaric replied.

"I think that I always believed you, but unfortunately I had to make a show of it for the others. If I just accepted you for who you were then I think Jacob would have succeeded in his plan." Caleb could not believe what they were saying.

"I see that you are very wise. There is no doubt that you deserve to be chief of the Heji," the words sounded condescending, but Abram did not take it that way.

"Now I believe that some better rooms are in order," Abram wanted to change the subject. "I am sorry for having to keep you in the cell. You will have proper accommodation tonight."

"Thank you," Alaric didn't think that there was anything wrong with the accommodation they had been given, but he was not going to question him. "I think that we need to talk further."

"Of course, but now is not the time. There are matters that I have to deal with." Abram started walking towards his house.

Alaric paused for a moment before he followed after. He wasn't sure if Abram had finished the conversation, but he was sure that the Heji had more to say.

"Will you show Marina to their new quarters?" he spoke over his shoulder to Caleb. "I wish to have a private word with Alaric."

"What is it you wish to discuss, chief?" Alaric asked when they were alone.

"This outsider, the one you call Na'garoz, how dangerous is he?" Abram asked.

"I think that you made the right decision not to go after him. He is extremely dangerous," Alaric explained.

Abram seemed happy with Alaric's answer. Alaric wasn't really sure why Abram had asked the question. He thought that his explanation the day before would have been enough. He did not paint a nice picture of the Dark Knight. The most important thing was that the Heji no longer associated him with Na'garoz. There was a greater chance of recovering the prophecy and the lost treasure with the aid of the Heji. At the very least they wouldn't hinder him anymore.

"I need to speak to you about the thief." Alaric thought that was the best way to describe Na'garoz.

"Of course we do, but now is not the time." Abram stopped outside his front door. "Today has been a day of revelations and I need time to think about it. I know our brains don't work as quickly as yours, but I believe that they can be just as effective, given enough time."

"Of course, Chief Abram, I did not mean to offend you." Alaric was surprised at Abram's profound statement.

What happened next surprised Alaric even more. The great chief started to laugh. It was a deep rumbling sound, but there was no doubt that it was laughter. Alaric wasn't sure what he was laughing at. He didn't think that he said anything funny.

"That is alright, no offence taken. Now I think that you should return to the village. I am sure that your friend will be waiting for you," Abram waited for Alaric's response, which he knew was coming.

"Thank you chief. When is it that we will talk?" Alaric was starting to get anxious. Now that he knew how close Na'garoz was he wanted to get after him.

"Patience, my small friend, there is still much to be said. You can not just go rushing outside unprepared. It is amazing you lasted so long. We will discuss a plan of attack in the morning. Until then you should rest and keep your strength up. I have a feeling that the next few days will be the hardest of your life, at least up until now." Abram didn't wait for a response this time. When he finished speaking he disappeared into his house.

Alaric remained standing outside the front of Abram's house for a few minutes. There was something in the tone of his voice that he didn't like. He wasn't sure what it was, but it was almost like there was an edge of impending doom. There was nothing that he could do except wait for morning. He had to admit to himself that his body was still tired and could use the rest.

Chapter 31: Plans made

The house they were given was much nicer than the prison cell, not that they thought the cell was all that bad. There were four rooms. The first room was a lounge area. In itself it was larger that the cell they had been staying in. Three doors led from the lounge room to three bedrooms. One of the bedrooms could have easily accommodated the two of them

Alaric found Marina lounging in one of the arm chairs when he returned. She was picking at a plate of fruit that sat on a small side table. When Alaric entered she looked pleased to see him. He had to admit that he was glad to see her as well.

"Caleb said we can move around freely now," Marina said.

As much as Alaric would have liked to explore the Heji's little world he really didn't have the energy. Although he had acted strong since he had woken he was still feeling the effects of the previous day. In the morning they would have to be after the Dark Knight and he would need all his strength. All he could do was rest for the remainder of the day. If Marina wanted to explore then she would have to do so on her own.

"That's nice," Alaric said as he found a comfortable seat. "I think I will just remain here." He didn't want to admit to Marina that he was still feeling weak.

"Come on Alaric. When are we ever going to get an opportunity to do this again? This is a once in a lifetime chance," Marina's voice was full of hope.

Alaric shook his head. "You should go and explore. I need to get some rest."

Hearing Alaric's words made her rethink her plans for the afternoon. It was obvious that he had not completely recovered and she didn't want to leave him alone, no matter how much she wanted to explore. The expression of concern and disappointment was clear on her face.

"Don't worry about me. I just need to rest some more. I'll be fine. You go an enjoy yourself. There is no telling what will happen tomorrow." His words were filled with doom and they didn't make her feel any better. "Please Marina, I'll be alright. I just need to spend some time by myself."

"Last time I left you alone, or fell asleep as it may be, you didn't end up real well. I think I'll just stay here."

Alaric sighed. He just wanted to be left alone. He needed to rest and he didn't think he could do so with Marina hovering over him. Despite the fact that she wasn't going to leave him alone there was something very comforting with her attitude. She was no longer acting like the spoilt princess from Darshival. Although it crept back every now and then it was almost gone. The thought made him smile.

"What?" Marina asked.

"Oh, nothing, I was just thinking." There was no way Alaric was going to tell her. "I appreciate your concern, but I really think you should go exploring." An idea came to him as he was talking. "At least would you check on the horses? Hopefully the Heji have been treating them well."

Marina had to admit that Alaric had a point. They would need the horses if they were going to escape the wasteland. There was no telling what had happened to them since they had been taken prisoner.

"Very well. I will see to the horses, but then I will return."

Alaric just smiled at her. She would do whatever she wanted, but for a short while at least, he would be left alone. As soon as Marina left the room Alaric closed his eyes and fell asleep.

Alaric woke with a start. He had no idea what time it was and he felt disorientated. The room was darker than when he fell asleep, but there was a light coming from somewhere. It took a moment before his senses returned and he remembered he was safe inside a house. As he looked around he saw Marina sitting at a small table. On the far side of the room a fire burned brightly.

"What time is it?" Alaric asked.

"It's getting late. You've slept for the rest of the day," Marina's voice was soft.

Alaric rose from his chair and walked to the table. His body felt stiff from the position he had slept in, but he still felt refreshed. All he could think about was food. He was famished.

"How were the horses?" Alaric asked as he started to eat.

"It looked like they were having the time of their lives. It's been a long time since they were able to eat fresh grass, although the grass itself didn't look overly fresh."

There was something strange about Marina's words that made Alaric put down the fruit he was about to eat.

"That is an odd thing to say. What makes you think the grass isn't fresh?"

"I don't know if that's the right word for it. Maybe sick is a better word, although I'm not really sure if that is correct either. What I would have thought would be lush, green grass had tinges of brown. The horses didn't seem too worried about it thought."

Alaric was starting to understand why the Heji were so concerned with what Na'garoz had stolen. When they were riding towards the village Alaric had noticed that there seemed something wrong with the forest. He didn't take much notice at the time, but upon reflection he definitely knew something wasn't right.

"Did you have a look at the rest of the forest?" he asked

Marina blushed for a moment. She had said that she was going to watch over Alaric, but that had not been the case. "After I checked on the horses I returned to see how you were," her tone was defensive. "When I saw that you were comfortable I took a stroll around the forest. I have to admit that the forest didn't look healthy, not that I know what it should look like."

Something was definitely not right. Alaric wanted to discuss things further with Abram, but knew that he would have to wait until the morning. There was nothing more he could do that night.

"I think we should get some sleep now. It'll be a long day tomorrow."

Marina didn't argue. It was getting late and she was more than happy to go to bed. Despite the fact that he had been sleep for most of the afternoon Alaric didn't think he would have any problem falling asleep again.

It was early in the morning when Abram came to see them. The moss had only just started to light the roof of the cavern. Alaric was already up, but Marina was still sleeping. In a way Alaric was glad. He wanted to speak with Abram alone, at least for a little while. The Heji Chief had arrived with Caleb.

"Thank you for coming so early," Alaric greeted the two Heji in the lounge room.

"Time is of the essence, for us too," Abram spoke. "Our world dies a little every day. If we cannot regain our treasure then our world will cease to exist."

Alaric looked at the floor in front of him. What he had to say was not going to be easy. He had only just gained the trust of the Heji and what he had to say to them could easily ruin it, but he had no other option. He had to be honest with them or else he was no better than the Dark Knight who had stolen their treasure.

"The treasure, can you tell me about it?" Alaric asked, although he thought that he already knew the answer.

"It is a band made out of gold metal. I would say it would wrap around your wrist quite nicely," he looked at Alaric's arms to accentuate his words. "Yes I would say that it would be a good fit."

Alaric assumed that the treasure was a bracelet, but that was not what he was asking about. "Is there a gem stone on the bracelet, maybe a green stone?" Alaric hoped that his guess was wrong, but he knew that it wasn't.

"Yes, on the top of the bracelet," Abram thought it was a strange name for the band of metal, but it wasn't important. "There is a small green stone. When we bring the bracelet out for celebrations the stone glows. We believe that it brings renewed life to our land." Alaric didn't think they knew exactly how right they were. "This is why we believe that our land is dying."

"I think you are right, but here in lies the problem," Alaric couldn't wait any longer. "I believe that the stone on the bracelet is in fact the Emerald *Stone of Power*. If you recall the…" Alaric saw the dead looks on their faces and thought that he had to explain, Abram had other ideas.

"Yes, I do remember your stories about the *Stones of Power*. I do not believe that our treasure is one of them." Abram could read between the lines. He knew exactly what Alaric was talking about."

"I hope that you are right, but I really don't think that you are. There is a reason why Na'garoz came to your land. I believed that it was just to take the prophecy out of my reach, but now I know otherwise. The prophecy would have told him where the next *Stone of Power* was and it led him here. I am afraid that I will need to take the stone with me when we find it," Alaric didn't know how else to explain it.

"Then how can you expect us to help you?" Caleb could not believe what he was hearing. "We should lock you up and not let you leave. Let's face it; your thief friend will only survive so long outside by himself. I wouldn't be surprised if his carcass is lying out in the sun as we speak."

"I can assure you that he is still alive." Alaric did not like Caleb's response.

"We can worry about that when we get the bracelet back," Abram's words surprised everyone. "If we argue then neither of us will get the treasure. For now our main goal must be the return of the bracelet."

Caleb did not like what Abram was saying. He was surprised that his chief was taking such a passive position on the matter, but there didn't seem to be a good way to ask him. There was a reason why Abram asked him to be present, but he didn't know how much leeway he would get.

"Are you sure that this is the right decision?" Caleb asked as he watched Abram's reaction closely.

"There is more to this than you know," Abram didn't sound upset at being questioned. "We have been getting rumours that the Scartlers are massing."

"That is impossible," Caleb could not believe what he was hearing. "They are solitary creatures. They only come together to mate and that happens very rarely."

"Now you can see why we need to broaden our perspective," Abram was calm as Caleb started to crumble.

"I am sorry to interrupt, but what is a Scartler?" Alaric was confused.

"You saw a Scartler when you were waiting for me. They are our enemy. Occasionally one will try its luck at raiding our home. On rare occasions they will succeed. Generally one by itself is not much of a problem, but if they are gathering?" Caleb let his voice trail off as he thought about it.

"We are strong in our land and Scartlers are just as dangerous in theirs. Outside in the desert they can be lethal. A young Heji is no match for a full grown Scartler," Abram explained further. "It is a worrying sign that they are joining together. If they are planning on attacking our village then I don't know what we will do."

"I do not believe that they are banding together to make an attack," Alaric added, now that he had a better idea of the situation.

"I don't mean to be rude, but you don't really know what you are talking about." Caleb wasn't in the mood for Alaric's opinion.

"Well I am afraid that I know more about the situation than you believe." Alaric did not like what Caleb was insinuating.

"Please, Alaric, tell us what you are thinking," Abram remained calm.

"Na'garoz is gathering an army. He now knows that I am here. I'm sure that he has guessed that I am with you."

"That is impossible. There is no way he could coordinate the Scartler into forming an army. They would eat him the first chance they got," Caleb retorted.

"He has survived in the outside world for this long. I think that he knows what he is doing. There is no doubt that if the Scartlers are gathering it is Na'garoz who is controlling them. He is goading us to go and get him. Things have just got a lot worse for all of us," Alaric's words gave no reassurance.

"This is indeed a bad sign," Abram said, not really knowing how to respond.

"You have no idea how bad this is," Alaric agreed with him.

"What is happening?" No one had noticed Marina enter the room. She did not like what she was hearing.

Alaric thought about what he was going to say. In the end he decided the truth was the best. Marina listened as he summarised what they were talking about. When he was finished she had a concerned, yet pensive look on her face. Alaric didn't know how she was going to handle the situation.

"There is not much we can do," she spoke slowly. "We have to attack and we have to attack now."

"I do not think that would be a wise decision," Caleb spoke again. "We can defend in our land, but we could not attack in the outside world."

It was clear that Abram had enough of Caleb's negative attitude. Alaric was the first to see it. He wanted to speak before Abram, but the chief got in first. "I would wish you would stop being so negative. It sounds like you have already condemned us to death and that is not the reason why I asked you to join us. There is a problem ahead of us and we need to work it out."

"I am sorry." Caleb had not even realised what he was doing.

"We have to use what we know to our advantage," Abram added.

The four of them sat in silence as they thought. There was information they could use, but they wanted to think about it first. It was Marina who was the first one to speak.

"Do you know where Na'garoz is right now?" She looked at Alaric.

Alaric closed his eyes to concentrate. Ever since he had broken the spell he had not been able to feel the prophecy at all. There had been too many distractions for him to be able to see if what he had done had worked. To his relief the sensation returned to him. This time is was more prominent. He could point to the exact location, but he refrained from doing so. His next problem was trying to judge the distance. With a little time the answer finally came to him.

"He is less than a day's ride. I would be surprised if he was more than two or three hours' away," Alaric spoke with his eyes still closed.

"Do you know if he has gathered the Scartlers to him?" Caleb was almost afraid to ask the question.

"I do not know," Alaric kept his eyes shut. He was still trying to get a better feeling of what was happening. "I can feel the prophecy. I know where the prophecy is, but as far as anything else I can't tell you. I think he has created another subtle spell to mask the location of the Scartlers."

"Can you break it?" Marina asked quietly.

"No!" he opened his eyes as he responded. "There is not enough time. He has played it well, but it is time for us to take a chance." Something had changed in his composure.

"We cannot rush this," Caleb spoke again.

Abram was watching the exchange closely. He noticed that Alaric had changed, although he did not truly know what it meant. He did not really understand the subtle changes in their body language, although it was clear that something had happened, he wanted to know what it was before he commented.

"We have no choice. We have to move and we have to move today," Alaric spoke with purpose. "We have already wasted too much time. The longer Na'garoz remains in possession of the prophecy and the Emerald stone the less likely we are of getting them back."

"What do you want us to do?" Abram resigned himself to the fact that Alaric would have to take command. He did not know how to organise a battle.

"You need to organise all the Heji who can fight and we need to venture outside," Alaric explained.

"Aren't you forgetting one thing?" Marina asked as the two Heji rose.

"What is that?" he asked when she did not offer up the answer.

"It will be getting very hot out there. I don't think that we would be able to survive," Marina didn't want to dampen everyone's spirits, but she a point.

"You can wear the pelts," Caleb spoke quickly, also not wanting to lose the momentum.

Marina shuddered at that thought. Since she had been able to bathe she did not want to wear those filthy things again. To make matters worse she didn't think that they would be suitable in battle. She was about to voice that opinion when Alaric spoke.

"I wouldn't worry about that. I will make sure everything is alright," his voice was filled with confidence, but it did nothing to reassure Marina.

"What does that mean?" she asked with a suspicious tone in her voice.

"You will just have to trust me on this one." He was not going to give anything away. "How long do you think it will take to gather the other Heji?" he asked as Caleb and Abram stood.

"I think we should be ready in an hour," Abram seemed confident.

"Good. Then we will meet you on top of the cliff," Alaric was happy with his response.

The Heji left without another word. Alaric could sense that Marina had more questions. He wanted to ready himself, but he knew that he would not get a moment's peace if he did not listen to her. This was the reason why he didn't want her involved in the meeting.

"How are we going to survive this?" her voice was thick with concern. "By the sound of it if those creatures are fighting on Na'garoz's side we don't have much chance."

"And that is not the worst of it," Alaric added in an ominous tone.

"What is that supposed to mean?"

"There are a lot more Scartlers than Abram thinks."

"How do you know that? I thought that Na'garoz was masking their whereabouts?" Marina sounded suspicious.

"That is not exactly true. Na'garoz wants me to know where he is and who he is with. That in itself means that I should not share the information with the Heji," Alaric explained.

"But they need to know what they are up against," Marina could not believe what she was hearing.

"I don't think that it would do any good. I don't think they really understand numbers all that well," Alaric explained.

"But if they do not have a chance of winning then why do we go to war?" Marina was confused.

"I didn't say we didn't have a chance of winning. We have a very good chance of winning. All I said is that things are worse than what they thought."

Marina didn't think that there was much point in taking the conversation any further. Alaric was being very elusive with his answers. She thought that he was just doing it to frustrate her and it was working. She wanted to get more answers, but it wasn't worth the headache. All she could do was rely on the fact that Alaric knew what he was doing.

There was one last thing Alaric had to do before they left. He needed to get the Jade dagger. He would need all the help he could get for the upcoming battle and he hoped the stone would be there for him.

Quickly he found the velvet sheath before he lifted the chest onto the table. He was glad that Marina was busying herself in her bedroom. There was no time for the stupid questions she would ask. All he had to do was open the chest and place the dagger in its sheath.

***

They found the horses grazing freely just outside of the village. They looked as though they had been enjoying themselves. The rest was doing them good. It had been a long time since they were able to eat and drink as much as they wanted. Alaric was a little concerned that they might be getting lazy, but when Adelanta saw them he looked ready. He pranced over to greet them and shook his head in appreciation towards Alaric. There was no doubt that he was ready for whatever lay before them. The mare didn't seem as enthusiastic, but nevertheless she was ready to do what was necessary.

Alaric and Marina arrived at the cliff face as the last of the Heji were being assembled. There were fewer of the creatures than Alaric had been expecting, and hoping for. At the front of the line were Abram and Caleb. They looked like they were ready for battle and were glad to see the two of them approach.

"We are assembled and ready for orders," Abram sounded a little too excited for Alaric's liking. When it was said and done, enthusiasm might be the only advantage they had.

"Is this all?" Alaric had to ask the question.

"This is all except for those who are either too old or too young to fight," Abram sounded proud of those before him.

Alaric had assumed that their makeshift army had been all males, but by Abram's words there were women as well. He took another look over the Heji, but he still could not pick the difference. Their thick hair covered anything that might distinguish between the two genders. He had to shake the thought from his mind. There were much more important things for him to worry about.

"Very good. I think that we should head out," Alaric waited for Abram to make the command.

"Now is the time that we stand up and be counted. Our enemy has wandered unhindered for too long. Some of us may not return from this day, but at least we can say that we took our destiny in our own hands," Alaric was surprise again at Abram's powerful words.

When he finished speaking there came a roar from the other Heji. Both Alaric and Marina had to cover their ears. As she did Marina felt something on the back of her neck. With the sound of the cheering Heji she almost missed it. She looked towards Alaric, but there was little expression on his face. Absentmindedly she scratched at her neck and thought that it must have just been an insect. It was an odd sensation, but there were more important things for her to worry about and she quickly put it out of her mind.

Abram did not wait for the cheers to die down before he started the climb to the outer world. Once he started moving the other Heji followed suit. They had no idea what was waiting for them on the surface and if they did they would not have been so keen to move. Alaric and Marina followed closely behind the Chief and Caleb. They did not think it was appropriate to walk with the chief, at least not for the moment. There would be time when Alaric would need to assume control, but until then he was happy for Abram to lead.

"What about the sun?" Marina asked as they neared the exit.

"Don't worry. It has all been taken care of," Alaric was not going to elaborate any further.

Marina shook her head. She knew that it was true, but that didn't make things any easier. Alaric had become distant and she did not like it. She wanted to remain in the loop, but for some reason he was trying to exclude her. There was something she wanted to say, but she knew that it wasn't the time. She would store it away and bring it up later.

Outside the sun was high in the sky. The heat beat down, but for some reason Marina did not feel it. She knew that the temperature would be reaching its extreme very shortly. It would not take long for their skin to start to blister and boil. The only problem was that Marina only noticed a slight change in the temperature. It was not right. She should have already been sweating profusely especially since she was only dressed in the light cloth of the elves.

It was not that she wasn't grateful for the protection, but there was more to it than that. Although she did not have much of an idea of magic, she did know that all spells took a certain amount of energy. She assumed that blocking the sun's heat would take quite a lot. She knew for a fact that Alaric would need all of his energy to fight Na'garoz and that worried her, but it did not seem to concern Alaric. The look of concentration did not falter from his face.

"Which way should we go?" Abram asked when all the Heji were out in the open.

Alaric thought for a moment longer before he spoke. "He is to the south," he pointed to add to his statement.

"Let's move out." Abram started to march to the south.

The Heji kept a steady pace. Abram was just as keen to get to the battle as Alaric. The more time they took the more advantage Na'garoz gained. Alaric was surprised that he was not more than a day's ride away. That was both a relief and a concern. He had a bad feeling that he was riding into a trap, a trap that could see the destruction of the Heji. If they did not win the war then it would not take long for the Scartlers to overrun the Heji's world.

They had been travelling for over two hours when Alaric suddenly called for a halt. Abram called for the Heji to stop. Once they had stopped moving Alaric rode to the front of the line. There were a few murmurs passing through the crowd, they did not like what they were seeing. It looked as though Alaric was trying to take control. Abram should have explained the situation better, but it was too late.

"They are just over that small dune." He pointed to the small rise in front of them. "We need to proceed with caution."

Abram referred the information to the rest of the Heji. He also made a point that if Alaric voiced a command that the Heji were to listen as if it came from his own mouth. Again there was low rumble from the Heji. Although they didn't like what they were hearing they would not go against their chief's wishes.

"What are you planning?" Abram asked when he was confident that the Heji would do what was required.

"I don't know," Alaric wasn't sure if he should have said that. "I can't see exactly what is going to happen. Once I see the layout then I will be able to tell."

His statement was not exactly correct. He knew that the Heji were just a distraction. He needed them to take out the Scartlers. Alaric and Marina had to focus on Na'garoz. He didn't know what the Dark Knight was planning, but he knew it would not be pleasant.

"Let's move into position." Alaric stared out at the horizon. He was not looking forward to what he had to do.

They started off again at a gentle pace. They didn't want to alert Na'garoz and his army of Scartlers to their approach. When they were running they made quite a noise. It was not necessary for them to be quiet, but any advantage was better than nothing. Although Na'garoz knew they were coming he didn't know their exact arrival time.

Alaric was loathed to crest the dune. He knew that the sight on the other side would be menacing. He was prepared for it, but he was not sure how the Heji would react. They were used to seeing Scartlers one at a time. What they were about to see would shock them. He just hoped that they would have the strength to keep going.

As they crested the dune the sight before them was worse than Alaric had expected. He did his best to control his nerves, but it was obvious that everyone else was shaken. His heart started to race and there was nothing that could stop it. He was beginning to regret his decision to bring the Heji to war. He had no idea what sort of enemy they were about to attack, but if what the Heji said was anything to go by then they didn't have a chance.

About half a mile in front of them was a sea of Scartlers. Alaric could only guess that there were a thousand of the creatures, just waiting for them. He didn't think that there would be many more than a hundred Heji standing behind him. He could feel their fear. He could feel them faltering. He didn't know if they were going to be able to make an attack.

"This is our time," he heard Abram's voice from behind him. There was nothing but strength in his voice. "This is our battle. We finish it today."

A great roar came from the Heji. Alaric wanted to look around, but he didn't want them to see the fear in his eyes. Only Marina could see that look from where she was. She also felt the same fear that Alaric faced and she also knew she would have to overcome it if they were going to succeed.

Behind the line of Scartlers, on a similar small dune, was Na'garoz. Alaric's vision suddenly focused on him, as if he was only a few paces away. He wore a dark robe with the hood covering his face. Although he could not see inside the hood he knew that there was a wicked smile on his face. The Dark Knight held up a book in his right hand. Alaric knew that it was the prophecy. He waved in front of himself, taunting Alaric to come and get it.

"You have to separate the Scartlers from Na'garoz." Alaric spoke as his vision returned to normal. "They will not attack without the Dark Knight controlling them. It is our best bet to defeat them."

"Don't underestimate the Heji. We are a strong race and we will fight to the end. As much as this started out as your fight, it is ours now. Our enemies have joined together and now it is time for them to die," Abram was not at all rattled by the sight in front of him.

"Well I guess there is nothing else for it. Let the battle begin," Alaric tried to focus on Na'garoz as he spoke, but it didn't work.

Chapter 32: War

Alaric and Marina moved out of the way of the Heji as they started their charge. They would not take part in the main attack on the Scartlers. There was little chance that they would be effective against the reptilian creatures. The battle would have to be fought by the Heji. Their fight was going to be much harder.

The charge started with a great roar from Abram, which was in turn followed by the rest of the Heji. The opposing army started their charge with an ear piercing screech from the Scartlers. Sand clouds blew up into the sky from behind both armies as they raced to meet each other.

Na'garoz made no attempt to join the fray. Like Alaric and Marina he stayed out of the battle. It was obvious that the fighting was just a distraction, the result of which would have no real effect on the outcome of their fight. Neither side made a move to advance. For the moment they were both happy to stay out of trouble.

Neither Na'garoz nor Alaric watched the battle, despite of the terrible noise that it made. Their eyes were locked on each other. Neither one wanted to miss anything he other did. Alaric thought that he could see a strain on the Dark Knight, although he still could not see anything under his robe. He wondered why Na'garoz didn't get involved in the fight.

Marina, on the other hand, couldn't take her eyes off the battlefield. The sight sickened her stomach, but she could not look the other way. The two adversaries charged at each other without a care for their own wellbeing. The first clash was covered in sandy dust and impossible to see from their vantage point. The sound, however, could easily be heard. A mixture of deep roaring and high pitched screeches rang out into the air.

When the dust settled Marina could see what see had only been able to listen to before. Her first instinct was to look away, but she couldn't. For some reason she could not look away from the horror. As she watched she recognised Abram at the front of the line. She didn't know how she recognised him as all Heji looked alike to her, but she knew that it was him.

The chief of the Heji was battling with two Scartlers. The creatures snapped at him with their razor like jaws and thick claws. They screeched as they tried to attack him. Marina didn't know how she could hear them over the sound of battle, but that really didn't matter. Abram swung his powerful arms at the attacking Scartlers. The move was purely a show of fighting back. As much as the Heji could crush a Scartler skull with a direct blow, he was not swinging hard enough. If he had he would have overbalanced and left himself wide open for attack. Instead Abram waited for his moment. He grabbed one of the Scartlers by the neck as it tried to bite him on the right leg. The move was bold as it left him open to attack from its large pincers as well as the other Scartler. The second Scartler then missed its opportunity. The first one snapped at Abram, but he held it at a safe distance. He used the Scartler he had in his right arm to strike at the second. The attack confused both of the creatures. The second Scartler started to nip at the first in an attempt not to get struck, not realising its ally had no choice in the matter. Marina almost laughed at the display.

The rest of the battle was being fought at a ferocious pace. The Heji were having the better of the fight, but they were having losses as well. The pure weight of numbers was proving to be a handy advantage. Marina diverted her attention from Abram when he slammed his fist into the Scartler's head. She thought she could hear the sound of shattering bone as he smashed the creature's skull. She instantly wished that she had kept her gaze on Abram. The sight that caught her eye was even worse. She just saw the end of a fight between a Heji and a Scartler. She did not know what had happened before, but she saw the result. The Scartler sunk its powerful jaws into the Heji's left thigh. Although it was not enough to bring the Heji down it was enough to distract him. With a snap of its mighty claws it took the Heji's head clean off. Once it had latched on there was nothing that could have removed it. With the Heji on the ground it did not take long for other Scartlers to come to investigate. Soon enough there were almost a dozen Scartlers feeding on the dead Heji. The sight made Marina start to gag.

Alaric noticed that Na'garoz was starting to show signs of strain. If it wasn't for Marina's reaction he would have missed the feeding frenzy happening on the battlefield. It took him a moment, but then he realised what was happening.

"He is controlling them," Alaric's voice was distant as he returned his gaze to the Dark Knight.

"Who is controlling what?" Marina was glad to hear Alaric's voice, although she had no idea what he was talking about.

"I can't believe I didn't realise it earlier," Alaric mused to himself.

"Would you please explain what you are talking about?" Marina knew there was some important information that he was keeping to himself.

"Sorry, I will try my best to explain." Alaric let his attention fade away from Na'garoz. "Na'garoz is controlling the Scartlers. Now to take complete control of all the creatures would take too much power for anyone, so he takes partial control, so to speak. He puts an idea into their minds. Creatures with low intelligence are easy to control. Once the idea is in their head they will follow it until a better idea comes along. As you can see a better idea has crossed their mind and now Na'garoz is struggling to maintain control." He pointed to the scene where the Scartlers were still feasting on the carcass.

Another two Scartlers were trying to join the party, but there was no room for them. The creatures were starting to fight amongst themselves. It was also happening at other places on the battlefield were a Scartler had managed to bring down a Heji. The distraction was not good for their survival.

"So what does this mean?" Marina said finding it hard to follow what Alaric was saying.

"It means that if we can break the control Na'garoz has over them then this war is over. The quicker that happens the better," Alaric explained.

Marina would just have to accept what he said. Although there were more dead Scartlers on the ground the Heji's numbers were quickly starting to dwindle. She did not know how much longer they would survive. With each death the battle became tougher and tougher.

Alaric closed his eyes to concentrate. He had wanted to keep his gaze on Na'garoz, but it would be much quicker with his eyes closed and time was of the essence. It would not take long for Na'garoz to realise what he was doing. There could be no other reason why he would have his eyes closed for so long, but Alaric didn't care. Once the Dark Knight knew it would force him to react. Whilst he was hiding behind his army of Scartlers Na'garoz had the upper hand. Either way Alaric was going to sever the connection.

It didn't take long for Alaric to find what he was looking for. The link between Na'garoz and the Scartlers was too big for him to successfully hide and in the end Alaric didn't think that he even made the effort. When he was comfortable with what he had to do he opened his eyes. As he did he heard a small scream come from Marina. He thought that something might have upset her on the battlefield, but when he looked for Na'garoz on the other side he realised what had happened. The Dark Knight was no longer standing on the opposite dune. He was now standing no more than half a dozen paces away. The sight came as a slight shock although he had to admit that he was not overly surprised.

"I am surprised that it has taken you so long to realise," there was a rasping tone to his voice.

Alaric ignored the jibe. It was obvious that he was trying to buy time. If he could control the Scartlers long enough to defeat the Heji then he would win. Alaric had to be careful. If he tried to undo the spell then he was sure that Na'garoz would release the spell and go on the attack. The situation had become both fortuitous and deadly at the same time.

"Give me the prophecy and the stone and I will let you live." If he was able to divert his attention then it would be easier to break the spell.

Na'garoz started to laugh. "You do not frighten me. I will destroy you. I warned you not to come here. Now you will feel my wrath."

It was Alaric's turn to laugh. Although there was nothing funny in the threat he knew that it would get on Na'garoz's nerves. With the sounds of the battle in the background Alaric knew that time was running out. It would not be long before the Scartlers would overrun the Heji.

"Does the Great Lord know that you are here?" he decided to go on a different tangent.

"What?" Na'garoz sounded surprised at the question. It was not something that he was expecting.

Even Marina was little surprised. She was more concerned with the reference to the Great Lord. She didn't think that it was appropriate in the current situation. She wanted to say something, but knew it would not be constructive. The last thing she wanted to do was draw attention to herself. She had never been more scared in her life. No more than a dozen paces from her was the thing of nightmares.

"I take it by your response that he doesn't know that you are hiding in the Southern Wasteland. I am sure that he would be interested to find out how weak you are." Marina understood where he was going, but it did nothing to believe her terror. "You have taken the first chance to run for your life. I do not think that he will be too happy when he hears that."

"Do not try and tell me what the Great Lord thinks," Na'garoz was starting to get upset. Alaric was surprised at how easy it was. "I have done more than any other of the Chosen. Tell me who has not only discovered a stone, but has control of the prophecy?"

"You have been away from the mainland for too long." Alaric was not going to divulge too much information.

"What do you mean? What has happened?"

"The Great Lord has secured power. I have been sent to bring you to his knees for justice," the lie was thin, but he didn't think that Na'garoz would see through it.

"No, it can't be true," there was panic in his voice. "I have served him well."

That was all the opportunity Alaric needed. He knew that Na'garoz was going through the different scenarios in his mind. He was too distracted to realise what Alaric was about to do.

The spell itself was not difficult to break. He did not need all that much time, but he needed some distraction. Before the Dark Knight regained his composure Alaric snapped the threads of his spell. He was so engrossed in what Alaric had told him that it took him a few seconds before he realised what had happened. The first sign that it had worked was the multitude of screeches coming from the battlefield. Alaric did not have to look to realise that the Scartlers were now running for their lives. He didn't know if they were smart enough, but if they were they would be wondering what they were doing in the middle of a war. Without the spell to urge them to fight they would go back to their solitary lives. The retreat was followed shortly by a great roar from the Heji. They were celebrating their victory.

"What is happening," Na'garoz looked down on the battlefield. He knew that his spell had been broken, but he had hoped the Scartlers would finish what they started.

"It is over, Na'garoz," Alaric almost laughed as he spoke. He couldn't believe it had been that easy.

"Nothing is over," he almost spat the words.

Before Alaric had a chance to react Na'garoz disappeared. Marina felt a shiver run through her body. Alaric knew exactly what had happened and he cursed himself for being so nonchalant. He had been so happy with his little victory that he was unable to see the big picture. His only advantage was Na'garoz did not have time to mask his spell. Alaric could see the magical residue. As he watched it an idea came to him. Before he could complete his thought he heard a great voice boom from behind him.

"We have won the war," there was something close to elation in Abram's voice. "I don't know how we did it, but we won."

"Congratulations," was all Alaric said. He was trying to regain the thought. He knew that it was important, but he just couldn't figure it out.

"What about you? I see that your friend is no longer here. Does that mean that you have recovered our treasure?" Abram was hopeful.

"Not yet," Alaric was starting to become annoyed with the questions. "You have done your job. You need to return to your home. There is nothing more that you can do here." Alaric pushed Adelanta a step forward. He didn't mean to be rude, but he could not carry on the conversation.

"I think you should do what he says," Marina moved closer so she could speak with Abram. "Your Heji have fought bravely. There is nothing more you can do."

"Surely there is something we can do to help?" Abram did not want to leave with the job only half finished.

"No," Alaric's voice was hollow. "You have done enough. There is nothing more you can do. This battle is between me and Na'garoz," there was something in his tone that made Abram listen.

"We return home!" Abram called at the top of his voice. It was so loud that Marina had to cover her ears, whilst to Alaric it seemed as though it was somewhere in the distance.

Their roar was a tremendous sound. It brought a renewed hope to Mariana's heart. The thud of the Heji returning home shook the ground, but it was not enough to break Alaric's concentration. He needed it to work out what Na'garoz had done, then it suddenly came to him.

"Caleb," Alaric noticed the Heji was about to pass him by.

"Yes, Alaric," he stopped, happy to speak to him.

"Would you take the horses back with you?"

"What? How will you get back without your animals?" Caleb asked.

"Don't worry about that. Please, just do as I ask," there was something in his voice that made Caleb react.

Caleb wasn't sure what Alaric was planning, but it was the tone in his voice that made Caleb do what he wanted. Marina could not believe what she was hearing. Without the horses there was no chance of them returning to the Heji's cavern before nightfall. She didn't know how long Alaric could protect them, but she didn't think it would be for very long.

"But Alaric..." Marina didn't know how to ask the question after they had both dismounted.

Caleb had already started to lead the horses away when Adelanta looked back at his owner. He wasn't sure what was happening. The last thing he wanted to do was to leave his master out in the desert by himself, but it seemed as though that is what Alaric wanted. The mare could sense Marina's concern, but she was too frightened of what the great beast might do to her if she disobeyed him.

"Trust me," Alaric replied. "We do not have much time. If Na'garoz has jumped again then I do not think that I will be able to find him."

Marina had no idea what Alaric was talking about. Na'garoz had disappeared. She looked around, but he was nowhere to be seen. She knew that Alaric could sense the prophecy, but without the horses they would not be able to track it down. Whatever Alaric was planning she hoped that he did it quickly. As the last of the Heji disappeared over the small dune she started to feel very alone. If they did not leave soon then there was a very good chance that they would die in the wasteland.

Alaric was staring at the place where Na'garoz had been standing. He could just make out the remnant of the spell the Dark Knight had used to escape. He knew he could duplicate it, he could see it in his mind. The only problem was being able to follow the same route Na'garoz had taken. It was those strands that he had to put together.

Slowly Alaric started to draw in the energy around him. He was surprised that the wasteland was full of magical life. He had thought that the entire place would be barren. A smile crossed his face as he drew in the power around him. Marina thought that he looked strange. She was beginning to wonder if he knew what he was doing.

The spell was a lot more intricate than Alaric had first anticipated. He had a new found respect for the Dark Knight. He was a lot more skilled than Alaric had originally given him credit for. He would have to be careful when it came time to attack. Creating the spell would drain a lot of energy from his body and coupled with the spell that protected them from the heat he would be extremely weak when he was finished. He didn't know how he was going to defeat the Dark Knight, especially since he possessed had the Emerald *Stone of Power*.

"Hold my hand," Alaric's voice sounded strained. He didn't know if it was necessary for them to be touching for Marina to be pulled along with him, but he did not want to take the risk.

"What are you doing?" Marina took a step closer, but did not reach out for him.

"I think that it would be best if you close your eyes," Alaric spoke through clenched teeth. "Now hurry, we do not have much time left."

The urgency in his voice was what caused Marina to move. She put her hand in his and closed her eyes. As soon as her eyes were closed she felt a sudden rush around her body. She thought it was the wind, but she really didn't think it felt like it. She wanted to open her eyes, but she had to believe in Alaric's advice. She was feeling more than the rush of wind. Her body was tingling all over. It was only a subtle feeling, but it was definitely there. The feelings only lasted for a few seconds before they were gone again. When the rushing sensation died down she opened her eyes. When she did she almost fell over. The scenery had completely changed. Instead of being out in the wasteland they were in a cave. A small fire in the middle provided the only light. On the other side of the cave was Na'garoz. He looked as though he was busy packing and didn't realise that they had entered the room. That only lasted a moment before he was obviously distracted. He spoke without turning around.

"It seems as though you are stronger than I gave you credit." He was playing with something in front of him. He was trying to do.

"It is unfortunate for you that is not the only mistake you have made. Now I think that the time for talking is over. Face your doom," Alaric tried to keep the strength in his voice, but it was obvious that he was weakened.

"Well I have a little surprise for you." Na'garoz was so concerned with what he was doing he didn't notice the weakness in Alaric's voice.

Before anyone could reply Na'garoz turned around. He had something in his hands, a small velvet pouch. It was the same material as the dagger's sheath and the rings pouch. Alaric knew instantly that the Emerald bracelet was inside. It was obvious that they were going to get straight to the point. He fingered the sheath on his belt, but he was not ready to reveal the Jade dagger.

"I think that you will find that I hold the advantage," Na'garoz might not have been so confident if he saw the ring on Marina's finger or if he had known of the Jade dagger.

Without a moment to waste Na'garoz opened the pouch and revealed what they were all expecting. Instantly the Emerald stone started to glow. As it did the Sapphire stone also started to glow. Marina hid the ring behind her back before Na'garoz could notice. The Dark Knight was too focused on the Emerald stone to worry about the other two. He was consumed with the precious treasure in his hand.

Alaric had to hold his hands to his ears when Na'garoz released the Emerald stone. He knew that the sound was inside his head, but the move was involuntary. There were two voices screaming inside his head. One sounded female, whilst the other was male. He knew what was going to happen next. If he was going to fight Na'garoz he would have to unleash the Jade stone. That would cause even more havoc inside his head. The two who possessed the stones did not seem to be having the same problem. Alaric flicked at the velvet sheath. He was loathed to open it, but he knew that it was inevitable.

"The time to end this is here, but this is not the place," with that Na'garoz promptly disappeared.

Alaric acted without thinking. He should have known that it was all a little too easy. The trail that Na'garoz had left behind was too obvious. It was easier to follow than the original trail of magic that Alaric used to find him. This thought never entered Alaric's head. All he could think about was catching the Dark Knight and killing him. He just had the presence of mind to bring Marina along with him as he blinked out of sight.

They were once again out in the desert. As soon as they blinked back into existence they were met by a force that knocked them both off their feet. Alaric took the full brunt of the blow. His head rattled and for a moment he had no idea where he was. He looked up to the sky and thought that he saw stars. His next thought frightened him. He suddenly remembered where he was and guessed what must have happened and was surprised that he was still alive. He could not believe that the Dark Knight would not have finished the job. He tried to lift his head, but he was still too shaken.

What he didn't see was that Marina, who was also struck by the invisible force, was still standing. Na'garoz had unleased the Emerald stone onto the two of them. It was the Sapphire stone that had prevented Marina from being knocked to the ground and protected Alaric from being killed. A protective blue light surrounded her.

"So it seems that the prophecy is true after all. I must admit that I had my doubts when I read about the 'beautiful partner' and the 'blue protector'. It took me a while to work out the scribble, but when I did it was really quite informative, but I didn't really believe that it was true. Now I see that I should have looked deeper into the words. There is one problem with your 'blue protector'." There was something in his tone that worried Marina. It was like he knew something that she did not.

"And what might that be?" she asked when it was obvious that he was not going to continue until she did.

His rhetoric was not doing him any favours. He was under the assumption, however, that Alaric was incapacitated and would be an easy kill. What he didn't know was that the some of the Sapphire stone's power also protected Alaric. His concentration was locked on Marina as his only threat. He did not think that she would be nearly as powerful as Alaric, or have the control over the stone like he did. Nevertheless he did not know who she was and that made her dangerous. She had survived his attack with the Emerald stone and that made her a worthy adversary, more so than the so called Chosen One.

"The stones draw power from the world around them." The Dark Knight said. "They draw on the life that their maker brought to the world. As you might have noticed there is no water here. The Sapphire stone will be weak and ineffectual," the Dark Knight almost laughed at his revelation.

For the first time Marina sensed that they were far away from where they had originally started. She could still sense that there was water underground, but it was a lot further away. She was not getting a good feeling from the Sapphire stone. There was panic in her heart and she wished that Alaric would return to his feet. She did not think that she would be able to defeat the Dark Knight even with the aid of the stone.

What Na'garoz said was true. The stones drew power from the world around them and the Sapphire stone thrive around water. What he failed to mention was that the Emerald stone drew power from the world of nature and the wasteland was void of vegetation. He was trying to use his words as an advantage. Fortunately for him Marina did not pick up on his ambiguity.

The Emerald stone in the centre of the bracelet started to glow. Marina knew an attack was imminent. She tried to bring the Sapphire stone to life, but she felt nothing. She didn't know how to waken the sleeping stone. All she knew was that if she did not do something quickly then she would be killed.

The next attack was more visible. A bolt of green light shot from the centre of the stone and flew directly towards Marina. Just before the light struck her she did the only thing that came to mind. She raised the ring to shield herself with the Sapphire stone. Just before the bright green light struck it suddenly stopped and froze in the air. The Sapphire stone was shining brighter than Marina had seen before.

"This cannot be," Na'garoz spoke between clenched teeth and he strained to push the light further.

Suddenly Marina could feel the water from under the ground becoming closer. It felt as though the watertable was slowing starting to rise. With the rising water she could feel the strength grow inside of her and the stone. She pushed out in return to force the green light backwards. Before it was half way back towards Na'garoz both lights suddenly blinked out.

"It seems as though you are stronger than I thought," Na'garoz did his best not to show his strain. He had already used a lot of his energy to control the Scartlers and to jump between locations. His two attacks had drained a lot of his reserves, but he still had enough to keep going. If nothing else he could draw on the power of the stone.

Suddenly things got worse for the Dark Knight. During their short battle neither of them realised that Alaric had returned to his feet. He looked a little worse for wear, but he was standing nonetheless. He had managed to keep the spell going that kept them from getting burnt. They were in the middle of the afternoon and if he dropped the spell then they would certainly die.

"It seems that you are not as strong as you claim to be. I am sure that Nyrra would be pleased to hear it." Alaric deliberately chose to use Nyrra's real name.

His plan worked. The reference to Nyrra's name annoyed the Dark Knight. No one was allowed to use the Great Lord's real name. His attention completely returned to Alaric totally ignoring Marina. She wished that she was able to conjure a spell to defeat him, but it seemed as though the Sapphire stone had gone to sleep again.

"When I bring him your corpse then he will know my true power. I will sit by his shoulder and rule the world with him," Na'garoz was happy to keep up the battle of words.

Both combatants were short on strength. All that Alaric had done had drained his energy. He had yet to reveal the Jade stone, which was his only advantage. What he didn't know was that Na'garoz was also suffering from the trials of the day. If he had known then there was a good chance he could destroy him. For the moment they were both happy to continue in such a fashion.

"I do not think that you will be leaving the wasteland alive. When I finish with you your body will rot in the sun," Alaric sniggered as he spoke.

It was at that point that Na'garoz realised that Alaric was planning the same game. The advantage was back in his court. Although he did not know how depleted Alaric was, he figured he had much more strength. It was time for him to go on the offensive again.

Alaric could feel the magical energy before he could feel the blows. The Dark Knight did not draw on the power of the stone for his spell. The attacks were weak, but effective. The blows came quick and were hard to defend. At first he tried to block with his arms, but that was pointless. The only way to block the blows was to draw on the remaining energy in his body. He was not quick enough with his spell casting to block all the blows, but it was enough to keep it too a minimum. Small bruises started to appear on his face and body. When it was obvious that the blows were not going to kill him Na'garoz stopped the attack. He was happy enough with what he had accomplished.

Marina watched Alaric suffer the blows and wished that there was something she could do for him. She reached out for the Sapphire stone, but again there was nothing there. The only thing that reassured her was that she could feel the water level slowly rising. She could not guess how deep it was, but she knew it was getting closer. When the water reached the surface she knew there was a good chance she would have the power to defeat the Dark Knight. She only hoped that Alaric would be able to keep him occupied until that time.

It was time for Alaric to reveal the Jade stone. He was panting for breath as he tried to recover from the Dark Knight's attacks. The last thing he wanted to do was to unleash the Jade stone, but he did not think he had any other choice. It would not be long before Na'garoz used the Emerald stone again and he did not think he would be so lucky the next time. Without the aid of Jade stone he was doomed and he couldn't rely on the Sapphire stone to save them again. He took a deep breath, but it was not enough to stop him from gasping for breath before he unlatched the velvet sheath.

The result of unleashing the Jade stone was completely different to what he had expected. He thought that his mind would be filled with a horrendous noise. Instead there was pure silence. In fact all external noises had also been extinguished. He could see the Dark Knight's mouth move, but no words reached his ears. He didn't know if it was a good sign or a bad sign.

"It's about time," the voice inside his head sounded a little offended.

"What are you talking about?" Alaric made a point not to move his lips as he used his internal voice.

"You were going to let Emerald and Sapphire have all the fun?" the voice asked a strange question. "Well I guess I shouldn't get offended. I am not renowned for my ability to attack."

Alaric was starting to understand the conversation. He wasn't sure what the right response was, but there was a question that he wanted answered. "You are the glue that brings everything together. Why would you need to attack?"

There was a short silence. Alaric thought that he might have offended the voice, but soon enough it started to speak again. "We all have the ability to attack, in one way or another. We just draw on the powers of our special abilities. Now I don't really think this is the time for a conversation. I believe that your enemy is attempting to insult you again."

Alaric was suddenly shot back into reality. He didn't hear the words of Na'garoz's last rant, but by the tone it was not pleasant. He didn't know how he should respond. In the end he decided that it was best for him to remain quiet.

"Well if that is the way you want it, then I guess I will just have to destroy you," Na'garoz raised the bracelet in front of him.

The Emerald stone started to glow more intensely. The strain was obvious on Na'garoz's face as he tried to control it, more so than when he had been attacking. Alaric prepared himself fort the impending attack. The Jade stone had already started to glow before Alaric knew what was happening. He could feel the power start to grow. The energy filled his body and rejuvenated his strength. He felt as though there was nothing he could not accomplish. His thoughts almost drifted away from the battle in front of him.

"What is happening?" the Emerald stone started to lose its intensity as Na'garoz struggled to regain control.

Alaric understood immediately the power of the Jade stone. It was absorbing the power from the Emerald stone. Alaric had no idea that it could do such a thing, but there was no doubt in his mind. It was the perfect opportunity for him to attack. As Alaric released the power that he had drawn from the stone the earth started to shake. He knew that he was drawing in a lot of energy, but he didn't care. He was going to make sure that Na'garoz did not survive.

Just as Alaric was about to consume Na'garoz in a ball of fire he heard a voice next to him. He could only just make out the words over the rush of energy passing through his body. "Remember the prophecy. If you completely destroy him then you will completely destroy the prophecy."

Marina was right. Alaric would have to be more careful if he was going to regain the great tome. At the last minute he changed the spell that he was going to release. Instead of consuming the Dark Knight in fire Alaric whipped up a dust storm. The small grains of sand whipped at Na'garoz, cutting into his skin. The attack was not enough to kill him, but by the cries of pain coming from inside the storm he knew it was effective.

When the storm blew away the Dark Knight was still standing. He looked worse for wear, but he was still on his feet. When it was clear that the storm was gone a grin appeared on his face. Although he had not heard Marina's words he was starting to understand why Alaric had not destroyed him when he had the chance. It was time for him to go on offensive again.

The sand storm blew away not because Alaric had finished with the spell, but because he had lost control. Even drawing on the power of the Jade stone Alaric was not able to hold the spell. He knew that his power was really starting to wane. Once he had defeated Na'garoz he still needed the power to return to the Heji's home. He didn't know if he could summon the energy for another attack.

Seeing Alaric so weak gave Na'garoz the extra strength he needed to conjure up another attack. Alaric thought that the Dark Knight had an unlimited source of energy. He didn't know that he was struggling just as much. The Emerald stone was not helping him as much as what he thought it would. It was as if the stone was deliberately trying to hinder his progress. He was not going to let that stop him from killing the Cursed One.

There was only time for one more attack. He knew that he would not have the power to create a second one. Na'garoz knew that if he could tap into the power of the Emerald stone then he would only need one spell. Alaric could also feel the struggle inside the Emerald stone. The Jade stone had already started to glow. It was the Jade's intervention that caused the Emerald stone to stop resisting Na'garoz's control. The Dark Knight felt the rush of energy through his body. Alaric could also feel the power emanating from the Emerald stone. He knew that he did not have much chance to survive the attack. He did not have the energy to front a serious defence.

"Can you feel it," Na'garoz opened his arms towards the sky as the power rushed through his body. He wanted to savour the feeling before he released the spell. "This is magnificent."

The delay was all that Marina needed. Throughout the exchange she had been concentrating on the rising watertable. It was water that she needed and it was water that would save them. Before Na'garoz had released his spell the water had risen to a level that Marina could use. The Sapphire stone seemed pleased that she tried to contact it. It was as if the two were one and the stone knew exactly what she was trying to do. Her body rushed with the power that the stone was drawing from the water. She was not as preoccupied with the feeling as Na'garoz was, but it was still distracting her from her end goal.

It was all too late when the Dark Knight realised what was happening. He had been too concerned with his own gratification than his surroundings. He knew that Alaric had been beaten, but he had completely forgotten about Marina. She was ready to attack and he had taken too long.

The ground in front of Na'garoz started to crack. It was the first sign of what Marina was doing. If he had not been taken by surprise he would have had enough time to attack Alaric. With the hole in the ground there was nothing to stop the water from making its escape. A geyser of water shot into the air. It was the water that would be the downfall of the Dark Knight. With all the power she had in her, or whether it was the stone itself, she pushed out at the waterspout.

Both Alaric and Na'garoz didn't know what she was planning on doing with the water fountain. They didn't think that she could do much damage, but Marina knew exactly what she was doing and that was all that mattered. She didn't give them much time to wonder. A small spout of water shot out from the main fountain. The powerful stream hit the Dark Knight square on the chin. The blow was enough to knock him from his feet. It was more the surprise than the initial blow that caused him to drop the bracelet.

Losing possession of the Emerald stone meant that he had to contain the power that he had drawn. If he was fresh then he might have been able to survive, but since he was battle worn he had no hope. There was no way he could contain the energy and he was no longer in a position to positively release any. At first a crack appeared in his chest. A bright green light shot out towards the sky. It ripped through his robe without hindrance. It took a second, but soon enough Na'garoz was screaming out in pain. Partly because of the physical pain, but also because he knew that he had failed to kill the Cursed One.

The pain had only just begun for Na'garoz. The small gash in his chest was not enough for all the energy to escape. He knew that there was more to come. His only chance of survival was to regain the Emerald stone. With great pain he rolled over and stood before starting back towards where he had dropped the stone. Before he came within arm's reach another shot of water struck him on the right shoulder. The blow was strong enough to knock him backwards, but not off his feet. As the water struck him it created another wound for the green light of magical energy to escape. Although he cried out in pain he did not let up. He had to make it to the stone. His life depended on it. He dropped to his knees after he took another step closer to his destination. The pain rippled through his body, but he could not stop.

The Dark Knight moved closer to the stone before he was struck again by the waterspout. He was struck on the left shoulder as he crawled. Again the blow ripped a hole in his skin that allowed the energy to pummel out of his body. He screamed in pain and dropped to the sand, but he quickly returned to his crawl. He was so close to the stone that he could not give up. A strained effort brought him a couple of feet further and well within his reach. A smile crossed his face as he reached out for what would save his life. Before he was able to clasp the bracelet another stream of water took his hand and pushed it away from the stone. He would not be dissuaded and reached out with other hand. Again he was struck with water. Each time he was struck another gash opened up. Marina had to jump out of the way as a bolt of green light shot directly at her.

A barrage of water struck out at the Dark Knight. Each time he tried to move forwards Na'garoz was struck by another bolt of water. It did not take long before he was rolling in pain on the sandy ground. All hope had quickly left his body. He knew that he was going to die. The only thing left he could do was try and make life difficult for the Cursed One. At least in death he could still serve the Great Lord, although he had to wonder if he had chosen the wrong side. With a painful effort he reached into his robe and pulled out the prophecy. Before he could do anything another shot of water hit his hand causing the prophecy to go flying through the air. It landed over a half dozen paces away onto dry dusty earth. If it had landed in the water then there was chance he would have succeeded in his final evil deed. He knew that there was no point in continuing towards the book. Even if he had the strength to reach the prophecy he knew that it would do no good. He didn't know whether it was the Sapphire stone or Marina, but either way he had been beaten.

The only thing left for Na'garoz to do was to die in agony. He rolled around in pain and cried out for the last time before the green light completely consumed his body. Once he was dead the light suddenly blinked out of existence. All that remained of the Dark Knight was a holey robe. His body had completely disappeared.

With Na'garoz gone Alaric dropped to his knees. He was panting strongly as he struggled to hold onto the spell that kept them protected from the scorching sun. Although he had managed to remain on his feet throughout the Dark Knight's ordeal, he could not have shown a sign of weakness.

The water spout slowly came to an end and the energy slowly left Marina's body. She was sad to let it go, but there was nothing she could do to hold onto it. The Sapphire stone was no longer shining. All she could do was rush to Alaric's side to make sure he was going to be alright.

"Are you alright?" it was a stupid question, but it was the best she could do.

"I'll survive. Help me to the bracelet," Alaric's voice was weak.

"I'll get it for you," she stood when she finished speaking and was about to collect the bracelet when Alaric grabbed her ankle.

"No," Alaric's voice was louder than it should have been. "I do not think that it would be a good idea for you to touch the stone."

Marina knew what Alaric was staying, but she could not believe that any true harm could come from it. Even in his weakened state his grasp was tight on her ankle. She didn't think that she would have a problem breaking his hold, but she wanted him to relinquish her on his own. It was not until she stopped her forward force did he let her go.

"Please, you have to trust me. You have to help me to get the stone," Alaric's voice had lost its strength.

Marina put his arm around her shoulder and assisted him to his feet. With the added energy gone from her body she was also starting to feel the strain. She would do her best to do what he said. There was no point in arguing no matter how silly she thought he was being. It would only serve to make matters worse. It was a slow walk to where the Emerald bracelet was lying in the sand. Marina was saddened to see that the water had already evaporated. She could feel the water table starting to return to its normal level.

When they arrived at their destination Alaric gently pushed her away before collapsing to his knees. The stone glowed softly as Alaric looked at it. He had already returned the dagger to its sheath and covered the stone. He didn't think that he had enough energy to control them both.

"Get the prophecy," he missed his manners. "We have to be going soon."

Not only did he want to move to where the prophecy was lying, he also wanted time to look at the Emerald stone before he collected it. It seemed as though it was gently calling out to him with its soft glowing. He knew that as soon as he touched it the words would come into his mind. That was one of the reasons why he did not want to pick it up. He didn't have the energy left to do what he needed to.

Marina quickly collected the prophecy and the bracelet's velvet pouch. She could feel the effects of the sun as Alaric's spell started to weaken. She didn't know how Alaric was planning on getting them back to the safety of the cavern. She, herself, had no idea where they were. She could not feel the safety of the cavern either. To make matters worse the watertable had returned to its normal depth. At least the water would have given her some comfort.

"What are you waiting for?" she asked when she returned and saw that he still had not picked up the bracelet.

"Shhh," was all the response she got.

The brush aside annoyed her, but she did not have the energy to scold him. All she wanted him to do was pickup the bracelet and take them back to safety. The longer they staying out in the wasteland the more chance they had to die. She knew that there was nothing she could do to rush him. She could tell how weak he was and she did not want him to die. She didn't know what she would do if he did.

Alaric slowly reached down and picked up the bracelet. As soon as he touched the band he felt a rush of energy through his body. His eyes flickered in his head and his body went stiff. The last thing he needed was a further strain on his body. Marina didn't know what she should do. There was a chance if she tried to help that she would only make things worse. That was a chance that she couldn't take. She had to believe that he knew what he was doing and that he was still safe.

"I see that you have power," another voice came inside his head. He did not know how, but he could recognise the difference compared to when he held the Jade stone. He was glad he had covered the Jade stone. He didn't think he could handle two voices inside his head at one time. It was bad enough with one.

"This is not the time or the place," Alaric tried to keep the strength in his voice. He was surprised at how easily it was to keep his mind-voice steady.

"I don't see any reason why not. Now is as good a time as any," the voice was not going to ease up.

The longer they stood in the open the more Marina could feel the sun starting to burn into her skin. She could see a great pool of sweat appear on Alaric's his face. A number of blood vessels also appeared on the sides of his head. He was trapped inside his mind and there was nothing she could do to help. She had to hope that whatever the battle was he was going to win.

"I told you that this is not the time. You do not have the power to overpower me. Now shut up and let's get out of here." It was more of a bluff than any real threat. Under normal circumstances he would have been able to overpower the stone. In his weakened state he would have to rely on the stone letting him go.

"Okay, I will give you a break," Alaric didn't like the sound of the voice. He knew that he was about to pay for his freedom. "Do no put me back in the prison. Wear me on your wrist until we have a chance to discuss this further."

Alaric didn't like the terms of the agreement, but he didn't have a choice. There was a risk involved, but it was better than staying trapped in his head. The thought of going back on his word crossed his mind, but only for a second. He knew that once he made the promise he could not go back on it. Of course he physically could have placed the stone in its pouch, but then it would cause further problems in the future.

"I will agree to your terms," Alaric didn't sound pleased, but that was more for the voice's benefit. "We will continue this conversation later."

As soon as Alaric said the words his voice returned to normal. He almost fell over as reality rushed back to him. He let out a deep breath that he had been holding since he had picked up the stone. He was grateful to be back, although the sudden increase in temperature was not a good sign.

"Put the bracelet in the pouch," Marina said as she offered him the pouch.

"No!" Alaric kept his gaze flat in front of himself. As he spoke he slid the bracelet over his wrist.

Before Marina could speak again they both blinked out of existence.

Chapter 33: A Chance to Rest

The Heji were surprised to see Marina and Alaric suddenly materialise onto the square where the celebrations of their victory had already started. Although they had lost a lot on the battlefield it was still a success. The Scartlers would think twice before they attacked again. The overall tone of the celebration was joyous. Those who had lost loved ones and were too sad to celebrate stayed in their homes, although that was only a small number.

As soon as they appeared Alaric collapsed to the ground. The day's ordeals had finally come to bear. Again he was left with no energy and struggling to live. Marina was worried. He looked worse than when he had unravelled Na'garoz's spell and he only just survived that. She was not positive that he was going to make it this time. She herself was also feeling the strain, but she wasn't about to give up. The only thing that was keeping her on her feet was the fact that Alaric needed help.

"We need to get him inside," there was panic in her voice.

The square was suddenly quiet as Marina spoke. The celebrations stopped. Although Marina didn't realise it the Sapphire stone had carried her voice so all the Heji could hear her.

"Of course," it was Chief Abram who spoke from his throne. "Caleb, take him to their house."

The large Heji quickly moved into action. He scooped Alaric up in his arms and made his way off the square. Marina followed closely behind, doing her best to look strong. The other Heji did not know whether they should continue to celebrate or not. It was obvious that Alaric was in danger of losing his life, but that was not really their concern. Their concern was the Emerald bracelet which he wore on his left wrist. They couldn't believe their chief did not order the bracelet to be removed.

"There will be time," Abram spoke to his congregation when he realised what they were all thinking. "For now it is a time of celebration." He needed time to work out what he was going to do with Alaric.

It would have been the perfect opportunity to remove the bracelet with Alaric semi-conscious, but the bracelet could not have been removed. As long as Alaric still wore it the Heji would not be able to take it from him. The stone would do anything in its power to remain in the man's possession. For the moment Abram was just happy that they had survived. What would happen next was a problem for another day.

Caleb placed Alaric in his bed before promptly leaving. He did not want to miss out on the celebrations. He was glad that Alaric had retrieved their treasure, but that was as far as it went. He had already risked his life to save the man and he wasn't going to miss out on the fruits of his labours. He knew that if he stayed then he would try and take the treasure from Alaric's wrist and for some strange reason that was not what the chief wanted.

Marina was glad that they were left alone. Once the Heji had left the house Marina collapsed onto one of the lounge chairs. She took a number of deep breaths in an attempt to relax. All she wanted to do was close her eyes and go to sleep, but she knew Alaric needed her and she was going to do everything she could to save him.

She took one of the water pouches into his bedroom with her. As before, when he had overdone things his body was dripping with sweat and his skin was pale. His lips were dry and cracked and his breathing laboured. If Marina didn't know him better then she would have thought that he was about to die. She knew in her heart that he would not. They had come too far for him to die now. They had achieved what they came into the wasteland for and it was time to return to the mainland. With any luck the war was already over and they could live out their lives in peace. She knew that it was a silly thought, but it was a pleasant one nonetheless.

At first she poured a little water into his mouth before taking a long drink herself. She knew that he was thirsty, but she did not want to choke him by pouring in too much. The next thing she did was strip him of his clothes. They were already drenched with sweat and she thought that they would be uncomfortable to wear. Once he was completely naked she washed his body. It seemed as though that as soon as she cleaned one part of his body another was drenched in sweat again. It would be an uphill struggle to try and regulate his body temperature.

She did her best to keep him dry, but it was a losing battle. In then end she had to give up. Fatigue was starting to take control. When she had finished caring for Alaric she did not have the energy to return to her own bed. All she could do was snuggle into bed with him. Even though he was still sweating profusely she was happy to have Alaric so close. She rested her head against his chest and fell asleep listening to his heart beat. The sound was soothing even though she knew that he was fighting for every beat.

In the morning she woke to find that Alaric was still unconscious. On the bright side he had stopped sweating, but his skin was still deathly pale. His breathing had not improved at all and his heart beat was still slow. She did not know how he remained alive. She didn't think that he was getting enough oxygen for his body to survive. That fact that he was still alive was a relief. The longer he survived then the more chance he had of recovery. That was what she told herself.

It took three days before Alaric was awake again. He still looked very weak as he slowly lifted his head from the pillow. Marina could not contain herself when she saw him move. She threw herself onto the bed and wrapped her arms around him. She could not stop the tears from rolling down her cheeks as a wave of relief flowed through her. She was starting to believe that he might remain in the coma for the rest of his life.

"What is happening?" Alaric's voice was cracked and weak.

"You're alive," Marina lifted herself from his body and wiped her face. "I didn't think you were going to make it."

Alaric tried to remember what had happened, but his memory was still sketchy. The last thing he could remember was facing Na'garoz in the cave. Then the Dark Knight had disappeared and that was all he could remember. The thought made him worried. If the Dark Knight had gotten away then there was no telling where he would be.

"How long have I been like this?" Alaric asked, the strength slowly starting to return to his voice.

"About four days." She rose from the bed as she spoke. She silently cursed herself for not getting him some water sooner. She also thought that he would be very hungry. She had managed to pour some water down his throat whilst he was unconscious, but he had not eaten since they had left to fight Na'garoz. "You must be starving," she said after she offered him the water pouch.

Alaric had not thought about food. It wasn't until Marina mentioned it that he realised how hungry he was. The thought of Na'garoz was still thick in his mind, but he thought that it could wait until after he had eaten. Regardless of what had happened he was in no state to do anything about it.

Marina smiled as she watched Alaric fill his stomach. He was able to sit up as he ate, which Marina thought was a great improvement. She didn't know how long it would take before he could rise from his bed, but he was alive and that was all that mattered. She did not care if they spent the rest of their lives in the Heji's cavern. As long as they were together she did not care.

"What happened with the Na'garoz? Did he get away?" Alaric lay down again when he had finished eating. His head was dizzy from sitting upright. He could tell that he still needed rest.

Marina had to laugh at the question. She was quite happy to explain what had happened. She of course over-embellished his role and left out what had happened with her and the Sapphire stone. She thought that he would only worry if he knew she was using the power of the stone. There would be time for conversation when he was back on his feet.

"That is a relief." Alaric thought for a moment. "Has Abram demanded the stone yet?"

"No," Marina sounded surprised; more so at her answer than his question. "Caleb looks in every day, but they have been content to let you rest."

"Hmm, that is interesting. I would have thought that they would have tried to take the bracelet off me as soon as we got back. I don't really know if this is a good sign or a bad sign," Alaric mused.

"I am sure it can only be a good sign," Marina replied.

"I think I should rest again." Alaric had a lot to think about. He didn't think that Marina was telling him the whole truth about what had happened in the wasteland. He didn't know what she could be keeping from him, but he figured that it was something important.

Alaric slept for the rest of the day. Marina was concerned that he might have slipped back into a coma, but his breathing was levelled and his heartbeat normal. She was confident that he was just sleeping. Marina slept in the same bed as him and even though he was getting better she had gotten into the habit and it would be hard to break. He didn't wake until the next morning and she made sure that she was up before him as she didn't want to make an issue of it.

In the morning Alaric was able to get out of bed. It was the first time he had stood since returning to the Heji's cavern. He was a little wobbly on his feet, but that didn't matter. His strength was returning and soon enough they would be ready to leave. The thought had been so far from Marina's mind since he was unconscious that she had almost forgotten where they were. The thought of leaving brought a new spring to her step.

"I must have a meeting with Chief Abram," Alaric stumbled slightly as he spoke. He hoped that Marina did not see.

"You are in no state to be going out." Marina saw what had happened. "Maybe in a day or two."

Alaric sat down before he spoke again. It was sweet that Marina was trying to look after him, but that was not going to help the situation. Time was getting away from them. He knew that Bern and the Alliance would be arriving in Jarrat soon and they would need his help if they were going to survive. He didn't know how long it would take them to get back to the mainland. He was still weak from fighting with Na'garoz. His memory was still hazy, but he could remember one thing. He knew how to jump through reality. Na'garoz had shown him how.

"We don't have the luxury of waiting. I need to speak to Abram today. Tomorrow we have to be on the move again," Alaric explained.

The jump from the Heji's cavern to the mainland would take a lot of energy, but there was no other way for them to leave. If they travelled like they had when they arrived then there was a good chance that they would get lost. He did not want to take the chance that the Sapphire stone would find them protection again. The quickest way for them to reach Jarrat was to jump.

"You stay here and I will go and find the chief," Marina didn't like the idea, but it was obvious that he was not going to let up.

"Thank you," Alaric wasn't sure how hard she was going to look, but he hoped that she didn't linger too long.

The light was bright outside in the cavern. She had not left their rooms since they had returned. It never ceased to amaze her how the moss on the roof could light the entire cavern. She quickly found her way up to the main square in front of the chief's house. To her surprise she did not pass any Heji on her way. She wondered where they could be. She started to become nervous as she approached the chief's house.

Marina waited as she reached the front door. She didn't know whether she should knock or go straight in. The truth was that she didn't think that she should be there at all. She wanted nothing more than to turn around and return to the main village. She knew that Alaric would see straight through her if she didn't at least try.

She raised her hand to knock when it suddenly moved open. She jumped in surprise and her heart started to race.

"Sorry if I scared you," Abram's voice was soft, or at least softer than usual. "I saw you standing there and figured that you had something to tell me."

Marina felt suddenly foolish. She had been worried that Abram would not want to speak with her. She knew that the Heji treated him with fear, awe and respect, but it was different with her and Alaric. The chief did not seem so scary after all.

"Alaric has asked if he could speak with you."

"Of course," Abram looked around. He seemed surprised that Alaric had not asked him himself. "Where is he?"

"He is still weak. He is back at our house." Marina suddenly understood why he had sounded somewhat confused.

A look of understanding crossed Abram's face, although Marina could not read its meaning. One thing that confused him though was why Alaric did not wait to be fully fit before approaching him.

"Okay then, let's go and see him." Abram was breaking all protocol in going to the outsider's house. The only time he visited a Heji in their home was when they were dying. If he wanted to speak with someone all he had to do was summon them. The other Heji would be shocked, but he could not hold on ceremony.

"Where are the other Heji?" Marina asked as they walked back towards the house.

"Today is a day of worship. They remain indoors for most of the day. Then they come out at dusk to celebrate," Abram explained.

Marina remembered the celebration when they first arrived. It was eight days ago. "So you do this every eight days?"

"That is correct. It let's us all relax and celebrate together. It is the way it has been since as long as I can remember. We have a lot to celebrate this time. Today there will be a lot of reflection, which always means the celebrations will be stronger."

Marina wanted to asked more questions, but they had arrived at the house. She was surprised at his candour. Since they had arrived in the Heji cavern the chief had been someone to fear. If they had not treated him with the right amount of respect they would be put to death. It seemed that since their return he was happy to speak to her as an equal. She thought that it might be due to the fact that Alaric had regained their treasure. She was scared at how he would react when Alaric told him that he would not be returning the bracelet.

Abram waited for Marina to open the door and let him in. She did not know whether it was Heji custom or if he was just being polite. They found Alaric sitting in the front room. He looked as though he was about to fall asleep. It wasn't until they stepped into the room that he realised they were there. He sat up instantly and tried to make himself look awake.

"What is it that you wish to discuss?" Abram came straight to the point.

"I need to leave tomorrow at first light. There are things that you need to know before we leave," Alaric started puffing when he finished speaking. He was trying to remain strong, but it was not working. Marina quickly moved to his aid when she realised how weak he still was.

"Our treasure, this Emerald *Stone of Power* of yours. I have been wondering how long it would be until you brought this up?" Abram was not going to give anything away.

When he finished speaking the stone started to glow softly on Alaric's wrist. It was so soft that only Marina noticed it. Alaric kept his gaze on the Heji Chief and vice-versa. She did not think that this was a good sign. She was sure that Alaric would not use the power of the stone again, which meant that the stone was coming to life on its own. She knew from experience that it would not be easy to control, especially in Alaric's weakened state.

"I know the stone means a lot to you and your kind," Alaric didn't really know how else to start. That was all he was able to get out before Abram started talking.

"It is more to us than just a mere trinket. It is the life source of our existence. All you see around you is due to that stone. Without it our lives would cease to exist. The Heji would slowly die out," Abram tried to keep the anger out of his voice, but it was hard.

Alaric knew that it was not going to be easy. He felt sorry for the giant beast. The Heji had helped him to recover the prophecy and now he had to take away their greatest treasure and possibly doom them all to death. It was that thought that made him think that it might be better if he left the stone in their possession. He was out to save lives not to take them. He didn't know if killing the Heji was any different to killing men. Suddenly with the thought in his mind his body went completely stiff. His eyes rolled back into his head and his eye lids started to flicker.

Marina gasped at the sudden movement. She had seen it happen before, although she did not know exactly what it meant. Each time her heart started to race and she wondered if he was going to recover. Abram was also shocked by the movement. He did not like what was happening. He wanted an answer to his statement.

"What is he doing?" Abram asked in a gruff voice.

"I don't know. Alaric!" she called out to him in a vain hope to gain his attention.

Alaric was suddenly in a dark room. There was no light at all. He couldn't even see his hand in front of him, though he wondered if his hand even existed in such a place. He looked around to see who had brought him. He knew the answer to the question, but he wanted to see for sure.

"What do you want from me?" Alaric called out to the darkness around him.

There was silence for a moment before a green light appeared somewhere in the distance. Alaric tried to see who was inside the light, but no matter how hard he tried to focus he could not. When his gaze drifted he thought he could see the figure of a man inside the light, but when he tried to refocus his eyes it disappeared again. The entire situation was frustrating.

"It is time for us to have that talk," there was a playful tune to the voice. "I do believe that was part of the deal."

Although Alaric wanted to get back to his conversation with Abram he figured that it would be pertinent to listen. "What is it that you want with me?" he asked his question towards the light, although he didn't think that it would make much difference.

"You have a power within you that I have not felt for a long time," there was no question, but the voice waited for a response nevertheless.

"I don't exactly know what you mean?" Alaric was not going to give away any free information about himself. He didn't completely trust the green light. He was getting a bad feeling that it was trying to trap him.

"Who are you?" there was annoyance in the voice for having to point out what it thought was an obvious question.

"I am Alaric," he kept his answer short.

"This will go a lot quicker without the combative attitude. I am not here to hurt you. In fact you might say that I am here to help you," the voice tried to take the edge out of its tone as it spoke.

"Then why don't you tell me why you have brought me here?"

"That will come in time. Now tell me how you came to hold such power?" the voice would not be suckered into Alaric's trap.

"The prophecy calls me the Chosen One," Alaric didn't want to tell the voice that, but he figured it would be easier that way.

"You know of the prophecy?" the voice sounded surprised. "Have I been asleep for so long?"

"I have the *Prophecy of the Stone* in my possession," Alaric ignored the rhetorical question. "It is the reason why I was drawn to this place," Alaric didn't want to reveal too much, but the words just kept coming out of his mouth.

"Well things are finally starting to make sense. What does my brother Jade have to say about things?" the question seemed strange, but for some reason Alaric knew exactly what he meant.

"He is helping me to gather all of you together. He knows that it is what he must do, even if he doesn't like it. He stays tucked away until he is ready to behave himself," Alaric had no idea what he was saying.

"I see. Then I suppose that I should play along as well," the voice sounded appeased.

"What is it that you can do?" Alaric wasn't exactly sure where the voice was going.

"There is no reason why the Heji can't survive without me being here. Sure their world has thrived with my help, but I have only helped with the prosperity because it pleases me to be around living plants. With the proper care their world will continue to exist."

It all started to make sense. The Emerald stone had only helped their world prosper. They had existed in their cavern before the stone arrived in their possession. He wondered at how they didn't know the fact themselves.

"I must admit that I do enjoy their praise of me. I have altered their awareness slightly. They truly believe that I am the reason why this world exists. It has served my purpose, but if you take me with you then I will release them from their bond," the voice answered the question, even though it was just a thought.

"Then I think we should get moving," Alaric was becoming excited. "There is not much time and we need to be on the move again shortly."

"Agreed!"

Suddenly Alaric snapped back to reality. It was a strange conversation inside his head, but it was better than previous conversations with the mysterious voices. He looked down at the Emerald stone and saw its glow was starting to become more intense. It grew and grew until its glow filled the entire room and washed them all with emerald light.

"What's happening?" there was fear in Abram's voice. It was the first time that either of them had heard fear from a Heji.

"It's alright. Just wait and you will see," there was something in Alaric's voice that was different.

He could feel the green light around him and he thought that it was magnificent. The pure power was enormous. He wanted to drink it in, but he knew that was not what it was there for. He felt a renewed power inside his body. It was the best he had felt since he could remember. He felt as though he could take on the world. He could not control the smile that crossed his face.

The look on Alaric's face made Abram nervous. He knew that the man had great power. He didn't think that Alaric would turn against them, but he had also thought that same thing about Na'garoz. He wanted to race out of the room, but something was stopping him. There was something in the back of his mind telling him that he should stay and see the result of what was Alaric was doing.

Marina was also concerned, but for a different reason. She could see the elation on Alaric's face and knew that it was due to the Emerald stone. She had felt the same when the Sapphire stone was in full flight. The last she wanted was for Alaric to lose his strength again. If they were going to leave then he would need all his power. The travelling would be hard enough and there was no telling what they would get into once they reached Jarrat.

The light grew and pushed out into the village. It ignored normal obstacles, such as roofs and walls. It spread, like a ripple on a pond, over the village. Once it had completely covered the village it then spread out over the forest until it blanketed the entire cavern.

Abram wanted to run. He did not know what was happening. He had a bad feeling, but he could not move. There was something going on that he didn't understand. Once the light had stopped moving a calm fell over him and he no longer had a feeling of dread. The change happened so quickly that he could hardly believe he had felt any other way. The problem that he had come to solve no longer seemed important.

Suddenly the light blinked out and the feelings that had come with it disappeared. The Emerald stone was completely dark. Alaric suddenly felt very weak again. He knew that the stone had given him a false sense of strength, but he wished for it to return. He hoped that whatever it had done had worked because he didn't think that he had the energy to fight with Abram anymore. What Alaric didn't know was that the Emerald stone had drawn on the power that it had given to him. When the light blinked out he was weaker than before.

"What were we talking about?" there was a certain amount of confusion in Abram's voice.

"The fact that you don't need the Emerald stone to survive," Alaric was quick to regain his senses.

Marina was about to speak. She thought that Alaric had also forgotten what they were talking about. When she saw the look on his face she knew that it was not the case. He had a very deliberate look on his face. There was a spark in his eyes that made her realise that he knew exactly what he was doing.

"I see," said Abram, the words didn't seem right, but he could not work out what it was. Slowly the words started to make sense and when they did he was a lot happier. "Of course it is time for the stone to leave. Its business is in your land, not mine. It will take some getting used to, but I am sure we will survive. Well it seems as though we will have something new to celebrate tonight. Can I offer to escort you to the festivities," there was something new in Abram's voice. There was a renewed hope, a sign that the future was going to be alright.

"As much as that sounds like a lovely offer I am afraid that I am going to have to pass. I am still exhausted from fighting Na'garoz. I need to rest before we leave tomorrow," Alaric explained.

"And what about you, my dear? Will you be joining us this evening?" Marina was surprised that he asked her.

"Thank you for your offer, but I should make sure that Alaric is alright." It was as good an excuse as any.

"That is a shame, but if either of you change your mind please feel free to come along," Marina thought that the chief of the Heji bowed his head before he left the room. It was not at all what she was expecting.

Once she was sure that he was not listening at the door Marina spoke. "What just happened?"

Alaric really didn't have the energy to explain, but he figured that he owed her that much. "The Emerald stone had a spell cast over the Heji. They believed that their world would collapse without it. I think it was a way for the stone to get the Heji to protect it. I am sure that it has done no real damage. Now that the spell has been released they no longer feel as though they will not survive without the stone."

Marina didn't like what she was hearing. It was hard to believe that the Emerald stone could take control of so many minds, seemingly effortlessly. It was not a good sign that Alaric kept the bracelet on his wrist. She was concerned that the stone was starting to take control of him.

"Don't worry." He read her face and knew what she was thinking. "The stone has no control over me, at least not yet."

Alaric sounded sure, but so had the Heji. The stone could be controlling Alaric without him knowing about it. She wanted to take it from him, but she remembered how painful it was when Alaric had taken the ring off her finger. She had to talk him out of it, somehow.

"Don't you think that it is time for you to put the bracelet away?" she made it sound as casual as possible. She even busied herself getting something to eat to add to the charade.

Alaric stared at the floor in from of him. He heard the words, but he didn't want to respond straight away. He felt that the question, however nonchalantly put, deserved thought. Marina wanted to ask again, but it would seem too forced if she did. Instead she would have to wait and hope that he decided to speak.

"I think you are right," he started, but did nothing to remove the bracelet.

When it was obvious that he was not going to take it off Marina spoke again. "If you think I am right then shouldn't you take it off?"

"I suppose I should," Alaric didn't look at her when he replied.

He made no move to take the bracelet off. Saying one thing and then doing the exact opposite was one of Marina's pet hates. She knew that he had been and was still going through a lot, but that was no excuse. The more she thought about it the madder she became. Eventually she could no longer contain herself.

"If you say you are going to take it off, then take it off," Marina spoke through clenched teeth. If she didn't she would have yelled at the top of her lungs.

Alaric didn't seem to take much notice her, which only fuelled the flames that were brewing inside of her. The princess was starting to come out in her again. If she had been treated in such a manner in the palace, by anyone except for her father, then they would be sent to the magistrate to spend a number of days in prison.

"You will listen to me when I am talking to you," she failed to keep her voice level.

"I am sorry," Alaric looked up for the first time.

Marina gasped when she saw his face. It was drawn and pale. Large black rings drooped under his eyes. He looked as though he had aged by twenty years. The sight only met her eyes for a moment, before he was back to normal. She blinked a few times to make sure what she was seeing was true. She was relieved to see that he was indeed back to normal, but was worried at the reason all the same.

"I cannot take the bracelet off, at least not yet. It is hard to explain, but you have to trust me," Alaric's voice was soft. "Now I think that I should get some sleep."

He rose from his chair before she had a chance to speak. It was obvious that he did not want to hear from her again. Marina wanted to comfort him, but she didn't know if that would be appropriate. She felt foolish for berating him like she did. She should have known that he wasn't being deliberately petulant. She had scolded him for no reason at all.

Marina stayed in the front room as Alaric walked into his bedroom. She wished that she could go and support him, but she knew that he didn't want that. The best thing she could do for him was to leave him alone. She would crawl into bed with him later without his knowledge.

In the morning Marina woke to find that Alaric was already up. When she rose she found that he was not in their house. A slight amount of panic filled her heart. Her initial reaction was that he had left without her. She did not know what she would do. She could not imagine living out the rest of her life with the Heji. The door suddenly opened as she was going through all the different scenarios in her head. The relief was clear on her face when she saw him.

"It is good that you are up," Alaric spoke as he entered.

"Where have you been?" was all she could say. She wanted to rush into his arms, but she knew that would be inappropriate.

"I have been getting the horses ready. We have to be on our way," Alaric sounded better than he had in a long time. If anything he sounded uplifted. His renewed spirits uplifted her own. "Are you ready to go?"

"Once I have eaten," Marina replied.

Alaric finished packing their things whilst Marina ate breakfast. He had to admit that the thought of leaving the wasteland was better than he had originally thought. Although the cavern was hospitable it was nothing compared to the mainland. He just hoped that things had not gotten worse since he had left. He wished that he had time to read the prophecy before they left, but he did not have the time to waste. There was no telling how long it would take for him to find the passage he needed.

"We have the meet Abram at the square before we go," Alaric explained when Marina finished her meal.

"Do you think that is a wise decision?" She was still unsure on how the rest of the Heji would take the news that they were leaving with their treasure.

"It will be fine," Alaric brushed off her concern.

They led their horses up the stone steps to the square. As they expected they were met by the remainder of the Heji. Their numbers were a lot less than what Marina thought they would be. The sight placed a sadness in her heart. It was a shame that the war on the mainland had to have such an effect on them. It was not their battle and yet they had bled more than anyone to date.

"Welcome, Alaric, Marina," Abram greeted them when they reached the square. "Thank you for coming here before you leave."

"I could not leave without saying goodbye. I could not have succeeded in defeating Na'garoz without your help," a broad smile crossed Alaric's face as he spoke. Marina could tell that he was speaking with fondness in his heart.

"Thankyou for your kind words, but I am sure you would have managed without us. It is I who should be thanking you for freeing us from our misconceptions," Abram brushed off Alaric gratitude and returned with more of his own.

The gratuities passed backwards and forwards for about fifteen minutes before Alaric finally ended things. It could have gone on for the rest of the day if he didn't. The day was already starting to slip away and they really needed to be on the move again. Alaric said one final goodbye before he mounted Adelanta.

"I thought we were going to jump?" Marina kept her voice low so only Alaric could hear.

"We are. I think it would be better if you mounted your mare. She we find it less disturbing if you are on her back."

Marina did as Alaric suggested. She didn't see the problem, but she had to take his word for it. As soon as she was mounted they promptly blinked out of existence. A cheer came from the Heji it was a mixture of relief that they were finally gone, but more so a cheer for what they had done. The life of the Heji would never be the same again.

Chapter 34: Planning for War

The army was starting to become restless. They had only been camped for a day, but that didn't matter. They had marched for nearly four weeks and they were ready for action. The command had spent most of the night trying to work out a plan of attack. With each new solution came the same problem. What would they do once they breached the wall? The Dark Knight who was posing as Prince Leroy was the thorn in their side. They did not know his true power and as much as they thought they could overrun him with numbers, they did not know how many men they would lose.

"We have to do something," Hulkan spoke firmly, with a touch of frustration in his voice. He stroked his thick brown beard as he spoke. It was all the dwarf could do to stop from slamming his fist down on the table. "We are risking a mutiny. Some of the soldiers are starting to lose faith in our ability to lead."

"The soldiers will do what they are told," General Jarwe's voice was brash. Despite the fact that there were no plans for war he still wore his steel breastplate. Unlike his silver breastplate there were no adornments on the one he was wearing for battle.

"That is all well and good, but this is not a regular army. Things have been tense ever since the army was constructed. Normal bullying tactics will not work," Wojtek voiced his opinion. Sorrell's advisor was not going to wait for his General to speak as he normally word.

"The Hondin Lel army will not desert," Hadar did not like what Sorrell's advisor was insinuating. The Duke was a commanding character and his voice boomed around the command tent.

"That is great, but where is the Hondin Lel army? I believe that you left most of it in your homeland," Sorrell wanted to defend his advisor, but his words almost sparked a physical fight.

The argument had been going all morning with no solution in sight. The only two who were quiet were Bern and Aimon. After the first repetition Bern decided to ignore the conversation. He figured that it would be obvious if something productive was said. Instead he was still thinking of how he could defeat Prince Leroy. He knew there had to be a way.

A lot had happened to Bern since he had left his quiet little life in Arsiliac. The farm and family life had suited his passive personality. That had changed quickly when they reached the Alliance. A strange entity was sharing his body and giving him vital information, but it had been quiet for days. Even with the aid of the entity he did not think he could defeat a Dark Knight.

Aimon chose to be quiet for a completely different reason. Whilst the command group argued amongst themselves there was no need for him to cause dissention. He thought his words would only bring them together. He was happy to sit back and watch them tear each other to pieces. He slowly ran his hands through his shoulder length, brown hair. It was satisfying to listen to them argue, but his silence would not last.

"This is your city Aimon," Jarwe's voice boomed over the rabble. The mention of Aimon's name brought Bern's attention back to the conversation.

"I am sorry. I don't know what to tell you. These are my people and I do not want to see them killed," Aimon had already prepared the speech.

"A lot more are going to die if we don't come up with a solution," all eyes moved to Bern. It was only at that point did they realise that their General had not spoken for well over an hour. Bern knew that Aimon was a Dark Knight and his jibe was not going to gain any results. He was just starting to become frustrated with his own lack of ideas.

"The only way I can see our victory is in a frontal assault to the castle. There will be casualties on both sides, but how else are we going to succeed," there was strange look on Aimon's face as he spoke. It was as if the words were coming unbidden.

Bern was suspicious of anything that came out of his mouth, but his words were not at all what he was expecting. There had to be something underlying in them. He couldn't risk confronting the Dark Knight. His only advantage was the fact that he knew who Aimon was and the Dark Knight was oblivious to that.

There was silence in the command tent as Aimon's words settled over the command group. They had not expected such a profound response. The Captain from Entero had no friends within the group, but they had to respect his knowledge of the city. Those who didn't know his secret only humoured him at Bern's insistence. What had caught their attention the most was his suggestion to attack his home.

"It is a last resort only," Bern was the first one to speak. "I have faith that Alaric will be here soon." He had hoped not to mention Alaric in the meeting. There was no telling when or even if he would return and he didn't want to give the others false hope.

"How can you say that?" Sorrell asked. "It has been over a month since we last saw him. We have no idea what he is doing. We do not even know if he is still alive. Despite your instructions not to look for him I know we have had riders sent out in search of him and they have all come back with nothing. It is like he has dropped off the face of the Seven Kingdoms."

Bern had to hide a smile at his statement. The General had no idea how true it was. There was little doubt in his mind that Alaric was somewhere in the Southern Wasteland or at least that he had been. Despite the fact that he didn't like knowing that the entity could take control of his body he really wished that it would take the opportunity to help. No matter what he did he couldn't call on the entity for assistance.

Sorrell's words brought another round of arguments bouncing backwards and forwards around the group. Aimon was glad that the attention had been taken off him. Bern also took the opportunity to think further. He was never given the chance to answer Sorrell's question, which he was more than happy about. He could feel that Alaric was getting closer and that was something he didn't want to explain, because he didn't know how he could. He knew that he had a connection with his old friend, but he didn't know the reason behind it. Each day that passed he could feel Alaric getting closer. He knew that it was only a matter of days before he was back. The only problem was that they didn't have a few days. He knew that by the next morning they would have to have made a plan of attack.

The afternoon was just as productive as the morning and that was to say not at all. When they finished arguing over one subject they quickly found another and never once found a solution. Bern was starting to become desperate. He had hoped that someone would have come up with a decent plan. It wasn't until after dinner that Richmond came up with the first real plan of the day.

"There is no other way around it. We have to move tomorrow or else the army will start to disband itself," Richmond only just started his oration before he was interrupted.

"I don't think that there is any point in repeating the obvious, but thank you for wasting our time," Jarwe had taken offence to Richmond throughout their last argument.

"Please, let him continue," it was the first time that Bern had spoken in well over an hour.

"Thank you." The room was suddenly silenced. "Tancred and I know how to get into the castle unnoticed. I think that if we can get into the castle and assassinate the Prince then there is a chance that we will have victory here."

"It is not like we have not already suggested this," Jarwe was still not happy with Richmond. "It's a suicide mission to enter the castle."

The arguments were about to start up again, but that would not help anything. Bern had been happy to let them go when it gave him a chance to think, but it was time for Bern to make a decision. Although he did not want to say what he was thinking there was no other option. He knew that Jarwe was correct. Without Alaric to battle the Dark Knight it would be suicide, but there was no other option. It was the only chance they had of avoiding a full on war. If they could rescue Eldred then there was a chance that he could fight the Dark Knight.

"We need to rescue Eldred and Alena. We will leave before first light." Bern's words silenced anyone who thought about speaking. "I think a small group has more of a chance of infiltrating the dungeons." It was time for Bern to decide who he was going to take with him. He knew that given a chance they would all volunteer. "I will take Richmond and Hadar." Bern thought they would be the two obvious choices. They had both been in the castle at one time or another."

"I do not think that you should go in with such small numbers," Wojtek suggested.

"I am sure that more numbers would help," Jarwe retorted.

It was clear that the arguments were about to start up again. It was the last thing that Bern wanted. He had made a decision and that was supposed be the end of it. It was clear that they had all accepted that they needed to infiltrate the castle, but that was not going to solve anything. Stealth was the key to a successful mission and the army still needed leaders to keep it in check.

"I have to come as well," Tancred said when the arguing died down. "The Lady Amilie is still in there and I believe that her life is in danger. I need to get her out."

Tancred missed the look that Richmond shot Bern when he heard his words. Richmond did not think that it was a good idea to take his advisor back into the castle. He was still under the influence of the Dark Knight Argoz and there was no telling what he would do. On the other hand it would be good to have one more body that had been inside the castle. In the end he didn't think that there was much of a chance keeping Tancred out.

"I am not happy, but you can come along," Bern conceded. "And that is it. This is no longer up for debate."

Bern did not like the situation at all, but he could hardly deny him. He still did not want to reveal Aimon's true identity and he would have to be very careful with Tancred. Their mission was going to be dangerous enough and it just became even harder. At least Richmond knew what was happening and would be able to keep an eye on his advisor.

"So what do we do with the army then whilst you are storming the castle? We still need to get them doing something," Sorrell was still not happy with the situation.

It was a problem that Bern had not figured out a solution for. He knew that his decision had only been piecemeal. It was the army that they needed to keep occupied. There had to be something that he could do to keep them busy. It took a few tense minutes, but the idea finally came to him.

"We make preparations to attack the castle," Bern blurted out as everyone was watching him.

"I thought that we decided that was not the answer?" Hadar was the first one to say what they were all thinking.

"That is the beauty of it. We don't need to actually attack the castle to keep the men busy. We need to build battering rams if we are going to break down the gates. That should give us enough to time to get into the castle and do what we have to do," Bern explained.

"And what happens if the army is ready to attack and you have not returned?" Hadar continued to ask the questions.

This time Bern had already thought of the response. The thought was not worth thinking about, but he now had no other option. There was nothing else he could do.

"Then you will have to attack. If we are not successful then there is no other option. We have to attack and try and free the people of Jarrat."

To Bern's surprise there was no argument. They were all happy that a decision had finally been made regardless of what it was. It was not the best of situations, but it was at least something. The soldiers would have a purpose and that would make life easier for everyone involved.

"I think we should tell the troops. I am sure they will be keen to make a start," there was renewed hope in Sorrell's voice.

"Just make sure that they cut the trees deep in the forest. We don't want them to know what we are doing in the castle," Bern added the unnecessary comment as the others were leaving the tent.

The only one who remained with Bern was Richmond. He had been waiting to speak with Bern ever since he agreed to let Tancred come with them into the castle. He didn't think it was a good idea. If Argoz was able to take control of his mind inside the castle then there was a good chance they would get captured. He really wanted to know what Bern was thinking. There was obviously something he was missing.

"I don't think that we should take Tancred with us. He is too much of a liability," Richmond spoke when he was sure that he was alone.

"I don't think that there is anything we can do about it. It looks as though he is determined. I'm sure the others accept our decision, but I'm not sure about Aimon. The last thing we want is for the Dark Knight to know we are onto him. If we can keep an eye on Tancred then we can make sure he doesn't get up to any trouble," Bern explained. "I don't think that there is any other option."

Richmond had to admit that Bern's words made sense. He didn't want to speak about his friend like he was a traitor. He would much prefer to be having the discussion with Tancred than Bern. He missed his advisor more than he thought that he would, but until he was free of the Dark Knight's yoke there was nothing he could do.

"So what do we do now?" he asked eventually.

"I think that it would be a good time to get some rest. We need to be in the castle before the sun rises in the morning," Bern explained.

Richmond did not want to leave the command tent. There was something secure about being inside the tent that would leave as soon as he left. The thought of walking out into the night air did nothing for him. He knew that he was just being silly, but he could not shake the feeling of dread. It was obvious that Bern wanted to be left alone and he didn't want Bern to have to tell him again.

Bern was wondering why it was taking Richmond so long to leave. He had to admit that he enjoyed the Lord's company, but it was time for him to think by himself. At about mid-afternoon he had lost the sense that Alaric was close. He didn't know what had happened, but he wanted to concentrate to get him back. The feeling had disappeared in the past, but never for so long. Whenever it returned he was always much closer than before, but there was still no sign of him.

Closing his eyes Bern concentrated on his surrounding. He could feel the wind blowing through the trees. He could feel the cold night air outside of the tent. He could sense the soldiers moving around the campsite. No matter how hard he tried he could not feel Alaric. It was as if he had been wiped from the face of the world. The thought did nothing to settle his nerves.

After he had tried to feel Alaric for almost half an hour he decided that it was time to give up. He had hoped that his old friend would arrive before they had to leave in the morning, but he thought there was very little chance that would happen. He even started to hope that the entity that shared his body would take over. There was more chance of success if the entity was in control, but he didn't think that was going to happen either. The entity seemed to come and go as it pleased. He didn't think it was the type of situation that would cause it to appear.

In the end Bern had to drag himself out of the tent. A good night sleep was the only thing that he had to look forward to and he doubted he would receive that. He was not looking forward to infiltrating the castle. The only plus was that they were finally doing something. There was a lot going through his mind and it would take him a long time to unwind. When he did finally sleep it was laboured and not very restful at all.

***

Argoz sat in his tent. Things were starting to change. He was surprised to hear that Bern was going to try and take on his brother. There was something strange about the man. He couldn't figure out what it was and it wasn't just the so called entity that showed up every now and then. He didn't think that Ra'naroz would have any problem in disposing of them, but he wasn't completely sure. There was something inside telling him that the man was dangerous. If they managed to rescue Eldred and Alena then there was a greater chance that Ra'naroz would not survive.

When it was all said and done he didn't really care if his brother lived or died. He had never really liked him. Since he had become the Prince of Entero his attitude had become even worse. He didn't know why Ra'naroz got to enjoy himself in the castle with the Queen, whilst he had to slum it in a tent with the army. Although he didn't care to be around the weak creatures it would have been more comfortable in the castle than what he was experiencing. He couldn't think what he had done to upset the Great Lord, but he was sure that he had done something to deserve it.

To get back in the Great Lord's favour he would have to get word to his brother that the attack was imminent. If he could stop things before they happened then there was a good chance he would gain favour. The only problem with his idea was that he was sure it would be Ra'naroz who would gain the favour. He didn't think that his brother would be gracious enough to tell the Great Lord that his success was due to him. He knew that his brother would take all the credit. That still didn't change the fact that he was sure if he kept the information to himself the results would be far worse.

He was relieved that Tancred was going into the castle. It would be the easiest way for him to get a message to Ra'naroz without blowing his cover.

Suddenly Argoz dropped to his knees and his head bowed down until it hit the ground. His body was completely stiff and he could not move. The initial shock had him confused, but it did not take him long before he knew what was happening. He didn't know whether to be excited or scared.

"Oh Great Lord," Argoz grovelled on the ground. "Thank you for gracing me with your presence."

Normally Argoz had to use the orb to speak with the Great Lord, but it seemed as though his master had found another way to contact him. That could only mean one thing. The Great Lord was roaming the Seven Kingdoms and his strength was growing. The thought brought both fear and elation to his heart, but he kept both from his mind. There were no doubts that the Great Lord would know exactly what he was thinking.

A sudden rush of pain shot through his body. Nyrra looked down on his servant with disgust. His Dark Knights had once been superior to all, but himself. For so long they had been lost from their path. They made him sick, but they were still the best he had. He did enjoy watching the creatures writhe in fear beneath him. He liked the fear that his presence commanded. He drank it like the creatures drank water, but that was not the reason he was there.

"I have a mission for you," his voice boomed inside of Argoz's mind.

"Anything you ask, Great Lord," Argoz felt his body relax, but he knew better than to rise without permission.

"The Cursed One will be returning soon," Nyrra wanted to spit at the mention of Alaric's title. "He is bringing a new woman with him. She is different. I do not know much about her, but I know that she is special to their cause."

Argoz did not know what the Great Lord was talking about. It was almost like he was unsure of what he was saying. The Dark Knight had never known Nyrra to be anything except confident. He was beginning to think that maybe one of his brothers was playing a trick on him. He was about to lift his head, but then he thought better of it. If he was wrong then the retribution would be unthinkable.

"Who she is, well that isn't important, it is what she has that I am interested in," there was a pause. "Get off the ground. Have some pride. You are one of the lucky seven to serve the Great Lord."

Argoz quickly rose to his feet, but he still kept his head low. He didn't want to risk looking the Great Lord in the eyes. It was obvious that he was not happy about something and he did not want to risk irritating him further. He knew the consequences of upsetting the Great Lord and he did not want to take that risk.

"Yes, Great Lord, tell me what you want and it shall be done," Argoz spoke quickly.

"She is carrying something with her, or more to the point I believe that she will be wearing something. I need you to take it from her and bring it to me," Nyrra explained.

"Of course, Great Lord, but what is it that you want me to take. What could such a woman possess?" Argoz hoped that he had not said the wrong thing.

"You will know it when you see it. That is enough for you to know at the moment." In truth Nyrra didn't know what it was. All he knew was that she had it and he wanted it. He was sure that it would be obvious, even to a lowly creature like Argoz.

"Of course, Great Lord." If the Great Lord did not want him to know then there had to be a good reason for it. There would be all the more glory for him when he succeeded.

"When you have it in your possession you must leave the army and come and deliver it to me," Nyrra continued.

"Where will you be?" Argoz asked slowly. He wanted to raise his head, but he could feel the Great Lord's eyes burning into him. He did not think that it would be a wise decision.

"You do not need to know that. When you have the item then I will contact you again. Do not fail me," Nyrra warned. "If you do not succeed then you will not live to celebrate our victory."

"Yes, Great Lord, I will do what you command," he was about to remain quiet, but he thought he would use the opportunity to big note himself. "The army is preparing to move against the castle. Some of the commanders are going to sneak in before dawn and try to assassinate Ra'naroz. Don't you worry. I will get word to him so he will be ready for the attack."

There was a pause as Nyrra thought on his words. Argoz wanted to speak. He wanted to explain further what was happening, but he had a feeling that was not the right thing to do. The Great Lord was still upset and anything could happen. The last thing he wanted to do was to bring down the wraith of the Great Lord on him.

"Do nothing," Nyrra spoke.

"I do not understand," Argoz was truly surprised.

"Of course you do not understand. That is why I am the Great Lord and you are my servant," there was a note of true disgust in his voice. "Ra'naroz has been too swept up in his persona that he has lost sight of what he was sent to do."

"But he is still in control of the Enteroites?" Argoz could have hit himself for speaking, but it seemed pertinent.

"He is too concerned with the pleasure of his perceived body. He enjoys spending his time with his pet Queen. Now that would be fine if he was taking care of his other tasks, but he has not. He knows that your army is on the edge of the forest. He should have sent out his soldiers to attack. There should have been carnage, by now. I do not wish for you to help him any further. If he is going to survive then he has to do it on his own," Nyrra's voice was firm.

There was now a new hope inside of Argoz. He had thought that Ra'naroz would be in the Great Lord's favour. Now that he knew he was not there was a chance for him to rise in the Great Lord's eyes. He had been a given a mission, albeit that he did not know what it was, and he was sure that it was important. He would sit on the Great Lords right hand when the war was over. He would receive the accolades that were promised.

"It will be as you say, Great Lord," Argoz was almost drooling with anticipation.

"Then you should get to work. I will contact you again soon. Remember that your life depends on it," with that last threat the image of Nyrra disappeared.

Argoz collapsed to the ground when he knew that Nyrra had disappeared. He panted as he tried to catch his breath. It was not long before a feeling of euphoria passed over him. It was something that Nyrra did to keep his followers in check. He loved to see them writhe in pain, but he also knew that they enjoyed other things. It kept them in tow and made them easier to control. He had learnt that a long time ago. A little reward, when deserved, went a long way.

There was not much for him to do. In fact there was nothing for him to do until the Cursed One arrived. He thought that he could cause a little more havoc before he left, but with what the Great Lord had told him he did not think it was a good idea. The Great Lord wanted Ra'naroz to suffer and he had no objections to that.

He was somewhat relieved that soon he would not have to play the role of the Enteroite Captain. Although he though he had done a great job he had a feeling that they were beginning to become suspicious. It was only a matter of time before they realised that he was not Aimon. When that happened he did not want to be around.

It had been a good night for Argoz. His unexpected meeting with the Great Lord had gone better than he anticipated. He could not remember the pain and suffering he had felt when he was in Nyrra's presence. All he could remember was the euphoric feeling that Nyrra had left him with. To his memory he had felt the same way throughout their meeting. He had done something right, because the Great Lord was trusting him with an important mission. He could not wait until the Cursed One brought this woman to him. He would take great pleasure in removing the unknown item. Then he would bring her great pain. He thought that would please the Great Lord, then he thought that he had not mentioned anything about torture. In the end he decided that if the Great Lord did not want him to torture the woman then he would have said so.

Chapter 35: A Dangerous Mission

Bern was the first of the four going into the castle to wake in the morning. He had not been able to sleep much. The thought of what the day had before them was worrying. They were embarking on a suicide mission. There was a good chance they would not see out the day. That was not a pleasant thought and had definitely not been an easy one to go to sleep on. He did, however, wake in the morning ready to go.

They met in the command tent. None of the other commanders were there. It was something that Bern had planned. Their place of meeting was secret. He knew that if everyone else knew where they were meeting then they would want to come along. It was not the most secretive of places to meet, but it did the job.

"Are we all ready to go?" Bern asked when the others had arrived.

There was a sombre yes, echoed by all in the tent. They had all been keen to volunteer the night before, but in the cold dark of the morning it did not seem like such a great idea. There was nothing they could do about it. They were already committed to what they had to do, even though it surely meant their death.

They all wore dark robes to help hide themselves as they moved across the field towards the castle. Once they reached the castle they would remove the robe to reveal the finery they wore underneath. Once they were inside they would have to look the part. If they looked like soldiers then they would be discovered before they reached the dungeons. They only weapon they wore was a light rapier, which wouldn't look out of place. The other three, although it wasn't their weapon of choice, seemed happy enough. Bern had only ever trained with a war axe or a broadsword, as was suitable to his build. If it came to battle he didn't think he would be any help with the lightweight sword.

"Then I think we should get moving. It will be light soon and we need to be on the other side of the castle before the sun rises," Bern stated the obvious, but he felt as though he had to say something.

Luckily the waning moon was covered by clouds when they stepped out of the forest. The area between the forest and the castle was completely empty. There was little light coming from the sky and they moved quickly through the darkness. It was only a matter of time before the clouds dispersed and the moonlight would give them away. Once they reached the far side of the castle it would not matter, but until then they had to be swift.

The morning air was cold, which Bern thought was fitting for the start of their mission. Sneaking through the cold dark of the morning seemed appropriate somehow. He couldn't help but feel doubtful about what they were doing. There was a small chance that they would survive, but he could not see how. He felt bad, because if he had no confidence then there was little hope that the others would. It was that thought that caused him to steel himself. Eldred and Alena had been prisoner for a long time and he couldn't imagine the pain they had suffered at the hands of the Dark Knight.

They moved in relative silence until they reached the far side of the castle and a moment of safety. The grey of dawn hit just as they disappeared around the corner. The added defence of the trees meant that they would not be seen from above. They were safe to wander around without fear of being seen. The only way they would be caught would be if someone was guarding the outside of the castle wall and Richmond had assured him there would be no one there.

Tancred took the lead when they reached the far wall. He seemed a little more certain than Richmond on where they were going. No one said anything when he moved on in front. He was on a mission and he wasn't going to be perturbed. Ever since they had left the open he moved with purpose. It was as if he could sense that Lady Amilie was in danger and he needed to rush to help her. Whatever was happening to her was his fault and he wasn't sure if he could live with himself if she got hurt.

"Should we say something to him?" Richmond asked Bern, keeping his voice low so Tancred could not hear him.

"What are you talking about?" Duke Hadar sounded suspicious.

Richmond shot Bern a look. He was not sure if telling Hadar was the right thing to do. Bern was not as suspicious of Hadar as Richmond was. The Duke had been stalwart when they were in Hondin Lel. He thought that he could trust the large man and he nodded for Richmond to explain the situation.

"The Lady Amilie helped us sneak into the castle when we were here. I think Tancred had a short, but passionate relationship with her," he was loathed to mention that fact. "We also believe that Lady Amilie has been taken prisoner. The chance that she is still alive is not great." Richmond chose to leave out the part about his mind being controlled by a Dark Knight. Bern was glad that he did so.

"That is not good. You should not have let him come along. We have a specific mission and that does not involve rescuing trapped maidens," Hadar had to grit his teeth to keep his voice low. It made his words sound harsher than they were supposed to.

"That is not for us to decide," Richmond's voice was solemn. "She helped us when she did not have to. If it wasn't for her help then we would not have so much information. I think that Tancred has every right to try and save her."

"But you said yourself that you think she has been captured. It has been over ten days since you left the castle. I hate to be the bearer of bad news, but I do not think that she will still be alive," Hadar controlled himself a little better as he spoke.

"I fear the same, but that doesn't mean that we shouldn't try. Eldred and Alena have been imprisoned for a lot longer and I have to believe that they are still alive. There is no reason why Lady Amilie's fate shouldn't be the same," Richmond hoped.

There was not much more to be said. There was nothing that could be done. An argument could, and more than likely would, alert the guards of their presence. If that happened then it wouldn't matter if Amilie was alive or not. Her fate would soon be theirs. The first key to their survival was entering the castle unnoticed.

When Tancred found the place where the stairs disappeared into the wall he did not wait for the others. He quickly disappeared into the dark. Richmond only hoped that he would not be stupid enough to enter the castle without them. In his current state he did not know what he would do. If the Dark Knight was in control of him then there was absolutely no telling what would happen. The fact the Tancred had found the stair without really looking was a concern. As he walked past he could not make out the marks he had made on the wall. Something was definitely amiss, but he kept his concerns to himself.

"Be careful. It is pitch black in the tunnel," Richmond warned as he let the other two down the stairs. His advisor had already moved out of sight when he disappeared into the earth.

When they were in the tunnel they could hear Tancred moving around in front of them. It was a good sign that he had not already exited the tunnel. Things were going to be hard enough as it was without Tancred making things more difficult. He wasn't thinking straight and he could lead them into a trap. They needed to look like they belonged and that meant they had to remain casual.

"We need to be careful on the other side. Once we come out of the basement we will be in the castle stables. I don't think that they will be on the lookout for people inside, but I don't really want to take that risk," Richmond explained. "We'll make our way as quickly and calmly as we can into the castle."

No one argued, but no one responded either. Richmond only hoped that they were nodding their heads and he just couldn't see them in the darkness. He tried to make his way past Tancred to open the door, but his advisor would not let him through. Richmond wanted to yell at him, but he knew that their voices would carry. He would have to wait before he berated Tancred.

Tancred did not wait for permission. He slowly opened the door and walked through. He found the sudden light hard on his eyes, but he was too focused to let it worry him. He would not be deterred from his mission. After waiting for the others to enter the basement he closed the door. Richmond was thankful that Tancred didn't run away from them. He was beginning to regret their decision to bring him along with them, not that it was his choice at all.

"I will take the lead," Richmond spoke softly. "You have to stay close, Tancred. We can ill afford one of us to get captured. If that happens then there is a fair chance that we will all be caught."

Tancred wanted to argue, but he knew that there was no point. He could move off when ever he wanted, but he also knew that they were there to do something important. He could not risk everything for Amilie, even though he felt responsible for what happened to her. Everything would work hand in hand. If they were able to kill the Dark Knight then they would be able to rescue Amilie. It was that thought and that thought only that kept him going. If he didn't think that way then he didn't think he would be able to contain himself.

"Let's go then," Richmond spoke when he was sure that Tancred was going to do as he was told.

Richmond led the way into the stables. There were a number of horses still stabled, but there were no people around. Bern thought they were either very lucky or they were about to walk into a trap. Either way they had no option but to continue. The further they walked through the stables the more Bern felt as though something was not right. He thought that the horses seemed to be nervous and that was never a good sign. He wanted to call out for the others to stop, but he didn't know what to say.

Richmond didn't wait when he reached the end of the stables. The large double doors leading out into the castle's main courtyard were shut. It seemed strange to Bern, but Richmond didn't notice. Without a second thought he pushed one of the doors open. As he did he quickly pulled it shut again. He almost got it closed before a sword blade was slid into the gap stopping it from being completely closed.

Everyone drew their weapons when they saw the blade. At least whilst they were in the stables they had the advantage. The stables were not wide enough to allow a lot of soldiers in at one time. It was a small consolation, but it was all that they had. Richmond wondered at who had tipped them off of their arrival. It was as if the soldiers were specifically waiting for them. He looked accusingly at Tancred, although there was no proof he could not think of anyone else. Aimon would have made more sense, but Richmond wasn't exactly thinking straight. His advisor didn't know what that look was for. He couldn't understand what his Lord was doing.

"There are too many of them," Richmond warned. As he did the door was pulled out of his hands. He took a number of steps backwards to prepare himself.

A soldier wearing the greaves of a captain walked into the doorway and stopped. He did not have his sword drawn and he did not look as though he was concerned. There were a number of soldiers standing directly behind him. They all had their swords drawn and looked as though they were ready for action. It was obvious that they were the reason why the captain was so confident.

"Lower your weapons. There is no chance of you making it out of here alive," the pure arrogance in the Captain's voice made Bern want to chop his head off, but he knew that it was not an option.

The other thought that ran through his mind was trying to escape, although he did not think there was much point in trying. The only option they had was to surrender. That was just as promising as the other two. He had to make a choice, but nothing was coming to mind.

"Drop your weapons or you will suffer the consequences," the captain drew his sword as he offered the ultimatum.

"Do as he says," Bern sounded defeated as he spoke.

"But…" Hadar let the word drift away.

Bern had already let his sword drop to the ground. There was no point in trying to mount an attack. Hadar was disappointed in Bern. He thought they could at least put up a fight. If the soldiers wanted them dead then they would not have offered the surrender. Even if they fought he didn't think that they would end up dead. He believed that they wanted to keep them alive and that at least was a promising sign.

"Very good," the captain moved aside as the soldiers collected their weapons. In doing so they were able to get in behind the group. "Now you will come with us."

None of them moved, even when the guards advanced. They were waiting for Bern to do or say something. They would not move without his advice, not that they had any other options left.

"Let's go," Bern commanded, at least it sounded as though it was their choice, even though they did not have one.

They all started walking out of the stables. Their weapons had been taken by the guards. At first, when they had been found, they thought that they might have been able to fight their way out, but when they saw how many guards there were they changed their minds. If they attacked then it would only be a matter of time before they were slaughtered. They also did not want to kill the soldiers. In the end they were fighting on the same side. All that had to be done was to secure their freedom from the yoke of the Dark Knight.

They were marched through the courtyard to the main entrance of the castle. Everyone in the courtyard stopped to see what was happening. Everyone, except for Richmond, kept their heads down as they were paraded through the square. He caught the eye of a well dressed man and nearly cried out when he recognised who it was. The Duke Xarles Dúc watched them carefully. When he realised that Richmond had recognised him he placed a finger to his lips. Richmond slowly lowered his head. There was a glimmer of hope. He did not know what the Duke could do to help, but at least there was a chance.

He wanted to tell the others, but he was afraid to speak. He took a couple of deep breaths to calm himself as they walked up the man stairs. He would just have to wait. When the time was right he would tell the others. Until then he would have to keep the sombre expression that the others shared.

Once they were inside the castle some of the soldiers had to fall back. The corridors were too narrow for them to remain in their current formation. Bern looked around for a chance to escape, but it would be a futile attempt. There was nothing that they could do. They would have to continue to the end and hope that an opportunity would arise.

Richmond's heart sank when he realised where they were being escorted. The guards were taking them towards the Queen's main chamber. There was no doubt in his mind that the Dark Knight would be waiting for them. There was little opportunity that they would get out alive. In the end they knew it was going to be a suicide mission. He looked over at his advisor, but he could not get a read off the man's face. It was as steely as it could be. He hoped that his old friend would not betray them.

They all continued to walk until the captain stopped outside the Queen's main chamber. He didn't look happy about having to knock on the door. He was even less impressed when he was called to open it. There was a sudden rush of cold air when the door was opened. It sent a shiver down Bern's spine. He knew that the Dark Knight was waiting for them.

"Bring them in," a cold voice spoke from inside the room.

The captain did not look happy. The last thing he wanted to do was to enter the room with Prince Leroy. He never liked to be in the same room as him. He made him feel very uncomfortable, but he knew better than to ignore a request from the Prince. Those who did usually ended up in the dungeon, a fate, that these days, was worse than death. He led his prisoners into the room. At least he was entering with good news. The only thing he hoped for was a quick exit.

"Who is this?" Prince Leroy didn't look up from what he was doing.

The Prince was lying across a bed that was covered with throw pillows. There was a half naked women lying behind him. There was a dazed expression on the woman's face. Her eyes were open but glazed over. Her long brown hair was a mess on the bed. The Prince looked back at her when he felt the bed move, but didn't give her any more attention. The captain was almost physically sick when he realised who it was. He had to look away, but in a manner that did not draw attention to himself. He had never seen the Queen in such a state. He doubted that anyone had seen the Queen in such a state.

"These are four men who we found trying to sneak into the castle. We believe that they are assassins," he could not look at the Prince as he spoke to him. All he wanted to do was to leave the room.

"Hmm. I see." The Prince still didn't look up at the prisoners. He seemed to be judging them without seeing them. Finally, after a long pause, he looked up. The expression on his face didn't change as he looked over them, until his gaze reached Bern. At first it was like he was trying to work out where he knew him from. When it dawned on him he tried to keep his composure, but there was something twitching on the side of he face. "Leave me," the Prince stood from the bed as he spoke.

"Yes, your majesty," the captain did not care that there were four unguarded prisoners alone with the Prince and his Queen. All he wanted to do was to leave the room and return to his duties.

The captain quickly left and shut the door behind him. Throughout the exchange Queen Oriana had remained on the bed, seemingly oblivious to what was going on around her. Bern tried his best not to look at her. Although he had never met the monarch before he felt something towards her. No one deserved to be in the thrall of a Dark Knight, let alone a queen. He could not believe that she was just lying on the bed with her naked breasts in full view of everyone in the room.

"Now before we get down to business it is time for you to have something to drink," Prince Leroy spoke directly to the Queen. It was the first time that he had acknowledged her since they had entered the room.

The Queen moved when she heard the Prince's voice. She didn't seem to notice the other four men in the room or the fact that she did not have anything covering her from the waist up. She moved across to a small side table. The only item on the table was a small pewter mug. She picked the mug up without looking what was inside and drank the entire contents before returning it to the table. When she had finished drinking she looked as though she became unsteady on her feet. Her legs shook slightly, but it was only there for a second. It was obvious to all that whatever was in the mug was causing her trance-like state. Bern did not think it was a very good sign. He was hoping that the Prince was casting a spell to control the Queen. If that had been the case then it would be draining his power, but a drugged drink would be doing nothing to it.

Queen Oriana moved back to the bed when she had finished drinking. Leroy looked as though he was very pleased with himself when she did. He could see the look of either horror or disgust, or a mixture of both from the four men. He didn't care which one, just as long as he got a reaction. He was already on the front foot and he planned on keeping things that way. Once he had looked at all four of their reactions he returned his gaze to Bern.

"So you thought that you could just sneak into the castle and assassinate me, did you?" His eyes were cold and there was little expression on his face.

"I guess I should have given you more credit," Richmond was about to speak after a short pause, but it was Bern who spoke first. "I thought that Nyrra's lowliest of servants would have been easy to dispose of."

Bern didn't know which of his insults cut the deepest, his calling the Prince the lowliest of servants or calling the Great Lord by his real name. The only clues were in his eyes. There was no reaction on the Dark Knight's face at all. Bern saw this as a good sign. It meant that he was starting to lose his calm. He was not able to keep complete control of his fake façade. It was a small victory, but it meant that Bern's presence was upsetting him.

"I don't think that it would be wise to make fun of me. It is the best way for you to end up in my dungeon. I don't know if you have heard the rumours, but it is better to die quickly than to end up in there. I am quite proud of the fear I have created," there was some movement returning to his face as he spoke.

Bern thought about another good response, but decided that it was just a waste of time slinging insults. He was not going to gain any advantage. He knew that Eldred and Alena were in the dungeons and if he mentioned their names then it would cause him to become defensive. Instead he thought he would get straight to the point.

"Very well, you have caught us. Now what is it that you want to do with us?" Bern sounded bored as he spoke. There was fear in his heart, but he could not let the Dark Knight see it. He wished the entity would come and take control.

"I think that my brother's pet should tell you." Leroy looked at Tancred.

There was an awkward silence before Tancred realised that they were all waiting on him to speak. "Why is everyone looking at me?" he asked, genuinely surprised.

There was another silence in the room as they all tried to figure out what was happening. Even the Dark Knight looked confused. He was waiting for something from Tancred, but there was nothing coming. Bern was the first one to realise , although he did not know the full extent of the betrayal he knew that something had happened.

"It seems as though your brother no longer has your back," Bern sneered. He almost started laughing when he finished speaking. "Now why is it that you think that Argoz is not warning you about our intentions?"

The mention of the Dark Knight's name surprised everyone. Tancred and Hadar did not know who he was referring to. His words hit Leroy like he had run into a stone wall. He had thought that Argoz's identity was still a secret. He wondered if the man in front of him knew his true identity. That was not something he wanted to consider. He knew that there was power in the man before him, but he didn't know how much.

"I am sure that there is reason why my brother has no new information for me. But that is not your concern now, is it? I think that you should be more worried about what I have in store for you." Again his face did not move, but there was hatred burning in his eyes.

"Yes, I suppose that we should get to the point," Bern sounded bored.

"What is going on?" there was a delay in Tancred's response. Ever since the Leroy had singled him out he was trying to work out what his importance was.

Bern shot Tancred a harsh look. He really wished that Richmond's advisor had not spoken. It was something he probably should have spoken to Tancred about before they entered the castle, but he didn't know he would take it. Especially with what the ramifications would mean. If he knew that he had betrayed Lady Amilie there was no telling what he would do.

"I see that you like to keep your people in the dark." Leroy could not understand why Tancred didn't know. If they knew the truth then there was no reason for them not to tell. He was confused and that was not a good sign. He needed more information before he continued. "You are the puppet of my brother," he sneered at Tancred as he spoke.

"What is he talking about?" Tancred spoke to his life-long friend.

"This is not the time," Richmond whispered.

"Oh, but this is the perfect time." Leroy said he used magic to hear what was being said. "The information that you shared with me the last time you were here was very useful. I don't know what I would have done without it." Leroy was enjoying himself.

"What is he talking about?" Tancred repeated the question, but for a different reason.

"I'm sure that there are more important things we can discuss." Bern had to keep the conversation away from Tancred. It was clear that Leroy was gaining the advantage.

"Your friend wailed when I tortured her," Leroy ignored Bern's words.

"What? Who?" Tancred was starting to panic. He didn't know what was happening, but he knew something bad had already happened and he had a feeling that he had been involved.

"The Chosen One is on his way here," Bern blurted out. He could not think of any other way to divert the conversation.

His idea worked. Leroy was no longer happy teasing Tancred. Something was happening that wasn't supposed to. If the Cursed One was on his way to Jarrat than he should already know about it. He wondered why his brother did not give him the message. He wondered why the Dark Lord himself did not give him the message. He needed to keep his attention on the man in front of him. As much as he was having fun toying with Tancred he had other things to worry about.

"You will tell me all that you know about the Cursed One," there was a new hatred radiating from the Dark Knight.

Bern wanted to breathe a sigh of relief, but he could not. He had to keep the conversation going the way that he wanted. He knew that he could not divulge any information about Alaric's movements, partly because he no longer knew where Alaric was. He had been unable to feel his old friend right up until the time they entered the castle grounds. The last time he had felt Alaric he knew that he was very close. He would be arriving in the next day or two. At least he hoped that was the case. If they failed then at least Alaric could lead the Alliance into battle.

"I am afraid that I am not going to be able to do that. If you want that information then you are going to have to work for it." As much as he didn't want to put the idea of torture into the Dark Knight's head there was not much else he could do.

"What is going on?" Tancred was still distraught. He had only heard the conversation as a background noise in his head. He wanted to know what he had done to help the Dark Knight.

"I can tell you that the Chosen One will rise up and destroy you," Bern spoke quickly so the attention would not return to Tancred.

Leroy started to laugh. "I do not think that your Chosen One," he spat as he said 'Chosen One', "will be any match for me. I have control of this castle and all the soldiers in it. Tell me what the Cursed One can do?"

The question was a crafty one, but Bern was ready for such tricks. He would not be taken by surprise. There was still a chance that they would be able to get out alive. If he could waste enough time then Alaric could arrive to save them. It was a long shot, but he was sure that Alaric would not leave them to die. The only problem was that time was against them. At least the Dark Knight thought that they had information. That would keep them alive a little longer, although it would not be pleasant. He was sure that torture would be on the menu, but if it kept them alive then it was their only option.

"He will rain down a horror on you that you could not imagine. Since the Evil One does not have your back anymore I do not think that there will be any hope for you. You will die a painful death and there will be nothing waiting for you on the other side." If only he could gain more time, was all that Bern was thinking of.

Leroy started to pace backwards and forwards. When he stopped he looked at the Queen lying on the bed, it diverted his attention, but he knew that none of the four were going to attack him. The sight of the almost unconscious and half naked Queen on the bed gave him an idea.

"I think that it is time to visit the dungeons," a smile crossed his face as he turned and looked at the others.

As much as Bern did not want to go into the dungeons it was always going to be their destination. If they had to go as prisoners, then that was the way it had to be. At least they would be closer to their main goal. It would give them a chance to figure out where they were holding Eldred and Alena. It was weak, but it was all he could think about to keep the fear in check.

"Well I don't think that there is any other choice." Bern didn't think that there was any point in delaying the inevitable any longer. He had run out of ideas.

"You sound brave, but let's hear what your friends have to say. I don't think they will share you enthusiasm once I start tearing strips off their bodies. You might think that you know what torture is, but you have no idea. The things that I can and will do to you will make you regret the decision that you have made," Leroy was rubbing his hands in a threatening manner. He looked at the faces of Bern's companions and could easily see their fear.

Bern hoped that they did not speak. The last thing he wanted was for the Dark Knight to know how much fear was in their hearts. He would feed on it and it would make him stronger. That was one thing that Bern did not want to happen.

"Well I guess that we should get going then?" Bern wanted to speak before anyone else decided to.

"Not just yet," the Dark Knight sneered.

Bern heard something drop to ground behind him. It was followed shortly after by two more thuds. As much as he didn't want to divert his attention from the Dark Knight he wanted to see what had happened. As he expected he found his three companions lying on the floor. It was obvious that they were unconscious.

"What about me?" Bern asked the obvious question.

"I have a better way for you." The Dark Knight moved towards the back of the room where there was a pitcher and a number of mugs.

Leroy took something from a small jar and stirred it into a mug of water. Once he was sure the contents had been dissolved he returned to where Bern was standing. He took one last look inside the mug before he handed it to him. Bern's first thought was to tip the water onto the floor, but he knew, in the end, that it would prove nothing. The Dark Knight would make him drink in the end.

"What is it?" There was still a chance to waste some time.

"I know that you are trying to pretend that you don't have any power inside you, but I know that it is there. This is a simple herb that will block you from reaching that power. The dose that I have given you will also knock you out for long enough to have you taken to the dungeons. You see I am not a simpleton like you seem to think. This will keep you nice and sedate until I need you." He waited for Bern to drink.

The last thing Bern wanted to do was to drink whatever it was. He knew that it would have the effect that Leroy said it would. Slowly he started to understand why Eldred had not been able to escape. He took a tentative sip and swallowed. There was a bitter taste to the water.

"Don't do it like that," the Dark Knight sounded annoyed. "Drink it all or else your friends will suffer the consequences."

There was nothing false in his threats. Bern was starting to wish that he had not brought the others with him. He should have foreseen what was going to happen. They would all suffer for his mistakes. If they lived they would have the memory of it etched in their minds. It would be kinder if the Dark Knight had just killed them and moved on. He didn't know if he wanted to survive the ordeal. With that thought in his mind he downed the foul tasting liquid.

He thought by the taste of the concoction that he would instantly bring the liquid back up. Instead it had a calming effect on his stomach. He thought that it would be a sickness remedy. That thought only remained inside his head for a moment. It did not take long for the true effect of the herb take effect. His head felt woozy. There was something strange about the room. He thought that everything looked blurred. Then it seemed as though he was looking at the room through a tunnel. He could not focus on anything. Just when he thought he had worked out what was happening everything went dark and he collapsed to the ground.

"Guards!" was the last thing Bern heard as he fell to the ground.

Chapter 36: The Dungeons

There was a strange, musty smell in the air when Bern regained consciousness. His head hurt and he didn't really know where he was. He could feel that his arms were hanging above his head. When he tried to pull them down he found that he could not. There was a dull pain in his shoulders, as if they had been overused. He tried to open his eyes, but they were shut tight.

It took almost five minutes for Bern to regain his composure. His head still ached, but he knew where he was. He was in the castle dungeons, chained to a wall. Now that he knew what was happening he was loathed to open his eyes, but it was the only way he would be able to gauge his true situation.

As soon as he opened them he wished that he hadn't. The urge to retch was overwhelming and there was nothing he could do to stop it. The taste of the bitter liquid was still in his mouth, which did not make things easier, although the sight that met his eyes was enough to do the job. He did his best not to get the contents of his stomach on himself, but he failed. Being chained up made it an impossible task.

He was in a small cavern, lit by a number of torches in wall sconces. Once he had finished retching he was able to look around. His three companions were also chained to the walls like he was. In the centre of the cavern was what had made him sick. A naked woman was chained to the roof. Her body was stretched to its limit with only her toes touching the ground. Her shoulders looked as though they had separated a long time ago. It was clear that she was dead and Bern thought that it was a small mercy. Her skin had been stripped, almost in its entirety. Bern couldn't imagine what it would have taken to cause such wounds. Along with the marks of a beating were also a number of long cuts. Patches of her hair had been ripped from her head. The manner of her torture was horrendous. He only hoped that some of the damage had been done after she had died, although he knew that it was not true.

A cry from the other side of the room indicated that Richmond had regained consciousness. It took a while for his screams to die down. He had obviously seen the poor girl in the middle of the cavern. He couldn't imagine what was going through his head. He knew that it was the fate that awaited them. If Alaric didn't arrive soon there was no other option.

"Are you alright," Bern asked when there was silence.

"What do you think?" by the sound of his voice it was obvious that he was trying not to retch himself. He didn't sound impressed by the question.

"You need to remain calm. If the guards know we are awake then they will come to torture us," although with the noise Richmond had made he doubted that it wouldn't be long anyway.

"That is easy for you to say. You do not know who that is," Richmond referred to the dead woman.

"Who is she?" as soon as he asked the question he knew the answer.

"That is the Lady Amilie. I don't think Tancred will be able to control himself when he sees this," Richmond was trying his best.

"What is this atrocity?" Hadar's gruff voice did not sound afraid.

"Keep your voice down," Bern warned. "This is a fate that will befall us sooner rather than later if we alert the guards."

"I don't think it will matter once Tancred joins us," Richmond sounded deflated.

"What do you mean by that?" Tancred was awake.

Almost as soon as he asked the question did he realise what Richmond was talking about. At first he was sickened by the sight in front of him, but it took him a moment to realise who it was. When he did he didn't want to believe that it was true. He could not imagine the pain she would have gone through to end up in such a state.

"What is this? It can't be," Tancred was starting to ramble.

They all knew that it was only a matter of time before he broke down. They only hoped that he did so in a quiet manner. That was not likely to happen. Richmond knew his advisor all too well and he knew that it was only a matter of time before he cried out.

Bern was surprised at how long it took for Tancred's emotions to come to the surface. When they did they all came out at once. His wailing struck their hearts. They could feel his emotional pain. The sight before them was sickening enough, but knowing the short lived relationship that the two of them had was heartbreaking. The fact that Tancred had betrayed her, but had not even known he had, was even worse. There was no doubt that there would be someone coming for them soon.

When his weeping died down they could hear footsteps coming towards them. They could make out two distinctly different sets of steps. Bern thought about playing unconscious, but he didn't think that there was much point. It wouldn't take long for them to realise he was faking.

The creature that entered the room first was not what they were expecting. The orglin was a skinny creature with patches of tangled brown hair all over its body. The only place that it didn't have hair was on its wrinkled head. Two small tusk-like teeth protruded up from its lower jaw. Its skin was a sickly grey leathery like covering. It walked with its back hunched over. It didn't look like it should be allowed to exist. It seemed as though the man walking behind didn't think so either. He kept control of the orglin with a chain with a collar around its neck. If it got too rowdy the warden would tug harshly on the chain.

The man was fitting for the job. He was large and Bern estimated that he was a least six and a half feet tall and if he was not at least half as wide Bern would be very surprised. He had a bald head and a number of large boils on his face. It looked as though the man had not seen the sun in years. Bern thought that he looked very accomplished at his job.

Once they were in the cavern the man let the orglin scuttle up to the hanging corpse of Amilie. To the disgust of the four prisoners the orglin started to lick the congealed blood on her body. To make matters worse the evil creature started to grab at her and hump her leg. The warden thought about pulling the creature off before he saw their reaction. The sight did not please him, but it was worse for his prisoners. The orglin seemed happy enough so he let the creature go.

After all four of them had been physically sick the warden pulled on the choke chain. The orglin held on for as long as it could before it crashed to the floor. He didn't seem happy to be interrupted. It had taken a large chunk out of one of Amilie's breasts. The flesh hung down in a sickly fashion. The creature stared at the meat and salivated. If any of the prisoners had anything left in their stomachs they would have brought it up.

"Enough," Tancred strained to free himself from his chains, but to no avail. "What is it that you want?"

The warden started to laugh. It was a nasally, guttural noise that didn't sound right. It was easier to make them break than he had thought. Although he did not realise the connection between the dead woman and his new prisoners, he knew that it had worked. He wished that he could have left her in position, but he needed the chains for his new prisoners. They would be brought out into the centre and tortured one at a time.

"I want nothing with you," his voice used the same nasal guttural tone as his laughter. "I am not here to get anything out of you. All I am here for is to make you suffer," he grinned as he spoke.

"I will see you dead before the end of this," there was a sharpness to Bern's voice that really didn't fit the situation. It caused everyone, except for the orglin, to look at him. There was a glimmer of hope in the hearts of the other three prisoners.

"I was warned about you." It took the warden a moment to realise who he was. "Don't you worry yourself, with the drugs the Prince has given you there is nothing you can do to stop me. You will suffer just like your friends."

The warden took a tentative step towards Bern. Even though he was sure that the drugs were working he was not completely sure. The last thing he wanted to do was to be taken by surprise. With his attention diverted the orglin took the opportunity to befoul the hanging corpse again. The distraction was all that the warden needed to stop his advance.

"Nasty creatures, but they serve their purpose," the warden spoke to himself as much as the prisoners.

As he yanked on the choke chain the sound of footsteps could be heard approaching their cavern. The orglin squealed. The warden didn't know whether it was from the chain or because it knew what was coming. Either way the creature retracted away from the corpse. Although there was little expression on the hideous creature's face Bern thought that he saw fear. It could only mean that it was the Dark Knight approaching. Bern didn't know if it was a good sign or a bad sign.

It wasn't long before Bern's suspicions were confirmed. The Dark Knight entered the cavern. He smiled when he saw that they were all awake. He was even more impressed with the expressions on their faces. Bern was the only one who didn't look deathly afraid. He could feel the fear that filled the room and it excited him. When he saw the corpse hanging in the middle of the cavern he realised why. He casually walked over it and started to stroke her cheek. It was as if the dead body was a house pet. He looked fondly at her before he returned his attention to the others.

"If it makes you feel any better she lasted a lot longer than I expected before she broke. She squealed like a pig for so long that I thought she was going to shapeshift," he laughed loudly at his joke.

"Your time for self-gratification will soon be over," Bern kept his voice level. The others wanted to shout, but they were too afraid. The time for their torture was imminent and they were happy to let Bern speak.

"I do not think that will be the case. You will beg for mercy before you tell me everything that I want to know," Leroy did not notice the edge to Bern's voice.

Bern was sick of talking to the Dark Knight, but he knew that it was the only way to keep them from being tortured. It was another chance to delay what they all thought was the inevitable. Although he still could not feel Alaric he knew that his old friend must be close. With any luck he would already be in the castle.

"The Chosen One is close," Bern closed his eyes in an act of searching. "You would be wise to leave why you still can."

"That is funny, because I know that you cannot feel anything. The Cursed One will not know where you are. No one is coming for you. You will live out the rest of your lives in pain in my dungeon, however short that may be."

"I hear that you like to keep your prisoners alive." It was the best chance Bern had to find out if Eldred and Alena had survived.

"As your friend can testify, I don't keep my prisoners alive." Leroy was not going to give up the information easily.

"That is not what I have heard. I hear that you are holding a couple that are important to your Great Lord." Bern nudged a little further.

It took a moment, but a look of knowing suddenly crossed Leroy's face. He had to admit to himself that his two prized prisoners had slipped his mind. For some reason the woman was important to the Great Lord. He had been given strict instruction that she was not to be killed. The Great Lord had not mentioned anything about the man, but he thought that it was better to be safe than sorry. To be sorry meant a fate worse than death, a fate that not even he could imagine. As long as they were alive there was no mention of what state they had to be in. He wondered if they were still being tortured. It was at that point he realised that he had been thinking for too long.

"I believe that they have been taken care of." He was not going to let them know their friends were still alive. He thought it would have a greater effect if they thought they were dead.

By the long pause and the strange look on the Dark Knight's face Bern judged that they were still alive. He was grateful for that, not that it meant anything for their own wellbeing. There was no escaping the inevitable, but Bern was still not going to give up.

"I can see right through you. I know they are still alive. I was right. You are too afraid to disobey the Great Lord," it was not much of an insult, but it was all he could think of.

"I see," it was the weak comment that returned Leroy's attention to the job at hand. "I think that you should be more worried about what I will do to you." He sneered at Bern. He had almost forgotten about the other three. "The question is who do I start with?" He walked past the others, watching them closely. "Cut that body down. I have had enough fun with her." He deliberately stopped in front Tancred when he spoke. In truth the body reminded him that he had lost control and killed her by mistake, but he wasn't going to let anyone know. "And she was so much fun," he whispered into Tancred's ear. "Give her to your pet. I am sure that it will have even more fun with her."

Tancred tried to hit the Dark Knight with his head, the only part of his body that was within striking distance. Leroy anticipated the attack and simply moved out of the way. He was glad that he got a reaction out of the man. It was obvious that the woman had meant something to him. It was time for him to have a little more fun before he got down to business.

"You know that without your information I would not have known that she was a traitor. So I suppose that I should thank you. I don't know if she would be pleased to know it was you," the warden cut the body down as Leroy spoke.

"You leave her alone," Tancred cried out. He could no longer keep his emotions inside. "You leave her alone." He thrashed around in his chains, in a futile attempt to break free.

Bern wished that Tancred would stop, although he understood what the man must be feeling he knew the Dark Knight was feeding on his anguish. There was nothing that Tancred could do. In the end it was a hindrance and it would not make him feel any better. He could not say anything because that would give the Dark Knight a further advantage. He had to admit he wanted to cry out himself when he saw the warden carry the limp body out of the cavern. No one should be treated in such a way, especially not in death. He was grateful that the body was carried out of sight.

The orglin followed its master with a hungry look in its eyes. No one wanted to think about what the creature was going to do when it was left alone with Amilie. It was not worth thinking about. What they had already seen was enough to last them a life time. The only problem was that it would be their turn soon enough.

"Now I think that it is time to get down to business," there was malice in Leroy's voice. "Tell me what the Cursed One is planning?" Finally the question was asked and their chance to escape torture. All they had to do was betray everything they were fighting for. The only problem was that they didn't know what he was planning. Alaric always kept his movements close to his heart.

The Dark Knight moved from prisoner to prisoner. He was trying to gauge a reaction by their fear. He knew instantly that they did not know. The only problem was Bern. There was no reaction and nothing to read, but it did was give him an idea. It was time for the party to truly get started.

"I see that you are going to be a tough group to crack," he looked at Bern as he spoke. "I think that we will start with… you," he spun around to face Richmond when he answered as the warden had returned.

The warden didn't need to be told. He knew to unchain Richmond from the wall and chain him in the middle. It was possible to torture him from the wall, but it would be more effective if he was in the middle of the cavern. The warden had no fear about Richmond escaping once he was unchained. Even if Richmond was able to outmuscle him he knew that Prince Leroy would be able to subdue the prisoner. Richmond also knew that there was no point in struggling. He had noticed the Dark Knight's reaction to Tancred's struggle and was not going to make the same mistake. His heart raced with fear. He wished that he was anywhere else. The panic was almost uncontrollable. Once he was chained again he knew that there was no escape. All he could do was pray for death. He prayed, but no one answered.

"Now I will give you one more chance to speak," he looked directly at Bern. He knew that there was no point in asking anyone else.

"Don't answer him Bern," Richmond tried to sound strong, but the fear cut through his voice. "I can take whatever they want to deliver."

His words caused the Dark Knight to laugh out loudly. It was valiant, he had to give the man that, but it was foolish. No one in the room believed his words. The other three men winced when they saw what the warden had in his hand. It was a wicked looking whip with three knots on the end. It looked as though it would easily strip the skin from the body. The warden deliberately stayed behind Richmond so he could not see what he was holding. The looks on his friend's faces did nothing to settle his nerves. He knew something terrible was about to happen.

Leroy made the warden wait. He wanted to savour the fear that was emanating from Richmond. He knew it would not last forever, but he wanted to make the most of it. The warden was also started to get restless. There was drool starting to build up in the corner his mouth. The anticipation was going to make him burst. Leroy took a one last deep breath and gave the order.

The warden didn't bother taking Richmond's shirt off. He knew that eventually the whip would do the job for him. A slight amount of drool dripped from his jowls as he swung the whip backwards. Richmond could hear the wind as the whip moved and he closed his eyes. The warden used all his strength to bring the whip down on Richmond's back. The whip cut through Richmond's shirt and his skin. The crack of the whip as it struck his skin made everyone cringe. Richmond had promised himself that he was not going to cry out in pain, but there was nothing he could do to stop himself. The pain ripped through his body as the whip ripped through his skin. He cried out in pain. The sound made everyone cringe again. A drop of blood flicked into the air as the warden brought the whip back again.

As much as Richmond hoped that was going to be the only attack he knew that it would not be. He had never felt a pain like it in his life and he knew that it was just the beginning. The second time the whip came down on his back the blow crossed the one that he had already received. The warden had not relented on the second blow. This time Richmond didn't bother about trying to hold the pain in and he let it all out in a heart-breaking moan. Sweat started to appear on his face and he started to breathe heavily. The pain was taking its toll and it had only just started. Richmond didn't know how long he was going to be able to take it. He prayed that he would lose consciousness. At least them he would not feel the pain anymore.

"Don't think that I am going to let you get off so easily," there was something joyful in Leroy's voice.

Richmond felt his eyelids start to close. A third blow struck his back. The words seemed like a distant memory. The cavern seemed as though it was a long way away. He could hear the noise come out of his mouth, but it sounded as though it was on the other side of the dungeon. He knew that his reality was slipping away. A smile crossed his face. It was almost over. He was about to slip into sweet unconsciousness.

Suddenly the reality sucked back to him as a fourth blow, just as powerful as the first, struck him. He cried out in pain and anguish. He didn't know which was the more powerful. He was fully aware of what was happening around him again. More to the point he was fully aware of the pain he was feeling. He thought he had managed to beat the Dark Knight, but he was clearly mistaken.

"I told you that you cannot escape. I can keep you here for as long as I wish," he laughed after he finished speaking.

He raised his hand before a fifth blow could be made. The warden was disappointed. He loved causing pain. It was the only reason why he rose in the morning. The new Prince had given him a new lease on life. He loved, what he thought was, the man before him. He also knew that there was no point in trying to continue without permission. The Prince had a strange power, but as long as he let him do his job he did not care.

"I will give you one more chance," Leroy spoke to Bern. "Then I will leave you to enjoy the company of my warden."

Bern had to seriously think about what Leroy was saying. He didn't so much care about his own wellbeing. He could take the punishment; it was the others that he had to think about.

"And if you are thinking that you can take the pain, remember that your abilities have been blocked by the potion. You will feel everything just like the others," Leroy warned.

He had to admit that he had forgotten about the potion. He thought there was a chance he could block the pain. He could not let that worry him. "You can do your worst. You will suffer when the Chosen One arrives. It will be that thought that keeps me going." He gave Richmond an apologetic look.

"It's alright. Together we will be strong," there was no strength to Richmond's words, but no one expected there to be any.

"It will take more than this to break us," Tancred added.

"We will laugh over your dead body," Hadar was not going to miss out.

Their words had a clear effect on the Dark Knight. He was not happy with the optimism. There was something very unsettling about it.

He could still sense the fear, but it was not as strong as it once was. He would have to administer some more pain. He was tempted to start punishing them himself, but the risk that he would kill them was too great. If didn't want to make the same mistake that he had done with Lady Amilie.

"Continue," Leroy said to the warden.

Even the warden was surprised at his command. He did not think that Richmond could take much more punishment. He enjoyed giving pain, but there was a limit. When nothing happened the prince looked at him. There was nothing else that he could do. He struck Richmond again and then once more and watched as he hung limp, still conscious. The warden didn't know what was happening. The man should have passed out a long time ago. No one could stand up to the pain he was dishing out.

The look on Richmond's face was almost enough to break Bern. The only thing that stopped him was his lack of knowledge. He thought that if he knew everything then he would talk. Since he didn't truly know what Alaric was planning he didn't think there was any point. There was no way to stop his pain. Bern tried to tap into the power that he knew was inside him. He had never done it before. He had always relied on the entity, but he had to do it himself. He reached deep down inside, but there was nothing there. There was nothing he could do.

"Is this all you have?" The only chance he had was to provoke the Dark Knight to punish him instead.

"You are right." Leroy motioned for Richmond to be let down.

As soon as his wrists were unbound Richmond collapsed to the ground. He did not have the energy to lift himself. He was lying in a small pool of his blood that had dripped from his wounds. On the ground under him his blood mixed with the pile of dried blood from many other prisoners. Richmond wanted to move, but his body would not respond. The warden had to lift Richmond back into position. The Lord from Bellarome hung limply in his chains. He thought that his shoulders would separate at any moment, but there was nothing he could do about it.

"You will be next," he pointed at Hadar and smiled.

"Are you afraid? Is that why you will not take me?" Bern was starting to become frustrated. He wanted to take the pain away from his companions.

"Ha, ha, ha..." he laughed out loudly. "You really want to take the lead?" He paused and let the question sit for a moment. "There will be time. Now it is your friend's turn to enjoy my hospitality."

Hadar clenched his teeth as hard as he could. He had seen what Richmond had gone through and he was not looking forward to it. Like with Richmond the warden waited a moment before striking for the first time. Hadar kept the pain inside for as long as he could, which was not long at all, before he let out a scream that shook the cavern. Only Richmond could truly understand the pain that he was going through.

Once they were done with Hadar they moved on to Tancred. Unlike the other two Tancred was happy to go into the centre of the cavern. He felt responsible for Amilie's death. They had only known each other for a short while, but he had felt connected to her. He didn't know how he had got her killed, but he knew that he had played a role. He wanted to feel the pain. He wanted to die and the Dark Knight could sense it. That took away some of the pleasure in his torture. He received just as much punishment as the others, but it was not as enjoyable for Leroy. He was surprised that his brother did nothing to protect him.

Once they were done with Tancred it was finally Bern's turn. He was grateful for such a small mercy. He had been forced to watch his three companions' brutal torture. He wished that he had information that he could share with the Dark Knight. At least that is what he told himself. It would have been a different decision altogether if he had.

"I think that will do for the day," Leroy spoke as the warden moved towards Bern.

The warden didn't look happy when he heard the words. He had been looking forward to punishing Bern. The man had been so keen to join him in the middle. Those who had false bravado he liked to punish even more. There would have been a different fate waiting for him. The look of surprise on Bern's face also irritated him. It was as if he was disappointed. It only made the warden want to hurt him more.

"What are you doing?" Bern asked as Leroy turned to walk away. "Are you that frightened of me that you will not punish me like the others?" it was a weak threat, but it was all that he had.

His words struck a cord with Leroy. He paused in mid-step before turning around. There was a hint of hope in the warden's heart. The Dark Knight took a slow step back towards the centre of the cavern. He looked at Bern carefully. There was a fire in his eyes. He wanted nothing more than to torture Bern himself. The upstart would feel the true power of the Dark Knight, but there was still something stopping him. No one ever begged him to be tortured and he didn't like surprises. It was the reason that prevented him from continuing. Then he remembered the reason why he was not going to have Bern tortured.

"No I am not afraid of you. How long do you think your friends will last being tortured, whilst you are left unscathed? I am sure that soon enough they will force you to tell me what they know. For now I think that you should have a drink and get some rest," there was a wry smile on his face as he spoke.

No one saw him pick up the mug that was now in his left hand. He walked to where Bern was hanging and reached out as if to pass it too him. He laughed when he realised what he had done.

"I guess that I will have to make you drink," there was malice in his voice.

He held Bern's mouth open with his right hand and poured the liquid down his throat with his left. Bern was surprised at the strength he had. It belied the body that he wore. There was nothing Bern could do to stop drinking. He knew that the mixture would take away his energy. He tried to fight against the feeling that was taking over him, but his eyes became heavy and his head started to swim. His entire body started to feel numb. There was nothing he could do. The potion was too strong for him.

The last thing Bern heard was the Dark Knight laughing as he walked away. The wicked laugh was over the sound of his three companions whimpering around him. Being strung out there was little comfort for them. Bern could only imagine the pain they had been through and what they were still going through. It was that final thought that passed through his mind before he lost consciousness.

Epilogue: Too Late

Duke X was panting when he reached the clearing with his fellow rebels. He had left the castle in such a hurry that he had not been able to change into his disguise. The other rebels took a moment to recognise him in his finery. There were a number of gasps as the connection was made between his real identity and pseudonym.

"Duke Xarles," a young woman, who had once been a washer-woman inside the castle, was the first to speak to him. "I can not believe that it is you."

"Save us Duke Xarles," a call came from within the gathered crowd.

"Enough! Where is Jerome?" he asked as he scanned the crowd

"I am here sir," Jerome raised his hand and pushed his way through.

Jerome was one of only a handful of people who knew that Duke Xarles was Duke X. He had been a supporter of the rebels ever since it began, but had only been an open member since the night his family had been slaughtered. The Duke had instantly taken a liking to him once he had joined his group. No one hated the so called Prince Leroy as much as Jerome. It was that hatred that kept him going. He organised the rebels as best he could. Xarles was grateful for his assistance as he had been struggling to keep control with the time he had to spend within the castle.

He smiled as his friend reached him, although it was more of a grimace than a smile. It was time for them to move into action. Since Lord Richmond had arrived he knew that it would not be long, but it had been over a week. The rebels were starting to become restless again, not to mention that their living conditions were substandard and they were running out of food. Xarles didn't know how long they could survive.

"We have much to do and no time to do it," Duke Xarles' voice was grave.

"But we are ready for battle," Jerome didn't understand what he was saying.

"It is true that the army has arrived, but that is not the battle that we will be fighting." Xarles was still trying to catch his breath.

"Then what have we been doing here?" Jerome did his best to keep his voice level, although his frustration was starting to rise.

"We are here to fight, but not the battle that we originally thought," Xarles' panting was starting to die down.

"You are going to have to give me more information. I don't have the energy to decipher the clues." Jerome was starting to become frustrated.

"I am sorry," he said as he composed himself. "The Prince has some new prisoners. I recognised two of the men. They were Lord Richmond and his advisor Tancred. I didn't recognise the other two, but one of the men held himself like he was of noble birth. The fourth was strange. He had a strength like nothing I have ever seen before. I can't explain it, but I know he is important," Xarles explained as best he could.

"I still don't understand what you are talking about."

"We have to rescue them," Xarles blurted out. "We can not let them be executed."

"If they have already been taken prisoner then I don't think that they are still alive. I know that we don't like to see anyone tortured, but I do not think that getting ourselves caught will prove anything." Jerome did not like what he was suggesting.

"I do not believe that they are dead. I don't know why, but I believe that are alive. If that is the case then I don't want to think what they are going through," Xarles added. "We have to draw up a plan of attack and we need to do it quickly."

Jerome still didn't think that it was a good idea. It was suicide to enter the castle. He felt sorry for the four prisoners, but he had more important matters to deal with. As much as Duke X was their founder and leader Jerome had a great deal of sway with the rebels. They had seen the work he had done whilst the Duke was away. The last thing he wanted was to cause a rebellion, but he would have to do what he thought was right. The irony was not lost on him.

"The castle soldiers outnumber us at least five to one, if not more. There is little chance of getting into the castle, let alone rescuing anyone. I do not think this is a wise decision. I think we should stick with the original plan," Jerome voiced his opinion.

Xarles was surprised with his confidante's reaction. It was the first time that he had disagreed with him. There was something strange in the man's face. It was like he did not trust him anymore. It didn't matter, however, he was still the leader of the rebels and they would have to do what he said. It was not the greatest of attitudes, but time was running out.

"We can get into the castle grounds. There is a secret way through the stables," Xarles tried to explain, but Jerome would not let him finish.

"That is all well and good, but what are we going to do once we are inside. There are too many soldiers. There is nothing that we can do. That is not the only reason. These soldiers are our kinsmen. The only reason they are doing what they are doing is because Prince Leroy has control over Queen Oriana. I hate to break it to you, but I think it is too late for those four," Jerome was firm.

Xarles had to admit that Jerome had a point. There was still the problem of losing once they were inside the castle. If they were all captured then there was nothing they could do and it would all be for nothing.

"The four of them are part of the Alliance," there was an idea coming to him. "I do not think it will be long before they attack. Once the soldiers are distracted we should be able to storm the castle. I know that it is still risky, but at least it gives us a chance."

Jerome had to admit that what they were planning would cause the death of many of their kinsmen. Storming the castle to rescue four prisoners did not sound good. They would lose a lot more of their numbers than he was willing to sacrifice.

"I do not think that I can let you do this." It was not what he wanted to say, but he had to look after his own.

Xarles was shocked by his response. He had trusted Jerome ever since he arrived. Now he was not so sure that he had made the right decision. He could tell that the situation was about to turn sour.

"I don't think that is your decision to make," he didn't know what else to say. "I brought these people together for a reason."

"And that was to return power to the Queen. It was not to rescue foreigners." Jerome started fingering the hilt of his sword.

It wasn't long before Xarles noticed what he was doing. He did not know what he was thinking, but he was sure that it was not a good sign. The last thing he wanted to do was to start an internal fight, but he could not back down. He knew that they had to rescue the four men. He could not explain why, but he never felt stronger about anything in his life.

"I do not think that is a wise decision," Xarles warned him. "I have many years of training with the sword."

Jerome suddenly stopped what he was doing. He could see the hardness on the Duke's face. He had been stroking the hilt of his sword absentmindedly. He had no intention of starting a fight, but he didn't think there was anything else to do. Despite being a trained soldier he didn't think he would be able to beat Xavier in a sword fight. For victory he would have to rely on the support of the other rebels. He was sure that he had enough support to continue.

"I don't think threats are going to get you very far," his hand gripped the hilt and he was ready to draw his sword.

Duke Xarles saw his move and knew that he would have to act soon. He did not want to fight his friend, but there didn't look as though there was any other option. The last thing he wanted to do was to create unrest, but he didn't think there was a way to talk himself out of it.

"If you are not going to see sense then I don't think that there is anything else for it," Xarles had enough.

Without waiting for Jerome to respond Xarles drew his sword. The sudden movement caught Jerome by surprise. If the Duke had decided to attack then he would have easily killed Jerome. He gave his friend enough time to draw his own sword and defend himself. Even with his opponent ready for battle Xarles didn't attack. He was still hoping that there was going to be another solution to their problem.

"What are you waiting for?" Jerome had to ask the question, although he really didn't want to know the answer. He made no move to attack and hoped that they would not come to blows.

It did not take long before some of the other rebels saw that they had both drawn their weapons. At first they didn't think anything of it, but when neither man backed down they realised that something was wrong. They started to gather around to see what the commotion was about. It was exactly what Jerome was hoping for. If he was able to gain enough support then the Duke would have to back down. There was no way that Xarles would kill him in front of so many people.

"Well I guess there is nothing stopping me now," it sounded as though Xarles was already defeated.

The tone of his voice did nothing to encourage Jerome. It was clear that the Duke was prepared to go through with his threat. There was something in that which made Jerome wonder at his passion. Although he didn't believe in risking their lives to save four strangers he was beginning to think that there was more to the story than what Xarles was letting on. Either way there was no longer time to discuss the situation. It was clear that the Duke was preparing to make the first attack. All Jerome could do was hope that he was able to defend long enough for someone else to step in.

***

Alaric and Marina suddenly burst into the reality. The arrival was so sudden and so unexpected that Alaric went flying over the head of Adelanta. He crashed into the ground, narrowly avoiding smashing his head on a rather large pine tree. Marina was able to remain on her mare, but it took a lot of control. She was confused as to why they had returned so suddenly. She had to admit to herself that she was not all that comfortable skipping through reality. Each time they had returned it had been different, but it had never been so rushed.

"Are you alright?" Marina dropped from her horse and rushed to his side.

Alaric remained face down in the dirt until Marina dropped to his side. She rolled him over so he was able to breathe. He looked as though he was unconscious, even though his eyes were still open. It took him a moment to snap back to reality. He looked up and was glad to see Marina's face. It had been a long journey and he didn't think he could have made it without her support. Her face turned from worried to concerned when she realised he was awake.

"What happened?" she sounded relieved.

"I don't know. I was following a feeling that was leading us to Bern when it just suddenly disappeared. It was at that time that we were shot back to reality," Alaric's voice sounded weak. "On the plus side I don't think that we are far from the army's campsite.

"I think we should rest here for a while," Marina suggested as she helped him to sit up.

"That sounds like a wonderful idea, but I don't think that we have the time. We have to keep moving. It is not a good sign that I can no longer sense Bern. I have a bad feeling that something very wrong has happened," Alaric tried to bring strength into his voice.

"That is all well and good, but you know how you get after travelling," Marina warned.

She did not think it was a good idea to keep moving. She knew that they were close to their destination, but she did not want to risk Alaric's health. They had tried to keep moving after their first jump and Alaric had nearly collapsed after the first fifteen minutes. He had then slept for a day and a half before his strength returned.

"I know, but I will be alright. We need to get to the campsite so I can work out what is happening. Once we are there I will be able to rest," Alaric would not be dissuaded.

"Fine, but I will be keeping a close eye on you," Marina did not sound happy, but she helped him onto Adelanta nevertheless.

***

"They have been gone too long. I hate to admit it but I think that they have been captured," Sorrell raised his voice as he reiterated his point.

"It has only been a few hours since they left," Jarwe sounded exhausted. "We have to give them more time. Besides, the soldiers haven't finished with the battering rams."

Ever since they had met over breakfast they had been debating the best time to attack the castle and each time it came back to the fact they were not ready to attack. Those who were opposed to taking the field were rueing the time when the battering rams were finished. It would be hard to dissuade the others.

"We have to do something. I am sure we would have heard from them by now if they were successful. They have been gone too long," Hulkan was worried about his friends.

Aimon watched the exchange and wondered what was happening in the castle. The easiest way would be for him to get in the mind of Tancred, but he didn't think that would be a good idea, besides the fact that he was struggling to sense his slave. He did not think that the others had found him. It must have been his brother trying to block him. He was glad that the Great Lord decided to leave him out of it. He couldn't think of anything better than Ra'naroz being destroyed. If they had truly been taken prisoner then there was not much chance of that happening. Either way it was a win-win situation for him. He had his own mission to keep him busy. If he was able to succeed, and he would, then the Great Lord would bestow him with gifts of unimaginable glory and power.

Suddenly they realised that someone had entered the command tent. No one knew how long they had been there listening, but they were glad for the distraction. When they saw who it was they were not sure if it was good thing.

Alaric was standing inside the doorway. He had his arm around Marina. At first the bulk of the room thought that they were a couple. When they took a closer look they realised that Marina was holding him upright. His face was pale and he looked as though he had no strength left. Suddenly and idea came to Aimon and it took a lot of self-control to keep the wicked smile from his face. It was a perfect opportunity for him to take out the Cursed One. He knew that the Great Lord had told him only to steel the treasure, but if he had known that the Cursed One would be in such a state he was sure that it would be allowed. As the thought passed through his mind he noticed that there was a ring on the woman's finger. The blue stone set in the middle of the band was unmistakable. He didn't know how he could not feel the power of the stone when she had entered the tent. As soon as he saw it there could be no mistaking the Sapphire *Stone of Power*. He knew that was what the Great Lord wanted. He had underestimated the power of the Cursed One's companion. There was a reasonable chance that if he tried to kill the Cursed One then she would kill him. That was a risk that he didn't want to take. His main priority was to remove the ring from the woman's finger. The ideas were already racing through is mind.

"Princess Marina, let me help you." General Sorrell rushed to their aid as he was the first to regain his senses.

Marina was happy that he took Alaric's weight. As much as she liked having Alaric in her arms she was starting to struggle. She moved to the table and took a seat. She was glad to be off her feet. She only hoped that there was a chance to relax, although she knew that there was not. At least there was still food on the table from their breakfast. She didn't hold on tradition as she quickly picked at the almost empty platters.

"My lady, do not eat the leftovers. I will have something brought for you." General Sorrell was in shock to see his princess act in such a manner.

"Don't be silly," she spoke between mouthfuls. "I am not the spoilt princess that I once was. I have seen things that even you cannot imagine," she continued eating once she had finished speaking.

Alaric looked flimsy in his chair. It looked as though he could fall over at any moment. He took a couple of seconds to compose himself before he started to speak.

"I must see General Bern," Alaric used all his willpower to bring strength to his voice.

There were some nervous looks across the table before Hulkan finally spoke. "He is not here."

"Where is he?" Alaric spoke before giving Hulkan a chance to continue.

"He has gone into the castle with Richmond, Tancred and Hadar."

All of a sudden it made sense to him; there no doubt in his mind that the four of them had been captured by Ra'naroz. He had felt something when he reached the campsite, but his mind was too busy on other things and he didn't realise what it was. When he started looking for it he could feel the magical energy emanating from the castle. It was still a subtle sensation, but with each passing day Alaric was becoming more in tune with the world around him. Whatever it was it was blocking his ability to feel his friends. Without that feeling there was no way to pinpoint their exact location.

"Alaric?" Marina spoke to him when he didn't answer. He had a glazed look on his face that worried her.

"Sorry." Alaric snapped back to reality. "What is the army up to? I would have thought they would have taken the battlefield by now." Alaric was trying to divert the attention from those trapped in the castle.

"We decided that it was not the best of ideas. The people inside the castle are not our enemy. They are under control of Prince Leroy and it is not their fault," Sorrell explained

Alaric had to admit that he had a point. It was going to be a matter of friend against friend. To make matters worse if the Entero component of the Alliance turned and joined their kinsmen then all hell would break loose. The unfortunate part was that there was no other option. If Alaric was going to rescue his friends trapped in the castle then he would need something to distract Na'garoz. A full attack on the castle would be perfect.

"I must go into the castle and rescue the others," Alaric's voice was weak.

Marina fussed at his side, but Alaric pushed her away, as gently as possible. The exchange was confusing to the others sitting around the command table. Something had changed between the two since they had left Kiarome, that was obvious.

"That is a good idea. Do you want anyone to go with you?" Jarwe sounded excited.

"No, I will go alone, but it will not happen today," Alaric's words dampened the sudden rush of enthusiasm in the tent. "I need to rest. We have travelled a long way in a short period of time. Hopefully I will have recovered by tomorrow. Trust me, gentlemen, when I say that I do not want to wait."

"There may be one problem with that," Sorrell began. "The army is almost ready to fight. They have been building battering rams to assault the castle. Once they are finished it will be hard to stop them from attacking."

"You have to. It the army attacks too early then all is lost."

Aimon listened to the conversation closely. He only wished that he could do something to provoke the army, but that was not what the Great Lord wanted. He returned his gaze to the blue stone inset in the ring on Marina's finger. When he looked up he realised that Marina was watching him with a concerned expression on her face. He quickly returned his attention to Alaric, although he had missed parts of the conversation. "They must move when I tell them to. You have to keep them in the forest until then."

"It will not be easy, but if they know we are attacking tomorrow I am sure that they will do what they are told," Sorrell sounded confident.

"Unfortunately that is the easy part. The hard part comes when you reach the field outside of the castle," Alaric was starting to pant for breath and again Aimon thought it would be a perfect time to attack him.

"I don't understand." There were nods and murmurs throughout the tent. "What is the point of leading the army out onto the field if we are not going to attack? We will leave ourselves open for their archers. They will be able to pick us off, one by one if they have to," Sorrell did not sound happy.

"For starters I need you to distract Na'garoz, the Dark Knight, the one you know as Prince Leroy. That is why you must take the field and not attack. You must provoke him. There is another reason, but I don't know what it is. I am too tired at the moment. Hopefully it will come to me before we have to attack," Alaric sounded as though he was becoming weaker and weaker.

"I think that is enough," Marina clearly noticed the deterioration. "You need to get some rest."

Marina helped Alaric from his chair. There were still many unanswered questions, but it was clear they would remain that way. Alaric did nothing to deter Marina. He knew there was something that he was missing, but he was not strong enough to struggle with her. He had to do whatever she wanted. He was grateful, though. He needed his rest if he had any hope of rescuing his friends and destroying another Dark Knight.

***

Eldred opened his eyes. The nightmare would not end. Every time he opened his eyes he wished that it had been a dream. He wished that it had all been a dream. He had lost count how many days they had been in the prison. It could have been weeks, months or years for all he knew. It didn't make any difference. All hope had gone. He thought that Alaric would have come for them by now. For all he knew the Chosen One had come and failed. He did not truly believe that it was true, but it was a distinct possibility.

Alena remained on the small bed in their prison cell. When they first arrived they had been sharing the bed, but Eldred let her have it. Her will had been broken. He could see that there was nothing left inside of her. He did not even now if she wanted to be rescued anymore. He had prayed for death himself and he was sure that she would have done the same thing.

The only saving grace was that the guards had seemingly forgotten that they were there to be tortured. The only problem with that was that their meals were not brought to them regularly. Although Eldred no longer knew day from night he thought that there were days on ends that they were not being fed. He had lost a lot of weight as had Alena. He doubted that either of them would have the strength to survive another beating. There was a chance that was the Dark Knight's plan all along.

The biggest surprise to him was that neither the Serpentant nor the Dark Knight had visited them in days, maybe even weeks. That at least was a good thing. Their punishments were a lot worse when one of them was around.

Although Eldred couldn't be sure, he felt that there had been a falling out between Viper and Ra'naroz. The Dark Knight had left Viper in charge of their torture and it was strange that he had not returned. At first he had come every day and then ever other day. Eldred had not noticed any change in his demeanour, but he was hopeful nonetheless.

Slowly he closed his eyes again. He could only keep them open for short periods at any given time. He did not have the strength for anything else. He could not remember the last time he had stood up. At first he had tried to exercise as best he could in the small cell, but eventually he ran out of strength. The best he could do was to check on his surroundings every now and again. He did not even know if he would have the strength to eat the next time they were given food.

Without the evil brew they had been forcing him to drink he was able to feel the power around him. It was a sickening, evil power, but it was there nevertheless. The only problem was he was too weak to use it. He knew for a fact that if he started to draw on the power it would drain his life completely.

His breathing slowed as he prepared himself to sleep again. At least he could save energy whilst he was sleeping. His mind was also able to escape the horror that had become his life and that was a godsend. The only problem with falling asleep was that eventually he would have to wake again. He hoped that next time he fell asleep he didn't wake up. That was the last thought that passed through his mind before he lost consciousness again.

www.ingramcontent.com/pod-product-compliance
Lightning Source LLC
Chambersburg PA
CBHW030925020726
47498CB00001B/123